CHARLES AYLING

For the Love of Man

Mindfield
PUBLISHING

Mindfield Publishing

(A Division of Taretimi Enterprises)

* Yenagoa: #1 Osomowo Otuzi Close, Off Big Church Street,

Tombia-Amassoma Road, Yenagoa, Bayelsa State.

Tel: +234-803-931-7950

* Abuja: Plot 34 Samuel Ladoke Akintola Boulevard,

Gark 2, Abuja FCT. Tel: +234-915-139-1999

* Makurdi: #2 First Avenue, Off Yogbo Road, North-Bank,

Makurdi. Tel: +234-701-290-5484,+234-802-611-4636,

+234-810-490-5391

* E-mail: mindfieldpublications@gmail.com

edoroso@gmail.com

* Website: http://www.mindfieldpublish.com

* Facebook Page: https://facebook.com/mindfieldpublishing/

First edition

This book was professionally typeset on Reedsy.
Find out more at reedsy.com

I dedicate this book to my wife Wendy. Without her input and support, this work would never have been written.

Contents

Other Mindfield Publishing titles by CHARLES AYLING   iv

I   Plan One

1   The Carpentry Ends   3
2   The Journey Begins   6
3   Baptism   10
4   Temptation   13
5   Rejection at Nazareth   17
6   Healings   24
7   The First Disciples   28
8   Choosing the Twelve   37
9   Lessons for the Apostles   51
10 Teaching and Proving   54
11 Mary, Oh Mary   70
12 Lessons   86
13 Many Miracles, Much Resentment   91
14 Prediction and Fear   104
15 Lazarus   120
16 Agony at the Last Supper   133
17 The Deed   141
18 Pain and Denial   149
19 Pilate's Dilemma   154
20 Agony Within   161
21 A Cross to Bear   169
22 Peace in the Tomb   176

| 23 | All is Not Lost | 180 |

II   Plan Two

24	The Near Future	195
25	Out of the Blue	200
26	The Assignment	208
27	The Interview	211
28	The Tale on the HD memory card	226
29	Blue	228
30	Proof	233
31	Eva's Miracle	236
32	Hard to Believe	250
33	Scars	254
34	It Begins	266
35	A Visitor	270
36	The Rally	278
37	The Promise	290
38	A Change of Program	297
39	Understanding	311
40	The White House Gets the Blues	316
41	The Red Visit	327
42	An Important Call	345
43	The President is Nuts	348
44	They Do Not Hear	352
45	Should All Roads Lead to Rome?	358
46	Nothing Has Changed	373
47	Return to Hope	391
48	The Gardener visits the Garden	398
49	Reflections to Come	406
50	The Final Chapter or is it?	408

III   Plan Three

51	Shock	417
52	Easter Morning	442
53	Devil May Care	449
54	Nothing to Preside Over	454
55	The President Moves On	470
56	An Important Lesson	480
57	Still Commander in Chief	496
58	More Discoveries	508
59	Holy Land	518
60	The Way to Flagstaff	535
61	More Survivors	557
62	The Last Stage	580
63	Unbelievable	588

Other Mindfield Publishing titles by
CHARLES AYLING

The Borneo Experience

THE BORNEO EXPERIENCE (2020)

Alfred, a young Army Captain involved in liberating the prisoners of war from the horrors of a Japanese prison camp in Borneo in June 1945, lives with these harrowing memories twenty years after. Half-heated about traveling to New Zealand on a new cruise liner to celebrate twenty years since the atom bomb was dropped on Japan, the new liner becomes wrecked by a freak tsunami resulting in Alfred and two of the ship's crew being washed up on deserted island in the South Pacific. He is cautious about forming any kind of relationship with one of the survivors, the crew's attractive ship purser, Avril who has other ideas. The other crew members do not help the situation. With hardly any water or food and no rescue in sight, Alfred takes the lead in their survival. Evidence of slave trafficking on the island becomes apparent while searching for water. Reverting back to his army training and obsessed with bringing these cruel pirates to justice, he discovers a former Japanese enemy is behind the child trafficking. Now, more determined, Alfred and his small crew manage to infiltrate, rescue and carry out the ultimate revenge.

Sunrise at Noon

SUNRISE AT NOON (2020)

On Tuesday, August 27th, 1895, Colonel John Rhodes, an Englishman with impeccable intelligence credentials and military experience is summoned to the Department of the Interior in Washington DC to be appointed as a US Federal Marshal with the unusual request of investigating a serious situation developing in Shasta County in Northern California. He is to delve into the troubling mystery of the disappearance of three previous Deputy Marshals and the local sheriff in inexplicable circumstances while investigating a series of illegal lynching.To add to the problem, there are strong rumors of a new gold strike in the sacred mountains belonging to the Shasta tribe. If John cannot prevent another uncontrolled gold rush it would mean an all-out war with the native population and probable obliteration.On the Pullman Express from New York to San Francisco on

Wednesday 28th August, 1895 Colonel Rhodes meets Bolete Forster, the strong-minded daughter of the wife of the Chief of the Shasta Tribe and the local Danish landowner Erik Forster the second. The 29-year-old is returning home to the Shasta tribe having left home ten years earlier to Europe where she's studying for her medical degree paid for by her rich Grandfather Forster living in New York. Rhodes and Bolete's encounter under traumatic circumstances draws them close together for the four-day journey and the rest of their immediate future.

Even though this unique story is based on historical and theological research, it is a work of fiction. Names, characters, places, and incidents are either from available scriptures and text or a product of the author's imagination. Any resemblance to actual persons, living or dead, events and locals is entirely coincidental.

I

Plan One

INTERPRETING THE DREAD

1

The Carpentry Ends

The muscular forearms blend into strong sensitive hands that have hardened over time from hewing and shaping wood. The same hands take hold of a nearby spoke-shave, one of the collections of basic wood tools gathered over the years for making simple furniture.

A shadow appears from the light of the doorway extending to the crude workbench. In response, the young man turns around. Meanwhile, a strand of light brown wavy hair falls over one eye. Concentrating on the figure in front of him, he brushes back the hair with his hand exposing warm hazel eyes, which crinkle in the corners from his smile of affection. The older man opposite leans in an awkward posture on a crude walking cane. By the look of anguish on his face, his back has given out again. Reacting to the older man's pain, the young man takes hold of a nearby high stool and places it next to his workbench. He then helps the ailing man mount the stool and positions the cane between his legs. Still leaning on his cane for support the older man's voice appears strained.

"I am sorry to bother you my son, I know that chair has to be finished today, but..."

Happy to take a break, the son interrupts and leans back against the workbench.

"You never bother me father. How can I help?"

Suppressing his rising anxiety, his father's grip on the cane increases.

3

"I – I have been talking it over with your mother about you giving up the family business and leaving us."

Having been through this conversation many times before, his son has to look away.

I know what he wants. I realize that me and my brothers John and James are the main breadwinners and my departure will put a burden on my parents...

Releasing a heavy sigh, he turns back to face his father.

"Father, you know I 'have' to go. I am being called. The mission starts now."

Observing the determined look in his son's eyes, tears of apprehension escape down the older man's cheeks.

"How do you know its 'God' calling you, and not your own restlessness?"

It grieves Jesus to witness the hurt in his father's eyes.

"I just know – that's all."

Suppressing a deep inward fear, Jesus turns to face his bench, places both hands on the almost completed chair, and then gazes out of the nearby window. After a thoughtful pause, he turns back to Joseph.

"I must get this chair finished. I promised Jacob the wine merchant he can collect it this afternoon."

Joseph is not listening about mundane matters, his fear and anger for the future is taking priority.

"Who is going to look after us when you're parading around the country pursuing this 'mission' of yours?"

Doing his best to keep his mind clear and his emotions steady, Jesus again looks out the window to absorb the beautiful day and the people of Nazareth going about their daily business.

"My brothers will collaborate for a while until I can arrange for us all to be together."

Now crying in desperation, Joseph's face becomes distorted with frustration. To relieve these painful emotions, he bangs his gnarled fist hard down on the workbench.

"I want us together – now! Here is our home, not some faraway place...
"

Biting his lip in sympathy and guilt, Jesus turns to face his father again. "Home is in your heart. Home is where you have love."

Reacting to his son's stubborn attitude, Joseph attempts to stand, but the stabbing pain in his back makes it impossible. Affected by his father leaning at a precarious angle against the bench, Jesus steps forward and grips his father's upper arms. Gazing into his dark brown eyes, Jesus supports him while turning him to lean forward over the end of the bench. The pain easing, Joseph stares at his son with a pitiful expression. His eyes bloodshot, his cheeks tear stained, Joseph's voice becomes resigned.

"What will you do first?"

Still uneasy by his father's stance, Jesus rests his hand on his shoulder.

"I will go into the desert. I need time and solitude so I can think and pray for what is about to come."

His pain returning with a vengeance, Joseph struggles in asking the inevitable.

"What is about to come? I don't understand!"

As Jesus slides his arm further around his fathers' shoulders, he is reminded of how thin and weak his father has become.

"To be honest, I don't fully understand fully. All I know is life has to be better than this? With all the persecution, corruption, hypocrisy and poverty among us, I sincerely believe God is telling me to bring hope."

Becoming weary and shaking his head with despondency, Joseph attempts to stand upright. Supported just by his cane, he is desperate to keep his balance and tries hard to hide his ceaseless pain. Unable to withstand his father's agony, Jesus embraces him. After kissing his father's forehead, he whispers in his ear.

"God loves you."

For a few seconds they stand as one. Dazed and a little confused, Joseph separates and takes two steps backwards.

"My back. It doesn't hurt. I have no pain!"

Leaning against his workbench for support, Jesus takes his father's right hand, kisses the palm and smiles.

"As I said, God loves you."

2

The Journey Begins

In the fifteenth-year of the reign of Tiberius, when Pontius Pilate is governor of Judea, the word of God has come to a man called John, the son of Zechariah. He spends his time traveling the desert around Jordan preaching a baptism of repentance for the forgiveness of personal sins. His physical presence is made more profound by his clothes, which consist of rough camel skin tied together by a crude leather belt around his waist. His unkempt dark hair and beard exalts a coarse wild look.

Jesus is sitting on a knoll observing John preach with enthusiasm to a curious crowd of about fifty onlookers. While absorbed in John's intense oratory, a man a few years older than Jesus and dressed in fine clothes, Jesus sits next to him and begins to converse in a well-educated voice.

"Do you know all he eats is locusts and wild honey? People are coming from all over to listen and observe other people confessing their wrongdoings. The unusual part is when John listens to them, he then dunks them underwater. When the poor soul can breathe again, John inform them they have just been baptized in the presence of God, and all their sins are forgiven."

While listening to this man and caught up in John's power of persuasion, Jesus is enthralled. He now knows how he will begin his mission.

"Tell me, sir, will he be here tomorrow?"

The older man looks up with interest at this intriguing young handsome face.

"I truly don't know, but he seems to be following the river."

Analyzing his next step, Jesus smiles and thanks the man. While standing and gathering his few scant belongings, he grips the man's shoulder as if to thank again, and then heads out into the desert.

Still inspired by John's teachings, Jesus finds a sheltered spot among some large boulders. As the evening sun begins casting long shadows he sits on his hand-sewn blanket, shakes his almost empty water bag and lifts it to his lips to drain the last few drops. Realizing he should have filled his water bag at the river, he looks up at the few stars now showing.

"Well God, this is a fine start to my mission. Now I will have to go back to the river. At least I have some food."

Resigning to the situation, he decides to pull out a piece of bread from his small bag.

A short while later after his food has been eaten and his thirst returns with a vengeance, he tries to ignore his parched throat by watching the sunset and the desert sky turning red.

"Oh, these desert sunsets are beautiful. God, what a beautiful place you have created. It's a shame that I'm going to suffer until the morning..."

Still in awe of his surroundings, and tuning in to the sounds to the desert, all is quiet except for a faint trickling noise. His senses stirring, he concentrates on this new sound, stands, and steps closer to its source. To his astonishment, he can hear running water amongst the boulders. Excited and relieved, he rushes back to retrieve his water bag. On returning, and peering closer in the fading light, he discovers clear running water trickling between two large boulders, and a gap just wide enough to fill his water bag.

Amazed by such luck, his water bag is now filled and his thirst quenched. Feeling better and appreciating this life saving spring, he lies down on the blanket and realizes something.

"God? Did you sense my suffering? Was it you that guided me here in the first place knowing there was a spring?"

Pondering on his questions, he stares up at the stars. After a minute, his mind wanders back to the last evening before he left home.

He had made a small bonfire in his workshop's back yard burning useless pieces of wood after cleaning out the shop and yard of scrap and rubbish. While crouching close to the fire, and his mind in a whirl about what the future may hold, he feels a pair of gentle hands stroking his back and shoulders. Knowing whom it is without turning around or saying anything, Mary his mother kisses the nape of his neck, and then sits down beside her son.

"Hello Mother. What brings you outside?"

Ignoring his mild sarcasm, she gazes at the fire.

"To see you of course! So, you're off tomorrow on this 'mission' of yours."

"It looks that way. Why?"

"I felt some tension in your shoulders. Are you really sure if this is right for you?"

As if embarrassed by her question, he stokes up the remaining embers.

"Oh, I am sure it's right. Maybe a little afraid."

She glances up at him to search his eyes, and then stares back at the fire.

"Afraid of what? It's obvious that God has chosen 'you' otherwise you wouldn't be so adamant. I expect you'll be given all the help and strength you need."

Appreciating her trying to alleviate his creeping anxiety, he places his left hand on her shoulder and observes her strong profile reflecting in the amber glow of the flames.

"All I know is that I have to do 'something'. I am being driven. My instincts tell me it will make a difference."

With an element of doubt, he removes his hand from her shoulder, and brings it up to her cheek. As if seeking reassurance from her, his fingers stroke her soft skin. In response, her pale brown eyes moisten in fear turning them into gold pieces reflecting off the firelight.

"Regardless of your uncertainty, I have a strong feeling that this is all meant to be, going right back to your birth and beyond. Do you remember back when you visited the temple in Jerusalem at Passover? You were only twelve years old, and went missing for three days. After us becoming distressed by your absence, at the time you said we didn't understand. You were right we didn't, but I knew then you were special. Now look at you, thirty years old and ready to change the world..."

His eyes stinging with burning tears of a loneliness he cannot fathom; Jesus looks up at the desert sky still hearing his mother's voice echoing in his head as fatigue takes over. As Mary's voice diminishes, he falls asleep.

3

Baptism

After a restless night, Jesus is heading back to the previous day's spot by the River Jordan. Occupying his mind and emotions with a strange mixture of excitement and trepidation, Jesus hopes John will still be at the same place as yesterday. To his delight, it looks as if John never left. Dressed the same, John is shouting to the heavens with the same enthusiasm as he dunks his new converts into the water.

Fascinated and yet apprehensive, Jesus walks down from the knoll and blends into the crowd.

In between each baptism, John bellows out.

"Repent, for the Kingdom of God is near."

Having pushed forward to be in front of the main crowd, a group of Pharisees and Sadducees are busy discussing the actions of this 'wild man' and are trying to decide what they should do about him. As if knowing their intentions, John turns on them; his face distorts with anger.

"You hypocrites stand there like a group of vipers looking down on me as some form of low life. You say to yourselves: we have Abraham as our

Father, so we have no need to repent, we are already righteous."

Continuing his rage, and with a touch of drama, John dips his hands deep into the water and lifts out two smooth, hand-size rocks.

"I tell you hypocrites that out of these stones, God can raise up the children of Abraham. The axe is already waiting at the base of the trees.

The ones that do not produce the fruit of repentance will be cut down and thrown into the fire."

Demonstrating his passion, he throws the rocks back into the water. The exaggerated splash emphasizes the spectacle.

"I 'baptize' with water for repentance, but after me a great and powerful one will come, whose sandals I am not fit to wear. He will baptize with the fire of the Holy Spirit."

John is so preoccupied by the reaction from the Pharisees that he doesn't notice Jesus stepping into the water behind him and stopping about an arm's length away.

While the main crowd is still mesmerized by John's fervor; a couple of lone voices shout a question.

"Once baptized what shall we do then?"

Exhibiting his frustration, John lifts a handful of water out of the river and throws it into the air creating a fountain.

"The man who has two tunics should share with the man who has none, and one who has more food than he needs, should do the same."

In response to this analogy, a puzzled, well-dressed man comes forward.

"I'm a tax collector. What should I do?"

John studies the man's expensive clothes before answering.

"Do not collect any more than you are required to do so."

As the crowd becomes immersed in this man's compelling teachings, a world-weary soldier comes forward.

"What about me?"

John inspects the soldier's well-worn bronze breastplate, and then replies with a stern expression.

"Don't extort money, and falsely accuse people. Be content with your pay."

As the atmosphere becomes fraught with a curious arousal, another voice shouts out.

"So, you're not the one that is to save us – the Messiah?"

His face flush with a new excitement, John turns to face the man in question.

"NO! As I have just said, I..."

He notices Jesus standing waist deep in the water. As if recognizing this man standing a yard away, John takes a deep breath, while his dark eyes widen in surprise. In response to John's startled expression, Jesus' eyes warm with a smile.

"Baptize 'me' cousin John."

Knowing full well who is standing in front of him, John's reaction is to take one step back, and then crouch in a submissive manor so the water is almost to his shoulders. In response to his cousin's request, his voice softens.

"I need to be baptized by you, and yet you come to me?"

Eager to continue, Jesus replies.

"Of course! Baptize me now!"

As a small dark cloud glides across the sun creating a somber atmosphere, John's instinct is to stand to his full height and place both of his hands on Jesus' head. He then pushes him down into the river until submerged. Pausing for a second while listening to the stillness of the crowd, John lets go and steps back as Jesus stands up with water cascading from his body. Jesus' eyes now alight with a new confidence and reassurance, steps forward to embrace John.

"God loves you cousin John."

Overawed, tears fill John's eyes.

"And you 'are' the one."

The crowd looks on in wonder as the dark cloud hiding the sun splits in two to create a beam of sunlight, which shines on Jesus. With everyone mesmerized by this 'specter', a white dove appears from nowhere and lands on Jesus' shoulder. Breaking the spell, someone shouts.

"It's a sign!"

The cloud soon evaporates, and the dove flies off as if it is all an apparition.

4

Temptation

His spiritual rebirth complete, Jesus returns to the desert.

"To feel complete in body and mind to begin my mission, I need to fast for at least forty days and nights. In doing so I will be cleansed and reborn."

Drinking the water from his discovered spring; the beginning of the fast goes well. The desert is cool at night, so that is the time Jesus meditates and prays.

By the twenty-first day, the temporary euphoria has gone, and the hunger pangs are becoming intolerable. It is through his will, and the strength of his prayers that is getting him through this ordeal. Meanwhile, Jesus has marked each day by scratching a line on a piece of sandstone resting by the boulders.

Today is the thirty-seventh. His weight has dropped drastically, his energy is at an all-time low, and painful hunger pangs gnaw at his insides. His prayers of desperation asking for the strength to get him through the next three days are crucial.

"O God! I must complete this fast. By doing so, I will be ready to face the upcoming challenge."

Sheltering in the shade of a large boulder, his mind drifts between the sleep of exhaustion and the willpower to stay alert to survive. After taking a sip of water, he hears a man's smooth deep voice.

"Would you like a fine piece of freshly baked bread to go with that spring water?"

Not knowing if his mind is playing tricks, Jesus shuts his eyes, places both hands hard against his ears, and shakes his head to remove the tempting thought.

"No! I will wait."

His senses are playing tricks. He can smell bread.

"Please God, if you're testing me there is no need. I won't let you down."

The sensation still present, he opens his eyes. The shape of a tall man silhouetted against the bright sun stands in front of him. He is breaking apart a small loaf of bread. A black headdress accompanied by a black robe covers his dark brown curly hair. His green eyes brighten as he flashes Jesus a broad genuine smile.

"Here, have some. Take the whole loaf. You look as if you need it."

He bends down and places the loaf between Jesus' legs, and then sits down beside a disoriented Jesus and gazes out into the desert.

"Pleasant spot you have here. Ideal for a fast."

Acting interested, he points at the natural spring.

"Not short of water I see."

Marshaling what little strength he has left; Jesus picks up the loaf and tosses it further away. In mock displeasure, the man in black glares at Jesus and stands.

"Tut, tut! That is a waste of good food. That could feed some poor soul."

Now exhibiting a mocking expression, he leans against the boulder in a casual stance.

"Talking of poor souls, I'm disappointed. You being the Son of God, I expected more of a strong adversary than a shriveling wretch crouching in the middle of the desert."

Not sure if he is awake or fallen asleep, Jesus' mind is in complete turmoil.

Is this a dream? Is this man a messenger? Oh God, don't let me give in. Not now!

Displaying a taunting expression, the man's green eyes seem to penetrate deep into Jesus' soul.

"Tell me? If you 'are' the Son of God, surely you could touch these stones lying in front of you and turn them into 'more' bread."

Knowing now this is no dream, Jesus dips into his non-existing energy reserves, and responds with as much anger as he can muster.

"Man doesn't live by bread alone."

Observing this young man's deterioration, the black hood turns away, and ponders.

"I agree. To have a rich and fulfilling life you need far more than bread. Let us put it another way. I have the power to give you the authority to rule the whole world in all its splendor and riches. Just think of what you could achieve with that power? The world belongs to me anyway, but I have the authority to hand it over to anyone I please, for a small price that is..."

Still not sure if this is a nightmare, Jesus is still repulsed by such arrogance.

"I worship and serve only God."

In response to this desperate statement, the man in black stands more upright and takes a step toward Jesus.

"Oh dear, you are a dreamer. Come! Stand with me. I want to show you something interesting."

The hooded man steps away from a tormented and confused Jesus and strides up a nearby slope. Now looking over a cliff top, and expressing a genuine smile, he holds out his hand to beckon Jesus.

"Join me my friend. Let us fulfill what is written."

Struggling in his mind whether to continue with this dreadful nightmare, Jesus finds he is unable to resist the man's invitation. As his fatigued body struggles to grapple with the rocks, his reluctance diminishes. Once standing, he then shuffles toward the awaiting dark robed stranger.

Now standing at the cliff's top, they both look down at the sheer drop. Seeing Jesus is unstable on his feet, the other man grips him by the forearm. The man's sincere flashing smile exposes a set of perfect white teeth.

"Now, if you are the Son of God, throw yourself off this cliff, and prove to me, as it is written, you can command the angels to come down and protect you by lifting you back to safety."

Giddy and weak, Jesus looks down at the sickening height, and then steps back.

"It is also written that you do not put God to the test. I also know who you really are – SATAN!"

His body shaking from his weakening fatigue, Jesus attempts to defy this man in black.

"You're here to temp me, and hoping I fail my fast, and then my mission. So, get behind me - Satan!"

The man in black stares at Jesus in mock astonishment, and laughs.

"Your mission? Don't make me laugh. You're going to die a useless, painful death. The only thing 'God' offers is the suffering of the flesh. I offer the 'pleasure'. If I were in your shoes, I know what I would choose."

Struggling to keep standing, and desperate in holding onto his dignity, Jesus turns his back to hide his burning tears of fear and exhaustion.

"You're not in my shoes. So, get behind me - get behind..."

His voice giving out, Jesus has great difficulty in shuffling back down the slope. Unaware, 'Satan' has gone.

Back at his crude camp, Jesus collapses onto his blanket. He lies there gasping for air and struggling to salvage his confused thoughts. After a minute of painful analyzing, he shuts his eyes and clenches his hands together.

"Oh God! Was that really Satan or was it you testing me? Or worse still, was it all in my mind? I am so tired..."

He lays exhausted as the sun goes down on the thirty-seventh day of fasting. As his mind drifts toward a restless sleep, he notices that the loaf of bread is still where it landed after he threw it earlier, shriveled from the hot sun.

5

Rejection at Nazareth

It is the last evening of his fast. Jesus is kneeling on his well-used blanket. His emaciated body is a black silhouette against the blood red setting sun. He listens to the night sounds of the desert that have been his comfort and companion for the last forty nights.

Now it is all finished, he takes a celebratory drink from his water bag. Relishing the coolness as it runs down his parched throat to his aching empty insides, he looks up to the darkening sky. Thirst now quenched, he places the water bag down on the blanket, and then puts his hands together entwining the fingers in a tight grip. #He then lowers his head, rests his chin on his chest, and begins to pray.

"Oh God, thank you for the strength so that I could survive this testing ordeal. I 'know' this is all part of your plan. Now, as part of that plan I must go back to Nazareth."

Now filled with relief and mild elation, he manages to dig down into his exhausted reserves of energy. Gathering up his few meager possessions, he begins to walk the best he can, through the cool night on his journey back home.

It is the early hours of the following morning; the dark sky is fading as daylight approaches to take over another blistering day. Jesus eases his fatigued sore body down onto the ground and sits against the wall of his house. His aching head resting against the wall, his exhaustion causes his mind to fade in an out of consciousness. Blurred and distorted images of the last forty days float in front of him like a toxic mirage. The temptations, especially the fresh bread, were the hardest to endure.

Now I'm home. All is well. Or will it? I have a nagging feeling I shouldn't be here, but where else can I go? Where do I start...?

He collapses into a heavy sleep.

Approximately one hour later, Jesus' younger brother James opens the back door of their house to smell the fresh morning air. He pauses for a minute by taking a couple of deep breathes, and then decides to step over the threshold to be outside. He stretches his upper body, pauses again, and then turns to return into the house. As he goes to enter his house, something catches his eye. He notices a thin dirty, haggard man asleep against his clean house. His curiosity aroused; he steps toward the disheveled man. Acting cautious, he puts his foot out to the man's boney legs. Thinking that this man may be contaminated with some disease, he prods the legs. Receiving no response, he prods again. Prodding harder this time, there is still no response.

Perhaps he's dead. Some poor starving beggar.

Becoming more concerned, James crouches down.

"Hey you! Go and beg somewhere else."

Jesus stirs. His bloodshot eyes hurt as they open. His cracked, sore mouth whispers.

"Is this how you treat a man in need?"

Exhaustion causing his eyes to close, his mouth stays open producing shallow breathing. Sudden realization sinks in as James recognizes his eldest brother.

"Oh my God, it's you! Jesus. what happened? Here, let me help you."

While bending forward to lift Jesus off the ground, James is shocked at how light his older brother weighs. He then carries him into the house toward his own bed. While still holding Jesus, James acknowledges his mother Mary who has just risen, and notices the disheveled man.

"Who have you their James?"

"It's Jesus."

"What?"

Becoming sick with worry, she goes straight to Jesus, now lying on the bed. Tears of concern filling her eyes, she crouches down to him.

"Oh, my son! What have they done to you?"

His eyes now open, Jesus offers his mother a weak smile and whispers.

"I am ready now Mother. I am clean in mind and body. All I need now is food and rest..."

Witnessing his eyes closing, this whole situation is confusing her. Her anxiety mounting, she decides not to ask questions, but help to alleviate the circumstances.

"Yes. Food! Quick James, milk the goat. Your brother needs milk. And find some fruit. I'll bake some bread."

Because of Jesus' weak condition, James obeys his mother's orders without question, and rushes off outside to presumably milk the awaiting goat. Mary takes a deep breath to stabilize her emotions, and then goes into another part of the house.

With all the humdrum noises going on around him, Jesus lies quite still. Whispering to himself, he looks up toward the roof of the house. His eyes fill with burning tears of relief and gratitude.

"God will provide, Mother. God will provide."

Three days have passed. Jesus is sitting outside on a crude wooden bench by the wall in the shade of the house. It is early afternoon and the sun is high. Everywhere is quiet in Nazareth. A short distance away, he can see a dog panting trying to keep cool in a small area of shade. They look at each other. Jesus feels for the dog; it reminds him of his ordeal just a few days ago. In a compulsion, the dog decides to trot the distance between them and join Jesus. Seeing there is some fresh bread and goat cheese left over from breakfast, the dog looks up at Jesus as if to plead. Stroking the dog's head, Jesus offers the leftovers to his new friend, who devours it as if it is his last meal.

Sympathizing with the dog, but still very tired, Jesus rests against the wall. His mind going over what he has to do next, he shuts his eyes and puts his imagination to work.

Tomorrow is the Sabbath. On many previous Sabbaths, I have read and quoted the Law of Moses to people in the synagogue. They have listened intently and nodded in agreement, but done nothing else. No questions, no discussion, nothing...

He opens his eyes and focuses on the temple roof, and mumbles under his breath.

"Tomorrow is going to be different. I'm going to wake them up to a new order. Help the people to find the true kingdom of God within themselves. For too long they have been going through the motions of the same rituals a thousand times without any spiritual advancement..."

Patting the dog as he rests his head on Jesus' lap, Jesus looks down at the grateful eyes.

"Helping the poor has been replaced by rampant greed. Hypocrisy and corruption has replaced sincerity. This, my friend, has got to stop."

Next morning, Jesus and his family are seated on the front row of the main hall in the synagogue. This is traditional for the person who is going to speak for that day. The rest of the congregation are gathered behind them. His stomach churning with apprehension, but tinged with determination, Jesus can hear some of the crowd gossiping about how he turned up just a few days ago delirious and emaciated. So, how can it be right and proper for him to address them today?

After all the preliminary customs and protocol, Jesus is summoned to talk. As he steps out onto the open floor, an attendant comes up to him and hands him an aged parchment scroll.

Everyone now quiet in anticipation, except for the occasional cough or throat clearing, Jesus pauses. While he is slow and careful in unrolling the delicate piece of history, he uses both hands in holding open the parchment. After a few seconds of deliberation, he scans his audience. Aware of all the eyes upon him, he hides his apprehension.

Something tells me this is not going to be an easy teaching session.

He focuses on the parchment and begins to read aloud.

"The full spirit of God is within 'me', because 'I' have been anointed to preach the good news. To ease the burden on the poor, to free the prisoners of persecution, recover the sight of the blind, and to release the oppressed..."

He takes a pause, and then is slow to re-roll the scroll, and hand it back to the awaiting attendant. While the attendant leaves to sit with the others, the atmosphere is a mixture of silent expectancy and curiosity. Sensing this, Jesus stands still, shuts his eyes, and raises his head toward the roof. Creating an aura of intrigue, he then opens his eyes, brings his head down and glares at his captive audience.

"Those are the words of the great prophet Isaiah. That scripture is 'now' going to be fulfilled by 'me'."

The silence in the hall is replaced by murmurings of shock and confusion.

Demonstrating his irritation, an elderly man is abrupt when standing at the rear of the group.

"I don't understand. Aren't you Jesus the son of Joseph, a mere carpenter?"

"Yes, I am.

"Then how come a mere carpenter without any formal teaching, claim that he has the same power of God as Isaiah?"

Jesus stares straight at the man hiding his feelings of disappointment at this reaction. His family is looking worried at this questioning, and at what is unfolding in front of them. Still hiding his dismay, Jesus answers.

"No prophet is accepted in their home town. Elijah and Elisha were not accepted in theirs, so they taught and healed in other places where they were greeted with respect and reverence."

Demonstrating his annoyance, another man stands. Jesus can tell by the splendor of his clothes that he is wealthy. Jesus eyes sadden at the man's accusations.

"You're 'definitely' not Elijah, Elisha or Isaiah! So, how dare you say you're the anointed one."

Agreeing with the wealthy man's denunciations, the rest of the crowd stand and shout criticisms and abuse at Jesus. Troubled by these circumstances, Jesus glances down at his family who are becoming apprehensive. Several men of different backgrounds and ages rush forward and grab Jesus by his clothes. Protecting their older brother, John and James, stand up and confront these men. As the whole situation becomes ugly, Mary stands and screams at the top of her voice so she can be heard above the din. Her voice is so angry with frustration at how they are treating her kind, caring son, she faces the crowd.

"You stand there and dictate to my son, saying that he thinks he is comparing himself to the old prophets? Who do you think 'you' are to treat him like this?"

As the hands let go. John and James stand in front of Jesus to protect him.

Concerned, an elder from the synagogue comes forward. His flowing robes give him that air of authority, as he raises his arms and faces the crowd.

"Please! This is the house of God"

He then turns to Jesus. Their eyes meet for a second, as he looks down as if embarrassed or even ashamed.

"Look. I think it would be better if you and your family move on. As you can see, you are not welcome here."

Angry at the elder, and to a certain extent, Jesus, Joseph rises from his seat.

"What is a matter with you all?"

His anger mounting, he begins to walk into the people, and pushing aside anyone who gets in his way of making a pathway for his family to exit. The environment is tense as Jesus' family leaves the building. While Jesus is last in line to leave, a hand grabs his shoulder. This sends a signal for others to do the same. A look of fear glides across Jesus' face as four men are now gripping onto him. Jesus' fear becomes unbearable as someone shouts.

"Blasphemer. Heretic!"

Someone else spits at him. The sputum now running down his left cheek, he doesn't resist as another voice shouts.

"To the hill. Up the hill!"

Others join in as they jostle Jesus out of the building up a narrow dusty road toward a nearby hill. His family looks on in horror and helplessness, as Jesus is being dragged up this hill causing him to lose his footing. They reach the hilltop that ends at a cliff with a sudden sheer drop below. The crowd, now hysterical with irrational fear, hold Jesus on the cliff edge. Jesus feels sick as the front of his sandals send dirt down hundreds of feet. More aggressive shouts come from the crowd.

"Throw him off! Let him die!"

While the rest of the crowd from the synagogue is now approaching, Jesus looks toward the sky and shouts.

"Forgive them! They are lost sheep, stumbling around in the dark without a shepherd."

His forgiveness being ignored, he digs deep inside and finds the strength to pull himself free from their grip. In doing so, his eyes blaze with a fury that has never been witnessed, while he turns to face them. For an instant, they become afraid and back away. Knowing now he has the advantage; Jesus points at them continuing his anger.

"Fools, idiots! One day your eyes will open and you'll see just how stupid and ignorant you really are..."

Not waiting for a reaction, he walks away toward his anxious awaiting family.

6

Healings

It is two days later. Jesus and his family have now moved to Capernaum, a town in Galilee. To survive, his brothers hire themselves out to do carpentry work, and general odd jobs, while Mary insists Jesus needs to recuperate more.

The day is Thursday, the day before the Jewish Sabbath. The time is evening; the whole family is sitting around a rough-hewn wooden table in the main room of a small rented house. The atmosphere is quiet and resigned.

Joseph breaks the bread for supper and passes it around the table. He breaks the silence by glaring at Jesus with angry condemnation.

"Why did you have to go back to Nazareth from the desert? The rest of us could still be there, in our own home, instead of this place?"

Hiding his irrational guilt, Jesus looks at his father, knowing deep down he is right. Sensing her son's turmoil, Mary cuts in.

"We are all together as a family, that's what counts."

Needing to keep the peace, she turns to Jesus, and places her hand on his forearm.

"Home is where the heart is. Remember?"

Agreeing with his mother and sticking up for his older brother, James gives his opinion.

"That's right Mother. If the people of Nazareth can treat us so badly after all the years we've lived and worked there, then they're not worth the effort of staying anymore."

Except for Joseph, a general feeling of consensus now fills the room. As Jesus takes some fruit from a carved wooden bowl in the center of the table, he needs to express his message to them.

"I'm going to teach in 'this' synagogue tomorrow. You're all welcome to come and be with me."

Mary, still resting her hand on his forearm puts on a brave face as she is still concerned at Jesus looking tired.

"We will always be with you. Your mission is what's most important."

Not happy with his wife's misguided loyalty, Joseph stands.

"Mission! Not that again?"

Suppressing his irritation, he goes over to the one outside door of the house, opens it, and lets in the evening light.

"I will be there tomorrow, but now I'm going for my evening walk."

He leaves and shuts the door, forgetting it was Jesus who cured his painful crippled back, now making it possible for him to go on these brisk walks to dispel his frustrations. Staring at the door, Jesus sighs, and offers his mother a resigned smile.

"I think I'll go to sleep early tonight. I'll need the strength for tomorrow."

Apprehensive at the dark shadows under his eyes, she returns the smile.

"I understand."

She always seems to understand, but hidden away is deep anxiety.

It is mid-morning on the next day. Jesus, appearing a little less tired, is in this new synagogue. Some people are seated while others are standing. All are listening with intent and interest to Jesus preaching.

"Repent now and all your sins will be forgiven, because the kingdom of God is at hand..."

As his preaching becomes more passionate and intense, the crowd expands. The word seems to be out. These people are becoming more curious as Jesus teaches his profound message with a confidence and authority not seen before. One man's voice is not so convinced, as he is heard from the center of the gathering.

"Ha! What do you want with us Jesus of Nazareth?"

Meanwhile, a young man pushes his way forward toward the front of the crowd. His dark hair and beard appearing unkempt, and his clothes being dirty and tattered, his pale brown eyes exude a wild look.

"Have you come to destroy 'us' now? I heard what happened at Nazareth."

His mouth dribbling at the corners with saliva, he comes right up to Jesus.

Their height and build about the same, he grabs Jesus by the shoulders and begins to shake him.

"I know who you are..."

A loud concerned voice interrupts from the rear of the gathering.

"Be careful Rabbi. That man is possessed by demons."

Shocked by the statement, John and James stand to protect their brother. Keeping the situation calm, Jesus nods at his brothers in reassurance. In the meantime, the young man's mouth begins to foam and he spits as he goes to speak. Sensing the man's inner turbulence, Jesus grips the man's forearms and stares into his eyes. The shaking becomes weaker, as the young man's eyes roll upward, and his face convulses, spitting out these words.

"The Holy one of God..."

He wants to continue, but mumbling unintelligible sounds spew from his mouth. The shaking becomes more violent again. Feeling the man's pain, Jesus is desperate to hold on to the man's arms to give him the peace he needs. With his eyes closed, and talking soft, sweat begins pouring down Jesus' face. Timing his emotions, he opens his eyes, and bellows out.

"Quiet! Come out of him!"

As if an unseen power has overcome him, the young man stops shaking. His eyes return to normal, and then close. His head drops to one side, his body jerks, and then doubles up and vomits. While continually retching until dry, the crowd looks on in astonishment as the young man goes limp against Jesus. Still holding onto the young man, Jesus grips even tighter so he can embrace him. For a minute, they are as one. The crowd, now silent, stares in awe at what they have just witnessed. Feeling the young man's strength returning, Jesus eases away, but still holds him at arm's length. After a few seconds of quiet, the man opens his eyes. His face calm, but alert, he gazes at Jesus in a new light.

"What happened? I feel at peace. My dreadful torment has gone."

Fatigue showing on Jesus' pale face, he releases him, and then places one hand on the man's shoulder; to support him and also his own fragile body.

"You now belong to God – who loves you."

Not realizing the effort Jesus had to put into this 'miracle' the crowd becomes joyful. Through his daze, Jesus can hear them muttering.

"What are these teachings? What is this power and authority that can get rid of evil this easily?"

Knowing it is not easy, Jesus collapses on a nearby bench. The young man now revitalized is eager to join the excited gathering, regardless of how his 'healer' might be.

Concerned by how pale and tired her son appears, Mary joins Jesus, and wonders if the energy her son is applying is worth the effort.

7

The First Disciples

It is the following morning; the sun has been up for a couple of hours. Jesus' younger brothers have gone to work for a local landowner. Finishing his breakfast, Jesus is reflecting on the way he helped the troubled young man at the synagogue yesterday, and the way he was under appreciated.

Did I do it for him, or to show the onlookers the power of God through me...?

His mother appears and sits next to him. Just aware of her presence, he feels her hand being placed on his head, and her soft voice reverberating in his delicate mind.

"Anyone at home?"

He returns the gesture with an amiable smile. Still looking down at the tabletop, he reacts further.

"I'm sorry, I was contemplating the next move."

"Are we leaving here then?"

Deep in thought, he turns to face her. While her eyes peer into his, as if trying to read his complex mind, he senses the bond between them is unbreakable.

His face turns serious, as he answers her question.

"No! You stay here for now with the family, while I go."

Her eyes show concern.

"Where are you going?"

Even though their eyes are locked, he takes on a faraway look again.

Releasing a heavy sigh, he turns away to look back again to the table.

"Further into Galilee. I need help with my mission."

She now looks down at the table.

"I can help you."

Listening to the plea in her voice, he feels a strong pang of guilt.

"I know Mother. I know I can always count on you..."

He turns his body to face her, pauses and puts his arm around her shoulders.

"I need a group of men that I can teach everything I know and feel, so they can carry on after I'm..."

"After you've what?"

Not wanting to answer, he stands and moves over to the one window in the room. His mind churning, he peers outside. She can see the morning sun illuminating his face in contrast to the dim room. Studying his strong profile, firm jaw and determined look, she can sense he wants to tell her something important, but finds it hard. She decides to wait.

"When 'are' you leaving?"

"This morning. My bundle is ready."

Suppressing her tears, the ache inside her is too much to bear. She goes to him, wraps her arms around his waist and rests her head against his chest. In the stillness of the room, she can hear his heartbeat through his coarse woven smock. He can feel the dampness of her quiet tears penetrating onto his chest as he rests a tender hand on her head. Noticing and becoming worried by his frail state, she squeezes him a little tighter.

"How will you live?"

Reacting to her pain, he strokes her head.

"I have a few coins saved. I have given myself totally to God, who I know will provide for me."

Not so confident, she is reluctant to unwind her protective arms from him. As she withdraws and wipes her face, she then sits on a nearby bench. Him racked with an irrational fear mixed with resignation, he leaves the room without saying a word, and goes into another part of the house.

Minutes drag by for Mary who now wonders what her son is doing and why is he taking so long. Her patience depleted, she gets up from the bench and walks in a soft manner through the house. She stops when she discovers him standing in the boys sleeping area. He is in the middle of the floor with his small bundle at his feet. His hands are clasped together hanging full length in front of him, and his head bowed down with his chin almost touching his chest. She cannot see if his eyes are closed or not, but can hear him talking in soft tones. Becoming aware of her presence, he pauses, and then sniffs, wipes his tear-filled eyes, and bends down to retrieve his bundle. He glances at her as if needing some extra strength. Reacting to his visual plea, her insides burst with emotion. She sees her tender little son from way back seeking reassurance, and needs his mother's love to make everything better.

"Are you ready now?"

As they embrace again, he kisses her on the forehead.

"Yes! I'm ready. I love you mother. Tell father for me."

While more burning tears well up in her eyes; her voice cracks with heart rendering emotion as she answers him.

"I will. I love you my son. I love you..."

After releasing her, he strides toward the door as if in a hurry, and then he's gone.

Mary stares at the closed door and wipes her eyes.

"Please God, look after him."

Later that morning, Jesus is sitting on a boulder relishing a piece of bread taken from his small store wrapped in his bundle. It is a beautiful clear day on the shore of the Sea of Galilee. A light breeze blows across the surface of the clear blue water creating tiny ripples. He can see fishermen coming and going from shore to sea, and then back again, observing that they don't seem to be catching anything. Finishing his bread, he bends down to pick up his bundle when a sudden, but faint familiar voice speaks quite near to him.

"Now, let me see. I suppose you're going to try to collect your little band of Brothers?"

Remembering the desert, Jesus turns toward the voice, but finds he has the sun in his eyes. The black robed silhouette that is blocking his view, speaks again.

"Surely, 'you' being the Son of God, already have the power to do and take as you please. So, why on earth do you need a band of followers?"

Just making out the green eyes and dark curly hair, Jesus now knows this is the same man as in the desert. His insides turn over.

Why always this test? Why the constant temptation?

With this dilemma torturing his mind, Jesus defies this black hooded man.

"Why do you bother with me? You must know I'll never listen or give in to your dark ideals?"

In reaction, the black robe bellows out a hollow laugh.

"You say that now. You haven't even started your 'mission' yet. You wait until a few months have painfully dragged by. The waste of time and frustration of dealing with ignorant, stupid little people, and having to painfully accept the debilitating fatigue from having to do so many 'miracles' just to 'prove' yourself to these aimless masses. You might want to reconsider if it's worth all the pain and trouble."

Remembering how tired he became after helping the young man release his 'demons', Jesus finds it hard to turn away.

"I know what I have to do!"

"You think you know what you have to do, or is it your ego telling you all this, and not God. Did you ever think of that? Of course not, you have this blind belief and vanity in yourself that God will forever be there for you. Is it also your vanity telling you that you need people around you to 'teach' your new way? Or, is it because you think when you die, your little band of followers can carry on your 'good works'? Admit it! You know they're not going to do that."

His insides now churning with a new doubt, Jesus hesitates for a second. *Could he be right?*

His body now beginning to tremble with uncertainty, he looks upward. *Oh God! Don't let me be tempted like this?*

As if coming out of nowhere, a new strength rises up within him. With growing confidence, Jesus lifts his right hand straight out in front and points with his index finger at the menacing green eyes.

"Go! You will 'never' win. Do you know why? Because I'm right and you're wrong."

The man in black's reaction is to laugh again. Still peering at Jesus, he continues his rhetoric.

"You go and collect your group of 'disciples' and teach them your way, your new order. I guarantee you will be let down and disappointed time and time again. Remember though, all is not lost. My original offer still stands."

Not listening, Jesus focuses his mind on the clear blue water. Now there is silence, Jesus hesitates. While he is cautious at turning around, he finds there is nobody. Becoming obsessed, he searches the immediate area, and then scans the horizon - nothing.

"Was that really Satan again, or worse still, is it all in my head?"

The new strength still flowing inside him, and with extra determination, he picks up his bundle and heads down toward the beach on the way to the fishing boats.

As he arrives at the beach, there are two deserted moored fishing boats. Jesus becomes curious as he looks around for the owners, and sees nobody. He does hear a soft, but gruff man's voice. His interest stirring, Jesus turns to the direction of the sound. Not far away, hiding behind one of the boats, two men are repairing their spread-out nets. Jesus studies the man that is talking. Being of medium height and thickset, his heavy arms and hands are struggling to repair a large hole right in the center of his net. His impatient character curses and swears at the frustration of being poor and not being able to afford a new, stronger net.

"Oh! This is hopeless Andrew. It looks like we'll have to share your good new net until we can catch a larger amount of fish. Then if we're lucky, I can afford to buy a new one of my own."

Andrew being the taller, more slender and lighter haired of the two men, his kind blue-gray eyes look on at his brother with an affection found from a long loyal relationship.

"That's fine Simon. You have the better boat - I have the better net, so, as always we make a good team."

Ignoring his brother's optimism, Simon sighs, throws down his tattered netting, and runs his hand through his thick black hair. His dark eyes crinkle at the corners as he smiles back to his younger brother.

"You're a good man Andrew…"

They become startled by a tall slender man dressed in an ivory course smock approach.

"Then why don't you go out to the deep water and put down your good net?"

Not taking in what this stranger is asking, the brothers glance up toward this new voice. Simon is the first to respond.

"Well sir, with all due respect, we have done just that, and as you can see, we have caught - nothing."

Ignoring Simon's irritation, Jesus steps closer. Sensing Andrew is the more rational of the two brothers, Jesus concentrates on him.

"Try again. Just once."

Unable to ignore this man's intense hazel eyes, Andrew speaks to his brother, but still keeps looking at Jesus.

"Let's give it one last try Simon."

Becoming impatient with his younger brother, Simon stands to his full height. His strong barrel chest becomes exposed by his open shirt.

"My dear brother! Don't you remember we have worked all night? I'm tired, and haven't the strength to go way out to the deep water again."

Conscious of Jesus now focusing on him, Simon has no choice but to lock eyes with this intriguing stranger. Becoming aware of Jesus' strong personality, Simon shrugs, looks at his brother's pleading expression, and changes his mind.

"All right sir. Because you have such faith that there is fish out there, I'll try. Right! Andrew my boat, your net."

Determined to prove his theory, Jesus steps into Simon's boat, while

Simon and Andrew collect the good net and tie it in position ready to drop when needed.

They are now far out into the deep water. The brothers experienced eyes scan the whole area for any sign of life to catch. His frustration being hard to suppress, Simon turns to Jesus.

"Sir! As you can see, there is no sign of any fish."

To relieve Simon of his exasperation, Jesus lets out a hint of excitement by extending out his right arm and pointing.

"There! Over there."

Not believing this man's intuition, Simon sighs as he adjusts the boat's rudder making the boat steer to port. They sail for another ten minutes to where Jesus has indicated. The brother's glance at each other, shrug and lean on the net expressing skepticism. To convince these brothers, Jesus' excitement becomes more profound.

"Here! Stop here. This is it!"

Simon mumbles with continual pessimism, while he and Andrew drop the net over the starboard side.

Not expecting any stroke of fortune, the boat gives a sudden jerk, and then leans heavy to starboard. All three men look at each other; they know what's happening. All three now struggle to pull the bulging, overflowing net onto the deck. Almost capsizing the boat in the meantime, Simon shouts with excitement as they pour the fish into the open hold. When the net hangs limp and empty, all three men stare with amazement into the hold opening. They gaze at each other as if this is all a dream. Taking all this serious, Simon shouts across to Andrew who is standing next to Jesus.

"Isn't this wonderful? At last no poverty, and I can now buy a new net."

Meanwhile, Andrew studies Jesus' face, which has now turned serious. Still caught up in his own euphoria, Simon shouts to Jesus oblivious of his expression.

"Sir! You have a great gift. Please stay with us and make us our fortune."

Jesus puts on a smile for Simon, but his eyes are serious.

"Simon? I can make your life far richer than this."

Simon's eyes widen even more.

"Richer than this? How?"

"I will make you fishers of men. Lay down your nets and come with me."

Simon looks astonished at such a statement.

"Follow you? To where and for what reason? Explain what you mean by fishers of men. Is it as profitable as catching fish like this?"

Jesus response to Simon's obvious question, is to offer a bemusing smile.

"All will become clear on our journey. Trust me".

Even though affected by the huge catch of fish, Andrew is drawn to something deeper in Jesus.

"It's all right Simon. This man knows what he's doing. I feel in my heart that our path is now with Jesus."

Simon is troubled by his brother giving in to this stranger.

"I don't know. I'm not so sure. I can't just give up my livelihood. Not now. What about all this fish?"

Expecting Simon's hesitation, Jesus answers.

"Give it to the poor and hungry. Look!"

As he points toward the now approaching shoreline. A large crowd of expectant people are gathering on the beach.

"Don't be afraid Simon. From now on you will catch only men."

To confirm the fact, and reassure, Jesus places his hand on Simon's shoulder, while Andrew is already preparing to beach.

The boat now securely moored; the growing crowd becomes excited at the free fish being offered. Curious by what is happening, two more fishermen join in the giveaway. To ease their puzzlement, Andrew explains to them the skills of Jesus, and that he and his brother are going to join him to become 'fishers of men.' Observing, the other two men, Jesus approaches the four fishermen. Finding it hide to suppress this new excitement, Andrew introduces the two men as James and John, sons of Zebadee. Making sure these other men are what he needs, Jesus looks into their eyes. After a second, he knows.

"Come. Follow me also, and you will all be that much richer."

The two new brothers look at each other in doubt, and then peer at Jesus, who in turn offers them a reassuring smile. Becoming caught up in this subterfuge, the two pairs of brothers, are drawn by Jesus' sincerity. Andrew, who is more convinced than the other three, places a hand on each of James and John's shoulders, while watching Simon begin to follow Jesus walking toward the town.

"I believe we have found the Messiah."

8

Choosing the Twelve

Several weeks have gone by. The four disciples are following Jesus as he demonstrates the power of his healing and teaching. By demonstrating what is 'expected' of them, the four men are having difficulty in under-standing – 'fishers of men.'

One quiet afternoon on the outskirts of Galilee, the five of them are resting under a large tree by the roadside. Jesus is teaching them an example of a 'parable' by using simple stories to get his message across.

"Everyone who hears me and puts my words into practice is like a wise builder constructing his house on a rock foundation, so when the rains come and the winds blow hard beating against this house, it will not fall or be damaged.

For those who listen to me and give lip service to what I say, is like a builder constructing his house on a sandy foundation. So, when it rains and the winds beat hard against this house, it collapses into a worthless heap of building materials - no use to anyone."

The four men are listening with intent. After a few minutes of reflection, Simon thinks he understands the story.

"By what you're saying sir is that we are the houses, and if we stand steadfast against those who disagree with us we won't collapse."

Hiding his disappointment, Jesus smiles and places his hand on Simon's shoulder with an affection of a brother. Needing to answer and explain, his heart goes out to this good, but impetuous man.

"Simon? You're half right..."

He glances around at the other three, while keeping his hand on a puzzled Simon.

Being the wiser brother, Andrew responds.

"Does it mean, if we really believe in your words and practice them when anyone who beats, accuses and claims hypocrisy against us, we won't falter? Because your words are our rock foundation?"

A warm smile of satisfaction spreads across Jesus' face in response. His eyes water with relief at Andrew's understanding.

"Correct, Andrew. My 'words' are the foundation. No evil will 'ever' deter them or us."

Even though his younger brother shows more wisdom than he, Simon shakes Andrews hand. Even though Jesus is expressing a mood of achievement, he is hiding his doubts at the slow progress.

While they all rest back and ponder over Jesus' words, they hear the sounds of hurrying footsteps coming toward them. As four men approach carrying a rough made stretcher, they stop in front of Jesus, and with care place the stretcher at his feet. A coarse woven blanket covers a sick looking young man in his early twenties. One of the four stretcher-bearers, a tall burly man of middle age and poor background, kneels down in front of Jesus, his eyes pleading.

"Rabbi, I have heard such great things of you. Please can you help my young brother? He can't walk for he's crippled. We've tried many times to see you, but you're always so busy."

Apprehensive by this new challenge, Jesus stands. In the meantime, the four fishermen look on sensing their master's anxiety. Because this is the first time since being with him that a situation like this has arisen, they witness their master acting confident, when Jesus places his hand on the burly man's shoulder.

"I am truly touched by your faith."

Out of the corner of his eye, Jesus notices a group of six curious Pharisees walking toward them. Thinking this may be a trick to test him, Jesus ignores these men of authority and concentrates on the young man lying at his feet. As if in defiance, he raises his voice so everyone can hear.

"Son? Your sins are forgiven."

The Pharisees coming closer, and overhearing Jesus' prophetic words, one of them appears to be their leader and steps forward. His eyes full of anger, he points his right index finger at Jesus with the intention of expediting his 'authority.'

"You are blaspheming! Who gives you the right to talk like that? 'God' is the only one who can forgive sins."

Feeling contempt at this insufferable little man, Jesus glares at him. Demonstrating his indignation, but hiding his fear, Jesus is reassured as his disciple's rally round behind him showing their loyalty and support. Knowing the four stretcher-bearers appear apprehensive by this tense situation, Jesus again takes the lead by taking a step closer to his accuser.

"Why are you saying such things? Which is easier to say to this poor boy, 'Your sins are forgiven?' or 'Get up and walk!' That is what you're afraid of? You 'know' I have the authority on Earth to forgive 'all' sins."

Ignoring the angry expressions of his accusers, Jesus crouches down to the crippled boy, places his right hand on the boy's forehead and his left hand on his lifeless legs. Jesus then closes his eyes and concentrates. Beginning to murmur under his breath, everyone, even the cynical Pharisees have no choice but to stay silent and focus on what is happening. Sweat now pouring off Jesus, he turns away from the boy and collapses onto the ground. While everyone gasps, and appears puzzled, Simon rushes to him, crouches, and then cradles Jesus in his arms. Meanwhile, the boy sits up stretching out both his arms.

"Can somebody please help me up?"

Two amazed, but confused men from the four stretcher-bearers come forward and take the boy's arms as he attempts to stand.

"Now let me go."

They do. Even though the lad is unsteady on his feet, he manages to put one foot in front of the other. After a few seconds, he begins walking. Unstable at first, but as each step progresses, so does his stride. He then turns back toward Jesus who is now in a sitting position supported by Simon. Grateful, the boy holds out his hand.

"Thank you for my life."

Glad to see his effort was worth it, Jesus takes the lad's hand and clasps it.

"Remember, God loves you."

The Pharisees, still standing silent, peer at each other as if searching for answers to this unbelievable circumstance. The older, and less aggressive one of the group approaches Jesus, who is now standing with the assistance of Simon. The Pharisee smiles with respect and holds out his hand. Sensing this man is sincere, Jesus takes the firm, dry hand. While he focuses on the man's kind brown-gray eyes, he notices the Pharisee does not look away while talking. Demonstrating a sure sign of sincerity and honesty, he wants to hear more from Jesus, as he makes a formal introduction.

"My name is Nickodemis. I would like to thank you for healing that poor boy and for letting us witness."

Becoming humble, he releases Jesus' hand, gives a slight bow and returns to the others of his group. Meanwhile, Simon expresses his contempt by spitting on the ground.

"Those hypocrites! Be careful sir, they're not your friends."

Jesus' energy now returning, turns and studies Simon's dark, troubled eyes.

"Simon, I appreciate your concern. Be assured, I recognize my enemies. And thank you for your support when I needed it most."

Simon displays his modesty by bowing his head in appreciation. He then looks back up to Jesus, noticing the previous anxiety has gone.

"Are you feeling stronger now sir? You seemed worried just before you laid hands on the lad."

Smiling to hide his weariness, and not giving away his fear that he could have failed the young man, Jesus rests his hand on Simon's shoulder. Still a little troubled, Simon continues to question.

"I've also noticed that every time you - err, help someone, you become very tired."

Still holding onto Simon's shoulder, Jesus slides his arm around Simon's shoulder giving him a slight hug.

"Everything has its price my friend."

Overwhelmed by it all, the stretcher-bearers leave with the healed excited boy.

Without giving any instruction, Jesus begins to walk in the direction of the town of Capernaum. Looking at their leader with wondrous respect, Simon, Andrew, John and James follow close behind.

Approximately an hour later, they all arrive at the town. Upon entering, Jesus, a few paces ahead, stops, and then leans against a nearby wall. Simon, still concerned by his master's weariness, glances at his brother, leaves the three men and goes up to Jesus.

"Are you all right sir? Can I help?"

Appreciating Simon's concern and offer of help, Jesus repays him with a warm smile.

"I'm fine. Just thirsty."

"I'll take you to the town well. The water is nice and cool."

Taking the lead in organizing assistance, Simon beckons to the others for help.

Now able to walk, but assisted, Jesus shows his gratitude at being supported each side by Simon and Andrew. Journeying further into town and arriving at the well, Andrew and Simon ease Jesus down onto the surrounding stone step. Still taking the lead, Simon wastes no time in drawing the much-needed water.

After everyone has drunk, and their thirst quenched, the four fishermen gather into a small group and begin chatting and sitting relaxed against the well. Not minding being left alone, Jesus is drawn to a tax collector's booth situated across the town square. His interest stirs as he observes an elderly man giving the tax collector some money. Feeling a touch guilty at leaving his new master, Andrew notices Jesus' gaze.

"That is my friend Matthew. He is one of the town's tax collectors."

Without acknowledging, Jesus stands and begins walking towards the booth. Curious at more strange behavior, Andrew decides to follow.

After thanking the gentleman for his tax payment, Matthew looks up to see a tall slim man arrive at his booth. Jesus offers him his hand.

"Why don't you give instead of just taking?"

Surprised by such a question, the collector's deep brown eyes connect to Jesus.

"This happens to be my profession".

Andrew stands nearby as Jesus reaches out and places his right hand on the collector's shoulder. Before Jesus has time to say what is needed, Andrew thinks it is time for an introduction.

"Master? This is Matthew."

For some irrational reason, Matthew cannot take his eyes away from Jesus. Keeping up the momentum with his hand still on Matthew's shoulder, Jesus turns toward his four other companions, and comes to the point.

"These four men have joined me in my mission. I would like you to join me also."

Even though mesmerized by this stranger, Matthew stares at his four friends for some sort of validation.

"Mission for what? How am I supposed to live?"

Still with his hand on Matthews shoulder, Jesus is gentle in maneuvering him out of the booth.

"The mission is to live by the power of God, who will provide!"

Becoming nervousness by this new challenge, and observing the eager nods of the others, Matthew closes his booth. In joining the others, he wonders if this is his last time at him being a tax collector. Lost at what to do next; he offers the men a proposal.

"As I'm venturing into the unknown, I can at least invite you all to dine at my house. I am having some friends and fellow tax collectors coming to dinner this evening."

Still apprehensive, he indicates for Jesus and his disciples to follow him.

An hour later, they are all being served generous helpings of choice quality meats, vegetables and fruit, all being washed down with large goblets of fine wine.

Over a period of time, Matthew's fellow tax collectors and friends gradually arrive to join them in the feast. Soon the vibrant festivities increase and overflow into the streets. The news soon spreads to the pharisees that Jesus, this new 'Prophet' is gaining a reputation. The Pharisees, still curious about this man, are becoming concerned that Jesus is dining with 'sinners' and decide to investigate.

Three Pharisees make their way to Matthew's house, to witness the mirthful festivities. Appalled by what they're witnessing, the leader for the three approach Simon.

"Why does your teacher eat and enjoy the company of tax collectors, and 'sinners'?"

Suspicious of the Pharisee's intent, Simon signals to Jesus. Noticing the familiar black robes, Jesus acknowledges with a smile, and wanders over to them. Continuing his easy fasard, Jesus slides his arm around Simon's shoulder. Irritated by such conduct, the Pharisee leader repeats his question. In reply Jesus' face turns from jovial to serious.

"So, you're wondering why I dine with tax collectors and 'sinners'? It's not the healthy who needs a Physician, but the sick. So, you go and learn what this means. I don't expect sacrifice, because I haven't come to call the righteous, but the sinners."

Enough said, he turns his back on them. Ignoring the frustrated men in black as the storm out of this 'Den of iniquity', Simon and Jesus return to the other guests.

During their walk away from these 'sinners', the Pharisees decide that from now on, they will keep an eye on this 'Jesus' and his few disciples. As they're now seeing him as a threat to their position in society, something has to be done.

The next day, still in the town of Capernaum at Matthew's house, Jesus and the now five disciples are seated on the floor in the center of the house.

Wanting to learn more, Andrew asks a poignant question.

"How is it that John the Baptist's disciples and the Pharisees all fast, but we don't?"

Jesus looks down at the handmade rug, then looks up and faces each one of his followers in turn.

"Fasting as you know is to cleanse the body, and hopefully the soul. So, let me put it this way, how can the guests of the bridegroom fast while they're with him celebrating? They can't. I'll put it another way; no one pours new wine into old wineskins. If they do, the new wine will burst the skins, so both wineskins and wine end up useless. No! You pour new wine into new wineskins. You here are the new wineskins, clean and unpolluted. I, by my teaching, is the new wine being poured into you. So, there is no need to fast..."

There is a loud knocking on the front door of Matthew's house. All heads turn as Matthew goes to answer the door. Standing there in the open doorway is a young man with curly brown hair and gray eyes. He glances at Matthew, but tries to look over his shoulder past him.

"Is he here?"

"Who?"

"The one Moses has written about. The prophet. Jesus of Nazareth – the son of Joseph?"

Hearing the questions, Jesus makes a point of standing up from the table.

"That's me."

Without any hesitation, the young man rushes past a bemused Matthew, and stops in front of Jesus. Staring into Jesus' eyes, he then crouches down in front of him.

"My name is Phillip. I have heard so much..."

"Stand Phillip. Let me look at you."

As the young man stands and faces his new mentor, Jesus' eyes search Phillip's face, as he lays on hand on his shoulder.

"Follow me."

Phillip's reaction is to crouch down again. This time, he takes hold of

Jesus' left hand, and places it against his own cheek.

"Oh, Rabbi! Thank you. I also have a friend waiting outside with all the other

admirers who wants to join you."

Infected by the young man's enthusiasm, Jesus smiles.

"Show him in."

Eager to be more involved, Phillip wastes no time in stepping toward the door. Leaning forward outside, he beckons to the crowd to someone out of sight. A few seconds later, a short, stocky, older man enters the doorway. As if entranced, his pale brown eyes stare at Jesus.

"Oh! Sir. You 'are' the son of God. The King of Israel!"

Becoming mesmerized, he comes forward and crouches in front of Jesus. Finding all this adulation a little embarrassing, Jesus pats him on the shoulder.

"Stand my friend. We are all equal here."

A little puzzled by the casual attitude, the man stands and faces Jesus.

"My name is Nathaniel from Bethsaida...."

Before he can finish, Simon interrupts.

"So are we. Welcome!"

Raising one eyebrow in irritation at Simon's impulsiveness, Jesus indicates for him to be silent. Biting his lip, Simon realizes his mistake.

"I'm sorry sir, you see...."

Jesus still indicates for him to remain silent.

"I understand. Now, after you have introduced Nathaniel to the others, I need to talk to you."

Releasing a gentle smile letting Simon know he is not really angry; Simon soon involves Phillip and Nathaniel into a deep conversation with the others. Knowing his master's need to talk, Simon does not waste any time in approaching Jesus.

"You needed to talk sir?"

"Simon, I must go into the hills tonight to rest and pray. I'll spend the whole night there. As you know we now have a lot of followers, so, I need the peace and quiet to decide on my final twelve apostles to help me for what's to come."

"I think I understand sir. Do you want us all to be on the beach tomorrow morning?"

"Yes. You need to let all the disciples know. I know this is asking a great deal of you."

"Don't worry sir. I will have everyone waiting for you by early tomorrow morning. You must have your rest."

Thankful for Simon's loyalty, the two men embrace.

"God loves you Simon. Oh, tell Nathaniel he's more than welcome."

As they separate, Simon is concerned by his master's frailty, as Jesus bends down, picks up his bundle, and departs. His eyes filling with thoughtful tears, he watches with a heavy heart, as his mentor exits the house. The others stop talking as they notice Jesus leave without a word being spoken. Matthew being of high intellect and strength of character, speaks out.

"Is everything all right, Simon?"

His instincts telling him otherwise, Simon puts on a smile.

"Yes. Fine. He's going to rest and pray. He also wants us to arrange to have all the disciples at the beach tomorrow morning."

Simon turns to Nathaniel.

"Nathaniel? He told me to tell you, you're more than welcome."

Jesus is now in the foothills east of Galilee. He has found a sheltered inlet to rest. It is getting dark and the full moon is rising. His energy dissipating, he leans back against a wall of rock. His aching body now screaming out for rest after the stress and responsibility of looking after so many disciples, he must choose the remainder of his apostles to make up the twelve he needs for this mission. His eyes becoming heavy with the need for sleep, he clasps his hands in an attempt to focus his mind.

"God? Give me the strength and guidance to...."

"Do you really think that will help?"

Jesus' body tingles with shock as the eerie familiar voice continues to echo throughout the immediate area.

"So, here we are with the final choice for your little band of brothers. I must admit your following is much larger than I was anticipating. But you wait and see, they will turn on you, or run like rabbits at the first sign of fear or persecution against them."

Even though exhausted, Jesus' anger gives him enough energy to turn toward this voice. Making out the familiar dark cloaked shape of Satan, his voice cracks with effort.

"Go away! There's no room for you here..."

Satan cuts in by letting out his usual hollow laugh. After a brief pause, he then speaks again.

"You still don't see it! You are the one that is going to lose, not me. I am still offering you the whole world - although with one 'small' condition."

Bursting with irritation and the newfound strength, Jesus stands. Glaring at the dark shape leaning with a casual air against the rock face, Jesus shouts in rage.

"You listen to me! In time I will eliminate you, and your kind, when my mission is complete..."

The anger in him is so intense that he lurches forward toward the black shape. Landing hard against the rock face, he stands back in a daze to find his own shadow against the wall reflected by the full moon. In desperation and becoming confused, he crouches down.

Was it my shadow all the time, or was Satan really here?

What little energy remaining, he collapses onto the ground. Lying on his side, a feeling of hopelessness overwhelms him. Again, he clasps his hands together.

"Oh, God! Talk to me! Give me the strength and wisdom I need in the task of choosing my Apostles. And most of all help me not be detoured by temptation."

Not feeling any better, he rolls onto his back feeling the coarseness of his threadbare blanket. Staring up to the clear sky, and focusing on the moon, his mind tries to concentrate in choosing the rest of his twelve Apostles. After a few seconds, he drifts into a restless sleep...

A long, single endless line of disciples is standing erect like solders. Standing at the beginning of the line, he takes two steps forward and turns to face the line of expectant faces. All eyes are focused on him as he begins to stroll to studying each face as he goes. Some seem to glow with a pale blue aura, while others are out of focus. The line seems endless as fatigue begins to overcome him. He stops, because cool water is flowing over his feet. The sea air feels refreshing against his face. He turns to find the line has gone. Six disciples remain. Their faces joyful and still surrounded by the blue aura. With their arms outstretched they walk towards him...

Jesus awakes with a start. He sits up.

I can still see the six faces from my dream. The remaining six Apostles?

Encouraged by a new feeling of certainty and confidence, he looks up at the moon.

"Thank you."

As if a burden has been lifted, he lies back down and falls into a deep dreamless sleep.

Next morning on the beach, which edges the Sea of Galilee near Capernaum, are well over a hundred waiting disciples. Some are sitting on or leaning against boulders, many standing around in small groups, while the remainder sit alone or in pairs on the ground.

As Jesus arrives, and goes straight to Simon who is with the already chosen apostles, his face is bright and clear after his lifesaving sleep.

"Good morning everyone, I see everyone is here."

Expressing his appreciation, he slides his arm around Simon's shoulder.

"Thank you, my friend, for arranging this."

Not waiting for a reaction, Jesus turns to the expectant crowd. While all the faces will their master to choose them for the honor of being his personal apostle, Jesus beckons to Simon, Andrew, James, John, Phillip and Matthew to stand behind him. After this is done, he then calls out to the remainder.

"For the past several months you have chosen to follow me and witness my mission and teachings. For this I am honored and eternally grateful. The more of you there are, the easier it will be to spread the good news."

Murmurs of agreement fill the air, as Jesus continues.

"As you know, to forfeit my mission, I need to choose twelve personal apostles to accompany me at all times. These twelve will go out into the world and lead the rest of you to teach and expand the Kingdom of God..."

He looks down, ponders, and then faces the expectant crowd.

"After a great deal of prayer and deliberation, I have chosen my final twelve. Six you already know, including Simon who from now on you will know as Peter, after the Greek word 'rock'. For he will be my cornerstone to build our new order - The Kingdom of God."

Simon now called Peter; smiles with tear filled eyes of gratitude. Jesus continues.

"Now I will call out the remaining six I've chosen. Then please come and stand here with your brothers."

He pauses while trembling with excitement, but feels empathy for the remaining disciples not chosen. Now focusing on his final choice, he calls out.

"Thomas, Bartholomew, James son of Alphaeus, Simon the Zealot, Judas son of James, and finally, Judas Iscariot. Will you please stand with your brothers?"

He pauses while the chosen few come out from different points of the crowd to join the other apostles standing behind Jesus.

Now everyone is in position, the remaining disciples watch Jesus as he turns to face them, wondering what is about to happen next. Sensing their disappointment,

Jesus speaks to them.

"For those of you not chosen; I love and cherish your loyalty. So, go now and tell your families, friends, anyone you meet, and tell them to come back here with you tomorrow. Because then I will explain the power and the good news of the Kingdom of God."

Feeling a sense of relief that this stage of the mission is now complete, and his trembling has ceased, he watches the crowd recede. After a couple of minutes of quiet, he looks skyward and whispers.

"Thank you."

With everything going according to plan, he now turns to his twelve apostles.

"Come and sit around me. I want to begin by giving you all the good news. Then

Later, you'll be able to spread it yourselves."

The twelve become apprehensive at the 'later' statement, sit in a semicircle in front of and facing Jesus. As Jesus sits and faces them, there is an atmosphere of tension and expectancy. Being the more educated apostle, Judas Iscariot is the first to speak. This does not surprise Jesus for he knows that Judas possesses the intellect to absorb and analyze his words, and therefore can explain to the others.

"Rabbi? I am curious about your last statement. Are we not to be with you always?"

Aware of the criticism, Jesus doesn't answer straight away. Instead, he turns to one side, and with his right index finger draws in the sand, and then looks into Judas' gray-green eyes.

"I will be with you forever, but you'll not be with me. There is a certain amount of time available for me to teach you everything. How long, I'm not sure, but not forever. It's all part of the mission."

The twelve sit in silence while trying to absorb and understand the profound meaning of Jesus' words.

9

Lessons for the Apostles

Minutes later, Jesus alters his sitting position. Turning again to one side away from them, he places his right index finger in the sand and begins to draw. As he concentrates on his hand, he begins to talk in earnest.

"The full commitment from you to me starts right now. From this moment on, I am going to teach you the secret to acquire the Kingdom of God."

In the meantime, Judas Iscariot is straining his neck to see the result of the drawing, but to no avail. Jesus then turns back to face them, sits upright with his hands resting on his knees.

"For those of you that are poor in spirit, you 'will' receive the Kingdom of God.

For those of you that mourn, you 'will' be comforted.

For those of you that are meek, you 'shall' inherit the Earth.

For those of you that hunger and thirst for righteousness, they will be filled.

For those of you, who are merciful, 'shall' receive mercy.

For those of you that are pure in heart, you shall 'see' God.

Bless those of you who are peacemakers, for you will become the sons of God.

For those of you who will be persecuted because of your righteousness, yours is the Kingdom of God."

He pauses, and then turns away to draw in the sand again. The twelve are spellbound, but worried by what they've just heard. Jesus stops drawing, looks up, and then peers at some individuals, sensing their doubts. Taking a deep breath, he continues to teach.

"The main thing that you being my apostles, you will be insulted, persecuted, and falsely told all kinds of evil against you. Because of me, you have to be strong, because your greatest reward will be receiving the Kingdom of God. You're the salt of the Earth, but if you lose your saltiness you will be of no use to me, yourself or anyone else. You're now the light of the world. So, don't burn your light undercover, let it be seen by others and spread goodness everywhere as in the Kingdom of God."

Noticing the glazed look in most of their eyes, Jesus begins to worry. Having no choice but to carry on, he continues.

"Don't do your good deeds or 'acts of righteousness' before the public, so obviously seen. When you give to the poor and needy, do it quietly, not by announcing it with trumpets as the hypocrites do in the synagogues. God will see you care for others, and you will be rewarded. The most important thing to remember, is when you pray, don't pray like the hypocrites who like to be seen to pray aloud in large synagogues and on the streets, in full view of the crowds.

"So, when 'you' pray, go to a private place and pray quietly from the very depth of your soul, not babbling just from your mind. Pray for strength and courage to carry out the word of God, and you will receive it..."

Still concerned by their blank expressions, Jesus swallows hard and continues.

"Pray for the well-being of others, and it will be carried out. God knows what you need, even before you ask.

"When you're in your greatest need, the most significant prayer is as follows:

Our god in heaven, hallowed is your name.
Your kingdom come, yours will be done on Earth as in heaven.
Give us today our daily bread.
Forgive us our trespasses, as we forgive those who trespass against us.

Lead us not into temptation, but deliver us from evil.
Forever. – Amen."

While absorbing Jesus' prophetic words, the apostles accompany him by murmuring 'Amen'.

Now silent, they all look at each other, wondering what next. Judas is more astute and is the first to comment.

"Rabbi, this is all wonderful and righteous, but very hard to do, as we are 'always' surrounded by continuous temptations."

Not rising to Judas' challenge, Jesus can feel the consensus of agreement from the others. Except Peter, who is abrupt when standing; shows his anger.

"Haven't you been listening at all? Our beloved teacher has just shown you the perfect way to live, and you come out with a stupid statement like that."

Realizing he is out of order, Peter sits struggling to quell his anger. Jesus becomes saddened by Judas' cynicism, and also by Peter's outburst. However, he continues.

"If you forgive those who sin against you, God will forgive you. If you bear a grudge or be vindictive, and not forgive others for 'their' sins, God will not forgive 'your' sins."

Peter nods in agreement, puts out his hand to Judas as if to apologize. Judas takes his hand, but his reaction is to smile, but not thinking he has to say sorry. Observing this behavior, Jesus admires Peter's actions and stands. Because he feels emotionally exhausted, Jesus glares at Judas, and then glances at the other apostles.

"We will meet back here tomorrow. It will be a demanding day. Now, I need to rest and pray."

After bending down to whisper a few words to Peter, he walks away toward the hills. In response, the twelve stand, bewildered, and have a tendency to congregate around Peter.

10

Teaching and Proving

Mary, Oh Mary

With a great feeling of relief, Jesus finds his enclave to rest. He collapses onto the ground, still holding his small bundle and water bag.

He lies still. A minute goes by as he gazes up at the early evening sky. Studying the shapes of two isolated dark clouds streaking across the deep red setting sun, his disturbed mind becomes erratic while going over the details of the day.

His body aching with draining fatigue, he drags his body to a sitting position, and takes hold of his familiar water bag. While putting the spout to his dry mouth, and relishes the cool water flowing down his parched throat, he stiffens at the sound of a sarcastic voice

"I bet that feels good after what you've been through today."

Knowing the voice, Jesus freezes. His insides turn over as he becomes cautious when lowering the water bag. A few paces away in the dim light, he can just make out the silhouette of a tall black hooded figure. The outline glides toward him and sits an arm's length away. The head turns toward Jesus, letting the setting sun reflect in the eyes, making them glow a shimmering red.

"Well, well. How are we? I see you have had to perform some really major 'miracles' lately, and 'still' your message is not getting through."

Too tired to fight, but still strong enough in his mind to resist, Jesus glares in silence, as Satan continues.

"Didn't I warn you it would be hard and frustrating? You see, the main trouble is that basically they're 'all' sinners. That's the one thing I know we agree on. Nevertheless, that's where any similarity stops. You want them to 'stop' sinning, while I want to 'encourage' them. You see, I make it too easy for them to give in to temptation, which unfortunately, leaves you with the impossible task of teaching them to resist."

The sun is almost gone. Satan's eyes have now turned to black holes in his pale face. Even though Jesus is exhausted, he rages at the arrogance of this complete evil sitting next to him. He raises his voice as if to drown out any weakness he feels.

"Your temptations are not just evil; they destroy a man's soul until he is unable to tell the difference between good and evil."

"That my friend is the whole object of the exercise."

His pale shadowed face distorts into a sardonic smile. His perfect formed teeth seem to glow in contrast to the immediate surroundings. Meanwhile, the rage in Jesus is sapping his remaining energy.

I must get rid of this evil before I disintegrate.

"I give a man's soul the strength he needs, because good will always be stronger than you. Evil is a bully; mean and selfish on the outside and 'weak' on the inside. So, the more temptation you offer, the more they need, and the more you cannot fill those needs, like a spiraling vortex into Hell. I offer a love that is clean, pure and endless, making man strong and courageous for . . ."

He leans back against the rock wall sweating and exhausted. Satan's voice reverberates.

"Like you feel now?"

Jesus is so weak; he is having a hard time in turning away. Placing his trembling hands up against his ears, at not wanting to hear anymore, he lowers his head, as Satan goes in for the final assault.

"Your 'love' is impossible for the normal person to achieve and hold on to. I will continually be there to get in the way. That's what I'm here for. I will 'always' win, because of their weakness and greed. Good will perpetually struggle like it did back in the Garden of Eden..."

He pauses to stare at the sun almost gone.

"As for you my friend, you haven't even started to struggle. Ha, Ha, Ha, Ha..."

The cold hollow laugh seems to bounce and echo off every nearby rock and boulder.

Now crouching, Jesus squeezes his head even harder to stop the evil sound penetrating his mind. Keeping in this position for a while, he opens his eyes. Noticing darkness has fallen, and everything is now quiet, Jesus senses the peace. Taking a chance by releasing the pressure from his aching head, he scans the immediate area.

No Satan? Nothing! As if the last horrifying moments never happened.

Still picturing the last painful minutes, doubt overwhelms him like a wet, cold blanket.

Was Satan really here?

Desperate for another drink, he grabs his water bag and gulps down several mouthfuls, almost heaving on its coolness. Thirst quenched, he sits, resting against the rock face; and looks skyward toward a starlit moonless night. His mouth trembles as tears of fear burn channels on his dusty face.

Is it true I am going to suffer a lot more?

With his mind in further turmoil, he rests his head in his cupped hands.

What am I thinking? Here I am worried what Satan says? He's always going to be there waiting for me to fail in my mission, but somehow, I will fight him with the help and the full power of the Holy Spirit.

With a renewed determination flooding through him, Jesus relaxes and unrolls his bedroll. Exposing a smaller bundle of food comprising of unleavened bread, goat cheese and dates, he eats just enough to conserve, and then drinks more water.

Satisfied somewhat, he lies his stiff body on his blanket bed, and stares up at the mass of stars, which shroud over him like a calm shroud. It is so quiet he can hear his own breathing. Being so tired, he cannot fall asleep. His nerves are tingling with exhaustion. Still looking up, his eyes again sting with tears, while his mind is fearful.

Oh God! I am so scared, vulnerable, and alone. Why is it so hard for people to understand such a simple message? Even my apostles are finding it hard. Satan, the messiah of evil is reveling in my struggle. Please give me the strength so I can complete my mission..."

His eyes become heavy; his body twitches with fatigue, as he falls into an uneasy sleep.

Her warm olive eyes seem to radiate deep into his soul. Her generous wide smile enraptures his whole being. Her thick long dark wavy hair falls in a sensuous fashion across his face causing his body to tingle in a way he has not experienced before. She pulls away, and laughs as if to tease, and then comes back by pressing her warm, voluptuous body against his....

He wakes up with a start. His heart pounding, his body soaked with sweat, even though the night is cool.

"Oh my God! What has Satan put into my head?"

Picturing the beautiful woman as if she is seared into his subconscious, he falls back into an exhausted troubled sleep.

He is falling into a vortex of fire entering a boiling pit. His mouth is so dry his swollen tongue fills his mouth.

Has Satan finally beaten me? Is this the road to Hell?

He awakens to a brilliant light accompanied by intense heat. He is finding it difficult to open his eyes. Gathering his thoughts and beginning to focus; he can feel the course woven blanket underneath him. Putting one hand up to his face, he tries to shade his eyes. The sun is beating down with no mercy.

It is past midday. I must have slept for over fourteen hours.

He struggles to sit up. His mouth is so dry, his tongue has stuck to the roof of his mouth. He begins to drink the warm, but refreshing water from his water bag.

Now refreshed, he concentrates his mind. He scans the local area for shade, but the clumps of boulders on sand offer nothing. He decides he must stand. His body stiff and painful, he struggles to grip hold of the nearest boulder to pull up to his full height. Now standing, he reaches for his water bag.

Well, what now? I have twelve days to find somewhere where I'm unknown and can rest, get strong again, and then rejoin Peter and the Apostles. I will go south to Samaria and find a quiet village, then return here.

With difficulty, he reaches for his blanket and the remainder of his little bundle to roll everything together. After tying everything, he places the bundle under his arm and begins to walk south.

Two days have now gone at walking through the dry rocky desert. Jesus' meager water and food supply has long diminished. He finds a sheltered spot to rest for a while. His parched mouth and gnawing stomach are sapping his remaining strength. He sits, leans back against a rock face, and reflects on his present situation. Looking around, it all reminds him of his first journey into the desert to fast for his first baptism.

Forty days and nights that I will never forget. How long ago was it now? It seems a lifetime away. I can still smell the bread Satan offered me. No devil's messiah today.

Feeling a little rested he stands, picks up his bundle and empties the last of the water bottle, and then continues walking south.

Four hours go by; it is late afternoon, and the sun is baking. Shading his eyes, Jesus stops on a small hill looking down to a shimmering valley. Through the heat haze, he can just make out a small village with the customary flat top sandstone houses interspersed with mature olive trees. Feeling somewhat hopeful, he staggers down the gravel hillside toward this welcoming sight. While struggling to keep his legs from buckling, he can picture the well in the village center. He can almost taste the water waiting for him.

He is here, leaning against the well. The last of his strength has now evaporated.

I must drink before I collapse...

The well is too deep. He is too weak to operate the bucket. In desperation, he falls down onto the hard ground. Leaning helpless against the rough sandstone wall of the well, he gazes at the stony ground.

Oh God. No more please. Not like this.

He drifts in and out of consciousness; light into blackness, then back to light. He can hear a soft woman's voice singing away in the distance, then a muffled splashing of water. He feels something cool and soft touching his burning forehead. This welcoming touch compels him to open his painful eyes a little to see a pair of curious olive eyes gazing back at him. Her voice seems faraway, as her soft even mouth form words.

"Are you all right sir?"

The stroking of her hand against his forehead, brings him into some kind of focus. His rasping throat struggles.

"Will you give me a drink?"

Her kind eyes turn from curiosity to challenge.

"You are a Jew. I am a Samaritan. Jews detest Samaritans."

Jesus hasn't the strength to argue and plead. His cracked lips cannot form the words he needs to say. Seeing him struggle, the warmth returns to her eyes. She then crouches closer putting one arm around his head for support. The next, he feels a cool wooden goblet pressing against his parched lips. Smelling the water, he manages to open his painful mouth just enough to allow the cool liquid to enter. Letting it roll down his flaming throat, she keeps giving him the water until he can't take anymore - for now. As she crouches even closer, the softness of her firm, heavy breasts support his head. Her natural scent wafting from her long, thick dark wavy hair enters his nostrils. As he focuses on her soft pale skin and warm mouth, it reminds him of something...

This is the woman in my dream. Is this another trick? Is SHE Satan?

Her soft welcoming hand is now resting on his chest. Strong, yet tender, she slides it up to his chin turning so he is facing her. The olive eyes now filling his view, her voice, a low, slight husky tone pulsates.

"Better?"

Afraid to be caught up in this apparition, Jesus nods. Grateful for her help and presence, and yet he fears it is still an illusion. Not so worried about him now, her gaze becomes stern.

"As a Jew, how can you ask 'me' for a drink?"

As the lifesaving water revives him, he is more able to sit up. She takes this as a hint that he is on the mend. She reacts by removing her hand from his forehead, but lets his head still rest against her breasts. Her warmth and softness now injecting strength beyond any expectation, something deep down inside of him assures him that this woman must be one of God's own creatures, not a trick from the devil.

"If you knew the gift of God, and who it is who asks you for a drink, you would ask him to give you living water."

Lost in her softness, he is unaware of her gaze turning to puzzlement.

"Sir, you have nothing to draw with, and this well is deep. Where can you get this 'living' water? Are you greater than our father Jacob who gave us this well and even drank from it himself, as did also his sons and his flocks and herds?"

Hoping this warm natured woman will understand, his face hurts as he tries to smile.

"Everyone who drinks from 'this' well will become thirsty again, but whoever drinks the water 'I' give will 'never' thirst. This water will be a spring welling up to eternal life."

His body becomes aware of a new sensation as she pulls him tighter against her.

Not wanting to let this intriguing man go, because the longer she holds onto him, the more she is aroused by his power of good. Wanting now to search his eyes for the truth he relates, she is reluctant for him to withdraw. As Jesus' eyes burn deep into her soul, her heartbeat increases, and her body aches for him.

How can this be? I have only just met him, but I know the bond between us is going to be for life.

Their eyes never losing contact, her mouth opens with a wide smile, exposing perfect white teeth in line with her handsome strong features, all expressing an emotion he has never experienced before. Her eyes soften more as she places her right hand at the base of his throat. Sending a shockwave throughout his body, he is overwhelmed by her natural scent as his eyes are drawn to her soft lips as she pleads.

"Please give me this water, so that I will never be thirsty again, and have to keep coming here to draw water."

Placing his hand against her cheek, their faces are inches apart. She shudders, relishing his touch, as his voice takes on a different tone.

"Go and tell your husband, and then both come back."

Her eyes harden in disappointment, as the ecstasy is withdrawn.

"I have no husband!"

Continuing to gaze into her eyes, he withdraws his hand.

"I know. Get the man you're living with now."

As irrational guilt overwhelms her, she begrudges pulling away to stand. In remorse she places her hands together tight against her breasts. Still facing him, tears flood her eyes.

"Yes, I have sinned. The man I'm living with is a brute. I've been beaten, raped, and abused in every way. I'm always the victim. It's my own fault. I have that effect on men. I love too much, so I get taken advantage of. All I want is to love and be loved. I have so much to give."

Perceiving every word, she is saying is true, his heart goes out to her. He wants to hold her in his arms.

This is my soulmate! She is going to be his closest confidant.

He indicates for her to sit down next to him. She does, but this time closer. As their bodies touch, he has an overwhelming need to embrace her. This new ache of yearning is now dictating his mood, and also giving him the strength, he needs for the future. He reaches up and strokes her cheek again. Her response is to take his hand in hers, smothers it in gentle kisses; each kiss adding to the mountain of desire to love her. Still gripping his hand, she places it against her breasts as if she never wants to let it go. Her expressive, but sad eyes gaze at him as if in a trance.

Is this a new dream? If so, I do not want to wake up.

"For a Jew to have this effect on me, I see you must be a prophet.

Our fathers worshiped on this mountain, but the Jews say we must only worship in Jerusalem."

Their eyes never break contact. Besides this deep yearning for her, a calm reassurance overcomes him that he can trust this woman.

She has the capacity to love and possesses the loyalty and strength that I need. She must leave the man she's living with and come with me.

"The trouble with you Samaritans, you worship what you don't know, and the Jews worship only what they do know. However, the time is coming when the true worshipers who fully worship God in spirit and in truth, are the only people God seeks."

Astounded by such passion and authority, the dreamlike gaze in her eyes turns quizzical.

"I know the Messiah is coming. When he arrives, he will explain everything to us."

Now content and somewhat revitalized, Jesus manages to stand. Without hesitation and still griping his hand, she stands with him. They now face each other with a small gap between them. Her perfume filling his lungs, he places his free hand on her shoulder, and then pulls her toward him.

"I talk to you - as him."

Her eyes widen in excitement.

This is beyond my wildest fulfillment. I am falling in love with the 'Messiah.'

Her instinct is to reach up and wrap both her arms around his neck. Pulling his head down so her lips brush against his. The kiss intensifies, then she withdraws to gaze deep into his astonished eyes.

"Oh, dear God, I have found you. Now I feel worthy of you. I want to give you all my love, my whole being..."

Witnessing her warm tears running down his face, he does not resist when she grips him even harder, and places her soft burning lips on his. On holding the kiss, she realizes her behavior and let's go. Withdrawing her arms, she then looks down to the ground.

"I'm sorry. I shouldn't have done that. Forgive me!"

Jesus doesn't care. He grips her upper arms and pulls her against him.

I want to be held and loved by her. This new experience is making me strong and whole, an advantage in facing my mission.

"Nothing to forgive. God loves you."

Her temporary shame dissipating, she lifts up her head, cups his face in her hands, and pulls down his face. Kissing him again on his mouth, she holds that position. While the earth stops and time stands still, her softness, smell, and passion flows through him like a torrent.

Needing to control this new passion, she is reluctant to pull away. The ecstasy never leaving their lips, she grips his hand and begins to walk away from the well.

"I know a house in the village where we can stay together. I will feed, take care of you, and love you forever."

Even though she has revived him, he is still exhausted. So, the thought of resting in her company for the foreseeable future, brings him relief, hope and comfort.

Ten days later, Jesus is now rested, loved and rejuvenated. Thanks to his new constant companion Mary Magdalene, he is standing in the prearranged place to meet his apostles.

It is a pleasant, cool sunny day. Sitting next to him Mary feels so natural being with the love of her life. After about an hour, Jesus' mother Mary, arrives, her face grave. Jesus' reaction is to stand, and wonder why the grief. On the verge of tears, his mother falls into his awaiting arms. Not explaining why, she is sobbing against his chest, the comfort of his hand stroking her hair calms her grief. After a short while, she pulls away a little to look up at him.

"Your father Joseph – died yesterday."

Guilt hits Jesus like a sledgehammer. Still holding his mother, he looks skywards, his eyes filling with tears.

"I should have been there."

Witnessing this tragedy, Mary Magdalene joins him at his side.

"You can't be everywhere at once."

His mother becomes curious toward this new woman in Jesus' life.

Observing her bloodshot eyes look at him, and then back to Mary, he announces the introduction.

"Mother, this is Mary Magdalene. Without her, I would not be standing here."

As the two women study each other, each one can sense they have the same love and caring for Jesus. Their instincts are to embrace each other. Before separating, Mary reassures the hesitant mother.

"You must be with us all the time now, and support Jesus with his mission."

"Yes. I intend too. Thank you for taking care and - loving my dear son."

Relieved the two Mary's have found a bond, Jesus looks with concern at his mother.

"Did he suffer?"

"No. He went peacefully in his sleep. However, he was never the same since you left home."

Guilt still pounding away, Jesus places a reassuring hand on her trembling shoulder.

"As Mary says, you must stay with us now, so we can all be one family."

Peter, Andrew, John and James accompanied by Judas; arrive in a buoyant mood. Witnessing Jesus talking to the two women, Peter stops and glares at the stranger. He knows Jesus' mother, but does not recognize the other woman. For a few seconds, this unsettles him for he has always felt he is number one in Jesus' eyes.

Becoming agitated, he turns to the others.

"Who is that woman? Why is he talking to her - in that way?"

He is even more put out when they notice the new woman kissing Jesus, and then leaving him, and bestowing a loving wave as she goes. The apostles glancing at each other without saying anything, they decide not to pursue the matter. On the other hand, Peter is still troubled.

Mary Magdalene is traveling back to her village to tell the people she has found the Messiah. Meanwhile, Jesus doesn't mention anything about his love for Mary Magdalene, nor his mother being with him on a permanent footing or the death of Joseph.

Becoming distressed at the loss, he tries to relieve his anxiety by sitting on the dusty ground, and begin drawing with his index finger in the sand.

While the other apostles arrive, making up the twelve, Mary, Jesus' mother, sits down next to her son. This sends a signal for the twelve to do the same. Some sit near, while others sit a few paces away. Peter and his brother Andrew sit close by opposite Jesus. Even though Jesus is rested, the two brothers notice he still looks thin. Still a little agitated, Peter needs to comment and prove his self-worth.

"Sir? Please eat something."

Ignoring Peter and still brooding over Joseph's death, Jesus, continues to draw without looking up.

"I have food to eat that you know nothing about."

Stunned and hurt by this brisk answer, Peter hides his feelings, and asks a different question.

"Have you just eaten then?"

Not answering, Jesus continues to draw. Amazed by their Rabbi's behavior, the twelve glances at each looking for an answer. Without looking up, and with a touch of irritation in his voice, Jesus answers.

"My 'food' is to do the will of God, who sent me to finish the work."

His mood becoming taut, Jesus looks up to twelve puzzled faces.

"Don't say there are four months more, and then the harvest? I'm telling you now, open your eyes and look at the fields, they're ripe for harvest. Even now, the reaper draws his wages. Even now, he harvests the crop of eternal life so the reaper and sower can be glad together. Thus, the well-known saying - one sows while the other reaps."

The atmosphere is strained. The twelve searches for reassurance from each other. The atmosphere is strained. Is there anything they can do to ease their master's burden?

Meanwhile, Mary Magdalene is convincing her village fold.

"You must come and see the man that knew all about me, and told me about my past. This 'is' the Messiah."

Receiving a good response, but not letting her true feelings for Jesus show, she says her goodbyes and begins to walk away toward her love. The village people are so taken by Mary's sincerity, they all decide to follow.

Jesus is still hurt and guilty about his father's death. To compensate, he continues with his stern lesson at his still confused apostles.

"When I went away to rest, I sent you out to reap. What you've not worked for, I have done. You reap the benefits of 'my' labor."

Realizing their teacher knows without them having to admit anything, they were unsuccessful in carrying out his request in healing and teaching in his name, the twelve bow their heads in shame.

Having made his point, all is quiet. Disappointed, Jesus relieves his frustration with a heavy sigh, and goes back to his drawing.

Minutes go by. There is a noise of a crowd approaching. Jesus looks up and sees to his delight, Mary Magdalene leading a large group of believing villagers to heading toward him. The atmosphere filled with expectancy; they gather around. Some mixing with the apostles, while others sit in small groups nearer to Jesus. Her excitement noticeable, Mary sits with Jesus' mother.

The familiar apprehension fills Jesus, as he stands to be in full view to everyone.

I need to explain more of my message to the apostles, as well as to convince these new arrived Samaritans.

Waiting for the right time when he has everyone's full attention, he begins.

"A farmer goes out to sow his seed. As he scatters, some fall on a path and are trampled, then birds come and eat the remainder.

Some seeds fall on rocky ground so when the seeds shoot, they come up and wither through lack of moisture.

Other seeds fall amongst thorns and weeds, which grow, but eventually, get choked.

The remainder falls on good fertile ground, growing up into a fine crop, a hundred-fold more than was originally sown..."

66

He scans the still expectant, but confused crowd.

"So, he or she, who has ears to hear, let them listen..."

Judas interrupts by raising his hand. Aware of the sarcasm and challenging in his eyes, Jesus is wary.

"Rabbi, what 'does' this story mean?"

His eyes blazing with frustration, Jesus turns on him.

They still don't understand!

"It means that the secrets of the Kingdom of God I've given to you before will be explained to these people in parables, so it's easy for them to understand. The problem I am having right now with you, is although you see me, you still can't see my message. Although you hear me, you still can't hear my message."

Embarrassed that this answer is meant for him and not the crowd, Judas sits back trying to blend in with the others. To quell his irritation, Jesus glances down to Mary and his mother. Both seem to understand by conveying to him smiles of encouragement. Enthused by their support, he faces the crowd.

"The meaning of this story, is the seed is the word of God. Those along the stony path are the ones that 'hear', but are tempted by the devil who takes the words from their hearts, so they can't believe and be saved. Those people on the rocks are the ones who receive the word with joy, but have no root. They believe for a while, but in a time of testing, they just fall away. The seed that falls amongst the weeds and thorns stands for those who hear, but go on their own way being chocked by life's worries, possessions, and riches, so, they don't mature. However, the seed that falls on fertile ground, stands for those with a noble and good heart, who hear the word and retains it, and by persevering, produce a bountiful crop."

Absorbing the parable, the Samaritans appear quiet, until a mature man stands. Dressed in clothes that gives him an air of authority, his voice echoes his enthusiasm.

"We no longer just believe Mary Magdalene's account of you, we've heard you for ourselves. We now know for sure you're the savior of the world."

Followed by an applause from the Samaritans, gives Jesus a new sense of hope, instead of the usual frustration. His reaction is to glance down at Mary who is busy joining the applause, and offering him a smile of encouragement.

In the meantime, two tired, haggard men join the crowd. One sits, while the other comes up to Jesus, his face troubled. The applause subsides. For a short while there is stillness, not even a stirring of the air, until the troubled man sputters out his grave words.

"Rabbi, I have some bad news."

He goes to whisper in Jesus' ear, but Jesus stops him.

"Tell this to the people here. The whole story."

Jesus decides to sit while the man struggles to put his words together.

"My name is Levi. I am a disciple of John the Baptist. Herod arrested John about a week ago because he was preaching that Herod should not be possessing his brother Phillip's wife Herodias. John kept on preaching, "It's unlawful." So, Herod put him in prison. Herod just wanted to kill John, but was afraid what the people would do, because everyone loves him, believing him to be a great prophet..."

As if relaying this message is too painful, the man hesitates. Meanwhile, Jesus can picture John in his mind from the day of his baptism. Now anxious about hearing this bad news, Jesus prompts the man to continue. Racked with emotion, Levi fumbles, while a fearful shout reverberates from the crowd.

"What happened?"

Rubbing his hands to relieve his nervousness, Levi continues.

"Well, on Herod's birthday two days ago, rumor had it that the daughter of Herodias danced provocatively in front of Herod, teasing and flaunting. So, in his mood of lust for her, he offered her 'anything' she wanted. She asked for John's head on a silver platter. Herod was extremely nervous about this request, but being so mesmerized by her sensuous beauty, her request was granted - by beheading John in prison."

Levi begins to tremble and cry, but takes control and continues.

"His bloody head was brought on a silver platter and given to the girl who then carried it to her mother..."

He pauses again, and wipes the tears from his eyes.

"We buried him this morning."

At hearing such awful news, stunned silence fills the air. Controlling his distress, Jesus stands, and embraces the grief-stricken Levi. No words being spoke, just the sharing of tears.

11

Mary, Oh Mary

With a great feeling of relief, Jesus finds his enclave to rest. He collapses onto the ground, still holding his small bundle and water bag.

He lies still. A minute goes by as he gazes up at the early evening sky. Studying the shapes of two isolated dark clouds streaking across the deep red setting sun, his disturbed mind becomes erratic while going over the details of the day.

His body aching with draining fatigue, he drags his body to a sitting position, and takes hold of his familiar water bag. While putting the spout to his dry mouth, and relishes the cool water flowing down his parched throat, he stiffens at the sound of a sarcastic voice

"I bet that feels good after what you've been through today."

Knowing the voice, Jesus freezes. His insides turn over as he becomes cautious when lowering the water bag. A few paces away in the dim light, he can just make out the silhouette of a tall black hooded figure. The outline glides toward him and sits an arm's length away. The head turns toward Jesus, letting the setting sun reflect in the eyes, making them glow a shimmering red.

"Well, well. How are we? I see you have had to perform some really major 'miracles' lately, and 'still' your message is not getting through."

Too tired to fight, but still strong enough in his mind to resist, Jesus glares in silence, as Satan continues.

"Didn't I warn you it would be hard and frustrating? You see, the main trouble is that basically they're 'all' sinners. That's the one thing I know we agree on.

Nevertheless, that's where any similarity stops. You want them to 'stop' sinning, while I want to 'encourage' them. You see, I make it too easy for them to give in to temptation, which unfortunately, leaves you with the impossible task of teaching them to resist."

The sun is almost gone. Satan's eyes have now turned to black holes in his pale face. Even though Jesus is exhausted, he rages at the arrogance of this complete evil sitting next to him. He raises his voice as if to drown out any weakness he feels.

"Your temptations are not just evil; they destroy a man's soul until he is unable to tell the difference between good and evil."

"That my friend is the whole object of the exercise."

His pale shadowed face distorts into a sardonic smile. His perfect formed teeth seem to glow in contrast to the immediate surroundings. Meanwhile, the rage in Jesus is sapping his remaining energy.

I must get rid of this evil before I disintegrate.

"I give a man's soul the strength he needs, because good will always be stronger than you. Evil is a bully; mean and selfish on the outside and 'weak' on the inside. So, the more temptation you offer, the more they need, and the more you cannot fill those needs, like a spiraling vortex into Hell. I offer a love that is clean, pure and endless, making man strong and courageous for..."

He leans back against the rock wall sweating and exhausted. Satan's voice reverberates.

"Like you feel now?"

Jesus is so weak; he is having a hard time in turning away. Placing his trembling hands up against his ears, at not wanting to hear anymore, he lowers his head, as Satan goes in for the final assault.

"Your 'love' is impossible for the normal person to achieve and hold on to. I will continually be there to get in the way. That's what I'm here for. I will 'always' win, because of their weakness and greed. Good will perpetually struggle like it did back in the Garden of Eden..."

He pauses to stare at the sun almost gone.

"As for you my friend, you haven't even started to struggle. Ha, Ha, Ha, Ha..."

The cold hollow laugh seems to bounce and echo off every nearby rock and now crouching, Jesus squeezes his head even harder to stop the evil sound penetrating his mind. Keeping in this position for a while, he opens his eyes. Noticing darkness has fallen, and everything is now quiet, Jesus senses the peace. Taking a chance by releasing the pressure from his aching head, he scans the immediate area.

No Satan? Nothing! As if the last horrifying moments never happened.

Still picturing the last painful minutes, doubt overwhelms him like a wet, cold blanket.

Was Satan really here?

Desperate for another drink, he grabs his water bag and gulps down several mouthfuls, almost heaving on its coolness. Thirst quenched, he sits, resting against the rock face; and looks skyward toward a starlit moonless night. His mouth trembles as tears of fear burn channels on his dusty face.

Is it true I am going to suffer a lot more?

With his mind in further turmoil, he rests his head in his cupped hands.

What am I thinking? Here I am worried what Satan says? He's always going to be there waiting for me to fail in my mission, but somehow, I will fight him with the help and the full power of the Holy Spirit.

With a renewed determination flooding through him, Jesus relaxes and unrolls his bedroll. Exposing a smaller bundle of food comprising of unleavened bread, goat cheese and dates, he eats just enough to conserve, and then drinks more water.

Satisfied somewhat, he lies his stiff body on his blanket bed, and stares up at the mass of stars, which shroud over him like a calm shroud. It is so quiet he can hear his own breathing. Being so tired, he cannot fall asleep. His nerves are tingling with exhaustion. Still looking up, his eyes again sting with tears, while his mind is fearful.

Oh God! I am so scared, vulnerable, and alone. Why is it so hard for people to understand such a simple message? Even my apostles are finding it hard. Satan, the messiah of evil is reveling in my struggle. Please give me the strength so I can complete my mission..."

His eyes become heavy; his body twitches with fatigue, as he falls into an uneasy sleep.

Her warm olive eyes seem to radiate deep into his soul. Her generous wide smile enraptures his whole being. Her thick long dark wavy hair falls in a sensuous fashion across his face causing his body to tingle in a way he has not experienced before. She pulls away, and laughs as if to tease, and then comes back by pressing her warm, voluptuous body against his...

He wakes up with a start. His heart pounding, his body soaked with sweat, even though the night is cool.

"Oh my God! What has Satan put into my head?"

Picturing the beautiful woman as if she is seared into his subconscious, he falls back into an exhausted troubled sleep.

He is falling into a vortex of fire entering a boiling pit. His mouth is so dry his swollen tongue fills his mouth.

Has Satan finally beaten me? Is this the road to Hell?

He awakens to a brilliant light accompanied by intense heat. He is finding it difficult to open his eyes. Gathering his thoughts and beginning to focus; he can feel the course woven blanket underneath him. Putting one hand up to his face, he tries to shade his eyes. The sun is beating down with no mercy.

It is past midday. I must have slept for over fourteen hours.

He struggles to sit up. His mouth is so dry, his tongue has stuck to the roof of his mouth. He begins to drink the warm, but refreshing water from his water bag.

Now refreshed, he concentrates his mind. He scans the local area for shade, but the clumps of boulders on sand offer nothing. He decides he must stand. His body stiff and painful, he struggles to grip hold of the

FOR THE LOVE OF MAN

nearest boulder to pull up to his full height. Now standing, he reaches for his water bag.

Well, what now? I have twelve days to find somewhere where I'm unknown and rest, get strong again, and then rejoin Peter and the Apostles. I will go south to Samaria and find a quiet village, then return here.

With difficulty, he reaches for his blanket and the remainder of his little bundle to roll everything together. After tying everything, he places the bundle under his arm and begins to walk south.

Two days have now gone at walking through the dry rocky desert. Jesus' meager water and food supply has long diminished. He finds a sheltered spot to rest for a while. His parched mouth and gnawing stomach are sapping his remaining strength. He sits, leans back against a rock face, and reflects on his present situation. Looking around, it all reminds him of his first journey into the desert to fast for his first baptism.

Forty days and nights that I will never forget. How long ago was it now? It seems a lifetime away. I can still smell the bread Satan offered me. No devil's messiah today.

Feeling a little rested he stands, picks up his bundle and empties the last of the water bottle, and then continues walking south.

Four hours go by; it is late afternoon, and the sun is baking. Shading his eyes, Jesus stops on a small hill looking down to a shimmering valley. Through the heat haze, he can just make out a small village with the customary flat top sandstone houses interspersed with mature olive trees. Feeling somewhat hopeful, he staggers down the gravel hillside toward this welcoming sight. While struggling to keep his legs from buckling, he can picture the well in the village center. He can almost taste the water waiting for him.

He is here, leaning against the well. The last of his strength has now evaporated.

I must drink before I collapse...

The well is too deep. He is too weak to operate the bucket. In desperation, he falls down onto the hard ground. Leaning helpless against the rough sandstone wall of the well, he gazes at the stony ground

Oh God. No more please. Not like this.

He drifts in and out of consciousness; light into blackness, then back to light. He can hear a soft woman's voice singing away in the distance, then a muffled splashing of water. He feels something cool and soft touching his burning forehead. This welcoming touch compels him to open his painful eyes a little to see a pair of curious olive eyes gazing back at him. Her voice seems faraway, as her soft even mouth form words.

"Are you all right sir?"

The stroking of her hand against his forehead, brings him into some kind of focus. His rasping throat struggles.

"Will you give me a drink?"

Her kind eyes turn from curiosity to challenge.

"You are a Jew. I am a Samaritan. Jews detest Samaritans."

Jesus hasn't the strength to argue and plead. His cracked lips cannot form the words he needs to say. Seeing him struggle, the warmth returns to her eyes. She then crouches closer putting one arm around his head for support. The next, he feels a cool wooden goblet pressing against his parched lips. Smelling the water, he manages to open his painful mouth just enough to allow the cool liquid to enter. Letting it roll down his flaming throat, she keeps giving him the water until he can't take anymore - for now. As she crouches even closer, the softness of her firm, heavy breasts support his head. Her natural scent wafting from her long, thick dark wavy hair enters his nostrils. As he focuses on her soft pale skin and warm mouth, it reminds him of something...

This is the woman in my dream. Is this another trick? Is SHE Satan?

Her soft welcoming hand is now resting on his chest. Strong, yet tender, she slides it up to his chin turning so he is facing her. The olive eyes now filling his view, her voice, a low, slight husky tone pulsates.

"Better?"

Afraid to be caught up in this apparition, Jesus nods. Grateful for her help and presence, and yet he fears it is still an illusion. Not so worried about him now, her gaze becomes stern.

75

"As a Jew, how can you ask 'me' for a drink?"

As the lifesaving water revives him, he is more able to sit up. She takes this as a hint that he is on the mend. She reacts by removing her hand from his forehead, but lets his head still rest against her breasts. Her warmth and softness now injecting strength beyond any expectation, something deep down inside of him assures him that this woman must be one of God's own creatures, not a trick from the devil.

"If you knew the gift of God, and who it is who asks you for a drink, you would ask him to give you living water."

Lost in her softness, he is unaware of her gaze turning to puzzlement.

"Sir, you have nothing to draw with, and this well is deep. Where can you get this 'living' water? Are you greater than our father Jacob who gave us this well and even drank from it himself, as did also his sons and his flocks and herds?"

Hoping this warm natured woman will understand, his face hurts as he tries to smile.

"Everyone who drinks from 'this' well will become thirsty again, but whoever drinks the water 'I' give will 'never' thirst. This water will be a spring welling up to eternal life."

His body becomes aware of a new sensation as she pulls him tighter against her.

Not wanting to let this intriguing man go, because the longer she holds onto him, the more she is aroused by his power of good. Wanting now to search his eyes for the truth he relates, she is reluctant for him to withdraw. As Jesus' eyes burn deep into her soul, her heartbeat increases, and her body aches for him.

How can this be? I have only just met him, but I know the bond between us is going to be for life.

Their eyes never losing contact, her mouth opens with a wide smile, exposing perfect white teeth in line with her handsome strong features, all expressing an emotion he has never experienced before. Her eyes soften more as she places her right hand at the base of his throat. Sending a shock-wave throughout his body, he is overwhelmed by her natural scent as his eyes are drawn to her soft lips as she pleads.

"Please give me this water, so that I will never be thirsty again, and have to keep coming here to draw water."

Placing his hand against her cheek, their faces are inches apart. She shudders, relishing his touch, as his voice takes on a different tone.

"Go and tell your husband, and then both come back."

Her eyes harden in disappointment, as the ecstasy is withdrawn.

"I have no husband!"

Continuing to gaze into her eyes, he withdraws his hand.

"I know. Get the man you're living with now."

As irrational guilt overwhelms her, she begrudges pulling away to stand. In remorse she places her hands together tight against her breasts. Still facing him, tears flood her eyes.

"Yes, I have sinned. The man I'm living with is a brute. I've been beaten, raped, and abused in every way. I'm always the victim. It's my own fault. I have that effect on men. I love too much, so I get taken advantage of. All I want is to love and be loved. I have so much to give."

Perceiving every word, she is saying is true, his heart goes out to her. He wants to hold her in his arms.

This is my soulmate! She is going to be his closest confidant.

He indicates for her to sit down next to him. She does, but this time closer. As their bodies touch, he has an overwhelming need to embrace her. This new ache of yearning is now dictating his mood, and also giving him the strength, he needs for the future. He reaches up and strokes her cheek again. Her response is to take his hand in hers, smothers it in gentle kisses; each kiss adding to the mountain of desire to love her. Still gripping his hand, she places it against her breasts as if she never wants to let it go. Her expressive, but sad eyes gaze at him as if in a trance.

Is this a new dream? If so, I do not want to wake up.

"For a Jew to have this effect on me, I see you must be a prophet. Our fathers worshiped on this mountain, but the Jews say we must only worship in Jerusalem."

Their eyes never break contact. Besides this deep yearning for her, a calm reassurance overcomes him that he can trust this woman.

She has the capacity to love and possesses the loyalty and strength that I need. She must leave the man she's living with and come with me.

"The trouble with you Samaritans, you worship what you don't know, and the Jews worship only what they do know. However, the time is coming when the true worshipers who fully worship God in spirit and in truth, are the only people God seeks."

Astounded by such passion and authority, the dreamlike gaze in her eyes turns quizzical.

"I know the Messiah is coming. When he arrives, he will explain everything to us."

Now content and somewhat revitalized, Jesus manages to stand. Without hesitation and still griping his hand, she stands with him. They now face each other with a small gap between them. Her perfume filling his lungs, he places his free hand on her shoulder, and then pulls her toward him.

"I talk to you - as him."

Her eyes widen in excitement.

This is beyond my wildest fulfillment. I am falling in love with the 'Messiah.'

Her instinct is to reach up and wrap both her arms around his neck. Pulling his head down so her lips brush against his. The kiss intensifies, then she withdraws to gaze deep into his astonished eyes.

"Oh, dear God, I have found you. Now I feel worthy of you. I want to give you all my love, my whole being..."

Witnessing her warm tears running down his face, he does not resist when she grips him even harder, and places her soft burning lips on his. On holding the kiss, she realizes her behavior and let's go. Withdrawing her arms, she then looks down to the ground.

"I'm sorry. I shouldn't have done that. Forgive me!"

Jesus doesn't care. He grips her upper arms and pulls her against him.

I want to be held and loved by her. This new experience is making me strong and whole, an advantage in facing my mission.

"Nothing to forgive. God loves you."

Her temporary shame dissipating, she lifts up her head, cups his face in her hands, and pulls down his face. Kissing him again on his mouth, she holds that position. While the earth stops and time stands still, her softness, smell, and passion flows through him like a torrent.

Needing to control this new passion, she is reluctant to pull away. The ecstasy never leaving their lips, she grips his hand and begins to walk away from the well.

"I know a house in the village where we can stay together. I will feed, take care of you, and love you forever."

Even though she has revived him, he is still exhausted. So, the thought of resting in her company for the foreseeable future, brings him relief, hope and comfort.

Ten days later, Jesus is now rested, loved and rejuvenated. Thanks to his new constant companion Mary Magdalene, he is standing in the prearranged place to meet his apostles.

It is a pleasant, cool sunny day. Sitting next to him Mary feels so natural being with the love of her life. After about an hour, Jesus' mother Mary, arrives, her face grave. Jesus' reaction is to stand, and wonder why the grief. On the verge of tears, his mother falls into his awaiting arms. Not explaining why, she is sobbing against his chest, the comfort of his hand stroking her hair calms her grief. After a short while, she pulls away a little to look up at him.

"Your father Joseph - died yesterday."

Guilt hits Jesus like a sledgehammer. Still holding his mother, he looks skywards, his eyes filling with tears.

"I should have been there."

Witnessing this tragedy, Mary Magdalene joins him at his side

"You can't be everywhere at once."

His mother becomes curious toward this new woman in Jesus' life. Observing her bloodshot eyes look at him, and then back to Mary, he announces the introduction.

"Mother, this is Mary Magdalene. Without her, I would not be standing here."

As the two women study each other, each one can sense they have the same love and caring for Jesus. Their instincts are to embrace each other. Before separating, Mary reassures the hesitant mother.

"You must be with us all the time now, and support Jesus with his mission."

"Yes. I intend too. Thank you for taking care and - loving my dear son."

Relieved the two Mary's have found a bond, Jesus looks with concern at his mother.

"Did he suffer?"

"No. He went peacefully in his sleep. However, he was never the same since you left home."

Guilt still pounding away, Jesus places a reassuring hand on her trembling shoulder.

"As Mary says, you must stay with us now, so we can all be one family."

Peter, Andrew, John and James accompanied by Judas; arrive in a buoyant mood. Witnessing Jesus talking to the two women, Peter stops and glares at the stranger. He knows Jesus' mother, but does not recognize the other woman. For a few seconds, this unsettles him for he has always felt he is number one in Jesus' eyes.

Becoming agitated, he turns to the others.

"Who is that woman? Why is he talking to her - in that way?"

He is even more put out when they notice the new woman kissing Jesus, and then leaving him, and bestowing a loving wave as she goes. The apostles glancing at each other without saying anything, they decide not to pursue the matter. On the other hand, Peter is still troubled.

Mary Magdalene is traveling back to her village to tell the people she has found the Messiah. Meanwhile, Jesus doesn't mention anything about his love for Mary Magdalene, nor his mother being with him on a permanent footing or the death of Joseph.

Becoming distressed at the loss, he tries to relieve his anxiety by sitting on the dusty ground, and begin drawing with his index finger in the sand.

While the other apostles arrive, making up the twelve, Mary, Jesus' mother, sits down next to her son. This sends a signal for the twelve to do the same. Some sit near, while others sit a few paces away. Peter and his brother Andrew sit close by opposite Jesus. Even though Jesus is rested, the two brothers notice he still looks thin. Still a little agitated, Peter needs to comment and prove his self-worth.

"Sir? Please eat something."

Ignoring Peter and still brooding over Joseph's death, Jesus, continues to draw without looking up.

"I have food to eat that you know nothing about."

Stunned and hurt by this brisk answer, Peter hides his feelings, and asks a different question.

"Have you just eaten then?"

Not answering, Jesus continues to draw. Amazed by their Rabbi's behavior, the twelve glances at each looking for an answer. Without looking up, and with a touch of irritation in his voice, Jesus answers.

"My 'food' is to do the will of God, who sent me to finish the work."

His mood becoming taut, Jesus looks up to twelve puzzled faces.

"Don't say there are four months more, and then the harvest? I'm telling you now, open your eyes and look at the fields, they're ripe for harvest. Even now, the reaper draws his wages. Even now, he harvests the crop of eternal life so the reaper and sower can be glad together. Thus, the well-known saying - one sows while the other reaps."

The atmosphere is strained. The twelve searches for reassurance from each other. The atmosphere is strained. Is there anything they can do to ease their master's burden?

Meanwhile, Mary Magdalene is convincing her village fold.

"You must come and see the man that knew all about me, and told me about my past. This 'is' the Messiah."

Receiving a good response, but not letting her true feelings for Jesus show, she says her goodbyes and begins to walk away toward her love. The village people are so taken by Mary's sincerity, they all decide to follow.

Jesus is still hurt and guilty about his father's death. To compensate, he continues with his stern lesson at his still confused apostles.

"When I went away to rest, I sent you out to reap. What you've not worked for, I have done. You reap the benefits of 'my' labor."

Realizing their teacher knows without them having to admit anything, they were unsuccessful in carrying out his request in healing and teaching in his name, the twelve bow their heads in shame.

Having made his point, all is quiet. Disappointed, Jesus relieves his frustration with a heavy sigh, and goes back to his drawing.

Minutes go by. There is a noise of a crowd approaching. Jesus looks up and sees to his delight, Mary Magdalene leading a large group of believing villagers to heading toward him. The atmosphere filled with expectancy; they gather around. Some mixing with the apostles, while others sit in small groups nearer to Jesus. Her excitement noticeable, Mary sits with Jesus' mother.

The familiar apprehension fills Jesus, as he stands to be in full view to everyone.

I need to explain more of my message to the apostles, as well as to convince these new arrived Samaritans.

Waiting for the right time when he has everyone's full attention, he begins.

"A farmer goes out to sow his seed. As he scatters, some fall on a path and are trampled, then birds come and eat the remainder.

Some seeds fall on rocky ground so when the seeds shoot, they come up and wither through lack of moisture.

Other seeds fall amongst thorns and weeds, which grow, but eventually, get choked.

The remainder falls on good fertile ground, growing up into a fine crop, a hundred-fold more than was originally sown..."

He scans the still expectant, but confused crowd.

"So, he or she, who has ears to hear, let them listen..."

Judas interrupts by raising his hand. Aware of the sarcasm and chal-lenging in his eyes, Jesus is wary.

"Rabbi, what 'does' this story mean?"

His eyes blazing with frustration, Jesus turns on him.

They still don't understand!

"It means that the secrets of the Kingdom of God I've given to you before will be explained to these people in parables, so it's easy for them to understand.

The problem I am having right now with you, is although you see me, you still can't see my message. Although you hear me, you still can't hear my message."

Embarrassed that this answer is meant for him and not the crowd, Judas sits back trying to blend in with the others. To quell his irritation, Jesus glances down to Mary and his mother. Both seem to understand by conveying to him smiles of encouragement. Enthused by their support, he faces the crowd.

"The meaning of this story, is the seed is the word of God. Those along the stony path are the ones that 'hear', but are tempted by the devil who takes the words from their hearts, so they can't believe and be saved.

Those people on the rocks are the ones who receive the word with joy, but have no root. They believe for a while, but in a time of testing, they just fall away.

The seed that falls amongst the weeds and thorns stands for those who hear, but go on their own way being chocked by life's worries, possessions, and riches, so, they don't mature.

However, the seed that falls on fertile ground, stands for those with a noble and good heart, who hear the word and retains it, and by persevering, produce a bountiful crop."

Absorbing the parable, the Samaritans appear quiet, until a mature man stands. Dressed in clothes that gives him an air of authority, his voice echoes his enthusiasm.

"We no longer just believe Mary Magdalene's account of you, we've heard you for ourselves. We now know for sure you're the savior of the world."

Followed by an applause from the Samaritans, gives Jesus a new sense of hope, instead of the usual frustration. His reaction is to glance down at Mary who is busy joining the applause, and offering him a smile of encouragement.

In the meantime, two tired, haggard men join the crowd. One sits, while the other comes up to Jesus, his face troubled. The applause subsides. For a short while there is stillness, not even a stirring of the air, until the troubled man sputters out his grave words.

"Rabbi, I have some bad news."

He goes to whisper in Jesus' ear, but Jesus stops him.

"Tell this to the people here. The whole story."

Jesus decides to sit while the man struggles to put his words together.

"My name is Levi. I am a disciple of John the Baptist. Herod arrested John about a week ago because he was preaching that Herod should not be possessing his brother Phillip's wife Herodias. John kept on preaching, "It's unlawful." So, Herod put him in prison. Herod just wanted to kill John, but was afraid what the people would do, because everyone loves him, believing him to be a great prophet..."

As if relaying this message is too painful, the man hesitates. Meanwhile, Jesus can picture John in his mind from the day of his baptism. Now anxious about hearing this bad news, Jesus prompts the man to continue. Racked with emotion, Levi fumbles, while a fearful shout reverberates from the crowd.

"What happened?"

Rubbing his hands to relieve his nervousness, Levi continues.

"Well, on Herod's birthday two days ago, rumor had it that the daughter of Herodias danced provocatively in front of Herod, teasing and flaunting. So, in his mood of lust for her, he offered her 'anything' she wanted. She asked for John's head on a silver platter. Herod was extremely nervous about this request, but being so mesmerized by her sensuous beauty, her request was granted - by beheading John in prison."

Levi begins to tremble and cry, but takes control and continues.

"His bloody head was brought on a silver platter and given to the girl who then carried it to her mother..."

84

He pauses again, and wipes the tears from his eyes.

"We buried him this morning."

At hearing such awful news, stunned silence fills the air. Controlling his distress, Jesus stands, and embraces the grief-stricken Levi. No words being spoke, just the sharing of tears.

12

Lessons

As John the Baptist's tragic death is still resonating, Jesus decides to take a break alone with Mary. Her having this ability to rejuvenate him from his creeping exhaustion, he asks Peter to meet him in three days in Jerusalem for the Feast of the Jews. Not taking this request as a matter of course, Peter is resenting the influence Mary Magdalene is having over his mentor. It is the love he has for Jesus that quells any negative feelings. Respecting his masters' decision, Peter arranges for him and the rest of the Apostles to meet with Jesus in three days.

Relieved to be able to take this rest, Jesus and Mary leave. Accompanying them both, his mother is also looking forward to being closer to her son, they make their way to a small rented house in Capernaum.

The following evening, Jesus' mother is happy in baking bread ready for the next day. With the glow of the stone wood fire reflecting on her contented face, her soft voice sings, while her hands knead the dough.

Jesus and the love of his life are lying close together on the floor in the back of the sandstone building. Jesus, with the back of his head being supported by a rolled-up mat, Mary is lying with her head resting on his chest. Listening to his steady heartbeat, her hand strokes the soft hairs in the opening of his smock.

"She sounds happy."

Jesus lifts his left hand, places it on her head, and by stroking, her lush curls glide through his fingers.

"She's always happy when I'm close to her."

Her eyes sparkling with happiness in the soft light, Mary lifts her head up to face him.

"That makes two of us."

His hand still stroking her hair, she leans forward and kisses him on the lips. Her soft mouth parting, she holds the kiss, and relishes this time, as if it is her last. After a few seconds, she is in no hurry to separate, as if teasing.

"I love you so much. You're my whole life. Without you I would just wither away and die, like a neglected blossom."

She would like to pursue her lovemaking and reach that pinnacle of ecstasy, but knowing he needs to rest, she lays her head back on his chest. and continues to stroke his hairs.

The sweet taste of her kiss still lingering on his lips, he senses that she wants to give more, a lot more. Reassured by her love, he is contented with his life, and the relationship with God. Even though the pangs of uncertainty still gnaw at his insides at what's to come, for now, he is happy.

His mind drifting into a pleasant haze, while his mother's soft singing and Mary's warmth and softness float into the distance...

There is a loud knocking on the main door. This startles everyone. As Jesus jerks upright, and disturbing Mary's comfort, he watches his mother wipe her floury hands on a nearby cloth, and go to the door. She pauses as another knocking commences. Biting her lower lip in caution, she opens the door to find two Pharisees standing in the night air looking regal in their fine woven black and gold robes.

Jesus strains his ears at the muffled voices. Mary lets them in asking them to stay just inside the door. Looking apprehensive, she creeps further into the house to find Jesus.

"There are two Pharisees here wanting urgently to talk to you."

Without replying, and feeling contempt for these people, he is reluctant to stand, especially after spoiling a rare period of comfort and delight.

Carrying a brooding expression, Jesus follows his mother toward the anxious men. The older of the two men puts out his hand.

"My name is Nickodemis and this is my companion, Joseph of Arimathea. We are sorry to disturb you Rabbi."

Being acknowledged as 'Rabbi' from these men, Jesus is finding it hard to control his contempt. Now remembering the kind eyes of Nickodemis from the past, he inquires.

"Didn't you witness me helping the young boy to walk? You came over to me."

"That is correct sir, which is one reason among many others why we need to talk to you."

Beginning to relax, Jesus beckons to a nearby table and benches.

"Why so late at night?"

Nickodemis looks down, as if embarrassed and ashamed.

"Fear does strange things to a man. We are risking our lives in seeing you tonight."

Understanding the men's dilemma, Jesus indicates further.

"Please sit."

While they all sit, the robed men make a point of sitting together, and opposite Jesus.

"So! How can I help you gentlemen?"

Hiding his anxiety, Nickodemis places both his hands on the rough tabletop. Noticing a slight tremor, Jesus reaches out with his right hand to touch and reassure. After a couple of seconds, the hand is withdrawn, and Jesus offers a relaxed smile. This being the signal to relax and talk, Nickodemis begins.

"Rabbi, we know you're a great teacher who has been sent by God. No ordinary man could perform such miraculous signs if God wasn't with you. Can you help us receive this power, so we can do good like you?"

Although admiring the sincerity of these men, Jesus is still cautious, and a little irritated.

"The truth is, to see and receive the Kingdom of God you must be born again."

Puzzled by this reply, the two men look disappointed. Meanwhile, the two Mary's are huddled together by the stone fire looking apprehensive. Seeing the women are not understanding this situation, Joseph pauses for thought before speaking.

"How can a man be reborn when he's old? Surely, he can't enter his mother's womb for a second time to be born again?"

Expecting this answer, Jesus conveys to them a bemusing smile while his eyes harden.

"Unless a man is born of water and the spirit, he can't enter the Kingdom of God. Flesh gives birth to flesh, but the spirit gives birth to the spirit. So, don't be surprised when I say 'you must be born again'. Look, the wind blows where it pleases. You hear its sound, but you can't tell where it's coming from or where it's going, so it is with everyone born of the spirit."

Still looking puzzled, Nickodemis asks the obvious.

"How can this be?"

Becoming frustrated by their lack of understanding, Jesus looks down, releases a heavy sigh, and then looks back up.

"You and your kind are Israel's teachers, and you don't understand this? You only speak of what you know, and testify of what you've seen, but still you people do not accept my testimony. I speak to you of earthly things, you don't believe me, so then how can you believe me if I talk of Godly things. No one has ever gone into the Kingdom except the ones that come from God like me – the Son of Man..."

Wary of the men's eyes glazing over with disbelief, Jesus continues.

"Just as Moses lifted up the snake in the desert, so I must be lifted up so that everyone who believes in me will have his soul and live forever. For God loves this world so much that I was sent to say to you all that whoever 'really' believes in me shall never perish, and will have a full rewarding life. I'm not here to condemn the world, but to save it, through God. So, whoever believes in me will not be condemned."

Jesus pauses, wondering if his message is getting through.

"However, for those who do not believe in me are already condemned.

Look, through my light, man can come out of the darkness. Unfortunately, people like the darkness, because of its evil. So, everyone who possesses evil hates the light. They will not come into the light for the fear of having their evil exposed. Whoever lives by the truth will come into the light. So, whatever they do, they do through God."

Dumbstruck by this profound statement, the two Pharisees are lost for words. In response, they glance at each other, and then gaze with helpless expressions back to Jesus. Joseph speaks first.

"We can see what you say is true, but if we explain this to the Jewish ruling council it will be counted as blasphemy."

His patience dwindling, and energy draining, Jesus stands. Exasperated at not being understood, he can't explain any more, and feels it's time for the Pharisees to leave. Taking the initiative, he walks to the door and opens it. Before stepping out into the street, Nickodemis puts out his hand to Jesus.

"You truly are Him. God help us all."

Gripping the man's hand, Jesus offers them both a broad confident smile.

"Yes! But God loves you."

Hesitant in stepping outside, and now skeptical of the future, the two Pharisees step out into the blackness. Watching the men in black fuse into the night, Jesus shuts the door, and then leans against it contemplating the frustration of the last several minutes.

Observing his pale tired face, Mary Magdalene rushes to him, wraps her arms around his waist, and leans against his chest.

"Fools! Good men, but fools."

Too tired to talk, Jesus musters up enough energy to stroke her hair and relish her company.

13

Many Miracles, Much Resentment

Three days later, accompanied by the two Mary's, Jesus meets up with Peter and the Apostles for the Feast of the Jews. With tears of joy, Peter goes up and hugs his mentor.

"We've missed you so much sir, we are all so lost without you. You give us such strength and inspiration when you're with us, but when you leave, our strength leaves also."

Understanding Peter's plight, Jesus places his right hand on his friend's broad shoulder, and with his left hand, wipes the tears off Peter's cheek.

"It's because you have faith in the man, but not in his message."

Embarrassed by this truth, Peter looks down. Determined to not let this slide, Jesus looks around at the other eleven doubtful faces.

"That goes for all of you! If you keep trying, there is still time for your faith to develop."

Knowing the two women in his life are sure of his true identity, Jesus stays silent and begins to walk toward the city. Appalled by his own shame, Peter looks at the others in earnest and indicates for them to follow.

They all arrive at a popular entrance into Jerusalem called the 'Sheep Gate'. Nearby is a pool called Bethesda, known for its healing water. Five covered columns surround the immediate area. Jesus sees a number of disabled, blind and sick people of all ages surrounding the pool. Taking in this dreadful site, he stops. Studying the empathy on Jesus' face, Mary Magdalene, stands beside him, but turns her face away with tears welling up in her eyes.

"What an awful place! Surely we can help these poor souls."

Without saying anything, Jesus pats Mary on the shoulder and heads to an emaciated middle-aged man lying on his mat by the pool's edge. Because Jesus is not known here, the rest of the surrounding sick ignore him, as he crouches down to the man. While Jesus looks into the man's hollow eyes, Peter taps Jesus on the shoulder, and then points away to his right. Curious, Jesus' eyes follow the hand and notices four black-robed Pharisees watching them at about twenty paces away. Without commenting, Jesus turns back to the invalid man.

"Do you want to get well?"

His brown eyes filling with tears of pain, the man struggles to look up at him.

"I have no one to help me into the pool when the water is stirred. While I struggle to get in, somebody else always beats me to it. This has been going on for years, but I believe God will send someone so I can be cured."

Jesus knows if this man were ever placed into this pool it would not cure him. The minerals might make him feel better for a while. In the meantime, Jesus glances in the direction of the Pharisees who are walking in earnest toward him. Turning back to the invalid, Jesus places his left hand on the man's wasted legs, and his right hand on the man's forehead. Jesus then shuts his eyes, lowers his head. While his lips form silent words, Mary looks on spellbound knowing what her love is trying to do.

Now used to Jesus' miracles, Peter is more anxious, as the men in black step nearer. Meanwhile, Jesus' pale face drips with sweat and his hands tremble, as he still holds on to the man. After a few more seconds, Jesus' head rolls to one side. Letting go of the man, he then collapses. Looking on in horror, Mary rushes over to Jesus. Irritated that Mary gets to Jesus first, Peter does the same. As they both crouch down to their master, Mary senses Peter's irritation and beckons him to help her lift Jesus into a more comfortable position. While this is going on, the invalid is now sitting up, even though a little confused and dazed.

Jesus opens his eyes, smiles with gratitude at Mary and Peter, and then looks at the man he has just healed.

"Get up! Pick up your mat and walk."

The man's instinct is to obey. His thin legs give way at first. On a second attempt, Mary Magdalene comes forward to help him. While putting her arm around his shoulder for support, she whispers in his ear.

"You're now well. Jesus the Messiah has just cured you."

Helping the man to stand, Mary senses the man is not realizing what has happened. She acknowledges Peter, as he leans forward to pick up the mat, and offer it to the man. Meanwhile, the Pharisees are approaching.

Still being supported by Mary, the man rolls up his mat, but is still unsteady on his feet, as he begins to shuffle away in a daze. In awe at what is happening, Mary turns to Jesus who is looking at her with sheer admiration and affection. The look irritates Peter, as a nearby voice bellows.

"Do you know what you have just done?"

Becoming annoyed by this rude interruption, Peter turns to the presumed leader of the group of Pharisees, and shouts back.

"Yes! We know. My master has just healed a poor invalid. A lot more than you hypocrites could ever achieve."

Unperturbed by this outburst, the young angry Pharisee is determined to have his say.

"It is forbidden for a man to carry his mat on the Sabbath."

Not believing what he has just heard, Peter bursts out laughing. At the same time, Mary and Jesus look at each other with concern that this situation could turn ugly. An even younger Pharisee steps forward making his way to the cured man.

"You know it's against the law to carry your mat on the Sabbath!"

Still dazed, the poor man leans against a nearby wall, shaking at this accusation. His words stumble as he answers in his defense.

"But sir! That man there said to me 'Pick up your mat and walk' and so I did. You see he has...."

The zealous young Pharisee interrupts him.

"Who is this man who told you to pick up your mat and walk?"

"I have no idea sir. All I know is that I can now walk. As before I couldn't."

Suspicious of this answer, the youngest Pharisee returns to his older colleagues, who are questioning Jesus. Now able to stand with Peter and Mary's support, Jesus addresses the Pharisees with a touch of anger.

"If you gentlemen wish to challenge or criticize me, I will meet you at the temple."

Surprised by this challenge, all the Pharisees agree. On leaving, Jesus smiles, while he hears them muttering with excitement and not looking back.

Later, as arranged, Jesus and his Apostles are sitting in the temple talking amongst themselves, when in walks the invalid that Jesus had healed earlier. He is surprised to see Jesus, so he scurries off in the other direction toward a prominent group of Jews. Astonished at the man's behavior, Jesus shouts after him.

"I see you're really well now. That's good, but stop sinning, because something worse may happen to you."

The Apostles laugh at Jesus' wry humor. The man looks embarrassed, but still he works his way over to the group of Jews catching their attention. Jesus can see the man pointing to him, probably explaining to them how he cured him on the Sabbath. This attracts many other Jews in the temple including the Pharisees. All now congregating into a larger group, they begin walking toward Jesus.

Sitting in a position at the top of the temple steps with his Apostles standing in a straight line behind him, Jesus becomes tense as the group approaches, ready to confront him. Recognizing the Pharisees from earlier, Jesus is prepared as the group stops at the base of the steps. After a short while of staring each other out, three of the group begins ascending the steps. Stopping three steps away, Jesus is still above them, even though seated.

A lone voice from the rest of the group shouts out.

"Who are you, and why are you doing things on the Sabbath?"

Within seconds, others join in with shouts of condemnation. Hiding his fear, Jesus feels threatened by this sudden hostility. Sitting next to Jesus, Mary Magdalene senses his mood, and grips his forearm to reassure he isn't alone. His Instinct is to place his trembling hand on hers.

Even though he has never spoken in Jerusalem before, his reputation has preceded him. His fear now subsiding, he stands in defiance of his challengers.

"To answer your question, God is always at his work, regardless of the day.

Therefore, as I work for God, I am always at work, regardless of the day."

Wondering if they want to understand, he pauses. His eyes blazing; he looks down, and then turns to his left to take three paces. He stops, and then turns back to the crowd who is now quiet and showing interest in this intriguing man. Sensing their interest, Jesus lifts his head up skyward and shuts his eyes for a few seconds. On opening his eyes, he lowers his head and glares at his audience.

"The truth is, the son can do nothing by himself. He can only do what he sees his parent doing. So, whatever the parent does the son does also…"

He looks down to his feet; pauses, and then looks back at his audience who can see tears forming in his eyes.

"You see! The mother loves her son very much and shows all that she does."

These emotional words are confusing the crowd and annoying the Pharisees, but they are still compelled to listen. Jesus' mother wipes away her own tears, as her son continues.

"So, just as the mother raises the dead and gives life, so the son can do the same to whom he pleases."

The silence is deafening, as he takes two more paces to his left and lowers his head again. He can feel the tension as every eye is focusing on him. The passion and strength of his own belief rekindles and fills his insides, while he raises his head again.

"Now! God doesn't judge, but has trusted all the judgment to the son."

His passion mounting; his voice bellows....

"So, you all shall honor the son as you honor the mother. He who does not honor me does not honor God."

The stunned silence remains, as the crowd glance at each other as if trying to understand this man dressed in a shabby ivory smock. Observing the confusion, Jesus pauses again. His passion still intense, he realizes these people are not fit to enter this grand building of worship. His response is to pace three steps to his right, to stand next to Mary.

Glaring at his audience, the tears of passion return to his eyes. Frustration mixing with the passion, his voice booms to every corner of the temple.

"I only tell the truth! Whoever hears my word and believes in God has eternal life within him and will never be condemned. For he who has crossed over from being dead within himself, to having a full and rich life, will forever be alive.

The time is near when the dead inside will hear my voice and begin to live. For as God is life, so it has been granted me to have life within myself. In addition, I have been granted the authority to judge..."

He stares at the curious eyes gazing at him in a mixture of wonder and uncertainty.

"Don't be amazed at what I'm saying. The time is near when all those who feel they're already in their graves will hear my voice and come out. Those who do so, will rise up to live. Those who have committed evil will rise up only to be condemned by me. As a mere man I can do nothing. I judge only as I hear, and my judgment is just. I seek nothing for myself, but only for God, who has sent me."

Still observing the stillness, he feels many in this crowd still do not understand his message. Contented that he has explained as best he can, he is at peace, confident in his mission, which is now beginning to climax. A loud shout breaks the still atmosphere. It is the young Pharisee from earlier, pointing his finger in anger at Jesus.

"You not only disobey the laws of the Sabbath, you also put yourself equal to God."

Witnessing this young man stirring the crowd with these new mixed emotions, Mary glances at the Apostles who now look uneasy at this new situation. Still confident, Jesus places his right hand on Mary's head to reassure that everything is all right. He glares in defiance at the accusing Pharisee.

"You! Who has never heard Gods' voice in your pathetic little life, or seen any form. Does the 'word' really dwell in you? For you don't believe me, for whom God has sent. You diligently study the scriptures, because you blindly think that will give you eternal life. These scriptures tell you about 'me' and yet you refuse to come to me to have life. I don't accept praise from men, but I know...."

His voice becoming even louder, he points to the main group of Pharisees.

".... that you do not have the love of God in your hearts. I have come to you in God's name and you still don't accept me. If someone else comes to you in his own name you accept him. So, how can you believe if you accept praise from each other yet make no effort to obtain the praise that only comes from God. If you believe Moses, you should believe me, because he wrote about me. So, since you do not believe in what he wrote, how are you ever going to believe what I say?"

As these new words shock the crowd into some form of understanding, silence fills the building. Even as this new phenomenon takes the pharisees by surprise, Jesus cannot say any more. Becoming drained of emotional energy, he has had enough of these people. Without any hesitation, he begins to walk down the large steps toward the crowd. Watching their leader, Peter, Mary and the Apostles take this as a signal for their departure. While they follow Jesus, the curious crowd splits in two to let them through.

Jesus keeps walking, his pace quickens, so and he can get as far away as possible from these hypocrites. In desperation, he stops nearby in a quiet street and rests against a rough stonewall. His trembling hands wipe away the sweat pouring into his eyes.

As the two Mary's approach him first, he looks up above their heads noticing with dismay the Apostles all arguing with each other as they approach.

"What are they arguing about?"

Mary Magdalene, still breathless after the vigorous walk, looks straight at her man with concern.

"Are you all right?"

He doesn't answer her question, because he is still anxious about the squabbling Apostles coming nearer. His mother sees the pain of faithlessness in his eyes.

"They are debating whether going to the temple this early was wrong, because your news hasn't spread here yet."

His voice full of disappointment, he glances at the two women for some sort of reassurance.

"I felt it was right. Didn't you?"

The women look at each other as if searching for the right answer. Instead, Mary Magdalene steps forward and kisses Jesus on his right cheek.

"If you feel it was right, then so do we."

Grabbing hold of his right hand, she stands close to him as the others arrive. They can hear Peter's voice bellowing above the others.

"Will you stop squabbling? We have to start sometime. Why not now?"

The pain easing at these understanding words, Jesus gazes with affection at his loyal fisher. On the other hand, Judas his opinion.

"I think it's too early to start teaching in Jerusalem. Look at the hostility."

Still frustrated with his colleagues and sensing Jesus' torment, Peter has not finished in explaining.

"That was hypocrisy, not hostility. They're afraid of losing their positions in this corrupt society..."

Listening to both sides, Thomas interrupts.

"This is hard teaching anyway. Who will 'ever' accept it?"

98

Listening to the doubt coming from his chosen twelve, Jesus lowers his head in despair.

I never realized before that even my close Apostles do not have any understanding of my mission. Only loyal Peter seems to understand – sometimes. Hiding his dismay, Jesus' tired face peers up at Thomas.

"Does all this offend you? Don't you still understand that it is the spirit that gives life, not the flesh. The flesh counts for nothing, the words I speak are the spirit, and they're the true life. Yet I feel most of you still can't or won't believe."

Out of the doubtful faces focusing on their Rabbi, Jesus' gaze turns to Judas; his voice tinged with anger.

"I tell you now that no one can come to me unless God has enabled him."

While listening to these profound words, Judas keeps Jesus' stare. After a couple of seconds, his eyes become troubled, so, he looks away. Jesus then turns to Peter, tears forming in the corner of his eyes.

"You don't want to leave me? Do you?"

Embarrassed by these circumstances, Peter's deep respect and love for his mentor is in no doubt, but he is often lost and confused at his teachings. He looks down, and then back up. His anxious eyes gaze at his master for an answer.

"Where shall we go sir? You're the only one who has the right words of eternal life? We here all know that you're the Holy one of God..."

Although appreciating Peter's words of assurance, tears of disappointment trickle down Jesus's face. His eyes meet Mary's concerning expression. He tries to offer her a reassuring smile, but can't quite make it. He wipes his eyes, takes a breath, lifts up his head, and turns back to his confused Apostles.

"Haven't I chosen you twelve? Yet I feel that Satan is still gnawing away at most of you."

The following weeks Jesus pushes himself hard; going from village to village, performing miracles and teaching his main message. However, he keeps away from Jerusalem. Each small town or village he arrives at, his reputation has preceded him. The crowds are also becoming larger with each destination.

Although this would seem an advantage, the people that wait for him seem helpless, like sheep wandering without a shepherd to guide them.

One such village, not far from Jerusalem, Jesus is in the center of the crowd relaying his message. As the people jostle for a better view of him, Jesus feels a tug at his smock. At first, he ignores it and carries on talking. Behind him is a distressed woman who has suffered from bleeding for twelve years. She has come to see Jesus to be saved from this awful disability. Plucking up courage for a second time, she attempts to pull on his smock.

"If I can just touch his clothes, I know I will be healed."

She reaches again, and grabs the bottom of Jesus' smock, holds it tight, and shuts her eyes in anticipation. A sudden feeling of fatigue overwhelms Jesus. He leans on Peter's nearby shoulder for support, and then notices the poor woman crouching still holding onto his smock. His voice trembles as he rests a hand on her shoulder.

"Whatever your illness, take heart. Your faith in me has healed you."

In the meantime, she looks down to find her bleeding has stopped. As tears of gratitude fill her eyes, she stands and wraps her arms around him. Her voice muffled by his clothes.

"Thank you, thank you."

News of these miracles has now spread to the whole region including Jerusalem. In Jesus' mind, he has to make a decision.

Now is the time to enter this city!

However, he needs to prepare his Apostles, because he has one more village to visit before his final entrance into the gates of Jerusalem.

Jesus and his Apostles, accompanied by both Marys' are now sitting in the village square facing a large interested crowd. One man stands near the rear; his silver beard and long robes give him an air of authority. His deep voice reverberates as he raises one hand.

"Who is the greatest, in the Kingdom of God?"

In replying to this searching question, Jesus looks around. He notices a child. Beckons to her to come over to him. Without any hesitation, the little girl of about eight years of age skips toward him. Jesus response is to squat down, and look into her bright olive eyes.

Her handsome aquiline features remind me so much of – Mary.

His heart filled with a yearning that Mary can fulfill, he places his right hand on the young girl' left shoulder.

"Unless you change and become like innocent little children, you will never find the Kingdom of God. So, whoever humbles like this sweet child, becomes the greatest in the Kingdom, and whoever welcomes this child in my name, welcomes me…"

He kisses the girl's forehead, glances at the fascinated crowd, and continues.

"However, if anyone causes one of these children who believe in me to sin, it would be better for the child to have a huge millstone around its neck and be thrown into the sea and drowned."

As he takes the girl's hand; her bright, expressive eyes gaze into his as if searching for that guarantee. Unable to reassure her in the way he wants, despair comes over him. Still holding her hand, his eyes turn toward the crowd.

"It's a shame what causes people to sin. Unfortunately, such things will always happen."

His hand returning to the little girl's shoulder, he stands and glares at the crowd.

"Woe betide the person when it does happen. If your hand or foot causes you to Sin – cut it off. Its better you're crippled and are saved, than have both hands and feet and be thrown into Hell's eternal fire. If your eye or tongue causes you to sin or lust, gouge them out and throw them away. It's better to have only one eye and no tongue and be saved, than have both eyes and your tongue be thrown into Hells eternal flame. So, let the innocent children come to me, for the Kingdom of God belongs to them."

There is a calm silence as Jesus' heartfelt words penetrate into the crowd.

All eyes are still focused on him, as the little girl looks up at him shading her face with her free hand. Mary can see the emotional affect this subject is having on Jesus. Being discreet, she stands and whispers in his ear.

"You look tired, you haven't slowed down in weeks. Let's go back to your mother's house in Capernaum and rest. We must be ready for your important journey back to Jerusalem."

While her words sink in, he looks around for Peter, to see him in deep discussion with Judas. Meanwhile, the crowd is becoming restless. Presuming Jesus has finished, the crowd appears disheartened, as they begin to dissipate. The little girl's reaction is to let go of his hand and run into the remains of a waiting group that must be family.

Saddened by his own failure, Jesus catches Peter's eye and beckons to him. Without hesitation, he wastes no time in approaching Jesus. Noticing the fatigue and despair on his master's face, he asks the obvious.

"Are you all right sir?"

Putting on his usual confident act, Jesus conveys to Peter a reassuring smile.

"Yes, I'm fine. Just a little tired. I am going to rest at my mother's house in Capernaum. I'll see you in two days."

Trying to hide his disappointment at not being with Jesus again, Peter conveys a smile that does not reach his eyes.

"Right, Sir. Two days then. At your mother's house."

Becoming discouraged, and beginning to turn away, Jesus touches Peter's shoulder.

"Thank you."

Without looking back and tears filling his eyes, Peter nods, and then walks toward the other Apostles.

After a long trek, Jesus and the two women in his life reach the house. It is dark. All Jesus can think of is how much he is looking forward to his mother's cooking and falling asleep next to his love, Mary. Nevertheless, some Jewish elders are waiting for him. While Jesus becomes annoyed by this intrusion, he is surprised by their humble and polite demeanor

"Rabbi, there is a Centurion's servant whom his master values very highly. He is sick and about to die. The Centurion sent us to find you. We know you stay here sometimes so we took a chance and hoped you would be at home. The Centurion is a good man. He loves our country and has built our Synagogue."

Even though Jesus is exhausted, he says farewell to Mary and his mother and walks with the Jews.

As they approach the grand house of the Centurion, a man approaches them before they can enter.

"Please sir; I'm a friend of the Centurion. He asks me to tell you he's not worthy of you to come to him, but says; just say the word and his servant will be healed, for he himself is a man under authority with soldiers under him?"

Surprised at this statement, Jesus acts accordingly.

"Tell the Centurion I haven't found such great faith in all of Israel. Tell him his servant is healed."

Entranced at such power to heal, and the Centurion's friend grateful, the Jewish elders thank Jesus and leave.

Now alone, and overwhelmed by exhaustion, Jesus' legs buckle. His head spins, as a shrieking sound fills his ears. Just as he collapses, a warm pair of arms break his fall, and are now laying him up against a nearby wall. His body begins to tremble, sweat runs down his face, as his eyes try to focus on who is helping him.

Mary Magdalene gestures to him not to talk, and holds him tight against her soft, comforting chest.

"Oh, my love, I followed you, I knew if you were to heal someone you would be exhausted."

The narrow street is dark and quiet. The sound of a dog barking in the distance breaks the silence. Supporting his weight, they make their way home.

14

Prediction and Fear

Being this an imposing situation, many of the Jewish elders and hierarchy have banded together to be allies, because of the rumors and gossip about Jesus performing great miracles, and claiming he is the Messiah the Jewish people have been waiting for. This is bad news for all the leading Jews. An order is sent out to find and question this Jesus.

Learning of this, Jesus decides to postpone his visit to the temple in Jerusalem for now. To him, the timing is not right to go on.

It is now evening; the whole family is sitting around the table for supper. Jesus' mother Mary is preparing a fine fish meal accompanied by fresh baked bread and fruit. Jesus and his two brothers face each other across the roughhewn table. Each Mary brings the food, lays it on the table, and sits each side of Jesus. Looking at his brother Jesus with concern, John decides to break the bread and pass it around.

"You ought to leave here and go back to Jerusalem. The people there are ready, as well as all the Disciples you gather daily. All these people can witness your miracles."

Listening with intent at his younger brother, Jesus glances at James.

"What do you think James?"

"No one who wants to become a public figure acts in secret. Since you're doing all these things, show yourself to the world."

Not wanting to hear this from his siblings, Jesus becomes forlorn as he glances at Mary, and then his mother for their reaction.

"The right time for me hasn't come yet. For you, anytime is right. The world can't hate you, but it hates me, because of what I testify about evil and what it does. You go to the feast with the others, I'm not ready yet, I'll stay here and rest."

Having heard Jesus' opinion, John and James glance at each other not understanding. As they get up to leave, they kiss their mother goodbye. Leaving behind an uneasy atmosphere, Jesus watches the front door close. Disappointed with his brother's reaction, he lowers his head. Mary Magdalene understands by sliding a loving arm around his bony shoulder. Appalled as he winces, she notices how thin he is becoming.

"I think maybe - they are right. Perhaps you should go into the city for the feast at the tabernacle, and show them who you 'really' are."

A little surprised by this statement, Jesus turns to face her. His tired eyes expressing his love, he reaches out to grip both her hands.

"My wise Mary. Perhaps you're right. I'll tell you what I'll do. I will go to the feast on my own, but in secret. Not many people know me there. I'll make sure it's safe, and then I will expose myself."

Admiring his courage, she leans forward and kisses him on his lips. After a couple of seconds of delight, she pulls away a little to search his eyes.

"If you're sure, I'll stay here, and wait for you."

Becoming more aware of the challenge ahead of him, she kisses him again; longer this time. After she separates, he nods and stands up from the table and leaves. With a heavy heart, Mary watches the front door open and close. The two women react by looking at each other and feeling the other's fear for Jesus' future.

John and James are sitting in the main temple in a quiet corner eating and listening to the general conversation of rumors and gossip. Nobody knows them, so they blend in unnoticed. While they mingle with the several hundred people already in the temple, a thousand or more are congregating outside. The main topic of conversation seems to be about their oldest brother Jesus. Quite near them the conversation is becoming quite heated.

"Where is he? Do you see him? Is he as good a man as they say he is?"

James winces at someone's reply.

"No! He deceives people by giving them false hope."

Ignoring the two brothers, some other people nearby people tend to express their opinions in muted tones, so as not to attract the attention of the higher Jews.

Unknown to his brothers, Jesus had arrived earlier. Halfway through the feast, Jesus makes his way unnoticed to the temple courts. Still not noticed, he stands on the temple steps. Being the same spot as last time, he shouts at the top of his voice.

"Hear me! With all this food, it's not Moses who's given you this bread, but God. He gives you the true bread...."

Curios heads turn, as the noise from the crowd evaporates. Now receiving the crowd's attention, Jesus continues.

"For the bread of God comes down and gives life to the world."

Members of the crowd react by beginning to mumble.

"Is this him?"

His face expressing sarcasm, one prominent-looking Jew shouts back to Jesus.

"Are you going to give us a miraculous sign, so all us here might believe you?"

Laughter erupts from some sections of the crowd. The rest wait for Jesus' reaction. As he is expecting this kind of demand on him, he acts calm and unperturbed.

Why is it so hard to convince these people who I am, and why I'm here?

All of a sudden, he becomes nervous. His hands tremble, as he raises them to explain again.

"As I have just said, the bread of God comes and gives life to this world."

The same Jew speaks out.

"I suppose from now on you give us this bread?"

Laughter erupts again. Even though the sadness inside him is overwhelming, Jesus acts undeterred.

What fools they are!

He looks up for a second by focusing on a beam of light piercing through a thin gap in the roof. Tears of frustration run down his face, as his lips move in silence. Digging deep into his withering courage, he faces the cynical crowd. The anger now filling him, gives him new strength.

James and John, his brothers, surprised by their older brother's presence, move in a discreet fashion toward Jesus just in case this crowd may turn on him.

Not aware of his brothers, Jesus eyes blaze, as he raises his arms to the crowd.

"Look! I am the bread of life. Those of you that come to me will never go hungry, and those who really believe in me will never be thirsty. I know many of you have seen me work, and still don't believe. All that God gives comes directly through me. Those of you who do come to me will never be turned away. I'm here not to do my will, but to do the will of God. While I'm on this Earth, I will lose none of the power invested in me. Therefore, everyone who looks at me and really believes, shall have eternal life."

The skeptics in the crowd of Jews begin grumbling. Not contented with Jesus' speech, they become restless and irritable. Aware of what is happening, John and James are now ready to protect their brother if needed. Meanwhile, the cynical Jews raise their voices among each other.

"Isn't this Jesus the carpenter, the son of Joseph? How can he say he comes directly from God?"

Jesus becomes aware of his brothers conveying to him smiles of reassurance. He reacts by nodding, and then making a point of glaring at the Jews.

"Stop grumbling to yourselves. No one can come to me unless the power of God draws them. No one shall see God unless through me, because I tell you the truth. For I am the living bread that comes only from God. This bread is my flesh for which I give life to the world."

Finding this new message strange, the crowd is now arguing with more aggression.

"How can you, a mere carpenter, give us his flesh to eat?"

In hearing this, Jesus becomes more passionate by shouting back.

"Unless you eat my flesh and drink my blood you will never have any life. Whoever does this, shall have 'eternal' life. Just as God sends me, and I live because of God, so those of you who feed off me, will live – because of me."

The crowd becomes quiet with a mixture of surprise and confusion. A lone Pharisee breaks the silence. His voice calm and inquisitive faces Jesus head on.

"How do you really know all this without having studied?"

Expecting this query from such a hypocrite, Jesus wastes no time in answering.

"All this I teach to you is not my own, it comes from God, who sent me. If anyone here is already doing God's work, he will know whether my words are true or not. He who speaks on his own does so for his own honor and ego. One who speaks and works only for God, will have the honor of God; for God is truth. Didn't Moses give you the law, yet none of you keep that law? So why are you persecuting me or even trying to kill me?"

Not so calm, the same Pharisee bellows back.

"You are demon-possessed. Who is trying to kill you?"

Jesus, now more defiant, and his anger giving him the strength he needs, becomes more aware of everyone now focusing on him, and waiting for the answer.

"I do 'one' miracle and you're all astounded, yet it's not enough. Then you're angry with me for healing on the Sabbath. The Law of Moses says you can circumcise on the Sabbath, and yet you pass judgment on me for healing the whole man on the Sabbath."

The crowd becomes quiet and attentive, as Jesus points to the group of black-clothed Pharisees. His voice now loud with passion, jabs his forefinger in the air.

"You need to reform your judgment. Those of you here who have followed me and witnessed my work, know where I'm from and who sent me. Therefore, I will remind you 'again' that I know God, because I am from God, who sent me."

Not wanting to believe this extreme message, some of the crowd erupts. While abuse and threats are thrown at Jesus, some hands try to seize him, but with the help of his brothers, they are repelled. However, the remaining crowd who does believe in Jesus' is preaching try to quell the noisy members. One tall man raises his hand to be heard. Jesus notices his tattered clothing and a look of poverty, as the man shouts to him.

"When the 'actual' Messiah comes, will he do even more miraculous signs than you?"

Not believing his ears at the foolish behavior of these poor lost sheep, Jesus reacts accordingly.

"NO! There will be no one else. 'I' am the one. I'm only with you for a short time to deliver my message, and then I go to God. You will look for me, but you won't find me. And where I'm going, you can't come."

Becoming confused, the same man shouts out again.

"Where do you intend to go that we can't find you? Will it be among the Greeks? Is that the place we can't come?"

Jesus releases a heavy sigh.

Why don't they understand? What am I doing wrong?

He replies. "Where I go streams of living water will flow, so those of you that believe in me shall drink this water of the spirit and will never thirst."

The crowd is now divided. Some want to seize and silence Jesus, while others want to learn more. These new 'disciples' are realizing that Jesus may be some kind of Messiah. Meanwhile, the worried Pharisees observing the effect Jesus is having on these new believers, decide to send a messenger to call out the temple guards to arrest him.

A short while later when the guards arrive, they hear Jesus' words, and observe the positive mood of the crowd. They refuse to arrest him. This opportunity enables Jesus, John and James to leave the temple.

Becoming more exhausted, Jesus decides to go to the Mount of Olives and rest, while James and John return to their mother's house.

Meanwhile, the temple guards report back to the chief priests and Pharisees whose anger, and now frustration is becoming obsessive.

"Why didn't you bring him to us?"

His abrasive manner annoying the priests, the highest-ranking guard steps forward.

"No one has ever spoken like this man."

His fury at them obvious, the high priest stands, and steps up to the guard.

"You damn fool! You mean you let him deceived you also?"

Seeing he is not getting anywhere; the priest dismisses the guards who make a point of marching off in a neat single procession. His anger mounting, the high priest storms around the center of the floor. His black and gold robes flow in the air, as he paces in a wide circle ready to question the rest of the priests.

"Do any of you rulers or Pharisees sitting here now believe in this Jesus?"

Before anyone can answer, he continues.

"No! Of course not! However, these mobs that know nothing of the law, are cursed by him."

There is a quiet pause, as Nickodemis steps forward. His kind, but determined eyes challenge the high priest, while positioning his stance on the center of the floor. His modest and quiet personality makes it easy for people to listen. Knowing the popularity of this man, the high priest scowls. Meanwhile, Nickodemis clears his throat to emphasize his soft, but clear voice.

"Does our law condemn a man without first hearing him, or find out what he's doing?"

His voice heavy with sarcasm, the chief priest's annoyance is clouding his judgement.

"Oh, I remember now, you're from Galilee. You should know above all people that no prophet has 'ever' come out of Galilee."

Witnessing the roar of laughter from his fellow high priests backing the one who is belittling him, Nickodemis feels hurt and betrayed. His emotions now turning to anger and shame, Nickodemis, controls this anger, as he bows out of this meeting and leaves.

Still resting at the Mount of Olives, Jesus is becoming weary as he leans against the trunk of a large olive tree. While he runs his hand over the smooth, gray bark, it brings a modicum of comfort as his mind races through the day's frustrations. Lethargy flows through his body in waves making him grip onto the trunk for more support. Unable to stand anymore, he slides down the tree until he hits the ground. Debilitating pain travels up his back as he attempts to rest. Praying for some relief, he gazes up at the moonless black sky. As every star twinkles back at him in a teasing manner, sadness overwhelms him. Stinging tears of dismay burn his eyes.

"Oh God - why? Why is it so hard? Why doesn't 'anyone' understand?"

He shuts his eyes to suppress the tears, when a familiar voice resonates.

"How do you expect them to?"

Fear and disgust forces Jesus to open his eyes. Confronted by the darkness, his eyes adjust to focus on a black undefined figure, hovering a small distance away. Knowing who it is, Jesus waves a tired arm in that direction.

"Go away! There's no space for you here."

Ignoring Jesus' request, the shape floats toward him as if to threaten, and then drifts away, as if to tease.

"Not here with you perhaps, but there is 'elsewhere', as you're now finding out.

That's why they don't understand you – I won't let them..."

The shape comes nearer. While it seems to envelope Jesus, he becomes cold, and afraid. The voice is now so soft and close it feels as if it is coming from inside his own head.

"This is nothing. Soon it will get 'devilishly' hard. Excuse the pun. To make it worse, you will be denied by a close one, and then betrayed, which will lead to your death. Not a year from now, but in a few weeks."

Stunned by this prediction, Jesus' body begins to tremble.

What am I hearing? How does Satan know all this? Why am I so cold?

"Go! Just go..."

Exhausted to the point of passing out, Jesus rests his heavy head into his shivering hands. The black evil presence just laughs at Jesus' feeble attempts to resist him.

"Look, my original offer still stands. You don't have to suffer like this. Just think, you would have no more letdowns with all these stupid people. No more trying to convince the ignorant masses. You can be a sovereign of everything with me right behind you; giving you strength and guidance..."

"Stop it! Stop it!"

Unable to resist anymore, Jesus presses his hands hard against his ears. He curls up on the ground, while his head hurts by the pressure of his own hands.

"Oh God I need you so much. Please give me the strength to carry on. I can't take much more."

Minutes drag by. No more voices. He releases the grip on his head, and looks up.

No dark shape. No Satan!

His anxiety leaving him, calmness covers him like a welcomed warm blanket. His shivering stopped, he leans back against the tree again, and looks up at the far away stars that shine down with a neutral dispassion.

"I must go back to the temple tomorrow. There are still many people who want to listen further."

From a mixture of fatigue and lack of food, his mind now goes blank. His body collapses sideways to the ground. Within seconds, he is asleep; a deep dreamless sleep.

It is now early next morning. With the effects of hunger, Jesus makes his way back to the temple courts.

To his surprise, the high priests are already there. Not wasting any time, and expressing a sarcastic sneer, the chief priest steps forward to confront him.

"I knew you would return this morning."

Anxious at this early confrontation, Jesus acts calm by conveying to the man in black a pensive smile.

"Many people from yesterday wanted to listen to me, but were stopped."

His black and gold robes flowing around his obese body, the man in front of him ignores this statement and turns away. While following this priest, the black mass reminds Jesus of the black mobile accumulation of Satan. His anxiety increasing, Jesus stops as the priest points to a dark corner of the stonewalled temple.

"Come! There is something we would all like to show you."

As he beckons to someone out of sight, two temple guards appear bringing in an attractive young woman. Jesus estimates she is probably in her mid-twenties. Her gold-olive eyes stare at him pleading for help. She can see she looks scared, and notices her plain coarse clothes look ragged compared to the Priests' and Pharisees fine woven garments. Glaring at Jesus for a reaction, the chief priest points an accusing finger at the poor woman.

"You see this young woman? She was caught in the act of adultery. The Law of Moses 'demands' we stone such a woman. Now what do 'you' say?"

Aware of the trap that being set for him, Jesus feels a pit in his stomach. So, they have a basis to accuse him, he doesn't answer right away. Instead, he crouches down to the temple's dirt floor and begins to draw with his left index finger. After a minute, he looks up at the fearful young woman, and notices nasty welts on the base of her neck. Continuing his drawing, he pictures a scenario of her being caught in the arms of a man who loves her instead of being routinely beaten and raped by her so called husband. Pondering, he looks down again, his index finger making grooves in the dirt. Aware that this delay in judgment is annoying the entire Jewish temple establishment, Jesus stops, straightens up, and conveys an accusing expression at this impatient audience.

"If any of you here is without sin, let him be the one to throw the first stone at her."

While the priests ponder this extraordinary statement, Jesus offers a reassuring smile at the young woman, as he crouches down again to draw.

Without even looking, he can hear the accusers grumbling to each other and leaving one by one until there is just Jesus and the young woman left. Now safe to stand, he reaches out to grip her slender forearm.

"Woman? Where are they? Is there anyone here to condemn you?"

Her handsome face expressing relief, she answers.

"No sir. No one."

"Then neither do I condemn you. Even though you have had a tough time, go now and leave your life of sin."

Trembling in front of him; tears well up in her eyes and pour down her face. Finding it hard to believe what has happened, she breaks down and sobs. His reaction is to wrap his arms around her as she rests her head against his chest. Her beauty reminding him of Mary, he strokes her hair and whispers.

"God loves you now."

In the meantime, the Pharisees return deep inside the temple. Grumbling and making threatening noises, one particular Pharisee shouts out in exasperation.

"He's tricked us again. Making us look like fools."

Joseph of Arimathea decides he needs to express his righteous opinion.

"We feel now that he has tricked us. In truth, don't you feel he has touched our souls, and sensing our guilt?"

Becoming irritated by the discord, the chief makes his comments.

"All right, all right. He made a point. As far as our own positions are concerned he is still a constant threat. We must get rid of him. Unfortunately, it's not a good time right now, because of his huge following. However, we could make him look wrong in the eyes of the law. If so, his following will evaporate overnight."

Murmurs of agreement follow. Joseph of Arimathea declines to comment. Meanwhile, Jesus enters the main hall speaking with new confidence.

"I am the light of the world. Whoever follows me shall never walk in darkness, but will have the light of life."

The sound of Jesus' unshakeable optimism causes the Pharisees to freeze.

"It's him, he's back! Perhaps this is our chance to challenge him properly."

The chief Priest indicates to the others to follow as he leads them toward the main hall.

Observing the Temple's authority forming a line barring Jesus to go further, he stops at a distance of about three paces. Sickened by their black and gold robes blending into one huge mass, Jesus glares at the chief Pharisee whose dark eyes still express sarcasm and contempt.

"So, you have returned again. You appearing as your own witness is unfortunate because your explanation and testimony will not be valid."

Knowing the law, Jesus sighs as he hears murmurs of agreement from the black mass. Jesus peers down at the floor as if searching, then he lifts up his head and offers the dark eyes a positive smile.

"Even if I testify on my own behalf it would still be valid, because I know where I've come from and where I'm going. However, you have no idea. You judge only by human standards. I pass judgment on no one. However, if I do judge, my decision is always right, because I'm not alone. I stand here with the one who has sent me."

The Pharisees glance at each other in confusion, and then back to Jesus. Not understanding a single word, because they see him standing alone, Jesus offers them another smile.

"In your own land it is written that the testimony of two men together is valid. Therefore, I'm the one who testifies for myself, accompanied by my other witness who has sent me."

Again, the Pharisees glare at each other, but this time frustrated and annoyed as Jesus is playing with their authority. A young zealous Pharisee reacts by stepping forward. Remembering him from the pool, Jesus expresses silent contempt as the Pharisee's red-brown eyes challenge him. His face ugly distorted with rage, he points to the empty space next to Jesus.

"Then 'where' is your witness?"

"You don't know me, or my witness. If you did know me, you would know my witness - who sent me."

All the Jews stare at Jesus dumbfounded. Their reaction is to huddle together and discuss among each other.

"He's playing with us. Treating us like idiots. He won't even tell us who or where his witness is."

Surveying their discord, Jesus raises his voice another notch so he can be heard above their murmurs.

"I'm going away. You will look for me and die drowning in your sins. Where I go, you can't come."

Still not understanding, the Jews huddle closer to each other.

"Will he kill himself? Is that why he's telling us that 'where I go you can't come?"

Enjoying the disorder, Jesus raises his voice even louder.

"You're all from down below, I'm from above. You're of this world, I'm not. 've told you that you'll die of your sins. If you don't believe that I'm the man I claim to be, you will 'indeed' die of your sins."

Becoming more agitated, another Pharisee steps forward. Jesus notices he is older, his face stoic and unemotional. The man's slate-gray eyes appear puzzled as he confronts him.

"Who are you?"

Undeterred by this man, Jesus answers.

"Who I've been claiming all along. I have much to judge you for. The one who sent me is totally the truth, so what I hear from that truth, I repeat to the world."

Shaking their heads, the Jews still do not comprehend. Their frustration is becoming so bad, it is surmounting to anger. Unfortunately, they are powerless to do anything, because the original small crowd who came in with Jesus is swelling so much that it is overflowing into the streets. Jesus senses the situation and knows that this is not the time they will take him. So, with extra confidence he continues his message.

"When you have lifted up the son of man, you will 'know' who I am, and that I speak with the one who has taught me, here with me now. I'm never alone, my truth stays the same."

Enthralled by his wisdom, many in the crowd behind Jesus are questioning to each other.

"Perhaps this really is the Messiah?"

Now on a roll, Jesus continues to raise his voice even more over the crowd.

"If any of you here hold my teaching, you really are my disciples. You will know the truth and be set free."

This is all too much for the Pharisees. The chief priest steps forward, his dark eyes angry.

"We are the descendants of Abraham, and have never been slaves to anyone, so how can you stand here and say we shall be set free?"

Expecting this reaction, Jesus pauses. The crowd goes quiet, now waiting for his reply. The Pharisees begin to feel more confident in their arrogance. They are sure they have trapped him this time. Jesus response is to turn his back on the Jewish rulers and face the swelling crowd. Raising his left arm, he knows he has their full attention.

"The truth is, you're all slaves. Slaves to sin. A slave has no place in the family of God. A son belonging has the power to set you free, and by doing so you will be free."

He turns back and faces the Jews.

"I know you're the descendants of Abraham, and yet you're ready to kill me."

The whole crowd gasps in astonishment. The Pharisees look embarrassed, realizing this man knows their real intentions. Ignoring their reaction, Jesus continues.

"Yes, you're ready to kill me, because you have no room for my words, which are from God. However, your intentions are from the father of sin - Satan."

The chief priest knows he is losing face to the crowd and is desperate. Although losing this argument, his arrogance and vanity will not allow him to give in.

"Abraham is our father!"

Hearing that name, Jesus' eyes blaze with fury, but tinge with sadness.

"If you're the true children of Abraham, you would not want to kill me. Abraham didn't do such things, so you're doing this through your real father..."

Frustrated at losing this argument, the chief Jew interrupts.

"We are not illegitimate children! The only parent we have is - God."

Becoming tired of this hypocrisy, Jesus stares in disbelief at this Jewish council.

"If you hypocrites think that God is your creator, then you should love me, because I am from God. It is God who sent me. Now I'm here talking to you, you find it hard to understand me. Is my language not clear to you? Of course, it isn't. Your language is of the Devil, because he's your master, not God."

The crowd now murmuring even louder, some agree, but some still puzzled, but all are concentrating on the angry Pharisees. Ready for any onslaught, Jesus continues.

"The Devil has been a murderer right back to the beginning. Never telling the truth, the father of lies and deceit. That's why you don't believe me now. Can any of you standing here prove me guilty of 'any' sin? Of course, you can't, because they who belong to God hear only what God says. The reason you don't hear me is that you don't belong to God."

This accusation is too much for the Pharisees. Their embarrassment will cause them to try anything to make Jesus look bad in front of this huge crowd. The young Pharisee, his face still flushed with rage, bellows at Jesus.

"You're the one possessed by demons, not us."

His fatigue becoming obvious, Jesus spits back.

"I'm 'not' possessed by demons. I honor God's word while you dishonor mine. I don't seek glory for myself, only for God. However, you seek glory only for yourselves. God is the judge. I tell you only the truth. If a man keeps my word he will never see death."

Observing Jesus becoming tired, the chief priest thinks he has found a weakness in Jesus' argument.

"Now we know you 'are' demon-possessed. Abraham and all the other great prophets died, and yet you stand there and say a man who keeps 'your' word can cheat death. Are you greater than our father Abraham? We think not. So, who do you think you really are?"

Knowing what this man is getting at, Jesus stands steadfast.

"If I glorify myself it means nothing. You, glorifying yourselves mean nothing. God is the one who glorifies me. You don't know God as I do. If I said I didn't know God I would be a liar - like you, but all I do is tell the truth."

Not wanting to look bad in front of this huge crowd, the group leaders huddle closer together in desperation. Wanting to confront Jesus again, but no words come to mind, they decide that Jesus is the ultimate sinner and they will prove it by killing him, but not right now.

Smiling with a sense of fulfillment, Jesus senses the standoff. With his words of truth now spoken, he turns toward and enters into the crowd. Intrigued by this new preacher, the crowd makes way for him to exit the temple.

15

Lazarus

After the standoff with the ruling Jews, Jesus decides to get some relief and cross the Jordan River with his Apostles where he was first baptized.

The area now deserted; Jesus sits on the same bank as before. The twelve plus his mother gather round in odd groups trying to find shade. Mary Magdalene positions next to her man. Always wanting to be of use, Jesus' mother stays with Peter and begins to organize the sharing out of what food and water they have.

Even though they are sitting close together, Jesus gazes at the river in deep thought. Noticing his mind is not with her right now, she becomes aware that his world is caught up in the clear blue river; sparkling as it pours over the various size rocks, and then flowing away into the distance.

"What do you see my love?"

The sound of her concerning voice jolts him out of his daydream.

"A great man who helped me start my mission."

His eyes burning from this memory of John the Baptist, he looks away to observe the rest of his loyal followers. Peter, his mother Mary and Andrew are chatting and retrieving food from a rough sewn bag. Judas is talking to the remainder in a formal tone. Although Jesus cannot quite hear the words, but he is aware of the concentration of his small audience.

I've noticed of late that Judas is not so critical of me. His intellectual manner has become humbler.

The shimmering desert creates a harsh backdrop against this vulnerable small group. The hot breeze is disturbing everything as Judas laughs, and then carries on his previous discussion. Mary is still studying her lover's eyes, as he turns to face her. As if conscious of her analyzing his every expression, he begins to draw with his left index finger as if she isn't there. The lines in the sand are not developing into any particular form, but his lips move in earnest.

"I 'am' the good shepherd, who will always lay down his life for his sheep. The hired worker is not a good shepherd. He doesn't own his sheep; they are not his. So, any sign of trouble or a sight of a wolf, he will just abandon the flock and run."

Sensitive to this new mood, Mary places her hand on his left hand, while studying the labyrinth of lines in the sand. He looks up at her, his tired eyes filling with burning tears, while his voice cracks with emotion.

"I 'am' the good shepherd. I know my sheep, and they know me. I 'will' lay down my life for them. I have other sheep that are not in the pen, but I need to bring them all in so they can listen and learn from me."

As his bottom lip trembles, he clears his throat. Meanwhile, the rest of the twelve sense this foreboding and gather round. Jesus peers at them all, scanning each pair of curious eyes, and then stopping at his mother. Jesus' eyes do not sway from his mother, but his stare turns into a distant gaze, and his voice becomes clearer and more precise.

"No one will take my life. I will lay it down on my own accord. I have the authority to lay it down, and the authority to take it up again. This I have received from God."

Astounded by this new proclamation, a remote stillness fills the area. A small dark cloud appears from nowhere gliding across the sun. Dulling the light, a sudden chill fills the air. Wondering what is happening, everyone glances at each other, and then back to Jesus. The whole atmosphere becomes sad, almost depressing as Jesus bows his head and mumbles. The cloud disperses; the sun shines again as before. His face more relaxed, Jesus stands and scans the horizon. After a few seconds of reflection, he grabs hold of Mary's hand to assist her up, and then they begin walking.

FOR THE LOVE OF MAN

The puzzled apostles look at each other for some sort of communal decision

"Where are we going now?"

An hour has passed. They are all approaching a small village not far from Jerusalem. A large group of people has gathered on the main road into the village.

As Jesus and his Apostles walk by toward the village entrance, a woman's voice shouts out from the gathered group.

"Oh Rabbi. It's you!"

A woman runs up to Jesus, and grips his hand in desperation. Recognizing her, he becomes aware as another familiar woman arrives. Jesus knows them as Mary and Martha, the sisters of his good friend Lazarus, whom he is about to visit. Still gripping his hand, both women are becoming distressed causing Jesus to be concerned.

"What is it?"

"Oh Rabbi! Its Lazarus, he's very sick."

Jesus hesitates as his eyes take on a glazed expression. To offer reassurance, he places a comforting hand on Mary's shoulder.

"Don't worry. The sickness will not end in death, but we will stay here a while anyway."

The two sisters are confused by this casual statement, but still hope he will cure their brother.

Two days have passed. Jesus is sitting with the Apostles; his mood is restless as he glances at Mary Magdalene.

"I think we should go back to Judea."

Puzzled by such a suggestion, Peter is determined to demonstrate his opinion over Mary.

"But sir? Don't you remember the Jews there tried to stone you?"

Jesus reaction is to glare into Peter's dark eyes.

"Are there not twelve hours of daylight? A man who walks by daylight will not stumble as he would do by night. So, if he walks by night, he will need a light to guide him. I happen to be that light."

With Peter becoming hurt by his master's rebuff, and confused by this latest statement, he can do nothing, while Jesus stands, and speaks to no one in particular.

"Our friend Lazarus has only fallen asleep. So, I think I will go and wake him."

Becoming puzzled by this new encounter, Matthew speaks up venting his frustration at his inability to comprehend Jesus' words.

"Master? If he sleeps, he will get better."

Understanding his apostle's quandary, Jesus relays a confident smile and lays his hand on his shoulder.

"Let's go to him and see."

They arrive to find Lazarus has already been placed in a tomb. Nearby, a large group of people are weeping, moaning, in mourning. Some comforting Mary and Martha for their loss, while others glare at Jesus. Her tearful eyes raging with anger, and frustration, Martha rushes up to him.

"If you were here earlier you could have saved him."

Unperturbed by the resentment, Jesus offers her a reassuring smile. Becoming a little calmer by his reassurance, she becomes resigned to the situation.

"I know even now; God will give you what you ask."

Gripping her trembling hand to keep reassuring, he looks deep into her troubled eyes.

"Don't worry. Your brother will rise from this tomb."

"Worry? I know he will rise again; in the resurrection, on the last day..."

Observing his calm manner is not working, he places both his hands on her shoulders. His intention to calm her further, his voice comes across soft, but determined.

"I am the resurrection and the Life, those who believe in me will live, even though they may die. Do you believe that?"

Not really convinced, she lowers her head to wipe her eyes.

"Yes, Rabbi. I know you're the Messiah who has come to this world, but..."

"Where have you laid him?"

She turns to her sister, bewildered, while Jesus' mood changes. Now tenser, he repeats the question.

"Where have you laid him?"

Becoming confused by this sudden strange behavior, Martha grips his hand and begins to pull him toward the tomb.

"Come! We will show you."

The rest of the group becoming curious, begin to follow.

"What is happening? Is he going to raise Lazarus from the dead?"

Jesus, now accompanied by an anxious and curious group, are now outside the tomb. Jesus' determined expression, but apprehensive eyes, stare in defiance at the tall entrance.

"Take away this stone!"

Within seconds, four burly men appear from behind Jesus ready to roll the heavy stone back in its groove. Querying Jesus' order, Martha is shocked.

"But Rabbi, our brother has been dead now for 'four' days."

Jesus ignores her and beckons the four hesitant men to remove the stone.

As the stone rolls away, a foul odor engulfs the crowd. Choking and coughing as the odor penetrates, the group move back to leave Jesus alone with Martha.

"Haven't I told you that you will see the glory of God if you believe?"

As if embarrassed, she bows her head, and then backs away joining the main group.

Now concentrating on the immediate challenge, Jesus steps forward to within a step of the rough-carved arched entrance. He leans forward to rest both arms on the edge of the opening. He takes a deep breath, lowers his head, and shuts his eyes. Mumbling so his voice isn't audible to any witnesses close by, he leans a little further forward.

"I know you can always hear me. I say this for the benefit of these people. They have to believe it is 'you' that has sent me."

A deathly hush creeps over the crowd as their eyes focus on Jesus.

His prayer finished; he pushes hard against the wall. His eyes still closed, sweat pours down his face, as he shouts.

"Lazarus? Come out!"

Nothing happens. He shouts again, this time louder.

"Lazarus? COME OUT!"

Jesus lets his tired arms drop by his sides. He can just about stand. Knowing what he is going through, Mary Magdalene works her way through the crowd to be near him. She knows what is going to happen next.

In the stillness, a shuffling noise can be heard from inside the tomb. A bandaged figure appears at the entrance. Pieces of linen hang off the figure like dead limbs on a dying tree. Gasps of astonishment come from the crowd, as Jesus manages to lift up his right arm and point to the crowd.

"Remove his grave clothes and let him go..."

His legs buckle. Before he collapses, Mary wastes no time in catching him. Supporting his weight, she then crouches down to support his head against her breasts and cradles him in her arms.

"Oh, my love. My love..."

Jesus opens his heavy eyes and tries to smile.

"I told you he was only asleep."

Hiding his shame at not helping his master, Peter beckons the Apostles to help and surround Jesus, as the crowd comes closer in awe at witnessing this great miracle.

Unfortunately, as always on these occasions, few of the crowd are there on behalf of the Jewish Council. Even they have to admit they are amazed at what they witnessed, but not happy with Jesus' ever-growing following. They leave to report to the Pharisees.

A high-level meeting is being called. Every high priest, pharisee, and council member is present. The atmosphere is tense, as they mumble questions to each other.

"What are we accomplishing? Why are we having this meeting?"

Irritable by the situation, Caiaphas steps forward to answer. To define his authority, his fine quality black robes, lined with gold and bright silver etchings reflect in the light. To attract everyone's attention, he strides around the floor in a flamboyant manner, flashing his green eyes with enthusiasm. His dark curly hair showing just under his jewel-studded headpiece, he stands with his hands on his hips.

"As you know, a meeting such as this is only called in a crisis or in a severe emergency. Today we have both. There is a man out there performing all types of ..."

He pauses so his intentional sarcasm comes across to his audience.

"... err, 'miraculous' signs..."

He pauses again, and listens with intent to the reaction of his fellow Jews. By using scare tactics, he hopes to rally their support.

"If we let him go on like this, every peasant, merchant and even some of you will believe in him. Then gentlemen, the Romans will come and take both our place, positions and even the Jewish nation."

Sure he has the Jew's agreement, he paces around the floor oozing confidence. Timing his moves, he turns back to face them.

"So, gentlemen; it comes down to this - that you know nothing at all. Don't you realize that it is better for you that 'one' man dies - 'for the people' than the whole nation perishes? I have always prophesied that this man will die so the whole Jewish nation will finally come together."

Before his fellow Jews can respond, he leaves the chamber as dramatically as he entered. Stirred by the speech, the remaining Jews gather round and are unanimous in deciding that the time is getting near to kill Jesus.

In the meantime, Jesus, still very tired, decides to withdraw to a village near the desert called Ephram.

A kind house owner lets Jesus, his family and the Apostles, have the use of his house for as long as they want.

It is the following evening; all the Apostles are sitting outside in a rough circle enjoying the cool desert air. While, they murmur among themselves, uncertain about their future, Jesus remains in the house.

Sitting on the floor, propped against a wall, his strength returning, Jesus welcomes Mary Magdalene's head resting against his chest. Aware of him needing more rest, she looks up to him and searches his eyes.

"You know it's Passover soon. Many will be going to Jerusalem for the cleansing ceremony to get ready."

Contemplating her words, he is enjoying letting her lush hair glide between his fingers

"I know. I've been thinking about it."

While he strokes her head, she shuts her eyes relishing his touch. Enjoying her warmth, a sense of dread overcomes him knowing this ecstasy will not last much longer.

"The ruling council will now be after my blood. So, it wouldn't be wise for us to go right now. Perhaps it will be best if we go back to Bethany to visit Lazarus and his sisters."

It is now six days before Passover. Jesus, Mary, his mother and his Apostles arrive at Bethany. His eyes filling with tears of gratitude, Lazarus greets him like a lost brother. Jesus also gets a hug from the two sisters, Mary and Martha.

A dinner is given in Jesus' honor. The whole village is out to greet them and celebrations begin. The few Jews in the village that are still working and spying for the ruling Council, take note that there are many more becoming followers of Jesus. Again, they report their findings to the high priests.

The Council decides enough is enough. Plans are brought forward to kill Jesus and Lazarus.

Meanwhile, after much food, wine and merriment, Jesus is relaxing in Mary and Martha's house. Lazarus is sitting next to him while some of the troubled Apostles are still outside discussing about their own future. Somewhat more confident, Peter, Judas and Andrew decide to be with

Jesus. The mood is jovial. Martha's sister Mary enters the room carrying a small clay bottle. Without saying a word, she kneels down in front of Jesus and removes his sandals. She then pulls out the stopper from the bottle, pours a small amount of good quality perfumed oil onto the palm of her hand, and begins to rub it onto Jesus' feet. As the whole room fills with the exotic odor, everyone is silent, while they watch in fascination at Mary's deed. A little jealous of this deed, Mary Magdalene crouches down next to Martha's sister, and indicates that she would like to carry on the ritual.

As she takes over, Jesus closes his eyes absorbing the well-known touch of Mary's delicate hands. It is becoming more personal as Mary is giving sensual pleasure to her man. As the rubbing and stroking become more intense, she lowers her head and begins to drag her lush wavy hair across his feet at the same time expressing strong signals of her deep love for him.

His eyes still closed, this intimacy reminds Jesus of the time he and Mary first met, and how he felt the ecstasy she is able to produce within him.

Judas, hiding his embarrassment and a little jealous by this deep personal activity, glares at Peter for support. Peter, not bothered at what is happening, he shrugs. Becoming irritable by Peter's apathy, Judas glares at Jesus.

"Rabbi, why isn't this expensive oil being sold and the money given to the poor? It must be worth a year's wages."

To calm his fellow apostle, Peter squeezes Judas's arm. Meanwhile, Jesus is reluctant to come out of his pleasant daze. He opens his eyes and looks up to quell Judas's concern.

"Leave her alone. It is meant that she shall save the rest of this perfume for my burial. Unfortunately, you will always have the poor among you. However, you will not always have me."

Peter nudges a confused Judas and beckons him to join the others outside the house. Judas still confused; they both leave without even looking back.

Still enjoying his daze, Jesus indicates Mary to continue. Although the initial pleasure of her skilled hands has abated; he relaxes by rationalizing his thoughts.

This is why I'm here. This is part of my journey to help these people understand....

Her hands now finished with his feet; he feels a squeeze on his forearm. As Jesus opens his eyes, Mary beckons him to Lazarus. His eyes full of tears, Lazarus kneels down to be closer.

"Rabbi, because you saved me, all this rejoicing is for you. The village all believes in you. They are going to Jerusalem to spread the word for you to return. This time in triumph."

In his euphoric haze, Jesus gazes into Lazarus's light brown eyes, and places his left hand on his shoulder.

"Go and tell James and John to go ahead into the next village. They will find a white donkey, tethered. No one else has ever ridden this animal, so tell them to untie it and bring it here to me. If anyone asks; 'Why are you untying this donkey?' Tell them it's for me."

Lazarus appears puzzled, but without question, he leaves the room followed by his sister Mary, who gathers up the bottle of perfumed oil. Still caught up in the remaining euphoria, Jesus leans back giving the impression he is still calm and relaxed. Mary Magdalene knows different. Even though she knows the effect her foot massage had on him, she can now see fear developing in his eyes. To calm his fear, she leans over to stroke his cheek. He reacts by taking her hand and pulling it to his mouth. Delighting in her hand being smothered with soft kisses, she raises up so she can rest his head against the welcoming softness of her warm breasts. Knowing this always calms his anxiety, she wants to give him strength, comfort, and most of all, herself.

As predicted, Jesus' brothers find the white donkey. The village is quiet and no one witnesses them untying the chosen animal.

On their return, James inquires to his elder brother.

"Why this donkey? Why not a white horse? A status you deserve."

Jesus looks at his youngest brother with affection to explain.

"My brother, I'm not a ruler. I'm going into Jerusalem as a humble servant and savior on a beast of burden, because, it is my burden to save."

Not looking forward to the oncoming challenge, Jesus mounts the donkey. His feet almost touching the ground, Jesus reaches across to Mary.

"I'm ready as I'll ever be…"

Fearful for him, she slides her arm around his shoulder. Noticing he is wet from sweating even though it is still morning and the air is cool, she kisses his cheek.

"This is it my love. Recognition at last."

His eyes becoming moist with tears of apprehension, he is unable to look at her.

"We will see. Whatever happens, this is still part of the journey."

As he sets off, she notices his ivory smock looks dirty and stained compared to the clean white fur of the donkey. Taking a deep breath to calm her own anxiety, she joins the others. The two Mary's and the twelve Apostles follow on foot in deep discussion hoping this entrance into the city will be better than the last.

They are now approaching the Mount of Olives, which is just before Jerusalem. People are beginning to line both sides of the road. A few wave, some throw palm fronds and flower petals. Some just stand and look curious. Others, expecting a grand messiah, see to their disappointment a tired-looking young man on a lowly beast.

As they are now nearer to the city entrance, the crowds are swelling and more palm fronds and petals line the route. Jesus is amazed as the people shout.

"You're the King, who is here in the name of God."

His nerves tingling in turmoil, Jesus hears others praise him.

"You're the Son of David. Peace and glory in the highest."

In the meantime, taking a dim view of all this, some Pharisees mix with the people. One is brave enough to shout to Jesus as he goes by.

"You should rebuke these followers. This is all blasphemy."

Slowing down and hiding his contempt, Jesus conveys to the Pharisee a beaming smile.

"If they all kept quiet, the stones would cry out instead."

This is not what the high Jew wants to hear. Ignoring the accumulating crowd, he leaves.

Jesus is now approaching the city's entrance. Hundreds of people are now throwing cloaks along with the palm fronds and petals. Overawed by the crowd's enthusiasm, he stops the animal for a minute, and stares up at the archway. The sun's rays now beaming down on his face, his eyes sting with fresh tears. As the surrounding noise of the crowd seems to drift into the distance, his eyes focus on the stone archway.

If only you knew, that on this day I bring you peace and love, and not conquest. However, it is hidden from your eyes. You praise me now, but the day will soon come when the enemies of the Jewish people will build a wall encircling you on every side. They will beat you and your children, trying everything, because you will ignore my message and deny who I am.

The roar of the crowd returns to his ears. He looks straight ahead, tears of apprehension now running down his face.

Working his way into the city, hundreds more people praise and shout to their new King. Meanwhile, a group of Pharisees mix with the crowd not far from the temple steps. Expressing a mixture of scorn and fear, they are begrudging while they witness this spectacle. Irritated, a high priest raises his voice above the noise to his companions.

"Look at all this! This is getting us nowhere. The whole world is going after this man."

Amongst the cheering, some of the crowd question the legitimacy of this exhibition.

"Who is this man riding a donkey?"

Others answer their question.

"This is Jesus of Nazareth, the Prophet."

Feeling the pressure of the crowd's expectancy, Jesus stops by the Temple steps, dismounts, and then turns to find that Mary and Peter are right behind him.

"It's time to go inside the Temple to conclude my message."

As they climb the wide steps, Jesus observes that all is not right. To start with, there is an array of merchants and peddlers selling their wares at the main entrance. Mary has never seen Jesus this angry before. She becomes nervous - almost frightened to see his gentle face turn ugly and distort with rage. Tears of righteous anger fill his eyes, as he storms into the temple.

Now inside, he pauses to survey the scene. To his horror there are merchants everywhere using God's house to buy and sell. In his rage, he tips over a nearby moneylender's table, much to the amazement of the lender. As the lender scurries after his cherished money rolling everywhere, Jesus grunts with the effort as he tips over more tables. While throwing pieces of furniture, boxes and smashing pottery, howls of protest come from the traders that fill the hall. While they gawp at him as if he is a madman, Jesus stands catching his breath in the center of the floor among a pile of debris. His body wet with sweat, his hands tremble with outrage as he raises an accusing finger at the angry and confused merchants.

"It is written; my house is a house of prayer, but all of you here are making it a den of thieves. The blind and the lame came here to hear me and be healed, and yet when you and your Pharisees saw and witnessed my work you become indignant and threatened. Now you allow all this!"

The atmosphere becomes still, as the odd settlement of debris and angry murmurs from the merchants echo throughout. Angry and sad, Jesus turns and leaves, as Mary and Peter meet him at the steps. Needing her comfort, he holds his arms out for her. Her heart bursting with sympathy and outrage, she comes to him and wraps her arms around his trembling body. Meanwhile, a large confused crowd gathers around as Mary helps him descend the steps to where the others Apostles are waiting with anxious faces. Jesus' pale drawn face looks at his loyal, but fearful followers with affection. He then whispers in Mary's ear.

"Let's go back to Bethany."

16

Agony at the Last Supper

It is now two days before the Feast of Unleavened Bread. Still in Bethany, Jesus is restless, which is worrying for Mary and his mother. Every time either one of them tries to comfort him, he tends to withdraw and sit by himself. Never witnessing his mentor act like this before, Peter is also concerned. Putting on a casual air, he approaches Jesus.

"Sir? Where do you want us to go and make preparations for all of us to eat the Passover?"

Because of his master's behavior, Peter is not sure whether his question is heard. In the meantime, Jesus stares ahead into empty space. Peter and the two women glance at each other with mounting concern. After a short while, Jesus' eyes begin to focus. He turns toward them, speaking first to Peter.

"Go into the city. A man carrying a large jar of water will meet you. Follow him, he will lead you to a house. When you see the owner of this house, ask him that the Rabbi needs the guest room, where he may eat the Passover with his Apostles? He should show you a large upper room, furnished and ready. Once in the room, you will make the necessary preparations."

Working out in his mind what to do, Peter nods. He then beckons to the others. Indicating for Judas and Andrew to join him, all three men leave the house.

It is now evening. Jesus arrives at the requested room with his mother, Mary Magdalene, and the rest of the twelve. Peter, Andrew and Judas stand with an element of pride by a large square table positioned in the center of the room. The warm glow of the oil lamps reflects on their faces. They are eager for praise from their leader, as the preparation of the room has to be perfect. Without a word being said, Jesus goes up to each man in turn, placing a thankful hand on their shoulders and conveying a grateful smile. After gazing at the table, he indicates for everyone to sit in their appointed a place.

While the twelve plus the two women jostle for their seats, Jesus remains standing. As there is one gap left between Mary and Peter, they all have the same puzzling thought.

Why isn't he sitting amongst us?

To satisfy their curiosity, Jesus removes his smock. Mary and Jesus' mother are shocked by how much weight he has lost. He goes over to a small table standing by a nearby wall. On the table is a large earthenware water jug and bowl with some folded clean towels. All eyes are on him, as he takes hold of one towel and wraps it around his gaunt waist. Arousing everyone's curiosity, he then pours some water from the jug into the large brown bowl. The sound of the water seems exaggerated compared to the stillness of the room. The spectators are captivated at what is happening, as Jesus carries the bowl of water to where Philip is sitting. Jesus indicates to Philip to turn around away from the table with his legs facing him. As Philip turns, Jesus kneels, removes Philip's sandals and begins to wash and dry his feet. Witnessing this unusual act, everyone in the room stays silent and puzzled. Knowing that somehow their master is going to perform this ritual on all of them, they all turn away from the table.

When Jesus comes to Mary Magdalene repeating the same procedure, he takes his time. Looking up to her, his tired eyes strain a smile as he takes one of her pretty feet and gives it a kiss. Even though she can see he is exhausted, her body still tingles at his touch. Through the ecstasy, a sad thought flashes through her mind.

I've just realized, we haven't been intimate for some time...

Finished with Mary, his attention now goes to Judas, who puts his hand out.

"Rabbi this is not right. We are here to serve you. Not you – us?"

Ignoring the plea, Jesus says nothing. While washing and gazing into Judas' questioning eyes, Jesus takes longer than with Mary. As Jesus finishes, he grips both of Judas's feet, shuts his eyes and whispers. On opening his eyes, he releases the feet at the same time giving them a friendly pat.

The next is Peter who grumbles while moving his feet away.

"No, sir! It's not right that you wash my feet."

Ignoring the protest, Jesus kneels, and peers up to him.

"You don't realize why I'm doing this. Later you will understand."

Peter is adamant. He moves his feet even further away.

"No sir! You shall 'never' wash my feet."

Still crouching, Jesus lowers his head. Releasing a quiet sigh, he looks up at Peter. His eyes now stern, it is his turn to protest.

"Unless I wash your feet, you have no place with me!"

Shocked out of his stubborn pride, Peter's eyes now lock onto Jesus. Understanding his master's request, tears fill his eyes, as if a heavy burden has been lifted.

"Then sir, don't just wash my feet, but my hands and head as well."

Relieved at Peter's change of mind, Jesus puts on a smile as if the request is unnecessary.

"There is no need. A person who has fully bathed only needs their feet washed, because their whole body is already clean."

He finishes, gets dressed and sits down at the table in the empty space between Mary Magdalene and Peter. Even though Jesus seems to relax, he does not say a word. Instead, he closes his eyes, lowers his head, and moves his lips in silence. Everyone around the table except Mary, looks at him mystified, and then glance at each other looking for an answer. Conscious of the atmosphere developing, Jesus now raises his head, opens his eyes, and turns to Mary. Offering her a reassuring smile, he then stares at the rest. The soft warm amber glow of the lamps makes his eyes appear luminous, as if he is trying to reach deep into their souls.

"Do you all understand what I've just done?"

Searching for an explanation, except Mary and his mother, they all again glance at each other. Sadly, Jesus knows his twelve Apostles do not understand. Again, the continuous frustration and hurt overwhelms him, but he continues to teach them.

"You call me Teacher or Rabbi. That is all I am. Now, your 'Teacher or Rabbi' has just washed your feet. I have set the example to you that no servant is greater than their master, nor is a messenger greater than the one who sent him. Now you know this, act upon it. Wash each other's feet, and you will all be blessed."

A short while later, the mutual foot washing has finished. As if searching for a real meaning, they again look toward their teacher. The mood now lighter, but still serious, Jesus places his hands together palms down on the table. Her instincts in tune with her man, Mary rests her hands on top of his. Sensing his mood of resignation, and their hands locked, he looks at the others in turn.

"My dear children, I will be with you only a little longer. You will look for me, but as I told the Jewish priests, where I'm going you can't come."

This statement creates a heavy undertone of anxiety. Their confidence in turmoil, everyone looks at each other to seek some sort of reassurance. Meanwhile, Jesus continues.

"I give you a new commandment. Love one another as I love you. Everyone you meet will know that you are my closest disciples, because you will show this love for each other..."

His anxiety more prominent than the others, Peter interrupts.

"Sir? Where are you going?"

"Where I'm going, you can't follow now, but you will later."

"Why can't I follow you now?"

Witnessing the painful doubt in Peter's eyes, Jesus hesitates. His eyes searching, he takes a look at Mary's delicate hands, and then looks back up to Peter.

"Peter? will you lay down your life for me? I'll tell you now, that before the cockerel crows you will have denied me three times."

Not believing his ears, Peter stares at Jesus. Stunned, he turns his head away filled with a mixture of disbelief and doubt. All eyes now on him, Jesus releases Mary's hands, and then slides his left arm around Peter's shoulders.

"Don't let your heart be troubled Peter. Trust in God and in me."

He pulls back from Peters' shoulder and places his hands together back on the table. This time Mary does not hold them. Jesus continues.

"Where I'm going there's many rooms. If there wasn't, I would tell you. I'm going to prepare a place for you. When your time comes, I will come and take you there so that you will know the way to where I'm going."

Becoming more confused, Thomas speaks out.

"Rabbi? We don't know where you're going. So, how are we to know the way?"

"Thomas? I am the truth and the life. No one goes to God unless through me. So, if you really know me, you will know God as well."

His confusion more obvious, Thomas scans the others for some kind of support.

"Rabbi? Show us God now! That will be enough for us."

Listening to the murmurs of agreement, makes Jesus' sadness even more profound. He reacts by his eyes hardening and his voice becoming sharp.

"Don't you know me by now Philip? After I've been among you all this time, and all that I've done, can't you see I have God within me? These words I speak are not mine, but God's. God and I are one, as you will be. You are 'all' the sons and daughters of God, not just me. I'm here to teach you, so you can do what I've done. God will do anything for you if asked. I will do anything for you if asked. It's just the same."

Observing his control over his frustration, Mary leans her head on his right shoulder, as if to support. Her heart being a turmoil of joy and dread, she senses bad times ahead. Appreciating her support, Jesus continues.

"If you really love me you will do as I ask. If you do, God will send you another Helper – 'The Spirit of Truth'. Unfortunately, this world will not accept, know or see the truth, but 'you' know the truth. I will not leave you like an orphan. I will come to you and offer strength. Soon this world will not see me anymore, but you will, because I will live in you as God lives in me."

Caught up in Jesus' sincerity, Judas is moved by these words.

"Rabbi? Why do you just show yourself to us and not to the world?"

Admiring Judas' intellect, Jesus studies him.

"Because if 'you' truly love me and obey my teachings, God will love you and come to you first. If the world doesn't obey these teachings, God won't come to them. Don't worry. You will be constantly reminded of my teachings and everything I've said to you. Peace, I leave with you. I'm telling you now before it happens, so when the time does arrive, you will believe me. That's why I've shown myself only to you. Unfortunately, this is the last time we can talk like this..."

Overcome by his own intensity, Jesus begins to sweat. He wipes his forehead with a now trembling hand, and continues.

"I have much more to say to you, more than you can bear, but like I said; when the Spirit of Truth comes; it will guide and help you in your grief. As I've said, in a while, you will not see me anymore, and then you 'will' see me."

Now devastated, and utterly confused by this latest statement, they turn to each other for an answer to the same question.

"What does this mean? We will not see him anymore, then we will see him?"

Witnessing their insecurity, Jesus sighs with regret, and now tries to reassure them.

"When I go, you will grieve, but your grief will turn to joy when you see me again. From that day on, you will understand, and God will give you whatever you ask for in my name..."

He's finished. After a pause, he dips his hands into a nearby bowl of water. The others take this as a signal to do the same. Jesus dries his hands and takes a small-unleavened loaf off the pile of bread in the center of the table and begins to break it up. He pauses again to close his eyes, and then opens them, while passing the first piece of bread to Mary on his right. He then places the remainder of the pieces into a nearby simple wooden bowl, and hands it to a troubled Peter. He looks at the bowl, takes out a piece of bread and passes the bowl around the table. Jesus smiles as he watches until everyone is now holding a piece of bread.

"Take this bread, because it is my body."

They all look at each other puzzled by this statement. Mary, Jesus' mother knows what to do by pushing her piece into her mouth. Followed by Mary Magdalene, and then Judas; the rest respond the same. Making sure all the bread is being eaten, Jesus now takes a jug of red wine and pours some into a plain wooden goblet, and then in turn offers it around the table.

"Take this wine, as it is my blood, which is going to be poured out for many. I will not ever drink the fruit of the vine until I'm in the Kingdom of God."

Not understanding what this means, they all take a sip anyway. Ending with Mary gripping the almost empty wooden goblet as if it is the most precious possession, she watches Jesus serious expression.

His hands now locked together, Jesus is silent, as he stares again at the tabletop. After a short while, he lifts up his head to face them. As his eyes scan the whole group, his voice is flat with no emotion.

"One of you here is going to betray me."

As an undercurrent of shock fills the room, their voices seem to speak in unison.

"Not I Rabbi! Who?"

The room descends into a silence of uncomfortable doubt. Everyone searches each other's eyes for the truth. In the meantime, Judas takes a small loaf off the pile, breaks off a piece and eats it. A little while later, he breaks off another piece. At the same time, Jesus does the same, and then dips his bread into a bowl of brown liquid in front of Peter. As Judas does the same, Jesus glares at him.

"The one who dips his bread with me is the betrayer."

Stunned, Judas drops his bread. It lands back into the bowl, and floats in the liquid. Paralyzed, his eyes gazing with a forlorn expression at the floating bread. Feeling every eye in the room focusing on him, he looks up to Jesus' tear-laden eyes.

"Surely, not I Rabbi?"

"Yes! It's you. Go now before it is written."

His face ashen in the glow of the lamps, Judas hesitates. Sick to his stomach, he finds it difficult to get up from the table. His body now drained of energy, and stiff with pain, he places a trembling hand to his now sweating face. His eyes fill with tears, as he turns and wastes no time in leaving the room.

A stunned silence fills the air. Jesus reacts by staring at the bowl, while his eyes turn blank and distant.

"It's better for him that he'd never been born."

After a short while, he looks at Peter who is shaken by this sudden turn of events. His dark eyes find it difficult to keep any eye contact on Jesus.

"I will 'never' disown you – Sir."

"I pray for you Peter that your faith won't fail."

As if unsure, Peter lowers his head, and then looks up at his master. His eyes moist with forming tears, he pleads.

"Sir, I'm ready to go to prison with you and even face death."

Noticing the weakness in Peter's eyes, Jesus sighs at the brave attempt. Now afraid that he might weaken, Peter tries hard to push it from his mind by staring straight at Jesus.

"As I said Sir, I will 'never' disown you."

The others murmur in agreement.

17

The Deed

Now someway from the others, Judas makes his way toward the building of the Sanhedrin. He stops at the main door. A guard appears and prevents him from going any further.

"Who are you - and what do you want?"

Sick to his stomach, Judas fumbles for a reply.

"I - I am Judas Iscariot. I need to see the High Priest Caiaphas."

"At this hour?"

"Yes! It's 'really' important."

Seeming to recognize, the guard eyes him up and down with suspicion.

"Wait here."

The heavy door opens, letting out a warm glow of light in contrast to the dark cold atmosphere outside. The door closes. The guard disappears inside.

His insides hurting and his body shaking with fear, Judas feels isolated and alone.

The guard is now with the priests. The young pharisee from earlier is curious.

"Is he one of them?"

"I'm sure Sir. He was walking right behind the one on the donkey today."

Pleased at this good fortune, the priests look at each other for the next step. The young pharisee barks an order.

"Bring him at once."

"Sir!"

Minutes later, a pale, tired-looking Judas is standing in front of the Sanhedrin. The head priest, Caiaphas, steps forward, and points an accusing finger toward a nervous Judas.

"You're one of them? One of 'his' followers? So, why are you here?"

On the verge of vomiting, Judas flounder for the right words. Before opening his mouth, an outside force seems to be pushing him beyond his control. All he can see is Jesus' bright hazel eyes commanding him to betray. Why? He tries to focus on this inquisitive priest looming in front of him. Judas clears his mind as much as he can, and stumbles out the words.

"I – I – err, think I can help you in your quest to...."

Not really listening to this wretch, Caiaphas interrupts. His devious mind is already planning the next move.

"Where is he now? Can you take us to him?"

The nausea overwhelming, his body hurting like hell, Judas hesitates.

"I...err..."

"Your 'deed' will not go unrewarded. We will pay you thirty pieces of silver."

Before Judas can react, Caiaphas beckons to someone out of Judas' vision. A tall, thin gray man dressed as a pharisee appears with a small black canvas pouch. As he comes up to Judas, his stoic face beckons him to hold out his hand. He then stuffs the bag into it. Feeling the edges of the coins, Judas grips the small bag. Before he can say anything, the man leaves. The 'deed' paid for, Caiaphas eyes blaze with expectancy as he steps forward.

"Take us - now!"

The high priest beckons to someone else out of sight. In no time at all, several tough-looking guards appear. Satisfied with his decision, Caiaphas stands close to Judas.

"How will we know who he is?"

His nerves at breaking point, Judas ponders in a daze. Caiaphas is losing his patience.

"Well?"

"I'll go up and kiss the one you want."

In the meantime, Jesus, the two Mary's and the rest of the Apostles have left the room of their last supper, and have made their way across the Kidron Valley to an olive grove known as the Garden of Gethsemane. A familiar place where they have often laid before, but this time they are all tired as the darkness fills the area like a heavy blanket. Except for the half-moon struggling to shine through some hovering clouds, the light is minimum amongst the big olive trees. Not at ease with the situation, Jesus stops at a particular spot.

"Stay here while I pray."

His pallor pale and his eyes expressing fear, he indicates to Mary Magdalene, Peter, and his brothers James and John to join him. Noticing his sudden change of mood, she slides her arm around his waist as they walk away from the rest. After a short distance, he stops and turns to her. Searching into his tired eyes, she becomes even more concerned.

"Can I help in any way?"

"Mary, I am a bit overwhelmed right now. I must pray. You, Peter and my brothers stay here and keep watch for me".

Still searching his eyes for some sort of reassurance, she grips his hand. It feels cold and clammy, sending the fear of God through her. Turning away, Jesus walks further on, and then stops. When he feels he is out of view from the others, he falls face down on the ground. The bitter taste of fear is unbearable. He wants to retch, but can't. He struggles to lift up to rest on his knees, and then huddles into a human ball. Clenching his hands together; he shuts his eyes hard enough to suppress the flow of tears. To ease the pain, he begins to murmur.

After a short while, he feels a light sensation, as if cool soothing silk fabric is flowing over his body. A calm serine voice close to his right ear accompanies the sensation.

"All this suffering, betrayal, and now the pain of death looming? For what? You could have had it all - with me right behind you. However, as usual, you carried on regardless, believing in your own stubbornness that you would change the world. People are not going to change. Why should they? Listen, it's not too

late. Come with me now, where power, pleasure and profit prevail."

After listening, Jesus knows who it is. He digs down to his dwindling reserves of energy in desperation to find the strength to resist.

"Oh God! I am so tired. Help me fight this evil temptation that wants to work and corrupt its way deep into my soul. Everything is possible with you. Please take this pain and burden from me so you can do what you want and not what I need."

At the corner of his eye he can see no sign of Satan. He relaxes, raises his head, and stretches his left hand toward a nearby boulder. Using it to raise his stiff body, he observes the half-moon is now higher in the sky showing him some light. Somewhat relieved, he returns to where he left the others. To his disappointment, he finds Mary asleep, and his brothers gone. A snoring sound echoes from behind a nearby large boulder. His dismay increases as he walks behind the boulder to find Peter fast asleep along with Jesus' brothers. His eyes moistening with sadness, he looks down on them with a mixture of sorrow and guilt at now having to wake them. He crouches down and nudges Peter.

"Are you asleep?"

Peter stirs, and then comes to. For a few seconds, he has to focus on where he is, and what's going on. As his bleary eyes try to concentrate on the dark shape leaning over him, realization sets in.

"I - I'm sorry sir, I..."

His tired eyes glaring at his trusted friend, Jesus finds it hard to scold.

"Couldn't you even keep watch for only one hour so I can pray that none of you will weaken into temptation?"

The sound of Jesus' voice wakens his two brothers. As James and John stir, they waste no time in standing. Riddled with guilt, Peter does the same. Gazing at these pathetic creatures, tears of distress fill Jesus' eyes.

"The spirit is willing, but the flesh is weak. I 'need' you to stay awake, and keep watch, so I can pray some more."

Suppressing his pain, he leaves them and heads back to his former spot. On his way, he sees Mary still asleep. His heart aching for her, he stops and crouches down to be near her. Admiring her strong profile, he whispers, while stroking her upper arm.

"My dear? This is the last time we'll be together. My heart is breaking at what is to come. Whatever bad things happen to me; I will always be yours."

Leaving her asleep, he strokes her lush hair, sighs, and then stands. With his heart filling with dread and foreboding, and knowing there is little time left, he kneels down by the boulder again and prays.

"Oh God, I'm so afraid at what lies ahead. I need your strength tonight more than any other time to cope."

Dread flowing through him like a black scourge, he bows his head and prays some more. This time, no voice, no answers, nothing.

Minutes later, he struggles to stand. Contemplating his prayers, and wondering if God has even heard him, he searches his mind.

Has my life been a waste up to now?

Loneliness and fear draining him of what little energy he has left, he takes a large breath, to relieve the lethargy. Having no choice but to return to the others, he heads back to where he left Peter and his brothers. Finding them asleep again, the stabbing pain of betrayal is unbearable. Out of sheer frustration, he kicks Peter on the thigh. Letting out a yelp, Peter awakens with a jolt. This in turn wakes up James and John. Their heavy eyes peer up at Jesus' exhausted angry face glaring down on them.

"Are you sleeping again? Enough is enough! You've let me down. The hour has come."

Wondering what their master is talking about, they all hear distant noises. While the sounds come closer, glimmers of light from flaming torches come into view. Knowing what is coming next, Jesus braces his anger. Frustration now melting into extreme fear, Jesus turns away from Peter and points to the oncoming threat.

"Here I am, betrayed into the hands of sinners. Stand all of you, here comes my betrayer!"

Bewildered by what is going on, the Apostles join Jesus. Scurrying behind him, as if he can offer them some protection, Judas appears. His face grave, his eyes sad with uncertainty, he is being followed by the temple guards mixed with an accumulated mob carrying an assortment of clubs and swords. Not wanting to be here, Judas stops a distance from Jesus and raises his right hand. Stillness fills the area. Jesus now resigned to the inevitable, stillness fills the air. He shouts to the mob.

"Who is it you want?"

Several voices react by shouting back.

"Jesus of Nazareth."

"I'm Jesus."

The distance between Judas and Jesus is too far for the torchlight's glow to reach Jesus' face. Sensing the mob is unable to see him, Jesus asks again.

"Who is it you want?"

Again, the mob shouts back.

"Jesus of Nazareth!"

"I've just told you, that's me. If it's me you're looking for, let these others go."

Causing his stomach to churn, Judas can hear the pain in Jesus' voice.

Why am I here? This is not what I want? Why am I being driven like this? I love my Rabbi.

Feeling an irresistible inevitability that he has no choice; he turns to the leading soldier.

"Bring the torches, and I will go and kiss the man you want."

With a heavy heart, Judas begins to walk with a heavy lethargy toward Jesus. His fearfulness and guilt heighten as he can hear footsteps behind him.

Their eyes meet. Judas' filling with tears, Jesus' tired and bloodshot. Judas' trembling hand grips Jesus' left shoulder. He can feel the bones when his lips reach up to his Rabbi's left cheek. Again, everything stands still as if frozen in time. His vision blurred by his tears; Judas withdraws.

"I did what you asked Rabbi."

Riddled with guilt and confusion, he moves back. Two burly soldiers come forward and stand on either side of Jesus. Hesitating as if they are not quite sure of their next move, do not notice Peter's anger at this meaningless injustice. Taking advantage of the lull, Peter comes toward Jesus and pulls out a sword from one of the soldier's belt. The soldier's reaction is to turn away, wondering what is happening. The next he feels excruciating pain as the sharp blade of his own sword severs his ear. The man screams as blood pours from the gaping wound. Becoming horrified at this, Jesus turns to Peter who is still holding the blood-smeared sword.

"Throw down that sword. It will not help my destiny."

He then takes hold of the wounded soldier's head, and covers the wound with his hand. The blood trickling through his fingers, Jesus shuts his eyes, and mumbles. The bleeding stops, the pain eases. The soldier, thankful to the man who has just collapsed next to him, indicates to his comrade to help this gentle man to his feet. While the other soldier agrees, they appear confused that it is obvious this man is no criminal.

Jesus now standing with full support, the mob closes in. Torches reflecting the bleak situation, a mood of guilt touches everyone as they witness this frail young man. Exhausted by the circumstances, Jesus gathers what little strength he has left.

"Am I leading a rebellion that you have to come for me with weapons? Every day when I was with you in the Temple courts, you didn't lay a hand on me."

His eyes filling with stinging tears of hopelessness, his voice breaks with painful anger.

"Of course, this is your hour when darkness is everywhere, and evil reigns."

While he stumbles forward, two more soldiers join to help.

Their guilt still remaining, the mob splits in two to let them through. The people bearing the torches follow in silence. However, they have all lowered their weapons. Helpless and still angry, Peter throws down the sword, as the others join him including the two Mary's. Without a word being spoken, Peter gestures to everyone to split up and leave. This they do except Jesus' mother who just stands in the shadows watching the glowing torches dissipate. Unable to control her trembling body and painful sobs, Mary Magdalene, experiencing the same pain, slides her arm around the other woman's shoulders. Embracing each other to relieve their anguish, they can still see the torches reflecting in the distance.

18

Pain and Denial

While Jesus' hands are bound tight behind him, the strips of coarse leather dig into his skin. Trying to relieve the pressure on his wrists by moving his arms, the soldier standing next to him grips his hard, warning him to be still.

They are standing in front of Annas, the High Priest, and father-in-law to Caiaphas. He is a tall, thin man, and his back arches forward when he walks. His silver hair and long beard gives away his age, but his green-gray, piercing eyes still have the ambition of a younger man, as they gaze with dispassion at Jesus' tired, sweaty face.

"Why do you walk around with your followers all the time, and why do you teach them to disobey our laws and create all this unrest everywhere?"

As their eyes lock, Jesus' chronic fatigue does not dampen the anger he feels toward these hypocrites.

"I can only speak the truth. I always teach in the synagogues or at the temple where all the Jews come together..."

He has to pause to take a breath.

"...I say nothing in secret. So, why question me like this? Ask anyone who's heard me? They know what I say..."

A sudden explosion of pain assaults the left side of his face. Jesus staggers to his right, but the soldier standing on this side supports him. Meanwhile, a young Pharisee has come forward. Through his pain, Jesus sees a pair of raging eyes glaring at him. The Pharisee is also rubbing his hand.

"Is that the way to answer a High Priest?"

Blood runs into Jesus' mouth, while struggling to explain.

"If I say anything wrong – then explain yourself. I tell you the truth – and you strike me?"

Nicodemus, who is sitting at the back of the group of priests, is revolted at the behavior toward Jesus. He has to turn away in disgust and leave the hall.

Embarrassed at this young man's behavior, Annas has to look away from Jesus, and glare at the young Pharisee. Indicating with his eyes for him to return to his seat, he notices the blood on Jesus' face. Not liking this situation, his attention turns to the soldiers.

"Take him to Caiaphas. Let him deal with this."

Meanwhile, Peter is in the main courtyard, which leads to the entrance of the Sanhedrin. He had decided to follow Jesus even though he feels helpless.

The night air is cold, so he stands near a fire that has been built. To one side of the building, he can see light coming from a door being opened. A woman servant of the priests closes the door and walks toward the fire.

"They've got that Nazarene in there. They must be in a hurry about something."

The words offering little comfort, Peter stands nearer to the fire. Now he is in plain sight, the woman glances in his direction.

"Aren't you one of those disciples who's with the one from Nazareth?"

Without thinking, Peter denies.

"Nah! Not me. I don't know the man."

A male voice is overheard from the other side of the flames.

"Didn't I see you at the olive grove earlier tonight? Yes, you were with him!"

Even though these questions are digging into his conscience, Peter struggles to act casual.

"No! You're mistaken. I was nowhere near the olive grove tonight."

In the meantime, Jesus is now standing in front of Caiaphas. Behind him, Nicodemus appears uncomfortable. Jesus glances at him with hope. Nicodemus' response is to reply with a look of cautious optimism. However, his instincts tell him this is leading to disaster. Caiaphas also knows what this situation will arrive at, but still has to go through the motions. Reacting to being here late at night, and is tired and irritable, he steps forward to stand near Jesus. Avoiding eye contact, he proceeds at 'going through the motions'

"There has been a lot of witnesses against you. Some are even quoting you will destroy this man-made temple, and then in three days you will rebuild it. What do you say about that?"

Not wanting to answer such a stupid question, Jesus just stares ahead. Caiaphas' reaction is to smirk and pace the floor in a flamboyant manner, and then stop. Looking straight at Jesus, he conveys another challenge.

"So, you're not going to answer me?"

Not waiting this time for any response, he paces again. His flowing robes giving off an odor of stale body sweat, Jesus can sense the man's frustration. With a sense of satisfaction, he still has some strength to fight these corrupt people. Meanwhile, the head priest stops close by, his odor filling Jesus' nostrils.

"Are you 'really' the Messiah, who has come here to save us all?"

Some sniggers can be heard among the group who are finding this scenario amusing, while Jesus does his best to answer.

"I am, and I will be sitting at the right hand of God."

Jesus notices a vertical blood vessel pulsing in the middle of the high priest's forehead, as Caiaphas' color rises. His eyes bulging with rage, Caiaphas grips hold of Jesus' smock and rips it almost halfway down to the waist.

"We don't need any more witnesses. What we have here is 'blasphemy", pure and simple."

While the Jews murmur in agreement, another priest steps forward

151

and slaps Jesus hard across his face. As Jesus staggers backwards, the soldier next to him prevents him falling. Another priest steps forward and blindfolds Jesus with a piece of dirty coarse cloth, causing the dust to fill Jesus' eyes. Now having to deal with this new blinding pain, Jesus weakens even further. Before he has time to adjust, a fist hits him hard in the chest. Staggering again from the heavy blow, the soldier pulls him upright. Now gasping for breath as the fiery pain engulfs his chest, Jesus is confronted by Caiaphas again. Pacing before Jesus, he raises his fist in anger.

"Take him to Herod!"

Outside, Peter tries to keep warm over the dying embers, but as he gazes deep into the dwindling fire, his mind keeps traveling back to the last few days. Hearing Jesus' voice echoing that he will deny him three times, his hands begin to tremble, as misery and helplessness overcome him. Meanwhile, a tall, burly man stands next to him, and stares at Peter with a curios expression.

"Hey? You were with him tonight! You're a Galilean."

Peter's tremble increases.

"I - I don't know what you're talking about."

The burly man leans closer with a look of triumph on his face.

"Your accent gives you away."

Peter's body now shaking, and his strength evaporating, he continues to stare into the embers.

Oh, Jesus, where are you? I'm so sorry.

"No, you're wrong. - I don't know the man."

While Peter turns away in shame, the door of the building opens. Two soldiers step out supporting Jesus between them, followed by two tired priests who wish they were not part of these proceedings. Drawn to the small group, Peter hears a cockerel crowing in the distance.

Even though he cannot see, Jesus turns his head instinctively toward Peter. The group then blends into the darkness. Overcome with more shame, Peter turns away and melts into the shadows, the cold adding to his pain as he curls up on the ground and sobs.

19

Pilate's Dilemma

Jesus' blindfold is removed, but his hands remain bound. He is now standing in front of Herod, who is full of his own self-importance, while perched on his throne. He acts flamboyant while standing and stepping down to get a closer look at the Galilean everyone has been talking about. Jesus' painful, bloodshot eyes try hard to focus as Herod approaches. Herod being shorter than Jesus, he has to look up to make any form of eye contact.

"So, you're he. I hear you can perform miracles - and things. Perform something for me now."

Unable to say anything, because his mouth and throat are so parched, Jesus remains silent. The several elders that are present, have a tendency to sneer as they shout.

"If you are the Messiah, tell us."

To answer, Jesus has to struggle to clear his throat.

"If I tell you, you won't believe me, and if I ask 'you', you can't answer."

The elders are not at all pleased with this profound, and confusing statement. Feeling left out of the proceedings, Herod returns to his throne and addresses Jesus.

"Are you then the son of God?"

Expecting this question, Jesus raises his head to look at Herod.

"You are right in saying I am."

Everyone in the room reacts by shouting in protest. An elder steps forward. His hard, gray eyes peer at Jesus as if searching. Not finding what he wants, he then turns his back on Jesus to face the group.

"Why do we need any more testimony?"

Relying on his rising anger to energize, Jesus answers that question.

"Yes! You do need to hear one more testimony. I say I'm the Son of God, because we are all children of God. That making you the sons and daughters of God, why question me when you ought to be questioning yourselves?"

Jesus takes advantage of the stunned silence to finish.

"I'm the Son of Man. I will sit next to God as you can if you open your hearts and let God enter, instead of Satan..."

Being interrupted by more shouts of protest, forces Herod to stand and have to raise his hand for silence.

"We've heard enough from his own lips. Take him to Pilate the governor."

Judas is standing at the front door of the Sanhedrin. It is quiet and still dark. He forms his trembling hand into a fist and bangs on the door. Straight away, a soldier opens the door.

"What do 'you' want?"

"Caiaphas. I must see him now!"

The soldier beckons him in, closes the door and leaves. As Judas hears the footsteps echo in the distance, different footsteps are approaching. The young priest arrives, his eyes showing signs of strain.

"Oh! It's you. What do you want?"

"I must see Caiaphas!"

"He's unavailable. Tell me your problem."

Judas' hand shakes as he hands back the bag containing the thirty pieces of silver.

"I've done the worst sin a man can do. I have betrayed innocent blood."

Irritated, the priest takes a step back refusing to accept the bag.

"What's that to us? That's your responsibility?"

To relieve his anguish, Judas throws the bag on the floor. The bag spits open, scattering the coins, as he turns to leave. Staring at the dispersed coins, the young priest shakes his head in bewilderment, while he bends down to pick up the discarded silver.

"Well, I can't put this back into the treasury because its blood money. I'll have to use it to bury foreigners in the potter's field as it's written."

His despair beyond control, Judas runs until he must rest against the nearest tree. The pain of guilt becoming unbearable, he looks up into the breaking dawn.

"Oh! Dear God, please forgive me. I love him."

His eyes filling with tears of desperation, he notices the sturdy branch just above his head. Without any hesitation or logic, he climbs the tree and sits on the branch. Satisfied that it can take his weight, he undoes the cord around his waist. His nerves now at breaking point, and his body shaking beyond control, he ties one end of the cord around his neck, making the knot as tight as he can bear. Having a hard job to grip the other end of the cord, his shaking hands wrap the remaining cord around the branch several times so that it pulls his head down to the branch. As he grips the branch, and rests his head against the cool bark, his eyes sting with pleading tears.

"Why did you make me do it? Why?"

Not hearing an answer, he rolls off the branch. The rope tightens, his neck cracks, his body now lifeless and free of pain, hangs from the tree.

At Pilate's chambers, the elders and high priests are collecting behind Jesus, as he stands in front of the Roman governor. Pilate is not happy at being summoned by these irate Jews at such an early hour. He is becoming more irritable and impatient at their continual shouting and accusations at this poor wretch in front of him.

Hoping the Romans will deal with this problem that is so vexing to the Pharisees, the young priest steps forward.

"We have found this man subverting our nation, opposes payment of taxes to Caesar and claims to be the Messiah, a King..."

Demonstrating his annoyance, Pilate signals for the priest to be silent. Expressing a touch of sympathy, Pilate faces Jesus.

"Are you King of the Jews?"

Sensing this official is not bias or threatening, Jesus answers.

"It is as you say."

Pondering at the answer, Pilate turns away. His mind in deep thought, he turns back to Jesus, searches his eyes, and then glares at the Pharisees.

"I find no basis for a charge against this man."

The stunned elders and Pharisees are not pleased by this verdict. Becoming irrate and annoyed, an elderly Pharisee steps forward. His silver beard appearing unkempt on his wrinkly, aquiline features, faces Pilate and points an accusing finger at Jesus.

"But Pilate, he stirs up the people all over Judea. He began in Galilee and has come all the way here with his so-called teachings."

Even more vexed, Pilate paces the floor. Again, his mind returns to deep thinking. To him this emaciated man does not look as if he is a threat to anyone. He stops pacing and faces the group.

"So, he is a Galilean. That is Herod's jurisdiction. Take him there."

Releasing a heavy sigh of frustration, he turns his back on them and leaves his chambers.

Their exasperation rising, the elders and Pharisees look at each other for some sort of solution to solve this 'problem'.

Even though tired, hungry, thirsty and in pain, Jesus cannot resist a smile of satisfaction at how the Roman official has put the Jewish hypocrites in their place.

Now he is back facing Herod again. In his usual flamboyant manner, Herod paces the floor. His head hurts; the effect of too much wine in the previous hours. He stops in front of Jesus, leans forward, and whispers in his ear.

"Please do one small miracle for me? Anything to convince these idiots?"

Hoping for an answer, he steps back. When there is no reaction from

Jesus, Herod raises his arms up in the air in dismay, and shakes his head. Disheartened, he beckons to two nearby soldiers. He whispers an order that Jesus cannot quite hear. He sees one soldier come and stand by him while the other one leaves the area. Within a short time, the other soldier returns carrying a purple bundle. After placing the bundle in front of Jesus, he removes a long knife from his belt. The small crowd gasp, as the knife moves to Jesus' back. Herod smirks as the knife cuts through Jesus' bindings with little effort. Meanwhile, Jesus is becoming puzzled.

They must be letting me go. But why?

To try and relieve the pain, he rubs his swollen wrists. The soldier then wraps the purple robe around Jesus and steps back to admire his handiwork. His eyes widening, Herod now stands and holds his arms out toward Jesus.

"Behold the King of the Jews."

While the Pharisees look at each other in utter confusion, Herod has the final word.

"Unfortunately, I am the King of the Jews. So, as we can't have two Kings, take him back to the Governor."

Pilate is even angrier with these Jews for bringing a bound Jesus in front of him again.

"I keep telling you people, I find no basis for your charges. And, by all accounts, neither has Herod. I have examined him in your presence and find he has done nothing wrong, 'especially' to deserve death."

This not satisfying the Jews, a Pharisee steps forward.

"If he were not a criminal, we would not have handed him to you."

His patience dwindling, Pilate paces the floor and looks down as if pondering. His mind working overtime, he glances up at Jesus, and then back to the floor. For the next minute, he keeps pacing, and then stops to turn and face the anxious Pharisees, who now seemed to have expanded into a far larger group.

"Take him and judge him by your own laws."

Exasperation taking over, the group shouts back as one.

"We have no authority to execute anyone."

With this request for death ringing in his ears, Pilate gazes into Jesus' eyes as if searching for an answer. As he speaks, his voice becomes soft; almost caring.

"Are you the King of the Jews?"

Now past ordinary exhaustion, and his body hurts so much that his drained mind cannot function clearly, Jesus knows what his fate is to be. However, there is still something deep inside him that wants to fight back.

"Is that your idea, or have these Pharisees convinced you?"

Still keeping his voice soft and calm, but now more determined that he does not want the Pharisees to hear, Pilate continues his questioning.

"Do you think I am a Jew? It is your Jews that have handed you over to me. What is it you are supposed to have done?"

Looking deep into Pilot's eyes, Jesus knows this man is trying to help.

"My kingdom is not of this world. If it were, my servants would have prevented my arrest by the Jews..."

Seeing a way out, Pilate interrupts.

"So, you are a King then?"

"You're right to say I'm a King. I was born into this world as a man to teach the truth to anyone who wants to listen."

The more he listens to this man, the more Pilate respects Jesus' sincerity.

"What truth?"

Before Jesus can answer, Pilate wanders over to the swelling crowd of Jews.

"I still find nothing wrong with this man. So, I will just punish him, and then have him released."

This is not what the expanding mob wants to hear.

"No! No! Crucify him!"

Surprised at such a demand for so little offense, Pilate turns away from them. Jesus can see the frustration on his face as Pilate paces the floor again while the crowd continually chants.

"Crucify him! Crucify him!"

Pilot knows he cannot upset the Jews too much, as these minor rebellions irritate Rome. He has been ordered to quell any sign of trouble to keep this part of the Empire quiet and orderly. However, this man is not a rebel.

All he does is preach about love for your fellow human being. It would be fine if everyone did that, then we could all go home...

He stops pacing and stands next to Jesus. Aware of the seething Pharisees, Pilate is determined to save this poor wretch.

"It is customary for me to release to you one prisoner at this time of your passover. So, do you want me to release this King of the Jews?"

Surprised and annoyed by this offer, the crowd answer by erupting.

"No! No! Give us Barabbas!"

Becoming dismayed at this swelling mob, who is so determined to sacrifice this poor man for a real rebel like Barabbas, Pilate indicates to the centurion nearby.

Jesus recognizes the centurion from having healed his loyal servant. Pilate speaks to his Roman comrade, out of hearing distance from the threatening crowd.

"Basic punishment. Take it easy, he has been through enough already."

"Yes, Governor. I understand."

His eyes full of sympathy, but his face remaining stern, the centurion approaches Jesus.

"This way."

20

Agony Within

Now resigned to his fate, Jesus is being led to the punishment area. They come to a heavy wooden gate. Jesus is taken through into a round stone courtyard. His stomach churns as he notices a heavy wooden round block placed in the center of the courtyard. The centurion leads Jesus past the heavy bloodstained block toward a smaller gate. While waiting for the next step of his fate, Jesus can hear voices. One deep, coarse man's voice shouting, as others laugh in response.

Three roman soldiers jump to attention at the sight of their superior officer entering their enclosed area. The centurion beckons to a stocky, muscular man whose scarred features send chills of fear through Jesus. The centurion leans forward toward the shorter man keeping his voice calm and low.

"Punishment duty. Basic – no more! Understand?"

"Sir!"

Beckoning the soldier to follow. The Centurion leaves, and stops a few paces away out of Jesus' hearing.

"Go easy on this one. Governor's orders. I'll be back in a short while to take him back."

"Yes, sir. Sir? Out of curiosity, what's his crime?"

The centurion becomes lost for words.

What is his crime?

"Oh, err, he's a Nazarene accused of - oh, just another prophet enticing the crowds. I'll be back."

Understanding and ready to perform his work, the soldier nods and returns to his other two comrades. While Jesus hides his fear, the soldiers study his thin aching body like lions ready to devour their fallen prey. His breath smelling of cheap wine and garlic, the taller soldier of the three stands close to Jesus.

"I know you. You're the one who came in a few days ago on a donkey..."

His eyes gleaming with excitement, he turns to the other two soldiers.

"Hey men. This is the King of the Jews."

The others react by conveying a loud burst of laughter. Forgetting their officer's orders, they begin to bow and spout sarcasm.

"We are honored, your Majesty."

While Jesus can feel the burning bile rising in his empty stomach, the heavy built lead soldier makes a point in bowing quite close.

"Hail, 'O' King."

Out of nowhere, Jesus' face explodes with excruciating pain as a heavy fist strikes his right eye and nose. He staggers, but somehow manages to stay on his feet. His eyes water and blood trickles from his nose. He cannot see properly as another flash of intense pain lands on the other side of his face. This time he staggers and bangs his head against a nearby wall and falls onto his left shoulder. His ears fill with coarse laughter, as the stocky leader has an idea.

"I know? The King should have a crown."

While the others shout in agreement, Jesus feels him being lifted up into a standing position. As he leans against the same wall drifting in and out of consciousness, something sharp and jagged is being forced onto the top of his head. He retches with the pain, as the blood pouring into in his eyes is blurring his vision. Meanwhile, a traumatic cracking sensation hits his chest as something heavy rams into it. A stabbing pain radiates through him as something hard lands between his shoulder blades. His will failing, Jesus falls onto the stone floor. As more blows to his head and body follow, Jesus blacks out. The lead soldier appears disappointed.

"Well, look at that? He's out cold. That didn't take much."

The same soldier prods Jesus with his foot.

"Basic punishment our commander says. Not on my watch. Right lads, let's get him to the block. We could do with some exercise."

With the other two smirking and nodding in agreement, they laugh and banter as they drag Jesus' lip body to the bloodstained block. While the two support Jesus, the leader barks out an order.

"Remove the robe. We wouldn't like to get it soiled. The colors wouldn't match."

Laughter follows again, as the taller soldier of the three removes the purple robe leaving Jesus' torn smock.

"Yeah! Especially with his 'royal' blood."

More laughter as Jesus comes to, and his blood-soaked eyes focus on dirt.

His bound hands now stretched out in front of him, his stomach is being pressed against the block, forcing his back to tighten and the skin to stretch.

Taking all this in his stride, the leader begins to hum a tune, while he goes to a nearby stand containing a selection of whips. In removing one, he sneers.

"Try this gentle one first. The Governor did say take it easy..."

Laughter echoes again as the lead soldier picks out a vicious looking whip. Making a point of studying the prongs covered with small metal blades, he sneers again.

"...Then work our way up to 'this' one."

Hearty agreement pounding in his ears, Jesus hears footsteps approaching. After a short pause, a pain so excruciating spreading across his middle back, it causes him to dry vomit. As another flash of intense pain caused by the fine leather prongs tear at his stretched skin, his plea is inaudible to his punishers.

"Oh God, give me strength...."

As the nightmare continues, another lash, and then another. His meager clothing is becoming ripped and soaked in blood.

After a short while, the pain is so bad that he is drifting in and out of consciousness. It has got to the point where he is becoming numb to the pain.

There is a pause, a respite, as Jesus is drifting back into some sort of awareness. He can hear heavy breathing quite near. Wondering how long he can bear this agony, his body begins to tremble, as he tries hard to concentrate on the voices.

"Let's try this one. I'm sure it'll break him."

"But the governor said easy."

"The governor isn't here, so whip!"

Fear tingling his nerve endings, Jesus hears footsteps approaching. Again, a pause, while focusing on the blood-soaked sand beneath him, he is dreading the next...

Oh, God....

A sharp, ripping pain tears at his already swollen back. The heavy metal-tipped prongs of the whip dig deep into the flesh, and then tearing it out, ready for the next lash.

God, why am I suffering this much? Are you leaving me now? For what?

Another vicious lash.

Oh, God, where are you...?

He passes out, as the centurion enters the main gate to the yard. Witnessing the atrocity, he rushes forward and grabs hold of the whip. His eyes glare in anger as he pulls out his own knife from his belt and hits the soldier across the head with the heavy handle.

"You animals! I said easy, not kill him. I will deal with you three later. This is the last duty you will ever do."

Knowing the hard-Roman system, the soldiers' faces turn ashen. Their pathetic lives are now worth nothing. His anger under control, the centurion barks out his last order.

"Undo him and clean him up."

Fearing for their future, the three do not hesitate. One throws a bucket of water over Jesus, distributing a cascade of pink fluid, while the other two untie and help him to stand, even though he is semiconscious. The centurion surveys Jesus with consternation.

"I am so sorry. Can you walk? I need to take you back to the governor."

All Jesus can do is nod, his parched throat cracks as he begs for water.

"Get this man some water - NOW!"

The taller soldier rushes to fetch a goatskin. He puts the spout into Jesus' mouth, letting the cool water flow. For a second, Jesus is reminded of when he first met Mary.

Oh Mary! I miss you...

The centurion beckons the soldier to stop with the water. Seeing his prisoner is now somewhat revived, he indicates to the nervous soldiers to leave and go back to their quarters. The centurion is gentle as he grips Jesus' upper arm and helps him to walk.

As they make their way towards the governor, Jesus looks up to the overcast sky.

God? I know you haven't left me; you are in this Roman officer.

They reach their destination. Observing Jesus is on the verge of collapsing, the soldier leans him against a wall to rest.

"Are you all right?"

Jesus nods, but he is in a bad way.

After a minute of rest, they enter Pilate's chambers to find he is frantic as he paces back and forth. When he notices the centurion, he stops and stares in horror at Jesus, being battered and bleeding. His eyes exhibiting sympathy tinged with anger, Pilate steps forward. His face tense, he looks at Jesus, and then at the centurion.

"This is not what I asked for."

"I know, Governor. I have dealt severely with those concerned."

Trusting his chief officer, Pilate's face relaxes a little.

"Good. Bring him toward this door so I can address this mob."

Jesus is helped to the doorway, which leads out into a large stone courtyard where the Pharisees, Elders and Jews wait with noticeable impatience. Demonstrating their obvious lack of sympathy, they shout and jeer when Jesus appears. His face stern with annoyance, Pilate raises his arms for silence, and then addresses the crowd.

"Look for yourselves. I have brought him to show you that he has been 'severely' punished. I am also letting you know I still find no basis for a charge against him."

A sudden stillness of guilt engulfs the crowd as they study Jesus. Although most of the crowd seem they have seen enough, the small hard core of Jews feels no pity or remorse as they erupt again.

"Crucify him, crucify him!"

Witnessing these hardliners, Pilate's answer is tinged with anger.

"You take him and crucify him. I make no charge against him!"

Hoping that is the end of it, Pilate turns his back on them, when a lone voice speaks out.

"We have a law, and according to that law he must die, because he claims he is the son of God."

His anger rising, Pilate turns to face the lone voice. The 'voice' is a tall, green-eyed Pharisee with flowing curly black hair, standing in the front of the crowd.

For a second, a stab of fear and uncertainty goes through Pilate. He tries to ignore the Pharisee and takes Jesus' arm to lead him back to his chambers.

"Where do you come from?"

Jesus is too weak to answer.

"Do you refuse to speak to me? Don't you realize I have the power to free you or have you crucified?"

His eyes filling with stinging tears of hopelessness, Jesus nods.

"You have no power over me unless it is given to you from above..."

He staggers as if about to collapse, and then reaches out to a nearby pillar.

"The ones who handed me over to you are guilty of a greater sin."

Knowing Jesus is right, Pilate turns. His back now facing Jesus, his mind in a spin, he ponders.

He is right. What can I do? This man hasn't broken any Roman laws; only upset some corrupt Jewish hierarchy.

He leaves Jesus resting against the pillar, and goes to face the crowd.

"I am going to free him. He has not offended Roman law."

The crowd's response is to erupt. The Pharisee with the green eye's shouts to Pilate above the noise.

"If you let him go you will be defying Caesar. Anyone who claims to be a King without your permission opposes Caesar."

Pilate knows this man is right, so he goes back into his chambers. Jesus is still standing, but his body is trembling, in a state of shock. Pilate is still sympathetic as he gazes into Jesus' bloodshot eyes. Pilate sighs, as he grips Jesus' arm and leads him outside to face this unforgiving mob.

As if this all a bad dream, Jesus notices the sun is now higher. He can feel the heat on his swollen face even though the sky is still overcast. Pilate, still holding Jesus, raises up his free hand.

"I give you your King."

Jesus glances down to the leering, determined green eyes, accompanied by a mouth distorted with evil.

"Take him and crucify him."

Pilate focuses onto this man with a mixture of disgust tinged with fear.

"Crucify your King?"

The Jews of the mob shout back with one voice.

"We have no King but Caesar."

Pilate faces a dilemma.

If I let this man go, I face a rebellion. If I crucify him, it makes me look bad, because I cannot find him guilty of anything. Rome may be tough and disciplined, but they always want to appear fair about running their empire...

The crowd seems to sense his moment of doubt and weakness by shouting even louder.

"Crucify him! Crucify him!"

Pilot's reaction is to step up to a nearby marble water stand. He dips his hands in the water, holds them there for a second as if to relieve his pain. He then dries them and throws the towel down in disgust, and faces the crowd.

"I wash my hands of this whole affair. I am innocent of this man's blood.

It's now 'your' responsibility."

Knowing he has won, the man with the green eyes smiles with satisfaction.

"Let his blood be on us and our children. Free Barabbas!"

21

A Cross to Bear

Jesus is being led away by the centurion from Pilate's chambers amid shouts and jeers from a triumphant mob. He is then taken through a stone tunnel, which ends at a large work yard where large wooden posts and cross beams are being made in haste to keep up with the demand of recent crucifixions.

They stop before entering the yard. A look of anguish on his face, the centurion draws out his long knife. Jesus stiffens as the sharp blade severs his bindings, bringing relief to his throbbing wrists. While returning the knife to his belt, the centurion looks deep into Jesus' tired eyes.

"I'm sorry."

"No need. This is all meant to happen. My God loves you more than you will ever know."

Embarrassed at not being able to help any further, the centurion lowers his head.

"Stand here while I sort out a beam."

As Jesus leans against the stonewall in the shade, the cool air gives him some slight relief to his burning soreness. He watches the centurion go over to a stack of finished crossbeams, lifts up several to inspect, and then discards them. He keeps doing this until he reaches one that is a lot lighter and drier. Doing the best he can to lessen Jesus' approaching destiny, he beckons Jesus over.

Now standing beside him, Jesus looks down at a heavy piece of wood almost as tall as himself. The centurion leans toward Jesus.

"This is the lightest one I can find. You have to carry your own cross beam. We are not allowed to help you."

Understanding the soldier's plight, Jesus nods. He then slides both arms around the beam, and with all his remaining strength, lifts it up onto his right shoulder. Wincing with the pain as the weight of the wood presses into his raw flesh and tender bone, the centurion feels sick at being unable to help this poor man.

They begin to walk out into the street that is leading Jesus to his final fate. Curious faces gather to watch. While the heavy load is becoming unbearable, he stumbles, and falls onto his already painful knees. While he peers down to the ground searching for some relief, burning tears of fear and despair fill his eyes.

"Oh God! Please don't fail me now."

With no help at hand, he has no choice but to carry on. With a supreme effort, he lifts up the beam, takes two more paces, and then collapses again. Meanwhile, a tall, dark skinned man standing nearby in the forming crowd comes forward to help. The Centurion stops him and grabs him by the shoulder.

"Leave him, he has to walk on his own, but you can carry his beam. What's your name?"

"Simon of Cyrene, Sir."

It is easy for Simon to pick up the beam and place it on his own shoulder. Jesus looks at him with love and appreciation, and then carries on his own struggle to walk.

More curious people gather and line the streets while watching this man walking to his death. No one shouts out, in either praise or defiance, because they know that this poor wretch is facing the worst death ever created by man.

After what seems a drawn-out amount of time, they arrive at the spot called 'The place of the skull'. A small hill, just high enough for all to see, but low enough to climb, erect, and dismantle the crucifixion frames. Two crosses are already erected with a single large pole in between. Jesus' insides tighten with fear as he notices a man trussed to each cross wailing in agony. The centurion beckons to Simon to lay down the wooden beam. Whispering thanks to Simon, Jesus watches him leave to and join the swelling crowd forming at the base of the hill.

Jesus strains to looks at the two men moaning in pain, as two soldiers lift the single central pole out of the ground, and lay it down nearby. Jesus looks up when he feels a firm hand on his left shoulder. The centurion motions him to step toward the pole. As he does just that, Jesus witnesses with a forlorn expression the two soldiers placing the cross-beam square onto the vertical pole. Fastening them together with long thick iron nails driven in with heavy bronze hammers, one of the soldiers provides a rough-hewn piece of wood with words burnt saying 'King of the Jews.'

At the same time, two Pharisees in the front of the increasing crowd see this. They babble to each other, and then one rushes away. His fear heightening, the two soldiers now grab Jesus by each arm, forcing him down onto his back against the wooden frame. The centurion stares down to him, his eyes filling with tears of remorse and sympathy. Attesting to his anguish, Jesus struggles to absolve the man's pain.

"Don't be sorry. As I said, this is all meant to be."

Meanwhile, the Pharisee who left the scene reaches Pilate's chambers. Noticing the man's agitated state, a guard stops him.

"What do you want?"

"I must see His Excellency."

"He's busy!"

"I must see him!"

Against his better judgment, the guard lets the Pharisee through. Pilate is sitting at his heavy table, his head resting in both hands. Sensing heavy breathing of someone in an agitated state, Pilate stares with a wary expression at the young Pharisee.

"What do you want? Haven't you had enough blood for one day?"

Looking apprehensive, the young Pharisee steps forward.

"You can't put that sign above his head."

"And why not?"

"Because it says he's the King of the Jews."

Controlling his temper at this unreasonable young man, Pilate stands.

"The man said he is a King. I've written what I have written. So, leave!"

He turns his back on the man in black as the guard escorts out the frustrated Pharisee.

Jesus is lying on his back, naked, but for his tattered loincloth. His arms are being stretched out across the beam of the frame. In the meantime, he stares at the sky, knowing what the soldiers are about to do next

"Oh God!"

Excruciating pain enters his right wrist and shoots up his arm into his shoulder. His screams have no effect on the soldier, while he pounds a heavy iron nail right through the Jesus' wrist bone and deep into the wood. As precious blood pools around the nail head and runs toward the ground, the painful procedure is repeated on the left wrist. The shock causes Jesus' body to shake, so the soldiers struggle to hold his legs down. While exhaustion helps to subside the shaking, the soldiers cross his legs by putting one foot on top of the other, and then push his legs up the pole until they create a slight arch. They then begin to drive in an extra-long nail through the bone of both ankles deep into the wood. The sound of crunching bone and ripping flesh is an everyday chore for these hardened soldiers. Meanwhile, agony of the searing pain and the loss of blood is making Jesus want to retch, but he can't. Even shallow breathing in this position is painful. Coming to terms with this horrendous fate, he closes his eyes.

As his mind drifts between waves of severe nausea, pain and exhaustion, a soft tender voice approaches.

"Well, here we are at death's door. In a short while, it will open for you. For what? If only you had accepted my previous offers you would not be suffering like this. What a waste. I saw great potential in you, but no, you had to refuse me in your usual stubborn way. Wouldn't it be nice if all this agony and strife were to vanish? Even now, I can still relieve you of this senseless suffering. Just say the word and all this pain will be gone."

Jesus shouts as he feels a lifting sensation.

"No! No! Satan."

The soldiers ignore the strange plea, as Jesus feels the cross being lifted up in a vertical position, and then with a heavy jarring thump, settle in the ground. The sudden excruciating pain sears through his body as all his weight is now pulling on the nails piercing his wrists and feet.

Having done their job, the soldiers now squat on the ground underneath the tall cross frame. After a few minutes, Jesus opens his eyes.

I can see Jerusalem. It seems to float as if on water. Where is Mary...?

He blacks out.

A sponge soaked in sour wine, held on a long stick from below is being pushed into his mouth. The shock of the acid brings him round and makes him want to vomit. The sponge is withdrawn. He can hardly breathe. His whole body is burning in agony. Jerusalem still looks as if it is floating. He tries to look down to see the Roman soldiers gambling over the purple robe. One of them peers up to him as a voice comes from his right.

"Aren't you the Messiah who's come here to save us?"

Jesus tries to turn his head toward the voice. Then another voice comes from his left.

"Why are you under the same sentence as us? We deserve our punishment, but not you. You've done nothing wrong."

Jesus cannot move his head to the left. He keeps it looking right. The man hanging on his right stares at Jesus with pain filled eyes.

"Just remember me when you enter your kingdom."

"Yes. I will remember you. Today you will be with me in paradise."

The clouds thicken. Stinging tears of pain fill Jesus' eyes as the inevitable approaches. Some people gather at the foot of the crosses. The Pharisee with the green eyes and curly hair shouts up at Jesus.

"You have saved others, now save yourself. If you are the chosen one, it should be easy for you."

One of the soldiers joins in the jest.

"If you're the King of the Jews, save yourself?"

Struggling to even take a shallow breath, burning tears run down Jesus' face.

"Oh God, forgive them. They don't know what they're doing."

Their faces ashen with grief, Mary Magdalene and Jesus' mother stand at the side of the small crowd. Trying to find some small relief, Jesus turns his head to his front. His heart turns over at the sight of the two women.

"Oh, Mary. Dearest Mother."

Jesus blacks out again. His mother shouts in anguish.

"Oh no, he's gone."

Mary Magdalene knows Jesus is still alive.

"No! Not yet."

Time drags on. Most of the crowd are now becoming bored and move away. All that is left is the centurion, the two soldiers, and the two women in Jesus' life. The sky is now dark and some light raindrops begin to fall.

Jesus floats back into torturous consciousness. For a few seconds, he is not sure where he is, and then the agony soon reminds him. He looks at his beloved and his mother, and cries out in desperation.

"Oh God! why have you forsaken me?"

Knowing death is near, he sobs. Rain mix with his tears. Light at first, then a full-fledged downpour. The two women huddle together trying to gain some comfort from each other.

Because the Romans dislike having bodies still hanging on the Jewish Sabbath, they always quicken the death on anyone still alive by breaking their legs. One of the soldiers is reluctant to grab hold of a heavy wooden club. He hesitates, and then offers the club to his comrade.

"Here, you do it. I hate this part."

"All right! Doesn't bother me. The sooner the better."

The soldier takes hold of the club and goes up to the first robber. With one heavy swing, he breaks both legs at the same time. The sickening cracking sound and the terrifying scream can be heard above the noise of the rain. Making sure the man is dead, he then goes to repeat the same procedure on the other criminal. Witnessing the screams, the two women reel in horror. As the soldier now prepares the club for Jesus, Mary screams.

"No, no!"

At the same time, a bolt of lightning cracks out of the black sky. The soldier freezes. The centurion steps forward and grabs the club.

"I think he's already dead. Give me your spear."

The dazed soldier drops the club and hands over his spear. Mary pleads with him.

"Please, no more."

"I have to make sure before anyone can take him down."

Mary turns away as the Roman dig's half the spearhead into Jesus' right side. As he withdraws, a mixture of blood and pale liquid pours out of the wound. Sure, there is no life left in this man, the centurion stands before Jesus displaying a mournful expression, as his eyes fill with tears.

"Surely this is a righteous man? Not a criminal."

He places a sympathetic hand on each of the women's shoulders to comfort them, and to some extent to forgive his helplessness.

22

Peace in the Tomb

The rain eases, the sky lightens; all is quiet. The only sound to be heard is water dripping and trickling away. It is approaching evening. Joseph of Arimathea and Nicodemus the Pharisee arrive, standing a small distance away from Mary Magdalene and Jesus' mother. Joseph being the wealthy wine merchant who had become a disciple of Jesus over the past year, turns to his long-time friend Nicodemus.

"My friend, this is a tragic day for our nation. A day when a righteous man is put to death, all because he preached love and exposed the hypocrisy and corruption of the Jewish hierarchy."

Sadness in his eyes, Nicodemus nods in agreement. He is holding a bundle of clean linen ready to wrap Jesus for the tomb.

As they approach the women, Mary Magdalene, her eyes full of sorrow, recognizes them and falls into Joseph's arms. While Mary receives a little comfort, Jesus' mother stands looking up at her son's lip body. Offering his few words of comfort, Nicodemus stands next to her.

"We went to the governor and asked if we can take Jesus down so we can place him in Joseph's family tomb. He readily agreed and gave us written permission. We then ask this centurion for help."

A short time passes. Jesus has been taken down from the cross and is now lying on a rough linen stretcher. At the centurion's insistence, Jesus is being carried by the two soldiers toward the tomb, followed by Joseph, Nicodemus and the two women.

The large round stone of the new section of the tomb has been rolled back. Inside, the soldiers observe the hollowed stone. Joseph enters, points to the hollow on the left reserved for the male, and instructs the soldiers.

"Place him alongside, please."

There faces solemn, the soldiers place the stretcher down on the stone floor and lift Jesus' beaten body onto the ground. Picking up the empty stretcher, they lower their heads in a mixture of respect and embarrassment, and don't waste any time in leaving.

His heart heavy with grief, Joseph stands over Jesus, and stares with a mournful expression

"You're at peace now my friend."

Suppressing his emotions, Nicodemus stands next to him, as the two women enter the tomb. Determined to be involved, Mary Magdalene comes forward.

"We want to help you prepare him."

Mary notices some large clay jugs against the wall. Knowing what they contain, she takes the jug that holds aloe and begins on her man by being careful in removing the crown of thorns. Sick at the sight of the deep jagged holes in her lover's forehead, she tosses the 'crown' in disgust near the tomb entrance. Running the tip of her fingers over the congealed blood, she strokes Jesus' head, as Joseph kneels down to join her. In an unsaid agreement, he washes the legs as she begins on his torso, paying particular attention to the wounds in his wrists and the damage done by the spear.

This soon done, they both turn Jesus to wash his back. Appalled and sickened at the sight of the deep lash marks, Mary places a hand on Joseph's arm.

"Let me do it."

Beyond feeling nauseated, Joseph stands, and heads to the tomb entrance.

While Mary continues to wash Jesus, she can feel warmth from the scourged flesh as the blood mixes with the liquid aloes. Imagining what he must have went through, her hands tremble. While she weeps, her tears mix with the blood and Aloe.

A short while later after the washing, Jesus' mother joins Mary and places the shroud on the ground in between Jesus and the hollow. The two men still suppressing their grief, lift Jesus onto the shroud.

When the wrapping is complete, the two men now place Jesus in the stone hollow. As Jesus' body relaxes into the hollow, a soft groan releases from his mouth. While they look at each other in shock, Mary speaks first.

"Is he...?"

Nicodemus, shocked as the others, tries to comfort.

"Bodies often do that. It is air trapped in the chest coming out through his throat."

Jesus is now embalmed in myrrh and shrouded according to Jewish custom. Nicodemus, still kneeling, places his gentle hand on Jesus' head. While closing his eyes and whispering a soft prayer, the others bow their heads to join him.

After a short pause, the two men leave the tomb. Meanwhile, Jesus' mother is still crying when she decides to join the men outside.

Besides her sorrow, Mary Magdalene's anger is taking over and giving her the strength, she needs. Unable to leave, she lies down next to Jesus. Her head resting on the cold stone near to him, she talks as if he is still alive.

"What now, my love? What do I do? All I know, I can't live without you. Is this 'really' the end? Somehow, I can still feel you, alive, our souls still entwined..."

Tears of torment filling her eyes, she struggles to stand, and then gazes down on him.

"God? Why 'have' you forsaken him?"

As she has always done in his time of need, she wants to hold him in her arms.

Oh, my love, how can I now face the world without you.

Reluctant to leave the tomb, she joins the others outside as evening approaches.

The two women watch in despair, as the two men struggle to roll the large stone back in place to seal the tomb. The four of them stand in silence; each in their own thoughts and pain, and then walk away.

23

All is Not Lost

Next day, some of the chief priests and pharisees go to Pilate. He is not in an amicable mood, because he is sick of the Jews and their constant demands.

"What is it you want - gentlemen?"

One of the younger priests' steps forward.

"We remember when he was alive deceiving everyone...."

Lost for words, he pauses. Pilate sighs with frustration.

"Yes, yes! What is it?"

"Well - he proclaimed that after his death he would rise on the third day. His disciples may come along and steal the body, and then claim he's risen. This final deception will be worse than all the others."

Imagining the scenario, Pilate thinks for a minute.

"All right. Take a guard and seal the tomb as you know how."

The young pharisee's face grins with satisfaction

"Thank you, your Excellency. It will save a lot of harm."

Pilate is glad to get rid of them.

"Yes – yes! Goodbye."

Sighing again with relief at being alone again, he ponders, and then walks to the main window of his chambers where can see most of central Jerusalem. The early morning sun is now rising, casting long shadows in the deserted streets. He focuses on the group of Jews he has just addressed walking down one of the streets in a joyful mood.

What a forsaken land. A land filled with strange people.

Very early next morning, the guard that has been placed at the tomb by the demanding Jews, leans against the large stone that seals it. He stretches and yawns, realizing that full daylight will not be long now, and his shift of duty will soon be over. The sky is more of a dark gray; a few stars are still shining, but the moon has gone. As the air is beginning to warm up, he decides to remove his heavy-hooded cloak, and lay it down beside him.

Inside the tomb is a different story; Jesus' eyes open to blackness.

Am I blind or is it the darkness of a tomb?

While his whole-body hurts and throb, his optimism returns.

If I can feel my pain, then I'm alive, and not dead!

The pain is unbearable, as he attempts to free his right arm from the linen shroud. Energy hard to come by, he waits and rests.

Oh, God. You didn't forsake me. I wish I could see.

Determined to free his right arm, he tries again. This time with more effort and a ripping of linen, his arm is free. After another rest, he raises his arm up and leans it to his right. His right hand landing against a flat stonewall quite close to him, he decides to try to free his left arm. With a little more effort, and further ripping of linen, his left arm is now free. Not dissuaded by exhaustion, he raises up his left arm, and moves it away to his left. When he hits nothing but empty black space, he lets his stretched arm fall until it reaches ground level.

I'm actually sunken into the floor.

The pain beginning to become unbearable, he rests some more. However, the excitement of being alive gives him a little more strength. This time, he attempts to roll onto his left side. The soreness from his wounds are so painful, he gives up half way. He rests again. His body burning, including his mouth and throat, he is forcing mind over matter.

I must try to get up and breathe properly.

With one more final effort, he manages to get on to his left side, and then using his right arm, grips a small crevice in the floor and crawls his way out of the hollow.

Exhaustion creeping over him like hot tentacles, he lays face down on the cold stone floor. Receiving some comfort to his burning wounds, his swollen tongue is sticking to his parched mouth.

Oh, Mary? I need your water right now. And oh, how I need you.

Still exhausted, his breathing is becoming painful and shallow.

Oh, God. Thank you for letting me live. Is this how my mission is meant to be?

As the excitement returns, his will to carry on enables him to lift up into a kneeling position. Either the effort, or what little energy he had, has dissipated.

Now, everything seems to tremble. Unable to keep his balance, he falls flat on his chest.

Oh no! Don't let me pass out now. Hang on, the tomb is shaking, not me.

Meanwhile outside, the guard drops his spear in fright. He cannot stand up; the vibration keeps knocking him to the ground. So, he stays there, his eyes fixed in horror as the large stone gives a sudden jolt, a snapping sound, and begins rolling back in its groove. The vibration stops. Not wanting to face the unknown, the frightened soldier flees in panic.

At the same time, Jesus is still lying face down on the floor. His body throbbing, his eyes hurt as he squints at the welcoming daylight.

Oh God, I'm free from this tomb. What now?

As he struggles to stand, he lets his eyes adjust to the light. Using what strength he can manage, he hobbles to the opening and peers out of the entrance. Seeing nothing and nobody, he shivers in the morning air. He looks down and notices what looks like a discarded cloak. Unsteady on his swollen feet, he steps outside and attempts to bend down to pick up the soldier's abandoned clothing. Now bent, he is unable straighten up. Besides being so stiff and sore, thirst is becoming a top priority. His body now cramping up, he has to bend his knees to be able to sit.

Now leaning back against the cold tombstone, he reaches over for the cloak and attempts to wrap it around him. He does not care as the odor of the Roman soldier fills his nostrils.

Poor man! Did he run from the earthquake? At least his cloak is keeping me warm – Do I hear water?

The noise of running water echoes nearby. Stirred by the sound, he can see a stone channel leading from a nearby well. Knowing he has a chance of not dying from thirst, he crawls on his hands and knees to the well. Before he can obtain any of the lifesaving water, he collapses. While the agony rips through his body in the exhausting attempt to raise up onto his knees and lean against the well, he shuffles a little closer.

All I have to do is reach out and cup my hands. Oh, beautiful water.

Managing to stretch his weak arms and cup his hands, he sinks his face into his hands and drinks.

Feeling the liquid refreshing all parts of his body, he glances down at his trembling hands. Not absorbing the mutilation, he is thankful just to be alive.

Oh God, thank you. I'm so tired. Is this what it feels like to rise again?

Now focusing on his hands, he is horrified.

Look at my swollen, bruised, and ugly wrists. Will they heal? Will I heal? Did I really die? Do I still have a mission?

While contemplating these questions about his immediate future, he realizes it is now full daylight. He looks around.

I am in a beautiful garden full of vines...

The air is becoming warmer, as the sun rises. To find relief, Jesus seeks the shade of a nearby olive tree. While he leans against the cool tree trunk, again, exhaustion overwhelms him.

No! I mustn't sleep. If I'm found, they will kill me for sure. I must hide...

A woman running up to the tomb attracts his attention. She shrieks as she sees the open entrance, and then disappears inside. He hears her scream. Jesus turns his head to get a better view. The woman exits the tomb; He can see it is Mary Magdalene exiting the tomb. Before he can gesture or shout, she runs off in the direction she came from.

Struggling to position his aching body, he hangs his head in disappointment.

"Oh Mary, my love. I'm right here for you."

His voice cracks with weakness and despair. The pain causing him to feel nauseous, he shuts his eyes. With the fatigue gnawing away at him, he floats into an uneasy sleep.

Not knowing how long he has been asleep; he is disturbed by voices echoing from a long way off. As the voices become nearer and louder, he opens his eyes trying hard to focus his mind. He can see it is Mary. She is back now with Peter, James and John. After entering the tomb, Peter returns outside holding the linen shroud against him. All looking shocked and confused, they talk in an erratic fashion for a short while, and then the two men leave in a hurry. Mary decides she wants to stay and wait. Appearing pale and strained, she sits down on a rock not far from the tomb entrance. After all this time Jesus has been watching her, the frustration is unbearable, because he wants to shout, but he is still too weak.

After a short while still watching, he notices Mary staring at the tomb's entrance in confusion. She then begins to sob. Jesus now exasperated, struggles to a standing position, and then begins to hobble toward her. As he gets nearer and his pain becomes more intense, her sobs become louder. Now leaning against the olive tree of earlier, he is behind her.

"Why are you crying?"

Without looking around, she answers.

"They have taken my love away."

Curiosity causes her to turn toward the voice. Because the rising sun is shining in her eyes, all she can focus on is the silhouette of a man dressed in a hooded cloak. Presuming he is the gardener, she pleads.

"Sir. If you have taken him away, tell me where he is, so I can go to him?"

His body now shaking in response to her plea, burning tears fill his eyes.

"Oh, Mary..."

Her eyes widen at the familiar voice. Wanting to get a better look at this man, she steps into his shadow. Even though his head is still covered by the hood, she steps nearer. Now focusing on his hazel eyes, her face exudes a mixture of disbelief, and concern.

"Oh, my love, it's you! You're 'not' dead. But how?"

Unable to contain her joy, she falls against him and wraps her arms around his waist. Relishing her smell and warmth, he winces with the pain.

"Don't hold onto me just yet. I'm not quite ready."

Realizing about his wounds, she is reluctant to withdraw. Instead, she takes hold of one of his hands, and is repelled at the heavy nail wound in his wrist. Her heart breaking, she reaches out for his other hand that he has placed on her head.

It's so nice to feel her hair again.

"Go and tell the others the good news."

She removes his swollen hand from her head to her lips. Wanting so much to heal and love him, she kisses the ugly nail hole.

"I still don't understand! When will you come and see us all?"

"Where are you staying?"

"At your mother's house."

"I'll see you all there tonight. I'll hide until then."

That evening, Mary, Jesus' mother and the eleven apostles are all gathered at the little stone house. Mary Magdalene has decided to wait outside. Waiting in the dark, she hears his weak voice.

"Mary?"

Her heart jumps.

"Yes, my love. I'm right here."

As he appears out of the shadows, she goes to hug him, but hesitates remembering his terrible wounds. Instead, she offers him a tender kiss on the cheek.

On her opening the door of the house for him, all the apostles stand as he enters. Standing just inside the front door, Jesus pushes his hood back, exposing his swollen and bruised face. To ease their troubled expressions, he raises his left hand.

"Peace be with you."

185

The room is silent as they all stare at him, disbelieving, foreboding and confused. Stunned, but joyous at the sight of her beloved son, Jesus' mother puts a hand up to her mouth, and her eyes filling with tears of concern. Needing to put them all at ease, Jesus leans against the table to keep his balance.

"Why are you all so troubled, and why do doubts rise in you? Look at my hands and feet? It's me, not a ghost who has no flesh and bones."

As they all still stare in amazement, he struggles around the table to sit.

"Do you have anything here to eat?"

Her eyes still full of tears, his mother appears with some cooked fish, bread and wine. Hesitating at first, Jesus begins to eat, and then sips the warm wine.

Observing his master's hands trembling while trying to eat, Thomas comes forward.

"Is it really you? I want to see the nail holes and the wound in your side."

Jesus responds by attempting to stand, but fails. Being helped by Mary, Jesus manages to stand, but winces in agony. Staring into Thomas's doubtful eyes, tears of anger fill Jesus' eyes, as he puts out his hands to expose the swollen wrists.

"Here, put your finger into the nail holes, and in my side and don't doubt ever again."

They all watch as Thomas examines the wounds. Embarrassed by his own cynicism, Thomas steps back to let Jesus sit. His face pale from the extra effort, Jesus points his trembling forefinger at them all.

"Now you've seen and believe. I bless those who believe, but haven't seen. Now all sit, eat and celebrate."

As if this is all a dream, Mary insists that Jesus stays at the house with her and his mother, while the apostles stay at Matthew's house.

The following evening the Apostles return to find Jesus appears a little stronger. He sits again at the table with Mary Magdalene on his right, and now Peter on his left.

Overwhelmed by it all, Jesus' mother brings bread and wine, which Jesus passes around. As she sits, his mother looks at her son in wonder. It is almost as if the crucifixion never happened. In the meantime, Jesus' eyes contain a faraway look as he turns to Peter.

"Peter? Do you love me?"

Appearing surprised, and disturbed at the question, Peter does his best to answer.

"Yes, sir! You 'know' I love you."

"Then feed my lambs."

Just as Peter tries to understand his master's request, Jesus turns away to look at Mary, smiles, and then looks down at the table. Pondering for a short while, he then gazes back to Peter.

"Peter? Do you 'truly' love me?"

"Yes, sir! You 'know' how much I love you."

Pleased with the answer, Jesus places his swollen hand on Peter's nearest shoulder.

"Then take care of my sheep."

Before Peter can respond further, Jesus turns away, glances back down at the table and drinks some more wine. The mood being somber, Jesus' mother still sees that distant look in her son's eyes. Jesus turns to Peter a third time.

"Peter? do you 'really' love me?"

"Sir? You know all things, and you know I 'really' love you."

"Then feed my sheep."

Just when Peter is about to contemplate his future, Mary leans her head on Jesus' shoulder. He does not wince this time. Instead, he surveys her fine chiseled features with affection. After a few seconds, he scrutinizes the others with concern.

"Don't leave Jerusalem. Wait for the gift from God, which you have heard me speak of many times. John baptized me with water, but in a few days you will be baptized with the Holy Spirit."

Andrew, who is sitting next to Peter, leans forward.

"Rabbi? Now you're back, are you now going to restore the Kingdom of

Israel?"

Fatigue eating away at him, Jesus leans back against the wall and looks at them all in turn.

"It's not for you to know what times are set for anything, but you will receive the power when God comes to you to spread the truth, as I've done."

While they all appear confused, Jesus sighs, and wonders if it is all worth the effort. Suppressing his frustration, he leans forward to make his point.

"Look, I was on that cross, and I was put into a sealed tomb. Now I'm here with you, as proof that God is within me as he will be within you – if you believe."

He struggles to stand.

"I'm now going to Bethany, up into the mountains so I can rest and pray, because I will be leaving you soon."

With each apostle glancing at each other for reassurance, Jesus turns and heads for the door. As if knowing the future, Mary Magdalene joins him.

All staring at the door being closed, sadness and confusion settles over the small group. Searching for guidance, they look to Mary, mother of Jesus, for that guidance. Sensing their plight, she stares with a mournful expression at the closed door with tears in her eyes.

Outside, Jesus has walked a short distance when he has to lean against the wall to rest. His rapid, shallow breathing alarms Mary. She gapes in horror as his wrists begin to bleed.

"Oh, my love! What's happening? What are we going to do?"

"Don't worry, I'm all right. Can you help me to Bethany?"

"Of course, I will. I want to be with you wherever you go."

It is now late at night; the stars are out and a full moon is giving them the light to find the hidden place he wants to be. As they rest, Mary is still in shock at having to support Jesus in every step to arrive here. She is still sickened with anger with him being put through all this unjust agony. Her focused mind begins to race as she helps him lie down.

After a few more days of rest I will get him to a safer spot, perhaps go back to my village and start again.

Wanting so much to love and care for him, she is careful when lying next to him.

While gazing up at the stars and listening to his shallow breathing, she can't shake of the feeling that this might be the last time they will spend together alone.

Not if I have my way...

For some reason she decides to sit up. On looking down at him, she discovers he is staring up at her. His lips tremble as he speaks.

"Stay with me for a while, and then bring the others here."

"Can you tell me why?"

Unable to say any more, his face looks ashen in the moonlight. Her concern heightening, she leans over him to study his face. As dark streaks appear on his forehead, from blood trickling out of the thorn holes, she lays her head on his chest. Listening to his heartbeat, which is soothing to her ear, she prays in her mind.

Oh god! Don't take him from me? Whatever your plan, make sure I'm part of it?

His heart beating steady, they both fall asleep.

When Mary awakens, the sky is breaking into a new day.

He's not here!

She sits up, fearful and shivering in the cold morning air. After listening for any sound of him, she hears his muffled voice from behind a nearby boulder. Her heart lifting, and knowing he is still with her, she comes around the boulder to find him curled up on his knees, praying.

"Oh God, take me now! I'm ready...."

Knowing Mary is watching, he stops. His tear-laden face full of fear, he gazes up at her.

"Go and tell the others there isn't much time."

Puzzled about there not being enough time, she crouches down and places her gentle hand on his back. He winces, but does not pull away.

Becoming confused by his behavior, she begrudges removing her hand. Instead, tears of confusion and fear fill her eyes as she places that hand in her lap.

"I don't ever want to be apart from you - anymore."

She begins to sob, as he reaches over and clasps her hand trembling in her lap.

"Please don't cry my love. We are 'never' going to be apart."

"Then why are praying for God to take you? I will take you to a safe spot and care for you as I've always done. Anyway, I have something important to tell you."

"Tell me soon enough. Now, please go and summon the others."

She appears hurt at his apparent indifference.

Why won't he listen?

"Why so urgent? I 'need' to tell you!"

His patience waning, he struggles to sit up. He grips her arm as she leans forward to help him.

"Please get the others."

After helping him stand, she is lost for words. Witnessing his troubled face, she then walks a few steps away, and stops. Her heart aches so much for him that she needs to tell him of their baby she is carrying.

Surely, God will let me do that?

On the verge of crying, she leaves to carry out his request.

Meanwhile, Jesus makes his way back to where they had slept earlier, and almost collapses. Overwhelmed by fatigue, he closes his eyes, and mumbles, as his mind drifts back over the past three years.

"What have I achieved? 'Nothing!' All right, I've helped a few souls and healed a few bodies. Where is everyone now? I thank you for Mary. Without her strength and courage, I don't think my 'mission' would have amounted to anything. Mission? mission for what? I had these wonderful dreams of wanting to change the world, get rid of evil. I tried, but what happened, not a thing! Nothing has changed. The corrupt Jews are still misleading the gullible people, and evil Satan is still rampant."

Tired by the memories, Jesus sips some water Mary has left him, and then again, he falls asleep.

The following evening, Mary arrives with Mary, Jesus' mother, and the eleven bewildered apostles. Jesus is standing in a forming mist, his face resigned and peaceful.

"Thank you for coming. This is the last time we shall all be as one. Please, can you form a semi-circle around me? I want to thank you individually for your friendship and loyalty."

As he goes along the line stopping at each one, he places both hands on their foreheads and gives a silent prayer. Peter is the last. With tears of appreciation, Jesus holds both of Peter's hands in his.

"Peter? You're my rock. It's you that will bring my sheep together."

He kisses Peter's forehead, and then moves away. When he comes to his mother, she is weeping in silence.

"This isn't goodbye mother, but a new beginning. Look after these children for me, because they will need all of your motherly courage."

He kisses her forehead, pauses, and then moves on to Mary Magdalene. He conveys to her a sincere smile, pauses to peer deep into her moistening eyes, and then turns back to the others.

"I am giving you what God has promised. Now is the right time for you to go out into the world and teach my message. Everything I've taught you is in God's name. Now 'you' go and teach in 'my' name. You will not see me in this form anymore, but I will be with you forever in spirit..."

As the evening mist thickens, he turns back to Mary Magdalene.

"Oh, my love. I will be in 'your' soul - forever."

Finding it hard to hold back her tears, she begins to cry.

"I don't understand! I can take care of you. Why now?"

"Please don't cry, I'm now going to be with God, as you will when your time is right."

To comfort her, he places his left hand on her abdomen, his right hand under her chin to tilt her head, and offers her a gentle kiss on her lips.

"This is the beginning of a new world. Tell our child about me and that someday I will return to reclaim that world."

While tears of impending grief roll down her face, the mist thickens even more. He then backs away until he is out of sight. Now engulfed in the heavy mist, his voice echoes.

"God loves you."

Minutes pass. A light breeze develops, dispersing the mist, leaving them silent and staring bewildered at the empty spot where Jesus once stood. Whispering through her tears, Mary holds her stomach.

"We love you."

II

Plan Two

PAINFUL PROPHECY

24

The Near Future

The dark office is filled with a smoky haze. An overweight man is sitting at an overflowing desk becoming frantic while hammering away on a keyboard. Glancing on occasion at the large flat computer monitor glowing in front of him, he puffs away at a heavy cigar, and chews hard on its end as his excitement mounts at what is coming up on the screen. Placed underneath the monitor is an antique finished bronze plaque with the inscription:

To Irwin Schulz – Champion of the Ridiculous.

He needs to pause to release a large puff of cigar smoke, which gives the monitor screen an eerie foggy atmosphere. His round face molds into a frown as his mind is trying to form the next and maybe the final sentence of his creative writing...

There is a knock on the door causing his honed focus to shatter. His reaction is to cough in a violent manner causing the cigar shoot out of his mouth and speed straight onto the screen resulting in a muted thud and a smear on the screen. In a form of desperation, he tries to clear his smoke laden throat.

"It's open."

The door squeaks open on its neglected hinges. His patience limited, Irwin gestures with a free hand to a nearby chair without taking his eyes off the screen. As someone comes in, they obey his gesture by maneuvering the nearby chair on the hard-wooden floor. At the same time, Irwin attempts to wipe the cigar smudge off the screen with his pudgy fingers, and then jams what remains of the cigar back into his heavy mouth. Regardless of whoever is sitting in his other chair, he carries on pounding the flat keys of the delicate wireless keyboard. Still managing to puff away at his now extinguished cigar, he has to talk through his teeth.

"Gotta get this crap finished or my ticker is going to reach its used-by date ahead of time over these damn deadlines."

Large sweat stains begin to form on his pale blue shirt, while he taps the last few keys. Now stopping, he leans his heavy weight back in his chair, and pushes his glasses back onto the bridge of his wide nose.

"There! That's this week's column finished."

Annoyed at what is left of his chewed-up cigar, he places it in a nearby overflowing ashtray, and then swivels around toward the waiting visitor. Although his chair is almost giving way, a brief look of recognition crosses his face as he pulls his glasses further down his nose. His pale blue eyes then look away as if searching for something. His swivel chair squeaks in pain as he turns to open a drawer. Rummaging, he retrieves a cigarette lighter, picks up his chewed cigar and proceeds to light it. Soon fogging the surrounding area with no regard for his guest, he lets out a rattling cough as he returns to face his monitor.

"Some call my writing bullshit, but at least it's my bullshit! The powers that be are clamping down on independent guys like me. 'Stick to the facts' they say. Whose facts? Theirs or mine? 'We don't want your asshole opinions' they say. My opinion my friend is the truth, as I see it. Isn't that what the truth is? As you see it? If the new editor doesn't like my 'truth' then that's his problem. I've had this column for fifteen years, and as you well know, I've built up a large following making this newspaper a good name and whole lotta money."

Satisfied in getting his complaint of his chest; he swivels back to face his visitor, who remains silent. Irwin looks again over his glasses and draws on his cigar stub. By doing so, he chokes. Becoming exasperated, he removes the stub, coughs again, which makes his face turn bright pink.

Aware of what the visitor might think, he regains his composure and flings what is left of the cigar stub into a nearby trashcan.

"Doc says I gotta quit! Damn it man, I've gotta have 'something' to help me get my 'truth' out on time."

Releasing a heavy sigh of frustration, he removes his glasses, wipes the sweat from his face with an old rag dredged from a nearby pocket.

"Anyhow, I appreciate you showing up on time! Many folks don't do that.

They want me to expose some bad guy or some greedy corporation by giving them plenty of helpful free publicity, and then they can't be bothered to show up on time."

His frustration easing, he jams his glasses back on his nose, swivels back to his desk and places both of his pudgy hands on a pile of disorganized papers.

He begins to rummage.

"That was an interesting phone call we had yesterday..."

Some papers fall on the floor. He curses under his breath.

"One of these days that jerk of an editor might be generous enough to hire me a secretary. Despite the millions I've made for this newspaper, he says he can't afford one since the Internet and social media is taking over all of the news. Ever get the feeling someone's out to get yuh?"

He finds what he is looking for. After a quick inspection, he holds up a pink sheet of paper in triumph.

"Gotcha."

While he leans back in his overburdened chair, he studies the rediscovered paper.

"Yeah that sure was one hell of a phone call..."

He begins to scan the paper

"Let's see...you're..."

He carries on mumbling. Satisfied with what he has read, he replaces the paper back on his cluttered desk, removes his glasses, and re-wipes his face with the same sweat-laden rag.

For some reason he decides to pull out a new cigar from a box next to the monitor. Regardless of his visitor, he shoves the cigar into his mouth, bites down hard, removes the cigar and spits the unwanted end piece into the nearby trashcan. After retrieving his lighter he goes through a ceremony of lighting this new cigar, puffs and fills the immediate area again with smoke. By doing this he coughs and coughs again. After about thirty seconds he swivels back to his patient visitor, and again begins talking through his teeth while still puffing.

"As you know from my writing, I am a big advocate of clean air. Unlike all those jerks out there polluting the hell out of us..."

He draws on his cigar, removes it, and then exhales a lung-full of smoke. By controlling the urge to cough again, he holds up the same piece of paper from his desktop and waves it around to clear the fog. Meanwhile, he has difficulty in clearing his throat.

"The trouble is, what you've given me is environmental stuff. To be honest, anything to do with the environment is a bum steer, especially since our beloved

Republican President and Congress has voted to shut down the E.P.A."

He turns to his computer and presses a key. The screen fills with data.

"Look at all this. Thousands of complaints about pollution and environ-mental damage. People getting sick and dying in the workplace, I could write every day until my ass turns blue. The trouble is - nobody cares any more about the little guy. It's always the ordinary Joe who suffers at the hands of the big moguls and corporations, and always will do, unless we have a revolution of some kind. Even after the Corona virus killed off millions of poor souls, we're still suffering. What I wanna know, where is God in all this?"

Becoming depressed by his own ramblings, he pauses, takes a final puff of his cigar, and then stubs it out in the overflowing ashtray. Again, he faces his visitor over the top of his glasses.

"Anyway, I like your angle - it's different. Yeah, I like it very much."

Becoming restless in his straining chair, he mumbles to no one in particular.

"Now where did I put that..."

He rummages through the mass of stuff covering his desktop.

"You're not there, so where are you, you little..."

With great difficulty he bends over causing his body mass to alter shape like a Jell-O falling out of a mold. Wheezing, he struggles to open several lower desk drawers.

"Come on man, where've you put it?"

Bending over as far as his mass will allow, the color in his face now rising to crimson, his eyes bulging, and each vein in his neck looking as if it is about burst, a small voice recorder falls out of his top jacket pocket, landing on the hard-wooden floor. With a mammoth effort, he retrieves it, and then with great difficulty, tries to regain something of his original posture. Happy to be holding the voice recorder, he splutters.

"Got yuh, yer little bugger."

His other hand desperate to grip the chair arm, the visitor reacts by rising from his chair to help, but Irwin manages to straighten up while the chair seems to squeeze down to half it's normal size.

"Thanks, young fella, but I've made it.

As a result of his effort, Irwin then goes into another coughing fit. Concerned, the visitor rises again. Irwin shakes his head and puts out a hand to stop him. He soon recovers. The visitor is reluctant to sit.

Seconds pass as Irwin checks the micro-digital voice recorder. Relieved it is still in full working order, he places it on a small clear space of desktop nearest to the visitor. Leaning back into the suffering chair, he looks at the visitor with a curious gaze.

"If what you say is true my friend, let's start from the beginning at what you predict is going to happen to this disintegrating world of ours and the poor buggars that hope to survive..."

He switches on the recorder.

25

Out of the Blue

The restless chanting crowd is growing like a malignancy. Hundreds of people are coming from all directions. As they mass toward a horizontal line of giant bulldozers in front of a deteriorating auto assembly plant, not surprising, the drivers have already vanished. A makeshift deck fitted with a podium has been placed right in front of the bulldozers. Several banners are on display inscribed in bold black letters on a yellow background:

'NO PLANT – NO SICKNESS.'

A middle-aged man dressed in overalls climbs onto the podium and attempts to talk into a microphone. The noise coming from the rumbustious crowd is drowning him out, so he turns to adjust the volume on a nearby amplifier, and then returns to the microphone for another attempt. He shouts.

"Fellow workers, listen to me!"

Because he is well known by the crowd, some of the 'fellow workers' nearer the podium begin to listen. Frustrated by the lack of attention, he shouts again.

"Listen! We don't need this evil plant here!"

A few more attentive listeners shout back in response.

"NO!"

Now he feels he is getting somewhere, the man in overalls communicates back.

"We know why, don't we?"

With a fair amount of agreement from the growing crowd, the man continues.

"We all know it's because the Federal Government is not accountable anymore. The corporations now make the rules for us slaves to follow, but the Feds choose to ignore them."

As the crowd expands, many more cheers are heard. Enthused by this support, the man carries on.

"Listen to me, my friends. They know by building a plant here to process this type of toxic waste, all types of sickness will occur."

More sounds of agreement are relayed. Enthused, the speaker raises his voice.

"Do the bastards care?"

The mass echoes their reply.

"NO!"

"Of course, they don't. All they're interested in is making..."

As if on cue, another large noisy crowd appears. Many wave banners stating

'NO PLANT – NO WAGES – NOTHING TO EAT'.

Riot police escorts this crowd, as several TV crews appear.

Frantic in assembling their equipment, their aim is to witness and report to the population at large. Knowing their audience will be transfixed in front of their T.V. sets, smartphones and computers right now, they are waiting for another episode of life's daily soap opera demonstrating a once great country, declining under the sagging weight of its own greed and constant corruption.

An attractive woman in her late twenties and of African dissent in is wasting no time in setting up her sound equipment, testing her wireless microphone, and then nodding to her camera operator. While he is focusing his lens on her upper body ready for transmission, he conveys to her a nod for her to begin. At first, she is a little hesitant, and as her confidence grows, she begins to address the faceless lens.

"This is Eva Brown reporting for Channel Six. I am standing outside this disused car assembly plant in Detroit, Michigan. As you can witness, I am having trouble making myself heard because of this huge emotional fraught crowd, made up of supporters for the government's new toxic waste treatment plant, and protesters who are against the plant by

attempting to surround the building..."

Attempting to get to a better position, she indicates to her camera operator to move further toward the podium. Satisfied she has a better view, she continues.

"If you've been following our extensive news coverage lately, you will know of the tremendous controversy that exists about plans to reopen this old car assembly plant as a Federal backed reprocessing factory for the toxic waste that is produced from the new bionic weapons being manufactured at several Government backed ordinance factories throughout the country. You can see behind me, the different banners supporting and opposing the project. The mood of these very large, two opposing crowds is becoming volatile.

The police, dressed in riot gear are arriving as we speak."

As she speaks, her camera operator turns to focus on the opposing masses who are now beginning to confront each other. Without any provocation, the 'Pro-plant' demonstrators begin to wade into the 'Anti-plant' crowd. While the 'pros' wield baseball bats and metal bars, the riot police make a feeble attempt at separating the two masses. The 'Pro' crowd appears far more aggressive than the 'Anti' crowd who are now just trying to protect themselves. It seems the police are subtle in helping the 'Pro' crowd by pretending to be unable to stop the two massive crowds converging on each other. With this 'uncontrolled' horror taking place, the camera lens focuses on people being knocked down for no reason, and then being trampled upon. Ear splitting screams can be heard above the roar of the angry, and yet confused crowd, as the camera zooms in and scans the ugly scenes. As the lens investigates, bright glints of knife blades instilling fatal wounds to any poor soul caught in their way.

Not having witnessed such carnage before, Eva Brown looks on in a trance, her hands shake around her lowered microphone. When her battle-hardened camera operator gives her a nod to proceed, this helps to break her daze. Bringing the microphone up to her face, she hesitates as her dry mouth refuses to find the spit to form her next words to describe and report on this morass of horrific violence.

"Th – this is frightening, terrible! People are falling everywhere! I've never seen such violence and carnage at a demonstration. The police have no control and don't seem to be doing anything to stop it. From where I'm standing some of the injuries look fatal. Surely, 'someone' has called for help to stop all this."

An additional disturbance causes the camera operator to focus on the podium. Eva follows with her eyes.

"Something is going on nearer the bulldozers. A man is trying to climb onto the podium, but others are attempting to stop him."

After a struggle, a tall young man manages to scramble onto the podium. Beneath him a mass of banners, metal bars, anything that can be used as a weapon are being pushed, bludgeoned, and bashed in all directions. With a sense of urgency, he grabs the microphone and shouts into it. Understanding that nobody can hear him, a police officer standing in front of the podium with his back to the young man is involved in a struggle with a banner holder. Meanwhile, needing to address the pandemonium, the young man is looking around as if searching for something. His eyes fix on the struggling police officer. He leans across the podium, bends down and withdraws the distracted policeman's gun from its holster. He fires a shot in the air, nobody hears him. Once again, he looks around the immediate area and then goes over to the amplifier, fiddles with some switches, and returns to the microphone. As he bites his lip in concentration, he cocks the revolver, places it close to the microphone, and then fires. The noise is so deafening as it is transmitted through the gang of heavy speakers that some of the crowd stop in surprise. Seeing the attention is insufficient, the young man fires again. Repeating the same deafening burst of fire, the mass of turmoil comes to a sudden halt. Taking advantage of the stillness, the young man grips the microphone.

"What in God's name are you doing? Why are you hurting each other like this? Look around you. These are your brothers, sisters, friends and workmates crying out in pain. Is this 'really' the way to get your opinions heard?"

A desperate voice cries from the crowd.

"We don't want to die of a deadly cancer."

Another voice shouts out with the opposite opinion.

"Our families are hungry. We need the jobs."

Others begin to join in with opinions flying everywhere. Some begin shouting abuse. The short period of peace diminishes and restlessness begins again.

As the young man's warm hazel eyes witness this with trepidation, his heart fills with dismay and sadness. His light brown hair sticks to his forehead as the sweat of frustration clings to his face. To pacify this crowd to get his point across, he raises the gun to the microphone. The police officer that has now realized his firearm is missing, begins to scramble up onto the podium. In the meantime, the young man cocks the revolver again. The police officer hesitates as the gun blasts again near the microphone. This in turn makes the crowd stop in its tracks; freeze framing the action of fists about to hit, iron bars about to maim, and knives in mid-stroke.

Determined to stop this madness, the young man demonstrates an authority in his voice.

"I 'command' you to stop this meaningless behavior right now! Instead of hurting each other why don't you help and comfort each other. Violence has 'never' solved anything. Deep down you all know that! Fortunately, I can show you a better way."

A lone skeptical voice shouts from the mass, and is echoed by others.

"Oh yeah? What way?"

His voice earnest with conviction the young man raises his free arm.

"I have been sent here to help you. This suffering is unnecessary. This is 'not' how it's supposed to be."

His crisp clear message seems to be having a calming effect on the crowd. Everyone seems to want to take an interest and listen. A light breeze develops out of nowhere causing his tussled hair to blow in such a way it exposes his face. His strong and yet kind personality comes across in such a way, he has them all in the palm of his hand. Realizing this, a warm smile glides across his face.

"I suppose it's a 'do unto others before they do unto you' sort of day today."

A few laughs are heard, the original meanness is evaporating, and weapons are being lowered. Pleased with his efforts, he smiles again in relief.

"As some of you might know, it's 'do unto others as you would wish them to do unto you' Unfortunately, this is mostly redundant."

He is amazed at how many of the crowd is still listening. His response is to peer at the concentrating eyes and continue.

"Did you know that all these problems before you can be solved? And I mean 'all'. This actual problem can certainly be solved, and 'both' sides can be victorious. I'm here to warn you that by following the 'wrong' way, both sides will be defeated. Now, go home to your families and loved ones, and I will make sure that those responsible for 'this' problem will be held accountable."

While his demeanor exudes authority and control, the breeze drops. Among the stillness his words sink in. For a few seconds everyone stands still...

The jarring of ambulances arriving breaks the silence. Paramedics jump out to help the injured and dying. The young man having somehow injected a sense of guilt into the crowd, some people rush to help, others disperse in a more tranquil manner, while the remainder comfort each other.

After observing this staggering set of circumstances, the TV anchor, Eva Brown brings the microphone back up to speak as her camera operator continues to scan the area, which minutes earlier was a gruesome battlefield.

"This is truly astonishing. We have witnessed something very extraordinary today. A young man coming out of nowhere has prevented this battle zone from turning into a major catastrophic blood bath. I don't know who he is, but he seems to be talkingfrom a position of authority, especially when he says, and I quote; 'that whoever is responsible for this problem today will be held accountable'. Right now, we're going to try and track him down to find out his true position."

While she gathers her portable equipment and begins to make her way toward the podium, the cameraman cannot resist filming the devastation as they go.

When they arrive at the podium everyone has gone. Disappointed, Eva asks a few passersby if anyone has seen the young man. Nobody saw him go. A trembling voice of a child shouts behind her.

"I did."

As Eva looks toward the source, a young girl of about seven years old with golden hair matted with blood, points at the other side of the bulldozers. Her tear-stained face stares up at Eva exposing her searching, tired blue eyes. Meanwhile, a screaming voice of panic is heard.

"Cindy! There you are."

A woman in her twenties, obviously the child's mother is crying with relief that she has found her lost loved one. In response, she crouches down and hugs her child.

"Oh, my baby – I couldn't find you."

The little girl's reaction is to cry. Realization coming to the fore, the mother touches the blood on the little girl's hair.

"You're hurt!"

Welcoming her mother's touch, the little girl ceases crying and reassures.

"No. I'm all right Mommy..."

A harassed paramedic arrives on the scene.

"You okay kid?"

He checks her head with speedy professionalism, and smiles with relief.

"You're fine. Must be someone else's blood!"

As he moves on seeking the owner of that blood, the two women stare at each other in thought. Holding her daughter's hand, the mother stands, and begins to walk away, but the little girl resists. Still gazing at Eva and the camera, she attempts to brush the matted hair from her face with a grimy hand.

"Are you looking for him?"

The mother becoming confused, and Eva astonished at this question, she answers.

"Yes, I am. How would you know that?"

Ignoring the question, the small child points in the same direction as before.

"I saw him go that way."

Having given the needed information, she turns to walk away with her mother. In the meantime, Eva is left standing in a daze. Her mind keeps seeing the grimy small index finger pointing the way. Coming to her senses, she straightens up her light gray suit and acknowledges the camera operator, pulls out an iPhone from her jacket, and taps the screen with a trembling hand.

"Hey Max - Eva. We lost him. I'm sorry. Did you get everything? Good. I know. I've lucked out on a great opportunity. Okay. See you back at the station."

Releasing a heavy sigh of despair, she taps the screen to close.

"Damn! My first big assignment and I blew it."

Resigned to this type of situation, her world-weary cameraman begins to pack away his camera.

"Never mind. It happens to us all. Got some great footage, though."

26

The Assignment

For a TV news boss, Max's office is plain and tidy, except for two flat screen monitors. The largest one is a smart 4K TV hanging on the wall behind his desk, and the other is a twenty-seven-inch computer situated in the center of his clean, bare desk. No frills, no mess that is what describes the character of the man.

Max Cowan is Jewish, fifty-five years old, five foot six inches tall, and bald. His face is stern, but warm. His dark brooding eyes show depth and compassion. He has been there, done it, and worn the T-shirt. He looks up as Eva knocks on his open door. He raises his voice while viewing the large TV screen.

"Enter!"

Apprehensive of his coming reaction to her journalistic 'failure', she enters the room followed by Mike, her cameraman. Revealing a welcoming smile, Max switches off the TV and swivels around in his chair to face them. Before Max can express an opinion, Eva spits out her words.

"I can't believe I missed him. One minute he was there and next…"

To pacify her, Max interrupts by holding up his hand followed by a sympathetic smile.

"No worries. We've found him."

Her emotions still riding high, Eva cannot quite take in what he is saying.

"You've what?"

"I said we've - found him."

"How?"

Intending to keep the mood calm, Max rises from his swivel chair. To prolong an air of professionalism, he saunters around his desk to where Eva is standing. To make her relax and feel comfortable, he places an affectionate hand on her shoulder. His eyes twinkle as the laugh lines on his face deepen, and his generous mouth widens with a warm smile.

"Look sweetheart, I've been in this business for over thirty years. I have contacts and moles everywhere. You? You're new at the job. Now you see with something like this, you keep your head and detach your emotions by moving in on your prey, and pounce when he's finished talking. If you had been nearer to the podium..."

He removes his hand and gives her shoulder a gentle pat.

"Not to worry, you'll get the hang of it. The main thing, we've got him."

As if exposing a well-kept secret, Max winks at Mike, who in return conveys to his boss an amenable smile. Observing this all-male strategy, and becoming more aware of these two media veterans, Eva struggles to regain her dignity.

"I appreciate you taking it so well Max. I'll certainly remember 'next' time."

His mood now business like, he steps over to a local street map positioned next to the hanging TV.

"That time is right now young lady."

To demonstrate his determination, he places his manicured stubby index finger on a section of the map.

"Here's our friend - on the corner of Nineteenth and Pine. It's an old disused church. It appears he's doing some sort of restoration work. Something to do with turning the place into a refuge for homeless and abused victims of society. Battered and mistreated wives and kids - that sort of thing."

Her confidence returning, Eva steps closer to Max to study the map,

"Is it a government backed thing Max?"

"Government? Hell no! They wouldn't be interested in this part of the city. Crime rate is too high. What made you ask?"

"This guy seems to talk with such authority. He was so sure of himself."

Max glances at Mike and conveys to him another wink.

"Good angles on the riot Mike. I want you to stay with Eva for a while. Help her all you can on this. Okay?"

"Sure Max. My pleasure"

While Mike offers Eva a reassuring smile, Max turns to Eva.

"You may have something on the authority thing. We've been jammed with calls wanting to know about this guy. The big networks and affiliates are also in town trying to track him down. But hey, being local, we're ten strokes ahead of them all. So, you two get your butts down to this old church, dig him out and interview. Preferably for the six o'clock slot."

His enthusiasm taking over his previous 'mood' he glances at his watch.

"Hell, we may even be able to do a news flash earlier! So, get going!"

Thankful for another chance, Eve glances at both men.

"I won't let you down this time Max."

In response to her gratitude, Max presence her with a disarming smile.

"I know honey – I know. Now get your asses outer here."

While Eva and Mike exit the office, Max rubs his hands together, and heads back toward his chair. Deep in thought, he leans over his desk, grabs a remote and switches on the large TV monitor. Pictures of the riot light up the screen showing the young man firing the revolver. Becoming entranced, Max sits down in his well-used comfortable leather chair, leans back and studies the big screen.

"I've got a strong gut feeling about you my boy. This is only the beginning."

27

The Interview

As the TV van cruises along a gray, rundown street scanning for their destination, Eva points out the church among some derelict buildings. Parking outside the disused church, they both stare at the surrounding area and wonder if this is the right building. Eva, still dressed in her snug fitting light gray suit, looks out of the passenger window, and studies this relic of past generations.

"St. Mark, 1865. I bet it was fine in its day. It seems every building around here is either empty, boarded up or waiting to be demolished. What a dump. The church looks deserted. I hope Max's intel was correct."

Feeling the same, Mike nods in agreement and shrugs.

"There's sure one way to find out."

While he opens his door, steps out and goes to the side door of the van to collect his equipment, Eva, still looking around, gets out and ambles up to the heavy, gothic sun parched front door of the church. Observing the rough texture of the door, she tightens her hand into a fist and knocks with her knuckles. Out of the blue and breaking the silence, she hears high-pitched screams. Becoming anxious, she cannot place the voices. As there is no response to her knocking, she tries to push open the door. It seems locked. The high-pitched voices appear again. Without any warning, a line of about a dozen young children come running out from a hidden alley somewhere, screaming and laughing. They speed past Eva as if she isn't there, and then disappear up the side alley of the gray church building.

Fitting his camera together, Mike seems unaffected.

"Is that some sign of life?"

Disturbed by the noise, and trying to act relaxed; Eva bangs again on the door, this time with the side of her fist. After a few seconds, they hear movement behind the door. A metallic scraping sound of a large bolt or lever is being slid across, accompanied by what sounds like a human grunt. The old iron hinges scream from years of neglect, as the large door eases open. Filling the doorway is a wide shouldered, tall man of about two hundred and fifty pounds. Reacting to this imposing sight, Eva steps back. For a few seconds, they stand gawping at each other. She figures him to be in his late twenties or early thirties. It is difficult to be sure, because his large, over-square face has no sign of life. It reminds her of a clay bust. Not letting her nerves get the better of her, she steps forward. At the same time, he leans his head to one side causing his long black hair to fall over his right ear.

"H - hello. Do y-y-you want to see Jesus?"

His voice sounding heavy with a slur, and his eyes appearing vacant, she has to stifle a nervous giggle, which ends up as an embarrassed smirk. The big man reacts by providing her with a puzzled frown and becomes a little agitated by adjusting the belt on his faded blue denim dungarees. Embarrassed by her own lack of decorum, she acts casual, but professional.

"I'm looking for the gentleman who was at the demonstration earlier today...."

Unaware of her predicament, he stands to one side and indicates.

"W - will you follow me, p - please?"

Before she can object, his huge spade-like hand engulfs hers, as he begins to lead her through the door. Mike, amused by it all, follows.

While being led through a maze of timbers, sheet rock, and general building materials, the big man stops at an old Gothic shaped door. Its old dark brown panels peeling and dirty, Eva witnesses the big man hesitate, and then with his free hand he is gentle in pushing the door ajar. The creaking hinges echo throughout the building, as he peers through the gap, and then pulls back with a satisfied grin that this is the correct place. He then opens the door wider causing further creaking of hinges. After taking a step into the room, Eva is taken aback. The room is large with a stone arched ceiling leading up to a small round central skylight. Her eyes are drawn to the light that shines through it. She follows the beam down until it reaches a young man dressed in paint-splattered jeans and a gray cotton tee shirt that has seen better days. Him sitting on an old wooden chair, the beam of light gives off an iridescent glow, while he holds onto a little three-year-old Asian boy sitting on his lap. Sitting and standing around him in various positions are about thirty other children of assorted ages and ethnic backgrounds. They are so engrossed in what the young man is saying, they are unaware of the big man still holding Eva's hand, and pointing into the room whispering.

"Jesus."

Thinking this is all rather strange and a little irritating, Eva tries to withdraw her hand, but with little success. Becoming aware he has company; the young man sitting stops telling his story and looks toward Eva. Offering her a welcoming smile that enlightens his handsome features, Eva's heart misses a beat.

He's even more handsome in the flesh.

His eyes then concentrate on the big man.

"Ahh Will. Who have you got there?"

Will's face coming to life, and still gripping Eva's hand, he does his best to explain.

"Th-these people w-want to see y-you."

In response, the young man whispers something to the little boy on his lap and places him on the floor. Eva, showing her annoyance at still being held by Will's strong grip, tries to step forward.

"I - I'm Eva Brown from Channel Six. This is Mike, my camera guy..."

Becoming more amused, Mike nods. Offering another smile, the young man stands, nods at Will, who then releases Eva's hand. Her reaction is to pull a face and rub back the circulation. As the young man steps out of the beam of light, he seems to vanish for a second. Then his hand appears

213

outstretched as Eva's eyes adjust to the dimmer light. While she takes it, the warmth traveling up her arm is disturbing. At the same time, he offers her a disarming smile; her palpitations increase. While reluctant to let go of her hand, he looks at Will.

"Thank you Will. Would you like to take our young friends here to the kitchen? There is that big box of cookies on the table that was donated earlier today."

With the sounds of gleeful expectation coming from the children, Will's square face produces a big childlike grin in anticipation of the treat to come. Meanwhile, the young man continues his directions.

"Then you can finish painting the hallway. Perhaps our little friends would like to help?"

With more sounds of glee, and offers of help by the surrounding children, the young man's face splits into an affectionate smile.

"You can all help Will while I talk to these nice people."

A sudden look of uncertainty overwhelms Will's face.

"Y-you sure you don't w-want me to stay?"

To reassure his close friend, the young man steps closer to Will, and places his hand on the big man's powerful shoulders.

"I'm sure. I'll be fine. You go and eat those cookies before they all disappear."

Satisfied the situation is safe, Will is still reluctant to leave. Encouraged by the remaining children of the treat waiting in the kitchen, he leaves. As the room empties, the young man looks at the open doorway with sadness. Wiping his eyes, he turns to Eva.

"That's William, my protector. He has no family. Just wandered in a few months ago, asked if he could help in any way. He's been here ever since."

Mike is listening to the excitable chatter of the children coming from down the hallway.

"He seems a bit..."

"Simple? Don't be fooled by his awkward speech. He has the strength of ten men, the heart of a lion and the innocence and honesty of a five-year-old. I love him deeply."

Reacting to this in-depth explanation of emotion, Mike and Eva glance at each other. As Mike raises an eyebrow, the young man's hazel eyes focus on Eva. His intense gaze makes her feel uncomfortable. Not used to men describing their feelings in such a way, she has to look away. A couple of seconds pass, his eyes turn to Mike who is now fitting his camera together. While he lines up the viewfinder, Mike inquires.

"He called you Jesus. Is that any significance?"

Evading the question, the young man's gaze returns to Eva.

"My friends call me Gus. Now what can I do for you good people?"

Eva has the man who seemed larger than life at the demonstration, now seems like a normal Joe.

What do I ask him?

Her inexperience beginning to show, her words stumble out

"Er, we covered you at the demonstration this morning. You did such a fantastic job in averting a major catastrophe that we wanted to follow up. Find out where you come from, who you really are - that sort of thing."

His response is to again focus on her.

"Well, to start with I'm trying to remodel this beautiful old church. Come, I'll show you around."

Before Eva can expand on her questioning, Gus wastes no time in leading them out of the room. While making their way through piles of old wood and masonry, Gus points to some aging planks.

"We hope to reclaim most of the wood."

Stopping by a large beam leaning precariously against a stone wall, he places his hand on a carved section.

"This particular piece is solid oak, over a hundred and fifty years old..."

The noise of excited children's voices interrupts as they begin to walk toward a makeshift kitchen. On his own agenda, Mike is busy working on his camera.

"Sounds industrious?"

They approach a half open modern looking door. Gus pushes it wide open to expose a wondrous site of children chanting and singing while painting various parts of the kitchen walls. His paintbrush resting on the edge of the table, Will is delving into the box of cookies. The children that are into singing in a serious way are doing less painting. Others are just watching and singing at the top of their young voices. As they notice Gus at the door, their faces seem to split in two as they convey to him innocent smiles of delight. The ones not singing race toward him with arms open. He strokes their young heads as they wrap their small arms around his legs and lower body. The others carry on painting, humming in time to their brush strokes. Will, with a half-eaten cookie in his mouth, keeps a protective eye on Gus as he heads further into the kitchen with these outsiders. Aware of Will's scrutiny, Gus faces a frustrated, but fascinated Eva.

"God's little innocents. If only man could stay this loving and honest as these children are…"

His eyes become intense.

"Why do you think man loses this innocence as he matures?"

Sensing the power of his personality boring into her, Eva feels vulnerable.

"I – I don't know. Should I?"

Mike, now operating his camera, observes Eva's quandary. He interrupts and gives his opinion.

"Perhaps life's too tough to stay innocent for long."

The intensity still there, Gus's face appears more serious for a second, and then his eyes soften.

"You may be right, but life's so beautiful - if you don't crack - or…"

He can tell these visitors don't quite understand his philosophy.

"…give in."

Becoming enthralled by this man, but confused by his rhetoric, Eva persists in keeping 'professional'.

"Don't let people corrupt you?"

Relieved he is making contact; Gus presents her with a heart-stopping smile.

"Yes, of course! Do 'not' give in to temptation."

His skeptical nature showing, Mike mumbles.

"Oh! That old cliché?"

His eyes becoming downcast, Gus turns toward the camera.

"Yes! I'm afraid it has become an old cliché, because standards of goodness have dropped so low that any evil has become the norm."

Even though he notices Eva is not accepting his opinion, Gus decides to carry on the tour.

"Come. I'll show you our first finished room."

While being gentle in releasing the children from his legs, Gus whispers in their ears. In response, they leap and skip away and are glad to be going back to the other children. In the meantime, Will climbs a ladder to carry on painting and cleaning, but still keeps a watchful eye on Gus.

As Eva and Mike are led to another part of the building, Eva inquires, while struggling to keep up with Gus' long strides.

"Where do all these children come from?"

"They're like Will. They have nobody, at least nobody who cares. Street children living amongst these derelict buildings."

Appalled by these circumstances, Eva's questions become more severe as they arrive at a recent restored Gothic door.

"Have you notified the authorities?"

Irritated by the question, his eyes glare, his face becomes stern, and his voice hard.

"What authorities? The present government? There is only 'one' authority I recognize!"

Becoming edgy by Gus's sudden change of persona, Eva forces her eyes away and glances at Mike who also seems a little unsure. Sensing their uneasiness, Gus attempts to relax.

"I'm sorry. You hit a raw nerve, but you'll soon understand."

He pauses for a second, puts on an amicable smile, and then opens the door.

"This is our first finished room."

Controlling his emotions, Gus leads them through the clean Gothic door into a bright, well lit room. The ivory painted walls are a prism of colored lights created by a round stained glass window positioned opposite the doorway. The sun's rays are beating through the stained-glass picture of Christ's head covered in bleeding thorns. The pain in his eyes is overpowering, as he looks up with hands closed in prayer. While Eva is drawn to the stained glass, she steps across the floor to be by the window. Mesmerized, she runs the tips of her fingers over Christ's eyes as if the glass could break at any time.

"It's beautiful! Look at the pain in those eyes."

His eyes moistening, Gus comes and stands next to her. As if to qualify, he rests his hand on her shoulder.

"It was a painful situation."

Her shoulder warm by his hand, she can't help but notice the stillness of the room. Just the soft whirring of Mike's camera as he points the lens toward the window, is not disturbing the atmosphere. Determined to change the mood, Gus removes his hand and clears his throat.

"Will restored it all himself. Such a great gift."

Still dazed by his presence, and disappointed at him removing his hand, Eva saunters around the rest of the room to keep up her interest. His camera still whirring, Mike follows.

She reaches a small dark oak desk and two wooden upright chairs, one painted green, the other stained dark brown. On noticing the rest of the room so clean, but bare, Eva has to ask.

"What is this room anyway?"

Enjoying her curiosity, Gus is willing to answer.

"I think originally it was the vestry. Now I'm going to use it as a counseling room. Sort of a one-to-one chat room."

Amused at the play on words, Eva looks at her watch.

"Could I chat – er - interview you now in this room?"

His amicable smile aimed to create a relaxed undertone, seems to bore deep into her subconscious.

"Sure, you can be my first one-to-one."

While his 'confidence' is causing Eva to be stricken with nerves, Mike positions his camera ready for the oncoming procedure. Being cooperative,

Gus takes it all in his stride, but is a little concerned at Eva becoming tense.

"What would you like me to do to make life easy for you?

Busy hiding her apprehension, Eva pulls the two wooden chairs in position so they face each other. Gus takes the lead by sitting in the chair facing the camera. Her face stoic with misgivings, Eva sits opposite, but out of view from Mike's lens. Eager to pursue and biting her bottom lip, Eva adjusts her microphone and recorder.

"Testing, one, two, three."

Gus conveys a relaxed smile, while Eva's nerves tighten as she positions her microphone at the ready.

"Now tell me Gus..."

Mike butts in.

"Hold it Eva! I'm sorry I have to fit on another filter. The stained glass window is affecting the color."

While Mike rummages through his bag for the correct filter, Gus stands.

"We can go elsewhere if you want, but the surroundings won't be so clean."

Ignoring Gus, Mike finds what he's looking for. Taking a few seconds to screw the new filter onto the lens, he then checks through the viewfinder. After another couple of seconds, he looks back up, and offers Gus an apologetic smile.

"Perfect! Sorry about that. You can start now Eva."

The delay is causing Eva to become agitated. Mike now relaxed, looks through his lens again. Enjoying the experience, Gus sits more upright, and repositions his chair.

"Heading for the six o'clock slot?"

Surprised at such a remark, she asks the obvious.

"Yes! How did you...?"

He answers by expressing a silent aura of understanding. Somehow this makes Eva relax somewhat. Confused by her own erratic emotions, she glances back to Mike and then faces Gus.

"I'm sorry! Are you ready?"

Gus is now more deliberate with his calm demeanor.

"I've been ready since I was born."

Ignoring the mild sarcasm, she checks the microphone again, checks her watch, and then clears her throat.

"I won't bother with preliminaries. I'll add them later back at the studio. I'll just ask you direct questions. If you decline to answer, I'll edit those parts later."

As she takes a breath, Gus's confident gaze puts her on edge.

"I'll give you anything you want."

Struggling to regain her composure, she begins the interview.

"This morning you took a great gamble by jumping up onto that podium, taking the police officer's gun and pleading with a murderous mob at the possible risk of losing your own life…"

Gus interrupts by laughing.

"Oh, I think maybe you're over-dramatizing it a bit? What I saw was a nasty situation developing…."

Her nerves becoming tense again, this time Eva interrupts.

"A situation? More like a goddam battleground. I mean people were falling, getting hurt. I tell you; I was really scared. Weren't you?"

Ignoring her mild profanity, he glares at her with such intensity, it is causing her nerves to become jittery.

"I was afraid! Not for me, but for everyone else. I saw what you saw. So, I felt something needed to be done. As I happened to be near the podium, I acted…"

Becoming irritated by his calm persona, Eva cuts in.

"Five people died this morning!"

His reaction is to release a heavy sigh and look down.

"I know. Tragic - very tragic…"

Her irritation mounting into anger, she cuts in again.

"How could you have known? You left the area when you finished talking…"

Mike interrupts by tapping her shoulder. Her nerves becoming more frayed by the interruption, her face becomes taut.

"What is it?"

Observing she is about to crack up, Mike points to the viewfinder. Suppressing the urge to scream and knowing this interview is going to be the ultimate failure, she is reluctant to obey her cameraman. While looking through viewfinder, she pulls away, glances at Mike with a quizzical expression, and then looks back into the viewfinder again for a little longer.

Amused, but becoming concerned by the hysterics, Gus leans back in his chair and folds his arms.

"Am I growing another head?"

Ignoring Gus's obvious sarcasm, Eva comes away from the camera appearing a little puzzled. As she sits back in her chair, an overwhelming sensation of being lost overcomes any concentration. Acting as if everything is on cue, she glances at her watch again.

"Where were we?"

Glad this attractive journalist is back in her chair, Gus answers.

"I was on the podium."

"Er-yes, I'm sorry. I'm making a complete mess of all this."

Gus's eyes expressing sympathy, his impulse is to reach across and touch her hand.

"You're doing fine. I'm enjoying myself."

Looking down at his strong and yet sensitive hand, she is aware of his warmth running up her arm. Disappointed when his hand is withdrawn, she tightens her jaw with the intention of being more composed. With Mike glued to his camera, she begins again.

"What you did this morning was a brave and sincere act. You seemed to have the confidence of someone who has the backing of a higher authority. I mean some of the statements you made, like..."

She looks down at some papers on her lap.

"I quote: 'I'm here to warn you that by following the wrong way both sides will be defeated, and those responsible will be held accountable' unquote."

His eyes exhibiting a twinkle, Gus pauses for a second.

"That's correct."

His casual and yet over confident attitude is becoming another irritation for Eva. Suppressing the need to vent her frustration, Eva raises her voice a notch.

"So, what Government department sent you to warn the crowd, and by whose authority will those responsible be held accountable?"

Not wanting to antagonize this attractive young woman who is trying to do her job, Gus looks away for a second. In deep thought he returns and stares hard at Eva. Transfixed by his eyes that are piercing straight into her, Eva is unable to look away while he reaches across and grabs her hand.

"Not a department - GOD!"

Still mesmerized by his expression, but annoyed at his flippant answer, she forces her hand away, pauses, and then decides to shoot back.

"God? What are you talking about?"

His 'confidence' turns to despondency.

"It's as I say. 'God' is my authority who will hold those responsible accountable. That's why I'm here. This is my mission."

This is not what she wants to hear. She envisions her 'scoop' flowing down the drain, and Max holding her responsible.

This guy's a flake.

Her frustration now showing, she snaps back at him.

"Mission? What mission?"

Understanding her reaction, his voice becomes grave, but sincere.

"To bring a warning."

Her irritation mounting and her patience waning, she spits back.

"What sort of warning? What the hell are you talking about?"

His patience never waning, he reaches out to her again. His grip on her wrist paralyzes her to the spot.

"Please hear me out. Believe me, I'm not nuts. I am telling the truth."

Having heard enough, she pulls her hand away and is finding it hard not to raise her voice.

"I'll ask again. What sort of warning? You're not making sense!"

Because of her inexperience, Eva realizes she is losing control, by breaking the cardinal rule of interviewing - don't lose your objectivity. A tear of disappointment escapes down her left cheek while she hangs onto her dignity by a thread. Although sensing what she is going through, Gus needs to carry on.

"My warning is to make it plain to all the world leaders that they have only one year to rectify these horrendous man-made problems - or else."

Unable to comprehend this man, Eva stands and knocks her chair over. As the last remaining shreds of her newsroom training dissipate, Gus looks up to her, and reaches out again.

"Just hear me out, 'please'. I will try to make you understand."

For a second, his pleading eyes remind her of the pain in the stained-glass window. Recuperating what dignity, she has left, it's her turn to release a heavy sigh, as she lifts back the fallen chair and sits back down. Still holding onto her hand, the pain in his eyes subside.

"My mission is to visit each of the world leaders and inform them of the grave consequences if they do not abide by my warning."

Resigned to her failure, Eva shuffles on her chair.

"So, what will be these grave consequences?"

With nothing to lose and not hiding the sarcasm in her voice, she continues.

"What if these world leaders don't oblige your request, or even want to see you?"

A pang of guilt rips through her insides when she sees his hurt reappear. He pauses to reply. The hurt goes, determination sets in.

"Oh, they'll see me all right."

While she becomes bored and frustrated with her failure, Mike is still glued to his camera. To relieve her boredom, she glances up at him, and is becoming more irritated while observing the fascinated look on his face.

Jesus, you would think he was filming something formidable for the first time. Why the amazement? The guy's just a flake!

Sensing he is losing her; Gus is still determined to carry on.

"I will inform these leaders that if nothing is done to alleviate the problems, the world, as we know it, will be destroyed."

Hearing these prophetic words, Eva has lost total interest in this man. Her eyes focus on a heavy knot in the floorboards. Conscious of the camera and ignoring Eva, Gus looks into the lens and continues.

"Three major events will happen. First, there will be earthquakes, hurricanes, tidal waves, and heavy floods, such as this planet has never experienced. You think that global warming is a problem right now, it is nothing compared to what's coming. When this ends, a new virus will surface causing famine, and plague. The corona virus was just a rehearsal. Millions of people will die. Then the final phase: fire so vast, the whole world will be ablaze, cleansing and sterilizing forever."

Even though she is now focusing on him, Eva's mind is beginning to switch off.

I've had enough of this crap!

Pleased at Mike still involved, while Eva has lost interest, Gus finishes.

"There will be survivors of course. The Chosen Ones! With help they will start again as it was meant to be in the beginning."

As Eva stands, she glares at Gus.

"Like the garden of Eden? I've heard enough! Look mister, Gus, or whatever your name is, my boss and I thought you might have been someone important from an authority or a Government agency. All you are is a nice guy who's a bit misguided..."

She wipes away another escaping tear.

"... I'm sorry we ever bothered you."

Filled with painful disappointment, she turns away.

I so much wanted this to go right.

Puzzled at why Mike is so mesmerized while still operating his camera, she barks an instruction.

"Okay Mike. Cut and wrap it. Let's go!"

Mike does not agree.

"Are you sure?"

"Of course, I'm sure – goddamm it!"

Her voice is even more impatient as she struggles with the microphone that is not cooperating in its case. Aware of her sense of failure and disappointment, Gus offers some comforting words.

"By the way, there is something that should interest you."

Her equipment still not cooperating, Eva is not listening. Meanwhile, Gus continues.

"Eva, you will be one of those survivors. You're lost now, but your heart is in the right place, and you will be shown the way."

Still ignoring him, and his words not penetrating, she takes her stuff and heads for the door. She glares back at Mike, indicating him to follow. He ignores her. Instead, he goes over to Gus and offers his hand.

"Interesting story. Thanks."

Gus takes his hand accompanied by a grateful smile.

"I hope you can use it. If not, don't worry, it's all going to happen anyway."

Demonstrating mutual respect, their eyes lock for a second. Hearing Eva leaving the building, Mike breaks away to go after her.

Remaining in his chair, Gus stares at the empty doorway, releases a sigh, and then looks up toward the stained-glass window.

The pain returns.

28

The Tale on the HD memory card

Frustrated, Eva throws the HD card down hard on Max's desk. He raises an eyebrow as a piece of plastic chips off the card's protective case and lands on his half-chewed doughnut. She is desperate to hold back her tears of her impending depression.

"There's your interview for the six o'clock news. I don't think…"

His face not giving anything away, Max leans back in his chair, acting casual.

"Didn't go so good, huh?"

He is meticulous as he picks off the piece of plastic from his doughnut. At the same time Eva's feelings pour out.

"Not so good? It was awful! The man's a total fruitcake. First, he says God has given him the authority to do what he likes. Second, he's taken it into his head that he's going to warn all the world leaders that if they don't do what he dictates, in twelve months we are all going to burn, die of famine, drown by tidal waves and hurricanes and…"

Expressing sympathy in his voice, he leans forward, and conveys to her a reassuring smile.

"Okay, okay! Calm down my girl. Let's look at the interview and judge for ourselves to see if he really is a fruitcake. No big deal. If on the other hand…"

Half listening, Eve is so wrapped up in her own familiar failures, she is unable to control more tears.

"Oh, man! I 'really' wanted this to be good."

While she grabs a handful of tissues from a box on Max's desk, and annoyed and surprised at the intensity of her own emotions, Max offers her an affectionate smile, and then beckons Mike for his contribution.

"I think you'll find it all very interesting, Max."

Such a statement from a seasoned cameraman makes Max sit up more in his chair.

"In what way?"

"You'll see when you view it."

By the expression on his boss's face, Mike takes a chance and sits down in a nearby chair.

Regaining her composure, but still remains standing, Eva is resigned to her fate. In the meantime, Max retrieves the card from the small chipped case, inspects it for further damage, and inserts the card into a slot in the side of the Apple computer and waits. As an instant picture appears on the monitor screen, Max and Mike watch with an intensity allowed for world changing events. Wondering what is so special, Eva glances at the two men, and then her eyes are drawn to the screen.

29

Blue

Exhausted, Eva enters through the front door of her small, two-bedroom apartment. Memories of the office computer screen still fresh in her mind, she leans back against the open door frame.

After all that drama, I'm so glad to be home...

Pausing for a minute, and then closing the door, the heavy click wakes Maggie the German born baby sitter, come housekeeper, come surrogate mother to Eva's young son, Ryan.

Startled by the noise over riding the TV, Maggie gets up off the well-used comfortable sofa. A little disoriented, she appears at the living room doorway and tries to straighten out her crumpled, well filled cotton dress. Just as Eva is hanging up her coat on a hook in the tiny hallway, which also leads into a small kitchen, she studies the kitchen cupboards wishing for new, modern ones. A faint odor of cooking interrupts her wishful thinking. To get her attention, Maggie clears her throat.

"Hello Miss Brown. How you do today?"

"Don't ask Maggie. I'm just glad to be home in my little hovel. Is Ryan okay?"

Now wide awake, Maggie becomes concerned by Eva's tired face. To compensate, she puts on an 'everything's okay' smile.

"Oh, he fine. He's alvays fine. Zat boy has such a sveet nature, he makes us all look bad. Right now, he is in his bedroom vatching his muzzer on zer six o'clock news vile he eating his favorite spaghetti. I have some for you as vell."

Relieved her home life is still fine and normal, Eva welcomes Maggie stepping toward her and sliding her arms around her taut body. As her arms tighten, her plump roundness seems to swallow up Eva's slender frame.

"Hard day my dear?"

Still enjoying the warmth and softness easing her aching body, Eva is reluctant to answer.

"Some. Strange also."

Pleased her hug has helped, Maggie is ready to let go. Her weariness overwhelming, Eva offers her an affectionate smile.

"You can go home now if you want."

"Sank you Miss Brown. I sink I vill. Zer spaghetti is in zer microwave."

Appreciating this woman beyond words, Eva plants a kiss on the other woman's fleshy cheek.

"Thanks, I'll see you tomorrow then?"

As Maggie reaches for her old camel hair coat hanging next to Eva's, her answer reassures.

"Yar! I'll be here."

While watching Maggie shuffle down the tiny hallway toward the stairs, Eva's mind is spinning after the events of the day. As she shuts the front door, she glances at a nearby mirror, and reels at how tired she looks.

"God, what a day..."

Hearing voices coming from one of the bedrooms, she walks toward the sounds and stops at a bedroom door. Listening to her own voice coming from a TV, she sighs and pushes the door open. Warmed by the sight of her nine-year-old son Ryan sitting on a large oversize footstool silhouetted against the giant flat TV screen that seems to fill the small room, she reaches out to touch his favorite yellow T-shirt, while he is busy eating Maggie's spaghetti, and absorbed in watching his mother at the demonstration recorded earlier. Not wanting to startle him, she hesitates, and then steps up to him and squats. His instinct is to turn and present his mother with a warm welcoming smile. Her heart turns over as his pale brown eyes inform her, he is glad to see her. Her affection obvious, she removes a small smudge of food just above his top lip. His mood is one of excitement.

"Hi mom, you're on TV again."

Her affection overwhelming, she ruffles his curly brown hair, and then sits on the same stool to be closer to him. Together they watch Gus pleading to the crowd.

"Who's that guy, mom?"

"Oh, just some guy. Nobody special."

The news ends followed by commercials. As she is not in the mood for anymore viewing, she picks up the nearby remote control and switches off the TV. Staring at the blank screen, she feels his head resting on her lap.

"Has my man had a good day?"

As he looks up to her, his big soft eyes seem to glow in the low light of the room.

"Okay, I guess. I've painted you a picture. Do you wanna see?"

"I'd love to."

Still excited, he hands her his empty dinner plate and scurries off under his bed to pull out a large piece of white cardboard. He places it face down on the floor in front of her, still with his hands on the cardboard. His excitement begins to evaporate, as his face turns serious.

"Mom? Why is it you're never at home anymore? I only see you a couple hours a day. You can never make it to my projects at school. Maggie always goes in your place. The kids at school say I'm lying in saying you're my mom. They say Maggie's really my mom."

Looking at the sight of his sad face creates a violent stab at her insides, and causes her eyes to fill with tears.

"Oh Ryan! You know I would love to be at home more."

Conflicting emotions tearing her apart, she stands. Her joints aching with fatigue, she places the dinner plate on a nearby sideboard, and then returns to her anxious son. With the tears now rolling down her cheeks, she drops down onto her knees to be next to the cardboard.

"Honey? Your mom has to work! This new job I've got with the TV Company is a golden opportunity for us to get out of this awful place and buy a decent house in a respectable neighborhood. So, at this time I have to work long hours so I can prove myself. You tell those dumb kids at school I 'am' your real mom..."

She leans forward to plant a gentle kiss on his forehead. Enjoying his smell, she then wipes her own wet cheeks.

"Now show me your picture."

A little subdued, he turns the picture over leaving it on the floor. Looking down she sees a typical child's drawing of a man in a dark red robe standing on a hill surrounded by many matchstick figures. The man has blue painted around his head. For some reason Eva pictures Gus's stained-glass window, as she stares at the drawing and saying nothing. Meanwhile, Ryan studies her face, and then points to the man on the hill.

"That's Jesus Mom."

Remembering Will at the church mentioning 'Jesus', Eva is still staring at the picture.

"Jesus?"

His face beginning to show frustration, he answers.

"Yes Mom. He's in the Bible. We're doing a project for Easter."

Still transfixed, her mind swimming, and Gus's voice filling her imagination, she is lost in the drawing. Puzzled by his mother's reaction, Ryan continues.

"He did many miracles Mom."

Becoming irritated, she snaps back at him.

"I 'know' who he is."

Observing the hurt overcoming over her son's gentle face, guilt overwhelms her for being so selfish.

Oh, Ryan! I'm so sorry. Something weird is happening to me. The last thing I want is to hurt you.

Controlling her own tears, she places her index finger on the man's head.

231

"The blue. Why the blue?"

"That's to show he's Holy. The Son of God."

She is so stiff and sore, she struggles to get up off her knees, so she can make her way to Ryan's neat bed. Troubled by Gus's hazel eyes penetrating her turmoil, she sits on the edge of the bed and rests her head in her hands.

"What's up Mom? Don't you like my painting?"

"I love it! Honestly. It's beautiful. You're so clever. Mom has had a very strange day at work. I'm a bit tired, I'm sorry."

"That's all right Mom, it's only a painting."

For some reason, she thinks different.

30

Proof

It is the next morning. Eva, still jaded after yesterday's letdown, is standing with Mike and another crew waiting in Max's office. After a few minutes of nail-biting anxiety, Max enters holding several sheets of paper. In a hurry, wearing his usual crisp white shirt, but missing the normal red tie, he scurries over to his desk. Wasting no time, he spreads the papers out on the desktop, and then sits in his chair looking straight at the crew members in front of him.

"Well folks, everyone who's anyone is taking a very keen interest in our new friend Gus. All the networks are taking into their heads to interview him."

Her perceived failed interview still fresh in her mind, Eva comments.

"They'll soon realize they're wasting their time."

Ignoring her sarcasm, Max's brown eyes smile at her and offers her a wink.

"Maybe, but at least we were the first, and thanks to Mike we've found something else. Here are your assignment sheets."

Max hands some papers to the other crew and some to Eva.

"As you can see, our new friend is holding a fund raiser for his refuge center tonight."

Still frustrated and annoyed, Eva spits back.

"So what?"

233

Ignoring her, Max continues.

"This guy is a smart cookie. As well as having the mainstream media's attention, the social media is going viral. So, he's using it all to his full advantage."

Her face forlorn, Eve bites her bottom lip, while studying her assignment sheet.

"So? What the 'hell' do I do?"

Still ignoring Eva, Max carries on talking to the other crew.

"Okay you guys, cover this story for the nine o'clock slot. Take your time and get some good footage. No screw-ups."

While Eva's insides cringe at Max's orders, and her confidence teetering, the other crew leaves. As they walk away discussing how they are going to handle the story, Max strides over to the door and closes it. Pausing for a second, he then hurries back to the front of his desk, rests against it, and gazes at Eva.

"I also want you and Mike to cover this one."

After yesterday, she can't believe her ears

"Why Max? Why me after yesterday's fiasco? I notice you've sent another more experienced crew. They won't take his bullshit!"

Still focusing on Eva, Max's eyes crinkle as he smiles with a determined glint.

"Forget the news aspect on this. After watching your interview, we three could be the only ones in the whole wide world who know about the blue aura...."

Anxiety taking over, Eva is skeptical as she interrupts.

"It was probably the stained-glass window next to him throwing the color onto his head."

Acknowledging Eva, Max ponders for a second.

"That did go through my thick skull Eva, so I thought I'd better get some more proof."

Not hiding her annoyance, Eva steps back from him.

"More proof? The guy's a flake. This time next week he'll have faded away and been forgotten."

Keeping his voice calm, but determined, Max stares into Eva's eyes as if searching.

"You may be right Eva, but I have a strange gut feeling about this guy, and I think you have too. Hence your emotional reaction. Call it an aging newsman's hunch if you like, but this is your next assignment. Trust me. I have good reason for wanting you two to cover this. Mike, use the same filter on your camera and we'll see what comes out."

Being the professional, Mike nods. Stunned by Max's trust and instinct in her, Eva's annoyance evaporates, replaced by a strange anxiety.

"Why don't you just send Mike? I'll just stay at home, so I don't screw things up anymore."

Wanting to calm her, Max rests a hand on her shoulder.

"Because I want you to be there. Call it another hunch. Besides, this is your baby. Anyway, what is it about this guy that gets you so uptight?"

Gus's eyes now penetrating her subconscious, Eva stalls for a second.

"I-I don't know. There's something about him."

His hand still on her shoulder, Max helps to calm her further.

"Look kid, if tonight fails, so what, no big deal. We'll forget all about it. As you said, it'll all fade away in a week and be forgotten. However, like you, I definitely feel something. The meeting starts at six o'clock. So, get down there early this afternoon and set up a good position. When it's all over, come straight back here with the recording for us to study, and then we'll take it from there."

He releases his hand.

"So, I'll see you guys later."

31

Eva's Miracle

It is 5:55 p.m. the following evening. The old gray church is crammed full of people. A mixture of newspaper, social media and TV reporters with camera crews are all elbowing and jostling each other to get a good angle in their viewfinders. Equipment is squeezed into every available nook and cranny. There are even extra lights and microphones plus several monitors being placed at convenient positions to facilitate any frustrated public outside. Police are everywhere trying to be discreet, while watching with the utmost diligence for any disturbances. The one unoccupied space inside the old church is a small stage, raised three feet high above the floor that used to be the altar area.

Will is having a hard job in controlling his nerves as he paces back and forth in front of this area to stop anyone from trying to clamber for a better view. Eva and Mike are in a good position near the front of the stage. Young Ryan, Eva's son, is holding onto her as if his life depends on it. Sensing his insecurity, Eva bends a little to talk to him.

"I'm sorry to drag you here honey, but with Maggie unable to take care of you tonight, I had no choice."

Demonstrating his sweet nature, Ryan looks up to her.

"It's okay Mom, so long as I can hang on to you, I'll be all right."

Her heart turns over with pride as she rubs his head.

"Sure honey, you just hang on."

Mike's honed instincts tell him to keep scanning the seething mass of bodies for anything out of the ordinary, while all waiting in anticipation of the unknown.

His face expressing a touch of apprehension, he glances at Eva.

"Sure is a big crowd. Max was right about getting down here early. Can you see our other crew?"

Being shorter than Mike, she is having a problem in scanning the hall.

"I can't see them. They're probably over on the other side. Do you have the filter ready?"

He taps the camera as an affirmative.

Everyone is caught off guard as a side door opens on stage left and Gus strides out exhibiting the confidence of a man on a mission. As he positions on the center stage, there is an explosion of camera and smartphone flashes, and an extra burst of TV lights, accompanied by excited and expectant murmurings as he adjusts his eyes to the glare being bombarded at him. His wavy hair seems to give off a fluorescent glow as it reflects against the lights. Meanwhile, a line of about twenty children come running out onto the stage from the same side door. Gus's face reveals affection as they sit along the breadth of the stage in front of him.

Soaking up the whole scene, Mike pans his camera, and then taps Eva's shoulder giving her the thumbs up sign without taking his eye away from the viewfinder.

In the meantime, Gus takes a step forward, almost touching a young Asian-looking boy sitting among the children. Eva recognizes some of the young faces from her disastrous visit yesterday.

Signaling everyone to be quiet, Gus raises his right arm. While the crowd falls silent, Gus begins his speech while studying his audience.

"I am truly honored, and to be honest, amazed at the support here this evening. I hope that this will enable my friends and myself to raise enough money to finish this H. E. L. P. Center. At least tonight I shan't have to fire a gun to get your attention."

Hearing the sound of muted laughter from the mass before him, he is confident he has their full attention. As several cameras keep flashing, a lone female voice shouts out.

"What do the initials H E L P stand for?"

To answer, Gus conveys to the woman, a since smile.

"It stands for assisting those in need."

His explanation sets of several laughs.

Meanwhile, a rough-sounding male voice comments behind Eva.

"I suppose he thinks he's a smart ass."

Controlling her disdain, Eva's sympathy for Gus increases, as it is hard for anyone to be confronted by a hardened, cynical media crowd. His nerves well hidden, Gus continues.

"No seriously. The word H E L P means – 'Here Everyone Loves People' which means 'everyone' and 'anyone' who is in need of help. Whether they be the homeless, the sick, the poor, the abused and exploited. Even the rich who are in need of help with problems that money cannot solve. Nobody will be turned away…"

A cynical voice bellows from the rear interrupting.

"What about the lazy bums who'll take advantage of you. The ones who just take, because they're too lazy to work."

Curious at the question, Gus peers toward the voice.

"We do not judge people whether they qualify for help or not. Their own conscience will dictate that."

The same rough voice behind Eva gives his opinion again.

"He's not only a smart ass, he's also very naïve."

Meanwhile, Ryan begins to tug at Eva's arm for attention.

"Mom? It's him!"

"Not now honey - later."

He tugs again. This time he raises his voice.

"But Mom? It's 'him'. The man in my painting."

"Later honey, later."

As other questions are being shouted at Gus, Eva cannot quite hear his answers or her son, because Ryan distracts by pulling away and pushing his way through the crowd toward Gus. Beginning to panic, she feels helpless as Ryan weaves in and out of pairs of legs, heading straight toward the front of the stage.

"Ryan? Come back here..."

Hearing Eva's voice above the crowd, and noticing Ryan coming to the stage front, Gus turns his attention.

"Ah! Here's a young man who understands."

As Ryan reaches the stage, puts up both his arms for someone to reach for him, all the attention in the hall now turns to him. With cameras flashing, bodies jostling for a better view as the children on stage reach down and pull Ryan up to join them, the heavy crowd pushes on forward toward the stage. After an exhaustive struggle to get to her son, Eva reaches the stage front. Becoming excited as his mother looks up at him, Ryan can't resist shouting.

"It's him Mom. It's Jesus!"

Honing in on Ryan, the crowd reacts by bursting into a roar of skeptical laughter. Now standing by an amused Gus, Ryan points to Gus.

"Can't you see it Mom? Can't you see the blue?"

In answering the question, a man's deep voice bellows out from the rear of the hall.

"I see it – I see it."

He begins to struggle to push his way in a frantic effort to get nearer the stage. Interested in this man, Gus pleads to the seething crowd as they turn their attention to this tall, thin pale figure, becoming desperate while elbowing his way forward.

"Please let him through. Here is another who understands."

Curiosity mounting, the media crowd keeps surging forward as they try to jostle for a better view of this man. Meanwhile, Eva is now pinned hard against the stage front with the full weight of the crowd bearing down against her.

The tall pale man reaches the stage. Breathless in his struggle to scramble up, the children dash forward to help him. His face absent of a smile or warmth, and ignoring the children, he stands an arm's length from Gus.

As Gus approaches him, takes his hand and shakes it, the thin man seems to be in a daze. His tattered dirty clothing and pale appearance makes him look sickly and grotesque under the bright TV lights. Showing his appreciation, Gus slides his arm around the man's shoulders and is gentle in turning him to face the crowd.

"See this poor soul. He has nothing in this world. Yet he came to me offering me the greatest gift of all - himself."

A cynical voice spouts his opinion to someone behind Mike.

"Well, here's his first lazy bum."

The pale man on stage gazes with a vacant expression toward the crowd. His pale blue watery eyes are in a daze, not quite registering what is happening. While he turns back to face Gus, the daze vanishes. An angry glare appears, which then turns into a snarl. His pale, gaunt features looking even more grotesque under the lights, he pulls away from Gus, and takes a couple of steps sideways. After a couple seconds, he stares hard at Gus.

"Who 'are' you?'

To the amusement of the cynical crowd, he begins pacing around Gus.

"Who are you 'really'?"

Surprised at the man's sudden change of mood and strange behavior, Gus's attention turns to Ryan, as he shouts to the man with fear in his voice.

"You saw the blue. He's Jesus!"

The tall man stops pacing, spins around to Ryan and bellows out a hollow, humorless laugh. He then stares at the captured audience, and again turns to glare at Gus.

"What blue? You're definitely 'not' Jesus."

More defiant, Ryan shouts out again.

"He is Jesus."

To the surprise of the crowd, the rest of the children respond by shouting in agreement. The man responds by spitting out his words and turning on Ryan.

"He's not! Jesus died for us over two thousand years ago..."

He points a bony finger toward Gus.

"This man is a fraud, a fake, an impostor, trying to make money like all the rest of the charlatans and blasphemers of this decadent world."

Acting protective, all the children on stage stand up and shout in unison at the pale man.

"No!"

At the same time, they surround the man. Will, who has been witnessing this scenario, takes an anxious step toward Gus, but is still out of sight from the audience. He appears fraught at his little friends surrounding this pale, haggard man who again points his accusing finger at Gus. Everyone becomes mesmerized as his deep, rough voice fills the hall.

"You're Satan - the Devil's Messiah!"

Feeling a heavy pang of sadness, mixed with pride as he watches his beloved children trying to protect him from this sick man, Gus flinches as the man pulls out a large knife from a tattered pocket. Still pinned against the stage front, Eva can't help but witness the heavy blade glint in the lights of the cameras, which are now flashing in frenzy at this sad, grotesque situation. Because of the pressure bearing down hard, her chest hurts.

The atmosphere in the building now turns to one of horror, as the man becomes vicious as he pushes away the children. Sensing trouble, two police officers at the rear of the building attempt to make their way forward through the mass of bodies. As they draw their guns, the pale man raises his arm. Gripping the knife as if ready to plunge, Ryan screams.

"No!'

He rushes forward and dives at the sick man's legs. Meanwhile, Will comes rushing onto the stage. While Ryan clutches the man, the two of them stumble toward Gus. At the same time, the two police officers take aim as the man falls onto Gus. As the knife plunges deep into Gus's chest, the guns open fire. The pale man spins ungainly as two bullets rip into his frail body. The knife handle sticking out of his chest, Gus falls toward the stage floor, and attempts to shout.

"No-no! Don't shoot. He doesn't mean to...."

Meanwhile, cameras are flashing with renewed frenzy, while voices of commentators are frantic as they shout their commentaries into their microphones.

His eyes welling up with tears of grief and fury, Will kneels and leans over Gus as if to protect him from any more pain. Reading his mood, Gus's voice stays soft and calm, and his eyes are resolute.

"It's all right Will. It's all right. Take me off the stage."

In front of this curios and yet stunned crowd, Will hesitates, and then lifts Gus as if he weighs just a few pounds, and then carries him with ease through the side door into a small room.

"Lay me down."

Will obeys. While he lays his dear friend on the bare wooden floor with the care of a mother with a child, within seconds, there is a commotion of reporters and camera crews scrambling up onto the stage heading toward the open door of the small room. Like a recoiling spring, Will stands and turns toward the door, his face distorted with emotional pain and anger. A man holding a microphone appears. Anger glaring in his eyes, Will's huge frame comes upon him, grabs him by the neck as others appear at the doorway. In one swift movement, Will lifts the man two feet in the air as if he is a rag doll. Tears streaming down his face, Will spits out his plea.

"You go! Leave us alone."

At the same time, while Gus is still lying with the knife sticking out of his chest, he witnesses the disturbance. The noise becoming louder as the media want better pictures, Gus turns his head to face Will.

"Will? It's all right. Come here."

Will hesitates, because he is torn between protecting his close friend and obeying his request. Reluctant to put down the shaking man who is still trying to hold onto his microphone, Will stares hard at the other Media.

"Y-You stay there. All of you!"

Not wanting to argue with a man of Will's size and mood, the crowd blocking the door stays put. As this is happening, a disheveled Ryan has pushed his way through all the legs and stays by the door. Offering Ryan, a cautious smile, Will goes back to Gus and leans over him.

A voice from the blocked door shouts.

"Paramedics are on their way."

Looking deep into Will's hesitant eyes, Gus whispers to him.

"Pull out the knife."

Looking down at the knife handle, Will becomes nervous. Hearing the bedlam off stage, Gus insists.

"Please Will. Do it 'now'."

Like a little boy being asked to do a major task, Will kneels and grips the knife handle with his powerful, but trembling right hand.

"Now Will. Now!"

Still gripping the handle, Will begins to pull at the knife. A puzzling frown spreads across Will's face, as the knife won't budge. His hand trembling a little more, he tries again. With a quick grunt the knife is free. Observing Will holding the knife in the air, the doorway becomes ablaze with flashing lights. The anguish becoming too much, tears of fear and relief pour down Will's face, as he stays kneeling over Gus.

"Help me up Will."

While Will's trembling hand drops the knife on the floor making a clattering sound that echoes in the now silent room, the faces at the doorway watch in fascination, as they witness Gus being helped to his feet. Giving Will a tight hug, Gus's eyes fill with tears of gratitude.

"I told you I was all right."

Will stares down at the knife, and then at Gus in astonishment.

"But–but the knife?"

Releasing his grip on Will, Gus looks at the curios faces filling the doorway.

"Cancel the paramedics."

As young Ryan rushes away from the door towards Gus, a reporter takes advantage and tries to follow. Like a streak of lightning, Will prevents him by pushing him back toward the doorway.

"I–I told you to stay!"

Relieved to see Gus is safe, but still puzzled, Ryan wraps his small arms around Gus's waist.

"I thought you'd be dead."

As his tears soak Gus's shirt, Gus places a hand on Ryan's head.

"You knew better."

Ryan' reaction is to squeeze Gus a little harder.

"In my heart I knew you couldn't be dead, but I was so scared."

Releasing Ryan's arms, Gus crouches down and wipes away the boy's tears.

"Don't be scared anymore. Your faith is so strong that it will never let you down."

Now standing with his arm around Ryan, Gus addresses the patient onlookers still crammed in the doorway.

"Well, everyone - I think we still have some fund-raising to do."

With Ryan holding onto Gus's hand, they head toward the blocked doorway. Still puzzled by this strange situation, and needing answers, the reporters and camera crews are clumsy as they try to move aside to let them through. With extra frenzy, cameras and smartphones are clicking and flashing as they head toward the stage.

Being caught up in the struggle, Mike follows with his camera that has been recording the whole event, but becomes concerned about Eva going missing.

As Gus and Ryan enter the packed stage, people gawp at Gus in amazement as he makes his way to center stage as if nothing has happened. Pleased to see their friend is all right, the children come rushing out of nowhere, screaming with delight. The whole building becomes abuzz with disbelief that Gus is standing there alive. While the children surround Gus for extra protection, the cameras continue to flash. Oblivious to the adults creating pandemonium, Gus tries to shout above the noise.

"Please can everyone clear the stage area so that we can continue with the rest of the evening?"

Eager to know more, the noise wanes as everyone scrambles to carry out his request. Looking for Eva, Mike works his way down onto the floor, settling near the stage front.

As Gus positions in his original spot on the stage, he gestures to the children to gather around him.

While all eyes are now on center stage, Gus reaches into his left inside pocket of his sports jacket with his right hand, and pulls out a small thick book. On raising his right hand, still holding the book, a smear of blood is visible on the black covering. He glances at the book in relief, and then peers at the audience.

"My workshop manual. Today it saved my life."

The reaction from the audience is a loud applause mixed with cheers of relief.

Caught up in this new excitement, someone shouts out.

"I keep mine in my car. I think I'll start wearing it instead."

As the audience responds with spontaneous laughter, Gus smiles with a pleasure that one gets being rescued from death. While waiting until the revelry subsides, he points the book at the crowd.

"This manual saves lives whether you wear it or not."

Not quite understanding his meaning, the crowd becomes more curious as Gus wipes the blood off the cover with his left hand, exposing bold gold lettering *Holy Bible*. Witnessing the irony, the crowd realizes and breaks into cheers. On lowering his right arm and replacing the Bible back into his inside pocket, he waits for the crowd to quiets down.

"The poor man. Is he okay?"

One of the police officers standing near the stage, reports.

"He is alive and is on his way to the hospital."

Sighing with relief, Gus looks upward.

"Poor man, he is the result of our broken society. He didn't know what he was doing."

The crowd begins muttering, while some people are puzzled, and others are stating that Gus ought to be angry about the attempt on his life. The minority seem pleased with the outcome, especially the children.

While onstage, Ryan, notices his mother's pained, vacant expression. As Gus continues to woo the crowd, a worried Ryan is discreet when making his way toward his mother. In the meantime, Gus is determined to get his message across.

"Are there any questions before I get on with my begging for your money?"

The tension now gone, and a more relaxed atmosphere apparent, a few laughs come from the crowd. Not wanting to distract from the crowd, Ryan stops heading to his mother. In the meantime, Gus continues.

"As you can see this great old church has wonderful possibilities for the new project. We owe it to the needy to finish..."

Becoming more concerned about his mother, Ryan creeps to the far end of the stage so as not to distract further from Gus.

Someone shouts to Gus from the crowd.

"Will you personally be running this center after completion?"

While Gus pauses to answer, Ryan reaches his mother. Gus answers the question,

"I will at first, but I have a far greater mission to complete...."

Never seeing his mother like this before, Ryan lays his hands on her hair. No response forthcoming, he then shakes her head. Still with no response, he is careful when lifting her head. When he sees blood streaming from her mouth, covering her notes sticking to her face, the look of fear spreads across his face.

Unaware of Ryan's turmoil, Gus continues.

"Where can these poor souls go? With so many government centers and benefits now cut, where are these victims of society supposed to get help... ?"

Caught up in own his pain, and tears running down his cheeks, Ryan screams while cradling his mother's head.

"MOMMY!"

Gus stops talking. Every pair of eyes in the building focus on this new heart-wrenching scream. Summing up the situation, Gus and rushes over to Ryan. After touching Eva's head, he pleads to the crowd,

"This woman is gravely ill. I beg of you to make room for her. Will?"

Being not far away, Will is already rushing toward the scene.

"Will, please lift this poor woman up onto the stage and lay her gently on the floor for me."

Gus turns to the crowd who are now fascinated by this new turn of events.

"Please move out of the way everyone!"

With athletic prowess, Will leaps off the stage and is gentle, but firm as his large hands persuade people to move to one side from Eva. A space created, his powerful arms then lift her like a baby to his shoulder level, and then place her onto the stage floor as if she is a delicate piece of porcelain. Fascinated by this new turn of events, the cameras begin flashing as the media jostles to get a closer look.

A voice shouts as an elderly man struggles to work his way toward the scene.

"I am a doctor. I can help."

While Will helps the doctor to maneuver onto the stage, the doctor wastes no time in kneeling down over Eva. Almost in a state of panic, he becomes frantic as he unbuttons her jacket and blouse. Sensing the doctor's plight, Gus is cautious as he kneels opposite him. Recognizing it is Eva, the TV anchor from yesterday's interview, he watches the doctor's trembling hands pull a stethoscope from his pocket. Witnessing severe swelling and bruising that is becoming more evident on Eva's chest, the doctor examines her. As a grave expression appears on his face,

Gus whispers to him.

"I think you will find she has several broken ribs, a punctured lung, and possibly a ruptured spleen, as well as acute internal bleeding."

Surprised and bewildered at such a quick diagnosis, the doctor stares at Gus as if lost. While fascinated cameras continue clicking away, Ryan begins to sob. Becoming prepared for what's to come, Gus places a reassuring hand on Ryan's shoulder.

"She's not going to die. Where's your faith?"

The doctor now in a helpless daze, and his voice breaking with emotion, looks at Gus in earnest.

"She has to go to hospital immediately. She is fading fast."

Gus answers him with determined glint in his eyes.

"She'll die for sure if you move her now."

Hearing this verdict, Ryan sobs even louder. As the agonizing cry fills the hall,

Gus slides his arm around the boy and lifts his tearstained face toward him and whispers.

"She is not going to die! Trust me!"

Riddling with confusion and fear, Ryan's trembling mouth replies.

"I do trust you."

Lowering Ryan's head, and being careful in moving him to one side, Gus turns to his attention to Eva.

After taking a deep breath, Gus leans over her, spreads both his hands, palms down, flat on her rib cage. The doctor's instincts inform him to move away a few feet. Now absorbed in what he has to do, Gus lowers his head and closes his eyes. Beads of sweat are now forming on his forehead, and his breathing is becoming heavier, as his concentration becomes more intense. As a deathly hush falls over the whole building, Gus begins to move his lips in silence. While the sweat drips off his saturated face onto Eva' chest, he leans over her further, and plants a gentle kiss on the forehead, and then whispers.

"God loves you."

To the surprise of the audience, he topples to one side, collapses, and rolls onto his back. While a sudden crescendo of clicking cameras, smartphones and flashing lights fill the building, the atmosphere is electric.

After a few minutes, Eva begins to stir. On lifting her weary head, she turns onto her side and attempts to rest on one elbow. After another minute of confusion, she then struggles to try and sit up. At first puzzled, and then realizing she is on the stage, she calls out.

"Ryan!"

"I'm right here Mom."

Glad the worse seems over, he rushes over to her, and wraps his arms around her as if to offer more protection.

"You okay, Mom?"

Still trying to gain her momentum, Eva sits up straighter.

"I think so honey. Why am I on the floor...?"

She looks down at her exposed bra.

"....and why am I undressed? Here, help me get up."

While Ryan helps his distressed mother rise to her feet, he hangs on tight making sure she is not going to fall. Embarrassed, her hands tremble as she begins to button up her blouse and jacket in front of the cascade of lights. Wanting to help, Will moves up behind her to act as protector. Meanwhile, the doctor goes over to Gus who is also struggling to get up on his feet. He conveys to the doctor a weak smile and gestures that he is all right. He then stands next to Eva, putting his arm around her shoulders, and wiping away the sweat from his face with his other hand. Not sure what they have just witnessed, the media cameras keep flashing and reporters are busy commenting on this amazing event. However, the object of their interest is now peering confused at the crowd, unaware that the man with his arm around her has just brought her back from the abyss of death.

32

Hard to Believe

It is the following morning in Max's office. Max and Eva are sitting in front of the wide computer monitor behind Max's desk watching the last couple of minutes of Mike's recording showing the previous evening's meeting. Eva has decided to wear her close-fitting purple suit, which in this case, does not match her despondent mood, as she studies the faint blue aura surrounding Gus's head, while he slides his arm around her shoulder.

Not wanting to prolong her agony, Max turns to his desk and presses a key on his digital keyboard. The screen behind him goes blank, as he leans back in his chair and studies Eva. Focusing on her anxious face, he keeps his voice calm and soft.

"I left it to this morning to view these pictures with you. Mike and I went through them last night. We came to a decision that it wasn't the stained-glass window that cast the blue aura; it's really there."

Becoming subdued, Eva stays silent. Viewing her with concern, he keeps his voice calm.

"How'd you feel?"

Not responding to his kindness, she snaps back at him.

"Fine!"

Regretting her response, she bites her lip.

"I'm sorry! I feel - I ought to feel lousy, but in actual fact, I feel good physically, but mentally and emotionally is a different story."

Unable to control her eyes stinging with fresh tears, she slumps back in her chair gazing at the dark, blank screen in front of her, which minutes ago showed her life being saved by Gus.

Understanding what she must be going through, Max stands and drags his chair around his desk to park it opposite her. He sits down, with their knees almost touching. This action makes her look down, causing her voice to crack.

"That's how he likes to sit."

"Who? Gus?"

"Yes. Isn't that strange?"

Wiping a tear off her cheek, she looks deep into Max's kind brown, but questioning eyes. Wanting to put her at ease, he holds both her hands, squeezes, and then let's go.

"What do you remember most about last night?"

"All I remember is struggling through the crowd after Ryan, and then a horrible sickening pain in my chest as I was crushed against the front of the stage. Then, kind of waking up on the stage, half dressed with this guy Gus lying right next to me!"

Looking away from him, she feels guilty for her irrational ingratitude. Still enquiring, Max continues with his calm persona.

"How do you feel after watching the recording?"

She looks up at him, as Max's questioning eyes keep staring at her.

"I don't know. I really don't know."

Not wanting to hear this, Max sighs, stands up, and goes over to the water cooler. As he pours a drink, she surveys his back. Realizing how lucky she is to have such a kind boss; a pang of affection comes over her. He returns with two cups of water, and then sits down opposite her again.

"So, you don't know!"

While she takes a sip of the water, he reaches out like a father to his daughter, and grips her other hand. This time, he keeps it there. Appreciating the gesture, she looks down at his hand.

That's what 'he' does.

Wanting to know more, Max continues.

"The guy kneels down and brings you back to life. And you don't know?"

Becoming frustrated by her reticence, Max lets go of her hand.

"How come you don't even feel grateful?"

"I'm sorry Max. The whole thing seems so unreal. Even though I've seen it on your computer, I'm still having a hard job in actually believing it happened."

While shaking his head in disbelief, Max manages to keep calm and smile.

"I suppose if you'd witnessed the miracle instead of being the lucky recipient, you might be more of a believer?"

She hesitates, and then shakes her head.

"I'm sorry. I really am!"

Keeping his patience in tact, he rises again. This time he goes to his desk, opens a drawer and retrieves a small piece of paper.

"Look, I want you to do me a favor."

He comes around his desk and hands her the paper.

"Take this check to him. Tell him it's a donation from the TV station towards his new center."

Her face stoic, she reaches up, takes it, and glances down at the check.

"This is your own personal check, not the TV station's."

"So? It's from me!"

"Its five thousand dollars!"

Max shrugs as he leans on his desk.

"I like the guy. I have a strong gut feeling about all this. Now go and see him, give him the check and thank him for saving your life. Okay?"

Wiping away a stray tear, she puts the check in her jacket pocket, and gets up from her chair. His affection for her being obvious, he slides his arm around her shoulder. Not threatened by this warm gesture, she welcomes his support. As he guides her toward the door, his voice seems to resonate.

"Do it now while it's early. Make it officially unofficial. You know what I mean, no crew, just you. Then report back to me. Keep it quiet. Just you and me.Okay?"

She nods, and plants a grateful kiss on his cheek.

33

Scars

"Yes. But don't let me stop you."

His face turning serious, he extracts a white
filled bag, tears it open, and exposes another burger.

"Looks rather wholesome as far as burgers go."

Him being his usual pleasant self, makes Eva smile. Any previous nerves are beginning to evaporate. Sensing her serious mood, he exaggerates his smile, while placing the half-exposed burger on the table behind him.

"I'll eat this later. I'll smother it in ketchup, The sky is overcast and gray, as Eva drives her ten-year-old blue Taurus toward the old church. Ignoring the few spits of rain on her windshield, her anxious mind keeps drifting back to the previous day's happenings. The meeting, the recording, and then total confusion of how she feels about Gus. A car horn breaks her daydream. Realizing she is wandering across the road into oncoming traffic, she grips harder onto the steering wheel. While swerving back into her own lane, her heart begins to pound, and her hands tremble as she grips the steering wheel a little tighter.

Now on a steady course, she decides to stop by a space near a newsstand. While switching off the engine, a debilitating feeling of fatigue rushes through her.

I must be more tired than I thought?

Slumping back in the driver's seat, she takes a deep breath and closes her eyes.

Those eyes of his. Its as if he is looking into my soul. I keep hearing him say – "God love you".

An inexplicable warm glow begins to fill her body. The fatigue evaporates, her energy returns. She opens her eyes. A bright light is filling the car. The sun has come out from behind the clouds.

She realizes that she is just a block from the old church, so she decides to climb out of the Taurus, lock it and head toward the church on foot. As she leaves her car, she notices a newspaper headline, 'Miracle Man at Fund Raiser.' Staring in fascination at the newspaper, she steps closer to the newsstand. Her eyes widen as she reads the headline. 'TV Reporter Eva Brown is brought back to life by Gus...' She can't read any more. The strong feeling of guilt is creating havoc with her insides, while the old man running the stand gives her a quizzical look. Not wanting to face anyone right now, she looks away, and then hurries off toward the old church.

The sun feels warm as it reflects off the old gothic church door. Before knocking, she gathers her thoughts, and then reaches for the doorknocker. Observing a slight tremor in her hand, she grips the knocker and bangs it three times. Seconds later, she hears a sound of a heavy metal bar being drawn back on the other side of the door. The door opens to reveal Will filling the opening. His vacant eyes study her with an intensity she remembers from last time. When sudden recognition lights up his eyes, he struggles to control his excitement.

"I-it's y-you."

Like an older sister, Eva offers him a smile of reassurance.

"Hello Will. Is Gus in?"

"H-he's just gone out to get a b-burger."

Overcome by intense disappointment, followed by resignation, she turns to leave without saying a word. Not wanting her to go, Will's large hand grips her forearm.

"No - no! Don't go. H-he'll be right back."

Not really wanting to leave, she puts her hand on his. Feeling safe by his warmth and strength, she turns to him and smiles.

"Okay. I'll wait."

As his large childlike face flushes with innocent excitement, he releases her forearm and grips hold of her hand.

"I-I'll t-take you to his ch-chat room."

Leading the way, his massive frame turns into the building, while he closes the heavy door. Without saying a word, or even looking at her, he begins to walk further into the building. With her following like a led child, they reach the room with the stained-glass window. With childlike exuberance, Will enters and pulls out a chair for her. She sits. He then pulls out another chair and sits opposite her. Surprised by the gesture, Eva watches Will sit.

This is weird. First Gus, then Max, now Will. They all sit the same way...

There is a pause, as she hears Will's heavy breathing. His voice sounding concerned, he speaks first.

"H-how are you?"

Overwhelmed by his huge physical, and yet childlike presence, she answers.

"I'm fine."

Not satisfied with that answer, his eyes turn sad.

"Y-you nearly d-died l-last night."

Realizing Will must have been a first-hand witness, a sinking feeling hits her stomach.

"So, I've been told."

There is another pause, Will's chair creaks under his weight. Becoming embarrassed by this kind inquisition, Eva has to look away. Her eyes now drawn to the stained-glass window; Jesus' eyes still reveal the pain. Echoing in the background, Will's words permeate her insides.

"I-it was Jesus brought you back to us."

Still staring at the window, and hearing the hollow words coming from her own mouth, she can't believe her ears.

"I know. I saw it on TV."

In a daze, she turns back toward Will, and notices him scrutinizing her.

256

A few feet away there is a sound of footsteps and pieces of wood being moved. Will's face reacts with childlike excitement.

"It's him."

As Will stands, the footsteps become closer.Eva's heart misses a beat when hearing Gus's concerned voice.

"Will?"

Ignoring Eva, Will rushes out of the room. Being left alone, she begins to feel nervous. Hearing the two men in the hallway, she is again drawn to the stained glass.

It's the eyes. They're so much like....

Gus appears at the door holding a brown paper bag. Seeing Eva sitting, Gus presence her with a warm smile.

"Well. Hello there..."

Will appears at the door behind him. Still looking at Eva, Gus instructs Will.

"Will? We must tidy that woodpile by the kitchen. It's dangerous when the children are here, and there is a contractor coming in an hour, so I don't want him falling all over it either."

Still smiling, Gus turns to Will, dips his hand into the brown paper bag, and pulls out a smaller white paper bag.

"Here. Some grub for you."

Will's grateful childlike expression says it all.

"W-with relish?"

Gus turns away from Will to wink at Eva.

"Yes. With relish."

Witnessing the warm banter between these two men, Eva becomes envious of their unique relationship. Happy with his food, Will wanders off. Presuming he is heading toward the untidy woodpile, Eva can hear the white paper bag being torn, and imagines Will's spade-like hands engulfing the relish-dripping burger in almost one mouthful.

Studying her dreamlike persona, Gus comes further into the chat room, closes the door and sits down opposite her in Will's chair. Continuing to study her, he pushes the brown bag toward her.

"Breakfast?"

"No, I'm fine."

"Sure? and then heat it in our new microwave."

Imagining him placing the whole package in the microwave oven, causes her to laugh.

"Don't forget to take it out of the plastic first."

Picturing the event, he joins her in the laughter.

"You mean I have to throw away the most nutritional part first?"

Enjoying his humor, and her nerves dissipating with her tension and anxieties, the laughter bursts out of her. Tears pour down her face, as the room becomes filled with the sound of their joy.

Eventually the laughter subsides. Searching her eyes, while he catches his breath, he speaks first.

"How do you feel right now? Right this minute?"

Even though more relaxed, the question throws her.

"I-I'm fine..."

"Fine? Have you noticed how people hide behind that word? If you feel lousy, you say – 'I'm fine', because you don't want to show anyone how bad you really feel. Now, when you do feel good, 'fine' isn't quite enough, but we still use it anyway."

Caught up in this jovial atmosphere, his hand reaches for hers. This time she doesn't resist. Instead his touch sends a mild electric shock throughout her body. Observing her reaction, he persists.

"I know how you feel. Physically you are fine. However, mentally you're...."

Becoming self-conscious and trying to control her obvious emotions, she finishes the sentence for him.

"Confused?"

As if an understanding is developing between them, he again searches her eyes, and tightens the grip on her hand.

"I'm glad you said it. You must feel terribly confused. One minute your chest is being crushed with such agonizing pain that it makes you pass out, and then there you are waking up in front of an audience, half dressed, with a man lying next to you feeling - fine."

Unable to sustain the eye contact, she looks down and observes her hand being squeezed and stroked with his other hand. Not wanting to hurt him in any way, her eyes return to his.

"To be honest, if I hadn't seen it on Max's computer, I would never have believed it. I remember vividly the sickening pain, and then sort of waking up with my blouse undone, my bra exposed and lying on my back with you lying next to me."

Picturing the scenario, he burst out laughing. Wondering what's so funny, her expression becomes serious.

What's the big joke?

Realizing that this conversation is no laughing matter, his laugh subdues to an even smile.

"I'm sorry. You have me there. I didn't realize how it would look from your situation. You see - I flaked out as well. That's why I was lying next to you..."

He hesitates.

"Unfortunately, every time I - well, never mind. You saw it."

Picturing the scene on Max's computer, she turns away, reaches inside her jacket to pull out Max's check.

"This is from my boss."

Controlling his curiosity and excitement, he unfolds the check.

"Wow! Tell him I really appreciate this. It will help me enormously. Please convey my gratitude. Since early this morning, I have had all sorts of envelopes with contributions dropping into the letter box."

"Well, you did put on quite a show last night."

Observing the sudden hurt appear in his eyes, she bites her bottom lip in regret. His eyes now puzzled; he stands up as if he needs to move away. Looking as if he is about to cry, he goes over to the window wall, pauses, and then turns to face her.

To her, his eyes and the eyes in the window seem to blend into one. Still holding the check, his eyes harden.

"Is that what you think? I put on a good show? A show to bring in the

259

money?"

As he turns away to face the window, it is obvious to her he is trying hard to control the hurt. Regretting her tactless statement, she watches him turn back to face her. His eyes are still full of pain.

"So, you being at death's door was just a golden opportunity for me to put on my act?"

The hurt in his eyes turning to anger, and then back to hurt again, he pleads.

"Look, your life was ebbing away. I did what I had to do. You could have been in a back alley with nobody around or in a stadium filled with fifty-thousand people watching; it's all the same to me."

Seeing his tears being held back, causes her to feel more wretched and guilty beyond words. With this new profound emotion overwhelming her, she stands, opens her arms and steps up to him. Not caring anymore about guilt or gratitude, she rests her head against his chest. Feeling his heart beating, and his smell enveloping her, she shudders as his arms slide around her shoulders. As if she has found something missing in her life, her voice is muffled against his shirt,

"I'm sorry. I'm so sorry..."

While embracing in each other's arms, the light from the stained glass window reflects on his face. Experiencing a new sort of turmoil, but savoring his warmth and smell, she is reluctant to pull away. Her face soaking with tears and her nose running, he reaches over to the table, looks inside the burger sack and pulls out some napkins. Offering her the tissues, she puts on a grateful smile, and proceeds to blow her nose and wipe her eyes.

"My boss went on at me earlier, telling me I should be grateful to you. Then he said he has a strong gut feeling about you."

Seeing she has finished with the napkins, he retrieves the sodden tissues and drops them in a basket by the table.

"Your boss sounds quite a character..."

His face turning serious, he grips her right hand.

"Do you remember me explaining that you will survive, because you have a good heart?"

She looks down at her hand and can't resist placing her other hand on his.

"Yes, I remember. Even though I didn't take much notice at the time or even understand."

With his other arm still around her shoulder, he guides her back to her chair. Feeling a little let down, by him withdrawing him warmth, she watches him sit opposite. Their knees almost touching, her voice now calmer and her tears gone, she is able to look straight at him

"Have you seen this morning's headlines? They're calling you the miracle man."

As a bemused look crosses his face, he looks away for a second. His expression changing to one of deep thought, his eyes return and focuses on her.

"Are you ready for me to talk now?'

She is taken aback by this question.

"What do you mean?"

As his face cracks into a wide smile, and his bright and mesmerizing eyes pierce into her, he answers.

"Oh, come on Eva. Your boss gives you a check, telling you to come and visit me 'unofficially', thank me, and then report back to him later. Is that correct?"

Not realizing it was so obvious, the truth of his statement stuns her for a second. Hiding her embarrassment, she tries not to sound too surprised.

"How did you know all this?"

Again, he smiles, and reaches for her hand.

"Because this is all meant to be. You have been chosen to get my message across."

"Why me? You seem to be doing a good job on your own."

As his eyes bore into her even more, she is unable to look away even if she wants to. To reassure, he gives her hand a squeeze.

"This is just a side show. The main message I told you earlier."

"You mean about the world being destroyed soon if we don't clean up our act and mend our ways?"

Hurt by her sarcasm, his smile vanishes.

"I can see you're having difficulty in accepting any of this, hence the cutting sarcasm."

Witness his genuine pain, her guilt returns. While she looks away, he continues.

"I can see you're finding all this a bit far-fetched!"

Unable to look him in the eye, he lets go of her hand.

"Was last night far-fetched?"

His voice seems to echo as her mind recalls last night.

What am I supposed to do now...?

She stands. Knocking the chair over, she glares at him.

"Look! This is all too much for me. I'm just wasting your time me being here. Whatever 'miracle you did to me last night, I really appreciate it. As for the rest, I'm still finding it difficult to take."

Understanding her confusion, Gus rises from his chair. Pausing for a second, he notices the reflection from the window shining on her pale mahogany skin. Admiring the warm glow, he is still aware that she still won't look at him. Not wanting to antagonize her, he reaches out to grab her hands. Her reaction is to pull away. Determined, he grabs her hands again.

"I want to show you something."

As she still cannot look at him, he releases her hands, and holds his own out, the palms upwards.

"As you won't look directly at me, at least look at my wrists."

Within seconds, she is drawn to a deep round ugly scar about the size of a large thumbnail appearing in the center of his wrists. She becomes mesmerized, as he turns his hands over, showing the same size scars appearing on the backs. Too stunned to react, she witnesses him lift his shirt to expose a deep ugly scar about four inches in length on his right abdominal region.

While her stomach churns and a strange fear runs through her, she has to withdraw from him.

"I don't know how you did that or what you're trying to prove..."

His eyes ablaze in frustration, he grabs her upper arms.

"I am the son of man. I was crucified over two thousand years ago to save man from himself."

Unable to resist his grip, and her turmoil increasing, she wants to fall into his arms, but something deep inside her still denies him.

" I guess it didn't work?"

His eyes still blazing, he is not letting her go.

"Precisely! That's why I've returned. But this time there is a time limit, and the rules have changed..."

He lets her go. As tears replace the frustration in his eyes, her resistance is waning. Because she cannot deny him anymore, her emotions are mixed. Experiencing a strange mixture of pity, desire, disbelief, she throws her confused body into his arms. Relieved she is beginning to understand – a little, he holds her tight.

Relishing the warmth and softness of her body flowing into him like a healing balm, the perfume in her lush wavy hair arouses some basic deep instinct from long ago. With both his hands he has a passion to stroke her head. He then grips her trembling face in his hands, and then kisses her forehead.

"I'm sorry. I shouldn't have said all that. I so desperately want you to believe me."

Not understanding what is happening to her, and becoming intrigued by his presence and scent, she slides her arms around his waist, and grips him tighter. Listening to his heartbeat, she so wants to believe him. Meanwhile, the emotion engulfing her now is a passionate sexual desire for him to make love to her.

What am I doing? What is happening?

Knowing she is losing it, she has to tear away and turn her back on him. Her breathing heavy, her heart pounding, and her irrational yearning for this man beyond control, she turns back to face him.

"Why pick on me? Their must be others who would be glad to fall at your feet and believe in you."

His emotions becoming awry, he studies her face.

What is happening to me? I'm experiencing feelings that I have never had to come across before. Not since Mary by the water well.

"All the same, I need you."

His body and mind screaming in conflict, he reaches out to brush her face with the back of his hand. She notices the scars have gone.

I also want you.

Trying to keep some form of composure, he steps closer. Her mind reeling, she is experiencing the same turbulence.

No, please. I will give in this time if you touch me again. I will surrender to you completely.

Instead, she takes a controlled step back.

"What on earth can I possibly do to help you?"

His eyes now turning from desire to a different form of excitement, places a hand on her shoulder.

"I want you to be with me always. You and your television company will get exclusives. The last time I chose twelve men, all of different backgrounds and education to spread my words, but now with modern communications, TV, the Internet, Social Media, you can spread the word a thousand times quicker. Now, go back to Max...."

"How did you know his name?"

As he shows her the check, her trembling eases. She begins to laugh, and cannot stop. All the frustrations and anxiety flow out of her until her stomach aches. Seeing the funny side, he laughs with her. This is when her body gives in, and she falls into his arms. Not caring about any consequences, she takes his hand and lays it against her left breast.

"Fill my heart beating for you..."

Her passion rising, she then holds his head in her hands. Searching his eyes for a reaction, her lips part as she fuses their lips together. Her hunger mounting, her mouth intensifies. His reaction accommodating, his arms pull her tighter toward him causing her breasts to tingle and her body ache so much that she knows he is the love of her life.

After a what seems like forever, he stops and is reluctant to pull away.

Oh, God. I haven't felt like this since Mary. What am I to do?

Confused by him separating, her eyes are still closed, and she is floating in a glorious daze.

Surely, he can't stop now?

His soft, caring voice breaks the spell.

"I need you to go to Max."

As her delightful dream dissipates, her eyes open to find him gazing at her.

"Go to Max? Oh – Yes – Max."

His eyes still engulfing her, he has to lean on the chair for support. Closing his eyes, he is using all his willpower to tear his yearning body away from her.

"Tell Max what you've seen and what I've told you."

He opens his eyes.

"I know it's hard for you now to understand, but you will, I promise. You will believe me – soon."

While she gathers her mind, which is telling her one thing, her body and emotions are screaming for another, she answers.

"Yes! Its what Max wants."

Her mind still reeling, she turns ready to leave. Acting calm, he grips her forearm.

"I am having a rally at the Hammers Football Stadium tonight. The Murdock Organization is sponsoring it. Please be there."

Still wanting to fall into his arms, she does her best to concentrate.

"I don't know. I don't know 'anything' anymore."

Tears appearing in her eyes, she heads for the door, opens it without looking back and leaves. He leaves the support of the chair and goes to the door. Listening to her echoing footsteps leaving the building, tears fill his eyes.

"Oh, Mary! You're still with me."

34

It Begins

It is a few hours later. The clock on the office wall points to 3 p.m. Eva is sitting in front of Max's desk still hung over from her meeting with Gus. Meanwhile, Max is pacing the floor. His excitement at fever pitch, he stops at his desk, turns and stares straight at her.

"You're absolutely sure that's what he said?"

The office phone rings. Displaying annoyance and frustration at being disturbed, he is abrupt when answering.

"Yes? Sure! That's fine. Don't forget, only three minutes!"

Becoming irritable, he bangs the receiver down harder than usual. He pauses, takes a breath, and glares again at Eva.

"Well?"

Eva can still hear Gus's caring voice and see the intensity of those eyes.

"That's what he said. 'I am the son of man! I died over two thousand years ago to save mankind.' How did I react to this mind shattering revelation? I was unkind to him."

Puzzled by her reaction, Max leans forward on his desk and stares at her with those dark 'Editor' eyes.

"Unkind?"

Eva is now becoming overwhelmed by this now familiar pang of guilt.

"Well, I said his dying hadn't worked. So, right in front of me, over two thousand years of despair overcame him. I have never witnessed such pain and frustration in a grown man. He admitted I was right, but he said this time there are conditions and..."

Her voice trails off. Max barks.

"...and what?"

She has to take a deep breath to answer.

"....and a deadline!"

As realization sinks in, Max stands up straight from the desk, and punches the air with a closed fist.

"I knew it - I knew it! Now tell me 'exactly' what you saw."

"Oh, Max, do I have to? I'm exhausted, and want to go home"

Ignoring her plea, he returns to pacing the floor. Raising his voice, it is obvious to her this is bigger than both of them. While pacing, he raises his voice.

"Tell me!"

The scene returning to her memory with a vengeance, Eva's voice is almost inaudible.

"I saw some scars appear on his wrists."

Max becomes incredulous, as he stops pacing.

"You what?"

Eva repeats it a little louder.

"The nail holes!"

His reaction is to pace again. With an air of triumph, he ponders. Her becoming exhausted, she flounders.

"I don't know if..."

The spring in him winding up, he stops her.

"Did he ask you to be with him at all?"

Still picturing the scene, she answers with an air of reluctance.

"Yes. He wants me to be with him all the time, and we can have the exclusives."

Max stops pacing.

"That's it then. That is what you'll do. I want you to be with him twenty-four hours a day if necessary, until God knows when..."

Max laughs at his own cliché.

"God will know when. Believe me."

Witnessing her boss becoming this excited is making Eva's stomach turn.

"You don't know what you're saying Max. This whole thing is far too big for me. I don't think I can handle it."

Having other ideas, Max comes around the desk, leans over her, and puts both hands on her upper arms. Looking straight at her, his voice is more determined.

"You 'will' handle it kid. You 'will' manage, and you 'will' succeed. Do you know why? The son of God chose you, and I am inclined to agree with his judgment. So, young woman, I don't want any more arguments or excuses."

As an awful sensation of fatalism creeps over her, she takes a deep breath of acceptance.

"What do you want me to do first?"

Satisfied she is 'cooperating', Max lets go. His face still flush with excitement, he reaches over to the rear of his desk and sorts through some papers, picks out a poster and hands it to her.

"This was emailed to me while you were seeing him."

Her hands trembling, she grips onto the poster, and glances through it. Meanwhile, Max continues his agenda.

"He's holding his first big rally at the Detroit Hammers Stadium, and guess who the sponsor is? The one organization that owns half of the world's biggest newspapers..."

Knowing who, Eva looks up from the poster and interrupts.

"I know. He told me."

Max stares at her in disbelief.

"Why the hell didn't you tell me?"

Begrudging all this, Eva throws down the poster.

"Because I don't want to go. That's why!"

Not wanting to hear this, his brown eyes plead.

"But it's you that's gained his confidence. You did say you'll be with him twenty-four hours a day?"

Even though fatigue is creeping over her in waves, Eva is still defiant.

"I never said that.You did!"

Max pauses for a second, and then smiles.

"Precisely."

Being taken over by a strong sense of resignation, she hangs on to he dignity.

"Do I have any choice?"

Affection being displayed in his eyes, Max keeps smiling.

"Afraid not! It's all part of the 'big' plan."

Accepting the inevitable, Eva takes a deep breath, and then releases it as a long sigh.

"I hope I can deal with your 'big' plan."

Full of self doubt, she begins to head toward the door. Before she can make it, Max strides forward and blocks her. His hand gripping her arm, she lowers her head to look down at the floor.

Oh, Gus. How am I going to cope with all this…?

Max's reassuring voice breaks into her despondency.

"He will make sure you can. That's why he brought you back."

She looks up to meet his eyes with a look that makes his hair stand up on the back of his neck. A look not seen since the beginning in the Garden of Eden.

35

A Visitor

Full of uncertainty, Eva is standing outside her apartment front door looking around the hallway at the other three apartments on her floor. The brass door numbers screwed onto the old paneled doors reflect in the single ceiling light giving the hallway an eerie glow.

Do you know, I've never met or even seen the people living behind those doors?

Her hands tremble from exhaustion as she struggles to open her handbag. Irritation adding to her already delicate state of mind, she rummages through its contents without success.

"Hell! Where are my keys?"

Her despondency flooding her in waves, she gives up and presses the buzzer. After waiting a few seconds without any response, she presses again. Still no response,concern is now added to the mountain of negative emotions flooding through her. As she goes to press it again, she hears a click coming from inside. Hiding her irrational fear and a sense of relief, she watches Ryan open the door.

"Hi Ryan, where's Maggie?"

Before he can answer, she pushes past him entering the hallway. A new fear now creeping through her, she looks around as if searching for something. Becoming worried by his mother's strange behavior, Ryan tries to reassure.

"It's okay, Mom. She's in the living room. We have a visitor."

Although her son's face is calm and relaxed, she snaps from this new anxiety.

"A visitor? Who?"

Not waiting for an answer, she storms into the living room, followed by a puzzled Ryan. She stops in her tracks at the sight of a handsome young man sitting next to a mesmerized Maggie on the old sofa. Sensing someone enter the room, he stops talking and turns to face Eva. Presenting her with a broad easy smile, he rises from the sofa with the ease of a tall, trained athlete. As his perfect white teeth draw her gaze; his tanned handsome face is framed by dark curly hair, giving him an impish air that could seduce any woman in an instant. His well-tailored dark blue suit appears natural on his neat muscular frame. As if she is alone with no one else in the world, he stretches out his right hand for her to take. Spellbound by his sexuality, she accepts his hand. Even though taken in by his demure, she is disappointed at his cold, clammy skin, making the handshake uncomfortable.

Hands separating, she is entranced by his emerald green eyes, which seem almost luminous in the soft lighting of the room.

"Eva, I believe. I'm Natas.. All my friends call me Nat."

Even though he is pleasing to the eye, Eva is becoming irritated by this man's intrusion. However, at the same time she is is drawn to his full sensual mouth, as he convinces her of his honest intentions.

"I have been having a wonderful conversation with this delightful lady here."

He looks down at Maggie who is still mesmerized and can't quite believe she is so close to this vision of masculine beauty. Confident of his winning charms, his eyes penetrate Eva's mood.

"And also your son. We have been playing on some new fun apps I downloaded for his computer - combined with my smartphone."

Coming aware of his coldness underneath the charm, Eva is becoming uneasy in this man's company. His green piercing eyes making it difficult for her to look elsewhere, Ryan's innocent gaze displays excitement.

"We've been on line, Mom. Nat's been showing me how to use the chat rooms, Twitter and stuff."

While alarm bells go off in Eva, her fatigue is crushing.

I don't want all this! All I want is a nice hot bath, hug my son and go to bed..

Out of concern, she snaps at her confused son.

"Ryan? Honey, please goes to your room."

"Oh, Mom?"

Still looking at Natas, Eva is listening to her son grumble, while he is reluctant to leave all the enticement.

"I do not appreciate you showing my son the dark side of social media – or

'Anything' else for that matter!"

His eyes take on a cool luster showing no reaction to her dislike. Instead, his charm increases.

"I wouldn't dream of corrupting your son's innocence. I was also hoping the beautiful lady standing before me would allow me an audience."

Even though his sex appeal is getting to her, Eva is not seduced. Instead, her anger mounting, she beckons Maggie as she forces her attention away from Natas' gaze.

"Excuse me."

Her body trembling with negative emotions and weaknesses, she walks back into the hallway, removes her coat and crams it onto the nearest coat hook. Worried about her long time friend, Maggie scurries after her. Mindful of Natas's gaze, Eva whispers to Maggie, out of earshot.

"Maggie? You 'mustn't let in strangers like this."

Surprised Eva's strange erratic behavior, Maggie realizes something deeper is lurking.

"I–I'm sorry Miss Brown! I did try and not let him in. He said he vas a friend of

Gus and needed to talk to you urgently. As you can see his charm got zer better of me."

Hearing Gus's name, Eva doesn't bother to reply. Her turmoil increasing, she turns to go back into the living room when she almost bumps into Natas, who is now standing in the doorway.

"I see I am the topic of conversation. I assure you Eva, my visit is purely an honorable one."

After receiving another flashing smile to disarm her, Eva glares at him straight on.

"So, you're a friend of Gus?"

His eyes darken for a second, and then resume the elusive charm.

"More of an acquaintance."

"So, what is it you need to tell me?"

His eyes brighten, but his voice takes on a smooth, and yet determined tone.

"I have come to give you a strong warning. Gus and I go back a long way..."

Not believing her ears, she interrupts.

"A warning? Warning against what?"

Gus now entering the equation, she is finding it hard to control her rising anger.

This guy is bringing out the worse in me!

Knowing the effect he is having on her, Natas remains calm.

"Not what - who! I am talking about Gus. I believe he has you quite close to him right now."

"Who I mix with or who I'm close to is 'my' business!"

Undisturbed by her outburst, his face remains calm, his smile cordial.

"My, he has got you turned up. I heard about the – 'miracle'. He is very clever with words you know. And oh, those hands."

As a picture of Gus's scarred wrists flashes through her mind, he is aware he has her confused. Pleased with his efforts so far, he continues.

"Look? I am your 'real' ally. I have come here to help you. All I am saying, do not believe every word he tells you."

Before she can react, he hands her a small card.

"Here, this is my iPhone number. You can call me any time - night or day."

While she stares at the card in a daze, he reaches into his other jacket pocket and pulls out a brown paper bag. His eyes glistening with satisfaction, he thrusts the bag into her hands.

"For you – Eva."

As Eva's imagination exceeds her rational mind, he is off walking toward the front door. On opening it, he pauses with his broad back facing her.

"Even if you loose the card, I will know 'exactly' where to find you."

Her stomach churning at the 'threat', she glances at the card again.

"It doesn't say what you do, or who you are. It just gives a number."

She is talking to nobody. He has gone, the doorway empty. Still holding the paper bag, Eva's instincts inform her that before opening the bag, she will come across a polished, perfect rosy apple. Repelled, and in no way will she ever take a bite, she trashes the bag. In the meantime, Ryan has crept out of his bedroom.

"Do you think what he said about Gus is true Mom?"

Still absorbed in the apple, she cannot hear him.

"Mom?"

Her mind clearing somewhat, she turns to him

"I'm sorry honey. I don't know. I'm a bit confused right now."

Witnessing his sad eyes on the verge of tears, she slides her arm around his shoulder and leads him toward the noise of dishes being handled in the kitchen.

Still caught up in the previous atmosphere, Maggie is talking to nobody while becoming frantic washing the dishes

"Now I'm all behind. I vish people vouldn't do zis to me. All I vant is a simple quiet life."

Listening to Maggie's strong and familiar accent, Eva can't help smiling as the tension of the evening is now ebbing away. Not noticing that she drops the card, as she slides an affectionate arm around the older woman's shoulders, her voice is calm.

"You can go home now. Finish off tomorrow."

"But Miss Brown, I am so behind."

"Tomorrow Maggie. Tomorrow!"

With a hint of impatience, she watches Maggie scurry around to retrieve her coat. At the same time, Eva feels guilty for speaking to her loyal friend in such a manner.

"Make it later tomorrow Maggie. Four in the afternoon will be fine. You can look after Ryan while I cover Gus at a big rally."

In hearing this, Ryan looks disappointed.

"Aw, Mom! Can't I go with you and see Gus?"

"Not this time honey."

Having to ignore her son's plea, she turns to Maggie.

"Don't let anyone in this front door, at anytime. Not even God!"

This makes Eva smile again. She feels better, still tired, but for some unexplained reason, relieved, and her old self again. While Maggie leaves and Eva shuts the front door, the apartment phone rings. Hesitant, she picks up the extension in the hallway and checks the caller ID.

Pay phone. Who the hell can this be?

"Hello?"

"Hello my dear, it is I."

Even though there is a little static on the line, she recognizes his voice. Sensing her hesitation, Gus continues.

"I hope I didn't call at an awkward moment."

She pauses.

How did he get my number? Why now?

"No, it's okay! What do you want at this time of the evening?"

Realizing she is on edge, the familiar pang of guilt hits her at the way she spoke.

Ignoring the tension in her voice, he answers with an amiable tone.

"I just want to know if you're all right. I had an overwhelming feeling you were in danger."

Natas coming to mind, she pauses again.

"No! I'm not in any danger. I'm fine."

Sensing she is lying, he is more direct.

"Did you have a visitor? A stranger in the last half an hour?"

She continues to lie.

275

"Err -oh! Just a friend of my housekeeper."

Why did I say that?

By the way he pauses, her instincts are telling her.

Dammit! He knows!

Instead of investigating further, he asks a poignant question.

"Ryan all right?'

Guilt rattling her nerves, she is abrupt in answering.

"He's fine!"

Becoming more concerned, he pauses again.

"You sure? You would tell me."

Exhaustion flowing through her like a torrent, she is even more abrupt.

"Look! I'm fine! Ryan's fine! Now, please hang up so we can go to bed."

His patience infinite, he answers with understanding.

"All right, I'll go. Tomorrow then. Sleep well."

Riddled with a sense of shame, she hears the click as he disconnects, and then the familiar dial tone. Her insides aching with further guilt, she hangs up, but still leaves her hand resting on the phone.

It was sweet that he was concerned for Ryan and me. Was he psychic? How did he know we had a stranger visit? Max would say he knows everything.

As she looks up from the phone, and withdraws her hand, Ryan is staring at her from the living room door. His inquiring eyes are puzzled as he walks toward her.

"Mom?"

"Yes, honey."

"That man, Nat, why was he saying all those things about Gus?"

Wanting so much to take him in her arms, she settles for kneeling down to him.

"I don't know honey There are a lot of things I don't know."

While she strokes his head, he looks at her with the ultimate love of a son toward his mother

"Did you believe him?"

Picturing those green seductive eyes, Eva sighs.

"I'm not sure, but we'll find out eventually. The truth has a sure way of coming out into the open.That's my job. Remember?"

Always reassured by his mother, Ryan flashes a back a questioning smile.

"Eva Brown, Investigative Journalist?"

"That's me."

See the funny side, she attempts to laugh, but her impending anxiety is getting in the way. Sensing her fragile mood, he hugs her. While his young head presses up against her soft comforting chest, her fingers tingle as she strokes his head. Her whole being now warmed by his presence, his words penetrate

"I love you Mom."

Hearing the words all mothers crave, tears well up in her eyes, and her voice cracks.

"I - love you - too honey."

As they hold on to each other, and the burning tears roll down her cheeks, he is reluctant to pull away, so he can look into her eyes.

"Mom?"

"Yes, Honey?"

"That man Nat, he didn't have the blue like Gus."

36

The Rally

The evening sun is casting long shadows in the packed football stadium. Large illuminated billboards are everywhere, advertising the fact that Gus is being sponsored by a major corporation .

On all the front rows of seats, hopeful people are on crutches or wheelchairs, all waiting that Gus the "Miracle Man" can cure or ease their suffering. Meanwhile, the big stadium clock reads 5:57 p.m.

All the media are placed in strategic areas so as to get the best angle for the sponsorship advertising, which is also a huge floodlit backdrop for the main podium. Eva and Mike for Channel Six are among the media doing a final check of their equipment. Sensing the tense atmosphere, Mike scans the stadium for some appetizing shots, while Eva begins to narrate in her soft, calm voice.

"Welcome to the Detroit's Hammer Football Stadium. This is Eva Brown for Channel Six. As you can see the stadium is packed. Sixty thousand people all waiting for the young man called Gus who is being named in many media outlets as the 'Miracle Man'. There are rows and rows of optimistic sick and disabled people sitting in a vane hope of being seen, or even just touched by him..."

The stadium clock now reading 6:00 p.m. and Gus stepping out from behind one of the huge billboards, distracts Eva's introduction.

As Gus and climbs onto the center podium with an air of confidence, hundreds of flashing cameras and TV lights go into action. Soaking up the atmosphere, Gus scans the expectant crowd. After about ten-seconds, he adjusts his microphone.

"Good evening ladies, gentlemen and children...."

As if on cue, about a thousand children come pouring out of the vast audience. Streaming down the long aisles toward the stadium center, their high pitched voices are full of the chatter and yelling of excitement. As Gus peers down at them with affection, they form a huge encirclement around the podium.

While the children settle, and everything is still, the mass audience is now focusing on Gus as he speaks with a clear precise voice into the microphone.

"Ladies and gentlemen! You see before you the innocence and truth of tomorrow. These young souls will be your leaders and servants in a clean new world. You may seem puzzled at a 'clean new world', but I assure you, it will be true, as I stand here before you relaying the most important message man has yet to receive about his future. These children see what many of you cannot, because they know who I really am. They are the chosen ones."

The crowd being mesmerized with curiosity, he pauses. His confidence oozing, his voice is calm, but determined.

"You see, I have returned, to give humanity a final warning. If the human race doesn't improve in a fundamental way to save this planet and themselves, the Earth as you know it - will be destroyed."

The stadium's atmosphere becomes electric with murmurings of astonishment and confusion. Having the crowd where he wants them, Gus continues by raising the pitch and volume of his voice.

"It won't be in the next ten years or even five. It will be in the next twelve months. You have ignored all the scientist's warnings about pollution, climate change and various pandemics, not to mention Government corruption, this is the final card in a stacked deck."

Letting this warning sink in, the audience becomes shocked as well as confused. As they mutter in disbelief, Gus pauses and lowers his head as if preparing for a final onslaught. Timing his pause, he raises his head. His tear-filled eyes focus on the crowd furthest away as if to make sure everyone in the stadium can hear him.

"Over two thousand years ago, I was harshly nailed to a crude wooden cross and left to die."

Hearing this hard to believe statement, the media continue to focus on Gus. At the same time, the whole stadium is demonstrating a further state of shock and disbelief. His voice becoming angry, Gus continues.

"I died for you! I took on your sins, knowing it was your only salvation. As people will never attain perfection, my painful death was futile. Because mankind betrayed me even more by not even caring, you let me down by not even trying to attain goodness. You just didn't get the true message. You have abused, exploited, and slaughtered each other, often in my name; all for your own greedy selfish desires..."

He pauses by soaking up the shocked feedback, and then continues.

"You all know the difference between good and evil. Unfortunately, you choose evil. Why? Because it's easier, and offers the illusion of instant gratification. For some inane reason you all find it a struggle to be good. You find it far simpler to be evil. Evil is far more tempting. Like a drug, the more you have, the more you need, and the more you are 'never' satisfied. I am telling you now that good is simple, clean, pure and honest, and it lasts forever..."

He pauses again to lower his head. Surprised that the whole stadium is so quiet, he presumes they are all waiting for the next in-depth message. Preparing his mind, Gus lifts his head to face the mass. His eyes scanning the vast audience before him, Gus continues.

"Unfortunately you haven't got forever to procrastinate. You have only one year. I can see from here that most of you are saying to each other; 'Who is this guy?' He's standing up here claiming he's Jesus. The man's a nut, a lunatic, and a blasphemer. Do you know something? Right now, I sincerely wish I were the latter, because it would be a lot easier, but I'm not. I am who I say I am; here to relay the final message to you. Enough is enough! It is now crunch time."

Meanwhile, in her private rooms at the White House, the President of the United States is watching Gus on television. Sitting together on a large soft sofa, fifteen-year-old daughter Julie is leaning against her.

"What do you think Mother?"

Determined to find some comfort because of an old back injury, her mother hides her irritant.

"I really don't know dear. I must admit he's fascinating to watch."

Not happy with that reply, Julie's expression changes to a frown.

"Do you remember what Daddy used to say when he was alive?"

Her mother is still facing the TV, but concentrating more on her back pain.

"Do you mean about Jesus coming back and warning us? Like in the Book of Revelations?"

Her voice raising a notch with excitement, Julie wastes no time in answering.

"That's right! He used to say all the time that the human race can't keep going on this way."

Even though still facing the television, the President's eyes take on a far away look.

"Poor John. His beliefs were a bit extreme at the best of times. You know that was always a point of disagreement between us."

Remembering those disagreements, Julie's face saddens at the fond memories of her dead father.

"Look mother! The children are now standing and holding hands."

While the camera zooms onto the happy faces of the children surrounding Gus's podium, the picture changes. Gus's face now even more serious and purposeful, continues his serious message.

"The final report to you is that I am going to visit every world leader and inform them that if they do not do something about mankind's horrible problems, the world will be destroyed. It's written that this will happen. However? Is it inevitable? Not necessarily so. It's up to you out there to make the changes and prevent the worst. The choice is yours."

The camera focuses on the restless crowd, who are now becoming confused. Meanwhile, a young man on crutches struggles to get up from his front row seat. Now standing, his face exposing grim determination, he stumbles his way forward toward the children.

"Show us now! Help us!"

He then collapses in front of the children.

In the meantime, the President's face is expressing concern.

"This is becoming a problem. I hope the paramedics are on hand."

Not hiding her exasperation, Julie grabs her mother's hand.

"Oh Mother! You see! Gus is going to help him."

Without any hesitation, and his face showing grave concern at what is happening, Gus comes down off the podium. As the children make way for him, he goes toward the fallen young man. The children form a protective wall around Gus as he kneels and takes hold of the young man and helps him to stand. At the same time, Eva narrates into her microphone.

"After delivering such a powerful message about time running out for us all, it will be interesting to see how he handles this new situation."

Meanwhile, the young man pleads as Gus wraps his arms around him.

"Please sir! Help me. These damned artificial legs are killing me. My real legs were blown off in that stupid everlasting war in Afghanistan. I just don't have the strength to walk on them no more."

While tears of pain run down his face, Gus releases his grip and holds the young man at arms length. Searching his blue bloodshot eyes, Gus can feel the fatigue and pain radiating from the young veteran.

"Do you 'really' believe I can give you this strength?"

"Yessir, I do."

"How do you know?"

"I can 'feel' it sir. My whole insides tell me."

Satisfied he can help, Gus presence him with a comforting smile.

"Then throw away your crutches and walk back to your seat."

Gus lets go. Standing unsupported, the young man trembles a little as he takes one step back. Leaning on one crutch, the crowd cranes to get a better view. As he stands more erect by taking his weight off the remaining crutch, Gus touches his shoulder.

"Go now. God loves you. Through me you have been given the strength."

Withdrawing his hand, Gus leans forward and takes hold of the crutches. While the young man gains confidence and takes his first unaided steps, Gus then hands back the crutches for the young man to carry. In the meantime, the stadium is spellbound, disturbed only by the camera flashes.

A strange feeling of déjà vu overcomes Eva as she attempts to narrate into her microphone. Unable to talk, she just stares at the young man walking with an unsteady gait, and carrying his crutches. The young veteran face now relieved of pain and misery, he stops, faces the crowd and raises his crutches above his head and shouts.

"I'm free...I'm free."

Caught up in this 'miracle', someone from the crowd stands and applauds with such enthusiasm, others join in. Many people just sit and stare, not quite believing whether this is genuine or just a trick. At the same time, a young woman has made her way down to Gus. As she kneels down before him, he can't help but notice her lank, thin hair falling over a pale sunken face, and her violet eyes sunk deep in their hollows. His heart aching to help, Gus crouches down to her. While reaching out and holding her, he feels sick with pity as his hands feel the bony back and shoulders. Welcoming his warmth, she lifts her head up to face him.

"Help me Gus. I'm sick.Real sick."

With his right hand, he is gentle as he pushes her hair back off her face. Keeping his hand on her head, he then strokes.

"Do you believe God loves you?"

Her reply is her eyes fill with tears, and her voice is somber.

"I don't know. Who would want to love me? Look at me, I'm wrecking my life."

The stadium now quiet again,, Gus's response is to take her face and cup it in both of his hands. Focusing on her pale olive eyes, his voice is soft and reassuring.

"I love you. I have 'always' loved you. There is no need for you to take drugs anymore to ease your inner torment. Now you have found a reason for living. So remember, from this moment, I am always with you and love you. Do you believe that?"

Looking into his eyes, burning tears well up in her eyes and run down her cheeks.

"I do. I do."

Within a couple of seconds, her face begins to brighten, her skin looks clearer, and a new look of self worth appears in her eyes. Witnessing this, Gus lets go of her face. He then stands, pulling her to her feet. Sliding his arm around her shoulder, he welcomes her grateful embrace.

"Now go and love others for me as I love you. And most of all, love yourself."

Her eyes now sparkling, she gazes up at him.

"I will. I will."

Planting a soft kiss of gratitude on his cheek, she turns and leaves.

In the White House, Julie is now sitting on the carpet right in front of the sixty inch TV screen. Her mother, the President, looking stoic, remains in the sofa.

"Well, Mother?"

"I reserve my judgment."

This pragmatic answer annoys Julie, as if all twelve-year-olds get frustrated at their parents.

"Are you going to see him when he visits you?"

Still concentrating on the screen, this question takes the President by surprise.

"We will see my dear. We will see."

The stadium clock reads 7:02 p.m. Eva is narrating again into her microphone. As half of her mind is on what she is saying, the other half is swirling with the memory of her being in Gus's arms. An irrational jealousy is taking over.

I should be in his arms instead of these people?

Because she stops talking, Mike looks away from his camera to see if his colleague is all right.

"You okay?"

Embarrassed at letting her emotions get in the way of her job, she nods. As Mike carries on with his work, she becomes tired all of a sudden. Studying the long line of sick people that are now waiting for Gus, hoping for their own miracle, she notices he looks tired as well.

Am I experiencing what he feels?

Her mind wanders back to their kiss.

I can still feel his lips...

She has to to take a deep breath to try and regain her focus so she can continue her narration.

"It is now just over an hour since the rally started. This man who calls himself Gus, who claims to be Jesus Christ, is helping a long line of sick and desperate people. Some in wheelchairs, some being helped by friends or family and others alone, all waiting to receive a cure to end their misery. I am now going to visit with the first happy young man that Gus helped."

Indicating for Mike to follow, he records as he goes. Arriving at the young man, she positions Mike for a good angle.

"So here, before me, the first person to be helped by Gus."

Placing the microphone between her and the young man, she presents him with a cordial smile that does not reach her eyes, and speaks into her microphone.

"Hello, sir. I'm Eva Brown for Channel Six News. Could I ask you how you are right now?"

His crutches discarded by his feet, the young man sits upright on the hard stadium bench, and looks Eva in the eye.

"Wonderful! Much stronger. These metal legs don't hurt me anymore."

Expecting this answer, Eva puts the microphone up to her mouth.

"So, you wouldn't say in actuality that he 'cured' you of anything?"

Taken aback by such a cynical question, the young man hesitates, as Eva points the microphone toward him.

"Well - I didn't have a disease, but he has freed me of intense pain. I feel I'm able to cope a lot more now. He's given me the hope and strength I needed, so I don't feel I'm a cripple no more."

Expecting this answer also, she offers the young man a shallow smile.

"That's wonderful. Thank you for talking to us."

As she indicates to Mike, her words sound hollow in her mind. Her heart believes, but at the back of her mind, she is still cynical.

Why?

While the sensation of holding Gus is still haunting her, she tries to snap out of this emotional entrapment and focus on the things at hand.

"I'm now going to the young woman who apparently has finished with drugs...."

Gus is exhausted. His pale sweating face appears ghostly under the harsh lights. As he finishes talking to the person he has just hugged, he can see the long line of burdened souls is never-ending. Gathering what strength he has left, he climbs onto the podium. With the children's help, he grips onto the microphone with his left hand, wipes the sweat off his face with his right, and then leans toward the microphone. Witnessing his pain and exhaustion, Eva's heart goes out to him.

I remember him looking the same when he was lying next to me on the stage floor.

Meanwhile, Gus is struggling to speak.

"Err – ladies and gentleman, I'm afraid that is all I can do personally for you tonight..."

As he takes a couple of breaths trying to continue, there are some boo's and jeers coming from the massive audience. While most of the suffering murmur in disappointment, Gus hangs on to the podium. Still gripping the microphone, the sweat drips off his face.

"I just want to say – that God loves you all, and there will be another time...."

He passes out and collapses. Meanwhile, some noises of concern come from the crowd, mixing with sounds of frustration, annoyance and disappointment coming from the waiting line. As Will appears from nearby, the children form a protective wall around Gus. Not wasting any time, Will lifts Gus up and carries him off behind one of the huge billboards to a nearby door. In the meantime, while Eva looks on with a heavy heart, Mike notices her mood and comes up to her.

"You okay?"

She doesn't hear him.

He tries again.

"You okay, Eva?"

Her eyes full of tears, she gazes up at him in a daze.

"I'm fine. Thanks Mike. Can you report to Max? I'm going to check on Gus."

In the White House, Julie turns to her mother with concern in her voice.

"Oh Mother. Poor Gus! I hope he's all right?"

"I expect the noise and the lights got to him dear."

Even more frustrated with her mother, because of her short sightedness, Julie raises her voice.

"Oh mother! You are such a brilliant President, having a gift for weighing things up and making the right decision, but sometimes I think you are completely out of touch with your feelings and the real meaning of life."

Never hearing such a profound criticism from her young daughter before, her mother raises one eyebrow in a mixture of astonishment and admiration.

"Oh come, my dear. For a mere fifteen year old, you're far to wise for your age. Gus fainted, that's all."

Her frustration mounting, Julie begins to pace the floor.

"Mother? He didn't just faint. He's exhausted from helping all those sick people. Every time he cures someone, he gives a part of himself until he runs empty. So, he has to rest to fill up again."

Still admiring the passion coming from her daughter, the President rises from the sofa and beckons Julie to her open arms. When Julie responds by sinking into her mother's warm embrace, the President strokes her daughter's hair.

"How do you know all this?"

"I don't know mother. I just feel what he feels – that's all...."

A voice from the TV screen distracts.

"It seems Gus is all right. We have been told by an aide that he is exhausted and will be fine after some hours of rest. I'll hand you back to the studio..."

Having heard enough, the President leaves Julie, grabs the nearby remote and switches off the TV. Her passion still smoldering, Julie turns to face her mother.

"There you are. I told you."

Her mind switching into another gear, Julie's mother ponders for a few seconds, and then goes to a side desk and presses a button on a black enamel panel. Within seconds there is a knock on the door.

"Come in."

A tall, broad-shouldered blond haired man in his early thirties enters the room. Dressed in a dark gray suit, the standard clothing for the Secret Service, the President observes he has a slight condescending expression on his face.

"Frank, isn't it?"

"Yes, Ma'am."

It is obvious to her, Frank does not like taking orders from a woman.

"Frank? Is my Chief of Staff still in the building?"

Frank's curt answer matches his facial expression.

"Yes, ma'am. I guess so."

"Please ask him to meet me in the Oval Office in ten minutes – if it's not too much trouble."

Ignoring his boss's sarcasm, he answers with the same attitude.

"Right away – Ma'am."

As Frank continues his air of contempt, he takes his time in turning away to exit the room. Not quite believing what she just saw, she makes a mental note for later, and then sighs. She then turns to her daughter.

"My dear? I am going to arrange a meeting with this Gus friend of yours."

Not quite believing her ears, Julie's face flushes with excitement.

"Oh, mother! You're wonderful. You will enjoy talking to him."

"I hope so dear. I sincerely hope so."

The stadium is now becoming empty of people. The billboard lights are turned off. The remaining illumination is the fluorescent lights in the tunnels leading from the stadium to the outside streets. Natas is at the largest e raising his voice to spectators as he hands out red printed flyers.

"The man is a fraud, a fake. Don't listen to him. Did you see anyone really cured with your own eyes? Did he bring anyone back from the dead? No, of course he didn't. Don't listen to him, he's dangerous."

37

The Promise

It is now 9:05 the same evening. Eva was desperate to speak to Gus after the rally, but couldn't find him. Mike told her he would go back to the station and see Max, while she decides to go to the old church.

Her blue Taurus stops outside the old church; she switches off the engine. The night air is still. The faraway traffic acts as a feint background roar . Not wanting to make any conspicuous noise, she is quiet while getting out of her car and shutting the door. She looks around, observing the dark gloomy street, which looks eerie and threatening. She shivers as she goes up to the big door of the church. To her surprise, the door is ajar. Wondering if she is doing the right thing, she places her hand on the old iron doorknob and pushes the door open further. She stops and listens. The sound of her own heart beating inside her eardrums is all she can hear. She pushes the door open a little more, and is about to ask if anyone is there, when a deep man's voice quite near booms.

"Who's there?"

While Eva almost jumps out of her skin, her hand lets go of the doorknob as if hit by an electric shock. Some dim lights come on. Will is standing nearby. His mass casts long shadows, creating grotesque, distorted shapes which mingle among the pieces of timber and building materials scattered around. Now recognizing the 'intruder', Will's serious expression turns into a warm smile. Her heart still pounding from the shock, she relaxes a little

"Oh - Will. Is Gus here?"

"He's a-asleep."

"Oh! I just wanted to see if he was okay, and maybe see him for a while."

His eyes showing a little anger at the interruption, Will hesitates and struggles to say the right words.

"D- don't you s-see, he n-needs his r-rest."

Disappointed, but can understand, she gazes with curiosity at Will's large square face. Noticing his eyes have calmed down, she becomes resigned.

"Okay. I'll leave."

Just as she is about to leave, a familiar voice lifts her heart.

"If you go I will be very upset."

As Gus's voice echoes throughout the building, a beam of light appears as a nearby door opens, turning the immediate area into a full blaze of light. Her heart now palpitating. Eva can see Gus's silhouette appear at the opening.

"I will also never talk to you again."

His voice reverberating, and her heart beginning to settle, she rushes into his opening arms. As her head falls against his chest, his arms wrap around her. Meanwhile, Gus indicates with his head for Will to leave. Realizing there is no threat, Will nods and is discreet as he disappears into the shadows.

Hearing Will shut the front door, Eva and Gus stand alone as one. Relishing his warmth and smell, she is reluctant to pull away to look into his eyes.

"How are you? I was worried."

Appreciating her concern, he looks deep into her eyes.

"Come and sit with me."

With one arm wrapped around her waist, he leads her into the illuminated room. On entering, she is surprised to see a clean, but sparse room with a single cot bed in one corner, a small table and two old wooden dining chairs in the opposite corner.

"Welcome to my palace."

Disappointed at him releasing his arm, he steps into the center of a well-worn green rug on bare floorboards. His warmthstill radiating inside her waist, she asks the obvious.

"Palace?"

His reaction is an exaggerated smile.

"Let me explain. One..."

He points to the ceiling.

"We have a roof over our heads. Two, we have a bed to sleep in..."

With the grace of a dancer, he glides over to the bed. Performing another graceful step, he takes her hand, and guides her toward the table and chairs.

"Here my dear is a full dining suite for two persons. What more does one need?"

Still holding her hand, her twirls her around, and then catches her in his arms. Surprised, but not threatened by the gesture, she sinks again into his chest.

"I love you Gus. I have never felt this way before."

Not replying, he holds her tight with one arm, with his chin pressing on her head. With his other arm, he strokes her dark wavy hair.

"I love you too my dear."

While tears of joy run down her cheeks and sodden his shirt, she lifts her head up to face him.

"I'm sorry If I act forward. I don't know what's happening to me."

His reply is to place his hand under her chin, and plant a soft kiss on her moist lips.

"You are awakening."

"Awakening?"

"Yes, you are awakening from the sleep of indifference, apathy, and insecurity. Your eyes are opening to what is coming."

Confused by this profound statement, she rests her head back against his chest. Even though unsure if he loves her in the same way, she is in a euphoric daze. Not caring anymore about the outside world, she is where she wants to be. The intoxicating smell of his open shirt and the irresistible urge of wanting him are overwhelming her. As he strokes her hair again, she squeezes him tight. Her whole body aching for him, she lifts her face to meet his. Her lips parting with this uncontrollable need, their lips fuse together. As their mouths open to greet each other, she is unable to control this overwhelming yearning. In a new frenzy, she pulls apart his shirt and begins kissing his bare chest and nipples. Sensing he is on the same page, she runs the tip of her tongue over the tanned skin. Working her way lower to his stomach muscles, she lays her hand on his swollen crotch.

He does love me!

Wanting her to go further, he cries out.

"Oh, Eva."

Unable to hold back any longer, her delicate hand begins unzipping his fly...

As if coming out of a dream, he pulls away.

"I can't!"

Bewildered, but still floating in a glorious haze, she attempts to place her hand again on his swollen crotch.

"Why? I can 'feel' that you want me!".

Suppressing his overpowering craving for what she is offering, he is reluctant to withdraw. Instead, he guides her over to one of the wooden chairs.

"I'm sorry.This just isn't right. It's all too sudden."

She sits. Bewildered, but still hankering, she hides her head into her hands.

"W-what are you saying?"

New tears of disappointment returning, she looks up at him and points to the cot.

"I love you! I want to do what every woman in love does."

Ignoring her plea, he drags the other chair so he can sit opposite her. Shaking with frustration, she gazes at his flushed face as he sits down opposite.

"I love you Eva. More than you will ever know."

"Then why…"

"Pull away? Refusing your offer?"

Their knees touching, he takes hold of both her hands.

"I have an enormous task ahead of me. It wouldn't be fair to you."

She does not see it that way, as she brings his hands up to her cheek, and then places them on her tingling breasts.

"My God! What more could you want? My whole body is aching for."

Her seductive warmth radiating up his arm is making it extra difficult in him releasing his hands.

"For two pins. I would lay you on that cot and…"

"Then why don't you?"

While she sits in a daze, he stands and paces the room.

"I've just told you. You will always be in my heart. Right now, I cannot offer you anymore than that."

Disenchanted, she stands and goes to the nearest wall. The pain becoming unbearable she faces the wall, and looks down at the floor.

"All I did was come round to see if you were okay after you passed out at the

rally, and I get all this."

Staring at her hour glass figure , the pain in his insides and the burning urge to love her is tearing him apart.

This is the first time in my life I have felt this way for a woman. Only my love for Mary Magdalene is anyway comparable. Last time Mary was with me all the time, was until my crucifixion and beyond. This time I'm torn between the love for Eva and my mission, which is graver than ever before…

He takes a deep breath to keep calm, and clear his head..

"As you can see I am now fi – oops, I almost used that word again."

As she is still facing the wall, his attempt to humor her is not easing the pain of yearning. Still trying to stay calm, he comes up to her. Standing close behind, his gentle hands reach out and grip her slender waist.

"I appreciate your concern by coming to see me. I still feel very tired,

294

but by morning I will be fi - recharged."

Realizing now how he must feel, she decides to be more positive by turning to face him. Looking down at his hands still hanging onto her waist, she then looks him in the eye.

"I 'think' I understand now how important your mission is. What I do know is that I love you now and will always love you. It must be difficult suppressing your feelings toward me, but its not half as hard as me aching with frustration and unable to fulfill my dream.That said, I need to sit down."

Finding it hard to release his hands, she moves away from him and sits in one of the dining chairs. The warmth of her waist now dissipating, he comes over to her and stands by the table. Both can't find the right words to calm their passion, until she decides to look up at him, and sound rational.

"How come you collapse every time you - help someone?"

Pleased she is making the first move, he takes her hand and sits on the table edge.

"Unfortunately, it takes an enormous amount of energy to help these poor souls. The more I do, the more exhausted I become.."

With the memory of her being 'helped' on the church stage, she stands, and faces him between his open legs.

"So when you - saved me, you completely collapsed."

Remembering that time, his face turns grave, and his eyes become tense.

"You were dying my love. It took everything I had."

Her need for him returning, she puts her hand up to his cheek.

"Doesn't God give you your strength?"

"Of course, but I am still a man. I feel and do as any man."

Her hand now stroking his face, she leans toward him and plants a soft kiss on his cheek.

"I know. Look at us now."

Her being this close and the kiss radiating, he is struggling..

"Unfortunately, my mission is more than any other man's."

Looking deep into his apprehensive eyes, her hand trembles a little as she continues to stroke his cheek.

"I'm scared for you."

Unable to take her closeness anymore, he reaches up to her hand and brings it down to his thigh.

"Don't be. I know this must be difficult for you. I also know it has not come at a good time in your life, especially after your husband deserted you."

This startles her.

"How on earth did you...?"

Ignoring the question, he continues.

"Now it's only you and Ryan, you threw yourself headfirst into your new job."

Still wondering how he can know about her private life, she looks at him in amazement. Studying his face for anymore surprises, she asks the obvious.

"Why me?"

Concerned her voice sounds fearful, he leans up off the table and pulls her towards him. Relishing her softness against him and her smell, he pleads.

"Because you are my last and only love. Please understand, I need you so much to be with me on this, I need your help in every way. When this is all over, perhaps we can become a couple again. I'll give you any strength you need."

His voice soft against her ear, he holds her even closer.

"Will you promise to help me?"

Suppressing how she really feels, she rests her head on his shoulder.

"You know I will."

While their bodies fuse together in each other's arms, Gus is already judging his moment of human weakness.

38

A Change of Program

It is the following day at 7:30 in the evening. The President is sitting in her favorite armchair positioned opposite the wide 8K,UHD screen television. Julie, her twelve-year-old daughter, is sitting on the floor leaning against this comfortable armchair by her mother's legs. While the President demonstrates her affection by stroking her daughter's dark brown wavy hair, she wants to relieve the tedium.

"Why on earth are you making me watch a trashy show like this? It's not as if I have nothing to do."

Biting her lip in anticipation, Julie turns to her mother.

"Mother? You know why!They've been advertising it all day..."

The commercials fade. The President releases the mute button on the remote control. As harsh music bellows out of the surround speakers, she adjusts the volume. A tall man in his mid-fifties appears on the screen. His dyed, short, cropped brown hair looks out of place on his pale, lined weary face. His capped teeth reflect as he smiles at the hyped-up studio audience. To attract more attention, he raises his deep rasping voice above the audience's cheers and whistles.

"Ladies and gentlemen! This is me, Walter Cameron, as usual on Mondays and Wednesdays with our hard hitting show: IS THIS TRUE!'"

Now capturing the audience's full attention, he lowers his voice to a more moderate tone.

"Modesty restrains me from telling you - but I will anyway. For the last six months this show has been rated number one across the nation..."

He times his pause while the audience show their appreciation by cheering and applauding; spurred on of course by the 'Applause' guy of the camera crew.

The audience now in his control, Walter speaks.

"I cannot imagine there could be anyone out there who have never seen me or this show before..."

He takes a another pause to let them all laugh, and then continues.

"I will explain for any new viewers how we work here. This show is live, and I mean 'live'. I do not mean taped live, or a five-second delay, but 'real' live. We don't want to edit or bleep out the naughty bits.What would be the point?"

His audience responds by more of the expected jeers and whistles.

Appearing comfortable at being in control, he continues.

"Stuff happens folks. As you may know, we invite a guest or guests that are in the headlines or the public eye. The more controversial these guests are, the better for the show. After all, we are here to find the truth. I ask direct questions. No beating about the bush, all to see if these people are honest and sincere, and not full of −b − baloney."

To allow more cheering from the still hyped up audience, he pauses again, and then maneuvers toward two sturdy leather armchairs. He leans against one and faces the appropriate camera.

"Tonight, our guest is a very controversial figure indeed. If any of you out there watched TV last night or were at the rally at the Hammer Stadium, you will know who I'm talking about."

Julie, still glued to the screen is now bubbling with excitement.

"It's Gus, Mother."

Mother strokes her daughter's head again. This time to calm her. Not wanting to be sitting in front of the TV looking at the trashiest show of the week, but as its for her daughter, she resigns to what's coming. In the meantime, Walter Cameron continues his agenda on the wide screen.

"He calls himself Gus. Please give him a big hand folks."

While Gus appears on screen wearing a faded blue tee shirt and jeans, there is an assortment of cheers and jeers as he makes his way toward the leather armchairs. Meanwhile, Julie shrieks.

"Oh Mother!Isn't he wonderful?"

Her patience limited , the President observes the camera scanning the TV audience and then zooming in for a second to a handsome young man with dark curly hair, a tanned complexion and green eyes. While sitting three rows back from the front center, his face expresses a calm smirk. The picture changes to a close-up of Gus, and then zooms back showing Gus and Walter sitting relaxed in the armchairs in front of a backdrop of a huge bright colored picture of Gus in a candid, passionate pose. Being the ego of the show,Walter speaks first.

"Welcome to our show Gus."

Gus's reaction after glancing at the curious crowd is to look straight at Walter.

"Thank you for having me."

Even though he is still talking to Gus, Walter looks away to face the camera.

"Now, as I tell everyone who comes on this show, we have not rehearsed, or are we scripted in any way."

Determined to make eye contact with Walter, Gus keeps looking to get Walter's full attention.

"That is correct."

Unnerved a little by his guest's direct gaze, Walter does make eye contact, but has a tendency to look away again.

"We also agreed earlier that I could fire any question at you, and that you will give me and the viewers an honest and direct answer."

"That is also correct."

Walter finds it easier to look at the camera, and not at Gus.

"There you have it folks. It's going to be a great show. So, don't go away. We'll be right back after the break."

Eva and Ryan are curled up together on the old sofa watching the same program. Her emotions on edge, and her mind in need of reassurance, she slides her arm around his shoulder to hug him. His reaction is to sink lower into her softness and rest his head against the front of her shoulder.

"Its great you don't have to work tonight Mom. We can watch Gus together." Listening to his genuine appreciation, tears of gratitude well up in her eyes. She holds him a bit closer so she can rest her chin on his short curly head. His smell filling her nostrils, she answers.

"Yes, honey. It's great."

The commercials end, the show returns, and Walter appears on screen. Trying to give an air of being relaxed, he taps into his experience in working the audience.

"Welcome back everyone. Tonight's guest is more unusual than normal..."

Still not looking at Gus, he appears troubled. Or, is it an act to throw his guest? In this case, he is hiding his annoyance by wondering if this audience has noticed how he is finding it difficult to look Gus in the eye. To compensate, he flashes another false smile at the camera, and then turns toward his guest.

"Well, Gus. I will start the ball rolling. By asking you two important questions. Question one. Are you 'really' Jesus of Nazareth....?" He pauses to raise his voice, emphasizing the sarcasm. "...who has returned to save the world?"

His bright hazel eyes not giving anything away, Gus is aware of the quiet audience waiting with bated breath for him to answer. Instead of catching Walter's eye, Gus stares at the audience, and keeps his voice calm.

"Yes, I am."

There is a few seconds pause while this answer sinks in, and then the audience erupts with a mixture of cheers, boos and jeers. Meanwhile, Walter smirks, and times his pause before interceding. Observing Gus unaffected by the loud reaction, Walter raises his hand to the studio audience. Being in total control, the noise abates until there is just a few murmurs and whispers remaining. Expecting this reaction, Gus remains undisturbed and awaits the next question. Aware of his guest continuing to stare him down, the presenter's smirk turns into a false smile. Gauging the audience, who is eager for the next onslaught, Walter continues with his false smile. Now appearing to make eye contact, and bolstered on by the occasional jeer, Walter looks Gus in the eye.

"Okay! For now we will presume you are who you say you are. Question number two. Is the world 'really' going to end in one year?"

As loud curious murmurs rebound from the audience, the camera zooms in for a close-up, as every eye is focusing on Gus.

"Only if everyone carries on in the same old way."

The puzzled audience falls silent, and become restless. In his element, Walter turns to them for more support. The smirk returning, he turns to Gus.

"Okay! What you're saying is that we all have to go to church on Sundays, and be good at Christmas...?"

The audience now laughing with him, Walter pauses, and changes tactics. He focuses more on the audience than Gus, by offering them a wink with his right eye and producing a sarcastic smile.

"How on earth can you save the world with your warning when - say ninety or even more percent don't even believe in you - or God or whatever?"

Anticipating the agreeing jeers from the audience, led by the handsome young man with the dark curly hair, Gus is still undisturbed by the question or the reaction. He replies before the audience quiets down.

"I know the percentages, but there is a lot more to it than that."

Now bored with the audience, Walter turns on Gus.

"More? Explain to us heathens what you mean!"

Enjoying the entertaining way Walter is trying to belittle Gus, the audience bursts into laughter. Waiting for everyone to calm down, Gus is learning to time his answers as Walter does his questions.

"As I have said, my mission is to 'warn', regardless of beliefs or culture. The human race 'has' to change. The corporate greed, global warming, and the suffering and abuse of ordinary people for power and financial gain has to stop."

Walter's reaction is to shake his head in disbelief and smirk again.

"All that sounds good in theory, but aren't you being a bit naïve...?"

Being led by the young man with green eyes, the audience begins to heckle and jeer. Drawn in by the provocative atmosphere, Walter takes advantage and continues by raising his voice.

"...sitting there and calmly issuing threat!"

Ignoring the jeers, Gus answers by raising his voice.

"No threats! I use the word 'warning'. But it has to start with the World leaders.

I am going to visit every powerful world leader, starting with your own President. She has kindly arranged for me to see her as soon as tomorrow."

The program cuts straight into commercials.

Meanwhile, in the White House, Julie turns to her mother

"I hate that Walter - Mother. I am excited for tomorrow. You will let me see Gus, won't you?"

Loving the enthusiasm radiating from her daughter, the President reassures by placing her hand on the young shoulder.

"Of course my dear. That is the least I can do, as you're the one that brought him to my attention."

The commercials finish, Walter appears on screen.

"Well Gus, as you have an appointment tomorrow with our 'beloved' President, it will be interesting to see how 'she' reacts to all of this. Our fine 'Lady' President is a touch kooky. She is not known for her listening qualities, so I hope she listens to you, or - we are 'all' doomed."

The audience reacts by bursting into laughter. Playing up to them, Walter changes his expression to a more serious tone.

"Now, on a slightly different note..."

He turns back to Gus.

"...it has been observed that you have performed som – err – miracles, quote, unquote."

Gus does not let the heavy sarcasm annoy or deter him.

"I have helped some people in need, yes."

Becoming irritated by Gus's calm disposition, and not rising to his bait, Walter pushes harder.

"I have also been informed that if the truth be told; you brought back Channel Six anchor Eva Brown from the dead."

In Eva's apartment, Ryan shouts out.

"He's talking about you Mom."

Gus appears onscreen in close-up.

"She was not dead! But she would have died, if she had been moved. So, I did what was necessary..."

Sarcasm continuing, Walter butts in.

"Oh! I did what was necessary? Boy - I like that one."

In the White House, Julie is becoming upset.

"Mother, they're mocking him."

Walter continues being relentless on screen.

"I don't know whether you know it or not my friend, but at this precise point in time there are at least one hundred million people watching this show. With such a great opportunity, why don't you prove to us right now on 'live' television that you are who you say you are. Go on; show us your real power..."

He turns to the audience like the showman he is, and raises his voice.

"....The power of God! Not just a small miracle, but something ''big' and magnificent in proportion to your outlandish claim."

The curly haired young man with the green eyes shouts out from the audience.

"He can't. He's a fake."

Seeming to recognize that voice, Gus turns to the audience. Now fired up like a mob, the impatient crowd begins to chant.

"Show us - prove it! Show us - prove it!"

Enjoying the power, Walter rises from his seat. Taking full advantage of this delicate situation, he steps over to Gus who is still seated, places his hand on Gus's shoulder, and raises his voice above the chanting, "Prove it to us right here and now to the millions of frustrated viewers that you really are – 'The Son of God'."

Caught up in the drama, the audience goes into an uproar with the young man leading them on. Wishing he wasn't here, and his face serious with apprehension, Gus rises from his seat.

Fearful for Gus, Ryan turns to his mother.

"Mom, what are they doing? He's not a circus act to perform tricks."

Hiding her own concern, Eva tries to calm him down.

"I guess they really want to know, honey."

"Like you, Mom?"

Back on the screen, the audience clamor out of their seats and begin charging toward the stage.

"Prove it! – Prove it!"

Sensing disaster about to happen, security guards rush on stage to protect Gus and Walter.

In the White House, Julie is so angry, she jumps up off the floor.

"Mother, this is disgusting. What is the matter with these stupid people?"

The President looks at her daughter, and then at the screen. She sighs in despair, and then answers.

"Unfortunately my dear, most people who have no faith are very demanding toward others who do have a faith. In this case they want instant proof."

On the screen, Walter is knocked over by some collapsing scenery. Gus is rescued and whisked off the set by a security guard. The screen goes blank. The show is canceled; replaced by commercials.

Backstage, Gus is shown into the Green Room, which is a small room situated adjacent to the studio. The noise of people tramping and shouting can still be heard everywhere. Making sure Gus is seated, the security guard becomes nervous.

"I've never seen anything like this before in my life."

While Gus tries to relax on a faded green sofa, he looks up in appreciation to the security guard who now seems lost. Standing by the open door, and not knowing what to do next, he gazes at Gus in a daze. Understanding the guard's situation, Gus asks a relevant question.

"How is Mr. Cameron? I saw him fall."

Still in a daze, the security guard turns to look out of the doorway to the empty hallway.

"I don't know sir. Perhaps I should find out."

Gus's reaction is to rise from the sofa, and step nearer the guard..

"Yes, you should. Don't worry about me. Clear the crowd. I can attend to Walter."

The security guard appears puzzled as well as dazed. Taking another glance at the empty hallway, he hesitates.

"I don't know about that sir. They may take him straight to...."

Interrupting, Gus walks toward him, and pleads.

"Do as I ask – please."

Overcome by an unusual trust in this man, the guard agrees.

"Okay. I'll try."

He disappears through the doorway. The noise seems more distant now, as Gus closes the door and walks back to the sofa. His thoughts are of the last twenty minutes and the disturbing familiar voice that heckled him from the audience.

In the White House still in her private rooms, the President is now seated behind a small desk speaking into her personal intercom.

"Frank? Could I see you for a minute? Thanks."

Julie becoming more agitated, is pacing back and forth on the carpet in front of the TV, now showing another program.

"I hope Gus is all right. That silly Walter Cameron, treating him like that..."

There is a knock on the room door. Frank enters. His face stoic.

"Ma'am?"

Not put off by Frank's cold persona, the President rises from her desk, but still stands behind it.

"I'm sorry to bother you Frank. Could you find out what the latest situation is concerning the Walter Cameron show?"

Special Agent Frank Jones tries hard to suppress a puzzled look on his face. His distaste of being, as he sees it, a black woman's messenger boy and gofer is hard to hide. The President as usual, senses his hidden attitude.

"Are you all right with that, Frank?"

"Err. - yes ma'am. I'll get communications onto it straight away."

"Thank you."

Not a happy man, Frank is at least discreet when leaving.

The television studio is now quiet, and the security staff has managed to clear the noisy crowd. Security guards are now focusing on a weak Walter Cameron lying on the green room floor. A kneeling guard holds a blood soaked towel on Walter's neck. Concerned about Walter's pallid complexion, the guard stares up at Gus.

"I've called for an ambulance to take Mr. Cameron to the hospital. It's his jugular vein, it seems badly ruptured."

Knowing what to do, Gus bends down next to him.

"There is no need for an ambulance."

The guard looks dumbstruck.

"But sir, he's bleeding like a pig. He needs urgent attention."

Gus glares at him.His hazel eyes beaming straight into the man's brain, seems reassuring.

"That is exactly what he's going to get. Now all you other guards make sure the studio is clear and locked, and then leave us! Thank you for your help."

The guards hesitate.

"Are you sure sir?"

Gus is short with them,

"Yes, I am sure! Now please go, and thank you."

While they leave, Gus turns to the kneeling guard.

"What's your name?"

"Fred."

"All right Fred, go into the bathroom and get another towel, and bring it to me - now!"

As Fred scuttles toward the bathroom, Gus takes over by holding the blood-saturated towel against the ugly gash on Walter's neck. A puddle of blood is spreading on the carpet as Fred returns, carrying a clean terry towel.

"Thank you Fred."

Walter's breathing is shallow, and his face a ghostly pallor, as Gus folds the new towel into four, and then places it on the oozing wound. Within seconds, the towel becomes crimson. Not appearing concerned, Gus lowers his head over Walter. Closing his eyes, he places one hand on Walter's forehead and his other on the towel. Pushing the towel firm against Walter's pale neck, Gus mumbles. The sweat drips off his forehead as he lowers his head and kisses Walter's temple. Transfixed by what he is witnessing, Fred is mesmerized by Gus soft murmurs.

"God loves you..."

Gus then collapses on the floor, next to Walter. Still transfixed, Fred witnesses the crimson towel fall off Walter, exposing a clean neck with a dried up wound. Fred snaps out of his trance and kneels next to Walter, who is now trying to say something. Walter's eyes now opening, and his voice soft and husky, he gazes up at Fred.

"Fred?"

"Yessir."

Walter tries to hold onto Fred for support, as he struggles to sit up.

"What am I doing in here? Why am I on the floor?"

He sees Gus lying next to him.

"What's he doing here?"

As Walter is being helped to the sofa, he notices all the blood..

"What the hell has been going on here?"

"Quite a bit."

While Gus is coming around, he becomes desperate in trying to sit up, but collapses again. Wanting to help, Fred crouches down to assist a weary Gus in sitting up. After a few seconds, he then helps him to the sofa. In the meantime, Walter is becoming bewildered.

"Will someone tell me what the hell's going on?"

Making sure both men are all right, Fred stands in front of them both and tries to explain.

"Well, sir, when some of the audience rushed on stage..."

"Yes, I remember that..."

Fred continues.

"A large piece of scenery fell on you giving you a nasty gash on your neck making you bleed some."

His patience waning, Walter feels his neck.

"What gash?"

As his fingers touch the dried up wound, he looks at Gus.

"All I can feel is a rough piece of skin. Did you get hurt?"

Fred speaks before Gus is able to answer.

"You see sir, you were bleeding real bad like, hell, and you were almost a goner, when - err..."

"Yes? What then?"

Fred points to an exhausted Gus.

"He cured you by stopping the bleeding. Geez, Mr. Cameron, you were almost dead. I mean, look at all the blood."

To study the huge bloodstain on the carpet and the blood soaked towels, Walter is a little unsteady when rising from the sofa.

"Is that...?"

"Yessir! It's all yours."

Becoming incredulous, Walter sits back down in the sofa with a heavy thump "Jesus Christ!"

Realizing what he has just said, he looks at Gus.

"Sorry! Hell! What am I saying?"

While Walter is in a state of shock, a phone rings. Fred rushes over to the opposite wall and picks up a dark green wall phone.

"Hello, security. Yes, Oh, I'll put you on to him."

With an excited look on his face, Fred beckons Walter to the phone. Puzzled, Walter takes it. He keeps his voice casual.

"Hello? This is Walter Cameron. Who? The President?"

He involuntarily stands to attention.

"Yes! Sure. Yessir – err - ma'am, I'm fine..."

He peers at Gus.

"He's fine also. Yes, I did get hurt, quite badly it seems."

He fingers the scar and turns again in awe at Gus.

"You could say it was a miracle ma'am. Thank you. I appreciate it."

Appearing a little shaken, he hangs up the phone.

"Well, gentlemen. That was our President inquiring as to my well being. She saw me get hurt on TV. Anyway, you heard what I said."

Calming down a little, he turns to Gus putting out his hand.

"Young man, I owe you a big apology. I hope you'll accept it, because I never apologize to anyone."

While Gus struggles to get up out of the sofa, Walter helps him and shakes his hand. As tears of gratitude fill Walter's eyes, he grabs Gus and hugs him.

"I owe you big time. I would like to put you back on my show again, and do you justice. You understand what I'm saying?"

Appreciating the hug, Gus smiles, and is reluctant to separate.

"I understand. I will need you soon. More than you realize."

Feeling. A little left out, Fred puts his hand out to Gus.

"I also would like to shake your hand sir. What you did tonight was beyond the call. If there is any way I can help you on this mission of yours, you know where to find me."

Appreciating the gesture, and the offer, Gus shakes his hand.

"Thank you Fred, I won't forget you. We all need to go beyond the call for what is to come. Well gentlemen, now I must bid you farewell."

As he heads toward the door, Fred beats him to it.

"Let me check to see if its safe."

Gus stands back while Fred unlocks the studio door, steps out and inspects the immediate area.

"Okay out here."

After taking few steps outside, Gus glances back to Walter and Fred with a wave. Never seeing Walter smile like this before, Fred is amused when Walter turns to face him.

"Well, Fred, it has been quite a night. Do you know, I feel quite hungry? How about you treating us to a pizza?"

"Sure."

"Just kidding, I'm buying."

Rolling his eyes in relief, Fred offers his new friend a bemused smile. As they leave the studio, and begin walking down the long echoing corridor, Walter stops and grabs Fred's forearm.

"Did you notice something about Gus, Fred?"

"What's that, Mr. Cameron?"

"He had a sort of blue haze around his head as he left."

"Yeah, I noticed that too"

39

Understanding

The old oak-rimmed clock on the wall of Gus's sparse room is showing midnight. He is laying on his back in his little bed staring up at the ceiling in a trance. While meditating, he is going through the events of the past few hours. His body stiff and sore, his energy low, but rising, he is startled out of his dreamlike state by a knock on his door.

"It's open."

While he struggles to lift his aching body to switch on the bedside lamp, the dooropens. Standing in the doorway, Eva's face is sad, and her eyes look bloodshot. Concerned about her predicament, he manages to stand and present her with a welcoming smile.

"Don't just stand there, enter."

Her eyes filling with fresh tears, she rushes into his opening arms. Relishing her warmth and her burying her face into his chest, he can feel his sweatshirt moisten with her tears.

"Hey? What's all this? You okay?"

His sweater now drenched, he strokes her hair until her weeping subsides. After a short while, she pulls away a little to lift her head up to face him.

"Thank God you're safe. I am so sorry."

Never seeing her this bad before, he strokes her cheek as if to wipe away the tears.

"For what?"

"I watched you being humiliated on that awful show tonight. Why did you let them do it to you?"

To answer, he holds her at arms length.

"I was expecting to be put through the wringer. However, some good did come out of it."

Aching for him, she resists his hold and leans back against his chest.

"Shows like that give TV a bad name. Max has been trying to get it off the air. Unfortunately, that kind of trash is hugely popular with the general public."

Thinking back to the show, he can understand. Not giving his opinion, he offers her a wry smile.

"Doesn't say much for the general public."

She responds by pulling away, and wiping her face with her hand.

"Isn't that why you're here? To straighten us all out?"

After a pause, he answers.

"Yes, I am..."

He leaves her to pull one of his little wooden chairs toward her.

"As you're here, can I offer you a chair ma'am?"

It is obvious to her, he is trying to put her mind at rest. She responds accordingly.

"Don't mind if I do."

While she sits, he grabs the other chair and places it opposite her. Their knees touching, he takes one of her hands in his.

"Better now?"

Wiping away an escaping tear, she nods, and searches his eyes for a warmer response.

"I heard through the grapevine that you saved Walter Cameron. Do you think he was worth it after the way he treated you?"

"It's not a question of worth. I don't pass judgment. He needed help, so I helped him..."

"Like you helped me?"

"Yes."

"I'm beginning to understand, but its hard."

Her heart palpitating, she brings his hands to her mouth and showers them with little gentle kisses, and then caresses them with her cheek.

"I wish I didn't love you so much, but I'm beginning to understand much more now. That's why I've come here to see you – to tell you."

As his eyes penetrate her soul, and seem to fill the room, she notices a small tear forming in the corners. Her heart feeling as if it is about to burst, she leans forward and plant a soft gentle kiss on his quivering mouth. Observing his eyes are now full of tears, she responds by standing and wrapping her arms around his neck.

"God knows how much I love you..."

She pulls his head into the softness of her heaving breasts.

"Why is it so hard for you to let me love you?"

Sensing his struggle, she releases him, and helps by conveying to him a reassuring smile.

"I'm sorry. I'm not being fair. I'm here for you in what ever capacity you require."

Missing her warmth, he looks up at her with a mournful expression.

"I'm sorry too for involving you this far."

Struggling to control this overwhelming passion, she acts casual while sitting back in her chair.

"I see you're going to visit the President in a few hours."

Grateful for her support, he wipes his eyes, and glances up at the clock.

"Ten o'clock literally! I suppose I ought to be getting some snooze time. I should not really show up at the White House with more bags than I need."

Blinking his eyes to make the point, causes her to smile. Even though the mood is lighter, her constant ache remains. After a pause, she gets up from her little wooden chair.

"Maybe I can assist in some way."

His body complaining, he takes his time to rise from his wooden chair. Leaning on the chair for support, he presence her with a reassuring smile.

"Oh, I'll be all right. Even though I may I have some convincing to do,

I'm actually looking forward to it. I know her daughter Julie will help."

Now her turn to reassure him, she touches his arm.

"All the media will be waiting on the lawn of the Rose Garden."

Preoccupied by thinking ahead, Gus makes a suggestion.

"I know one way you can help me! Is Ryan all right?"

"Sure. He's in the car sleeping. I couldn't leave him at home alone."

His imagination working overtime, a broad smile of relief spreads across his face.

"That's perfect. Can I take him with me to the White House?"

Wondering what he is up to, she gives him a puzzled look.

"How can he help you?"

His face now brimming with excitement, he grips her face and plants a soft. Kiss on her forehead.

"Ryan knows who I am. As Julie also knows, it is to be hoped that together they will convince Madam President."

Even though he seems confident about tomorrow, she can't help but notice the dark shadows appearing under his eyes. To make sure he rests, she makes her way toward the door.

"I'll have you son ready for you. How do you know about the President's daughter?"

Not giving anything away, he conveys to her a wry grin. Realizing straight away, she shakes her head.

"I don't know why I ask such dumb questions."

His grin turning into an affectionate smile, Gus replies.

"I guess that comes from working for television."

Even though she appears more relaxed, he knows she is struggling with her emotions. He goes to her as she reaches the door. Exacerbating her reluctance to leave him, she grips his forearm

"I will drop Ryan here just before eight o'clock on my way to the studio. Is that okay?"

"That's wonderful."

Still struggling, a late thought enters her mind.

"Oh, there are two things I have to tell you before I go."

"Oh?"

"The first thing, Max has set up a website, Facebook page, and a twitter account for you. It's called – The Right Way to Go, dot Com. I will operate them for you. That's if you don't mind?"

"Of course I don't mind. It all sounds so good. Please thank Max for me. The second thing?"

She hesitates, looks away for a second, and then turns back to face him.

"I know now you're Jesus, but I love you as the man standing here in front of me; not someone who lived over two thousand years ago."

For once he is speechless, but his eyes express it all.

"One day you will understand. Until then, I'll see you tomorrow or rather today."

Regardless of what he is trying to explain to her, the urgent need to love him is her top priority. Before she leaves, the irresistible urge to kiss him takes over.

His lips still radiating her warmth, he leans against the open doorway as tears of foreboding begin to fill his eyes again. Watching her elegant body sway toward the front door of the church, he shuts his eyes, making the tears roll down his face.

I love you Eva! Be patient my love; all will be revealed.

40

The White House Gets the Blues

The President is seated behind the famous large walnut desk in the Oval Office. For some reason she feels nervous. To counteract this disposition, she begins to tidy her desk, even though she didgeridoo same action ten minutes earlier. Meanwhile, Julie is gazing out of the West window. She also is restless, excited and nervous all in one. Rolling her eyes with exasperation, she turns to face her mother.

"Mother that is the third time you have rearranged your desk!"

"I know dear. You know how I like things to be just right. It leaves less room for criticism."

As she squares up the last item, there is a knock on the main door. Acting relaxed and in control, the President leans back into her heavy desk chair, and calls out.

"Come in!"

Demonstrating the same ill-disguised arrogance, Frank stands just inside the open door.

"He's here. Shall I send him in?"

"I presume you mean Gus."

"Yes - Ma'am."

"Show him in then - please."

With the same casual air, Frank turns, opens the door wider, and exits. On closing the door, Julie steps up to her mother.

"Mother? You must get rid of Frank. He has no respect."

"I will dear, but it's not that easy. The trouble is I understand how hard it must be for him to take orders from a woman, especially a black woman...
"

There is another knock on the main door.

"Come in."

As Frank enters with Gus and Ryan, the President rises from her desk and comes around with her hand stretched out for a formal greeting. At the same time, Frank turns to leave, but the President stops him.

"Frank! I wish to see you when our guests leave."

Frank's reaction is to just about nod, and then begins to leave. Not accepting Frank's casual, and intimidating attitude, the President insists on being heard.

"Did you hear me Frank?"

He stops in his tracks with his back still facing her. He is reluctant to answer.

"Yes – Ma'am."

While he leaves and closes the door, Gus smiles at the President.

"Your man seems to have a job satisfaction problem."

As the President shakes his hand, grins back at him, and notices his piercing hazel eyes, she reciprocates..

"More of a job attitude problem I'm afraid, which I will deal with appropriately..."

Gesturing her daughter to come and stand next to her, she presence Gus with a deeper, sincere smile.

"Anyway, it is a pleasure to meet you. This is my daughter Julie."

Just as Julie's excitement is bursting out of every pore, her soft hand trembles as she holds it out to greet Gus.

"It's so good of you come."

"My pleasure Julie. I know all about you."

In replying, her voice almost squeaks as the words try to leave her tight throat.

"You do?"

317

"Yes! And this is Ryan, a very good friend of mine."

Being shy in front of such famous company, Ryan steps forward.

"Hi."

Taking an instant liking to this young lad, Julie forgets any decorum and slides her arm around his shoulder. As everyone in the room seem lost for words, Julie takes the lead by releasing her grip on Ryan and going straight to Gus.

"Thank God you've arrived...."

Before Gus realizes what is happening, she throws her arms around his waist and buries her face into his chest. Overwhelmed by the trust of this young girl, he places hishand on her head.

"Yes, Julie. I have arrived."

After a few seconds, she lifts her head to face him.

"Thank you for being here for us."

After a friendly pat on the head from Gus, she is reluctant to let go. Seeing Ryan appearing a little lost, she goes back to him and wraps her arm in his. In the meantime, she becomes aware of her mother's embarrassment at her exuberant behavior.

"I'm sorry Mother, but I'm so happy!"

Needing to control this tenuous situation, Julie's mother turns to Ryan with a look of recognition.

"Aren't you Ryan, the son of the Channel Six anchor?"

Ryan answers with a wide toothy grin.

"Yeah. Ain't it great?"

Still caught up in her own swirl of excitement, Julie blurts out.

"My father...."

She hesitates, and then looks at her mother's tight expression.

"Shall I tell Gus what Father always used to say?"

Hiding her irritation, she snaps back at her daughter.

"Gus doesn't want to hear all that, dear."

His eyes awash with affection, Gus's reaction is to gaze at Julie.

"You mean your father, John?"

Failing to keep her surprise in check, Julie's mother's eyes widen.

"How did..."

Ignoring the surprised expression, Gus continues by looking into the President's hesitant brown eyes.

"Your husband was a very perceptive man. His death was unfortunate."

As the memories of her beloved father come flooding back, Julie's eyes sadden. With a burst of emotion, she turns on Gus.

"Why didn't you save him if he was so special? Like you saved all those other people?"

The President's face tightens at her daughter's outburst.

"Julie! Where are your manners? You don't talk to a guest like that!"

Julie's reaction is to burst into tears, put her hands up to her face and turn away.

"I'm so sorry. Please forgive me. I just loved him so much."

Somehow understanding her pain, Ryan slides his arm around her, while Gus steps up to her, and rests his hand on her shoulder.

"I love him also. He is at rest now, no more pain or suffering. He is now within you guiding your heart to do the right thing, which is important now, because you have to carry on his message for me. You, Ryan and all the other children, who see me as I really am, are the ones that hold the future..."

There is a knock at the door. Without waiting for the usual permission to enter, the door opens and Frank walks in wheeling a trolley full of refreshments. His stoic expression challenging his boss, his eyes soften a little.

"I thought maybe some refreshments were in order, Ma'am."

Hiding her surprise, the President conveys to him a grateful smile.

"You thought right! Thank you Frank. Please place them by the window will you?"

As he pushes the trolley over to the window, he nods to Julie's mother, as if he has just won a long standing confrontation. Taking his time, he turns, smiles at everyone, and then heads for the door to leave. While the President is analyzing Frank's new attitude, Ryan is the first to reach the trolly and say something.

319

"Ooo, cookies, and sandwiches, and...."

Reminding her new friend where he is, Julie pats him on the shoulder. While the President surveys the scene, she and Gus can't help but grin at Ryan's impulsiveness.

"All right, children. If you care to help yourselves while Gus and I talk. Please do not drop crumbs on the Oval Office carpet."

Julie's response to the 'order' is to whisper to Ryan.

"Ever have that feeling you're in the way?"

Ryan rolls his eyes in agreement.

"Many times. Let's eat."

Just as the eager children dip into the food trolley, the President guides Gus to an upright armchair.

"Please."

As Gus sits in the leather comfort, she drags up a smaller chair and sits opposite him. Her knees almost touching his, he is surprised at the sudden informal behavior. Endeared by the closeness, he studies her while she is settling on the chair. Her lush, dark brown wavy hair has highlights of gray, which catch the light. Her trim, but well covered frame now comfortable, her steady eyes search into his. As the earlier nervousness is disappearing, she looks down as if she were a shy young girl instead of a woman in her early forties.

"I hope you do not think this is strange behavior for a President? I find this is my favorite way of talking close to someone. My beloved father taught me as a young girl and I have done it ever since."

Intrigued her old habit coincides with his, he can't help but offer her a reassuring smile.

"Me too."

Meanwhile, Julie and Ryan are busy filling their young mouths with edible goodies. In between bites Julie whispers to Ryan.

"Can you still see the blue?"

Having no trouble in swallowing a bite of ham sandwich, Ryan answers.

"Yeah, I always see it. It's odd. It's there, but it's not there. Do you know what I mean?"

"Yes. I know."

While they continue enjoying the food, the President is talking in hushed tones.

"I have been following your activities very closely recently. To tell you the truth, I'm amazed, and yet confused at what I've seen and heard."

"In what way are you confused?"

"Well, I heard what you did to Ryan's mother, and how well you handled that awful demonstration, but..."

Sensing she is having a hard time accepting all this, Gus places one of his hands on hers.

"I do what I can to help while I'm here, but the big message starts here – now!"

Feeling a new burden, she drops her head for a couple of seconds, and then raises it to meet his gaze.

"Yes, I know..."

As if an unbeatable bond is developing, she lays her free hand on top of his.

"I want you to tell me everything, so I can do what I can to help."

In the meantime, Ryan and Julie are pretending not to listen. Their new bond unfolding, and not wanting to be overheard, Ryan whispers to Julie.

"They're doing the big talking now."

Crunching on a crisp cookie, Julie whispers back.

"I know. I expect it's about Gus's warning."

Helping to reduce more ham sandwiches, Ryan whispers back.

"My mom believes him now. She didn't for a while, but I always did."

Expressing in her eyes the warmth toward this nine year old boy, Julie agrees.

"So did I."

Meanwhile, Gus leans closer to the President.

"As I've been saying all along, the greed, corruption, persecution and exploitation, of the majority of the world's population has got to end. It is up to you and the rest of the world's leaders to come together to strike it all out. Otherwise, 'everything' is going to end – in one year."

With a sudden sensation of impotence racking her insides, she stares into his blazing eyes.

"But a year? That's hardly anytime at all?"

Ignoring her sudden lack of fearlessness, Gus continues.

"In the slow grind of politics this is true. But these politicians must rise to the occasion. This is the 'final' big picture."

Her vulnerability seeping through any confidence she once had, he responds by squeezing her hand with an affection he hopes will strengthen her resolve. Until that happens, a look of helplessness appears in her eyes.

"I could talk to Congress by introducing you and beg them to pass new laws or even declare a state of emergency. Unfortunately, we would both be laughed out of the building. The other world leaders would face the same predicament.

The few good people who are fighting for what is right, are always struggling. The few, strong hard liners are corrupt; the rest are apathetic, or powerless. But, for a few loyal friends, most of Congress resents me. I am in power because I was elected Vice President. I moved into this office under the worst scenario of the President being murdered by an extreme white supremacist organization. I always believed that trumped up former president who has ruined this country, was behind the killing, but have no proof. I am also resented as a young - black woman - in a white man's world..."

She pauses to get her mind straight.

"And another thing, most people do not believe who you really are. All right, they have seen you – 'do' things, but to say you are Jesus Christ who has come back to warn the World - is a hard pill to swallow."

His illusions becoming a little shattered, Gus appears shaken by her statement. Undeterred, from his ultimate goal, Gus compensates.

"I understand it's not easy. But do 'you' believe who I really am?"

While still holding her hands, she fumbles to find the right words.

"I...."

Needing to step up the pressure, he commands.

"Look at my hands."

As her confused face looks down, the nail scars begin to appear on his wrists. She has to let go, as if his hands are too hot to handle. Her eyes now filling with tears of confusion, she places one hand up to her face as if she is ashamed of her doubt. With the other hand, she touches the angry scars with the tip of her fingers, as her tears drip onto his skin.

"I am so sorry I doubted. It really is you! But you are just a man."

"I was 'only' a man over two thousand years ago."

As the scars begin to fade, she rubs her tears into his hands.

"My powers are so limited and...."

While Julie has been listening with Ryan to all this 'big' talking, she seethes with frustration, and calls out to her mother.

"Mother? You are the President of the United States of America. You tell them what to do!"

Agreeing with his new found friend, Ryan demonstrates his excitement.

"Yeah! You tell 'em!"

Enthused by the youngsters, Gus looks deep in to the President's hesitant eyes.

"I will 'give' you that power. The strength to do only good. With this power and strength you have never known, you will lead in such a way that people will see you, as they ought to see you, a person of principle and right."

Ryan calls out.

"God bless the real America!"

Her doubt dissipating and a new confidence taking over, a strong sense of vision appears in her eyes. Her energy returning, she rises and begins to pace the lush carpeted floor.

"I will talk to Congress. No, I will 'tell' Congress enough is enough. The greed, suffering and exploitation have got to stop – NOW!"

As the children continue to cheer in excitement, Julie shouts.

"Yes, Mother! Yes!"

Becoming more caught up in this fervor, Ryan shouts in agreement.

"Yeah! Go for it!"

Her mind now racing, she stops pacing and looks at Gus.

"How are you going to travel to Europe, Asia, Russia, etc, with your message...?"

Before Gus has a chance to reply, she comes up with an idea.

"I know. I will supply you with Air Force One and all the assistance you need."

While Gus is amazed at such an offer, Ryan and Julie hold hands and do a little dance of joy around the floor, cheering as they go. Still in a daze, Gus tries to focus his mind.

"I am overwhelmed by your generosity and kindness."

Her enthusiasm overflowing, she turns to him.

"It is 'I' who is overwhelmed. I can see it all now. My husband kept saying that now was the right time for you to return and I just used to laugh at him. I was so blind."

Clenching her fists with this new vigor, she continues pacing the floor.

"While I get things going this end with Congress and the UN, I want you talk to the other leaders or whomever you need to talk to. When you return, I will arrange for you to address the UN General Assembly."

Still pacing, and deep in thought, she stops and looks at Gus.

"How about a meeting with the World Council of Churches?"

Admiring this woman in a new light, he asks the obvious.

"You can arrange that?"

To answer, she offers him a radiant smile that fills the room with her new confidence.

" Of course! The World Council of Churches is having their annual meeting here in the US at the new Madison Square Garden in New York, on the day before Good Friday. The reason the meeting is larger than normal is that this year is their eightieth anniversary of its conception. So, every Christian denomination will be there. Another reason they're in the Garden is that Muslim, Buddhists, Hindu and every other religion known to man has also been invited, in the belief that the wisdom of all these faiths put together may somehow bring peace and order to this hopeless collapsing world."

Visualizing the concept, Gus can see the challenge and opportunity that the meeting affords him, but is hesitant.

"Unfortunately, I know what the outcome will be, but I'll still be there."

Observing his hesitancy, Julie and Ryan come up to Gus and hug him in a way to give him the strength he needs. Appreciating their support, his eyes moisten, as he stretches out his hand to Julie's mother.

"I really cherish your support, and everything you are doing for me."

Gripping hold of his hands, she replies with the same emotion.

"Time is a scarce commodity right now. I will have you driven straight to Air Force One. In the meantime, I will contact my press secretary to publicize that you are traveling to see other world leaders with my blessing."

Even though nervous about the immediate future, he pulls this wondrous woman toward him and kisses her hands.

"I am, for always, your servant, as well as your strength."

The warmth of his hands radiating up her arms, she gazes into his grateful eyes.

"I am forever in 'your' debt for helping me to see clearly again. Thank you."

Reluctant to let go of his hands, she leans over her desk and presses a button on a panel. Within seconds there is a knock on the main door. The President responds.

"Come in."

Frank enters. He closes the door with his usual casual air and relaxes as he faces his boss.

"Ma'am?"

Now she is the President again, her pose becomes more formal.

"I want you to arrange for my guest here..."

Beckoning to Gus.

"...to be taken speedily to Air Force One, and see that he wants for nothing. Contact me as to the time of the final arrangements."

Frank's face turns from his usual casual arrogance to complete surprise.

"Air Force One? Ma'am?"

"Yes, Frank. Air Force One. NOW!"

Dumbfounded by this different woman, he hesitates before obeying.

"Yes, er – Ma'am!"

He looks at Gus, indicating the door.

"This way. Please - Sir."

While an astonished Gus heads to the door, the children step back and move toward the President. Before leaving the office, Gus stops and turns to face the President for one last acknowledgment. Now standing in between the two children, with her hands resting on their young shoulders, she conveys to Gus a final smile of appreciation, and encouragement.

"I will make sure Ryan gets home safely. It is not going to be easy for you out there."

Gus's smile fades to a look of mild apprehension.

"Being right never is."

As the door closes, the President crouches down to the children.

"Well? How did I do?"

Ryan can't help but chuckle.

"Like a real President – Ma'am."

While they all laugh together, Julie pauses expressing concern, and faces her mother.

"Mother?'

"Yes, dear?"

"Did you see the blue?"

Still crouching, she focuses on the children's inquisitive expressions.

"Yes, dear! When he first came into the room."

41

The Red Visit

The President is seated behind the famous large walnut desk in the Oval Office. For some reason she feels nervous. To counteract this disposition, she begins to tidy her desk, even though she didgeridoo same action ten minutes earlier. Meanwhile, Julie is gazing out of the West window. She also is restless, excited and nervous all in one. Rolling her eyes with exasperation, she turns to face her mother.

"Mother that is the third time you have rearranged your desk!"

"I know dear. You know how I like things to be just right. It leaves less room for criticism."

As she squares up the last item, there is a knock on the main door. Acting relaxed and in control, the President leans back into her heavy desk chair, and calls out.

"Come in!"

Demonstrating the same ill-disguised arrogance, Frank stands just inside the open door.

"He's here. Shall I send him in?"

"I presume you mean Gus."

"Yes - Ma'am."

"Show him in then - please."

With the same casual air, Frank turns, opens the door wider, and exits. On closing the door, Julie steps up to her mother

"Mother? You must get rid of Frank. He has no respect."

"I will dear, but it's not that easy. The trouble is I understand how hard it must be for him to take orders from a woman, especially a black woman..."

There is another knock on the main door.

"Come in."

As Frank enters with Gus and Ryan, the President rises from her desk and comes around with her hand stretched out for a formal greeting. At the same time, Frank turns to leave, but the President stops him.

"Frank! I wish to see you when our guests leave."

Frank's reaction is to just about nod, and then begins to leave. Not accepting Frank's casual, and intimidating attitude, the President insists on being heard.

"Did you hear me Frank?"

He stops in his tracks with his back still facing her. He is reluctant to answer.

"Yes – Ma'am."

While he leaves and closes the door, Gus smiles at the President.

"Your man seems to have a job satisfaction problem."

As the President shakes his hand, grins back at him, and notices his piercing hazel eyes, she reciprocates..

"More of a job attitude problem I'm afraid, which I will deal with appropriately..."

Gesturing her daughter to come and stand next to her, she presence Gus with a deeper, sincere smile.

"Anyway, it is a pleasure to meet you. This is my daughter Julie."

Just as Julie's excitement is bursting out of every pore, her soft hand trembles as she holds it out to greet Gus.

"It's so good of you come."

"My pleasure Julie. I know all about you."

In replying, her voice almost squeaks as the words try to leave her tight throat.

"You do?"

"Yes! And this is Ryan, a very good friend of mine."

Being shy in front of such famous company, Ryan steps forward.

"Hi."

Taking an instant liking to this young lad, Julie forgets any decorum and slides her arm around his shoulder. As everyone in the room seem lost for words, Julie takes the lead by releasing her grip on Ryan and going straight to Gus.

"Thank God you've arrived...."

Before Gus realizes what is happening, she throws her arms around his waist and buries her face into his chest. Overwhelmed by the trust of this young girl, he places hishand on her head.

"Yes, Julie. I have arrived."

After a few seconds, she lifts her head to face him.

"Thank you for being here for us."

After a friendly pat on the head from Gus, she is reluctant to let go. Seeing Ryan appearing a little lost, she goes back to him and wraps her arm in his. In the meantime, she becomes aware of her mother's embarrassment at her exuberant behavior.

"I'm sorry Mother, but I'm so happy!"

Needing to control this tenuous situation, Julie's mother turns to Ryan with a look of recognition.

"Aren't you Ryan, the son of the Channel Six anchor?"

Ryan answers with a wide toothy grin.

"Yeah. Ain't it great?"

Still caught up in her own swirl of excitement, Julie blurts out.

"My father...."

She hesitates, and then looks at her mother's tight expression.

"Shall I tell Gus what Father always used to say?"

Hiding her irritation, she snaps back at her daughter.

"Gus doesn't want to hear all that, dear."

His eyes awash with affection, Gus's reaction is to gaze at Julie.

"You mean your father, John?"

Failing to keep her surprise in check, Julie's mother's eyes widen.

"How did..."

Ignoring the surprised expression, Gus continues by looking into the President's hesitant brown eyes.

"Your husband was a very perceptive man. His death was unfortunate."

As the memories of her beloved father come flooding back, Julie's eyes sadden. With a burst of emotion, she turns on Gus.

"Why didn't you save him if he was so special? Like you saved all those other people?"

The President's face tightens at her daughter's outburst.

"Julie! Where are your manners? You don't talk to a guest like that!"

Julie's reaction is to burst into tears, put her hands up to her face and turn away.

"I'm so sorry. Please forgive me. I just loved him so much."

Somehow understanding her pain, Ryan slides his arm around her, while Gus steps up to her, and rests his hand on her shoulder.

"I love him also. He is at rest now, no more pain or suffering. He is now within you guiding your heart to do the right thing, which is important now, because you have to carry on his message for me. You, Ryan and all the other children, who see me as I really am, are the ones that hold the future...."

There is a knock at the door. Without waiting for the usual permission to enter, the door opens and Frank walks in wheeling a trolley full of refreshments. His stoic expression challenging his boss, his eyes soften a little.

"I thought maybe some refreshments were in order, Ma'am."

Hiding her surprise, the President conveys to him a grateful smile.

"You thought right! Thank you Frank. Please place them by the window will you?"

As he pushes the trolley over to the window, he nods to Julie's mother, as if he has just won a long standing confrontation. Taking his time, he turns, smiles at everyone, and then heads for the door to leave. While the President is analyzing Frank's new attitude, Ryan is the first to reach the trolly and say something.

"Ooo, cookies, and sandwiches, and...."

Reminding her new friend where he is, Julie pats him on the shoulder. While the President surveys the scene, she and Gus can't help but grin at Ryan's impulsiveness.

"All right, children. If you care to help yourselves while Gus and I talk. Please do not drop crumbs on the Oval Office carpet."

Julie's response to the 'order' is to whisper to Ryan.

"Ever have that feeling you're in the way?"

Ryan rolls his eyes in agreement.

"Many times. Let's eat."

Just as the eager children dip into the food trolley, the President guides Gus to an upright armchair.

"Please."

As Gus sits in the leather comfort, she drags up a smaller chair and sits opposite him. Her knees almost touching his, he is surprised at the sudden informal behavior. Endeared by the closeness, he studies her while she is settling on the chair. Her lush, dark brown wavy hair has highlights of gray, which catch the light. Her trim, but well covered frame now comfortable, her steady eyes search into his. As the earlier nervousness is disappearing, she looks down as if she were a shy young girl instead of a woman in her early forties.

"I hope you do not think this is strange behavior for a President? I find this is my favorite way of talking close to someone. My beloved father taught me as a young girl and I have done it ever since."

Intrigued her old habit coincides with his, he can't help but offer her a reassuring smile.

"Me too."

Meanwhile, Julie and Ryan are busy filling their young mouths with edible goodies. In between bites Julie whispers to Ryan.

"Can you still see the blue?"

Having no trouble in swallowing a bite of ham sandwich, Ryan answers.

"Yeah, I always see it. It's odd. It's there, but it's not there. Do you know what I mean?"

"Yes. I know."

While they continue enjoying the food, the President is talking in hushed tones.

"I have been following your activities very closely recently. To tell you the truth, I'm amazed, and yet confused at what I've seen and heard."

"In what way are you confused?"

"Well, I heard what you did to Ryan's mother, and how well you handled that awful demonstration, but..."

Sensing she is having a hard time accepting all this, Gus places one of his hands on hers.

"I do what I can to help while I'm here, but the big message starts here – now!"

Feeling a new burden, she drops her head for a couple of seconds, and then raises it to meet his gaze.

"Yes, I know..."

As if an unbeatable bond is developing, she lays her free hand on top of his.

"I want you to tell me everything, so I can do what I can to help."

In the meantime, Ryan and Julie are pretending not to listen. Their new bond unfolding, and not wanting to be overheard, Ryan whispers to Julie.

"They're doing the big talking now."

Crunching on a crisp cookie, Julie whispers back.

"I know. I expect it's about Gus's warning."

Helping to reduce more ham sandwiches, Ryan whispers back.

"My mom believes him now. She didn't for a while, but I always did."

Expressing in her eyes the warmth toward this nine year old boy, Julie agrees.

"So did I."

Meanwhile, Gus leans closer to the President.

"As I've been saying all along, the greed, corruption, persecution and exploitation, of the majority of the world's population has got to end. It is up to you and the rest of the world's leaders to come together to strike it all out. Otherwise, 'everything' is going to end - in one year."

With a sudden sensation of impotence racking her insides, she stares into his blazing eyes.

"But a year? That's hardly anytime at all?"

Ignoring her sudden lack of fearlessness, Gus continues.

"In the slow grind of politics this is true. But these politicians must rise to the occasion. This is the 'final' big picture."

Her vulnerability seeping through any confidence she once had, he responds by squeezing her hand with an affection he hopes will strengthen her resolve. Until that happens, a look of helplessness appears in her eyes.

"I could talk to Congress by introducing you and beg them to pass new laws or even declare a state of emergency. Unfortunately, we would both be laughed out of the building. The other world leaders would face the same predicament. The few good people who are fighting for what is right, are always struggling. The few, strong hard liners are corrupt; the rest are apathetic, or powerless. But, for a few loyal friends, most of Congress resents me. I am in power because I was elected Vice President. I moved into this office under the worst scenario of the President being murdered by an extreme white suprematist organization. I always believed that trumped up former president who has ruined this country, was behind the killing, but have no proof. I am also resented as a young - black woman - in a white man's world..."

She pauses to get her mind straight.

"And another thing, most people do not believe who you really are. All right, they have seen you – 'do' things, but to say you are Jesus Christ who has come back to warn the World - is a hard pill to swallow."

His illusions becoming a little shattered, Gus appears shaken by her statement. Undeterred, from his ultimate goal, Gus compensates.

"I understand it's not easy. But do 'you' believe who I really am?"

While still holding her hands, she fumbles to find the right words.

"I...."

Needing to step up the pressure, he commands.

"Look at my hands."

As her confused face looks down, the nail scars begin to appear on his wrists. She has to let go, as if his hands are too hot to handle. Her eyes now filling with tears of confusion, she places one hand up to her face as if she is ashamed of her doubt. With the other hand, she touches the angry scars with the tip of her fingers, as her tears drip onto his skin.

"I am so sorry I doubted. It really is you! But you are just a man."

"I was 'only' a man over two thousand years ago."

As the scars begin to fade, she rubs her tears into his hands.

"My powers are so limited and...."

While Julie has been listening with Ryan to all this 'big' talking, she seethes with frustration, and calls out to her mother.

"Mother? You are the President of the United States of America. You tell them what to do!"

Agreeing with his new found friend, Ryan demonstrates his excitement.

"Yeah! You tell 'em!"

Enthused by the youngsters, Gus looks deep in to the President's hesitant eyes.

"I will 'give' you that power. The strength to do only good. With this power and strength you have never known, you will lead in such a way that people will see you, as they ought to see you, a person of principle and right."

Ryan calls out.

"God bless the real America!"

Her doubt dissipating and a new confidence taking over, a strong sense of vision appears in her eyes. Her energy returning, she rises and begins to pace the lush carpeted floor.

"I will talk to Congress. No, I will 'tell' Congress enough is enough. The greed, suffering and exploitation have got to stop – NOW!"

As the children continue to cheer in excitement, Julie shouts.

"Yes, Mother! Yes!"

Becoming more caught up in this fervor, Ryan shouts in agreement.

"Yeah! Go for it!"

Her mind now racing, she stops pacing and looks at Gus.

"How are you going to travel to Europe, Asia, Russia, etc, with your message...?"

Before Gus has a chance to reply, she comes up with an idea.

"I know. I will supply you with Air Force One and all the assistance you need."

While Gus is amazed at such an offer, Ryan and Julie hold hands and do a little dance of joy around the floor, cheering as they go. Still in a daze, Gus tries to focus his mind.

"I am overwhelmed by your generosity and kindness."

Her enthusiasm overflowing, she turns to him.

"It is 'I' who is overwhelmed. I can see it all now. My husband kept saying that now was the right time for you to return and I just used to laugh at him. I was so blind."

Clenching her fists with this new vigor, she continues pacing the floor.

"While I get things going this end with Congress and the UN, I want you talk to the other leaders or whomever you need to talk to. When you return, I will arrange for you to address the UN General Assembly."

Still pacing, and deep in thought, she stops and looks at Gus.

"How about a meeting with the World Council of Churches?"

Admiring this woman in a new light, he asks the obvious.

"You can arrange that?"

To answer, she offers him a radiant smile that fills the room with her new confidence.

" Of course! The World Council of Churches is having their annual meeting here in the US at the new Madison Square Garden in New York, on the day before Good Friday. The reason the meeting is larger than normal is that this year is their eightieth anniversary of its conception. So, every Christian denomination will be there. Another reason they're in the Garden is that Muslim, Buddhists, Hindu and every other religion known to man has also been invited, in the belief that the wisdom of all these faiths put together may somehow bring peace and order to this hopeless collapsing world."

Visualizing the concept, Gus can see the challenge and opportunity that the meeting affords him, but is hesitant.

"Unfortunately, I know what the outcome will be, but I'll still be there."

Observing his hesitancy, Julie and Ryan come up to Gus and hug him in a way to give him the strength he needs. Appreciating their support, his eyes moisten, as he stretches out his hand to Julie's mother.

"I really cherish your support, and everything you are doing for me."

Gripping hold of his hands, she replies with the same emotion.

"Time is a scarce commodity right now. I will have you driven straight to

Air Force One. In the meantime, I will contact my press secretary to publicize that you are traveling to see other world leaders with my blessing."

Even though nervous about the immediate future, he pulls this wondrous woman toward him and kisses her hands.

"I am, for always, your servant, as well as your strength."

The warmth of his hands radiating up her arms, she gazes into his grateful eyes.

"I am forever in 'your' debt for helping me to see clearly again. Thank you."

Reluctant to let go of his hands, she leans over her desk and presses a button on a panel. Within seconds there is a knock on the main door. The President responds.

"Come in."

Frank enters. He closes the door with his usual casual air and relaxes as he faces his boss.

"Ma'am?"

Now she is the President again, her pose becomes more formal.

"I want you to arrange for my guest here..."

Beckoning to Gus.

"...to be taken speedily to Air Force One, and see that he wants for nothing. Contact me as to the time of the final arrangements."

Frank's face turns from his usual casual arrogance to complete surprise.

"Air Force One? Ma'am?"

"Yes, Frank. Air Force One. NOW!"

Dumbfounded by this different woman, he hesitates before obeying.

"Yes, er – Ma'am!"

He looks at Gus, indicating the door.

"This way. Please - Sir."

While an astonished Gus heads to the door, the children step back and move toward the President. Before leaving the office, Gus stops and turns to face the President for one last acknowledgment. Now standing in between the two children, with her hands resting on their young shoulders, she conveys to Gus a final smile of appreciation, and encouragement.

"I will make sure Ryan gets home safely. It is not going to be easy for you out there."

Gus's smile fades to a look of mild apprehension.

"Being right never is."

As the door closes, the President crouches down to the children.

"Well? How did I do?"

Ryan can't help but chuckle.

"Like a real President – Ma'am."

While they all laugh together, Julie pauses expressing concern, and faces her mother.

"Mother?'

"Yes, dear?"

"Did you see the blue?"

Still crouching, she focuses on the children's inquisitive expressions.

"Yes, dear! When he first came into the room."

It is now four hours later. Ryan is anxious while watching his mother live on Channel Six. Maggie the housekeeper is sitting nearby, sipping hot black tea. The screen shows the President's Air Force One Boeing 797 stationary at an undisclosed airfield. Ryan's concentration becomes more intense as the camera scans a massive gathering of children accompanied by parents in a cordoned-off area away from the airplane. Ryan blinks as his mother narrates.

"As this crowd, so full of anticipation, are focusing on Air Force One, the official

jet of the President, we know that the President herself offered Gus the

free use of the plane to go anywhere he needs to spread his important message.

If you were watching earlier, the President held an urgent press briefing."

The screen cuts to a recording of the briefing. The President is standing at the familiar podium. Her tone is reflecting calculated urgency as she explains to the press.

"During my meeting this morning with this extraordinary young man, proved to

me that his sincerity and his message to the world are of the utmost seriousness.

To help him in his supreme goal to help mankind, I have offered him the use

of Air Force One, of which I might add is being paid for out of my own pocket

and not the taxpayers."

The screen fades and returns live to Air Force One. Eva continues her comments.

"There is much opposition anyway in the House and Senate against this President,

because of opposing politics, and now this..."

The doorbell rings, Maggie jumps, as her concentration is broken. The doorbell rings again. Maggie pulls a face and becomes reluctant, while struggling to get up out of the comfortable old sofa. Meanwhile, Ryan is still engrossed watching the program, although half listening to Maggie shuffle toward the door in her bedroom slippers. At the front door, while she peeps through the spy hole lens, Ryan glances back at her.

"Who is it Maggie?"

Maggie does not answer. As if in a trance, she opens the door to expose Natas. Handsome as ever, and standing with one arm leaning against the doorframe, he flashes Maggie a beaming smile.

"Hello Maggie? How are you?"

While she fumbles to answer in her thick Bavarian accent, Natas pushes past.

Still in a trancelike state, Maggie closes the door, and then shuffles up to Natas.

"I am not supposed to let...."

"I know Maggie. I know. But it is 'I' Nat. Your friend."

As he bombards her with his dazzling smile; performed by perfect white teeth, his green, hypnotic eyes bore right into her. Causing her mind to stop functioning, she is finding it impossible to resist him. In the meantime, Ryan is still riveted to the television screen.

His mother speaks again, while the background picture is still showing Air Force

One.

"There is no sign yet of the President or Gus arriving. The pilots and crew have

already boarded...."

Natas interrupts Ryan's concentration.

"Well, hello Ryan. Watching Mom?"

Not seeming disturbed at seeing Natas, Ryan glances in his direction.

"Yeah. She's at Air Force One!"

"Yes, I see. Our friend Gus seems to have strong powers of persuasion over our

dear Madam President."

Trying to concentrate on the screen, Ryan is casual with his remarks.

"No? She just saw his blue."

Hear this, Natas's eyes glimmer with irritation, and his face muscles tighten. Controlling his urge to argue, he soon relaxes into his false, sweet charming manner by placing his right hand on Ryan's shoulder.

"Of course, you were there this morning at the White House. You saw it all."

To get into Ryan's mind, Natas removes his hand, and then crouches down behind the sofa so his head is level with Ryan's. Hiding her uneasy qualms about this visitor, Maggie shuffles to the sofa and sits next to Ryan. Meanwhile, Natas leans his head forward over the top of the sofa so his mouth is just a couple of inches away from Ryan's right ear. So, as to not spook the lad, he keeps his voice at a low ebb.

"Do you want to know something interesting about Gus?"

Still focusing on the TV screen, Ryan is half listening,

"About what?"

Suppressing his irritation, Natas moves an inch closer. Maggie is now becoming more interested in Natas than watching the TV. Not to disappoint her, Natas raises his voice a little.

"The blue as you call it, is a trick. I can do that."

Obtaining Ryan's full attention as well as Maggie's, Natas decides it is time to stand.

"Oh yes! It is that easy. Better still, I can do other colors too. Shall I demonstrate?"

"Okay."

Natas now stands away from the sofa, and goes to the center of the room.

"How about I do my favorite color - red?"

Maggie appears perplexed.

"Red? Sat is zer color of zer...."

"Devil? No Maggie. That is all fairy tales. I am just trying to prove to you that it

is all a trick. He can do blue, I can do red. Look, I will now demonstrate."

While he stands erect in the center of the room, his athletic body seems to grow taller as he puts his hands together as if in prayer. He mumbles, as his eyelids close in slow motion. The room seems to grow darker, and even the TV screen dims when a faint crimson aura appears over the top of his black curly hair. His green eyes reopen, appearing florescent in the dim atmosphere. As Maggie almost jumps out of her seat, while Ryan appears nervous, Natas then shuts his eyes, and the aura is gone. The room seems to brighten as Natas opens his eyes again. As if a stage act, he offers his audience the trademark-flashing smile, and charm exuding from every pore.

"There! Simple."

A perplexed Maggie trembles as she attempts to stand up from the sofa. After the second attempt, she glares at the visitor

"It made you look - evil."

Natas's response is to burst into a roar of false heavy laughter that fills the room, while Maggie and Ryan exchange uneasy glances. After few seconds, the uninvited guest quiets down, with his top lip curls into a sneering smile.

"That was the object of the exercise my dear."

Becoming agitated by this man, Ryan stands up.

"What? To look evil?"

Observing his audience's rattled response, Natas strikes a more casual pose to give the impression of sincerity.

"No, no! Let me explain. Gus happens to give out a blue aura. Right?"

Not trusting this man, Ryan is emphatic.

"Only those who believe in him can see it. Those who don't - can't."

As the boy is getting on his nerves, Natas has to be careful in choosing his words.

"All right! Look at it this way. Human beings have been indoctrinated over the

years to think that a blue or white light is somehow holy and righteous, and red

is connected to Hell and damnation...."

341

Caught up in all this, Maggie interrupts.

"Zat is true."

Having her in the palm of his hand, he expands.

"It has all been a big con Maggie. Gus, as you call him, is very clever. He has

perfected the method of producing the blue aura and is frightening everyone

out of their wits by saying the world is going to burn. Now, to me that sounds

more like the Devil himself."

Natas takes one step back as if he is an actor on stage, ready to finish his major performance.

"Me, my friends, I am the complete opposite. I give you warmth. I fulfill your

treats and utmost fantasies. I let the world flourish. Does Gus do that? No, his

message is doom and gloom. Now with me, there is fun, amusement and

profit. Everyone gains."

Not convinced, Ryan still challenges him.

"I don't know. I'll wait and see."

He turns away from Natas and jumps back on the sofa to listen to his Mom. This causes anger to creep into Natas' eyes, but he keeps his rising incense under control as Maggie is still scrutinizing him.

On screen, Eva's voice is rising with excitement as the President and Gus appear. Now concentrating on the screen, Maggie sits next to Ryan on the sofa. Infuriated by the interruption, but drawn to the screen, Natas remains standing behind the sofa, as Eva continues.

"The President is now leading Gus to the steps of the plane, as he waves to the

hundreds of excited children and curious parents."

While this is happening, the camera scans onto many little hands waving back, and smartphones and cameras flashing from the parents.

Meanwhile, Natas' veins on his forehead are swelling, as his anger and distaste increases.

"Children! So, that is his little plan. Using their innocence, and corrupting their

sweet little minds. Unfortunately, they will all end up like their parents who are

all like lemmings, falling off the cliff of fatalism and apathy, then crashing into

the dark abyss of stupidity."

On the screen, the President approaches a positioned microphone.

"I stand before you today on the threshold of an exciting new era. This young man standing next to me has been sent to save us from making any

more mistakes...."

Natas splutters with anger as he spits out the words.

"You're making 'your' biggest one now, 'Madam' President!"

She continues.

"His message informs us, if we do not get things right within a year, it is the

end for us all. So, as a first step..."

Natas is still fuming.

"See what I mean? He has her completely fooled."

The President continues on screen.

"I hope that by giving 'my' personal support the whole world will learn of his

sincerity. I would like to emphasize again that the use of Air Force One is being

paid for by me personally and 'not' by the taxpayer."

As the screen shows more pictures of children waving and parents becoming more involved, Natas bangs his fists on the back of the sofa.

"Fools! Imbeciles!"

Trying to control his rage, he steps back from the sofa. His handsome face now contorted and ugly, Ryan and Maggie appear nervous, as they turn back to stare at him. After a couple of seconds, they look at each other, as if searching for clues to why this strange man is so outraged. Seeing his audience becoming hesitant, Natas forces a relative calm demeanor.

"This idiocy has to stop. The world will never be the same again if he is allowed

to continue. I have not worked for an immeasurable amount of time to mold this

world to where I want it, just to see everything destroyed by 'him'. My worldly

task is almost complete. I will not allow him to ruin it."

Ignoring any reaction from his audience, he strides away, and heads for the front door. On opening it, he pauses and turns back to glare at the two confused faces. Realizing he is letting down his guard, he flashes them his most charming smile.

"Forgive me my friends, my outburst was unforgivable. Normally I am a man of

extreme virtue. I am afraid I get extremely angry at gross hypocrisy and deceit.

Until my next visit, I bid you farewell."

Leaving the door wide open, he is gone. A little shaken, but more curious, Ryanjumps off the sofa and runs toward the open door. He scratches his head in wonder, as he looks down the long hallway outside the door.

"Where'd he go?"

In the meantime, Maggie is struggling to get up off the sofa.

"Shut zer door Ryan and bolt it. I feel deadly cold, as if I am lying in my own

grave."

42

An Important Call

According to Eva's bedside clock, it is 5:45 a.m. next morning.. She is fast asleep. Her iPhone rings. After the third ring she stirs. Not recognizing the caller, she studies the small screen, while her trembling hand lifts the phone from the bedside cabinet.

"H-hello?"

Gus is on the line.

"Eva?"

She does not recognize his voice.

"Who is this?"

"It's me Eva. How are you?"

She now knows its Gus.

"Oh Gus? I'm sorry. You seem so far away."

"Well, if you count the Atlantic Ocean, I suppose I am."

Rubbing her eyes, she switches on to the speakerphone.

"Are you okay?"

"Yes..."

Staring at her reflection in a nearby mirror, she smiles at the irony.

"I'm fine. I think."

Not liking what she is seeing in the mirror, she yawns.

"Where are you?"

"I'm speaking from this hotel in Brussels. I'm sorry for calling you so early, but I'm about to speak to the European Parliament. It so happens to be their monthly standard meeting, so with some persuasion from our President and the newly elected British Prime Minister, they have given me thirty minutes to speak."

Picturing the scenario, and knowing how cynical politicians are, she puts on a confident tone.

"That's wonderful. It sounds as if things are not going to be as tough as you first thought."

"I'll soon find out."

"Is the Air Force One crew treating you okay?"

"It couldn't be better."

He pauses as if he has doubts.

"Eva?"

"Yes? What it is? Are you all right?"

"I am going to the Vatican tomorrow."

"Oh! That should be interesting."

"Yes, very interesting. There are a few things they need to know..."

There is a pause. Sensing his misgivings, Eva talks first.

"Gus? You still there?"

"Yes, I'm still here. Eva, I'm going back."

The seriousness of his voice makes her stomach turn over.

"Back? Back where?"

"Israel!"

Feeling his mounting anxiety, it is her turn to pause.

"I don't want you to go! I mean - won't it be too traumatic for you - after last time?"

"Yes, it will be, but I have to go, before - anyway. How is Ryan?"

"He's good. He's still fast asleep."

"Good. I had a bad feeling last night. I felt he was in grave danger."

"No! He's all right. I haven't spoken to him since yesterday morning, but he appears to be okay."

"Good. You know how I love you both."

"I know. We love you too."

While memories of them together at the church flood her mind, he breaks the spell.

"I'll call you later. I expect you'll hear and see everything over the media in the next few hours."

"Oh yes! You can guarantee on that."

"I'll talk to you later then – bye."

Her heart turns over as she hears the familiar click, while she hangs up. The sound of his voice still haunting, as if fearful for what is about to come, she notices a slight tremor in her hand as she lays the iPhone back on the cabinet. Her insides churning with apprehension mixed with the constant longing, she rolls back into the bed and pulls her knees up to her chin like a nervous child. Looking out of her bedroom window, she gazes at the sun beginning to break through into a new day.

"God? Please take care of him for me."

43

The President is Nuts

It is three hours later in the Oval Office. The President is sitting behind the grand desk in the shadow of many famous past Presidents. Before her is Nigel Steinberg, the Chief of Staff. A career politician who has risen up in the ranks of the Civil Service and Democratic Party, and at fifty-six years old, he is at the peak of his career.

Right now, he is furious, while pacing back and forth in front of the grand desk. Trying to act the professional, he glares at the top of her desk, which is covered with copies of all the national daily newspapers, arranged in a neat precise order for the President to observe.

"What are you thinking - Madam President? Why on earth didn't you call me first?"

His pudgy little face is becoming crimson from the effect of his pacing and controlling his irritation. She, on the other hand is acting calm, and being patient with her Chief of Staff. Hiding his exasperation, he points to the top of her desk.

"Look at the papers, and the Internet Madam. The social media is having a field day. I dread to think what all the major networks are going to churn up."

By disturbing the precise order, his hand trembles as he picks up the first paper.

"The Washington Post! Your great supporter has headlines saying —

348

'The President is Nuts'."

His hands trembling a little more, he puts that paper down, and picks up another. This time it is the LA Times.

"What about this gem? 'How Dare She? Who Does She Think She Is?' They are all the same, except the Wall Street Journal, which has just put a small column at the bottom right hand corner of page one, 'President Lends Air Force One to the Man they are calling Jesus'. Which I thought was a bit strange."

Hiding her impatience and keeping calm, The President leans back to enjoy the comfort of her armchair.

"Why strange?"

"Well, they are out of line with the others."

Her irritation leaking a little, she raises her voice a notch.

"So, you think that because the Journal had the sense to keep neutral, that's strange? What is strange, is you strutting around like a frightened hen, clucking away and acting as if your eggs have been stolen. It so happens that as President I asked you to stay on and be 'my' Chief of Staff, because you ably held that position for the late President. Is that correct?"

"Well, yes but...."

"There are no 'buts' Nigel. In return I expect your support for my decision on this matter, like you would have done for him."

He gawks at her in complete astonishment. This is not the woman who was often indecisive as Vice President. Now she has gone the complete opposite. Who is 'this' woman? Wanting to keep his job, he sits opposite her, and decides to use a more conciliatory tone.

"I am sorry Ma'am if I got carried away, but you have made the presidency a laughing stock. Even if 'you' pay for this crazy guy's trip, Air Force One isn't your personal property to lend out as you please."

Releasing a little more of her irritation, she sits up straight and stares straight into his watery brown eyes.

"It belongs to the presidency! As I am the President right now, this is in America's best interest. I would say this 'crazy guy's trip' as you call it, is the best investment this aircraft has ever made."

Not waiting for a response or worse an argument, she gets up, pushes her armchair aside and strolls over to the nearest window. The sun is shining outside. The rays are reflecting off her lush brown hair, giving her a deep translucent look. Drawn to her beauty, he watches her take a deep breath, preparing for another verbal barrage. Instead, she turns to face him offering him a serene smile. Her face calm, and her eyes confident, she leans on her desk, and looks him in the eye.

"Nigel? I don't care what anyone says or thinks. In my mind, I have made the right decision, which is the only important thing for me right now. Gus is out there right now delivering the most important message 'everyone' needs to hear. And all you're worried about is what the media says?"

Relieved she is being kind to him, he responds with a likewise answer.

"The trouble is Ma'am it isn't just the media. Only a small minority of Congress and the public polls share your opinion. The vast majority thinks..."

She butts in to emphasize her passionate conviction.

"Thinks what? Because Congress has a Republican majority, what ever I say or do won't 'ever' get their agreement. As far as any public polls go, I don't look at them. I have to make decisions using my own convictions and be guided by my conscience."

He flinches as she takes a step forward toward him. He feels the need to grip the chair arms for support, as her manner is so determined.

"I know who he really is, and I am going to use all the power and clout I have to help him. So, get on to our UN Ambassador and coordinate with her for the next meeting of the General Assembly. By the way, when is the next one?"

His mind racing, he has to think and focus.

"Next Friday, I believe."

Relieving the pressure on him for a while, and her mind switching into top gear, she begins to pace the room with a sense of purpose.

"Today is Wednesday. That gives us ten days. Isn't that Good Friday?"

"I believe so, ma'am."

She stops pacing and glares at him.

"Is that your favorite noncommittal phrase? Nigel? Please give me 'definite' answers, not - I 'believe' ones."

"Yes, Ma'am. Ma'am? Do you realize how long it takes to organize such a meeting?"

"Of course I do Nigel. So, you had better hurry up and get started. Before you go, get in touch with the World Council of Churches. They're having an important meeting this next Thursday. I want Gus to talk to them."

As he stares at her in sheer astonishment, he is overcome by nervous exhaustion, compared to being told he has to climb Mount Everest by lunchtime. A little unsteady on his feet, he struggles a little to rise out of his chair, and then shuffles across the Oval Office toward the main door. Observing his wind being knocked out of his sails, she stares at him.

"Are you all right, Nigel?"

"I believe so Ma'am. I suddenly feel a bit tired."

Realizing she might have been a bit too demanding for a mere man to absorb, she strides over to him, and conveys her best smile. She then places one hand on his fat little shoulder.

"You will do it okay Nigel. I have great faith in you. I 'know' you won't let me down..."

She removes her hand, and then strokes his chubby pink cheek.

"So, let's get started."

"Yes, Madam President."

While he goes to open the door, her command penetrates.

"Nigel? Report to me only. Do you understand?"

"Yes, Ma'am."

His shoulders stooping a little as he exits, she watches him shut the door. Now alone with the deathly hush of silence, she contemplates what she has done. Not regretting any of her decisions, she turns and walk toward the window where the sun is still shining. Gazing at the lush green lawn, she looks upward toward the clear blue sky.

"I won't let you down Gus. I have your promised strength."

351

44

They Do Not Hear

It is 5 p.m. in Belgium. The European Parliament has been in session non-stop for over six hours and everyone is rather jaded. Many topics were not voted on because of the lack of agreement. The grand, half-circular main debating chamber is almost full. The speaker rises. He is situated at the front of the main stage area just below the guest podium. To hush the proceedings, the speaker shouts, "Order" into his microphone. As the house takes time to quiet down, the Speaker now addresses the house.

"We have a 'short notice' guest speaker for you this evening. Many of you may have been watching recently your television, computer screens, and social media learning about this young man. I have been informed he is going to deliver us an important message that is in 'everybody's' interest. I strongly suggest that you listen to him, because lately this house is becoming increasingly divided..."

The house responds by erupting with a mixture of protests and sporadic applause. His face exhibiting the strain of his position, the Speaker shouts in defiance into the microphone.

"Order. Order!"

As the house subsides into an uneasy peace, he resumes his speech.

"Please welcome - Gus..."

To demonstrate his position, the Speaker applauds with enthusiasm he hopes can arouse. A few scattered members of Parliament do likewise, while the rest frown.

As Gus enters, he is exuding enough confidence in hope it will be contagious enough to convince this cynical audience. While he steps onto the grand open stage, and then walks up to the ornate oak podium, his white casual shirt with a brown tie to match a pair of light brown chinos, look a little out of place compared to the dark suits below.

The TV lights beam down on him as he stands and adjusts his eyes to his new surroundings. The house is now quiet. The atmosphere is one of curiosity and suspicion. As he adjusts the podium microphone, and then rests both hands onto the podium, he scans the large audience. Pondering for a few seconds to gather his momentum, he speaks.

"I sense among you at this momentous gathering, a majority of souls reluctant to be here today. Not just to listen to me, but a general reluctance to even represent your constituencies and countries. Therefore, by you being in this state of mind, the ideals of a united Europe seem forgotten. However, I do feel a few good hearts among you for which I am most grateful."

'The few good hearts' lean forward, eager and receptive, while the remainder of the audience exudes animosity. Sensing this is going to be hard work to get his message across, he pauses for a second. Scanning the scene, the feeling of déjà vu is overpowering. A flashback of the Pharisees in the temple at Jerusalem, eager to prove him a fake, preys on him.

"Without going into boring details, most of you know why I'm here, but for the benefit of those who don't, it is to deliver a very simple, but important message."

Pausing as if to recharge, he then raises his voice.

"Get things right 'now', or regret it later!"

The audience is becoming agitated, and comments are flying. Raising his voice another notch, he continues.

"You are the European Union! In having no borders, no barriers and united as one, is a major achievement. However, being united as 'one' is a myth."

He holds us his hand to quell the increasing vocal opposition.

"As Britain left you because of your inane bureaucracy, I hear rumors of other states thinking the same. Why is that? Is it because of greed and inefficiency?"

He pauses to pick up a gold colored coin.

"Now in front of me I have six, one Euro coins, out of the fifteen that are in circulation. Each about the same size and color."

He picks up one coin as if to study it.

"At a quick glance they all look the same, but when you look and study them more closely, all is not what it seems."

He lays the coin down for a second; stops and studies his audience. The restless of the audience coming across, he is struggling to hold their attention.

"A long time ago I studied a coin such as this. I had been asked; should the people of Palestine, which then was occupied by the Roman Empire, pay taxes to the occupier? I asked for some money of the day, I was handed a Roman coin. I asked the people of that time, whose head was on that coin? Their answer was 'Caesar's'. I therefore said to them; just give Caesar what belongs to him and give to God what belongs to God. I can see by your faces, that you are saying to yourselves; 'What is this man talking about? What is all this to do with us?' Although you are not occupied, I can tell much from your coins. In the past the Euro was universal; now these six coins in front of me do not show a united Europe under God, as you once proclaimed. They are all different. Each country has its own Euro coin showing that nobody is really budging from their own sovereignty. If the 'so-called' united Europe cannot agree again on a universal coinage issue, what hope is there? You are all supposed to be Christian countries, but your coins show otherwise."

The confused audience rumbles with murmurs and protests. Gus pauses, ready to give another onslaught on a more desperate topic. His voice now calmer, but still determined, he continues.

"The declining United States of America and Europe combined, still consumes a third of what the world produces, all at the expense of the third world. Now we have China, the most powerful country in the world. With they're huge armed forces and a population expanding at an alarming rate, it will need another planet Earth to satisfy its lust for natural resources..."

Gus lowers head as I'd the emphasis his point.

"This delicate planet of ours is being raped of all its goodness. It would not be quite so bad if this wealth were shared evenly, but as it happens, five percent of the world's population owns ninety percent of its wealth..."

He looks up at the arched ornate ceiling as if drawing strength to carry on this difficult task.

"Something is very wrong here. So, what is happening to the other ninety percent of the world? I'll tell you; they're living on the edge, a meager existence and suffering with vast numbers on the verge of starvation. Did you know the West on its own 'throws away' more than the rest of the world consumes. To me that is the 'ultimate' crime against humanity. On top of all this, we have Global warming, and pollution of land and sea that is beyond putting right. All created by this greedy, wealthy ten percent."

Not wanting to listen to something they already know, the audience is becoming noisy and on edge. What can they do? Who is this upstart telling them what to do?

As Gus continues, he has to raise his voice above this agitated crowd.

"The irony is that this insatiable ten percent and the majority of the Western hemisphere have the highest rate of heart disease, diabetes and cancer over the rest of humanity. Do you know why? It is gluttony, greed, self-indulgence and selfishness. These people have to go on diets to lose weight. Go and live in a so called third world country and live like the 'natives' - you'll soon lose weight."

Now the crowd is insulted and even louder with its protests, Gus has to shout even louder his final barrage.

"Help your neighbor, don't exploit him! Teach and equip him to rid the world of corrupt governments and corporations. Do not pander to these builders of devilish empires for the sake of a quick buck. This is your last chance. Mend your ways in this next year, or you will all be finished."

Having heard enough of this upstart, the audience is now a mob. They stand and jeer, booing at him and throwing insults. A small handful stands up and applauds, but they get pushed to the floor.

Natas is grinning with a sense of satisfaction, while watching this grim turn of events on his latest super-smart wide screen television. He is lying on a massive king-size bed surrounded by three scantily covered voluptuous young women sprawling all over him. Their hands are everywhere, while he concentrates on the screen.

"Look at him, what an idiot. Doesn't he realize he is fighting a losing battle? A battle that I have been winning for years. Do you realize my beauties that my mission is almost complete? The world is practically at my fingertips. Just a small amount of time and it will all be mine. Isn't that so?"

They murmur in vague agreement while running their hands over his naked muscular chest, and then kissing and fondling every area of skin, all working their way down to his ultimate pleasure point.

"What is he offering the poor masses? He calls it love! That has always been an illusion. Sex and money makes this stupid world go round. Is that not right, my darlings...?"

They murmur and moan, more in pleasure than agreement, as they find what they want. Their intensity increases as he reaches that pinnacle of pleasure. Still fondling him and knowing their master is now satisfied, they now concentrate their lust on each other...

Meanwhile, the noise on the screen is overwhelming. Gus is being rushed off the podium just as the members of Parliament seem to go insane and stampede onto the stage.

In the Oval Office, the President's tears are streaming down her face, while watching the same events on her television.

"Oh Gus, what a mess. You're not getting through to them. They can't see...."

There is a knock at the door. Surprised, she turns the sound down with her remote, and then wipes the tears off her face.

"Come in."

Further surprised, her eyes widen as Frank enters.

"Are you still here Frank? I thought your shift finished hours ago."

"James is tired Ma'am after organizing many of the arrangements with Air Force One. I volunteered to do a double shift."

He pretends not to notice her tear-streaked face.

"I appreciate that very much Frank. I have been watching Gus getting crucified by the Europeans."

"Yes, Ma'am I know. It's a shame. I think he has something."

"Frank? He has everything! I hope the world sees it before we all perish."

"Yes, Ma'am."

"I'm sorry Frank. What did you want?"

"Just to inform you we just got a message from Air Force One. They will be flying to Rome within the next two hours."

"To visit the Vatican?"

"Yes, Ma'am."

Natas has his own agenda. He switches off the TV and is reluctant to pull away from his three joyful, entwined playmates.

"I have an important job to do now girls. Something I should have done eons ago. I have been far too tolerant."

Leaving the three disappointed beauties, he strides into an adjoining bathroom and slams the door shut. His jaw clenching with anger, he looks up to the ceiling.

"You have lost! You will not destroy this world, because you love it too much. It is your creation, remember? You would have done it years ago if you really wanted. Now it is too late. You have missed the boat. I have won! I am going to destroy you for your weakness. Your so-called love and compassion is a myth! I am going to get rid of your Gus as easily as swatting a fly on a hard concrete wall."

His green eyes blazing with cool fury, he turns to look in the wall mirror, and bellows out a wicked laugh. A laugh that has echoed throughout time.

357

45

Should All Roads Lead to Rome?

It is 10 p.m. the next morning. The soft lit room in the Vatican is decorated in the utmost opulence. In the center of the room is a grand circular table constructed from exquisite woods. The top consists of the finest Italian veneer marquetry, and lacquered to make it a priceless antique. Around this beautiful table are four high cardinals dressed in their superb quality red silk robes. All are earnest in discussing a current problem. A young priest appears out of the shadows, and whispers in the ear of the older one of the four. The cardinal nods in acknowledgment. The young priest then leaves and disappears back into the shadows.

There is a sound of a heavy door opening, a murmur of voices, and the same door being shut. A tall man appears dressed in cannon's robes. The black and red silk shimmers in the low lighting, as Natas offers the four cardinals his most charming smile. The smile soon goes, his mood becomes serious, as Natas steps nearer the cardinals.

"Thank you for agreeing to see me gentlemen at such short notice. I have come to you in great haste, direct from America via London, to warn you 'and' the Holy Father of this charlatan called Gus. I have seen him personally 'perform'.

He is nothing but a fraud."

The cardinals glance at each other, as if searching for an answer to these unfound accusations.The older one frowns as he responds to Natas.

"Are you really sure of what you are saying? All we have heard is good things about him."

Another cardinal peers up at Natas, expressing his concern.

"We hear he can heal. Even your own President is backing him."

Natas is finding it hard to control his frustration with these stupid old men.

"Don't you see? That's his plan. Win over the meek and gullible of this world, and then carry on his ambitions. You know my friend that is exactly how Satan works. It is well known that he can even imitate 'God' to get what he wants."

The four seated men ponder and nod. Natas' patience is wearing thin as the four murmur to each other in reluctant agreement. Now somewhat enthused, Natas is eager to continue.

"The man is a fake, a blasphemer as well as – 'evil'. I have personally made it my own crusade to follow his every move. Hence, my visit here today, because I am a man of the true faith - like you gentlemen."

He can see that he is not quite convincing these elderly cardinals. To ease his frustration, he begins to take his time in walking around the table.

"Look gentlemen...."

The oldest cardinal stops Natas by grabbing his arm. Their eyes meet. Hiding his anger at these old fools, Natas concentrates on presenting him with his best smile, while easing his arm from the firm grip. The cardinal does let go, but does not smile back to Natas.

"You say you personally witnessed this healing?"

"Yes! Every one! I even talked to the poor hoodwinked souls after-wards."

Becoming interested, one of the cardinals wants to be involved in this unusual conversation.

"What was the general outcome of your inquiries?"

Taking advantage of the question, Natas leans on the table in between two of the gentlemen, and then stares hard at the inquiring cardinal.

"They were all mind over matter. Any confident doctor could have done the same."

Making his point, he stands away from the table, and then looks away not to expose his mounting irritation. While pausing to regain his calm posture, he turns back to face them. The beaming smile now fixed into place, he glides around the table again like an actor building up to his finale.

"Look, monsignors, let's face it, the man is an egomaniac who 'says' he is one thing but is 'really' something else. The man is trying to fool us all. In my humble opinion, he is just 'plain' evil."

Hoping his opinion is sinking in, he stops walking and looks down at them. His breathing heavy with excitement, his mind races.

Surely, I have convinced them by now?

His gray dull eyes showing a hint of sadness, the eldest of the cardinals looks up at him.

"The Holy Father is keeping an open mind, but between us here at this table, we think he is skeptical."

Releasing his exasperation, Natas bangs his fist on the table, causing the four monsignors to jump.

"Of 'course' he is skeptical. Look! If God was going to send his son back to Earth, he would surely have let 'us' know, give 'us' a sign – 'us' being the leaders of the 'true' church."

The four cardinals react by glancing at each other with a: 'he has a good point' expression on their faces. In the meantime, the young priest returns again out of the shadows. He drifts with discretion up to the eldest cardinal and whispers in his ear. The old man answers with a thoughtful nod, and with a wave of his hand, dismisses the young cleric. As the young man blends again into the shadows, the cardinal informs his fellow monsignors.

"He is here gentlemen, awaiting an audience with his Holiness."

Thinking he is on the verge of convincing these cardinals, Natas has to control his anger at their complacently.

"Surely you are not going to allow...?"

The eldest cardinal raises his hand to quiet Natas's outburst.

"At this moment, he is being taken to His Holiness's private chambers."

360

Gus is standing outside an ornate wood carved door. The young priest standing nearby offers him an encouraging smile, while he knocks on the door. There is a pause for a second, and then a muffled voice answers on the other side of the door.

"Come in."

The young priest smiles again at Gus, as he opens the door, and indicates for Gus to enter.

At first glance, the room appears dark. All the windows are covered with heavy drapes, as glimmers of light try to force their way into the small gaps in between the heavy burgundy fabric. Gus's eyes adjust to the dimness, as he focuses on someone in the center of the private chambers. The Pope is sitting on a heavy carved fifteenth century walnut armchair. He is dressed in his familiar white and ivory robes. Gus can hear the door close behind him as he steps forward toward the Holy Father. On first sighting, he notices how frail he looks by the way he is haunching over and leaning to one side on the arm of the chair. The robes give off a ghost like reflection in the limited light.

As Gus approaches him, kneels and takes the Pope's left hand to kiss the famous ring, he can't help but notice the gnarled and deformed knuckles from years of painful arthritis. While Gus kisses the ring, a frail Brazilian accent comes to Gus's ears.

"Why do 'you' kiss my ring?"

Puzzled by the question, Gus gazes up to a world-weary face, accompanied by sparse silver hair showing from under the little scull cap.

"Because I am your servant and the ring is the symbol of your position."

Although the Pope's blue eyes are still sharp, and the strong aquiline features have not weakened with age and illness, Gus can still sense a disillusioned man. On letting go of the old man's gnarled hand, Gus rises, and takes notice of the same hand being pointed across the room to a nearby chair. Wanting to please and honor this poor soul, Gus grabs the chair, and places it in front of the Pope.

Now sitting opposite each other, and their knees almost touching, Gus's hazel eyes are finding it hard to receive any eye contact.

"I really appreciate you giving me this audience."

The Pope answers with a hint of sarcasm.

"By what I hear, it should be 'you' giving 'me' an audience."

Gus is realizing that the leader of the largest Christian church is jealous of his presence.

"It doesn't work that way. I am your servant, not a person of rank and position."

The Holy Father becomes agitated by this statement.

"Are you implying that the Church should not have leadership?"

Not wanting to inflame an already sensitive situation, Gus tries to explain.

"What I am saying is...."

Gus stops as he observes the Pope gripping his hands together, and moaning in sudden pain.

"How long have you suffered this condition?"

Venting his frustration, the Pope is still rubbing his hands.

"Many years young man. I have tried everything. An array of drugs, herbs, hypnosis, and even acupuncture to no avail. I am afraid it is getting worse."

Feeling the man's pain, Gus reaches out, and is gentle in taking hold of his hands. The Popes instinct is to resist, but Gus hangs on, and then begins to massage. Embarrassed by his own weakness, the Pope again attempts to pull his hands away. Gus's determination to ease this man's suffering, he keeps rubbing the swelling knuckles.

"Have you tried prayer?"

"Of course I have. I pray every day, but as you can see – 'nothing'!"

"Perhaps your prayers aren't sincere enough?"

"What?"

To answer, Gus releases the diseased hands, and with a deft movement, realigns his grip so his palms are upwards, and the wrists on show.

"Look at 'my' hands."

Still wanting to free his hands, the Holy Father ignores him. Gus insists.

"Just look at my hands!"

The Pope is reluctant to look down and witness the nail scars appearing on Gus's wrists. As the scars bloom, his eyes widen in disbelief.

"Oh, very clever. I suppose, you can bring God down from heaven to stand right here, in front of me, and talk to me personally?"

Hurt by the cruel sarcasm, Gus hides his pain by gripping onto the Pope's hands with determination.

"He's here already, but you're not seeing or listening."

Becoming irritable by such a suggestion, the Pope tries again to pull his hands away, but the effort in doing so is just too much to bear.

"Please just let me go."

Refusing to let go and needing to convince this man who he is, Gus raises his voice.

"Why are you denying me? 'Believe' what you've just seen. You cannot pretend otherwise. That is just what your church has been doing over the last eighteen hundred years – 'pretending', using my name in vain for your power over people instead of humbly serving them."

Still determined, Gus softens his voice.

"Put it another way, do you 'believe' God can heal you?"

The old man hesitates. He really wants to believe.

"I – I...."

Keeping his voice soft and calm, Gus continues.

"You, the head of the largest Christian church, hesitates? Isn't your faith deep enough to pray for your sick and tired body to be healed?"

Whether it is shame or embarrassment that he has lost his faith, the Pope makes a final attempt to pull his hands away.

"Please. I – I..."

Gus stares deep into the other man's eyes.

"Pray with me! Pray from the depths of your soul for the relief from this everlasting pain."

The pain now excruciating, Gus's grip tightens on the old hands.

"PRAY!"

In desperation, the Pope screams out in Portuguese.

"Oh God! I can't stand it anymore! Please 'help' me?"

While Gus still grips the hands, he shuts his eyes, as beads of sweat appear on his forehead. At the same time, tears of agony and confusion stream down the old man's face, dripping onto his robes.

Becoming overwhelmed by this now familiar fatigue, Gus releases the hands, and slouches back in his chair. Meanwhile, the Holy Father stops crying. In a reflex action, he wipes away his tears with both hands. Realizing he is free of pain, he rises from the heavy armchair with no effort.

"I have no pain!"

Flexing his hands and raising his arms above his head, he strides around the room like a young man.

"This is amazing! My hands and body have no pain!"

Not quite believing this is happening, he gazes at Gus.

"It's a miracle!"

Weary after his endeavor, Gus strains to answer.

"God loves you. Your plea for help has been answered..."

While Gus shuts his eyes to recuperate, the rejuvenated Pope makes his way back to his heavy carved armchair opposite Gus. His sharp blue eyes now sparkling with new life and optimism, he reaches across and places a now painless hand on Gus's head.

"What is that blue I can see around your head?"

His work not having been in vein, Gus opens his eyes in joy and relief.

"It is 'I'. Now do you believe?"

With humility, His Holiness takes Gus's hands in his. Observing the nail scars are still showing, he brings the hands up to his mouth to kiss the scars.

"I am so sorry for doubting you. Please forgive me. You had to perform a miracle before I could believe."

Memories of previous skepticism flooding his mind, Gus hides his cynicism.

How many times have I heard that one?

"With all the political bureaucracy in your daily life, you just lost your way. Now you're back. I hope with a different, more positive attitude."

Seeing Gus's point, and wanting to make up for years of neglect, the Pope lets go of Gus's hands. In doing so he notices the ugly scars disappearing. His energy firing this new enthusiasm, he rises from his seat and begins to pace the room.

"What should I do now?"

His energy returning somewhat, Gus leans forward in his chair.

"I want you to publicly recognize me and tell the world my message."

"We all have one year to get things right?"

"Yes,"

"A major task. You must realize that these days my guiding hand is usually ignored?"

"Now you have a new hand that they cannot ignore."

They both smile at the irony, but Gus is serious.

"If you are determined, God will give you the strength."

Pondering, the Pope sits back in his armchair.

"Then what?"

To answer, Gus indicates to their surroundings.

"Look around you. All I can see here is the extreme 'over-the-top' opulence built up over the centuries. It's not necessary. It is offensive to God when the wealth in this building alone could feed starving millions in the poor underdeveloped countries. I tell you this, start now by distributing that wealth to heal and feed the sick and needy. 'The meek shall inherit the Earth'. That is always part of my message. Only the 'true' followers will survive what is to come..."

A phone rings nearby. Enthused by Gus's message, the Pope springs out of his chair and strides over to his desk to pick up the phone.

"Hello? Yes! There is? All right.We will be right there. Thank you."

As he replaces the phone, and looks at Gus unable to hide his joy, his new hand trembles with excitement.

"It seems that you being here has leaked out. There is a huge crowd gathering outside in Saint Peters Square. I want you to join me on the balcony and let the world see us together. After, we will celebrate with some refreshments."

His enthusiasm abound, he goes to a nearby wall, grabs an ornate hanging rope, and gives it a tug.

"That is the first time I have been able to do that."

Gus beams back to him.

"Just think, this is only the beginning."

As a pair of heavy burgundy drapes open, exposing a crescendo of light coming from the tall pair of white painted French doors, Gus holds his breath in anticipations, as he attempts to stand. Rubbing his pain free hands together in expectancy, the Pope gestures Gus to follow him as he opens the famous tall doors.

His full strength not yet returning, Gus hangs onto the back of his chair to catch his breath. Demonstrating his concern, the Pope stretches out his hand to offer support. Gus smiles in appreciation as he grips it, and then follows the other man toward the doors.

The huge crowd roars as Gus and the Holy Father open the famous doors and step out onto the historic balcony. Many in the crowd realize that their Pope is not crippled with disease anymore when he raises his arm, taking Gus's hand with him.

Meanwhile, nearly five thousand miles away in Max's office, Max is sitting upright behind his desk becoming mesmerized by the television screen on the wall behind his desk. Eva is anxious, while sitting on the corner of the desk staring at the same screen. Becoming absorbed in the picture, Max raises his arms in joy.

"Gus has done it! That poor old bastard of a Pope could never stand up straight let alone raise his arms like that."

Becoming captured by the image, her heart goes out to Gus.

Another miracle? He looks so tired.

"Look at the crowd. They all know. Isn't it amazing?"

Deep in thought, Max leans back in his chair.

"It's a pity he has to convince people by having to perform a miracle."

The usual pang of guilt hits Eva.

"Look how exhausted he appears."

On the screen the camera scans the happy faces of the expanding morass of jubilant souls filling up Saint Peter's Square. The Pope, still holding Gus's hand, leans toward a microphone attached to the balcony. The camera zooms in on him.

"This young man standing next to me has come back to save us all. Through his crucifixion over two thousand years ago he took our sins upon his shoulders. Since then, our sins have become so intolerable, we don't deserve to be any redemption. As we are not trying to follow God's plan, we 'must' listen to Gus's words and obey his warnings against our greed, corruption and self-destruction. It is up to us all here and everyone around the world to help him finally get rid of this evil. Let us pray the Lords Prayer..."

Tears fill Eva's eyes as she witnesses thousands of people on the screen move in unison. While they kneel or bow their heads, the Holy Father begins the well known prayer into the microphone.

Elsewhere inside the Vatican, the Cardinals are becoming anxious as they pace the floor of the grand room. Each searching deep into their own thoughts and consciences, Natas stands by the main door, shouting out to the Cardinals in sheer frustration.

"I warned you gentlemen that he would pull the wool over His Holiness's eyes. He has to be stopped or generations of our church tradition will have been wasted."

Letting Natas' plea sink in, the cardinals stop pacing. Glancing at each other in search of an answer, they then gaze at Natas who is still shouting.

"Not only will the Roman Catholic Church, as we know it, end, but you gentlemen may be out of a job. Until then, I bid you farewell. I have a Holy Quest to finish."

The older men stare at the door, as it opens and releases a dim ray of light, which fills the room. While he exits and the door closes, the shadows return, and the worried Cardinals pace again.

In Max's office, Max and Eva are still entrenched by the pictures from

Rome. In the meantime, a young skinny youth enters the office through the open door. He pulls a face at the screen, as he reaches across Max and leaves a sheet of paper on the desk. Ignoring the lad leaving, Max and Eva look at each other, and peer down at the paper. As Max retrieves the paper and reads it, his eyes widen.

"It's all arranged! Gus is to address the UN General Assembly next Friday. My, she has been working hard."

Curious and becoming a little anxious, Eva wonders.

"Who has?"

"The President."

"The President?"

"Let me read this email to you."

"Okay, I'm sorry."

"You don't have to be sorry with me. Now, the President has also arranged for Gus to speak at the World Council of Churches annual meeting on Thursday."

Having a hard job to quell her irrational anxiety, Eva is deep in thought.

"Isn't next Friday, Good Friday?"

In response, Max glances at a nearby calendar hanging by the main window. Running his pudgy index finger along the calendar, his face tightens, and his jaw muscles clench.

"You're right. It is!"

His sudden serious tone causes even more concern for Eva.

"Are you worried Max?"

"I don't know. But I just felt a coldness hit my insides."

"Well, before your insides get too cold, Gus is going to Israel first."

As if being hit by an electric shock, he turns away from his desk in a jolt. Using his hands against the back of his chair for support, his brown eyes become ablaze with concern.

"Israel? How do you know?"

"He called me just before his disastrous meeting at the European Parliament."

His mind twisting and turning from this new bombshell, Max begins to pace the floor. After a few seconds of mind churning, and his eyes still blazing, he stops, and then looks at Eva.

"After what happened last time? I wish you'd told me earlier. The Israelis haven't changed."

"I know, but that's what he wants. His exact words were – 'I must go back'."

Adjusting to this new trepidation, Max glares up to the ceiling and clenches his hands together.

"God? Please don't let history repeat itself."

With anxiety still troubling her , Eva is more confident.

"I think it'll be different this time."

Meanwhile in the Vatican, the Pope and Gus are still acknowledging the enormous crowd that is now overflowing Saint Peters Square and beyond. While the cheering becomes tumultuous, the Pope smiles at Gus in a gratitude that to him will be impossible to equalize.

"Let's go back inside now."

Even though lifted by the enthusiasm of the crowd, Gus is still tired. He nods in agreement, while the both give the people a final wave, turn, and step back into the room through the open doorway. Now in a daze, the Pope closes the door and pulls the cord that operates the heavy drapes. As the room becomes dim and the shadows return, Gus collapses into the nearest armchair. Demonstrating his concern, the Pope lays his hand on Gus's shoulder.

"Are you all right my friend?"

Considering his fatigue, Gus's drained face looks up at him with a new and sincere friendship.

"I'm fine. Just a bit tired."

The Pope's reaction is to walk in haste to a nearby desk and press a button.

"My, it feels good to be normal again. As promised, I will get you those well-deserved refreshments while you rest..."

He goes to sit, when there is a knock on the door. Gus is impressed by the quick service.

"My, that was quick."

Not waiting for the customary invitation, a priest with a message enters the room. Gus watches the young priest hand the Pope a sheet of paper. The Pope's eyes widen as he reads the paper. After a few seconds, he is polite when dismissing the priest, who at this is holding the door open for the incoming refreshment cart.

A priest of African origin enters the room pushing a fine brass inlaid trolley full of all types of fruit, sandwiches, and drinks. The Pope is polite again when thanking the bearer of the cart, who now exits. Still holding the paper, he turns to Gus.

"A message from your President. An email straight from the White House."

As he hands Gus the printed email, he marvels at his own strength and agility, while, he pushes the stocked trolley over to Gus. Becoming absorbed in the email, Gus gazes up at his new friend.

"She has done it! She has got me to address the World Council of Churches next Thursday followed by giving a speech to the UN General Assembly on Friday."

Energized by the news, Gus is able to stand. Not so bound over by this news, the Pope touches his arm.

"Do you know what day it is next Friday?"

As if pouring cold water on a warm thought, Gus's face turns serious.

"Yes! I know."

Sensing the trepidation, his Holiness grips Gus's shoulders with both hands.

"Do you realize the similarity to before?"

"You mean the World Council of Churches compares to the Pharisees?"

The Pope's bright blue eyes fill with tears.

"I don't know, but I am afraid for you."

"Don't be. I have right on my side. Just pray for me and begin delivering the message while I'm gone."

"Gone? Gone where? You must stay here and rest until next Thursday!"

Gus is gentle as he pulls away from the Pope's tender grip. He then pours two glasses of red wine from the trolley. Becoming fascinated, the Pope watches Gus tear off a piece of bread from a sandwich, passes it to his Holiness and take a piece for himself.

"Eat this bread, for it is my flesh."

Engulfed in this new sense of purpose, they both eat the bread.

"Drink the wine for it is my blood."

They both down the small glasses of wine. Becoming caught up in this 'communion', tears of wonderment stream down the Holy Father's face. As Gus replaces the wine glasses on the trolley, and then holds his arms out to the Pope, he falls into his arms and sobs. His words muffled against Gus's chest, he grips Gus extra tight in their embrace.

"Oh, what a fool I have been. What idiots we have all been."

Feeling his shirt becoming wet with tears, Gus is gentle when pulling his friend away to arms length.

"You are now my Peter, my rock. Like I said, your mission starts here. Spread the message while I go back to Israel."

The Pope becomes shocked while wiping away his tears.

"The email said nothing about Israel? You cannot go! It is too risky. Israel? That poor country is in a permanent state of siege and sorrow, brother killing brother, suicide bombings...."

Gus lets go of him.

"I know, but I must go before..."

Noticing a small statue on a nearby decorative table, he steps towards it, and picks it up. It is a small porcelain of Mary holding the baby Jesus. As a puzzled Pope comes up to him, he caresses the statue.

"Beautiful, isn't it?"

"I believe the oldest one in existence."

"Good, then this is the one I need."

"Need? What for?"

As Gus is still clenching the small statuette in his hand; his warm hazel eyes seem to glow in the soft lit room.

"For centuries, Mary, my mother, has been revered out of context. It is time to put things straight and take her home."

46

Nothing Has Changed

The following day Gus is aboard Air Force One, which has just landed at a secret Air Force base in Israel. While the plane taxis into a designated position, Gus gazes out of the window by his seat. His heart is filling with so many emotions, so many memories, that he is a little disturbed by a line of about two dozen soldiers standing in precise unison with their weapons in the 'ready' position. An instant flashback reminds him of a similar a line of immaculate Roman soldiers with their spears at the ready. His mind still drifting, a tap on his shoulder brings him back to the present. He looks up at the attractive attendant standing close to him showing a fixed smile.

"Sir? They are waiting for you. You do realize you only have four hours?"

Hiding his disappointment, he offers her a polite smile.

"Four hours? My, how times haven't changed."

Her face displaying a puzzled look as he rises from his seat, she makes room as he reaches into the luggage locker above his seat and retrieves a small package.

While he walks to the exit, takes a deep breath of apprehension and steps out of t into the bright sunshine, the soft voice of the attendant seems to reverberate.

"We will wait for you."

Becoming more aware of the tense situation, he conveys to her a reassuring nod, and then slides the small package into his inside pocket of his jacket.

A young, self-assured Israeli officer appears in a brisk manner, and approaches Gus delivering a firm military salute. His Hebrew accent is obvious.

"Major Yosef Rabin. I am your - guide."

Gus offers him his hand.

"For the next four hours?"

"Yes. I'm sorry. That is all my superiors will allow. I have a vehicle waiting..."

He indicates for Gus to. Follow him to a nearby camouflaged, dusty jeep. They both climb into it, and then the Major turns the ignition key. As the engine bursts into life, and a few crunches of the gears resonate, they drive off. Holding the steering wheel with his left hand, the Major salutes the standing guard of soldiers. As they seem in no hurry to drive by, the troops stand to attention. Gus is impressed, but it is daunting at the same time.

"Impressive welcoming committee."

"I wouldn't say welcoming, more security. Just in case!"

Gus is beginning to feel irritated at this man's casual attitude.

"Just in case of 'what'?"

"Precautionary! I'm sorry."

Gus now developing a pit in his stomach, they drive along the dusty dirt road for a few minutes, and then Major Rabin stops the jeep outside a small, white flat-roofed cement house. His mood changing, he turns to Gus.

"This is my house. Please let me offer you a cool drink, before we start the tour. It will only take a few minutes."

Becoming drawn to this man's sudden sincerity, Gus thanks him with grateful smile.

"I would like that, thank you."

Pleased by the gratitude, Yosef Rabin is the first to climb out of the jeep and head toward his front door. As Gus follows, he becomes curious by the local desert landscape. On entering the little house, and shutting the door, Gus notices how the inside is cool and stark with a few basic pieces of furniture, and some loose rugs on the bare wooden floor. Still absorbing his surroundings, he sits in a nearby sofa that has seen better days. Meanwhile, Yosef comes in from what Gus presumes is the kitchen, carrying two bottles of cold beer. He sits down next to Gus and hands him a bottle. Appreciating the coolness of the glass, Gus smiles and takes a swig.

"I see you're not married."

"Is it that obvious?"

"Yes. Not having a woman around, it looks bare – empty of any emotion."

Yosef is surprised at the accuracy.

"You are right. My life is empty."

As Gus stares into he other man's cool, dark brown eyes, Yosef tries to look away. but finds it difficult. Gus keeps staring, and his voice reassuring.

"Your life is empty now, but from this moment on, your life is going to be full and rewarding."

Even though taking a liking to this stranger, Yosef is becoming wary, but transfixed.

"How?Who are 'you' to tell me such things?"

"Didn't your superiors inform you? Did you not wonder who was being carried here on Air Force One?"

"I was told, just two hours ago, that I had to pick up a man from Air Force One and show him the famous religious sites in Jerusalem or anywhere else he would like to go…"

"Within four hours?"

Yosef's eyes turn away from Gus. For some strange reason he feels ashamed and embarrassed at that part of his orders. Gus senses his predicament.

"Didn't you find that a strange order?"

"Yes, I did find it a bit unusual, especially when it involved the famous

Air Force One. However, you have to understand, Israel is now in a permanent state of siege. Palestine is now a sovereign nation and part of the UN. For various reasons we are given all kinds of strange orders, which I do not question."

Liking this man more by the minute, Gus rests his hand on Yosef's arm.

"My friend, the Jewish race has always been in a state of siege..."

Gus takes another swig of his cold beer. The strong consistency makes him choke. Understanding the predicament, Yosef pats Gus on the back to help relieve the choking.

"That is Israel's beer for you. Harsh at first until you get used to it."

"Like the countryside around here."

They pause for a few seconds while Gus attempts another swig. Determined not to waste another drop, this time he is successful at draining the whole bottle. Glad of his own effort, Gus then puts down the empty bottle on a nearby coffee table.

"I don't suppose any of the general public know I'm here."

"Not that I know. It is all very secretive."

Gus smiles at the irony.

"Like the ingredients of your beer?

Forgetting his military discipline, Yosef has to laugh at the comparison. Realizing time is marching on, he looks at his watch, and then eases out of the sofa.

"We need to get going. Time is precious."

Agreeing, but still frustrated, Gus rises.

"More than you'll ever realize."

Yosef's reaction to such a statement, is to convey to Gus a quizzical glance, and pause for a second in thought, before dumping his beer bottle on a nearby shelf, and heading out of the front door. Knowing he is penetrating this major's subconscious, Gus follows.

As they climb into the jeep, Yosef switches on the ignition. Again, he looks at Gus as if reflecting. His eyes focusing on a distant thought, he shifts the gear stick into first gear as the worn engine roars into life.

"I will take you to the Wailing Wall first, then to the other sites, and if time allows..."

"You mean I can go somewhere else?"

Yosef can't help but smile at Gus's sarcasm.

"Of course."

While traveling the bumpy road, Gus surveys the bleak desert countryside with some feint recognition. As they pass the natural landmarks, his mind drifts back and forth, observing that some of the countryside has changed, but so much is familiar. He then studies Yosef's profile while he concentrates on the precarious driving conditions.

Yosef can't be much older than me...

The Israeli's jaw keeps clenching as the jeep hits a bump or a small crater in the road. Gus attempts to shout over the noise.

"My father's name was Joseph."

Without taking his eyes off the way ahead, Yosef smiles, not hiding his pride.

"A Good old Jewish name. Yosef is the Hebrew pronunciation of Joseph."

A pang of longing for his previous childhood hits Gus. He pictures his earthly father's strong hands fashioning a piece of wood, and how they worked together with his two brothers making simple furniture of the day.

As they enter a more modern asphalt road, Jerusalem appears on the horizon, raised up on a hill. Gus feels his heart rate increase, as they come to a checkpoint, where some Palestinian Arabs are being questioned. Gus is surprised that his jeep is waved through.

While they drive closer to the ancient city walls, they pass other Arabs on foot. Gus's instinct is to wave. Yosef ignores them. Within minutes, they arrive near the Wailing Wall. Yosef stops the jeep, switches off the engine, points at the wall.

"You go down there and turn left."

"Yes. I know the way."

Yosef's reaction to Gus's unusual response, is to stare at him.

"Okay. I will wait for you here."

"You trust me not to run off?"

Yosef's serious expression cracks into a wide smile. His strong white teeth is a contrast to his dark tanned face.

"I trust you, but you would not get very far. I have ten plain-clothes men watching your every move."

"Very reassuring."

His body becoming stiff by the rough journey, Gus climbs out of the jeep. To release the tension in his body, he stretches his back, and then brushes the fine dust off his clothes.Without saying another word, he walks to the famous area.

On arriving, strong flashbacks enter his head.

I remember the old temple. Greedy merchants selling their wares, and me losing my temper by throwing merchandise around and destroying stalls...

He forces his mind to focus on 'now' as he walks to the top of the steps that show the vast historical area. He can't help but notice all the tourists enjoying a trip of a lifetime photographing everything for their own posterity. He also observes the groups of Orthodox Jews in earnest discussion. Their familiar black suits, hats and braided hair tails are in striking contrast to the casual dress of the tourist's who are photographing them.

With mixed emotions, Gus makes his way down the steps. On his way, he passes a group of tourists debating the safety factor. News of a suicide bombing in a Tel-A-Viv marketplace has reached them.

As Gus reaches the wall, a group of four young armed Israeli soldiers stretch out arm in arm forming a wide line, leaning their heads against the Wall, praying and chanting. Further along, Jewish men tap their foreheads against the sand colored stone, reading prayers from their little black books, and pushing pieces of folded paper into the cracks of the Wall. Past them, Gus can see a smaller section where the women are repeating the same rituals. Mesmerized by the pieces of paper sticking out of the wall, he suppress the need to shout.

You don't need to do that. I'm here. You don't have to push your scribbled prayers into the wall.

Knowing he would be ignored or even laughed at by such a gesture, he whispers under his breath.

"You poor souls. I'm here. You didn't know it the first time, and you don't know it now."

Nothing has changed. No one takes any notice of the most important sightseer in two thousand years, as he makes his way through the tourists and Rabbis.

Arriving back to where Yosef is waiting, he becomes aware of Gus's dejection.

"You all right?"

"I guess. Where to now?"

"The Garden of Gethsemane would be the easiest."

Hiding his despondency, Gus climbs into the dusty transport.

"Yes. Let's keep it nice and easy."

Ignoring his passenger's sarcasm, Yosef starts the Jeep and proceeds to the next destination.

The British, taking their biannual turn with the Americans, are on duty at the Garden of Gethsemane. They too, fail to note the important sightseer as he converses with his driver at the entrance to the Garden, and then turns to wait in line to pay his entrance fee. No one notices that despite the dry heat, the visitor is sweating more than normal. While wiping a hand across his brow, no one sees him hold his chest as if in pain. Meanwhile, the guides are busy gathering the tourists into little groups ready to enter. Trying hard to keep his equilibrium, Gus now has his ticket and joins a group. His guide, dressed as if from the bygone years of colonialism, exudes efficiency. His English voice is crisp and precise, as he indicates for the group to move forward.

"Welcome to the Garden everyone. As we proceed in an orderly manner, I will be pointing out characteristics that make this site the most authentic. Please follow me."

While trying to keep up with his group, panic attack symptoms over-whelm Gus. Not willing to wait for him, the rest of the group push past him. The guide notices the straggler.

"Come along old chap, don't dilly-dally, you're holding up the troops."

Not wanting to hold up the group, Gus makes a supreme effort. The guide's mouth continues to move, but Gus cannot hear him. In the meantime, the excited group walks by water well excavations that point to the ownership by a wealthy wine merchant, but Gus does not see them. He sees the Mount of Olives as men are sleeping, swords glistening. He hears shouts and scuffles, as the guide leads them to some railings at the side edge of the Garden. Proud of his knowledge, the guide continues.

"See that, ladies and gentlemen? Another sign we are at the correct location."

He leans over the railings and points past the Garden boundary to a rock face.

"The Skull of Golgotha for those of you who know your Bible, the Garden is mentioned as being close to that landmark."

The rivers of sweat blinding Gus have now run to his mouth. It tastes of blood, as his desperate hands grip the railing. A blue and white bus swings by and blocks out the view of the 'Skull'. The guide is not impressed by the interruption.

"No regard for history, but there you are. Right! Let us about turn and let us head for the most amazing site you'll ever see."

Gus is still gripping the railing, as the guide approaches.

"Are you all right old chap? Heat getting to you? We will be in the shade in a minute once we are inside the tomb. You won't want to miss that. Imagine, you'll be looking at the spot where Jesus lay. Of course, we've had to put railings up inside. Too many hands wanting to touch, and all that. It was wearing it away. Nevertheless, you'll get the feel of it all. What that poor man went through, just for us. Hard to imagine the pain. Here, take my arm. I'll help you, old chap."

Touched by the guide's concern, Gus is almost delirious.

"Andrew, my other rock."

"No! George is the name."

The guide's little group is becoming impatient while still waiting by the Garden tomb. The sight of the tall slim man with faltering steps, hanging onto George's arm does not stir them. A woman with heavy make-up and dyed blonde hair is becoming more annoyed.

"We've missed our turn to go into the tomb."

The guide is not sympathetic toward the selfish woman.

"We won't have to wait long madam. It will give me time to describe a few more things to you."

Ignoring a few more disgruntled voices coming from his group, George helps Gus sit on a nearby bench, and then carries on with his program.

"You will notice that the outside of the tomb has been reinforced in certain areas. The groove where the stone was rolled is wide, consistent with the biblical description of a heavy stone being used as a door. Matthew, Chapter 28, Verse 60. I would like you to take note of the notice on the new wooden door.

'He is not here, for he is risen".

Although Gus is unsteady as he rises to his feet, his voice is commanding.

"Then enter the tomb! Not with sadness, but with joy. Not with hopelessness, but with hope. There is 'still' time to act!"

As George studies the speaker, he is aware that the impatient woman is not listening. Instead, she shouts out.

"Finally! It's our turn. About time too."

Determined to make her way to the tomb, the guide interrupts by holding up his hands.

"I think in all fairness, we will let this young gentleman lead our group"

Not happy with this new arrangement, she sulks as Gus approaches the tomb. Hiding his trembling, he lifts his feet over the ledge of the groove, and then over the threshold. As if in awe, the group follows. His mind in a daze, Gus manages to walk to the far end of the tomb, stops and turns. Watching the group coming in toward him, he is calmed a little by the coolness of the surrounding rock, but he is sweating more than he should. His instinct tells him to turn to the right and lean against the black prison style railings. Meanwhile, the guide is busy explaining.

"The tomb is in two halves. Looking to your right through the railings, you will see the smaller final resting places for the female members of the household."

After countless tours, George is still overwhelmed.

"Now, if you turn to your left, you will be looking at the final resting place of our Lord Jesus Christ."

Never getting used to this part of the tour, his emotion is too much to bear.

"Please - meet me outside - when you are ready."

The group is left to think their thoughts, absorb the reality of what they are seeing, and make peace with their God. In the meantime, Gus feels he is suffocating. His clothes feel tight and the linen shirt is constricting his breathing. Memories come flooding back.

The searing pain as I woke, the blackness of the tomb, the ground shaking violently,and the light entering as the stone rolled back. The cool hollowed out resting place looks inviting. I wish I could tear down these railings, lie there and sleep forever...

A far away voice tears into his thoughts.

"It's finished."

Gus is still focusing on the resting place. He mumbles under his breath.

"I know."

Unaware George is insistent toward Gus, his voice seems faraway from Gus's trauma.

"It's finished, the tour is finished, and the next group is waiting."

Still not aware of George's insistence, Gus is struggling to breathe. In desperation, he pulls at his sweat laden linen shirt from under his jacket. Ripping a piece off and throwing it through the bars, George stares down in disbelief as the piece of linen settles in the shallow grave. The constriction gone, Gus can breathe. His heart lifts and his strength returns. Gus feels euphoric, as he steps out of the tomb into the bright sunshine.

Taking no notice of Gus, the impatient woman is informing the new awaiting group of her doubts.

"John Lennon once said the Beatles were better known than God. I believe that!"

Overhearing these caustic words, the hope Gus felt is short-lived.

Attracting the attention of the crowd, the woman continues with her opinion.

"What's God ever done for me? Nothing!"

Their interest growing, the new group wait before entering the tomb. Noticing their fascination increasing, she continues.

"I've worked hard all my life and got nowhere. All God's given me is a spouse with crippling emphysema and me with cancer."

Pulling out a cigarette, she becomes aware of Gus staring at her.

"As for you, keeping us waiting in this heat. If you're sick, you should have stayed at home."

Her poisonous words are like the spear at his crucifixion, thrusting into his body. Gus doubles in agony. While clutching his right side, the group watch in horror as he collapses to the ground. His head catches the ledge of the groove. Blood streaks down his forehead and neck. More blood seeps out from underneath his wrist as he holds onto his side. His other hand, lying outstretched toward the group, begins to bleed from the wrist. The group becomes transfixed, and stand motionless, like blood sport spectators. Fear and concern taking over, someone screams and then another shouts. Yosef appears. Assessing the situation, and becoming frantic while pushing his way through the ever-growing crowd, he shouts in desperation.

"Move back! Please move back."

As no one is moving, in further desperation he pulls his automatic from its holster.

"I said move back!"

Ignoring the gun, the impatient woman is jolted out of her fear of blood and kneels down to Gus.

"Me and my big mouth. Here, I'll get you sorted out in no time. I've got just the thing in my handbag."

Yosef and an accumulating crowd watches her pull out some traveler's tissues and some moist wipes.

"Here we are dear. Always prepared. Like wearing clean underwear. Know what I mean?"

As she raises a tissue over Gus, the bleeding stops. Like a receding river, it dries up and all traces disappear. The crowd gasps. Yosef is confused. He saw blood, 'everyone' saw blood. Meanwhile, Gus looks up at the woman, now wiping the sweat from his hands and face with a moist tissue. The fragrance of the tissue fills his nostrils.

"Do you know who I am?"

"I really don't care who you are love. You could be on one of those soap actors for all I know. That's not the point! You were just someone needing help."

Looking into the woman's olive eyes, he grips her arm.

"Thank you – Mary."

Her reaction is to laugh and look at the curious crowd.

"Poor man. Must be concussion. My name is June."

Not believing what he has just witnessed, Yosef looks down at the scene, and taps June's shoulder.

"I'll take over now."

He assists June to her feet, and helps her into the dissipating onlookers. Keeping his voice low, he bends down to be closer to Gus.

"I came to find you. We are running late. Do you think you can stand if I help?"

As Gus reaches out his hand, there is no hole in his wrist. The crowd applauds as Gus stands. Presuming they have been witness to some sort of special effects, it was all worth the ticket money.

Game over, the crowd begins to melt away, just as Yosef's cell phone rings. He answers in Hebrew, nods a few times, and then ends the call.

"We just have time to visit the Sea of Galilee."

Half listening, Gus is staring at June. She is bent over the trashcan by the bench, throwing in her new cigarettes one by one. Remembering her conflicting complaints and also her kindness when needed, he whispers.

"You're healed."

Viewing from their hot and dusty vehicle, the giant inland freshwater lake looks cool and inviting to both men. From their parked position, pulled

384

off the road, they can see the vast sweep of water curving around the town of Galilee. Across the water, the angle of the sun has lit up the Golan Heights. Their majestic cliffs hiding the signs of ravage and heartbreak. Yosef becomes defensive,

"The fresh water from the Golan Heights is our life blood. We need possession or Israel dies."

Even though listening, Gus remains silent.

Yosef interprets this as condemnation.

"You would have done the same!"

Gus removes his gaze from the tormented Heights and gazes at Yosef. Observing his desire for understanding, Gus grips the other man's forearm.

"I feel everybody's pain and misery. The Palestinians that are being driven from their homes to make room for more Jewish settlements, the thousands of homeless and hungry Arabs in refugee camps seeing no future. I feel for them all."

Yosef lowers his head, as if ashamed.

"I don't always agree with the politicians. I'm just a soldier..."

Resting his hand on the soldier's shoulder, Gus reassures there is no resentment.

"Your chance will come to put things right. In the meantime, can you drive through the town? I know of a jetty."

Thankful for the kind gesture, Yosef is surprised by the request.

"You know a jetty? How come?"

Gus not being inclined to answer, Yosef takes the hint.

"Okay. We drive."

While they travel past the quayside fish restaurants teeming with tourists eating fish, Gus becomes fascinated at the fish in the lake swimming against the sea wall hoping for a morsel of bread. The tourists are generous, tossing handfuls of crumbs to the already well-fed fish. Gus smiles at the irony of eating and feeding the same species at the same time.

There are certainly more than five loaves and two fish this time.

The traffic thins out as they approach an old jetty. When told to stop, Yosef is curios as Gus gets out of the jeep first and strides ahead. At the beginning of the jetty, he turns to look out over the blue water. He is careful as he picks his way along and over the large boulders, which lead to an aging fishing boat, which have been used in this area for thousands of years. At the water's edge, Gus leans over medium size boulder to stare down at his reflection. After a couple of seconds, two more, and then another two faces appear to join him. In comparison tp Gus's clean shaven appearance, the reflections have long hair and beards. His mind filling with heartfelt memories, Gus's eyes fill with tears. A sixth reflection is now staring back at him.

"Yosef? If I asked you to give up your job in the army and leave your home to travel with me, would you do it? Or would you think I was mad?"

Being taken by surprise, Yosef sidesteps the question. Becoming entranced by this unique stranger, he feels the need to be diplomatic.

"When I saw you bending over the water, I thought you were being sick. After your fall in the Garden and all this heat..."

His voice trails off as Gus stands up straight and gazes at him with a compassion meant for close friends.

"Don't worry about me. I'm not sick. I just saw some old, dear friends."

"Where?"

"In the water."

Yosef is becoming concerned by these bizarre observations.

"Maybe we should get back to the jeep. I don't want you getting sunstroke. We can stop off for a cooling beer."

Remembering the first beer with Yosef, Gus reflects

"Sounds good. But first I have another question for you."

"Really?"

"It was in this area over two thousand years ago, I met the men who became my apostles. I asked them the same question. If they would give up everything to be with me?"

Yosef's concern at whether Gus 'is' getting sunstroke, he acts considerate, and indicates to the Jeep.

"Yes. I know the story."

"Then you must know who I am? Haven't you seen enough today to realize?"

Being a practical army man, Yosef does not want to offend, so he continues to act thoughtful.

"Sir? I have seen many visitors come to Israel and go a little crazy. Believing they have been sent by god for the second coming, we call it 'The Jesus Syndrome'. We believe it is a sickness..."

Needing to convince this good man, Gus interrupts.

"Yosef come with me for just a little while. Let us sit on that old boat."

Without waiting for a reply, Gus negotiates his way along the boulders, and with one hand keeping the boat steady, he climbs over the edge and sits.

"Join me!"

Extending his hand to an irritable and confused Yosef, the boat creeks and groans under the weight of the two men. The seats are worn by many fishing trips. Gus notices the design has not changed over the years. Meanwhile, Yosef is becoming anxious and frustrated as he peers at his watch. Ignoring Yosef's tense expression, Gus is reassuring.

"At this moment, it is as if time has stood still. Look at me Yosef."

Used to accepting direct orders, Yosef is reluctant, but meets this man's gaze.

Although Gus has his attention, he knows he has to be more convincing.

"You're a good man with a kind heart. You often battle with your inner turmoil, especially since your wife and daughter died."

Yosef's eyes widen in wonder, tinged with shock.

"How the hell do you...?"

Gus's answer is to lean forward and take hold of Yosef's hands, while their knees touch.

"Three years ago your wife and nine-year-old daughter were killed in a senseless bombing near Jaffa. Your father-in-law committed suicide over the tragedy. God felt your bitterness and your anger."

Yosef trembles and begins to sob.

"God was nowhere to stop it! It should not have happened!"

Understanding this man's grief, Gus continues.

"You cannot use God as your scapegoat. It is man, trying to control his own destiny by turning away from God. Remember, you were God's chosen people, and you blew it."

Unable to concentrate on Gus's truth, tears of self pity still pour down Yosef's face.

"They were completely innocent! Just visiting a sick friend. Many people died that day."

Wrapped up in the other man's sorrow, Gus squeezes Yosef's hands a little tighter.

"I know. I was there crying with you. I am always there with the pain and the joy, but nobody wants to listen anymore. They prefer the easy pleasures of the devil, and he is winning them all over to him."

Looking down at their hands, Yosef is beginning to be caught up in Gus's message.

"Is that why you have returned?"

"Yes! One year to get it right, or it's all over."

Relishing the warmth of Gus's hands, Yosef wipes his face with his sleeve, and then refocuses back on the other man's intense hazel eyes.

"What is that blue aura?"

Warmed by the observation, Gus stands, and releases his grip on the other man's hands.

"Its good that you can see. Now we must act!"

As if a heavy burden has been lifted, Yosef becomes earnest.

"I have always believed as it is written, that our Messiah shall come to rid the world of evil and destruction."

"Well my friend, he has arrived, and you're looking at him."

"No one will believe you. Look at me? It is like...."

"History repeating itself?"

Avoiding to answer, Yosef looks at his watch.

"Its time to go. It's you that have much to do."

Still not sure if Yosef is convinced, Gus becomes somber.

"Yes. I'm afraid you're right."

Both now in a thoughtful mood, they climb out of the old boat, then make their way to the dusty jeep. As the engine starts as if in pain, they look at each other now as old comrades, and a new understanding.

Fifty minutes later, at the airfield where Air Force One is patiently waiting, an anxious Colonel is pacing back and forth. He stops, glares at his watch, and then scans the horizon. Nothing obvious to catch his attention, he turns again to pace.

As the Jeep appears out of nowhere, the sentry at the gate is abrupt when standing to attention. As the jeep screeches to a halt, and engulfs everyone in a cloud of dust, the anxious Colonel leans over the hot vehicle, and shouts in Hebrew.

"Cutting it a bit fine Major!"

Yosef's response is to salute and smile with a hint of sarcasm. The Colonel beckons to the sentry to lift the barrier, which he does in an instant. His eyes retaining the smile, Yosef gives the sentry a quick salute and heads off toward Air Force One.

They climb out of the jeep, pause, and look at each other with a new kind of understanding. Observing their dust covered clothes, they both burst out laughing.

Not bothering to brush his uniform, Yosef looks at his watch.

"Look at that! One minute short of four hours. Not bad for a man that had lost his way."

While they both laugh again and embrace, Yosef whispers in Gus's ear. "What do I do now?"

Enjoying the other man's warmth and sincerity, Gus whispers back.

"You can tell everyone the truth, or you can just ignore and forget."

"I cannot do that! Not now, but I am so scared..."

The colonel's voice bellows in Hebrew just a few yards from them.

"Major! They have to go - NOW!"

"Yes, sir."

Gus is the one to loosen the embrace.

"God loves you Yosef. You will be shown the way and the strength to overcome your fears."

"Thank you – my brother."

As they separate, Gus grips his hand, and then reaches inside his jacket and pulls out the small package and hands it to Yosef.

"Shalom."

While reluctant to climb the stairs to enter Air Force One, Gus turns before entering. He sees a curious Yosef unwrap the package. His eyes take on a faraway look as the statuette of Mary is revealed. In response, Yosef raises her to his lips, and plants a gentle kiss.

With a heavy heart, but also a sense of satisfaction, Gus waves goodbye as Air Force One takes off, leaving mother and his new brother on the tarmac.

47

Return to Hope

It is now evening. The sky is dark and overcast with heavy cloud. Having just stopped raining, the airport lights reflect off the asphalt making it appear like a large black lake as Air Force One taxies toward a designated landing bay. Security being tight, military and civilian police have surrounded the whole area. Allowing for a section of the airfield to be cordoned off for the public, hundreds of excited children accompanied by their parents are waiting. Their steamy breath can be seen in the cold damp air, as media crews beam their spotlights on the huge aircraft as it comes to a stop.

Thinking Gus is returning direct from Rome, the TV commentators are speaking into their microphones, and offering the viewers a short history of the young man about to exit the plane. Meanwhile, the crowd is becoming anxious as the minutes tick by, while they watch a portable staircase being pushed into place. There is a sigh of excitement as the aircraft passenger door opens and a flight attendant appears. The tension increases as she fastens the door, and then returns inside the plane. Now there is a pause of expectancy, when Gus appears. Light beams focus on him as cheers and cries from the welcoming crowd echoes as he waves and descends the steps. Media frenzy increases as the crowd's excitement reaches a climax when he reaches the asphalt.

Much to the surprise of the crowd, the President appears with her daughter and two secret service agents out of a nearby building. The crowd erupts as Julie leaves her mother and runs up to greet Gus with a hug.

Tears filling her eyes and running down her cheeks, Julia's mother resists the hug, but grips his hand with both of hers.

"You made it then?"

"Thanks to you."

His tired face glad to see them both, Gus slides his arm around Julie's shoulder as all three face the crowd as if one person. Wiping her eyes with one hand, the President grabs Gus's hand with her other and raises it as if he has just won the world boxing championship. The crowd roars again in full approval.

Fatigue now creeping into every muscle, Gus turns to her.

"I must go to them. Is that all right?"

"Of course. I'll wait here for you by my car, ready to take you to the White House."

Reluctant to let go of her hand, he puts on a smile, as he strolls over to the enthusiastic waiting crowd. He first notices Eva commentating into her microphone with young Ryan huddling up close. Not wanting to ignore the rest of the crowd, Gus heads straight for her. The noise is deafening as children shout for him accompanied by adults waving, taking photos, and waiting for any sort of personal contact. By the time he reaches Eva, she has switched off her microphone and reaches out to him. Glad to see her, he grips one of her hands and reaches down to kiss Ryan's head. Being caught up in the excitement, Mike is still recording, as tears fill Eva's eyes.

"You're safe my love."

Never losing his love for her, his eyes seem to sparkle a little, as he gazes down at her.

"Of course! Thank God, and Madam President. What is important, how are you?"

"I'm fine now you're okay."

The noise interfering with their thoughts, she turn toward the rest of the people behind the cordon.

RETURN TO HOPE

"They're all waiting for you. Go to them. They love you now, like we do."

Sensing a hint of jealousy in her voice, he plants a kiss on her cheek, and then peers at the crowd.

"How did they all know I would be here?"

Ryan is surprised at the question.

"You're famous! Or didn't you know?"

Becoming overwhelmed, Gus shrugs and rubs Ryan's head. Offering them a grateful smile, he leaves and heads toward the others.

At the rear of the crowd, a young man in his early twenties with short-cropped blonde hair, which looks metallic under the lights, is dressed in an expensive tan leather jacket, crisp white shirt, and neat pressed chinos. This clean-pressed young man is discreet as he maneuvers among the crowd. Unknown to the distracted mass, he is careful when extracting men's wallets from their trousers and women's purses from their bags. After a while, he rests and checks the zipper on his small duffel bag, which acts as a holdall for the stolen goodies. Delighted by his supply, he again maneuvers through the crowd. Aware of Gus talking and shaking hands with all the admirers, the young man continues with his endeavors.

Focusing on an ultimate prize of a bulging purse lying on top of an elderly woman's open shoulder bag, he glides in unnoticed.

This is so easy. It's almost a shame to take it. Where's the challenge?

As he reaches out toward the irresistible temptation, a strong hand grips his shoulder. The pickpocket gives out a surprised yelp, which is drowned out by the crowd's enthusiasm. His reaction to ease the pain radiating through his shoulder is to turn and see a military policeman.

"Think again boy."

The 'boy' freezes as Natas keeps a viselike grip on the young man's shoulder. Not wanting to create a disturbance, he drags the young man to a nearby wall where they disappear into the shadows.

"So? What have we here?"

Before the young man can retaliate, Natas grabs and unzips the duffle bag with one hand, while still holding the thief by the neck with his other. This being more painful, the 'boy' hisses through clenched teeth.

"Screw you!"

Natas' response is to squeeze harder, causing the younger man to howl in pain. As the older man's green eyes glow in fury, he relishes the fact he is scaring the young man to a jelly.

"What is your name boy?"

"Sid – Sidney Pot – Potter."

Now getting somewhere, Natas releases his grip. Sidney's instinct is to flee, but Natas doesn't give him that choice. With lightning speed he forces his knee up against the young man's groin, leaving him paralyzed to the spot.

"Now, what am I going to do with you Sidney?"

"You could just let me go."

Being insulted by such a request, Natas's knee increases the pressure, making Sidney sweat with the pain, and his hot breath streaming out in plumes. At the same time, Natas places his left hand palm down on top of Sidney's blond head.

"I see you have a sense of humor. I like that. Now – let us see."

Natas closes his eyes and concentrates.

"I see you have an extensive criminal record and no living relatives. How

Interesting?"

On opening his eyes, Sidney is drawn to their fluorescence.

"How the hell did you know?"

"It does not matter how I know? The main thing is I can put you away for at least ten years."

Sidney's basic instincts tell him this MP is not what he seems.

"You won't, because you would have whisked me away by now."

Admiring the boy's defiance, Natas' eyes beam into him.

"Do not be so sure young Sidney. I have the power to do what I like with you."

"You're nuts!"

Irritation setting in, Natas's knee increases the pressure.

"That's a good one coming from a small time loser who has to steal old ladies' purses to survive. Come! I have a real job for you."

On removing his knee, Sidney gives a jerk as if to flee. With lightning speed, Natas grips Sidney's upper left arm so hard, the pain makes Sidney give up.

"What sort of job?"

"Let us say there is fifty grand in it for you. So, let's go."

Natas achieving want he wants, he and Sidney disappear around the back of a building into the night.

Gus has finished shaking hands, smiling and talking to the crowds. Escorted by a patient secret service agent, he makes his way back to the President's big black Lincoln, known as the beast. Gus acknowledges her as the agent beckons him into the open door. Savoring the relative quiet inside the car compared to the enthusiastic clamber of the outside, Gus collapses back into the plush comfort of the leather seating. Sitting at a discreet distance, she pats his hand with affection.

"Tired?"

"A bit."

Julie, her excitement obvious, and sitting the other side of her mother, leans over to get a better view of Gus..

"We saw you on TV with the Pope. It was on all the stations, the networks and going viral on all the social media."

Appreciating the comfort, Gus, lifts his head up to extend his gratitude.

"I hope the commentary was friendly, because the European Parliament speech was a disaster. I completely lost it."

As the 'beast' begins to drive away, the President is mindful of the crowd.

"Let's give them one last wave."

His head hurting and the fatigue creeping further into his body, Gus hides his predicament by leaning closer to the window and presenting the crowd with his best smile, and wave. Holding on until the beloved crowd is out of sight, he then sinks back to his former position, and shuts his eyes. Trying not not push him too hard, she grips his hand, and keeps her voice low.

"How was Israel?"

"Under the circumstances it turned out to be good. However, it was also sad and extremely painful."

Needing to know more, she suppresses her eagerness, by squeezing his hand.

"The European 'disaster' went better than you realize. My sources inform me there is a lot of support under the surface for you."

"We pray and hope."

Unable to quench her enthusiasm, Julie leans across her mother again to get a better look at Gus.

"How has Israel changed since – well - last time?"

Gus opens his eyes and reaches across to her with his open hand.

"From what I saw in four hours, the country has changed a lot. The people have worked very hard in agriculture and infrastructure, but their attitude and outlook on life is just the same."

Mother and daughter gripping the open hand, Julie asks first.

"In what way?"

"Its like a time warp. For example, I overheard a tourist complain that a man outside the Church of the Holy Sepulcher was falsely saying no one could go in the church unless they paid him first as a guide..."

Exhaustion crawling over him in waves, he shuts his eyes.

While the big black Lincoln travels in silence through the night, it begins to rain. The windshield wipers go on. The back and forth rhythm is hypnotic, as the President breaks the silence.

"The World Council of Churches meets tomorrow at ten a.m. in Madison Square Garden. I have made all the arrangements. You will be staying at a hotel not too far from there, and will be looked after and protected. At eight-thirty you will be picked up and driven directly to the Garden. Your speech is booked for ten-thirty. Everyone is expecting you."

Having listened, Gus opens his eyes, and gazes at her in admiration.

"I can see why you're the President."

Appreciating the compliment, she squeezes his hand again.

"I strongly feel that this is God's plan. It so happens I am the right person in the right place at the right time. Will 'you' manage okay?"

To reply, he offers her a smile of appreciation.

"You try to stop me..."

He falls asleep.

48

The Gardener visits the Garden

New York's Madison Square Garden has always been famous for world champion boxing tournaments and sporting events. However, in recent years, it had been run down with lack of use. The occasional rock concert would revive it, but then it would just sit there looking dark and seedy. A new enterprising Mayor was elected. He got together with local and national business people to rejuvenate the 'Garden' to its former glory and beyond. Today is the first big event in the new Madison Complex. The World Council of Churches has decided to have their annual meeting in the new assembly hall.

An anxious Gus is waiting for his cue, and yet he is excited by this challenge of confronting this mass of clergy with a hope that they will accept his message. His nerves tingling, he tries to relax back into the armchair and close his eyes.

Relishing the silence, his mind drifts back a couple of thousand years when the Pharisees challenged him.

When they asked me if I really was the Son of God, I remembered the frustration, the sadness, and the hypocrisy of these 'righteous' upholders of the Temple....

The door opens. A quiet shushing sound against the new plush carpet fills Gus's ears, as a young priest enters and walks toward him.

"We are ready for you now."

Gus pulls a face, as he lifts his trembling body out of the chair.

"Yes! To crucify me?"

"Oh, no sir. We are all eager to hear your words."

Gus's mind now concentrating on the present, his eyes focus on the priest's familiar face.

"You were at the Vatican. Am I right?"

As his life is always in the shadow of his elders, young priest becomes embarrassed at being recognized.

"Aye. You're right."

Still a little overwhelmed, he puts his hand out to Gus.

"I hope that lot out there appreciate who you 'really' are."

His Northern English accent sounding pleasant to Gus's ears, he shakes this young man's hand.

"Do 'you' believe who I really am?"

"Aye, I do. But the masses in that hall...?"

He points toward a wall.

"I don't know. Look how you had to convince the Holy Father. Do you have to perform miracles every time to persuade these - people?"

Curious at this young priest's skepticism, he releases his hand.

"If I have to - yes."

As if searching for more, the young man peers into Gus's hazel eyes.

"I saw how exhausted you got after performing just 'one' miracle."

Thankful for the understanding statement, Gus presents him with a congenial smile and places his hand on his shoulder.

"I know - I know. Well? Lead the way Macduff. A lamb to the slaughter."

The new Assembly Hall is more like an indoor stadium. Seating ten thousand bodies at maximum capacity, today it is about half full. As Gus follows the priest down a narrow aisle, he observes the seats banking up at a steep angle from a small staging area in the center of the Hall. On the floor of this area, there is a round carpeted stage with an ornate wooden podium at its center. As Gus arrives near the podium, the tense atmosphere hits Gus like a sledgehammer making his stomach turn over.

Sensing his anxiety, the priest touches Gus's arm in reassurance, and leads him to the podium. As they arrive, the priest whispers as he points to two switches, one red and one blue.

"The red one operates the moving stage and the blue one switches on the microphone."

Gus's eyes penetrate the young man's steady gray eyes, as he whispers back.

"God loves you, and thank you."

"Thanks to your sacrifice."

Satisfied he has done his part, the priest is reluctant to leave. Seeing him disappear into a nearby tunnel, Gus positions his nervous body at the podium, turns, and scans his curious audience. High up, he can see a section for the TV and media. The silence is deafening, as he whispers.

"Give me the strength to convince these people."

Taking a deep breath, he presses the blue switch bringing on the microphone.

"Good morning everyone. I am now going to switch on the revolving stage, so I can go around in circles while talking to you."

Listening to several voices laugh, Gus can feel the atmosphere lighten a little. His sweating hands grip the podium while his mind races, but remains focused.

"I am deeply honored that you have set aside a time for me. Here inside this beautiful reconstruction, we can all let God enter inside of us."

Even though appearing lighter, the atmosphere is still one of suspicion.

"This is how it has to be. God is not out there floating on a big fluffy cloud looking down on us like ants. Nor is he in a huge computer bank with his angels pushing buttons giving out e-mails, Facebook messages or tweets in answering our prayers."

Mumbles of confusing can be heard, accompanied by the occasional cough.

His confidence mounting, Gus's mind is becoming razor sharp.

"God is only within you, if you let it happen. I feel right now that a vast number of you haven't really let God into your hearts. You are only 'saying' you have."

The reaction from the audience, are mumbles of protest while the stage keeps turning, and Gus continues.

"Throughout the ages when a disaster happens, people always say – why does God allow this to happen? It happens because, as you learned people know, in the beginning man chose freedom of choice. There is a heavy price to pay for free choice. Many of you don't realize that when you do let God into your soul, miracles do happen, and problems are solved. Unfortunately, you as God's so called representatives have not been getting this message across."

The atmosphere is becoming tense. Natas is sitting in the Roman Catholic section, smirking and willing Gus to screw things up, as Gus continues, "The battle between God and the Devil goes on. Humankind causes most of the tragedies by letting 'evil' into their lives. However, the rescue workers, doctors and nurses that follow to clean up the mess of these tragedies, have let God into 'their' lives. Unfortunately, time is now running out. Man has had over two thousand years to make his choice and get his act together. He has failed dismally by not even trying to get it right. I know some of you here who have taken God into your hearts, feel hopeless, because evil seems to win every time. Your hopelessness is well founded. Evil 'is' taking over everywhere, because collectively as leaders and fishers of men, you have let your petty squabbles and self-serving interests stand in the way of the big picture. The branches have failed the vine."

Natas smiles in satisfaction as the outcry surrounding him grows louder. To compensate, Gus increases the volume of the microphone.

"You have probably been watching the media lately and followed my actions. A few of you here recognize the truth and believe who I am, but most of you do not. So, for the benefit of the latter, I will now repeat my message to you so that your eyes may be opened. This beautiful planet of ours has 'one' year. One year only, for man to expel evil from his heart and put right 'all' that is wrong with the world. The key my friends is here in this very hall. First, dogma, hypocrisy, and being on your own agenda has to go. Because you are out of touch and out of date, I see empty churches. The dwindling faithful are worried sick about their crumbling expensive massive cathedrals, huge synagogues and gold mosques. Your flocks are bewildered, frightened, alone and most of all, let down. In that environment, Satan is having a field day. So, I say to you, open up your hearts and let God in NOW! It is that simple."

Becoming tired from the mounting tension, Gus can feel the atmosphere is becoming divided. He notices nods and murmurs of agreement from the smaller churches, but resistance from the larger ones.

"Be open to new ideas. Teach in the way people can relate. Use modern communications, e-mail, web sites, the social media, and continually question your own motives. Teach that forgiveness is a gift with a price tag attached. 'Go away and sin no more.' The main obstacle has not changed. Love one another..."

Feeling the unease building, he pauses to sharpen his mind, and then continues.

"All these things you must teach by 'example'. That has been your biggest failing. Your 'example' has fallen short. Tomorrow I go to address the UN General Assembly and tell them the same message. After one year, this world as you know - it will be destroyed. Only the 'true' believers will survive to start again, as it should have been in the beginning...."

Without warning, a strong, harsh voice bellows out from the audience. The media focus on Natas. Enjoying the attention, his eyes seem to glow in the dim light.

"You have no right to be going around scaring everyone like this. What proof have you got that this so-called catastrophe is going to happen?"

The aggravation becoming more intense, others join in.

"Yes! Tell us."

Knowing his adversary, Gus hesitates to find the strength to retaliate.

"Ladies and gentlemen, lets be honest. You all 'know' the final battle between good and evil is beginning right now in this fine building. I have it on Divine authority, as surely as this podium turns, so will your fate."

The large churches laugh, the smaller ones look nervous. Taking full advantage of the confusing situation, Natas shouts back at Gus.

"Divine authority? That sounds exceedingly grand. Next, you will be saying you are a God yourself. Admit it now; you are just a publicity seeker who does clever tricks. You're a fake, but we will forgive you, as long as you – 'sin no more'. Then we can all go to lunch."

The majority of the audience react by laughing, while the minority feel sorry for Gus. His response is to grip the podium, until his knuckles turn white with fury. Gus's eyes now ablaze with righteous anger, he shouts in defiance.

"Get you behind me!"

The audience now shocked into silence by the well known judgment, the podium turns away from Natas. The anger in Gus's voice still apparent, he is determined to continue.

"I suffered for you two thousand years ago in a way that was so painful, none of you here could ever imagine. I took 'your' sins on 'my' shoulders, I forgave you all by giving you a chance to obtain salvation. I knew you would still sin, but unfortunately you have sinned to such an unrepentant low, that enough is enough. It is crunch time! Accept God into your hearts 'now' or perish forever."

For a few nail biting seconds the silence is deafening. The stillness is broken by a single boo, followed by several jeers, and then loud heckling erupts and takes over. All followed by an overwhelming slow handclap.

Throughout the world, viewers are riveted to their small screens, televisions and computers. Max is in his office with Eva and Mike, focusing on the screen in front of them. Tears of empathy and frustration roll down Eva's face, as Mike grips her hand for comfort.

In the White House, the President is watching with her daughter Julie. They both are reacting the same by wiping tears from their faces.

"Mother, this is terrible. Look how they are treating him. It's monstrous, and they are supposed to be the world's religious leaders."

The President strokes her hair, sharing her daughter's anguish and frustration. "None are as blind as those that don't want to see, my dear."

Overcome by distress and worst of all failure, Gus presses the red and blue buttons together on the podium. The stage stops turning and the microphone is switched off. Doing his best to come to terms with this turmoil, he wastes no time in heading for the tunnel. Almost falling over the young English priest who helped him earlier, Gus hides his emotions.

"Oh! I'm sorry. I didn't see you."

As they look into each other's eyes, Gus notices tears running down the priest's face, and anger filling his voice.

"Those idiots! Are they 'all' so bloody blind?"

As Gus places a trembling hand on the priest's shoulder to help reassure the young man's fear, he can hear a mixture of shouts and jeers way back in the hall.

"Not all. Some can see. Walk with me. Let's get out of here."

While Gus grips hold of the priests arm for support, they increase their steps. Coming to the tunnel entrance, Gus is becoming tired and has to lean more on the young man,

"What is your name my friend?"

"Garth – sir."

Admiring the humbleness and a hidden strength of this young priest, Gus offers him a warm smile of gratitude.

"Father Garth? Right now I need all of your strength, wisdom and love."

Never being complimented like this before, fresh tears sting Garth's eyes.

"I have only been a full priest for a few months."

Walking toward the end of the tunnel, Gus stops and rests a little. By placing both his hands on Garth's shoulders, he searches Garth's gray eyes.

"My dear brother. You're one of God's rare children, and have gained more wisdom and love in those few months than all that seething mass in there put together. Forgive me. I'm tired. I shouldn't talk this way. There 'are' many good people in that audience, but unfortunately they are severely outnumbered."

Overcome by this new relationship, Garth leads Gus out into a lobby area that is deserted. The soft lighting emphasizes the pale pastel colors and gives artificial warmth that is challenged by the harsh outdoor daylight showing through the main glass-paneled doors. Taking charge, Garth speaks first.

"Where would you like to go now?"

Reviving a little, but depression racking his mind, Gus responds.

"I think I will walk to the hotel that the President kindly provided for me, and rest. I need to clear my head for tomorrow."

While Garth hears frantic voices from the stairs and the elevator buttons are flashing, he makes a serious suggestion.

"It's not safe to walk. The media has already left the hall. Moreover, there may be some crazy nut out there waiting for you. Hurry! We'll take my car. You may need to change your hotel."

As they run toward the small parked car, Gus turns to look back at the beautiful new building now tainted with evil and indifference.

What now? More failures?

49

Reflections to Come

Gus is lying on a plush king-size bed, eating a well made beef and salad sandwich, supplied by room service. He sips a glass of milk in between bites.

The television opposite his bed is on. A news flash, showing his painful experience at the World Council of Churches meeting. The outdated phone on the nearby bedside cabinet startles him as it rings. He becomes hesitant as he picks up the handset. Wondering who it could be on the other end, as he is not expecting anyone to call, he is reluctant to answer.

"Hello?"

A strong familiar female voice answers.

"Gus?"

"Ah! Madame President. How are you?"

"I'm fine. How are you? Are you enjoying your sandwich?"

"Thank you, it is wonderful and so is the room."

She laughs to hide the seriousness of it all.

"The safe house is reserved for special guests."

"I really appreciate you having a car waiting for me at the back of the hotel."

"After watching you suffer on the media, I realized that anyone wanting to cause trouble for you would see you heading for your hotel. So, we took the necessary steps to avoid an embarrassing situation. I would have used a helicopter to get you out of there if needed..."

She pauses for a second, and then her voice becomes serious.

"Have you any gut feelings how it's going to go tomorrow?"

Thinking of nothing else, Gus ponders the question.

"All I know is that I'm in God's hands. What ever will be, will be."

Becoming concerned by his fatalism, she remains positive.

"I will pray for you 'and' I will double check the security I ordered is carried out to the letter."

Picturing her on the other end of the line, he becomes humbled.

"How will I ever be able to repay you?"

As her own confidence grows, the joy in the President's voice reverberates.

"Well, for a start? After your speech, you can have dinner with me at the White

House. So, I'll see you in the morning then."

Without needing to reply, he hears the familiar click, then the electronic dial tone. His mind in a whirl, he replaces the phone back on the side table.

As he finishes his meal, the television shows commercials. He watches for a while, fascinated by how things never change in the world of commerce. Having seen enough, he reaches across for the remote and presses the power button - all is now quiet.

Contemplating what is to come, he lies back relishing the firm comfort of the bed. While he stares up at the ornate ceiling feeling guilty at staying in such opulence, apprehension of the daunting day ahead overwhelms him.

"Oh God! Give me the strength I'll need..."

He prays further, and then falls asleep.

Other people are praying too. The media are praying that they can find him, so they can meet their deadlines. The hecklers from the meeting are praying that he is struck down before he can cause any more division. Some nonbelievers are hedging their bets by praying for the first time. Natas has better things to do. His voluptuous playmates in bed are the main challenge he wants tonight.

50

The Final Chapter or is it?

It is the following morning. The UN building is glinting in the pale morning sun. It has rained most of the night giving the building an almost fluorescent glow against a patch of dark clouds.

Security is tight. Police cordons and checkpoints are everywhere. A little out dated newsstand nearby has the latest edition morning papers.

Miracle Man Talks at UN and *The Fake Meets the Flakes?*

Inside the UN building in a small room next to a janitorial storeroom, two men in pale blue UN Security uniforms are pinning on their plastic I.D.s. Sidney Potter is nervous and becoming restless.

"How the hell did you get these uniforms, and the I.D.s?"

Irritated by this pipsqueak, Natas conveys to him a cold hard stare.

"It is no concern of yours how I got them."

To ease his frustration, he checks Sidney's uniform like a drill sergeant on parade.

"You will never make a Marine, but you will have to do."

Natas also checks Sidney's firearm, and then his own 9 mm automatic. He switches the safety catch on and returns it to his holster. He feels tense, yet excited.

I have waited an eternity to have this irritant now calling himself Gus, to be removed forever.

Sidney demonstrates his nerves by pushing a cigarette into his mouth. Before he has a chance to light up, Natas snarls and smacks the cigarette away across the room, almost knocking Sidney over.

"What the hell do you think you are doing - you cretin? Can't you read all the 'no smoking' signs? Do you want to attract attention to yourself 'and' to me?"

Controlling his rising anger, he grabs Sidney by the scruff of the neck and almost lifts him off the floor.

"What on earth did I ever see in you?"

To answer the question, Sidney gives Natas a twisted smirk.

"Like attracts like?"

Not wanting to spoil his well laid plans, Natas lets him go. As Sidney attempts to straighten his spotless uniform, Natas's eyes pierce into him.

"All Right! Let us go through again what we have to do. I know for certain that he has to come past this door on his way to the main hall. He will be escorted by a security guard. I will be observing through the door crack. When they are in full view, we will rush into the hallway. I will kill the guard, while you shoot the man called Gus. It is that easy."

Sidney does not think so. He ponders for a second.

"If its that easy, why don't you kill this Gus guy, while I kill the guard?"

Clenching his jaw in exasperation, Natas stops and thinks.

This creep is not as stupid as he seems. Like does attracted like.

"He will recognize me."

"So what? He'll be dead anyway."

Not used to being questioned, by human beings that are eager to carry out his little games, Natas flusters.

"Look, I am rewarding you fifty-thousand dollars for a minute's work."

"So you say? I haven't seen the green of your money yet? Anyway, what about the other security guards and the noise from the guns?"

Natas' anger is increasing by the second at this boy's intelligent remarks.

The silencers! I have forgotten the damn silencers!

Floored by his own incompetence, Natas stumbles for an answer.

"Stop whining! It doesn't matter. It takes at least three minutes from when the alarm goes off for a person to travel from the main security bank to reach this area. By then we will be long gone."

Uneasy by the other man's sudden lack of confidence, Sidney shuffles from one foot to the other.

It is not the shooting that bothers me. I can kill without blinking an eye. It even gives me a buzz. It is this Natas guy. Something doesn't quite fit. He's too tense, as if there's a chance of failing.

Natas senses his companion's uneasiness.

"Is there a problem? Because if there is, it's now too late to worry. He will be here in fifteen minutes."

Needing this lad, Natas turns on the charm.

"So, do as I say my friend, trust me, and you will be well rewarded."

As Natas gives out his best smile, Sidney shrugs, sits down on a nearby hard metal chair, and dry smokes an unlit cigarette.

Although he is sitting in a comfortable armchair in a plush room normally reserved for heads of state, Gus is finding it hard to relax. His mind keeps floating back to that warm day riding a donkey into Jerusalem and visualizing how joyous, cheering crowds escorted him into the city, by throwing palm fronds and cloaks down in front of him.

"I want you to escort Gus along with the regular security guard."

It is the President talking to Frank, her Secret Service agent. Gus comes out of his daydream to see them standing by the door. Meanwhile, Frank answers the President.

"You know I'm not supposed to leave your side."

Knowing he is right, the President bites her bottom lip.

"I know Frank. I am just being extra careful. You're the most experienced agent

I can trust to protect Gus. Send James in to cover me."

Not liking this request, Frank's burly shoulders seem to shrink a little. To ease his anxiety, she reaches out and grips his forearm.

"Today, the President is not the most important person."

"Yes, ma'am."

His face tense, Frank glance at his watch.

"Five minutes to go."

"Okay Frank. Come back in five minutes with James."

"Ma'am."

As Frank leaves the room, Father Garth enters. He appears apprehensive. As he is invited as a friend, the President turns to him. Her face breaks into a warm smile as if to reassure him.

"Thank you for supporting Gus."

She then steps toward Gus, and reaches out for his hand. Hiding his own anxiety, he accepts her warm hand like a friend in need.

"Not long now."

Max, Eva and her son Ryan are in Max's office. Max, unable to his anxiety is busy channel surfing. All the news stations are previewing the upcoming event. Eva can't help thinking why she has not seen Gus for days.

He hasn't called. He always calls. The last time was at the airport on his return from Israel.

Hoping he is all right, she is overcome by a sudden intense feeling of dread and loneliness.

Is this how he is feeling right now?

Meanwhile, Max is fidgety. Becoming more anxious, he glances at his watch.

"Couple of more minutes."

Ryan is keeping occupied by doodling on a scrap piece of paper, while Eva looks over his shoulder. All she can see is Gus's name written repeatedly in his young boy printing. She ruffles his short curly hair.

"We miss him. Is that why you've written his name a lot?"

For a nine year old, he comes out with a mature pragmatic answer.

"Not really Mom. I've always wondered why he didn't call himself Jesus like before...?"

Max butts in.

"I've been trying to figure that one out as well."

Tension is mounting in all the newsrooms, as they inform the whole world there is one minute to go.

Frank enters Gus's room with James, the other agent. For some irrational reason, Gus is reluctant to stand and leave the welcoming comfort of the armchair.

"Its time?"

"Yes."

As if frightened to let him go, the President looks into his eyes, takes hold of Gus's arm, and gives it an extra squeeze.

"Make or break time."

"Make, I hope."

Ignoring protocol, she kisses him on the cheek, and is reluctant to let him go.

Without looking back, Gus leaves the room followed by Frank and Garth, who both glance back to the President, offering her reassuring smiles.

At the hallway entrance, a regular security guard joins them. He is a tall well-built African American football player type. His bright white teeth seem to fade away his facial features.

"The name is Wesley, gentlemen. I am here for your journey down the great corridor. Many a famous world leader has walked these floors into destiny."

Frank, Garth, and Gus exchange glances as Wesley enthusiasm beckons.

"This way - sirs."

Little do they know, they are beginning 'their' journey into destiny.

Ryan shouts, transfixed at his writing

"I got it Mom!"

Not really concentrating, Eva replies.

"Got what honey?"

In the small room, Sidney is staring at Natas in disbelief as he strips off his blue uniform.

"What's the hell's all that you've got on underneath?"

Natas ignores him.

Gus, Garth, Frank, and Wesley enter a slight bend in the corridor. His gun at the ready, Natas has the door open a crack. Still curios why the change of clothes, Sidney is right behind him. As Natas hears the distant footsteps approaching, he whispers to Sidney.

"Here they come. Get ready!"

Still feeling uneasy, Sidney is reticent in drawing his automatic firearm from the holster and releasing the safety catch.

Excited by his discovery, Ryan is emphatic in showing his mother.

"Look Mom! His name. It starts with G and then ends in 'us'."

While Max and Eva are concentrating on the TV screen, Eva is only half listening to her son.

"What do you mean honey?"

His nerves tingling, Natas can now see Gus and his protectors come into full view. Gripping his gun, he taps Sidney on his arm.

"Now!"

As they both rush out the door, the group freezes. Wesley and Frank's instinct is to reach for their firearms. Natas beats them by firing two bullets in rapid succession. The first hits Frank's forehead, causing him to spin backwards against the wall. The other bullet finds its way straight in between Wesley's eyes. He falls straight back onto Garth, causing him to fall, as if being pushed by a truck. Both Frank and Wesley die with a look of astonishment on their pale faces. Stunned into realization, Gus stares at the familiar man dressed as a Pharisee.

"You?"

Ignoring Gus's observation, Natas turns to Sidney,

"Shoot! Kill him!"

Sidney's bland response is to aim his gun at Gus's chest. Observing Gus's fatalistic expression, he hesitates. This not being the plan, Natas barks at him.

"Shoot! Idiot!"

Looking into Gus's calm eyes, Sidney can't squeeze the trigger. His patience running out, Natas puts his own gun at Sidney's temple and fires. As blood, bone, and brain splatter the nearby wall, Sidney seems to lift off the ground before he falls.

Trapped by the weight of Wesley's body, Garth can see the menacing black robes moving closer to him. Knowing Natas' intentions, Gus pleads.

"No more! Kill me. Its what you've been wanting all these years."

As Natas turns away from Garth, a wailing alarm siren now fills the building. Gus's hazel eyes turn defiant as they lock onto the hesitant green ones. For a split second, the finger on the trigger trembles. Natas then fires.

Ryan is proud when he shouts to his mom.

"Look Mom? It starts with God and ends with Jesus - Gus!"

Gus falls back. Shouts drown out the alarm. The whole building begins to shake and walls start to crack wide-open, crumble and fall as people are screaming in terror.

Outside, New York is being swallowed up by it's first ever mega-earthquake. The waterways are on fire. There is no 'one-year to get it right'. Now is the beginning of the end.

III

Plan Three

THE FINAL TESTAMENT

51

Shock

Everything is black. The rumbling, crashing and shattering, mixed with mind-bending vibrations has ceased. All Garth can feel is the pressure of the heavy weight bearing down on his chest making breathing very difficult.

How long have I been lying here?

The lack of oxygen is making him light headed.

If only I can get this weight off me and see what is happening? Gus? Is he all right? Oh God! Help me.

The whole area begins to vibrate. A heavy rumbling is shaking loose what masonry there is left standing. The pressure lifts. Light appears as Garth stares straight up to a heavy clouded sky. To relieve his need for oxygen, he inhales. His mind now clearer, he focuses on the immediate situation.

Gus and the shooting!

He struggles in pain to a sitting position and scans the immediate area. The desolation is unbelievable. To his confused eyes, it seems that the whole of New York is flattened to a moonscape of rubble. Remembering the shooting, he looks across to the heavy UN guard called Wesley that had been crushing him earlier. Tears of sadness filling his eyes, Garth observes the gaping pulp that used to be the back of the man's head. His eyes travel down to the bloody mess that was once a strong muscular back.

He saved my life.

As the nightmare comes flooding back of how this friendly man was shot, which seems only minutes ago, Nausea replaces the tears. His head swims as bitter bile enters his throat making him lean over and retch.

After a short while, his empty stomach aches, as small droplets of water contact the back of his neck. Looking skyward, light rain fills his eyes. He tries to stand, but with nothing to hold on to, he falls onto his knees. The rain increases. Hopelessness overwhelming him, the stinging tears return.

"Oh, God! What is happening? What have you done? Where's Gus?"

Now becoming drenched, he attempts to stand again. Making sure of his balance, he pauses, and then focuses on the enormity of the surrounding devastation. There is no noise, just a light whisper from the rain. Adding to his fear and desperation, shivering is setting in.

Not now! I don't want to die of hypothermia before I can find Gus.

The rain masks the tears of his fear as he closes his eyes and bows his head.

"God? What now? Have you a plan, or is this really the end and you have forsaken us?"

Wrapped up in his own helpless self pity, there is a tugging at his soaked Priest's smock. Slow in becoming aware, the tugging continues. Now mindful, his bloodshot eyes look down to his left, and sees a young boy not much older than seven years. His dirty blond hair is sticking to a blood soaked face that has one swollen eye shut and the other one is a blood shot blue. Hope rising, Garth crouches down gripping the boy's shoulders.

"Where are your parents? Have you 'anyone'?"

The boy is unable to answer. His response is his open eye begins to fill with tears.

"The poor boy is suffering from shock."

Becoming more hopeful, Garth turns around to the direction of the new voice. What he sees is a short stocky man looking bedraggled. His clothes are torn and dirty. Accompanied by a woman of African origin, in her late twenty's or early thirties, is standing about two feet behind him. Her black wavy hair being matted and caked with blood, and her mahogany skin riddled with a mass of tiny cuts and grazes, she gazes at Garth in desperation. What was once an expensive dark blue suit is now hanging off her in shreds. While they hobble closer to Garth, he notices that she has one shoe and her bare foot is bleeding. Glad to come in contact with another survivor, the man rests a trembling hand on Garth's shoulder.

"We saw him come out of that hole."

Trying hard to be strong through his constant shivering, Garth peers in the direction of the man's arm pointing to a mass of rubble. Meanwhile, the boy grabs Garth's hand. Tugging at it, he points to the same hole. As the four of them stumble toward the rubble, they soon discover that it is obscuring a large crevice, which opens wider the nearer they get. They stop. Standing at the edge of a solid downward spiral vortex, Garth wipes the rain from his tired eyes as he tries to focus on this huge opening, which looks as if the ground has been gouged out with a twenty feet diameter corkscrew.

The boy let's go of Garth's hand and begins to descend the 'hole' by scrambling down a narrow ledge, which forms the shape of the spiral. Not knowing what to do, Garth glances at the woman standing next to him peering down.

"Perhaps he has people down there?"

Her eyes full of fear, she turns her head toward him.

"Have you seen 'my' son?"

Before Garth can reply to this impossible question, the man grips hold of his arm.

"What's happened here? Where is everyone? One minute we're in my office watching TV and next, all this."

Her mouth begins to quiver, and more tears well up in her eyes.

"My son was with us. We were all together. Now I don't know where he is. Can you help us find him?"

Trying to control his shivering, and fatigued at the hopelessness of it all, he acknowledges.

"Of course I will help you. Let's follow this boy first. Both of you stay here..."

She has other ideas.

"I'm coming with you! Maybe my son is down there with other survivors?"

The two men look at each other for an answer both realizing that this poor woman needs relief from her grief. In desperation, she grips Garth's hand for him to lead her down the narrow ledge. Not feeling that brave, Garth indicates to the man to stay above ground.

To Garth's relief, the hole is not as deep as it originally appears. Now standing on the level concrete platform, the boy's face expresses relief on seeing the two adults heading toward him. Before Garth can reach him, he notices a large steel girder caked in crushed concrete looming above the boy. While creaking noises are reverberating everywhere, hundreds of pieces of debris are finding their final resting place. Garth's eyes adjust to the dim light as he reaches out to the boy who in turn points toward the dark unknown before them. Fear crossing her face, the young woman grabs Garth's other hand for support.

"What is this place?"

"It looks like part of the subway."

Still gripping Garth's other hand, the boy begins to lead them into the foreboding Subway.

Making good progress, they find the platform seems relatively clear. A few chunks of rubble lying around, they walk around with ease. The worst damage is on the rail track. Heavy concrete chunks, steel beams and loose rubble form an ugly, unstable wall piled up to what was once a ceiling. Glancing at each other for support, they walk a little further. An eerie glow appears. A dim yellow light filling the immediate area. Garth can just see an outline of a train being crushed by all the damaged building materials. The yellow glow is coming from a ripped gas main that must have been ignited by a spark during the actual disaster.

Hope appearing on his face, the boy stops and points to a gap the other side of the flame, and then looks up to the two adults, as if they might be able to achieve some impossibility. The glow from the gas is making the tears from his eyes look like liquid gold as they trickle down his dirty face. Wanting to help, Garth strains his eyes trying to focus beyond the gas pipe.

"He's pointing to a gap in the rubble. There might be someone."

Her hopes rising, the woman lets go of his hand and begins heading toward the gap. Wondering what she is doing, Garth hesitates.

"What are you doing?"

"To find some survivors."

As she rushes past the gas pipe, she trips. Her remaining shoe has got lodged in a hidden crack in the platform. Her emotional agony increasing, she squeals. Fearing the worse, Garth lets go of the boy's hand and runs toward her. Meanwhile, a loud creaking above causes Garth to stop just as he gets to the woman. Their eyes widening in panic, both look up to see the ceiling of rubble is beginning to change shape as if some invisible force is stirring it. She screams as she becomes desperate in trying to free her trapped foot.

"It's all moving! We'll be crushed!"

As the moderate creaking is now turning into loud screeching, Garth keeps calm and crouches down to take hold of her trapped foot. Yanking it out of the shoe, he then stands, and slides his arm around her waist. Turning her away from the flame, he encourages her to run. Leaving her shoe behind, she grips his hand again as the noise stops, and the roof caves in. They fall over from the vibration, while the rubble lands a few feet away.

They lay still as the dust around them settles. Now there is no further noise, Garth lifts his head up first to observe a small mountain of concrete and steel girders mixed with a mass of bricks. The whole scene becomes lighter as daylight radiates down. Happy to be alive, she gazes at Garth in gratitude, and then appears worried at the huge pile of entangled steel and concrete.

"Where's the little boy?"

Praying the boy is safe, Garth struggles to stand as he studies the pile. In the meantime, she stares at the pile dreading the worse. As if thinking the same, they both scramble toward the destruction. They discover there is still enough room for them to work their way around the pile to be back where they started. To their relief, the boy is alive, and standing a few feet away. As the woman cries out in solace, she goes to him and crouches down. Tears of mixed emotions fill their eyes, as they embrace. He shivers with fright, while she holds him tight and is gentle while stroking his head trying to keep him warm and calm him down. Even though she is glad for the little boy, a painful picture of her son Ryan keeps flashing through her mind.

Where are you Ryan?

A gentle hand touches her shoulder. For a split second her hopes rise. Garth keeps his voice level and calm.

"Is he okay?"

Wiping her tears, she nods as Garth pats her shoulder, and indicates they ought to keep moving.

Making their plight easier, the platform is clear for about another hundred feet until the area turns into a tunnel. Wary of the dark opening, they stop and glance at each other for support.

What now?

Taking the lead, Garth is cautious as he steps forward leaving the other two looking at him with a mixture of uncertainty and curiosity. He stops after a few feet of entering the tunnel entrance. Straining his eyes to adjust to the gloom, he can just see an outline of a window giving off a dim light.

As he moves forward, the window becomes nearer, but now it blends into a larger square mass. Needing to see more, he keeps moving forward. His eyes having to adjust to the dim light, he recognizes the shape. A train trapped in this tunnel, he keeps edging forward until he reaches the train. Fearing the worse, he peers through the back window. He can see the lights are still on, but are dim. Presuming this is the last amount of power from the backup batteries, he feels his way around to the side of the train coach.

Squeezing along the wall of the tunnel, he stops and squints into a side rear window. Wondering if the dim light is playing tricks on his eyes, he looks for someone or something, but there is nothing, no one.

Perhaps nobody got into the rear car.

His progress slow, he works his way down the black tunnel to the next car. Straining his eyes to look through another window, he can see something on the floor.

It looks like an abandoned holdall. There are still no people. Maybe it's just an empty train.

He struggles to creep further down to the next car, and gapes through another window. The sheer surrounding blackness seems to make the dim light inside the coach appear brighter. His focus is drawn to the end of the car where he can see a dark mass heaped up as high as the car's ceiling. His heart palpitating with apprehension, Garth slides down further to get a closer look. His eyes hurting from the strain, he is unable to move. His body becomes cold and clammy, by a pair of blank eyes staring back at him from the middle of the black mound.

My God! There are people trapped in there!

His aching eyes follow the line of stacked people up to the ceiling where it looks like a trap door or a vent.

They were panicking, while trying to escape...

From nowhere, a breeze blows onto his head. He shivers at the sudden coldness, and his stomach churns in fear. It is not just a gust of air, but a mixture of gas and air. Garth gasps and chokes at this change in the environment. Knowing speed is of the essence, he struggles in desperation to work his way back to the rear of the train. As he reaches relative daylight, he notices the killing breeze evaporates. He takes a chance by breathing in what he thinks is fresher air and heads toward where he has left the others.

Already shivering with cold as well as fear, he looks around to find nothing.

Where are they?

With all sorts of negative thoughts rushing through his mind, he decides to call out.

"Hello?"

Hearing a shuffling sound his hopes rise, as the boy comes out from behind the new formed rubble pile, followed by the woman. Relief rushes through Garth as the woman comes up to him. Her eyes full of concern, she asks the obvious.

"Are you all right? What's down there?"

"Not a pleasant sight I'm afraid. There is another broken gas line somewhere near the train, and somehow the gas got into the cars and..."

Visualizing the horrific pile of souls trapped in the coach, burning tears form in his eyes as his shivering becomes worse. To help elevate his suffering, she grips his forearm.

"Do you mean they're all..."

"Yes! And, if we don't get out of here fast, we will be joining them. When that gas meets up with the already ignited gas main, this whole place is going to blow."

Without hesitation, she slides her arm around his waist to comfort and steady him.

"Then, let's get going. We have survived this far, so I would like us to live a 'little' bit longer."

All thinking the same, the two of them plus the little boy hurry to make their way back to the main hole, and then begin to climb the precarious spiral wall toward the surface. Halfway, Garth has to stop and rest. The effort of walking around the vortex is making his head spin. Seconds go by, and some of his strength returns, he takes a deep breath. With a mixture of strong will and determination, he manages to climb to the top. The woman, holding the boy's arm is right behind him when Garth scrambles onto the surface. While the waiting man helps them all up, Garth notices how drawn he looks as he begins to talk.

"Any luck?"

Garth and the woman shake their heads.

The rain has stopped. The evening sun is glowing red on the horizon sending dark eerie shadows across the moonscape of New York.

After they have walked about twenty yards from the hole, Garth stops. He gazes at the warm sky and shivers again with more tears filling his tired eyes. In desperation he falls to his knees. Pressing his hands together, and curling his fingers tight, he lowers his head. On hearing him mumble, they become nervous at their 'savior' collapsing on them. The two adults and the boy stand behind him becoming scared as Garth shouts.

"Oh God! What is happening? Where are you? No more suffering - please."

All of a sudden, the ground begins to rumble, and then the area from where they have just come from, explodes with a giant 'whoosh'. Garth stops praying as the others turn to the sight of a twenty-foot high flame, gushing out of the spiral hole.

Then it is gone, leaving the immediate area glowing in the evening light. Not wanting to look at the cruel cremation, Garth keeps kneeling. In despair, his head is now resting in his hands. Full of concern, the woman crouches down next to him and rests her hand on his back.

"It looks like the two gases met after all and ignited."

Garth responds by raising his head and wiping his tear-streaked face. Admiring the courage shown by this attractive woman, Garth gazes at her as if searching for an answer to this devastation. A young frightened voice from behind Garth says it all.

"Was that God answering you?"

Both the woman and Garth stare at the boy in amazement, while the older man shows his affectionate by rubbing the boys head.

"He spoke!"

Still kneeling, Garth opens his arms and beckons to the boy. Much to Gus's delight, he falls into his arms. For a few seconds they are still and quiet. In contrast to the quiet surroundings, the boy begins to sob against Garth's shoulder. As a sense of hopelessness creeps over them all, the man speaks first.

"What now?"

Still comforting the boy, Garth looks up at the night drawing in and a full moon rising.

"At least the night looks clear. So, we need to find some sort of shelter and hopefully some food and water. I don't think I can go on much further."

Forgetting his own weakness, Garth stares down at the sore bleeding feet of the woman, and then surveys their local vicinity. Some twenty yards to their right, he notices the remainder of a concrete wall that stands alone about six foot high and approximately ten foot long.

"Let's head for that wall over there. It will give us some sort of privacy."

Her own creeping exhaustion taking its toll, and now hearing this wild suggestion, she snaps back to him.

"Privacy from what? There's nobody here! I don't think there is anybody left. I need to find my son. You 'promised' me."

Sympathizing with the priest, the older man is becoming disturbed by his friend's outburst.

"Steady on kid. The guy said he would help us. Its too dark and dangerous now, and we're all exhausted. I say lets find shelter for tonight and we'll set off in the morning and look for Ryan."

Thankful for the input, Garth looks at them both with a mournful expression. Unable to find the strength to handle any conflict, he lowers his head, struggles to stand, and begins walking toward the surviving wall.

Realizing and regretting hurting the priest's feelings, who is trying his best, she curses under her breath. The numbness of the original shock now wearing off, and the sheer reality of losing 'everything' now sinking in, she hurts all over, and is pining for her son Ryan and Gus.

The two men clear a small area in front of the wall enough for them to lie down. Needing to search for some sort of planking or sheets of plywood to give them shelter, Garth begins searching through the rubble. Indicating for the others to stay by the wall, the woman obeys and sits down on the cleared grass area. The boy joins her and lays his head on her lap. Watching Garth struggle through the rubble, she strokes the boy's matted hair, hoping to bring them both some sort of comfort. As the boy soon falls asleep, the older man stands and leans against the wall for support. Even though exhausted, he is curious watching the priest wander through the rubble.

"That poor guy. I think his God has forsaken us."

Determined to find something, Garth has traveled about one hundred yards when he discovers another hole. This is not a vortex, but a man made one. The evening light is fading fast as he looks down at a pair of open metal doors that is supposed to cover an underground cellar.

A ray of hope filling his tired insides, he crouches down to take a better look. Observing a small flight of concrete steps going down into blackness, he becomes cautious. As he begins to descend, a familiar smell hits his nostrils.

Body sweat! Maybe survivors?

As his feet touch level ground, the smell of humans persists. Pain hits his eyes as the whole area lights up.

"It's a priest!"

While the young girl's voice brings hope to his ears, Garth has to shield his face as the light comes nearer, and another young voice reverberates.

"I told you we are being looked after."

The beam from a large chrome flash light now guides the way for Garth to approach a nearby wall. Adjusting to the new light, Garth focuses on a small group of children ranging from mid-teens to a nine-year-old boy of African origin. The girl holding the flashlight comes forward. Her soiled face showing tear streaks, her eyes widen in hope.

"Oh Father! We are so glad to see you. Have you come to rescue us?"

Without answering, Garth walks among them to make sure this all real. In touching some heads, and checking if they are okay, he asks the obvious.

"How did you all get here?"

The older girl holding the flashlight has no trouble in answering.

"We were in the school bus on our way home, when all of a sudden the bus started shaking and things fell on the roof."

"What sort of things?"

Before the girl can answer, a seven year-old boy of Asian origin, steps foreword.

"Buildings! Whole buildings it was. It was horrible!"

427

While tears well up in the boy's eyes, Garth strokes his damp, cold curly hair.

"So how did you all get down here?"

The girl with the flashlight answers.

"It was all very strange. The driver stopped the bus and then shouted..."

His imagination running wild, the Asian boy interrupts.

"More like a scream. It was horrible!"

Not perturbed by the interruption, the girl continues.

"Get out! He said. We're all going to die."

As murmurs of agreement come from the other children, the girl with the flashlight continues.

"The driver hurried out as a large piece of building crashed down on the back part of the bus. Lucky there wasn't anyone sitting there, so we thought we had better leave as well."

While more murmurs of agreement follow, Garth asks the obvious question, as a sudden stillness fills the cellar

"Is the driver here?"

Needing to still be involved, the Asian boy goes to speak, and then hesitates. After a couple of seconds his courage returns.

"It was horrible! As the driver left the bus, a whole piece of wall came right down on top of him...."

Trying not to picture the sad incident, Garth's stomach turns over. Meanwhile, the boy carries on.

"We all only just made it out of the bus, when it vanished. We didn't know what to do, stuff was falling everywhere. So we just walked a way and after a while we found this place, the doors were open as they are now. This flashlight was lying on the steps."

Commiserating their anguish, Garth takes hold of the flashlight.

"You were very lucky."

A little red haired, freckled face girl comes forward with a resolute expression.

"It wasn't luck. It was God! Gus said that what ever happens, God would always look after us - if we were good."

Almost dropping the flashlight at the mention of Gus's name, Garth is becoming endeared by her large bright blue eyes looking pronounced compared to her grubby face.

"You know Gus?"

"Yes, we are his children, he looks after us…"

With one voice they point to the nine-year-old African boy.

"Except him. He joined us a little while ago."

Just hearing Gus's name, gives Garth a lift, a little extra needed energy. He focuses the light beam all around the cellar. All is empty except for a green painted, rusty metal door. Curious, he moves toward the door, grips a large metal doorknob and attempts to turn it. Unable to make it turn, he tries again. With all the rust surrounding the knob, Garth's limited fortune is dissipating fast.

Oh God. Give us a break!

The African boy stares at the door.

"Try just pulling it. I tried it earlier. It seemed to move a bit."

Welcoming the positive attitude, Garth gives the flashlight to the nearest pair of hands, which now shines onto the doorknob. Determined to help these children, Garth grips the knob with both hands. Using what strength he has left, he jerks it hard toward him. An excited voice shouts from the group.

"It moved!"

Not telling if it had moved or not, Garth takes a deep breath and tries again. Now more excited, the same voice shouts a little louder.

"It moved again!"

His arms aching from the effort, Garth feels the door give a little. Determination mixed with a sense of achievement, he gives the door one last tug. It moves halfway open, and then jams on the concrete floor. The light beam finds its way into the opening. Garth peers after the beam to see it landing on a stack of shelves. Glad he is discovering something that may help to keep them alive, he turns back to the holder of the light.

"Hand me the flashlight. This looks interesting"

With the flashlight in his hand, and murmurs of encouragement behind him, Garth eases through the narrow opening.

Realizing this is a storeroom, not a large storeroom, he observes the walls are bare unpainted concrete, covered by metal stacking shelves on all four walls. His enthusiasm mounting, Garth shines his light onto the full shelves and is overwhelmed by gratitude by what he sees. Before he can say anything, another voice shouts in wonder from behind him.

"Look at all this stuff?"

While still exploring the merchandise, Garth can hear the rest of the children coming into the room. Several murmur with relief to each other as they survey clothes, several types of canned food, bottles of water and juices accompanied by a vast assortment snack bars and packets. Before he can take all in, Garth turns to face the children.

"It looks as if we have been lucky and discovered a basement below a store that now no longer exists".

Although trying hard to listen to him, the children are becoming restless. While they gaze at the sweets and goodies on the shelves surrounding them, Garth keeps up the momentum.

"We can use this room as our base for now. So, as we go out and search for more survivors, we will have something to offer them. There are three people waiting for me right now, up above. Now, I want you to wait right here while I go and get them."

He lingers the light beam onto all the shelves as if searching for something extra. He stops when he finds more flashlights in a carton. As the group look on, he retrieves two, checks to see if they work, and hands one to the African boy and the other to the eldest girl.

"I'm going up above now. I won't be long so don't touch anything until I get back."

Not wanting to leave the children, and still holding the original light, Garth makes his way back up to the devastation.

Allowing his eyes to adjust to the darkness, he notices the air is still and a little cooler as he looks up to the moon filled sky. He focuses the light beam to where he thinks he left the others, but somehow the scenery looks different.

Where's the wall? Shall I shout for them?

Shivering again with the cold, he becomes nervous and self-conscious as if someone else might be out there.

How far did I walk?

Forcing his mind back to that wall where he left them, which was not more than fifteen to twenty minutes ago, he decides to bear right. Anxiety creeping through him, he walks for a few more minutes focusing the light beam on anything that looks like the wall. Becoming worried about the children, panic is now adding to his already anxious state.

Perhaps I ought to call out.

"Hello!"

As no response is forthcoming, he walks a little more, and then calls again.

"Hello?"

He hears a muffled cough. In desperation , he shines the light on the immediate area.

It's as if they've vanished.

The scenery that resembles anything like he remembers is some planks of wood leaning on an angle against some concrete. The light beam now deciding to grow dim, he switches off the light. The same coughing as earlier sounds louder.

There it is again! It's coming from behind those wood planks.

Hoping it is the same people, Garth scrambles over the rubble and pulls two of the planks away and then switches on his light. While the beam falls on three nervous faces, Garth is relieved to find his friends huddling each other to keep warm. The little boy begins coughing again.

"I'm so sorry. I couldn't find you. I was looking for the wall."

Her body stiff from fatigue and now the cold, the woman stands. Holding the boy's hand, and looking glad to see Garth, the man struggles to stand.

"You were gone for so long that I pulled up some of the loose planks lying around and made a shelter. Where have you been? We were getting worried."

"I'm sorry I was so long. I have found some more survivors. A group of children."

"That's wonderful. Where are they?"

"Not far from here in an underground cellar. Guess what, the cellar is full of supplies."

Even though the news is good, the woman begins to shiver and then cry. Offering her some hope, Garth grabs her hand with both of his.

"I promise we will find your son tomorrow."

Knowing her patience will not last until then, she hides her torment.

"Show me these children."

As soon as they arrive at the cellar entrance, Garth enters first. Shining his flashlight onto the concrete steps, he holds his hand out to the woman who is now holding the boy's hand. The light fading a little as a small cloud glides across the full moon, and the flashlight dimming, they form a chain to descend the steps until they reach the closed door. Garth's heart lifts as he hears the muted voices of the children. As he pulls the door open, the children hold their breath. Seeing it is Garth, they relax. His flashlight fading fast, Garth leans against the open door.

"Can someone hand me a fresh light please."

The instant the flashlight is put into his hand, the beam reflects onto the children's faces. Seeing the African boy, the woman's insides turn over.

"Ryan?"

Recognizing the voice, the boy strains his eyes.

"Mom?"

"It's me honey!"

As he steps forward, and she reaches out to him, everyone is quiet as they witness this heart rendering reunion between mother and son.

"Oh, Mom."

While tears of relief and joy pour down both their faces, Garth is overjoyed. Observing the other children looking on with curiosity, Garth slides his arm around her shoulder. Reluctant to let go, young Ryan releases his grip and turns to his new anxious companions.

"This is my Mom."

At the same time, the man steps forward into the light.

"Hi Ryan."

"Uncle Max! You're safe too."

"Yeah, I'm safe. How the hell did you get here?"

"I'm not sure. I think something knocked me out. When I woke up, I didn't know where I was, so I just kept on walking until I found these guys."

The red haired, freckled face girl comes and puts her arm around Ryan's waist.

"It was God guiding you to us so you could be safe."

Now an atmosphere of hope fills the small storeroom, the children begin to chatter with excited voices. Her hell now gone, Ryan's mother turns to Garth. Gripping his hand with gratitude, she leans forward and plants a kiss on his cheek.

"I'm Eva. And this is my boss, Max."

Never been kissed by a woman since his mother, Garth offers them both a welcoming smile.

"I'm Garth. Isn't it strange that we never mentioned our names earlier."

The two flashlights the children are using are beginning to dim. Garth reacts by stepping forward to make an announcement.

"Okay everyone. It's a miracle we are here, and so far we have managed to survive. We have to now organize ourselves and decide what we want do next.

The first thing I suggest is to take stock of these supplies and work out how we're going to use them..."

One of the children cries out.

"Can we eat something now, and then go to sleep? We are all very tired."

Another voice expresses the same opinion.

"We could take stock tomorrow?"

Realizing he is pushing too hard, Garth hesitates.

I want to organize to survive, and all they want is to eat and fall asleep.

"Okay, but let's just check what we have here first."

In front of some impatient faces, he shines the flashlight onto the shelving. Searching for anything of use, the beam settles on a large cardboard carton, sitting on a top shelf. Standing on tiptoes, he just manages to lift the box down to his chest and drops it to the floor. The all gather round and stare with curiosity, waiting to see what is inside this latest treasure trove. Guessing it is clothing, Garth opens the carton, and reaches down to pull out a dark blue anorak. He opens it out to show everyone.

"We have here a box of anoraks. Large size only."

Succumbing to cold and exhaustion, Eva, demonstrates her joy at the find by standing close to Garth.

"How many are there?"

Without commenting, he begins pulling out all the remaining clothing, counting as he goes.

"How many of us are there?"

Eva does a quick count.

"Twelve."

Garth pulls out the final jacket.

"Twelve it is."

Cheers fill the room as Eva hands round the clothing. Being – one size fits all, there is lots of discussion how the anoraks will fit, depending on the size of the person. The smaller children become engulfed. The bigger children, the jackets fit more like overcoats. Eva's is a bit on the large size, while Max's is a bit tight. The one anorak that fits well belongs to Garth.

As Eva rolls up her son's sleeves, Garth takes stock of the situation by going round and checking each child. Thanking heaven for small mercies, Garth decides to addresses everyone.

"I'm sorry that most of you are somewhat overwhelmed by the size of these Jackets. At least you're warm and dry..."

He reaches over to a nearby shelf and takes off a box of granola bars.

"Here! Take two each of these bars and eat them now. They should last you until breakfast tomorrow. Meanwhile, us grown-ups are going to talk about our immediate futures. So, if you children would like to find

434

anything on the shelves that you could use as a pillow, grab it and make yourself as comfortable as you can. We have a big day tomorrow."

Eva shoots him a quizzical look as the older children search for anything that will do as makeshift pillows. In the meantime, Garth indicates for Eva and Max to join him to go outside.

Outside, nothing has changed, except the air is colder. While Max and Eva watch Garth sit down on the top step next to the open metal doors, with his head resting in his hands, they become concerned. Wanting to help, Eva sits next to him, while Max sits the other side. Releasing a heavy sigh of despondency, Garth looks down at Eva's bare, sore feet.

"We must find you some shoes. Did you see any in there on the shelves?"

"I didn't look. I was too worried about the children."

Garth reaches across to her lap and grips her grubby hands.

"You've found your son!"

Appreciating the gesture and liking this priest more by the minute, her eyes sting with fresh tears.

"Thank God! And thanks to you."

Overcome with emotional and physical exhaustion, Max rests his head in his hands. Garth slides his arm around Eva's shoulder, hoping it will bring her some sort of comfort, and maybe help him at the same time. As her tears flow, her reaction is to rest her head on his shoulder. The sound of Eva's sobs echoing throughout, they sit like this for a few minutes wrapped in their own thoughts.

After a minute or so, she decides to sit up. After releasing a heavy sigh, she wipes her face on the sleeve of her new jacket.

"So, Father Garth? What now?"

"I wish I knew."

"Can't you do a prayer or something?"

His arm still around her shoulder, he withdraws to look her in the face.

"I think we're beyond that now."

Surprised by his answer, she looks up and stares at the full moon.

"Gus would know what to do."

Hearing Gus's name again, Garth's hope rises again.

435

"Did you say - Gus? The children know him as well. Do you - or did you know Gus?"

Even though she is looking straight at him, her eyes take on a glazed look, as if she somewhere else.

"Yes, I knew him. I worked with him for a short while for Max through Channel Six. I am or was a TV anchor that was unfortunate enough to fall in love with him."

"Wow. I first met him at the Vatican, and then I accompanied him at the UN when all this happened. Do you realize it was only a few hours ago? Do you think he's alive?"

Hearing enough, Max raises his head.

"He has to be! This is all his doing."

"What do you mean?"

"He told us that he came here to warn us all that if we did not mend our ways in one year, the world would end."

"Did you believe him?"

"I did, but the young lady here had her doubts."

Her mind flooding with personal memories of her love for Gus, Eva has her say.

"I disbelieved him at first. After a miracle, I came round to realize. What about you?"

"I had no doubt who he was. But all this?"

Fatigue overwhelming Garth, he rests his head back in his hands. It now Eva's turn to slide her arm around his shoulder. Meanwhile, this is all too much for Max. He again rests his weary head in his hands.

"We are all too exhausted right now to make any sensible decisions. So let's get some sleep and we'll talk it over in the morning."

Still comforting Gus, Eva conveys an inquiring look at her boss.

"We have to tell the children something?"

Listening to the muted chatter of the children, Max lifts his head and does his best to produce a comforting smile.

"Do you know what mystifies me?"

"What?"

"Finding these children that know Gus, and all these supplies, gives me an eerie feeling that this is some part of a master plan."

Listening to the older man's prophetic words, Eva takes the lead by standing first.

"Well, these children will be wondering what us adults are up to."

Next morning, after a restless, fitful sleep, Garth is the first to wake up. Having laid out on the cold concrete floor, he is having trouble getting his stiff and sore body to cooperate. He is managing to sit up and lean back against the shelves without disturbing the children. He can see daylight seeping through the half-open doorway, creating a soft warm light covering the children. Eva begins to stir. She rolls onto her back, opens her eyes, and then realizes where she is. She attempts to sit up, but fails. Understanding her predicament, Garth does his best to crawl over to her.

"You all right?"

"I think so. I've never slept on such a hard cold floor before. God, I'm sore."

"They say you get used to it."

"Whoever 'they' are."

Ryan wakes up and is glad to see his mother.

"Morning Mom."

Thankful to see her son is all right, Eva offers him a pensive smile, and then stares at Garth.

"So, what now? 'Father' Garth?"

Ignoring her sarcasm, and having to shoulder this new responsibility, he puts on a brave face and offers her the best smile he can manage. Disturbing the quiet atmosphere, a buzzing noise vibrates from Eva's pants. Becoming startled, her instinct is to search her pant's pocket, pull out her smartphone, and gaze at the screen lighting up in pale blue.

"It's my phone, but I don't understand..."

Garth peers at the screen.

"What's flashing on the screen? It might be other survivors."

Unable to answer, she just stares transfixed at the screen.

"I don't understand. There can't be any service now…"

"What does it say?"

Her hand trembles, as she hands Garth the phone. Studying the flashing screen, he becomes puzzled at the display in large white letters: *Follow the Sun.*

"Follow the sun? What does that mean? It must be some electrical thing. As you just said, there is no service any more. No towers, nothing."

Her mind becoming focused, she snatches the phone from him, and gazes at the screen.

"How do we know for sure? There could be others out there trying to communicate?"

Meanwhile, Ryan has been listening to all of this adult conversation and has come to his own conclusion.

"Mom? It's God telling us where to go."

While this is going on, little Miss redhead is awake and decides to join in the conversation.

"That's right! God! That is why we are here. We are all the chosen ones. The ones Gus said he needs for the new world."

The mention of Gus again, Eva and Max stare at the little girl in utter amazement. They then glance at Garth for some kind of verification. As Eva is still dumbstruck, Garth needs to speaks first.

"Well, I suppose that's one idea. Any 'other' suggestions?"

The phone screen now gone blank, Eva pushes the phone back in her pant's pocket.

"My suggestion is, she may be right. Gus said to me once that I would survive because I had a good heart. At the time I thought he was nuts, but now I miss him."

Absorbed in the discussion, Ryan agrees.

"So do we all, Mom."

All the children are now awake and listening. Several raise their hands and ask the same question at the same time.

"Can I go for a pee?"

Realizing different priorities are taking over, Eva and Garth look at each other and laugh. Eva is the first to comment.

"Life goes on. Well kids, you had better go up top and do it there. Girls first. Don't worry about privacy, because there isn't any. Come right back when you've finished."

As the children scurry up the steps leaving the three adults, Garth is looking apprehensive.

"We've got to talk!"

Making sure the children are safe outside, Eva agrees.

"Yes, we do. Have you any ideas for today?"

"I 'know' Gus is out there somewhere! We either need to find him or let him find us. Before we leave, we have to stock up with as much as we can all carry."

Listening with a foreboding expression, Max stares at the supplies.

"Where do we go then?"

Garth turns to Eva for an answer.

"What did it say on your cell phone?"

"Follow the sun..."

The children interrupt by returning from their ablutions and begin looking at Garth with hungry faces. Garth studies them with affection, noticing how comical they all look in their oversized anoraks, but also knows what great kids they are. None of them exhibit any selfishness toward each other considering the circumstances. Studying Garth's doubting expression, Eva goes and stands with her son Ryan. Demonstrating a mixture of pride and appreciation, she slides her arm around his shoulder. Still sore and stiff after a lousy night's sleep, Max joins Eva.

Even though hungry for some breakfast, the children are being patient, as everyone is looking at Garth for further instructions. Becoming more aware of this latest responsibility, Garth ponders for a minute, and then speaks.

"Well guys, this is the position. First, we can't stay here. I know we have been fortunate in finding these supplies, but they will soon run out. Second, having received the uncanny cell phone message telling us to follow the sun, which to my pea brain means to travel west. It's obvious that we cannot go east, because we will drop into the Atlantic ocean."

Finding this amusing, the children begin laughing. Hiding his creeping anxiety at the uncertain future, Garth pauses to let the children settle, and then continues.

"So, when we've organized ourselves in carrying as many supplies as possible, we will leave here, follow the sun, and hope we'll find Gus on the way. Will you all line up now, so Eva and I can sort out some breakfast and find a way for us all to carry the necessary food and water for the journey."

Ryan taking the lead, the children form a line. Amongst the supplies, they manage to find enough clothing, shoes, knapsacks and holdalls to carry dried snacks, water bottles and flashlights with spare batteries.

After a few minutes, everybody is now ready. Munching their breakfast granola bars, the children are in a positive mood, and sensing an adventure ahead. More aware of this commitment, Garth can only hope they are being watched over, as he leads everyone up the stairs into the unknown.

When on top, he does a final check on everyone just to satisfy his own tormented mind. Eva not feeling any better, so, when Garth comes to on check her, she confides in him.

"It's now off into the unknown. Are you scared?"

"Terrified! At least the children are taking it well."

"Yes, and they're such good kids."

"They should be, they're the chosen ones - remember?"

Ignoring his sarcasm, Eva searches Garth's eyes for the reassurance they all need to survive this ordeal.

"Lets get started. Everyone's ready. Oh, by the way, do you know what day it is tomorrow?"

"No! I'm sorry. I've lost track."

Not pursuing the matter, Eva watches Garth look up to survey the clear sky. Estimating the sun's position, he turns to where he thinks they should be facing and points.

"This way guys."

With Garth and Max taking the lead, the rest follow behind with Eva at the rear. Ryan's face turns anxious when he looks up at his mother.

"Do you know its Easter Sunday tomorrow."

"Yes. I know!"

52

Easter Morning

Her olive green eyes seem to bore right into his soul, while her generous wide smile enraptures his whole being. Her thick, long dark wavy hair, falls across his face as she leans over him offering a sweet kiss. Before the kiss can land, she pulls away laughing, and then comes back, pressing her voluptuous body against....

His heart pounding, Gus wakes up with a start. His body is soaked with sweat even though the air is cool.

Oh God! Mary. After all this time, you are still a part of me.

His eyes open to darkness. Straining for some sign of light, he gives up and pictures the recent dream.

Those eyes! The eyes of Mary Magdalene!

A sudden yearning loneliness covers him like a dark shroud. Adding to that, he begins to shiver.

Oh, Mary. Am I on my way to be with you? Is this really the final end?

Hopelessness adding to shivers, he cries out loud.

"Oh God! Have I let you down that much, you decided to go ahead and destroy evil and the World anyway - without me?"

Self-pity adds to his turmoil.

"I don't blame you. Let's be honest, I didn't really know if I could have ever managed to succeed in achieving such a goal - in one year...?"

He now feels tired and sleepy.

The final sleep, which will take me to her....

The warm sun is shining full on his face. Mary puts out her hand for him to take. He is eager to accept, and enjoys it's comforting softness as she treads backwards. Making a point of pulling him toward the sun, her sweet mouth keeps opening as if giving him instructions. Unable to hear, the same words are repeated as she points to the sun. Still unable to hear, the sun is getting nearer. Now feeling the intense heat, she is still pulling him forward. In desperation mixed with confusion, he tries to ask her what she is doing, but his throat is too dry.

Mary, stop! Give me your water from the well.

She does stop, and releases his hand. Her expression turning to frustration, she grips his head in both her hands, gazes deep into his eyes, and whispers in his ear.

"Just follow the sun."

Her soft warm lips fuse against his hesitant mouth. The intense yearning for her increases as she separates, while her sweet lips form other words.

"She is not me!"

In an instant she is gone. The bright sun remains, but shrinking. Shrinking until it is a small glow. He feels cold.

Oh Mary! Don't go. Not now!

Gus wakes up again to blackness. Shivering and soaked with sweat, the intense memories of the tomb at the Skull of Golgotha come racing back. He raises both hands, moving them in all directions to check his immediate surroundings. Unable to touch anything, he can feel a sharp familiar pain in the right side of his ribs.

The spear wound? Am I back in the tomb?

His mind begins to clear.

No! It's his bullet that hit me! Thanks to the vest the President gave me, it looks as if I'm still alive. Is SHE all right?

After a struggle, he manages to sit up. His hands laying palms down, he can feel the cold concrete floor.

It does not feel like the UN corridor.

Honing his concentration, he tries to sense his immediate environment by shouting.

"Hello!"

An immediate echo bounces back.

It seems like an underground basement. What's going on? What do I do now? There must be a way out!

He decides to try standing. First, by getting on his knees, his body feels as if it has been hit all over by a sledgehammer. After a few seconds, he eases his aching body into a standing position. Becoming more aware of his senses, he feels a draught of cold air hit his face.

This is what it must feel like to be blind. Am I blind?

Stretching his hands out in front of him, he struggles to shuffle forward into the draught. Straight away, he stumbles across pieces of broken concrete. Within a few minutes, he reaches a large concrete column. As he feels his way around the pillar of concrete, he notices that it is crumbling and the reinforcing steel is exposed.

There seems to be a great deal of damage down here.

Being cautious, he continues into the draught. Minutes go by when he comes to a full stop. His hands now touching smooth metal, he feels his way around this new surface.

It feels like a vehicle of some kind. This must be an underground parking lot. How did I get here?

With a new sense of hope and relief, he feels his way around to what seems like the driver's door. After a little more fumbling, he comes across the door handle. Running his fingers over the shape to picture in his mind what type of handle, he attempts to open the door. As there is no movement, his new found hope soon dissipates.

It must be locked. What did you expect?

He tries again. With a little more effort, the door does give way. The hinges squeak as the door opens wider, and a smell of stale air and leather hits his nostrils. No internal lights coming on, his fear heightens.

God. I hope I'm not blind. It is so black everywhere.

Not letting his fear dissuade his determination, he tries to focus his mind.

I have to find the switch for the vehicle's lights, to prove I can still see.

His hands tremble a little in anticipation, as he fumbles his way around the steering column finding the ignition.

No keys! What did you expect?

He carries on searching the dashboard - no light switch. Becoming frustrated with a ting of fear, he goes back to the steering column. He finds the indicator lever, and moves it about. Still nothing. Slumping back into the driver's seat, he then grips the steering wheel with a sense of desperation.

I have to get out of here! If only I could see SOMETHING? I will try one last time by feeling every square inch, starting from the left.

Beginning from the driver's door, he uses his left hand to glide over the dashboard surface. Within seconds, he finds something. Trying to picture in his mind, the raised circular disk of about two inches in diameter, and eighth of an inch in height, the tip of his finger can feel the center of this disk. A slender, raised piece with slight indentations register on his finger tip.

Feels like a rotary switch of some kind...

He turns it to the left. A dinging noise comes on at the same time as the concrete wall in front of the windshield fills with light.

Bingo! The light switch. I can see!

He gazes out of the car window in fascination mixed with shock. It is a large underground parking lot, half filled with a variety of assorted dust covered vehicles. He catches sight of his reflection in the rear view mirror. He cringes at his face covered in dust, and then focuses on a line of congealed blood on his forehead.

Not thorns this time.

The headlights still on, he chooses to climb out of the car and study his immediate surroundings. The draught he felt earlier is still coming in his direction, so he decides to walk into it and perhaps find his way out. First, he begins to walk with caution around the parking lot examining some of the other uncrushed vehicles.

Maybe I might be lucky and find one that is unlocked with the keys? Yeah, right!

After trying several locked cars and trucks, despondency is approaching and the headlights from the first car are beginning to dim. A few vehicles are still left unchecked, so he carries on. When he treads on something hard that is not concrete, he looks down in the dim light to see his right foot standing on a digital car key.

I don't believe it!

Becoming excited, he bends down to retrieve the small remote. On studying the black oval plastic, he notices the make of vehicle.

Land Rover. Let us press this little button.

A four-wheel drive SUV standing almost opposite him, lights up and gives out its own electronic signal. Excitement turning to relief, he walks toward the vehicle. As he approaches the Land Rover, a ting of guilt at using somebody else's car, even though the owner may now be dead, plays on his conscience. Pushing his feelings aside, he opens the driver side door, climbs up and soon becomes comfortable in the driver's seat. As he checks the mirrors, he notices the vehicle is almost new with a low mileage on the speedometer.

I am either very fortunate or this is all meant to be.

Using the digital remote, he presses the button again, which lights up a larger button just below the steering wheel. He presses this button, and is pleased when the engine begins to purr.

Now let us find the way out through this mess.

He puts the gear into drive and then pulls away at a slow speed toward what looks like an exit.

It's been awhile since I drove something like this.

He soon approaches a bend that blends into an upward slope. Being cautious, he carries on until he reaches the top of the slope. Seeing the way out, his hope fades as he comes across a mixture of rubble and sheets of roofing blocking his exit.

Now what?

Putting the gear stick into park, and leaving the engine running, he looks out of the windshield, and wonders.

I must get out of here! Surely this is all meant to happen, and this is just a temporary glitch?

Trying not to get frustrated, he notices just below the blockage, a closed emergency fire door in the concrete wall on his right.

I wonder?

Focusing on the door, he scrambles out of his seat, leaves the engine running and the headlights on full beam for maximum light. Rushing toward the door, he pushes the emergency bar, and to his regret nothing moves.

Perhaps if I push the bar down hard and lunge at the door at the same time, it might open?

This is what he does. To his astonishment and relief, the door flies open. Even though relieved to be free, and enjoying the bright cool sunshine, his horror, as the sun reflects the scene of devastation hits him hard. While trying to absorb the sight of pulverized parked cars, fallen masonry and heavy concrete beams, tears of shock fill his eyes.

Oh God! What have you done?

Regaining some form of self-control, he looks around to see where the blocked exit might be. What looks like an exit, is covered with sheets of roofing, weighted down with rubble. His mood turning to rage, he goes to the pile, and begins throwing the manageable pieces of masonry and concrete clear of the roofing, so he can pull some of the sheets clear.

Within ten minutes, every part of his body hurts, but is thankful that he has managed to clear an area large enough for him to drive the Land Rover through. Even though he is tired and sore, his rage dissipates, and his mood becomes more positive, he scrambles down the ramp toward the waiting vehicle.

Once out of the ramp, he maneuvers the car around all the obstacles until he reaches an area that seems like it was once a road. Still effected by the devastation, he stops and rests for a while.

Trying to get his mind into some form of equilibrium, it is difficult for him to accept the demolishment. Scanning the flattened horizon, the occasional low wall breaks the view. His eyes focus on such a wall. The boards leaning against it look out of place.

Someone has made a shelter. That means survivors!

His hope rising, he drives with care over to the site, to find it is empty. Feeling disheartened, he carries on driving at the same pace, while observing everything around him in anticipation of finding someone. Up ahead a pair of metal doors have been flung open. Curious, he stops, looks, and then gets out of his car.

Now standing at the top of the opening, he surveys the concrete steps that go down to a half opened steel door. His instincts tells him to descend the steps and enter the storage room the other side of the door. Standing by the open door, he notices the discarded granola bar wrappers and empty plastic water bottles.

Someone has been here in the last few hours.

Stepping into the room, he inspects the shelves, and tries to imagine how many people were here.

This must be part of a store. Whoever was here did not take much. These shelves are still well stocked. That means there were only a few, and they have no transport.

Looking around the shelves, he decides to fill his Land Rover with as much from the shelves as it can hold, so he will have enough supplies for anyone else he might come across.

Ten minutes later the back of the car is now full, and Gus is strapped into the driver's seat. Contemplating before setting off into the unknown, he stares out of the windshield.

God? What is your plan? Do I have to discover it one step at a time? Well, so far so good. At least for me. What about my children? Eva, Ryan, and the President? These good people should have survived. As always, I am entirely in your hands.

Taking a deep breath, he puts the gear into drive. Making sure the sun is in the right position for him to face westward, he sets off.

By the way, thanks for these supplies.

53

Devil May Care

Her liquid green eyes bore deep into his insides. Her black, thick wavy hair falls onto his face in a seductive manner, as she leans over him.

Look at that body! I must have her.

He reaches out, but she moves back - just out of reach. Teasing in a way that would send any man into a frenzy of lust, she tilts her head back and laughs as if mocking. Carrying on this 'game', she comes back. He reaches out again, but just so his fingertips can brush against her breasts. The overwhelming urge to take her is driving him mad with frustration.

Why is this beauty teasing me so? I cannot move to get near her. She keeps calling out and beckoning...

Natas wakes up to a voice crying out. He tries to move, but a heavy concrete beam is lying across both of his lower legs. He can feel sensation, but no pain, meaning the beam is resting its full weight on something else, and he is just jammed between the beam and the floor. Some sort of metal sheeting covers his upper body.

It seems I do not have a fracture, so all it needs is someone to lever the weight up an inch, and then I can pull myself free. Who is this person shouting? Perhaps they can help?

The man's voice is becoming fainter. He seems to be moving away. In desperation, Natas shouts. The voice shouts back. There is a sound of footsteps coming closer. Natas shouts again.

"Over here!"

The footsteps come closer, and then stop. Natas can hear heavy breathing.

"I am right here."

A large sheet of roofing covering Natas, is removed. As daylight fills his eyes, Natas focuses on a tall, large red haired man dressed in a tattered UN security uniform. His patience running thin, Natas stares up at the man offering him his best, grateful smile. Being of amiable character, the big man smiles back.

"How long you bin here man?"

"It feels like forever. Can you get me out of here?"

Even though weary, the man studies the situation, scratches his head, and then leaves. Not expecting this sort of reaction, Natas begins to panic.

"Hey? Don't leave me here. Come back!

Trust me to get an imbecile for help.

Within minutes, the man returns with a piece of heavy steel re-bar. He places the end of the bar about twelve inches under the side of the beam nearest to Natas.

"I will probably be only able to lever this bar once. So when I say 'go', you go. Okay?"

As Natas nods in appreciation, the man grips the bar tight with his strong grubby hands. Gripping the bar, he bends his legs and places his powerful shoulders under the bar as if ready to lift.

"Right. Go!"

With every muscle taught with effort, he levers the steel bar. With a heavy grunt of effort, he manages to lift the heavy concrete beam high enough to take the pressure off Natas' legs. When the man sees Natas is free, he lets go of the steel bar, causing the beam to land back with a heavy thump. As the dust settles, the two men glance at each with relief and a sense of satisfaction. Bruised and sore all over, Natas tries to brush the thick dust off his black robes. Curios by this man's costume, the man puts out his hand.

"The names George."

Receiving George's hand with his usual limp handshake, Natas spits out some dust.

"Call me Nat. What day is it?"

"Its Easter Sunday. You some kinda priest?"

Now George has served his purpose, Natas is reluctant to reply.

"Yes. Easter Sunday - mmm. I have been out since Friday. So, this is resurrection day for me too."

Not quite understanding this priest's humor, George stares at him with a puzzling expression.

"I'm sorry mister. You got me confused at all this. You bein a man of the cloth, can you tell me what thuh hells goin on?"

Ignoring the comment on his Pharisee robes, Natas is again reluctant to answer.

"If you need to know, hell is the right word for it my friend. Your God did this. The whole world is destroyed. Wiped out!"

Thinking that this disaster has effected this robed man's reasoning, George reaches out and grips Natas's shoulder in sympathy.

"How do you know? What are you talking about? Why? What for? Why have we survived?

"Because we are the chosen ones."

"I don't understand mister. Chosen, for what?"

Natas' green eyes flash with manic excitement mixed with irritation.

"Us. I – err - we, the survivors are chosen to run this new World."

Scratching his head in confusion, George persists with his questions.

"From what I can see, all the people have gone. There is nothing out there to run.

"Ah, but there is. You stick close to me and you will discover your true destiny."

Too tired to take any more of this strange man's ravings, George is just glad to be alive, and be able to help where he can.

"What ever you're sayin, we need tuh find some transport to go where ever we're supposed to go. If you know what I mean Jellybean."

Becoming irritable at this simpleton, but needing him for now, Natas controls his intolerance by flashing him a sincere smile.

"Yes. I know exactly what you mean. Two great minds think alike. As you say, we need a vehicle. So, let us get going, and 'find' one."

Stepping around and over the rubble with his manic energy, Natas makes his way out of the immediate area. Still puzzled by this predicament, George can't help noticing while trying to keep up with this guy, how theatrical he looks with his black robes flowing in the cool air.

An hour has passed. Both men are becoming weary as they stroll along a main road strewn with abandoned vehicles and fallen rubble. Both are trying the doors of different cars and trucks when...

"Ah-ha!"

Natas has found an unlocked Hummer. Banking on a winner, George scurries over to inspect the prize.

"It's even got the ignition remote. The previous owner must have fled in a real hurry."

George goes around to the rear and opens the back door.

"My God! Look at all this stuff."

Still irritation by George's childlike enthusiasm, Natas puts on another smile and wanders round to see what all the excitement is about. On finding a crate of twelve, one liter bottles of spring water, a box of canned tuna, and a cool box containing frozen beef patties and hot dog sausages, Natas has to laugh with a sense of satisfaction.

"God has nothing to do with it my good friend. When this person or persons unknown were on their way to have a barbecue or something, it was abruptly cancelled. Now it will not be wasted."

Ignoring Natas' ramblings, George wastes no time in opening two bottles of water. Offering one to Natas, he is a little disturbed when Natas takes it without a hint of thanks.

"Now we have to decide where we are going."

Even though he might appear a little slow, George knows what to suggest.

"We can't really go east because we'll hit the sea. North will still be too cold. So, I reckon we ought to go west."

Controlling his impatience, Natas heads forward to the front passenger door.

"Yes, that is what we will do. George? You get in the driver's seat and make sure you follow the sun."

54

Nothing to Preside Over

At the first noise of gunfire in the UN building, the President was soon hustled away by James, the relief Secret service agent and pushed with no ceremony into the armored limo known as the 'Beast'.

Now trapped inside by falling rubble, the President with her daughter Julie is anxious as they watch James, who is frantic in operating the satellite radio transmitter without any success.

"I'm sorry Ma'am, there doesn't seem to be anyone out there. At least not with a phone or radio. The batteries are also getting low."

The desperate President is trying hard to stay calm for the sake of her daughter.

"Thank you James. Give it another thirty minutes to get out of this - tomb and then it will have to be plan B."

Not knowing what plan B entails, James acknowledges and carries on calling on the radio.

"This is Exeter. come in 'anybody'."

Becoming anxious, Julie is crouched up in the back seat watching the sweat pour down James's anxious neck.

"What is plan B mother?"

"To remove ourselves from this stifling environment and find out what or who is left out there."

Meanwhile, George is cautious while driving the Hummer on the remains of what was once a freeway. While being careful when maneuvering around piles of debris and deserted vehicles, he becomes more curios and a little scared.

Where're the bodies? There's nothing!

While Natas is also keen in observing all the damage, he taps George on the arm.

"Stop here for a minute. I want to try something."

After stopping, Natas studies the unusual instruments on the dashboard. He then unclips a larger than normal cellphone, and gazes at the blank screen. Wondering what this man is going to do next, George witnesses Natas press a side button and then tap the screen. In a second the screen turns a bright blue, and another screen on the dashboard lights up to a pale green. As if striking gold, Natas' phone hand shakes with excitement.

"This is some form of satellite radio phone and GPS system. Of course! The satellites are still up there, bleeping away and transmitting to anyone who can receive and use them."

Wondering how this can possibly help them, George scratches his head.

"Big deal. How's it goin tuh help us?"

Not listening, Natas taps an icon on the phone screen causing the dashboard screen to form a circular pattern, and static appear out of nearby speakers. His face twitching with a manic excitement, Natas turns to George.

"I have a feeling this is an abandoned Secret Service vehicle. Direct contact to the White house."

George yawns, and is not impressed.

"I doubt if there is a White House. How'd you know it belongs to the Secret Service? With all that barbecue stuff in the back it could be anybody's?"

Becoming more irritated by this semi – intellectual, who keeps doubting, Natas' anger is getting hard to control. However, for now George is still useful. This being so, he conveys to George the best smile he can muster.

"George? With this type of communication system on board, it must be

Government or Secret Service. As for the stuff in the back, who knows? Thank your lucky stars I found that food. So, with you driving and me scanning the airways we might get somewhere."

Becoming resigned to his new, strange companion, George shrugs, puts the Hummer into gear, and begins to drive.

"Where to?"

Before Natas can answer, the speakers' crackle and a voice comes through.

"This is Exeter. To anyone out there?"

Natas almost drops the phone with the shock of hearing another voice. He has to take a deep breath to stay in control. Acting confident, but his hand trembling, Natas appears calm as he replies.

"Come in Exeter. I can hear you loud and clear."

Silence.

"This is Exeter. To anyone out there."

Observing his 'confident' companion floundering, George bursts out laughing.

"You didn't press the transmit button on the side of the receiver. Press it down all the time you're talking."

Becoming annoyed at his own ignorance for not realizing his simple error, and even more exasperated at this moron for pointing it out, Natas presses what he presumes is the correct button.

"Come in Exeter. I can hear you loud and clear."

He releases the button and waits.

Come on idiot. Answer!

"What is your position and the code of the day?"

He answered!

Natas' hand trembles a little with excitement as he presses the transmit button.

It is a Government car!

"All I know is, I am in a flattened New York and I do not have a clue about any code."

"Who are you and how did you acquire this vehicle?"

Natas stares in disbelief at the phone.

This man is an idiot!

"My name is Nat. I - err - we are survivors of this terrible disaster. We found this car abandoned, so naturally we commandeered it, so we can perhaps find other poor souls."

Figure out that one - idiot.

The idiot answers.

"We appreciate your concern for yourself and others, but you are in the possession of Government property. I have located your position. If you look on the GPS screen in front of you, there is a marker giving your position. You need to travel southeast to meet up with us. We will help you when you arrive. Please keep your phone on, and thank you for doing your duty as an American citizen."

George is amused.

"Once a Government man, always a Government man."

Natas is not amused. He is trying hard to focus and not look a fool in front of George.

"Do you know where Southeast is?"

"Yeah, I think so. You thinking of goin there?"

"You heard what the man said. He can help us when we arrive."

It is George's turn to focus.

"Do you know somethin? I bet they're no better off than we are. That original call sounded pretty desperate."

"You may be right. We are in a good position what ever we do. The tank is almost full and we have food to eat on the way. So, let us be good citizens and make our way to these fine Government people and see what happens."

Julie jumps off her seat in realization that there are some people out there. As the President clasps her hands together in thanks, James leans back in his seat, relieved they are not alone.

"It won't take them long to get here. By the GPS, they're not very far. Then what do we do – Ma'am?

"Perhaps they might have found Gus or have news of him."

Her optimism overflowing, Julie needs to express her opinion.

"Gus 'is' alive. I know it! This is all planned. He said this would happen."

Her weary, anxious mother is not so convinced.

"He said it would happen after a year, if nobody mended their ways..."

Being supportive, James says his piece.

"Well, it looks as if God or whoever thought otherwise, and got the job done quicker. We presume any survivors out there are some sort of chosen ones to start again, but hopefully better this time."

Looking at James with surprise and admiration. The President can't help but react.

"Let's hope you're right James."

In the meantime, Gus has traveled about five miles, when he sees three adults and about ten children. The group stop in surprise and delight, when they hear the engine noise approaching. Recognizing them, Gus sticks his head out of the driver's window.

"Anyone for a lift?"

Eva screams with delight when she sees driver. Garth reaction is to put his hands together in thanks, while Max gazes in wonder. The children all cheer and cry with relief, as Eva and Max go to him first. She places her trembling hands up to his face, as tears of joy pour down hers. Still not believing his eyes, Max puts out his hand to him.

"We meet at last. You survived, and with a car."

Eva begins to tremble in disbelief.

"Oh God! You did survive."

"Only the best for you my dear."

Surrounded by the children, Garth stands behind them.

"We all knew you would make it and find us."

Now lost for words, Gus scrambles out of the Land Rover and kneels down to the children.

"How is my flock?"

Ryan steps forward.

"Happy now you're here. We were beginning to worry."

Laughing at the humor, Gus stands, and rests both hands on the children's heads.

"Well, it looks like the Garden of Eden is coming earlier than originally proposed. I have received a message that we must follow the sun. That means we go west..."

Trying hard to calm down, Eva interrupts.

"My cell phone flashed the same message."

Gus looks surprised.

Mine came in a dream.

"That proves it then, we are being guided and looked after. So, from now on, don't any of us worry..."

Acting calm, as if this is all meant to be, the red haired girl with the big blue eyes interrupts.

"I keep telling everyone that its God looking after us. You always told us that. If we are always good to each other, God will 'always' be there for us."

Humbled by wisdom beyond her years, Gus looks at Garth and Eva to verify.

"Yes.You are right. I did say that. I do believe we are being looked after. Otherwise, what is the point of it all?"

While there is a pause for reflection, Gus continues with as much enthusiasm he can muster.

"All of you cram into the Land Rover as best you can. We'll drive out of the city area and stay overnight in the country..."

For a few seconds, Gus is overcome by the sudden burden at the enormity of it all. Putting on a brave face, he indicates to everyone.

"All right everyone. All aboard."

As all the children and Eva manage to squash in amongst the supplies, the three men cram side by side in the front. Gus sits in the driver's seat and looks around to check that everyone is secure.

"I'm sorry it's a bit cramped back there. It's only for now, until we find a larger van or even a bus. Then, we will change over."

As Gus slips the gear into drive, and is careful in driving away, he mentions an observation to Garth sitting nearest to him.

"I think the children are looking at this as a bit of an adventure."

Even though worried about the future, Garth can't help but smile.

"Perhaps that's how it's going to be. A new life with plenty of adventure."

Max is not quite so enthusiastic.

"Not too much of an adventure - I hope."

Ignoring Natas and his strange mannerisms, George is now heading southeast. Slowing down to go around abandoned or wrecked vehicles, he notices a raggedy looking man trying to get into an abandoned car.

"Hey look! There's a survivor. I'm goin to look."

Still involved with the GPS unit, Natas is not looking, but comments anyway.

"Do what you must. I suppose it will look good to be carrying survivors when we arrive at our unknown destination."

Ignoring his companion's cynical behavior, George guides their Hummer at the man leaning against a battered vehicle. George offers the man a wide smile, as he winds down his window.

"Hi guy, we're goin to get help. Get in the back."

The man is so exhausted, he is unable to talk as he struggles to climb into the rear of the vehicle. Without a word of complaint, the man rests back and under his breath, gives thanks. Sighing with resignation, Natas turns and conveys a cordial smile to the beleaguered man.

"There is some water at the back. If you reach over the seat."

Becoming annoyed at Natas' casual attitude toward this poor man, George decides to get out of the hummer, and give the man a bottle of water.

"We'll stop soon and have ourselves some grub."

As George returns to his seat, Natas is becoming irritated again with George.

"Hurry up George! Time is of the essence."

Ignoring Natas, George emphasizes his reply and winks at the new passenger, smiles and clips on his seat belt.

"Yessir!"

It is now three hours later. Gus has decide to park on a lonely stretch of highway by a wooded area. Relaxing for a minute, and the sun now shining through his windshield, he becomes aware to the north of him is an abandoned school bus that has rammed up against an overturned full size Wal-Mart Truck and trailer. Next to the bus is a dented mini van with a large round man leaning up against it with his arms folded as if waiting for someone. Weighing up the possibilities of this extra transport, Gus jumps out of the Land Rover. Observing the situation, Max, Garth and Eva exit the Land Rover, and wait so as to not wake the sleeping children.

Unable to see the man's face, because he keeps looking down at his feet, Gus approaches the waiting man.

"Hello? Are you okay? Can we help?"

The man's weary expression changes into a stunned look, as Gus reaches out to him.

"Its you! You said it would happen. And it did!"

Lost for a second, and then recognizing the man, Gus grips his upper arm.

"Irwin Shultz! I don't believe it."

Tears of relief fill Irwin's eyes, as he embraces Gus on impulse.

"Would you believe I still have that recording, but I can't play it."

Remembering the 'interview', Gus smiles at the irony.

"How long have you been here?"

"About an hour. I commandeered this battered mini-van when I saw these kids sleeping inside this bus. So, I thought I would stand guard until help arrives. And here you are, the man who predicted it all."

Not wanting to go back there, Gus focuses on the present.

"I don't think there will be any help arriving. Have you seen anyone else?"

"No one."

Becoming more aware of his extending burden, Gus looks through a side window of the bus. Curios, the other three join him. Relieved at what they see, are six Native American children huddled together on the wide back seat. Observing the children are in school uniform, Garth comments first.

"No sign of a driver. The keys are still in the ignition."

Meanwhile and wanting to help, Eva opens the driver's side door.

"We need to see if we can get this bus going, because there is no way we can carry these children in our present transport."

Nodding in agreement, Gus climbs into the driver's seat and looks around the immediate area to access if there is any damage.

"Garth, Max, can you check the front to see if the bus is stuck or locked up against the truck? Eva and Irwin? Can you sit with these children for a while, so they don't get frightened when they wake up? Which will be soon, if we can get this bus going?"

While waiting for Eva and Irwin to go and sit at the back of the bus, Garth and Max waste no time in checking the front of the bus for any damage. Seeing there is no obvious damage, Max gives Gus the thumbs up, and then comes to the driver's side.

"Looks okay to me. Maybe a few small dents under the head light. Otherwise, all seems good."

Thanking Max with an appreciative smile, Gus grips the steering wheel.

"Thanks Max. Well, here goes."

With one hand still on the steering wheel, he turns the keys in the ignition. The engine responds with a single click. Cursing under his breath, Gus tries again. This time, there is no response from the engine.

God? Why is it always so hard?

Hiding his frustration, he reaches down to pull the lever that opens the bus's hood. It springs up with ease, and is now covering some of the windshield. Garth and Max now peering at the silent engine, Gus sees their heads disappear for a minute, and then reappear giving him the thumbs up. Taking this as a signal to turn the key again, Gus accommodates. As the engine bursts into life, much to everyone's delight, Gus gives his two comrades a salute of appreciation.

In the meantime, the children stir, and gaze at Eva and Irwin in bewilderment. Suppressing his excitement, Gus turns to them, and speaks over the noise of the engine.

"Don't be alarmed we're here to help you."

The six children consisting of five boys in their early teens and one girl about sixteen, is the one that seems to be their leader.

"Who are you? What is happening?"

Eva's response is to reach out to her, and grip her hands.

"We are with Gus. Any of you hurt?"

Still a little lost at what is happening, they all shake their heads. Eva reassures.

"That's good. Where is, or where was your home?"

After a pause, the girl answers with a proud reply.

"We are Navaho. I am Chief Silver Eagle's daughter and these are my cousins. We were on our way home from school to our lodgings when all hell let loose and tossed us all around."

"What happened to the driver?"

"He got thrown out. We've been here since."

The noise of the bus engine has also woken the children in the cramped Land Rover. Thrilled that their lives are turning in a positive direction, Eva and Irwin leave the bus to help the other children out of the Land Rover.

Without any hesitation, they all run to the bus. Ryan being in the lead, enters the bus first, and is happy to find the other children all ready sitting in the back. With no hesitation, he beckons to his friends to follow him, so they can team up with these new comrades.

After closing the bus's hood, Garth and Max climb into the bus. Max sits next to Gus and Garth sits behind him.

"It was a loose wire from the battery. This is a stroke of luck, a bus that works and now a truck full of stuff. Let's hope it's not full of furniture or something useless like that."

Gazing at the Wal-Mart truck in front of them, Gus presence Max with a reassuring smile, and places his hand on his shoulder.

"Have faith my friend. You should realize by now that we are being cared for. I think you will find there will be enough supplies in that truck to get us to our destination."

Max still has his doubts.

"Destination? Where are we going?"

"West! We are following the sun – remember? But first, I am going to reverse this bus to be clear of that truck, and then we are all going to stock up. After that, we are going to have a bite to eat, and then drive until it gets dark. I hope that puts you out of your misery."

Liking Gus more by the minute and accepting his fate, Max joins Garth as they jump out of the bus to watch Gus reverse the vehicle until it is well clear of the trailer. To their surprise, this causes the back door of the trailer to spring wide open. Drawn to all the excitement, Ryan decides to join the two men, who are now staring in amazement at all the supplies packed in the open trailer.

"There's enough food in there to feed a whole city."

At Gus's instructions, everyone has evacuated the bus to stare in wonder at this latest find. With a mixture of relief and certainty, Gus addresses them all.

"I want us to give thanks for this bounty that has come our way. This is not just good fortune, but help that is being given to us for our final mission. The mission that started over two thousand years ago is now going to be finally accomplished. Now, what I would like is for you all to form a human chain. I will unload the trailer while everyone helps pack everything into the back of the bus."

With Gus unloading the useful supplies, the children passing each package along the chain, and the adults doing the stacking, in a short time they manage to fill about a third of the bus. Satisfied with the amount, Gus now stops unloading.

"That will do for us. There is plenty left for any more people that will come by. When we've finished packing, let's gather some wood and make a small fire, eat and rest for the night. Tomorrow we will be ready to carry on our mission."

Meanwhile, Natas has been concentrating on the little screen in front of him, while George is becoming weary by driving around in circles and being unsuccessful in finding the 'Beast'. Their new male passenger falls asleep, as the speakers crackle.

"This is Exeter. Come in Nat."

Natas jumps in response, grabs the phone, and presses the transmit button.

"Nat hearing you loud and clear - Exeter. Where the hell have you been for the last few hours? We have been going around in circles trying to pick up your signal."

After an embarrassing pause, James replies.

"Sorry about that fellas, but my batteries are running low, so I had to switch off to give them a small recharge. You are only about a quarter of a mile from your destination. From now on, I will give you the precise directions for you to arrive safely. Unfortunately, we are in an unusual situation, so please do exactly as I say and we will have no problems."

"I understand, Exeter. We are on our way."

We have been buzzing round like a bee looking for a flower, and he needs a recharge. So much for governing the New World.

Natas smiles with a sense of satisfaction, and then looks at George to validate.

"I have a feeling we are on our way to see Madam President."

"How'd you know that?"

"Trust me George, I know. I have been waiting for this moment. From now on you are now part of my destiny."

With the sun going down, Gus and his new family are seated around an open camp fire made from pieces of deadwood scavenged from the surrounding wooded area. The adults are opening cans of fruit, beans and meat, and handing them out on paper plates accompanied by plastic silverware. Observing the warm glow of the fire reflecting off the

465

children's happy faces as they chatter and appreciate the cold food, Gus looks again from one face to the next.

God? I believe we're going to make it.

Holding a plate for both of them, Eva sits down next to him.

"Penny for them?"

Still caught up in the situation, he turns to her. The firelight, now shining on the side of her face, he is drawn to her attractive profile.

Eva? You are one beautiful lady.

"I was thinking that we 'are' going make it."

"Of course we are. As you said, what's the point? We have to make it! This is all part of the mission. The thing I would like to know is why do we have to travel? Why can't we just start here and set up our community."

Remembering his prophetic dream about following the sun, Gus ponders.

"Good point! I cannot answer that one just yet. All I know is what I feel, and as this is far bigger than me, there is a reason why we have to travel to a prearranged destination to conclude this chapter of the mission."

Not quite understanding, she looks down at her plate, but her mind is not on food.

"Prearranged by God?"

"I presume."

Intrigued by this adult conversation, Ryan puts up his hand to ask a question. His mother acknowledges, but he points to Gus. Gus smiles and responds.

"Yes, Ryan?"

"The rest of us have been talking and are wondering if this is Revelations."

Taken aback by this mature question from such a young boy, Gus tries his best to answer.

"In a way, yes. All I know is that I have to complete this mission so the world can carry on, as it was originally conceived. Remember, that when the Bible was first written it was an assortment of books and scrolls, written approximately between fifty and two hundred AD. The Bible you read today is the abridged version edited by the Roman Catholic Church when the Roman Empire took the Christian Religion as its own. The Bible is a rough chronicle of Jewish history and yours truly."

Becoming involved in this deep discussion, Garth raises his arm.

"I think the best lesson you ever taught was, the meek shall inherit the earth..."

Sitting next to Garth, the Navaho girl raises her arm with the same pride as before.

"My tribe is 'not' meek! So, how can that be right?"

Understanding the girl's confusion, Gus presence her with a congenial smile and tries to explain.

"That has always been misinterpreted. It doesn't mean being timid. The 'meek' have humility, and are unselfish, kind and sincere. Who better to inherit this great planet of ours. You must also remember that there are survivors all over the world right now, waiting for this mission to come to them..."

Gus is distracted by a woman appearing out of the woods accompanied by two young oriental girls. Their faces become lit up by the glow of the fire, but the woman's face is still in darkness. Anxious about these newcomers, Gus beckons her to come forward. As she moves closer to the fire, Gus freezes to the spot as her face comes into view.

My God! It's Mary! It can't be?

Then he remembers the words Mary Magdalene said in his dream.

She is not me!

Meanwhile, Eva is becoming concerned by Gus' reaction to this woman.

"Gus? What is it?"

Still gazing at the woman, he is having trouble in answering.

"Oh - err – nothing. She reminds me of someone I knew a long time ago."

Eva is troubled and a little jealous by Gus's change of mood, as he stands and goes to greet the new arrivals. Gazing into her smoky green eyes, he is speechless as the woman accepts his hand and offers him a radiant smile.

467

"I am Madeline and these are the Chang twins."

His stomach turns over at the remarkable resemblance.

The hair? Her warm mouth, and those eyes?

Coming out of his trance, he lets go of her hand and turns to the others.

"Let's welcome our new friends, Madeline and the Chang twins. Give them food and drink. Anything they need."

His mind in a new turmoil, Gus walks to the bus and leans against it trying to calm down. Observing Gus's behavior, and the women's beauty, Eva is reluctant to leave the others to join him.

"Gus? What is the matter? You look as if you've seen a ghost."

"I have! That's Mary. And yet it isn't."

"You're not making sense. Do you know this woman?"

His unease increasing, Gus rubs his face with his trembling hands to try and stay calm. Not wanting to alarm Eva with this new emotion, he leads her further away from the bus, out of earshot of the others.

"I had a dream while I was coming round after all this devastation. Mary was telling me to follow the sun and she also told me that 'she is not me.' Meaning that this woman is not her, but it is her - in every detail. The love of my life!"

Thinking she was the love of his life, Eva, is feeling hurt and confused. Her reaction is to grab his hands, and look straight into his eyes. Keeping her. Voice calm and soft so not to attract attention,, she makes her point.

"I thought I was that once. You must know you're still the love of my life."

Relishing the warmth of her hand, tears of irrational guilt form in his eyes.

"I'm sorry. I know how you feel, and you know I love you. It's just the shock of seeing her and instantly going back all those years and remembering how she loved carried my child."

Listening to all this, Eva is becoming agitated at Gus losing focus.

"This is 'not' Mary Magdalene! It is a resemblance, that's all. You treat her like all the others. The mission comes first. Okay?"

Still holding her hands, he leans toward her and kisses her pensive mouth.

"You're so right, as always. That's why I love you so. We ought to all now get some sleep."

With his arm around her shoulder, they stroll back to join the others.

55

The President Moves On

George and the survivor passenger are standing outside the acquired Hummer looking at a large pile of rubble reflecting in their headlights. Natas is inside the vehicle, operating the radio.

"Come in Exeter. We are standing exactly where you directed us, and all we can see in this darkness, is a pile of rubble. What do you advise?"

Moron!

"That is correct Nat. We are in the 'Beast.' The President's personal vehicle, underneath the said rubble. I am speaking to you now in strict confidence. The President and her daughter are with me..."

As the radio becomes feint, Natas has trouble trying not to laugh.

A buffoon and the beast.

"I understand. How can we help?"

There is no answer, so Natas climbs out of the vehicle and informs George in a casual, and sarcastic manner.

"Underneath the 'said' rubble is the President, accompanied by her daughter and a Secret Service - person."

George and his companion gasp in amazement, scramble over to the rubble and begin gripping lumps of concrete and throwing them to one side.

Inside the armored car, James is desperate in still trying the radio.

"Sorry Ma'am. It looks like the batteries have finally died."

Thinking she can hear something outside, Julie pushes her ear against the inside wall of the car.

"Listen! I can here movement outside."

Outside, Natas is enjoying watching these two unfit men struggle to make a dent in the mountain of rubble.

What fools they all are.

Regardless of Natas not lending a hand, George discovers a space in the rubble.

"I've hit something."

Natas still looking on as if witnessing a second rate movie, he watches the two men become frantic, while concentrating on this new area. After a short while, part of a window appears. Julie is waving. Pleased with his efforts, George beckons to her to open the window a little.

Natas is even more amused by all this.

I'm surrounded by fools and idiots!

"They can't, the windows are thick, solid and bullet proof. Tell them to switch on the ignition, put the car into first gear and literally drive 'out' of the rubble."

Obeying his new master, George mimics a game of 'charades' to explain to Julie that they need to just drive out of the rubble.

Still amused by all these theatrics, Natas holds his breath, as the President's limo roars into life. George and his companion come back to stand with Natas, while the mountain of rubble collapses due to the 'Beast' appearing at a slow speed exiting the rubble like a newborn from its mother.

Now clear of the pile, the car stops. There is a pause. Still amused by these comical events, Natas sees a man dressed in a dark crumpled suit ease his stiff body out of the driver's door. Ignoring the witnesses, the man scuttles around to open the front passenger door. With dignity, the President exits her car. At the same time, the rear passenger door opens on its own. Natas' eyes widen when he sees an attractive teenage girl come into view.

Trying to keep up some sort of dignified appearance, the President stares

471

at the three men standing opposite her.

"Thank you for coming. You could have ignored our request and gone your own way."

Sure of her delicate situation, Natas offers her his most endearing smile.

"Madam President! How could I- we - have possibly done that when our country – or - our world is in it's greatest need."

Impressed by this handsome man's sincerity, she does her best not to show her vulnerability.

"That is very noble of you - err..."

"My friends call me Nat, Ma'am."

"Nat. Yes. Very noble. The thing is, what to do next?"

The survivor standing next to George raises his hand.

"Might I make a suggestion, Madam President?"

"Yes, of course - err..."

"Fred, Ma'am. I was a security officer at the NBC building or what's left of it. Anyway, to answer your question. I think we ought to try to find Gus."

Hearing that name, Natas almost chokes. Being the man he is, George pats him on the back, but still looks at the President.

"I quite agree Ma'am. I'm sorry, me name's George, and I'm a security officer for the UN building or what's left of it."

At the mention of the UN building, Natas' chocking turns into a full-blown coughing fit. George continues to pat his back.

"You okay old chum? Want me tuh get yuh a drink?"

Of course I am all right, you idiot. Stop banging my back.

Putting on a big show of acknowledging George''s kindness, Natas regains his composure.

"Yes! I am fine now. Thanks to you George. I am sorry for the interruption Madam President. When my close friend Gus was mentioned, I lost it, if you know what I mean."

Expressing sympathy, the President moves nearer, and grips Natas' arm.

"We totally understand. He is our close friend as well. Has anyone any ideas of how we might find him, if he is still alive."

Astonished by her mother's complacency, Julie glares at her mother.

"Of course he's still alive! All this is because of him. Anyway, I can feel he's still alive. We just have to find him."

Admiring her courage, and her beauty, Natas conveys to Julie his sweetest smile. Noticing he is making an impression, he turns to her mother. Still smiling, but with no admiration, he puts on the charm.

"I had an unusual dream this morning while I was in a state of semi consciousness from the devastation. I was informed by an angel that I had to follow the sun. Go westward. That is where we were heading when you contacted us."

Taking in this information, the President begins to pace.

"James? Have we still got the satellite capability in the Hummer to pinpoint a car live on the map?"

"We have got a fifty square mile capacity Ma'am. If we know roughly the direction Gus is traveling we can track him. On the other hand, we can be tracking any vehicle on a certain road, but we still won't know whose driving."

Not the answer she is looking for, the President stops pacing and looks at Natas with a curious stare.

"In your dream, you think you need to go west..."

Before Natas can reply, Julie interrupts.

"Like my dream!"

Raising an eyebrow at the interruption, her mother peers at her daughter with a touch of sarcasm.

"What dream is that dear?"

"When I was last asleep, I dreamt I was traveling on a long straight road with the sun setting directly in my eyes. There was sand everywhere. Like on a beach."

Liking this young girl by the minute, Natas joins her.

"Probably the desert. Arizona or California. But why?"

Ignoring Natas, the President answers her.

"It was only a dream my dear."

Admiring the young girl, but becoming irritated by her mother, his jaw clenches in frustration.

Small-minded idiot. I must take charge.

"I think it is a very important dream. It must be - because it coincides with 'mine'. I also suspect Gus has had a similar dream, as he and I are 'so' close. Therefore, I strongly suggest that we all make our way to the western desert. According to Moses - Ma'am."

The President is dumbfounded at being spoken in such a way. His arrogant manner is irritating her. Not showing her annoyance, she smiles back to him in a cordial manner.

"Well, as we seem to have a clue as to where we 'might' be heading, unfortunately, the 'Beast' is effective for what it is designed for, but not much use to us now..."

She glares at Natas with her eyes, but her mouth remains amicable.

" - I suggest we use the Hummer, stock up on as much food and supplies as we can carry on the way, and then travel west until we can find some suitable transport that can carry other survivors who might have the same idea."

Natas's reaction to this 'woman' standing in front of him, is to bite his lip and smile.

You will not be giving your orders for long – madam!

Taking the initiative, James begins making his way toward the 'Beast.'

"I'll start collecting what gear we need. If someone here can help me stock up the emergency rations and siphon the gas out of the limo into the Hummer...?"

As George and Fred waste no time in volunteering, there is a cold silence between her an Natas. While watching the men transferring the supplies, Julie becomes aware of her mother's anxious mood. She seems lost, as she stars into nowhere with a vacant expression. Never seeing her mother like this, Julie goes to her.

"Are you all right Mother?"

"Yes, dear. I – err - must take some important papers - and the nuclear football. Especially now, as we are going out into the unknown."

Rolling his eyes at such a ludicrous statement, Natas turns away.

Nuclear football? You stupid woman, there is nothing left to blow up! I must take charge – now!.

Offering the two females his most charming and confident smile, he turns to face them.

"Have no fear ladies, I am here at your service. I am desperate to find our friend Gus, as you are. We have a lot to do together. The world is entering a new era as never before. It is up to us in this moment of conception to bring fourth a life of true love and goodness for all."

Yeah right!

Astounded by such a profound statement, Julie and her mother stare at Natas, searching his face for the sincerity they need. Liking him more than her mother appears to, Julie speaks first.

"What is your religion? I am trying to decide what your robes are for."

Being taken by surprise at such a question, Natas hides this new irritation.

This attractive snip of a girl is no fool. I want to know her more – far more. For now, keep it casual. My time will come.

"It is Jewish my dear. I thought it appropriate in the circumstances, as the Jews were the original chosen people. Those Jews who might have remained on this planet are still the chosen ones - along with the rest..."

"So, you're a Rabbi?"

"Once, but not now. Just a citizen of the new order."

Mother and daughter glance at each other for a reaction. Neither receiving one, they decided to leave and help the others. Keeping his frustration in check, Natas watches them through a haze of incense.

Damn you! I will keep these robes on until my mission is complete, and the world is finally and deservedly MINE!

She leans over and kisses him on the lips. Her soft mouth sends spasms of electricity through his body, as her warm lips then brush his cheek on the way to his ear. He can feel her sweet breath as the familiar voice whispers.

"Keep going toward the sun until you come to the desert. My love will be waiting. Meanwhile, remember, she is not me."

Gus wakes up. He is lying on his back, and his eyes are staring at the stars. His mind is still on Mary telling him to go to the desert.

Where in the desert will she be waiting?

He can hear steady breathing close to his left. He turns to face Eva sleeping. His heart turns over while studying her serine features. Unable to resist the strong need, his lips fuse against her warm mouth.

Oh Eva! Oh God!

It is the early hours of the following morning. Natas' small group has traveled out of the built up areas and made camp on the side of the road by some open farmland. The President cannot sleep. Her mind is restless as she wanders around watching the others sleep in their various positions. Some still in the Hummer, while Natas seems content to be on his own several yards away under a large isolated oak tree. However her distaste for Natas, the President is pleased with the few supplies they have, and how well everyone has cooperated. Relishing the cool night air, she leans against a solitary fence post, as her mind keeps journeying back over the last two days.

We will find you Gus....

Concerned her mother is not sleeping, Julie comes up to her.

"Mom? You okay?"

Her mother stares at her. Startled, but controlled, she replies

"Can't you sleep either?"

"You woke me as you left the vehicle."

Her mother comforts her by sliding an arm around her daughter's shoulders.

"I'm sorry!"

At the same time, she stares ahead at the night sky. Her eyes filling with tears, she has a need to communicate.

"To answer your question? No! I'm not okay. Yesterday I was President of a great country. Now? Nothing! All because of one man telling us what to do and supposedly trying to put the world to rights."

Never having seen her mother this low before, Julie commiserated, but still has her say.

"Mother! You're talking about Gus, our savior and dearest friend. We are going to find him and start a new world order. An order of selflessness and giving."

Tears running down the President's cheeks, she turns to her daughter.

"Do you 'really' believe that?"

"Of course! Don't you? Why do you think you survived? You managed to escape into the limo just before the UN building collapsed. Don't you think that was meant to be?"

Becoming melancholy, Julie's mother turns back to face the horizon.

"I don't know any more."

"You saw the blue!"

"The blue...?"

As the sky begins to turn lighter in the East, Julie plants a soft kiss on her mother's cheek.

"Never mind. Start of a new day Mother."

A rustling noise behind them attracts their attention. Julie's mother sighs with relief to see it is James as he comes up to his boss.

"We're all awake and ready ma'am. George and I are going to take it in turn to drive. We'll stop and have a bite to eat in a couple of hours. Nobody seems to want cold tuna this early."

Still wrapped up in her own emotions and staring at the horizon, the President doesn't answer.

"Ma'am?"

She turns to him.

"I am sorry James. Yes. That will be fine. What time is it?"

He can see the tears.

"A little after five, ma'am."

"We will be right there. Thank you."

Uneasy about his boss appearing distressed, James nods and leaves to go to the Hummer. Julie and her mother look at each other as if searching for the right answer. No words are spoken as Julie slides her arm around

477

her mother's waist, acting as a support, while they follow James.

The soft, caring voice in the darkness sounds familiar.

"Come my friend, it is time for you to return home. Enough is enough. The world can be yours if you share it with me and my son. A place of goodness and love, as it was meant to be in the beginning. You left me once in conflict, but now it is all over. Come back to me. All is forgiven."

"You would have me back? Like the prodigal son?"

"Of course! We love you. You are always welcome, my lost friend."

"How do I do this?"

"I will send you the light..."

A bright light fills everywhere accompanied by a violent tremor.

Natas wakes up with a start. The bright sun is shining in his face and Fred is shaking him.

"Wha – ? What are you doing?"

"Sorry bud, but you were rambling in your sleep. Almost delirious."

A little disoriented, Natas sits up straight. Rubbing his eyes and getting used to the light, he has a need to talk.

"God was talking to me."

Getting used to this strange guy's ramblings, Fred acts interested.

"Really? What was said?"

"I was asked if I – oh - you wouldn't understand. Anyway, where are we?"

"Somewhere on interstate forty. It is now seven o'clock and you have slept the whole time since we left."

His mind now focused, Natas turns to look out of the rear window and observes the President and her daughter are standing outside with James and George. All seem cheerful while eating some tuna out of the cans.

Fools! If they only realize who I am and the power I have, especially now that God wants me to return to the fold. For the time being, I will be part of God and these poor idiots, until it suits me to do otherwise.

Acting out his pleasing persona, he scrambles out of the vehicle and joins the others. Realizing he hasn't eaten for days, he grabs a can of tuna and makes sure he is standing next to the President while stomaching his cold breakfast.

"Good morning Madam President. I am sorry you and Julie did not sleep that well."

Hiding her distaste for this man, she puts on an amiable smile.

"It's nice of you to comment. I see you managed to grab 'another' couple of hours on the journey."

Ignoring her sarcasm, he keeps up the pleasantries.

"Oh, I have no trouble sleeping. It's amazing what a clear conscience can do."

"Really? I do believe you were restless in your sleep this morning?"

He pauses while finding it hard in swallowing the fish.

God was calling me you stupid woman.

With his own hint of sarcasm, he answers.

"On rare occasions I have one of my prophetic dreams. Nothing important for you, but necessary to me."

Not wanting to expose his secret, he changes the subject.

"So? What is the next move?"

This continual sarcasm annoying her, her instilled professionalism keeps her controlled, as she answers with a strained smile.

"To carry on, find Gus and some more food and water. What we have now will not last very long. Maybe we'll find another car, or even a bus so we can pick up more survivors on the way."

Not bothered too much about other survivors, he offers her his most congenial smile.

"Sounds good to me. When do we leave?"

"Right away, when James plots a map on the GPS."

While they all clamber aboard the Hummer, and be seated as before, George the driver clicks on his safety belt and turns to the others.

"Everyone comfortable?"

Hearing his passengers all murmur okay, he puts the gearshift into first gear and enjoys the power of this heavy vehicle continuing their journey.

56

An Important Lesson

Garth is taking his turn to drive. He crunches the gearshift on the bus into a lower gear to help the vehicle drive up a steep hill. Aware of Gus and the others laughing at his pathetic driving, he turns to Gus to retaliate.

"All right you lot! I know I'm no bus driver. At least we're getting somewhere. Does anyone know where we are? I haven't a clue, except we're still going westward."

As the bus reaches the top of the hill, Gus rises up from his seat and stands behind Garth for a better view. In front of them lies a whole community that looks as if it has been flattened by a tornado. While the bright hot sun beats down making the area look even more desolate, Garth points to a lone building standing out of place about two hundred yards away to their right.

"What's that?"

Resting his hands on Garth's shoulders, Gus strains his eyes to look.

"It looks like a church."

"It might be an omen? A piece of genuine holiness saved from all the horror."

Releasing his grip, Gus pulls a face.

"I don't believe in omens. Drive up there, and we'll find out."

Meanwhile, Madeline is listening, and gives her opinion.

"There could be some survivors sheltering inside."

Gus is not so enthusiastic.

"Maybe."

As the bus pulls up outside the church, Gus turns and faces his apprehensive passengers.

"Everyone sit tight while Garth and I investigate to see if there are any survivors in this building."

While Gus and Garth disembark, Madeline can't wait to leave her seat and move to the front of the bus to get a better view. Remembering what Gus told everyone earlier, Eva watches this other woman and wonders.

"What are you doing?"

"Just want to see. This is so exciting!"

Assuming this church has been built in the last few years, by its square construction, Gus can see it is mainly red brick and high arched windows inserted with various stained colored frosted glass.

The two men stand outside the heavy arched front door, as Gus grabs the heavy brass doorknob, turns it and is cautious when opening the door. Compared to the outside world, Gus is astonished at everything inside so clean and untouched. As if approaching a time warp, they both enter at the same time. Pausing to survey this strange circumstance, they both take their time in approaching the alter. Behind them an excited female voice breaks the eerie silence. Knowing who it is, Gus, becoming irritated, turns to see Madeline standing in the doorway.

"It's beautiful."

Before Gus has a chance to respond, she hurries down the aisle toward the two men. Gazing into his eyes, she grips Gus's hand.

"I know you told us to stay in the bus, but I couldn't resist the temptation to come and see for myself."

Now flirting with her eyes, she pulls her hand away. With a provocative sway of her hips she wanders up to the alter, turns to face the men and leans back against the carved wood.

"This is so intriguing that this holy building has been spared. There must be a good reason for it?"

Doing his best to hide his annoyance by this inciting behavior, and her able to stir old memories and desires, Gus tries to focus.

There is a reason all right, and you're not part of it.

Spreading her arms out across the alter like a woman with enticing intentions, she raises her arms and stares up at the ceiling as Gus approaches her. Before he has a chance of quelling this ludicrous situation, she shrieks at him.

"Gus? Why don't you give a service of thanks for this sacred building, because it's been saved?"

His annoyance turning to anger, Gus, grips her right forearm.

"Not now – Madeline."

She pulls away from his grip and glares at Garth.

"You can do it? You're a priest!"

Becoming disturbed by the woman's erratic behavior, Garth stares at Gus looking for an answer. Before Gus can make a rational decision, a door opens, right of the alter. Two young men dressed in dark tee shirts and faded jeans come through. One of them is wearing a bright red baseball cap, and carrying a bulging holdall over his shoulder. The other young man smiles and looks straight at Gus as if to challenge.

"Well hi there you guys. It seems we all survived some sort of quake. You passing through or about to stay?"

Sensing all is not what it appears, Garth blocks their exit as the two young men edge up the aisle. Exhibiting a side Gus hasn't witnessed before, Garth is determined not to budge.

"What's in the bag?"

"Oh! Just a few knickknacks. Personal stuff."

By the guilty expressions on their faces, Garth knows they are lying. Meanwhile, the holdall becomes snagged against the edge of a pew. The young man wearing the red cap pulls hard on the bag to try to release it, but the top rips open. Spilling some contents onto the floor, all four of them stare at a silver chalice, a heavy gold crucifix and a cash box that has just opened exposing an assortment of paper and coin money. Having seen enough, Garth bends down to retrieve the crucifix.

"You're thieves, as well as liars."

Believing a mere priest is going to stop them, the one with the red cap speaks up.

"What you goin to do about it? Call the cops?"

Becoming intrigued by the situation, Madeline steps forward.

"There are no cops! No world either. Just us, or a few like us. We are here to make a new world. Isn't that right Gus?"

Before Gus can answer, she carries on talking.

"However, we forgive you. Anyway, all that stuff is valueless now. Isn't that right Gus?"

Ignoring her, and the two men staring at her in bewilderment, the two young men begin to edge their way toward the door. Red cap spits back at Madeline.

"You're nuts woman."

Gus takes hold of the crucifix.

"No! You're finished if you escape out of that door."

"You're all nuts! We're goin..."

They rush to the front door, hesitate, and then step outside. Within a second, a bright white light beats down on them, causing them to disintegrate. In shock, Garth gawks at Gus, and then with caution approaches the doorway. Still shaken, he stops and looks outside.

"What was that? They've vanished into thin air. One-second they were there, then next - poof, gone."

Madeline's face now pale and her eyes expressing fear, she stands next to Gus.

"You knew that would happen if they went outside! That's why you warned them."

Gus does not reply. Instead, he looks up to the ceiling of the church and closes his eyes. After a few seconds, the ground begins to shake and parts of the building start to collapse and fall onto the floor. Proving his point, Gus shouts to Garth as he grabs Madeline's hand.

"Time to leave! She's going to fall."

As Gus rushes out of the crumbling church, and pulling a confused

Madeline with him, Garth joins them.

While they head straight for the safety of the bus, the church collapses within itself. As a pile of rubble and loose timbers remains, Madeline hugs Gus to hide from anymore noise. Meanwhile, everyone in the bus is staring transfixed out of the windows in horror and fascination. Except for Eva, she is annoyed with Madeline at the way she is commandeering her man. Her response is to rush out of the bus to take hold of Gus' free arm. Now glaring at Eva, and still holding onto Gus, Madeline looks away.

"Why Gus? Why?"

Angry at such a stupid question, Eva glares at Madeline.

"Give him a break! He needs to sit down first."

Appreciating her protective instincts, Gus indicates with a smile to Eva that he is fine.

"Come inside the bus and I'll tell you why."

While everyone becomes settled in the bus, Gus is still holding the gold crucifix. He then sits in the driver's seat, and faces the curious and bewildered faces.

"I expect you would like to know why all this has happened. There are three lessons to be learnt here. First, we are no longer in charge anymore. Any sin committed without any form of repentance, will be treated this way. If those thieves had apologized and felt genuine remorse, they would be still with us. Second, that church was left standing for a reason."

He makes a point of staring at Madeline who is now sitting next to an still angry Eva.

"Unfortunately Madeline, you fell into the trap by wanting to have a religious service, just because a beautiful building was saved. As I have 'always' said, the people make the church, not the building. Finally, if any of 'us' stray from the narrow path, we will suffer the same fate as those thieves."

Wanting to make an impression, Madeline raises her hand.

"So you're saying that church was deliberately left standing by God to teach us or any other unfortunate soul who might have wanted to stop by."

Not wanting to answer, Gus has to acknowledge.

"Yes!"

Being the woman she is, she is still not satisfied.

"If those men had left the church with the stolen goods earlier before we arrived, would their fate still have been the same?"

"Yes. Any other questions?"

Glaring at Madeline, the Navaho girl raises her hand.

"The simple fact is that if people are genuinely good and not pretending to be, especially when others are watching, God won't make them disappear. By the way, my name is Mary Morning Star."

Admiring this gutsy Navaho native, Gus's eyes show affection, as he returns her question with a smile. In the meantime, Madeline is still not satisfied.

"That makes God a dictator! It all sounds too crazy for me."

Becoming concerned about Madeline's consistent attitude, Gus is reluctant to answer.

"Crazy is over reacting. This new world does not need laws, police or military, because we are all like-minded. Working and living for each other and the common good, instead of oneself, is the new order. Just think how it must feel to have no fear of being persecuted or being bullied. To know that every human being you see and talk with from now on is your friend. A world without enemies or evil."

Absorbed by this discussion, Ryan, Eva's son raises his hand.

"I was bullied at school. Do you think the white light will have zapped the bully?"

Gus replies firmly.

"If he never repented, yes,"

Letting Madeline know she has a mind of her own, Eva raises her hand.

"Why did God do this now? You were supposed to go and talk to the world leaders and get things done to make a better life for us all, not let it all be destroyed. So, what happened?"

With venom in her voice, Madeline interrupts.

"Don't talk to Gus that way! You know who he is, and that he 'was' trying to make a better world."

Not liking the way these two women are heckling each other, Gus focuses his mind for the sake of the others watching.

"This whole situation is hard for anyone to understand. I came back to warn the world that if things don't change, such as poverty, greed, corruption and persecution, the world will be destroyed in one year. Some of you here know of my mission, but unfortunately, it was taken away from me at the UN. God decided to step in. So, here we are starting from scratch, taking everything gradually. The Garden of Eden - part two."

Becoming more drawn into this discussion, Mary Morning Star raises her hand.

"If God is going to run our lives now, will Jesus ever return?"

Surprised by such a question, several of the children answer her in unison.

"Gus is Jesus!"

"I'm sorry I didn't know. I knew you must be someone special, because I keep seeing a faint blue around your head."

Touched by this girl's innocence and fortitude, Gus conveys to her a smile of appreciation.

"I thank you all for your patience and understanding. I will do my best to explain everything as we continue on our journey..."

The Chang twins raise their arms and talk in unison.

"One more question please? Can we have lunch now before we carry on our journey?"

As Gus nods to Garth who makes his way to the rear of the bus ready to hand out some sort of lunch, everyone laughs except Madeline and Eva.

Meanwhile, Natas' group has stopped by a massive tangle of flyovers and underpasses, which have collapsed in the great quake. Anxious not to keep stopping, James is busy studying the GPS with the President. Natas is outside the vehicle alone deep in his thoughts looking at all the damage.

What a mess you have created. Was all this destruction quite necessary? If I agree to come back into the fold can you make life a bit easier for me?

Meanwhile, George and Fred are all still inside the Hummer discussing the present situation. George is doing most of the talking.

"Well? What now? It looks like journey's end out there."

Not liking this new anxiety spreading, the President overhears and cuts in.

"We know where we are. We are calculating an alternate route to take. So, relax and be patient."

Becoming depressed by her mother's anxiety, Julie decides to sit next to George.

"I wish we could find Gus. It all seems so futile without him."

On impulse, George slides his arm around her shoulder to offer her some comfort.

"We'll find him girl. I'm dying to meet this fella. All I've heard is you guys saying how wonderful he is."

Fred laughs for a second, and then his face turns serious.

"Don't worry about Gus he has the almighty helping him. It's 'that' person I'm worried about."

While he points to Natas outside, who is walking among the ruins, Julie gazes out of the window. Detecting a sorrowful expression on Natas' face, she jumps up from her seat.

"I'm going to see him. He looks lonely out there."

As she makes her way out, the two men glance at each other, shrug, and then focus on James, who is becoming pleased with his own efforts.

"I have a fix Ma'am. We are at the junction of interstate eighty-one and interstate forty, which is perfect, because forty is what we want. The question is, how to get on it with all this mess in the way."

Listening and wanting to be more involved, Fred speaks up.

"Where does the Interstate forty go?"

"To Phoenix or what's left of it. Then on to interstate ten to make our way to the Californian desert."

"Have you seen any other travelers on that radar of yours?"

"No, not yet. We still keep looking."

Absorbing the situation, the President looks over to them.

"We should be setting off again. Where is my daughter?"

The men point outside.

Now standing next to Natas, Julie searches his eyes for some reaction.

"What a mess!"

He turns to her and offers her a genuine smile.

"The whole world is in a mess my dear. It is up to us, and any other survivors to now put it right."

"Do you think we can?"

He turns away to study the damage again.

"Of course we can. We are the chosen ones! Remember, we have God on our side."

"You sound so cynical."

He turns back to face her. His bright green eyes softening as he places a gentle hand on her shoulder.

"Young Lady! I am going to let you into a secret. You see, God and I go back a long way. Even further than Jes – er - Gus. I am the ultimate fallen angel. We had a big disagreement and was expelled from the holy order. But alas, I have been asked to rejoin the fold as the prodigal son. All is forgiven. As you can now witness, I have been saved."

Becoming mesmerized by his intense eyes and the warmth of his hand radiating through her body, she reaches up and touches his hand.

"The only fallen angel I know of is Luci...."

A voice shouting from the Hummer distracts. It is Julie's mother.

"We're going now."

Knowing the effect he is having on this innocent soul, Natas leans forward and plants a soft kiss on Julie's forehead.

"Mother's calling! Please keep this to yourself my dear. You are a sweet girl, and that is what I need right now. We will talk more later."

While they stroll back to join the others, Julie mulls over in her mind what has just taken place.

Is this handsome man really what he says he is? Or is he just a man, who is lost and trying to find his true soul? Whichever it is, I will do my best to help him.

The sun is low. The clear sky and quiet evening air makes the difficult driving conditions bearable. Gus appears concerned as he observes the fuel gauge indicating the tank is getting low. He turns to Garth who is sitting in the first seat opposite him.

"We're getting low on fuel. Have a look in that compartment near you by the door to see if there is a map or something. I feel lost. I know we're traveling west, but my senses tell me we need to go more south, and then go west to get to the western desert."

Garth opens the compartment and rummages through it's contents which includes, a flashlight, some odd wrenches, old candy wrappers and a dirty looking AAA map book of the USA. He flips through the pages until he reaches the main interstate map.

"Where do think we are?"

"I know we've traveled about five hundred miles..."

"According to this map we should be approaching Chicago. If we're near there, we should look for the interstate fifty-seven to Memphis, then we go west to..."

Garth feels a tap on his shoulder. He turns to find Mary Morning Star standing near.

"You go west on the interstate forty to New Mexico, stop at Gallup for my people, and then make your way to Phoenix by way of Flagstaff where you get the interstate ten to the Californian desert."

Appreciating Mary's efficiency and determination, both men nod in agreement.

The bus reaches a hilltop. Before them lay the remains of a large decimated urban area. Appearing distressed, Gus stops and switches off the engine. His face looking serious, he then turns to everyone and points to the windshield.

"The devastation we left in New York was terrible. The damage down there in Chicago is just as bad. We are going down there to find people, stock up on supplies and fuel our bus or find another form of transport. Therefore, please be aware that who ever we meet will be in a state of shock and suffering as we were. So, being here to help is our mission. Any questions?"

As no questions arise, Gus puts the bus into gear.

Now heading toward the unknown, the evening twilight emphasizes the structural carnage. The eerie sound of the bus's wheels crunching on loose rubble, echoes in the stillness. While Gus maneuvers the bus around the obstacles, Ryan sees something.

"Over there. It looks like a small fire. Maybe a camp fire?"

With the thought of finding more survivors, Gus steers the bus toward the smoke plume. As they get nearer, Gus can see a group of about a dozen people huddled together. Just as he stops the bus and opens the door, the weary group around the fire turn and face the bus. Focusing on the bedraggled group, Gus is astonished that they are all children. The oldest one of the group looks a little apprehensive as he or she approaches the person who is driving the bus. On removing a hood, his cold dirty face breaks into a smile of relief.

"Have you come to rescue us?"

Sympathizing with these poor souls, Gus smiles back and clambers out of his seat. On disembarking the bus, followed by Garth, Gus slides his arm around the young lad's shoulder.

"How many of you?"

The lad responds by beginning to shake.

"I'm not sure sir. It was terrible! We were in the school playground when the ground started shaking and everything began to collapse. Then these bright lights came out of nowhere making nearly every one disappear. It was horrible!"

Unable to control his tremors, the lad collapses into Gus' arms and begins to sob. In the meantime, Gus indicates to Garth to check the rest of the group. Reacting to Gus's kindness, the sobbing ceases. As the lad wipes his eyes with his grubby hands, Gus asks him again.

"How many are with you?"

"I think about ten sir. But where have all the others gone?"

"Don't worry now. I'll explain later."

Gus and Garth gaze at the assortment of cold and frightened children. Their ages seem to range from about five to fifteen. Besides the young lad with them, the reminder of the children stare in disbelief as they huddle toward the dwindling flames. Realizing this may be what most survivors will be, Gus tries to put their minds and fears at rest.

"We are here to help you...."

"Yes, we are going to help you start a new life."

Needing to be involved, Madeline steps down from the bus, and stands next to Gus. Arousing his usual irritation, Gus raises an eyebrow, but lets it pass. Feeling her arm slide around his waist, he continues to question the children.

"Have you any food and water?"

The eldest boy with them points to a mountain of nearby rubble.

"There's a load of stuff under that rubble. We managed to find a way in there."

Being tactful in removing her arm, Gus whispers to Madeline.

"Madeline? Please can you take these children into the bus and take care of their needs."

"Yes of course! We will help them all we can."

Both men watching her lead the children toward the bus, Garth sighs and delivers a quizzical look.

"I can't quite understand that one."

"Oh, I can."

"You'll have to enlighten me."

Keeping the atmosphere light, Gus smiles at his loyal friend.

"I will, don't you worry. Now we have to check out the pile of goodies in this rubble. Did you bring a flashlight?"

Garth shows him the flashlight from the bus.

"We have to help as much as we can."

Gus is finding it hard not to laugh at Garth's sarcastic imitation of Madeline.

They come to a gap in the rubble. Garth entering first still holding the light, the first thing that surprises them both is how the damaged structure is still holding up. The heavy wooden floor has somehow been squeezed up to form a dome, which is supporting the outside crumbling walls from falling into a basement full of supplies. As Garth scans the huge basement area, his light reflects on large oil drums, sealed pallets of bottled water and crates of canned and general goods.

"This looks like a civil defense storage facility. Where in case of a national catastrophe, these goods can be handed out to survivors."

"We certainly qualify for that. Lets take a look?"

They both climb down a wide flight of concrete stairs, leading down to a stack of forty-gallon oil drums. His hand trembling with excitement, Garth shines the light onto a label stuck on the side of one of the drums.

"Diesel fuel! Ideal for the bus."

He then shines the light on a stack of cardboard cases.

"Emergency military rations - MRE's. Probably the same type as the armed forces use. It's all good stuff, same as the water over there."

Astonished by the find, Gus goes over and studies the pallets of water.

"We need to get some more transport. The bus is not going to be enough. There must be a way out of here for a truck or something to have brought this stuff down here originally. Let's look around for an entrance."

With the help of the flashlight light, they walk down a long aisle situated between hundreds of stacked pallets. After several hundred feet, they come to a wide metal double door. Remembering his first experience with this type of door, Gus pushes the emergency bars. The doors open with ease to expose another storage facility.This time several heavy-duty military trucks fade into the darkness.

"Bingo!"

Not quite believing his fortune, Gus climbs into the first truck to look for a light switch. He finds one and turns it on. The whole area lights up, showing six covered open five-ton trucks and various maintenance areas. At the far end of the facility, another pair of doors is in view. His hands trembling with eagerness, Gus climbs out of the truck and points to the doors.

"There's our entrance. Perhaps we may be lucky and drive out of here loaded up. Luck may not be it. I reckon this is part of the grand plan."

Garth smiles at the thought.

"I always had an inkling this is all meant to be."

With the light of the truck behind them, they walk toward the doors. When they arrive, Gus pushes the emergency bar on the right hand door. As it does not budge, he tries again. When that doesn't shift, he tries the other door. It opens with ease onto an open ramp leading up to street level. Seeing the first door is a little distorted by the weight of the rubble, they both manage to push the first door wide enough for a truck. Being a pleasure working as a team, Gus pats Garth on the back with appreciation.

"This is it my friend. We bring the bus here. Unload what supplies we have left onto one of the trucks, and then keep filling that truck with what we can use from here. From now on, the bus will be for passengers only. Then we need to load the fuel drums on another truck."

Garth's reaction to such a task is to blow into the air.

"Those drums weigh a ton!"

"I know. I am sure you will find that one of the trucks has a lift. That will be our fuel truck. I also think you'll find a hand fuel pump somewhere near the drums or in one of the maintenance areas. That small office in the corner over there will have all the truck keys."

"Are you sure you haven't been here before?"

Gus has to laugh, but underneath he is deadly serious.

"As I have always said, this is all meant to be. You bring the bus around here and tell everyone the good fortune. As we are taking out time, I expect they're getting worried. In the meantime, I will organize these trucks."

His head buzzing with mixed emotions, Garth goes back to the others. Finding them all mulling around stretching their legs, Garth begins to explain their find and what needs to be done. At the same time, Gus explores the little corner office to find some keys.

It is now approximately two hours later. The bus has been cleared to carry passengers. Two trucks are full with fuel, food and supplies. As the three vehicles are refueled and ready to go, everyone is tired, but exhilarated, as if it is all like an adventure.

Now ready to go, and awaiting instructions from Gus, they all group together in anticipation. Weary, but grateful, Gus rubs his smudged and grimy face, as he leans against the bus for support.

"Well guys, thanks to you all pitching in, we are now ready to go all the way to the Californian desert."

While the adults are glad its all systems go, the children cheer. Waiting for the enthusiasm to wane, Gus continues.

"We will stop along the way to pick up more people like ourselves. Now, we need to rest. So, find anywhere you can to sleep for tonight. Tomorrow morning we will have a good breakfast, and then we will be on our way. Garth and Eva will drive the trucks, I will drive the bus and Madeline will be esponsible for the food. Any questions?"

The red head girl raises her hand.

"It is not really a question. It is just to say – I think I speak for everyone here, thank you for finding us all..."

Her eyes filling with tears of gratitude, she has to pause for a few seconds. Gathering her momentum, she continues.

"Thank you also for looking after and guiding us. Would it be too much for you to give us a prayer?"

Tears fill Gus' eyes as the group murmur in agreement. He wipes his eyes, sniffs, and clasps his hand together.

"Dear God. Thank for bringing us this far and the help you have provided for our important, upcoming mission. We are all ready to do your work, and will not let you down. Amen."

The group pauses at the 'Amen', and then begin to disperse. Most looking for a suitable place to sleep, decide to go to the bus. Garth climbs into the cab of the fuel truck. Watching him stretch out on the full wide seat, Gus also notices Eva accompanying the children to the bus. She catches his eye and offers him a warm smile. Before he can respond, she enters the bus and sits in one of the front passenger seats. Observing his slow reaction, Madeline hangs back as she also watches everyone enter the bus and settle in their seats. Acting casual, she walks up to Gus, as he leans against the supply truck.

"So far, so good?"

Suspecting her motives, he is reluctant to answer.

"The plan seems to be working."

Keeping her voice low, she stands close enough to him so he able to smell her natural perfume.

"You didn't expect it would?"

"I don't know. I suppose I have doubts and fears like anyone else."

"You are 'not' anyone else. How can you have fears? You're the Son of God. You have the power to 'make' it all happen."

Her perfume filling his lungs and her closeness disturbing, he hesitates. Surprised and annoyed at this strong statement, he also becomes rattled as places her hand on his bare forearm, and looks him in the eye.

"I'm sorry Gus. I spoke out of line. It's just that I care for you. More than care! Like she did!"

"She?"

"Yes! I remind you of her. I saw your face when we first met. You looked as if you had seen a ghost. A ghost of a past, tender love."

Becoming stunned by this observation, he is unable to reply. In response to his slow reaction, she continues.

"I want to be that love. I want to be your Mary Magdalene!"

In the meantime, Eva is staring out of the bus window, anxious and a little jealous at the way Gus is floundering at Madeline's advances.

No Gus! Not her! She'll only hurt you.

57

Still Commander in Chief

Her delicate hand is reaching out to him. In desperation, he grabs it. Aroused by the softness and warmth, her soft and seductive lips add to the sensation. Shaping and forming words he cannot hear, he must get closer. His whole body now aching with the need to hold her, he now can hear her words of love.

"You must come back to me. I need you here. You know you have been forgiven. It is now time for your return."

Still holding his hand, she pulls him toward her. As if in slow motion, he gets closer. Now where she wants him, her other hand reaches out and is gentle in stroking his forehead. His whole being now tingling and aching in a desire never experienced before, her face is irresistible. He can smell her perfume, as her lips part, and almost touch his wanting mouth. As if to tease, she pulls away to his right ear. The disappointment too much to bear, he begs.

"Please, no! Hold me, so we can have paradise together."

Still teasing, she whispers in his ear. Feeling her warm breath, but still unable to hear any words, he feels her grip his head. Making sure that he must understand, her piercing hazel eyes glare into him and her lips move again.

"You must come back to me now. Or otherwise...."

As a heavy blue mist covers them, he gasps for air while her hands grip his throat.

No, do not kill me. I want to come back. I want to be with you...

He begins to choke as salty liquid enters his mouth...

Natas wakes up to find Julie holding his sweating neck in both her hands. She is saying something, but he cannot hear above the rumbling noise in his head. He glares at her without recognition, while the sweat stings his eyes. He can now hear her shouting above other voices.

"Nat? Are you all right?"

"I – er – yes. I...."

While she has a tender touch when wiping his face with a tissue, he focuses on her soft young mouth.

Kiss me...

Realizing he is not dreaming, he glares into her concerned eyes and grips her hand.

"I must go back. She needs me."

"Who needs you? There is nothing to go back too."

Gathering his senses, he manages to sit up. He then shakes his head to try to get rid of the noise. Then he realizes the rumbling is not in his head, but coming from the rough ground that they are traveling over. Meanwhile, Julie stops wiping his face. As nobody in the car is taking any notice of them, she tones down her voice, as if it is just meant for him.

"You were having a bad dream. You were rambling and kept on saying no. I found it all a bit scary."

Appreciating her concern and still focusing on her mouth, he offers her a warm smile and kisses her hand, which he is still holding. Now drained of emotion and energy, he kisses her hand again and rests it on his chest.

"Yes. I was dreaming. A similar one to the last, telling me again to return. You remember? I told you."

"Yes! I remember."

"We will talk about it later."

"Okay."

While Julie is reluctant to withdraw her hand from his warm grip, her mother turns to look at her daughter. Not commenting on the closeness to Natas, she shouts above the noise.

"James has picked up some signs of life, so we are investigating. Is Nat okay? He's been out for hours."

Conveying to Natas a wry grin, Julie nods to her mother that he is all right.

Thirty minutes later, they are in a dry and dusty rural area. Observing the dust flying up off the Hummer, Natas hides his irritation, as James shouts out.

"That looks like something?"

In the distance, coming into view, they can see a skyline of destroyed buildings of various sizes and construction. As they approach, an army truck pulls out from nowhere and blocks their path. Fred's reaction is to put his foot hard on the brakes causing the Hummer to skid to a halt. Letting the dust settle, they all witness a soldier dressed in pale desert fatigues and with sergeant's stripes on his sleeves, step out of the truck cab. Carrying an automatic machine pistol, he is cautious when approaching Natas' group. Standing a few paces away, his dark mahogany face appears nervous, but his tone is calm.

"Hi guys? You lost?"

Sensing the fear in the sergeant's eyes, the President steps out of the front passenger side of the Hummer, and stands in a formal pose by the door.

"What is your name sergeant?"

Recognizing his commander-in-chief, the sergeant stares at her in disbelief. Lowering his gun, he salutes, and then gives out a loud whistle. Six more armed soldiers appear out from the back of the truck and fall in behind him.

"Staff Sergeant Thomas, Sir, I mean President - Ma'am. These are what's left of my company and the whole camp. What the hell happened Ma'am? It seems we were attacked by aliens and some sort of earthquake. We don't get quakes in Oklahoma, only tornadoes."

Noticing the soldiers are putting on a brave face, she takes charge.

"At ease Sergeant. What is your outfit?"

"Oklahoma National Guard, Ma'am."

"Have you plenty of supplies?"

"Yes Ma'am. They somehow escaped the damage. We've been loading up one of the trucks with food and water to keep it safe."

"Well, done. How many trucks do you have?"

"Two big trucks and one Humvee."

Seeing it is safe and his boss is in charge, James and the others decide to climb out of the Hummer and walk around to stretch their legs. James stands next to the President and speaks in a discreet manner.

"If it is all right with you ma'am, I'll take over now. I will go with Sergeant Thomas to check out what supplies they have, and what we can use and maybe find some shelter for the night. It will be getting dark in about two hours."

Relieved to to have James's reassurance, she nods in agreement, and leans against the Hummer.

"Water, Madam President?"

Surprised by Natas' offer of a bottle of water, and her daughter accompanying him, she has no choice but to accept.

"What now Mother?"

Conveying to Natas a reticent smile, Julie's mother grips the bottle and unscrews the cap.

"James is checking out the supply situation, and then we will bed down for the night."

Noticing Natas seems agitated and restless while she drinks her water, she is also aware that her daughter is beginning to become a little too familiar with him.

"Julie? Will you please find James for me and ask him if he needs any help. Then take your time in coming back to tell me. Nat and I need to talk."

Aware of her mother's disapproval of her new relationship with Natas, Julie pulls a face and is reluctant to obey. As her daughter heads toward James, the President turns to Natas. Even though she offers him a cordial smile, her eyes are serious.

"How are you feeling now?"

"Oh, just a reoccurring bad dream. It's nothing, I assure you."

"That's too bad. We don't want you getting down, especially now."

"Oh no, I am not getting down. I never get down. I think the dream is some sort of subconscious thing that will sort itself out."

While listening, she ponders, and stares into his eyes.

"Good! I hope your subconscious does not involve my daughter getting hurt in the process. I have observed the way she looks at you. She is just a child!"

Before he can react, she turns away to go and join the others. While watching her back, he becomes defiant.

I love her also, Madam President.

Julie's mother joins her daughter as she watches the men finish loading the trucks with fuel, tents and general supplies. Not wanting to alienate her daughter, she slides her arm around her young, but athletic shoulders.

"You okay?"

Her mind elsewhere, Julie does not react. Her mother tries again.

"I see you're becoming quite attached to Nat."

"I like him. He confides in me."

"In what way?"

"Oh - personal stuff."

Needing to know more, she shows her affection by giving her daughter's shoulder a light squeeze

"Not too personal I hope. Just be careful my dear. Even though you look mature for your age, you are still under age, and he is almost old enough to be your father."

Becoming agitated by her mother's grip and attitude, Julie pulls away.

"Oh mother! You still don't get it!"

Before the President can rectify this delicate situation, Julie marches off. At the same time, James approaches her, holding a clipboard.

"I have a complete inventory of all the supplies packed, and there's a large underground storm shelter where we can sleep tonight."

As her mind is still on her daughter, his boss does not hear him.

"Ma'am?"

"Oh! I'm sorry. I was miles away. My daughter."

Having witnessed the conversation, James understands.

"She's at a tender age. She will become a fine woman – like her mother."

Not wanting to expose her vulnerability, she becomes the President again.

"Precisely! Now? What were you telling me?"

While James re-explains, Julie hunts out Natas, who is now wondering with an aimless expression around the camp ruins. His mind is preoccupied as Julie approaches.

"Find anything valuable?"

Startled, he turns to face her.

"What?"

"Did you find anything valuable or interesting among these ruins?"

His green eyes seem to cloud over in a glaze.

"There is nothing of value left anymore. The world is one big uninteresting barren ball. No more fun, no more...."

"Yes?"

"Nothing."

Sensing her confusion, he places his hands on her shoulders to reassure. His hypnotic eyes stares at her with such an intensity, she surrenders.

Oh, Natas! What are you doing to me?

As if reading her thoughts. He answers.

"You my girl are 'really' one of God's children. Full of love and totally incorruptible. An angel of mercy. You only see the good in everything. Am I correct?"

"Well, yes. Don't you see good in people?"

"Oh yes! I am the ultimate in telling who is good and who is bad. Now there is only good, I have nothing. No excitement, no..."

Becoming more entranced, she interrupts.

"Why not go back? God will supply what you're searching for."

His eyes soften, as he leans forward and plants a soft kiss on her vulnerable lips. After a few seconds of electricity, he withdraws his arms, turns away and ponders. Her heart palpitating from the kiss, she gazes at his back. Admiring the way his broad muscular shoulders blend into his narrow youthful hips, her body tingles for more of him.

Is this what love feels like?

His eyes bright and focused, he turns back to face her.

"I will go back! But you will have to help me."

Joyous with a new sense of purpose, she grips his hand, as if scared to let him go.

"I 'will' help you. I will do 'anything' to save and lo..."

Knowing what she is about say, he leans closer to her. Ready for another tender kiss, she shuts her eyes in anticipation. The kiss landing on her forehead, she becomes disappointed. Knowing this and in control, he lifts her hand up to his mouth and holds it there for a few seconds. While his lips brush her knuckles in such a way, to her, surrender is an understatement. His voice seems a long way off, while her mind floats.

"Remember, all this is 'our' secret. Nobody else would understand how we feel towards each other. I think now we should join the others before they catch on."

He is crawling uphill in the sand. For every two steps he makes forward, he falls back one. Impossible to progress, his frustration adds to the heat and his thirst.

I must rest! What am I doing here? Is this the end of the journey? Where is everyone?

He hears a woman's voice.

'I'm here! Look up, you can see me.'

He does what she asks, but the burning sun is in his eyes. Adding to his frustration, he hears the voice again.

"I'm right here, just a little bit further and you will be here."

Without looking ahead, he becomes desperate as he scrambles upward in the sand. Making a little headway, he stops for a short rest, and then he is frantic to continue.

I must keep going. So tired...

Helping him forward, a strong hand grips his upper arm. Grateful to his rescuer, he looks up and can't believe his eyes.

Mary! You found me. Oh thank god. I thought I was lost forever, never to see you again.

He is now in her arms as she supports his head, and is smothering him in soft kisses on his forehead, cheeks and finishing at his lips. Not wanting this ecstasy to stop, he becomes disappointed as she withdraws, and whispers in his left ear.

"I am here forever. Always for you my love."

Caught up in her smell, and his body yearning for more, her whisper continues.

"I will never let you go. You will always be mine."

Not sure if he is still dreaming, Gus is laying on his back opening his eyes to darkness.

Someone is on top of me!

Now knowing he is not dreaming, because he is being smothered with real kisses, he rolls over on his side to free the weight. Finding Madeline gazing up at him, he cannot believe his eyes.

"You! What are you doing? Why – aren't in the bus with the others?"

Reaching up to touch his face, her eyes seem luminous in the dark.

"I just wanted to lie beside you when you are asleep. I was drifting off when you started talking. You were saying you were lost. You seemed afraid. So, I comforted you."

Becoming disturbed by her closeness, he sits up.

"I'm sorry. I shouldn't have been so hard on you."

Her eyes still penetrating, she now sits up close to him.

"Its me that's sorry. I lost control. You see..."

Her full mouth fuses against his pensive lips. Keeping her lips against his for a few seconds, she then withdraws.

"...I love you..."

Before he has time to react, she gets up and runs toward the bus, and then vanishes into the darkness. Confused, but annoyed by his own weakness,

503

he takes a deep breath. Trying to gather his thoughts, he lies on his back again and looks up at the stars.

"Oh God. Is it true in what she says, or is she using me for some secret agenda? That's impossible! There is no more evil. You took it all away."

His eyes shut, he tries to relax, but all he can see is Mary Magdalene's face merge with Madeline's. Disturbed even further by his emotions getting the better of him, and still unable to relax, he decides to stand and stretch, to relieve the stiffness of his joints.

"You can't sleep either?"

He turns to find Eva standing a few paces away. Her pale blue dress blends well into the night. As he moves toward her, a light breeze fills his nostrils with her scent. Instant memories of their past closeness comes flooding back making his emotions even more intense.

"No. I had a strange dream."

"Yes I know. She's standing the other side of the bus - crying."

Appearing confused, he hesitates.

"I must go to her. We can't have this sort of thing happening."

As he begins to step away, she grabs his forearm.

"That's exactly what she wants! You go to her now, she'll have your emotions on a lead. She will tug you anyway she wants."

"How can you say that? She said she loves me. I can't see her suffer."

Not wanting to show her anger at his nativity, she grips his arm even harder.

"She will not suffer! We 'all' love you. She is no exception. You know how much I love you, and I'm giving you my life so you can complete your mission to help us all. She will have to do the same!"

His emotions in disarray, and knowing she is right, Gus opens his arms for her. She responds by falling into his familiar embrace. For a while, she is back at the old church, wanting him until it hurts. She is unsuccessful in hiding her love and begins to cry. Feeling her tears soak his shirt, her grips her harder. Neither moves to end this blissful few minutes, until he notices the dawn breaking on the horizon.

"Sit with me for a while and watch the sun come up for a new day.

Another day in our new life."

She wipes her face and nods, as he lowers her down with him onto the ground. In the meantime, Madeline is hiding by the rear of the bus witnessing the tender scene, Clenching her fists in a jealous rage, her mind begins to scheme.

So that's how it is? Goody two shoes know how to get around him. Forget it Bitch! I'm going to be his Queen. From now on, I am going to be goodness itself and make sure he and everybody else knows it.

As the sun rises, and the daylight penetrates the windows, she can hear movement in the bus.

I can start right now by doing my designated duties.

It is now an hour later. Everyone has eaten and performed their necessary ablutions. Gus goes up to Madeline and thanks her for doing a good job with the food. She returns the complement by presenting him with her sweetest and most humble of smiles.

Gus and Garth have mapped out their next stage of the journey. A five hundred and fifty mile trip south to the Memphis area. There they will rest for the night, and then drive another four hundred and eighty miles to Oklahoma City. If they can average five hundred miles a day, they should get to their final destination in about three to four days allowing for picking any survivors and stopping at Gallop, New Mexico to check on the Navajo for Mary Morning Star.

Natas' group is now ready for the next stage of their journey. The soldiers are already waiting in the vehicles. Fred and George are in the Hummer waiting with Natas and Julie, who are sitting next to each other at the rear. The President is still outside having deep conversation with James her Secret Service agent.

"Can we go south to Dallas? I would like to check out Fort Hood. There must be some survivors there. After all it is, or was one of the country's largest army bases."

Not that keen on the idea, James unfolds a map and concentrates on a particular section.

"It will take us about two hundred miles out of our way. On the other hand, if there are more survivors and supplies, it will be worth it."

Appreciating his cooperation, she grips his forearm.

"Let's do it then."

Obeying without question, James acknowledges, folds the map and escorts her to their awaiting transport.

Before they set off, the President informs the others of her intentions.

"Instead of keeping on Interstate Forty, we are going south to Dallas, and then to Fort Hood to check on survivors and supplies. After inspecting the area, we will stay the night and if all is well, we can then proceed on interstate ten to our final destination."

Everyone is amiable and accepts the plan, except Natas, who raises his hand.

"When we reach the 'final' destination, what are your plans for us all then?"

Surprised by his question, and again annoyed by his sarcasm, she puts on a cool demeanor.

"It is not a question of 'my' plans. I am no different from any of you. I just want to find Gus and make a better world for all of the remaining survivors."

Before Natas can retaliate with more sarcasm, Fred raises his hand.

"Madam President, I thank you for your leadership in getting us through this far. I 'know' we will find Gus, because this is all meant to be. Others, like us, all over the globe are going to make this a better life than has ever existed before."

On impulse, George and James applaud. Julie peers at Natas, wondering why he is not overjoyed like his companions. He senses her doubt. So, he offers her a warm smile and whispers in her ear.

"Don't get too carried away. We have a long way to go yet. Anything can happen. God has not finished with us yet. You my dear will be safe, because I am here to love and protect you."

By him giving her forearm an affectionate squeeze, his action alleviates her doubts. Loving this enigmatic man, she returns the affection with a warm grateful smile.

58

More Discoveries

Even though all the main highways are scattered with thousands of abandoned vehicles, James and the National guard trucks behind, manages to weave through and around these obstacles with little trouble.

Arriving at Fort Hood, everything is in ruins and abandoned. In normal times, the entrance to the army base would have maximum security. Today, James is being cautious as he leads the little convoy through an opening beside the main gate.

The main administration block has a few remaining walls, but all the smaller buildings have gone. There are many abandoned tanks, trucks and cars all scattered around like toys, as if a child has got bored playing and tossed them aside. There is no sign of life.

After about ten minutes of maneuvering around the devastation , the President touches James' arm for him to stop driving. All the vehicles now stopping, the President turns to her companions.

"I apologize for bringing you all this way. I am distraught we haven't seen anyone. Normally there would be at least fifty thousand combat troops plus all the employees who work here…"

A sound of a gunshot and a bullet whistling over the top of the Hummer distracts her. James's trained instinct is to pull down his boss to safety. Another shot is fired. This time the bullet ricochets off the front bumper. While holding down the President with one hand, James becomes cautious as he peers out of the windshield, when another bullet penetrates a fender.

"What are they doing? Can't they see we are not a threat?"

Several more gunshots are fired. This time, behind them. The National Guard in the truck behind is retaliating. Shaken and shocked by the situation, the President pulls away from James.

"We need something white to show we mean no harm."

Fred, who is still sitting behind the President, wastes no time in removing his jacket, and then takes off his soiled white shirt.

"Take my shirt Ma'am. I'm sorry it's not cleaner."

He passes it to James. Excepting the shirt, James opens the front passenger door.

"I'm going to make my way to our friends behind us to tell them to stop firing. Perhaps we can make sense of all this by one of you start waving the shirt.."

With the prowess of a trained athlete, James hands the shirt to his boss, and rolls out of the door and disappears from view.

After a couple of minutes, the gunfire from the National Guard ceases, but the sporadic shooting from the ruins continues.

Becoming exasperated, Natas slides out of his seat and makes his way to the President. Without any form of explanation, he takes the shirt and encourages her to crouch behind the driver's seat. With no explanation, he then opens the driver's door and jumps out. Waving the white 'flag', Natas walks with cool determination toward the gunshots. As bullets are bursting all around his feet, Julie screams.

"Oh God. They'll kill him."

Suspecting different, George sits next to her.

"I don't think so. They're warning shots. He would be dead by now if it were for real. That guy has certainly got guts. I underestimated him."

Her heart in her mouth, Julie can see the gunfire has stopped as Natas moves further toward the ruins.

"I didn't. I think he's wonderful."

The President now sitting back in her seat observing the situation, has her say.

"We will soon see just how 'wonderful' he is."

Putting on a broad non-threatening smile, Natas has found who is firing at him.

"Okay guys, everything is all right. In that car is the President of the United States or what's left of it. We are here to help you. So, put your guns away and tell me who you are."

In front of him are three young soldiers pointing their automatics rifles in his direction. Behind the three, another twenty young soldiers appear. All looking scared, but seemed relieved help is at hand, their leader steps forward. Still holding his gun at the ready, Natas notices the two stripes on his arms.

"I am Corporal Luis Santoro. I am sorry for shooting at you. If I had known it was the President..."

He lowers his rifle and glances at the rest of his men to do the same.

"After the invasion, these men and women were chosen to guard the base against looters while the rest formed a convoy and left."

Trying not to laugh at this ludicrous situation, Natas keeps smiling with reassurance.

"I assure you there has been no invasion..."

The corporal is insistent.

"We saw white beams of light everywhere. An earthquake like you've never seen before. Who has done this? It was very strange how the white beams seem to choose who it took down. It would leave one person, and then vaporize several like I never seen before...."

Hiding his irritation and continuing with his relaxing charm, Natas steps forward and places his hand on the lad's shoulder.

"Where did the convoy go and what supplies and good transport have you got left?"

Controlling his own fears, Corporal Santoro tries to gather his thoughts.

"The convoy headed west. There are still plenty of stores, and I think what vehicles are left, there must be some still functioning."

Glad to hear all is not lost, Natas removes his hand and glances at the rest of the pale faces.

"Good. All of you split up into smaller groups and retrieve at least three good size trucks. One for fuel and tools, one for food and general supplies and the third to carry you guys, because you are all leaving with me – er - us."

The corporal is still hesitant

"Sir? what has happened? We can't disobey our orders to stay here."

His smile dissipating, Natas becomes insistent.

"Believe me, no one will be coming back here. You do realize the President in that vehicle is still your Commander in Chief. She has top priority Corporal. I have some National Guardsmen with me who will help you."

Unable to see anything, and still anxious for Natas, Julie continues to look out of the window. After another minute, she notices Natas reappear still holding the white shirt. On impulse and ignoring what her mother might say, she rushes to the car door, jumps out and runs up to him.

"You're safe."

Touched by her concern, he slides his arm around her shoulder.

"Of course, my dear."

Relishing the warmth of his arm, she grips his hand.

"You could have been shot!"

"I do not think so my dearest. You see - I am invincible."

He plants a reassuring kiss on her cheek. She grips his hand a little tighter.

"Who are they?'

"Just some confused young soldiers. It seems a convoy has left here heading west leaving these few behind."

As they reach the Hummer, James is standing outside not hiding his relief and annoyance.

"How many?"

Natas withdraws his arm from Julie, and throws Fred back his shirt.

"About twenty or so. I never counted. No officers only a corporal. I offered our National Guard to help them get some more transport for carrying extra fuel and supplies."

Natas senses James is still annoyed at him.

"Did I do something wrong?"

"Yes! You shouldn't take risks like that. You could have endangered all our lives."

Julie notices Natas' eyes turn hard as he remains cool while talking back to James.

"Look! I certainly did not take any unnecessary risks. I calculated that all the 'bad' people have now gone, and we would certainly not be harmed. These few souls needed help. Therefore, I offered."

Meanwhile, Julie's mother leans out of the door.

"Everything all right James?"

"Er - affirmative Ma'am. Nat here has discovered about twenty soldiers, no officers. It seems a convoy of survivors has already left. I – er - we are going to help them with the National Guard we have."

Relieved that her original decision to deviate from their original course has paid off, she offers Natas a weak smile of thanks.

"Let's get going then. Also, we need to find somewhere for us to shelter for tonight.

A weary James acknowledges.

"Will do."

It is now several hours later. Two large working trucks have been found. One has been filled with fuel and supplies. The second one is half-full of tools and equipment, making room for passengers. In the meantime, everyone has gathered around a small bonfire, trying to find some comfort against the cold evening air.

The shock that to pick up the pieces of what is left of this world overwhelms these survivors . The soldiers and the National Guard have a tendency to sit together.They seemed to have accepted Staff Sergeant Thomas as their immediate leader. Sitting opposite in between Natas and her mother, Julie smiles at James, Fred and George, as they huddled together. She then turns to Natas and studies his handsome profile while he gazes at the flames with eyes that appear gold.

"What are you thinking, Nat?"

He acts as if he hasn't heard, but after a brief pause, he turns to her. His eyes returning to their natural green, his voice sounds soft against the crackling of the fire.

"Oh, about what the future might bring."

Listening, Julie's mother looks away from the fire to Natas.

"What is your conclusion about the future?"

His eyes harden while still looking at Julie.

"We all know what Gus wants."

The President is becoming annoyed at his evasiveness.

"Isn't that what we all want? A clean honest world!"

"Depends on your point of view."

Julie is becoming puzzled by the man she is falling for.

"I don't understand. There can only be one point of view. That's why all this has happened."

For a second, Julie witnesses his eyes harden again, and it is scaring her. He realizes he has let his guard slip. To compensate, he grips her arm with a tender hold, and offers her his most sincere smile, while keeping his voice low.

"For some inane reason, we think all this is God's wrath. God alone, causing a massive global earthquake and sending down white light to exterminate bad humanity and leaving only the good behind? It's ridiculous. How do we really know?Normally in all major disasters, there are always some survivors, which in this case, is us. It is the law of averages. As we have no contact with anyone else, how do we know what the rest of the world is doing? This might only be local to this part of the world. Who knows?"

Absorbing these poignant words, nobody says a word. Interrupting the lonely noise of the fire, Julie raises her hand to speak.

"What about Gus? He 'said' this would all happen."

His eyes blazing, Natas reacts by staring hard at the hot embers. His

513

voice has a hard edge as he raises the volume.

"Gus? For the benefit of you here, that have not heard of this man, I will explain. He entered on the scene a few weeks ago, doing a few 'miracles'. He then convinces our beloved President here to lend him Air Force One. While he tours around the world preaching that if we do not give up our wicked ways the earth as we know it, will be destroyed..."

The President interrupts by raising her hand.

"I believed him and I still do. You're not being entirely fair."

One of the soldiers nearby raises his hand.

"Many us saw him on TV. He seemed a good guy."

Ignoring the positive comments, Natas glares back into the flames.

"We still do not know if he is alive or not. So, this conversation is irrelevant. The question is, what do we do when we reach our destination? No one knows why the Californian desert was chosen. I can think of a lot more pleasant places to start a new world."

Now becoming upset with Natas, Julie answers.

"It is because many of us have had a dream."

Being drawn into this discussion, Sergeant Thomas raises his hand.

"I've been having this dream that I'm traveling down this long empty highway.

Each side of the road is nothing but sand and at the end of the road, way off in the distance is the sun. But as I get nearer, the sun starts to change to a more cooler color, and then looks as if it is floating on water."

All at once, everyone around the fire begins saying they have had a similar dream. Cannot believe his ears, Natas is abrupt when standing. Clenching his jaw in frustration, he begins pacing around the fire and shouting in reaction.

"All right! So, you all have had a similar dream. What does that prove?"

Surprised by his reaction, all goes quiet, when Julie's mother stands to confront him.

"It means, young man, we are all 'meant' to be here, and you are being very negative. If you want to go off on your own, nobody here will stop you.

However, if you decide to stay and be part of the team, please join in and help."

She sits down again as Natas stops pacing and looks as if he is considering her proposal. As he steps nearer to the President, he looks hard at Julie as if searching for support. In seeing the fear in Julie's eyes, he becomes humble and offers a sincere smile.

You are not going to get rid of me that quick, Madam President.

"Please accept my sincere apologies. I was totally out of line. I myself have had a few dreams, as you know, which is why I am here - to help you."

To recapture their attention, he begins to pace again.

Fools! I will have you all in the palm of my hands by the time we arrive.

In his flamboyant manner, he stops and faces the fire.

"I have one major concern! Who is giving us these dreams and drawing us towards this particular destination, and for what reason?"

Julie becomes impatient while raising her hand.

"It's God!"

His eyes blazing at the sound of that name, Natas turns away so he can compose his anger. After a couple of seconds of inner struggle, he turns back trying to keep his expression amicable.

"God? How did you come to 'that' deduction my young lady? Why would 'God' almost destroy the world just to drag us few to a - forgive the pun, a godforsaken place like the Californian desert? It has no logic."

Not liking the way this discussion is leading, the President raises her hand.

"I think my daughter is right. My instincts have always told me that Gus was someone special and it turned out that he was. I 'know' he is alive right now. I can feel it. He will be just as puzzled as we are, why all this has happened. However, I think he has had a message of some sort to go where we are going. Where we will all meet up and the truth be told."

Natas insides cringe as she finishes.

Over my dead body!

Fighting his inner struggle, Natas puts on a relaxing air, and offers mother and daughter the most genuine smile he can manage.

"You could very well be right Madam President. Tonight though, we all need to get some sleep for our next part of this intriguing journey."

There is a mumble of agreement as everyone stands and makes their way to some form of makeshift shelter. Natas hangs back. While he gazes into the dying embers, Julie's soft voice behind him brings him into focus.

"Why are you so much against God?"

As if floundering for an answer, he carries on looking at the dwindling fire. Now focusing on the question, he reaches out his hand, while his eyes turn to a blazing red from the reflection.

"I am not 'against' God. As I told you, I am wanted back to rejoin the fold."

Spellbound by this intriguing man, she takes his hand and sits next to him.

"Then go back."

His eyes returning to green, he brings her hand up to his mouth.

"I am seriously considering it. If only I knew if Gus was alive or not?"

"Does it bother you if he is alive?"

"Yes. It bothers me - a lot."

"Why? He is the Son of God. When we see him, 'he' will accept you back."

As if to trying to find the right answer, his lips smothers her delicate hand with soft kisses.

"I wish it was that easy. Let me tell you something my dear. He and I have always been at odds with each other. He has always been the favorite, while I have always been the black sheep of the family."

Aroused by the softness of his lips, Julie peers into his eyes

"You do realize you weren't taken away like millions of others. So, you have been spared for a reason, like the rest of us. I didn't believe you when you told me you were a fallen angel. I think you're lost. Otherwise, you would be in hell with all the others."

He rests her hand against his chest, and stares into her eyes.

"My dear, I 'am' in hell. 'My' world is destroyed. Everything I have schemed and worked for - has gone. I have nothing."

Enjoying the warmth of his chest through her hand, she is desperate to please him.

"Well it goes to show you one thing, you haven't the power that you thought you had. Therefore, if I were you I would cooperate and be a member of the team and when we finally meet Gus, I will speak to him and he will accept you with open arms to be his brother. Then God will take you back."

Keeping her hand against his heart, his green eyes fill with tears.

"Do you think it will be that easy?"

She takes a bold step by bringing his hand to rest against her left breast.

"Yes! It will be that easy."

Still holding his hand, she brings it up to her mouth, holds it there for a few seconds, and then rests it in her lap.

Listening to the hub-bub of the others settling down for the night, her mother is leaning against a truck becoming more concerned at her daughter's behavior toward the man she is uncertain about.

59

Holy Land

The straight road ahead seems to have no end. The sand on each side is blowing little threatening spirals that come up to the road, and then pull back at the last minute. The sun is blazing, its rays are beating down with no mercy.

Mary grabs his hand. Her eyes glowing with excitement, her lips begin to move.

We are almost there my love.

As her voice fades, the sun seems to enlarge, and turns into deep magenta.

Mary? Where are you? Don't leave me now, just as we are so near!

The light is now unbearable. Hurting his eyes, he moves his head away toward the ground. Now he can hear other voices.

Is this another dream?

As Gus awakens and turns his head back to face a bright morning sun, everyone is moving around looking busy. Still reflecting on the dream, he sits up, rubs his chin stubble, and then stands. While stretching his aching body, Garth approaches holding the map.

"Guess what, I had that dream again. This time the sun changed color."

"That's strange! So did I. It just woke me up."

Holding back his excitement, Garth holds out the map.

"Today we should make it to Gallup to visit the Navajo reservation."

Sensing his friends controlled enthusiasm, Gus studies the grubby map.

"Good. I have a strong feeling there will be quite a few survivors to pick up."

"What makes you feel that?"

Gus looks up from the map, and gazes deep into Garth's open honest face.

"The American Native Indians are God's forgotten people. Even before the Jews were the 'chosen' ones, the American Indian always worshiped the Great Spirit.

They were thousands of years ahead, while everyone else were bowing to stone statues or performing human sacrifices to some imaginary effigy.

These Indians only took from the earth what they needed – like taking a handful of water from a lake to quench their thirst instead of draining the whole lake for industrial purposes and profit. They kept everything in perfect balance. It all changed for the worse when the greedy white 'Christians' drove them from their lands, causing them severe hardship and misery."

Picturing the history, Garth becomes thoughtful as he folds up the map.

"Tell me something? Why haven't we found more survivors?"

While they stroll toward the others who are waiting by the bus, Gus stops to answer.

"I've been thinking the same. We've traveled over fifteen hundred miles and we only have these few souls."

As if searching for a rational answer, Gus looks down and shuffles his foot about in the dirt.

"All that I do know, most people who are with us are having the same type of dream. Others elsewhere, who are also having the same dream are probably making their own way to the desert from different directions. Has it ever occurred to you that there are only a special few that need to come on this journey? So, when all is revealed, these people will go back to organize the rest who are awaiting the outcome. We won't really know the truth until we arrive at our destination."

Meanwhile, while Eva is staring at the two men in deep conversation, Madeline stands next to her.

"What fate are they deciding for us now?"

"So far they have done fairly good."

"So far!"

Controlling her irritation, Eva turns on Madeline.

"What is it with you?"

"Nothing sweetie! It's that I can't wait to get to where ever we are 'supposed' to be going. Most of all, I can't wait to be alone with Gus."

Jealousy adding to her mounting irritation, Eva frowns.

"Don't bank on it - girl! He's going to be a busy man who won't have time for any of 'that'. Take my word, I know, I've been there. You'll have to love him from a distance like the rest of us."

Unable to keep calm, Eva leaves her and ambles toward the men. Glaring at Eva's back, Madeline's mind is reeling.

That's what you think – girl!

As Eva approaches the two men, She smiles and gives them a mock salute.

"All present and correct General! We're all ready to go. As breakfast today is a protein bar, I have left you one, accompanied by a bottle of water on the bus driver's seat."

Admiring this beautiful and caring woman, Gus gives her an impulsive hug.

"What would I do without you?"

His warmth and smell intoxicating, for a few seconds she floats, and then drops down to earth.

Not wanting anyone else to read her expression, she whispers back.

"It's nothing. That's what I'm here for. You know that."

"I know. Thanks"

After a soft kiss on her cheek, they separate. Hiding her tears, she turns away to join the others on the bus. Being obvious how Eva feels for Gus, Garth commiserates by patting Gus on the shoulder as they walk toward the fuel truck.

As Eva is instructing everyone to board the bus, she glances at Gus in hope he looks back. He does, especially after saving her life at the old church, and having to refuse her love for a bigger quest. Bringing him out of his daydream, Garth touches his shoulder again.

"Why don't you let me drive the bus and you drive the fuel truck? It will give you a break."

Half listening, Gus agrees. With his mind still on Eva and the dream of Mary, he is not focusing on Garth's suggestion. Observing his friend and mentor is not quite right this morning, he makes a further suggestion.

"Are you all right? If you're not up to it, I can get Max to drive the bus and I can drive the truck."

Coming out of his daze, Gus looks at his loyal friend and conveys to him a grateful smile.

"I'm fine. I'll drive the truck if you don't mind driving the bus. Thanks for your concern. And thanks for everything."

Each understanding and in tune with the other, they separate. Each going to their chosen task, Madeline focuses on Gus climbing into the truck.

Not long now my love!

The sun is setting as Gus' little convoy turns off interstate forty highway toward the community of Gallup, New Mexico.

Mary Morning star is sitting behind Garth as he is driving. Giving him directions as they make their way through the devastation of flattened single story buildings and cluttered roadways, Mary taps Garth on the shoulder.

"Stop! What's happened?"

Shocked by what she sees, she begins to cry. Becoming fond of this beautiful girl, Garth does not hesitate in getting up from his seat to comfort her.

His clothes becoming wet from her tears, and her warmth and smell getting through into his subconscious, he is reluctant to withdraw when Gus enters the bus. Summing up the situation, Gus inquires.

"What's up? Is she all right?"

With his arm now around the girl's shoulder, Garth turns to him.

"She is devastated by all the destruction."

Unable to control her impending fear, Mary wipes her eyes.

"Where is everybody?"

As nobody can answer, Gus makes a suggestion.

"Is there anywhere that any survivors can shelter?"

Her hands trembling, she tries hard to concentrate.

"Only the old caves, up in the hills. They were used years ago for storing food for the winter."

Planting a light kiss on her forehead to calm her, Garth then climbs back into the drivers seat.

"Show us the way lass. We'll find your folks."

Relieved at Garth's leadership, Gus leaves the bus, and then climbs back into the fuel truck cab.

Meanwhile, Mary still sits behind Garth and scans the area, while the bus continues the perilous journey. Out of nowhere, a young woman appears. Standing in the middle of the dirt road just ahead of them, she waves both arms. As Garth stops the bus, the woman appears desperate as she runs toward the drivers side, just as Garth opens the door. Not believing her eyes, she stares straight at him.

"You a priest?"

Before Garth can answer there is a mixture of shrills and shrieks coming from the back of the bus. Mary cries out with relief as she rushes out and throws her arms around the Navajo woman. Curios and a little sad at so few survivors, Garth and Max step out of the bus to join them.

While the two females talk in a mixture of English and *Dine*, it is obvious they must be family. Witnessing the proceedings with interest, Gus climbs out of his truck and walks over to join Garth and Max. Becoming aware of the gathering crowd, Mary turns to them and introduces the woman.

"This is *Ne-zhoni-tas-chizzie*. Pretty swallow, but you can call her Tizzy or Sally."

Already attracted to these young women, but when Garth focuses on Tizzy, he becomes mesmerized by this young exceptional beauty. Observing her jet-black hair tied back into a long ponytail, which blends with her rich bronze skin. Her hourglass body being covered by a snug fitting sweatshirt and denims increases his interest so much, his hand trembles, as he indicates for her to shake it. As she receives his hand with a firm grip, her bright hazel eyes produce a smile that bores right into his soul. Witnessing Garth's reaction, Gus and Max smile at each other. They also shake her hand, and can see why their friend reacted the way he did.

Becoming aware of the sun going down, Gus slides his arm around Garth's shoulder to relax him, and then looks at Mary.

"Shall we find the rest of your people? It will be getting dark soon and we need to set up camp."

Wanting to become more involved, Tizzy taps Mary on the arm and points to the hills.

"There are over a hundred in the caves. There is plenty of room to park your vehicles."

Gus is leading the convoy as they approach a makeshift settlement of shacks made from an assortment of damaged building materials. He notices many young people helping a few older ones. Some of the younger ones are patching the little shacks with sheets of corrugated steel, while others are stoking small bonfires for cooking. He also notices some domestic animals: goats, cows and chickens all wandering about.

The convoy stops and everyone disembarks. Tizzy shows Mary and the Indian children from the bus to one particular hut that is more traditionally built than the others. In the meantime, Gus, Garth, Max, Irwin and Eva form a group to discuss details of what to do next. As Madeline isn't invited, she makes sure she joins them to give her opinion.

"Look at them all! Do we have enough room and supplies for them all?
Eva turns on her, but halts her anger.

"We will always have enough for whoever is with us."

Annoyed by Eva's answer, Madeline turns to Gus for support.

Not wanting any friction, Gus agrees with Eva, but consoles Madeline.

"Eva is right. We will never refuse anyone, even if we have nothing. However, I understand your concern."

Appearing hurt at not being supported by Gus, Madeline hides her anger, as Tizzy returns and stands next to Garth, but talks at Gus.

"I will introduce you all to our Chief, *Atah-besh-keh-he*, Silver Eagle. He is also *A-zay*, our Medicine Man."

As she begins to walk toward the traditional building, she indicates with her eyes for Garth to follow. Becoming more entranced by this beauty, Garth beckons the others.

"I think she wants us to follow her."

Understanding Garth's dilemma and glad of it, Gus demonstrates his affection by patting his dear friend on the back, while they follow Tizzy.

As they all enter the building, Tizzy leaves. Inside, there is a small brass oil lamp hanging off a roof support releasing a warm eerie glow, which reflects down to a silver haired man sitting cross-legged on a hand woven rug against the far wall. Dressed in light moccasins, jeans and a fine leather shirt, covered in traditional Navajo markings and beadwork on the shoulders and front, he appears formal and aloof. Standing next to him is Mary with her hand placed with respect on his shoulder, like a traditional photographic pose. Mary smiles and indicates for the visitors to sit on the floor rug opposite.

The five visitors sit down on the rug making themselves as comfortable as they can, about an arms length from the older man. Devoid of any emotions, the silver haired man just stares straight ahead, not registering any particular individual.

Before she speaks, Mary is gentle in tapping the man's shoulder.

"This is my Father, Silver Eagle. He is our Chief, Medicine and Holy man.

You may have noticed he is blind so therefore I'm his eyes."

She sits, as Silver Eagle puts out his hand toward his visitors. Presuming this is a signal for them to reciprocate, Gus leads.

When all the hand shaking is finished, the Chief places his hands on his cross-legged knees and lowers his head as if in prayer. After a few seconds of silence, he begins to chant. Becoming intrigued by the 'performance', the six glance at each other. Realizing this is some form of welcome introduction, they all concentrate on the chief as he stops chanting and stares toward them with a blank expression.

"I welcome you to my *to-altseh-hogan*, my camp. I sense among you a great one who has been sent to save us. I also sense love among you, which is good. Do not worry about your other children, Tizzy is taking care of them as we talk. Please relax as we have much to discuss."

In the meantime, Madeline is becoming fidgety and cannot relax.

All this over a bunch of goddam Indians.

Making the excuse that she wants to go and check the other children, she whispers to Gus. Hiding his annoyance at her disturbing such an important situation, he acknowledges and makes his apologies to the Chief.

"We appreciate all that you are doing for us Silver Eagle, but Madeline is anxious for all the children we brought and she also wants to help Tizzy."

The Chief's expression stiffens, as he nods and waits for Madeline to leave.

"Be careful! That one has her own agenda. For now, we must discuss our destiny. All the children and adults you see here have had the same dream. A long straight road stretching into the sun, and then the sun changes color. Is that right with you?"

Becoming more entranced by the wisdom of this man, Gus Answers.

"Yes. We have all had the same dream. It is common consensus among us all that we need to go to the Californian desert where the hot springs are. I suggest that we stay here just long enough to organize the transport and supplies, and then leave as one convoy."

Silver Eagle's response is to lower his head in thought, touch his daughter Mary on the knee, pause and gaze in Gus's direction.

"I need to *be-ke-ya-ti*, to talk over with the one that is 'Him'."

Garth takes the initiative and indicates to everyone, except Gus to leave.

Now alone, Silver Eagle indicates to Gus to come closer. As Gus sits with their knees touching, the chief then takes hold of Gus' hands, and feels them. Picturing them in his mind, he then lays them back on Gus' knees. After a slight pause, he leans forward and spreads his hands on Gus' chest. Pausing again, he feels his way up to his Gus's face. While the sensitive fingers explore Gus's features, Gus does not move a muscle, while his face is being pictured in the chief's mind. To his surprise, Silver Eagle pulls his hands away with a kind of urgency.

"You 'are' the one - sent here to us from the Great Spirit. Why have you taken so long? Why not years ago before millions of innocent souls had been slaughtered?"

Not letting Gus answer, he goes quiet and lowers his head in thought. He mumbles, and lifts his head up again to face Gus.

"We must *ah-hi-di-dail*, come together to create a new and purer world."

As if their souls are blending, they sit and hold hands. Their knees still touching, Gus begins to sweat as he senses the other man's suffering.

"You found Mary in a garbage tip fifteen years ago. You were not blind then.

You took the baby in and cared for her. You could sense she was someone special."

Hiding his surprise at this man knowing his personal history, Silver Eagle draws a deep breath to steady his emotions.

"She was sent to me from the Great Spirit, as my wife and I could not bear children. It was sad that my wife soon became sick with jealousy. She felt I was doting on my precious new daughter more than I loved her. I told her we must *ah-hi-di-dail*, come together and my love for her was just as strong. She said she now hated the child and would drown her. I tried to explain to her that Mary was from God sent to us to bring us joy and prosperity. The day I found her, it was early morning and there was only one star still shining in the early sky so I named her Mary Morning star. My wife would not listen, so in a rage she snatched the child and went to the well to drown her. We fought and I rescued the baby. She then cursed me and my ancestors and said I will never see Mary grow up. She then threw herself down the well, where she drowned. Next day I woke up blind as she had cursed me. I have her demon in me never to be freed until I die."

Needing to help this great man, Gus releases Silver Eagle's hands, and takes the initiative by placing his own hands against the chief's face. With the lightest of touch, he lays his fingers on the unseeing eyes. The chief does not move, as Gus begins to pray under his breath. While his hands begin to feel hot on the face, Silver Eagle cries out as if in pain. Meanwhile, Gus collapses. While Silver eagle's eyes weep heavy with tears, he lifts his head up and opens his eyes. Making out a shimmering dim light through his tears, he realizes it is the oil lamp hanging from the roof. His reaction is to shake his head and rub his tear-laden eyes with the back of his hands. Realizing he is no longer blind, he notices Gus lying on the floor.

The demon has gone! Her curse has been lifted. This man 'is' from the Great Spirit.

More tears of gratitude fill his eyes, as he touches Gus's sweaty forehead. With a sense of urgency, he stands, goes to the door and shouts.

"Help me someone!"

Garth and Max are with Tizzy helping with the children when they hear the pitiful cry for help. Wondering what has happened, Garth and Max rush to the dwelling. Tizzy and Mary follow. When they enter the building, they find Silver Eagle weeping and Gus lying on the floor with his eyes open in a daze. Sensing what has happened, while witnessing the chief's eyes appearing clear, Garth goes straight to Gus to sit him up.

"What happened?"

Gus reaches up, touches Garth's cheek and smiles with a sense of achievement.

"The demon has fled."

As Garth and Max help Gus stand and assist him out of the hut, an anxious Eva is waiting. At the same time, Tizzy and Mary are staring at their chief who is still standing by the doorway.

"Don't worry my children, the curse has been lifted. I can see you all."

Knowing what has happened, Eva goes to Gus, but looks at Garth.

527

"He has just done a healing. I know, I have witnessed it before - first hand."

Listening, Silver Eagle turns to her.

"This man from God has given part of his soul to rid me of my curse."

Mary's reaction is to rush into his arms.

"Oh, father! Isn't it wonderful?"

Taking a breath and filling his nostrils with her natural perfume, he pushes her away to arms length to inspect.

"Mary? Is this you? My, you are more beautiful than I ever pictured..."

In all the excitement, he becomes aware of Tizzy standing nearby.

"Is it you Tizzy? My, you are quite grown up."

His hands trembling, he looks upwards, as tears of gratitude run down his face. Becoming humbled by the experience, his voice fills the room.

"Oh God! Thank you. I am now fulfilled and ready to do your work."

Meanwhile outside, Gus is still being supported by Garth and Max, while he is sitting on a crude wooden bench. Eva is becoming more anxious while watching him coming round and regaining his strength. Gus shows his thanks to the two men by smiling with appreciation. Sensing Eva's anxiety, he offers her a wink to calm her.

"I think things will be much better from now on..."

Puzzled by such a statement, Eve is a little confused as he turns to face Mary coming out the doorway. Her eyes full of tears, she comes up to Gus and wraps her arms around his neck and whispers in his ear.

"Thank you for everything."

Now looking at Eva, Gus inquires, while patting Mary's head with an overwhelming sense of affection.

"How is everything? I'm afraid I got a bit distracted."

Controlling her own emotional need of wanting to be in his arms, Eva wastes no time in answering.

"Very good. They have quite a few supplies they rescued from the stores and three good pickup trucks. More to the point, how are you feeling?"

"I'm fine. You know how that goes."

"I'm afraid I do. Look, I must finish helping Madeline. We'll have some food in about an hour."

As Eva and Max leave, taking Mary and Silver Eagle with them, Garth gazes at Gus in adulation.

"I am so honored to be your friend and servant, and to witness these marvels. I feel so inadequate compared to you."

Loving this young Englishman more than his own life, Gus slides his arm around Garth's shoulder.

"Don't 'ever' talk this way again. You're my right hand. I love you. Your companionship and loyalty is what gives me my strength. That's how I manage to help these people by you taking much of the burden for me. There is no way I could have come this far without you. Do you not realize that you have been chosen to be my number one?"

Becoming overwhelmed by humbleness, Garth lowers his head and begins to cry. This makes Gus give him a hug and whisper in his ear.

"You are forever my dear brother."

Wanting to look Garth in the eye, Gus holds Garth at arms length and offers him a warm, grateful smile.

"I hope I didn't interrupt anything really important by this little distraction?"

Warmed by his friend's usual humor, Garth has to smirk.

"Tizzy and I got all the children organized for tonight in the shelters."

"She is quite a girl. I see you both hit it off."

Garth blushes at the truth coming out.

"She's wonderful. I need to talk about it with you."

"What for? Love at first site is wonderful. I envy you."

"Envy me? Why? I'm a priest. We're not allowed to fall in love, because of my church."

"What church? You're not a priest anymore! You're a son of God. The same as me and the rest of us all. Look my lad; love her how you want. You have my blessing."

Never experiencing this kind of love before, tears of relief and gratitude fill Garth's eyes.

529

"Thanks! Thanks a lot."

Overwhelmed by this new sense of freedom, he ponders for a few seconds, and then comes to.

"I – I'll go and help the others then."

Before Gus can reiterate, Garth rushes off to join the others.

For a minute, Gus feels alone and yet contented, as he stares out to the darkening horizon. Picturing Garth's happy expression, which stirs up memories of Mary, and now Eva, he wonders what the next step of the great plan is to be.

I hope Garth has found his soulmate.Anyway, two more day's journey and we'll be there. Then what...?

Madeline's voice behind him breaks his concentration.

"There you are!"

Before he has a chance to focus, she wraps her arm around his.

"Gee, I'm exhausted. What a load of work."

Hiding his irritation, Gus continues to stare at the horizon.

"Don't do so much. As there are more people in our group now, spread the work out. Everyone needs to do their share."

Her reaction is to squeezes his arm a little more.

"I do it because I want you to love me – like you did Mary – and now Eva."

Controlling his mounting irritation, and still not taking his eyes away from the horizon, his face hardens.

"Please don't put yourself in the same category as Mary Magdalene or Eva!

I can see you're trying, but there always seems to be a motive behind everything you do. However, when you 'finally' give yourself to others without thinking about your own position first, I will..."

Becoming annoyed that he wont face her, her eyes blaze with jealous fury.

"You'll what? You'll love me then? You will bed me as your wife like you did Mary?"

The mention of Mary in this way causes his face to distort with anger.

As he turns to face her, she flinches. Never seeing him like this before, and thinking he is going to slap her, she turns her head to one side. His response is to bring his arms up to grab her shoulders. She stiffens in fear, but is determined not to show it by facing him. As his eyes bore right into her, his voice becomes soft, but defiant.

"I cannot 'bed' anyone. This mission is far bigger than any of us."

While she stands her ground, the anger leaves his face. To demonstrate her feelings, she reaches up and grabs each of his hands.

"I'm sorry if I love you!"

Before he can react, she moves up close so their bodies touch.

He's weakening. I have him now, so I can wait. I will make a big point of apologizing.

"Please forgive me Gus. My love for you is so strong that I lost control. You're right. I will forget about my own needs and give myself to the others on this historic mission."

She takes her time in withdrawing, and plants a soft kiss on his cheek.

"If you could get inside me, you would understand how I feel."

Glad she has made her point, and sensing he is watching her walk away, she sways her full hips a little to encourage his doubting mind. As she sidles up to Eva, she makes a point of giving Eva a hug before she helps with the food.

Meanwhile, becoming more annoyed at his own weakness toward Madeline, Gus turns back and gazes again at the horizon. From the West, there is still a glow from the sun even though it has gone. He releases a sigh of resignation, as he sits on the ground. The sunset bothering him, he lowers his head, clasps his hands together, and prays.

As Garth and Tizzy are working so well together, he has a tendency talk while she listens. Standing as close as she can to him, she smiles, and feels optimistic that there seems to be a future for them all - maybe.

The food is ready. There are three bonfires with about forty people sitting around each fire all chatting, as if this is all meant to be.

A strong awareness of the desert trips of long ago, Gus wanders off to eat his food by a large boulder.

Today is different from then. There is now hope, and no Satan trying to coerce me away from my mission.

While eating from his paper plate of delicious corned beef hash and Indian fried bread, he once again stares at the horizon.

It is still glowing...

Someone comes and sits next to him. Silver Eagle slides his arm around Gus's shoulder to demonstrate his affection.

"This is *ben-bih-ke-as-chinigh*. What's written my friend is the end of the *chindi*; the devil. From now on man will finally be at peace with himself. However, why have I only a small fraction of my people left?"

Understanding the chief's grief, Gus turns to face his new friend.

"Because, enough is enough. The majority of the population of this planet had sunk so low, the time had come to act. Evil must go and innocence remain. I came here to warn the World, to give it one year or else. It turned out to be 'or else.' I feel I'm to blame, I should have done more."

Releasing his arm from Gus's shoulder, the chief stares at the horizon.

"You had an impossible task. Now *ut-zah*, it is done. We now must *yah-tay-go- e-elah*, make good. I remember my grandfather telling me as a young boy that everything around you is *ba-has-the*, important. Nothing should be taken for granted. He also foretold that a good man sent from the Great Spirit would come and change the World as Jesus tried to do in the Bible, but this time it would be different...

He studies Gus's frowning profile, and then picks up a piece of fried bread.

"At the time I thought it was strange talk, but now I can see what he meant. But this?"

He takes a bite from his food and concentrates on the horizon.

"All I have left of my whole nation are the few souls we have here. It seems like mass murder. Everything that God is against. Even though I was blind when all this happened, I could still hear the screams and feel the carnage and destruction. It was as if hell had broken loose..."

Tears run down the chief's face as he lowers his head to sob. Wanting to relieve this good man's pain, Gus slides his arm around his friend's shoulder.

"I can't cry for those who've been taken, but I can certainly help the good people that have been saved. That is the reason I'm here. I didn't manage it over two thousand years ago, but with God's help, I'm going to succeed this time."

Absorbing these profound words, Silver Eagle raises his head and looks into Gus's eyes as if searching for that something extra.

"How can you be so sure there is no more evil left on this desolate world?"

"Right now, I don't know, but when the mission is complete, there will not be any evil. Why am I so confident? Because there are two more stages to go through. Fire and absolution."

Silver Eagle's response is to point at the glowing horizon.

"You mean like that? That my friend is the mother of all prairie fires."

A new doubt creeping into his insides, Gus stares transfixed at the sky.

"I thought the sunset was lasting too long. This must be the second stage approaching. It's cleansing as it goes. To save our skins, we have to find shelter for everyone here, and all our supplies. NOW!"

Trembling with urgency, Gus stands and points to the caves.

"Can we get everything in there?"

Taking this 'urgency' in his stride, the chief conveys to Gus a smile of confidence.

"We will have no problem in parking the fuel and supply trucks in the caves, and all the people, but not the bus. I suggest we drive the bus up that dirt road which leads to higher ground and park it until the fire has passed. There is one thing we have in our favor; there is no foliage in this whole area, so there is nothing to burn. We just need to shelter from the heat."

Becoming a little bewildered, Gus gazes again at the glowing horizon.

"How long do you think it will take the fire to get here?"

"In my experience of previous fires smaller than this, I would guess by the early hours."

Becoming anxious, Gus rubs his face.

"We'd better get started then."

60

The Way to Flagstaff

A few miles east of Flagstaff, Arizona, Natas' group is traveling along Interstate Forty. Fred, who is driving the Hummer, notices the sun setting to a vivid horizon.

Making sure he is not hallucinating, he rubs his eyes and shouts back to his passengers.

"Look at that sunset guys. It looks as if the horizon is on fire."

Curious, Julie peers out of her window.

"It's beautiful. Mother? Look!"

Showing little interest, her mother glances out of her window.

"Yes, dear. Very pleasant."

Natas not so sure, gets up from his rear seat and works his way toward the driver. He then stops, and kneels next to James, who is also admiring the colorful sky. Concentrating on the glowing spectacular, Natas reaches across and grips Fred's shoulder.

"Stop the car!"

Not liking Natas's tone, Fred is slow to respond. Becoming irritated by Fred's reluctant attitude, Natas raises his voice.

"I said stop the car! That is no glorious sunset! The earth is on fire!"

Finding it hard to accept Natas's dramatics. Fred obliges by bringing the Hummer to a grinding halt.

Meanwhile, sounds of screaming brakes behind them can be heard as the

535

rest of the convoy screeches to a sudden stop. With mixed emotions, and annoyed with Natas, James jumps out of his side of the vehicle carrying a pair of binoculars.

Once outside, James brings the glasses up to his face, and focuses on the horizon. Becoming apprehensive by James's silence, The President and Natas join him. His face exhibiting dread, James lowers the glasses.

"It's as if the whole countryside is alight."

Without asking permission, Natas takes hold of the binoculars and inspects the scene ahead.

"It is not just this area. Like I said, it is the 'whole' world on fire."

Coming out of her complacency, the President appears shocked at such a blatant statement.

"What do you mean by the whole world?"

Suppressing his irritation, he turns to her.

"Madam President? You are witnessing the 'second'stage of the proceedings, which will result in the beginning of our new world - and new order."

"I don't understand."

Natas' false patience is diminishing.

You will woman. You will!

Acting calm and deliberate he begins to explain to his skeptical, but curious audience.

"The first stage of the new order was the earthquakes and the sudden evaporation of all the bad wicked people. The second stage is fire. The whole world will be ignited to cleanse and sterilize. We will be left with a new shiny world, devoid of any contaminates that would infect the new order."

Disbelieving, the President stares hard at him.

"How do you know all this? And is there any more stages?"

His eyes showing no emotion, he gazes in her direction as if any respect for her position has evaporated.

What fools you all are. Let's keep trying.

Wanting to show his exasperation, he thinks better of it and now appears concerned.

"To your first question, I know, because - I know. The answer to your second question is yes. There is one more stage."

The final showdown with me ending up on top.

Keeping his final stage a secret, he now becomes complicit by scanning the glow again.

"Might I suggest we hide somewhere where we won't get incinerated?"

James, who is trying to keep his head, turns away from Natas toward his boss.

"Ma'am? We are in the Grand Canyon area. There are many places here where we can shelter from any burning vegetation."

With the strain of it all showing in her tired eyes, she puts on her brave official face.

"Go to it James! Get us all to safety. It looks as if we don't have much time."

It is now an hour later. James has found a small private dirt road that is used for park ranger use. The convoy has to be cautious, as it climbs the precarious narrow track. Going through a wooded area, which leads to a large clearing free from any vegetation, the road ends near a steep cliff edge.

Now several hundred feet up from where they started, a vast panoramic view of a wooded valley stretches out below. In this clearing there is a single storey abandoned ranger station, which is about the size of a standard three-bedroom bungalow.

The first thing on the agenda is for James to peer through his binoculars at the fiery horizon, which is now a few miles away.

In the meantime, Staff Sergeant Thomas takes the initiative by leading two of his men to inspect the ranger station. While James takes charge at his end, he hands the glasses to Natas.

"It goes as far as the eye can see. It looks as if the whole country is on fire."

Hiding his exasperation, Natas enforces his opinion as he studies the fire.

"As I said, it is the whole world. If you look beyond the flames you can just make out streaks of lightning."

James is puzzled and is becoming tired of Natas's dramatics.

"What does 'that' mean?"

Knowing James is losing his edge, Natas smirks as he answers.

"The mother of all storms."

A few minutes later, Staff Sergeant Thomas reports to James.

"Sir? We have checked the building and found no personnel. The whole place seems to have been abandoned in a hurry. There are some supplies of food and there is water on tap. In addition, there is a generator and an air conditioner, which I think we are going to need when the heat from the fire hits us."

Keeping his fatigue hidden, James acknowledges.

"Thanks Sergeant. I think it might be a good idea to round up everyone and get them situated in the building."

Standing alone and becoming quite amused, Natas watches with curiosity as the soldier goes up to the rest of the group and shepherds them into the small building. At the same time, James leaves Natas to join the others.

Still holding the binoculars, Natas turns again toward the impending fire and raises his glasses.

So far so good. I think the cleaning action of yours is a bit much, but that is what's written, I suppose. Good idea of yours in having the storm to follow. Washes everything nice and clean to start afresh.

His face serious, and his eyes intent, he lowers the glasses and looks up at the dark sky.

I have not heard from you lately. Any more dreams? Am I still on borrowed time? And where is your delightful son? The one who was going to put this evil world of mine straight. You do know I shot him. He should be dead, or did you protect him again, so there will be some sort of a final showdown between good and evil?

His mind in a turmoil, he brings the glasses up to his eyes to focus on the horizon.

*Oh, it is all so melodramatic and pathetic. Why did you bother to save me? You could have zapped me like all the other scum. Do you **really** want me to return as your prodigal?You have that much faith in me?*

In the meantime, Julie is quiet as she stands next to him.

"Looking for anything in particular?"

Not wanting anyone to be with him right now, he hides his annoyance. Seeing it is Julie, he offers her a genuine smile.

"How did you guess? You, young woman are supposed to be in that building. I think we had better join the others before we are fried."

Demonstrating his affection, he slides his arm around her shoulders and guides her to the ranger station.

It is now an hour later. The heat from the fire is becoming intense. Natas, James and Sergeant Thomas are becoming anxious as they stare out of a large heavy window designed for the park rangers to observe the nearby canyon. The rest of the group are looking out of other windows or resting in the additional rooms.

James now has the binoculars. Tension adding to his fatigue, he raises the glasses to witness this extraordinary event a few hundred yards away.

"The rangers knew what they were doing by building a station in this vicinity. The fire is now surrounding us, but we're unaffected. Thank God!"

Witnessing the same trauma, and hiding his fear, Thomas murmurs in agreement. Becoming intrigued, but peeved by these annoying circum-stances, Natas borrows the glasses and scans the flames.

God has nothing to do with your safety. Who do you think started the damn fire? You're all fools!

He lowers the glasses just as a heavy streak of lightning flashes across their view.

"Well, here comes the storm to clean up the mess left behind."

His hand trembling, James scratches his head while still gazing out of the window.

"It's amazing how the storm is following the fire. It's like an act of God."

Natas does not wish to comment as he hands James back the binoculars, turns and walks away almost bumping into a fearful Julie.

"Oh! Sorry my dear. I never saw you there."

Her eyes searching his taut face, she grips his forearm.

"I've been watching you look out of the window. You're not happy with all this, are you?"

As if she has hit a raw nerve, he is discreet as he maneuvers her to a quiet corner of the room.

"Of course I'm not! Look at all the destruction? It is all totally unnecessary."

"Isn't it supposed to help us with the new order of things."

"Depends on your point of view."

"Obviously you are still torn between staying and going back..."

Julie's mother appears.

"Someone leaving?"

Noticing the dark shadows under her mother's eyes, Julie answers.

"No mother. Nat here is saying we have to wait at least twenty-four hours before we can travel again. Isn't that right Nat?"

"Er – yes! That is correct. You see, with the storm, the dirt road we came up on will be become too soft for the trucks. Therefore, I suggest that we wait and rest until tomorrow before we leave."

The President appears skeptical as she searches his eyes. As if to prove a point, she slides her arm around her daughter's shoulders. In return, Natas conveys to her his warmest smile, before leaving them to go and join the others in another room. Standing nearby, James nods to his boss and follows Natas.

Now alone, Mother and daughter step closer to the large window to observe the downpour and lightning. Staring hard at the scene, the President appears vulnerable.

"If I hadn't seen all this with my own eyes, I wouldn't believe anything like this could possibly happen. Its extraordinary."

"No mother. It is God's plan for us to start in a new clean world."

Julie's mother's hand trembles, as she rubs her tired face and tries to hide her tears.

"Everything is gone! We have nothing left to work with."

To demonstrate her sympathy, Julie slides her arm around her mother's waist.

"Mother? We have 'everything' we need. Why do you think we are being helped along the way? Take this building for instance. Why wasn't it destroyed like all the others?"

"Because it was meant for us?"

She gazes into her daughter's eyes, as if searching for more answers.

"You're so much like your father. That's just the sort of thing he would say."

In desperation, she gives here daughter a hug and whispers in her ear.

"What I want to know, where's Gus? He would know all the answers. He must be alive, otherwise none of this makes any sense. I mean - he started it all by coming back..."

"I 'know' he's alive Mother. I can feel it."

Julie feels her mother loosen her firm grip, but still holds on. Keeping her voice low, her mother asks another question.

"What about this Nat you're so friendly with? Who is he? Where does he come from? I feel uneasy when you're alone with him."

"Please don't worry. The reason I'm close to him is that he is the only one here hat's anyway connected to Gus."

Everyone in Gus's group has now sheltered in the Navajo caves with the trucks. Gus, Garth, and Silver Eagle are outside becoming anxious at the glowing horizon looming closer. As Garth is becoming transfixed by the color of the sky, Gus shows his affection by placing his hand on Garth's forearm.

"What are you thinking my friend?"

"I'm amazed and a little scared at what I'm witnessing."

"I feel the same, even though I know this has to happen. Right now, there are thousands of little groups just like us all over the planet watching and thinking the same thing."

Silver Eagle looks away from the glowing sky and focuses on Gus.

"None of the other groups have you. So, why us?"

Taken aback by the question, Gus tries to answer.

"I don't know why. I have to be somewhere. I know I'm being guided. So right now, I go by how I feel, like a gut instinct. Instinctively I know you both have God within you, like me. I can also feel that both of you will lead these good people and help them to build a whole new existence - without evil."

Garth becomes alarmed by such a profound statement.

"Does that mean you won't be staying with us for long?"

Gus replies by giving Garth's arm a light squeeze.

"I will always be with you - in spirit. Eventually, when this mission is complete here, I will be needed elsewhere to find people like yourselves and guide them to become leaders. Remember originally, I was supposed to tour the world and convince leaders of nations to get their act together. As we know it was taken out of my hands."

In reply, the Indian Chief shakes his head in confusion.

"When we all arrive at the required destination, how long do my people and I have to stay there before we come back home – here?"

Gus's response is to reach out and place a reassuring hand on the Indian's shoulder.

"My dear friend. The choice will be yours and your people's. There is a good reason we're all being guided to a bleak spot in the Californian desert. When we eventually find it out, we will all be free to live anywhere we want."

Three hours later, the fire has reached Gus' group. Silver Eagle was right in his estimation. The fire is bypassing them, but no one could ever imagine the storm that is following.The downpour and lightning is so intense, the three men stare in wonder mixed with fear.

542

To their relief, the storm soon passes, and all is now quiet and still. Garth takes a few steps to the cave entrance and looks up to the clearing sky and listens to the remaining drops of water falling from the roof of the cave entrance.

"I think I'll check the others, then we can decide what we're going to do."

Observing the eastern horizon still glowing and mixed with lightening, Silver Eagle nod in agreement and looks at Gus for more reassurance.

"I want you to tell me why all this is happening? I can just manage to take in the earth quakes and the beams of white light that vaporized most of my people, but why this as well?"

Gus does not mince his words in explaining.

"It is written that when the end of days comes, man will be punished for his evil and perish. Only the chosen ones will remain, and then the world will be cleansed of all evil, so that whoever is left can start anew."

Silver Eagle is not convinced.

"People need to be guided and led to make a fresh beginning. What about foodand shelter? Right now, there is nothing!"

To further reassure this doubting man, Gus places an arm around the chief's shoulder to help ward off his fears.

"My friend, there is so much stuff out there waiting for the few that are left that we can all manage for at least two years while we get organized in growing food and building communities. The main thing that you've forgotten is that all this is part of a great new plan. We will not be allowed to suffer because this is now the new Garden of Eden..."

Gus is interrupted by Garth running up to them. The anxious look on his face tells them something is wrong.

"It's Madeline! She's gone."

Becoming shocked and a little angry, Gus tries hard to hide his aggravation .

"What do you mean? Gone!"

Observing the strain on his friend's face and the disappointment in his eyes, Garth does his best to explain.

"She took off during the storm with the pickup truck that was at the front of the cave. She was already sitting in it while the fire was passing. When the rain began she started the truck and left."

On hearing this, Silver Eagle shows his disgust.

"I told you that one was on her own agenda. So much for the 'chosen' ones, all being good and righteous. Someone slipped up on that one."

Disappointed, he struts away in the direction of the caves. His own doubts showing, Garth turns to Gus.

"Why would she go like that? Where can she go? She took the only empty truck that we were going to use for carrying passengers. Now we'll have to squash everyone into what we have left."

Half listening, Gus is disturbed by Silver Eagle's reaction to Madeline's disappearance.

What happens if he's right? How many more 'slip-ups' are there?

Hiding his fears, he refocuses on Garth.

"I don't think it's anything to worry about. She is an independent woman, and there may be a good reason for her to go. We'll find out eventually.

However, for now we must all get some sleep, because tomorrow is a new day."

She is standing on the edge of a massive crater. Her eyes are focused on the deep center. She scans the whole area, which is barren of any vegetation.

"Magnificent isn't it."

She turns to the direction of the smooth male voice, to see a tall handsome man in his thirties dressed in black. Standing just a small distance away on her right, he looks down into the depths before him. He then turns his head to look at her.

She freezes at his smile, which emphasizes his beautiful green eyes. His dark curly hair reflects in the glow of the bright desert sun. He walks the distance between them, stopping just a few inches away. She feels as if she is melting as his presence is overwhelming her. Seeing the effect he is having, he reaches out to touch her forearm.

"You found me then? My love!"

He then takes both her hands and brings them up to his full lips. Bewitched by this male specimen of manhood, she focuses on his sensual mouth caressing her trembling hands.

"Yes! I have found you."

Her whole being now engulfed with a desire so strong she wants him to take her now. Tuning in to her craving emotions, he lets go of her hands, and slides his arms around her. Waiting for him to take her, she is not disappointed when his lips fuse against her burning mouth. After a few seconds of tingling delight, he withdraws for a few seconds, and searches her eyes for confirmation. She feels deprived, and then becomes satisfied as his head leans toward her neck. The floating she feels is from the glorious sensation of his soft warm mouth brushing the yearning skin. As he continues, she closes her eyes in ecstasy. Picturing his green, tantalizing pools, she is more than willing to submit in letting his gentle hands fondle her tingling breasts and lower her to the ground...

Madeline awakens. She is somewhat conscious of her hands gripping the side of the seat so as not to fall. The dream is still vivid, as she becomes aware of her own voice.

"Oh my God! You're so beautiful."

Now wide awake, she notices the sun is breaking the eastern horizon. She takes a swig of water from a nearby plastic bottle and relishes its coolness. She is reluctant to clear her mind of the handsome man for whom she was willing to give her all.

This is the future for me. I know it! He is my true love. Sorry Gus, I had to leave you. I wanted you so much, but you weren't interested in what I had to offer. Your mission was far too important.

To relieve her frustration, she rummages through the glove compartment, and then searches in the door pockets. She finds a crumpled map, opens it and spreads it out on her lap. It shows most of New Mexico and Arizona. While studying where she had just left, her mind wanders back the last few hours.

I was sitting alone in the truck after helping everyone get to safety before the fire. I remember becoming aroused by the sight of the flames followed by the lightening and rain. Feeling isolated from the others, and not belonging with them, I had the impulse to join the fire and bathe in the excitement of the storm. As if pulled by an unknown power, I started the truck and left. Driving in the storm, I was so absorbed in the power and yet unaware of its dangers. When the storm passed, I felt elated, but fatigued. Having to stop the truck, I fell asleep...

She studies the map closer to find her bearings, and then she sees it. The Arizona Meteor Crater.

That's my dream! That is where he will be. I estimate it is about a hundred mile trip to that crater.

The excitement pumping through her veins cause her hands to shake, as she folds the map and returns it to the door pocket.

After a minute of deliberation, she grips the steering wheel and stares out of the windshield. Willing her mind to think straight, she turns on the ignition. The fuel gauge registers two-thirds full. Turning the key, the engine roars into life. Checking her rear view mirror, she puts the truck into drive and maneuvers it back onto interstate forty.

"I'm coming my love. Don't leave without me."

He is standing by the crumbling edge, looking down into the vast circular chasm.

Surely, this must be the spot. The place your fury hit, demonstrating your frustration at your failed and flawed creation...

He senses he is not alone. Someone appears on his left.

Is it her? The angel you promised to bring me back to you?

His heart palpitates while walking the short distance so he can stand by her. He is now looking deep into her eyes.

My, you 'are' beautiful.

Her expression is relaying to him her rising passion.

Do I deserve such an 'angel'?

Experiencing a desire so powerful, he can feel his heart pounding in his head...

Natas wakes with a start. Julie is being gentle while tapping his forehead.

"Wha – ? What's the matter?"

To calm him, she strokes his forehead.

"You were restless with a bad dream."

Not wanting to show his irritation, he sits up in his sleeping bag.

"Actually it was a good dream. An angle had come to take me back."

Staring into his magnetic eyes, an irresistible impulse makes her lean forward to kiss his forehead.

"Time to go. Here is some breakfast for you."

He glances at the plate of beans and biscuit, and then gazes into her eyes.

"We can't go. I must find this angel!"

Julie studies his confused face and places the breakfast on his lap. Being so close, her impulse to kiss him further is suppressed.

"Are you sure it's her and not just wishful thinking? You do realize I could be that angel?"

His eyes widen as she grips his hand and places it against her left breast.

"Feel my heart beating for you my love. I want to take you with me in this new world."

As their lips meet, his guilt at enticing this beautiful young woman is bothering him. Reluctant to withdraw, he strokes her cheek.

"You would do that for me?"

Enjoying the warmth of his hand, she is reluctant to remove it from her breast.

"I love you Nat. What ever you plan, take me with you."

His conscience bothering him even more, he plants a soft kiss on her cheek and stands.

"My dream wasn't just about the angel, we are going to the wrong place. The destination we need has a large crater."

As she stands to be with him, she grips his forearm as if to reassure.

"None of us has had that dream."

Her being so close and her natural perfume filling his lungs, he is becoming agitated.

"Do you not see girl? We all dreamed of a big circle, which we thought must be the sun. No, it is this crater."

Becoming troubled by his closeness, an anxious Julie turns away and goes to see her mother.

The president who is now in deep conversation with James, smiles at her daughter approaching. Meanwhile James continues his concern.

"That's what I dreamt Ma'am. A big crater surrounded by many people all with their meager possessions."

"I don't know James. Nobody else has dreamt that."

Tuning into their discussion, Julie interrupts.

"Nat has. He just told me."

Julie's mother faces her daughter and notices a serious looking Natas standing behind her.

"Is it true – Nat?"

His expression pensive, he steps closer to the President and grabs her hand, as if his life depended on it.

"Yes, Madam President. It surly is true."

She turns to James for some form of sanity, so a proper decision can be made in this new turn of events.

"What do you think James?"

"You know what I think. Perhaps we ought to ask anyone else here if they have had a similar dream. If they have, we can go to the Arizona Meteor Crater. It's only about fifty miles south of here, so it wouldn't be much of a detour. If it's wrong, so be it. If we are right, there will be survivors there."

The president turns to everyone in the room.

"I know this sounds a bit strange, but can any of you tell me if last night you dreamt of a large crater in the ground with survivors waiting."

Four hands go up, two soldiers, Fred and Julie.

"Sorry mother I thought I was the only one that had the dream until Nat told me his."

Know what has to be done, the President looks at James.

"The crater it is then."

Gus' group is now ready for another day. Having a truck short, means cramming all the children in the bus, and the others sitting where they can, scattered among supplies in the rest of the vehicles. The Indians are sad and uneasy that they have been persuaded to leave their ancestral home for an unknown adventure.

Still skeptical, but trusting Gus, Silver Eagle sits behind Gus who is driving the bus.

"Where to now young man?"

"Flagstaff is the nearest city. Being about a hundred and fifty miles, it will take us most of the day to get there. Then we'll rest for the night."

His mind still in turmoil, Garth is sitting next to Silver Eagle.

"I still can't get over Madeline running off like that and pinching one of the trucks."

Hiding his own annoyance, Silver Eagle shuffles in his seat.

"She has the devil in her. She will cause trouble wherever she goes. Just let us hope there is no more like her. Otherwise, all this upheaval is for nothing."

Getting ready to start the bus, Gus is thoughtful, and hides his concern.

"You're right Silver Eagle on one thing, but wrong on the rest. You're right to say she has been corrupted by the devil. However, I feel confident she is a one off. Therefore, I assure you this is not all for nothing."

Natas' group has arrived at the crater and to their surprise, there are people parked in small areas on the west side of the crater near the road. Julie shouts with glee as the Hummer heads their convoy.

"Just as I told you, more survivors."

As they get closer, they can see at least seventy men, women and children sitting in three separate groups. As most of the accumulation are children, they run and play back and forth between each group.

As the convoy stops on the road, Natas and James gaze out of their windows studying these survivors. In return, a few of the adults wave as if in anticipation.

James is the first to comment.

"They look as if they have plenty of vehicles and supplies. It feels as if they are expecting us."

Staring out of her window, the President disagrees.

"How is that possible? We haven't communicated with anybody."

Becoming excited that her dream has been forthcoming, Julie gets up from her seat.

"I'm going out to see them and tell them who we are."

Before her mother can stop her, Julie jumps out of her side door and rushes toward the nearest group. Anxious by her daughter's impulsive behavior, the President shouts to James.

"James? Go to her! She might need help."

"Yes, Ma'am."

Natas smiles, as he becomes amused by the circumstances.

It is you that needs help woman. Not your daughter!

He steps out of the Hummer before James and hurries up to Julie who is now in deep conversation with a burly six-foot man in his forties. She smiles as Natas approaches.

"Nat? This is Peter Becker. He has led these people all the way down from Oregon."

Hiding his normal irritation of the burden of welcoming even more survivors, Natas offers the affable man his best and sincerest smile, and shakes hands.

"Glad to know you all sir. You all must have had the same dreams."

"So it seems. What happens now?"

Needing to be included, Julie's mother comes to join them. Peter's jaw drops when he recognizes the country's leader.

"Ah! Madam President. All is not lost then. Do we still have a Government? Moreover, can 'you' explain to us here, what's going on?"

To answer, she puts on a brave face.

"We do not have any Government. The only thing we seemed to have fathomed out about this whole situation is that we are being controlled by a higher power."

Pondering for a few seconds, Peter rubs his chin.

"That's what most of us think."

Apprehensive, James joins his boss. Assessing the uncertain situation, he offers Peter a reassuring smile.

"How long have you all been here?"

"We arrived yesterday. A few others were here already."

Distant dust being caused by an aging pick up truck, causes Peter to look eastward.

"Here comes another."

The pickup grinds to a stop. Everyone stares with curiosity while the dust settles.

A young woman dressed in tight denims and snug fitting tee shirt that can arouse any man's imagination, climbs out of the truck, stops and returns their stares. Assuming she is in safe company, she then begins walking toward the group. Him focusing on her swaying hips and the rest of her, Natas experiences a strange sensation.

She is the 'angel' from my dream!

As she gets closer to the group, the woman can't help noticing the tall, handsome man dressed in black. Her stomach turns over.

It's him! The one in my dream. I've found him.

Smiling first at Natas, she puts out her hand.

"Hi. I'm Madeline."

Becoming a little jealous, Julie can see that Natas is attracted to this new interloper. To dispel such emotions, she wastes no time in pushing in front of Natas.

"Hi. I'm Julie. This is my mother.The President of the United States!"

Madeline is surprised for a second, but soon realizes the impotence of the position.

"Sorry you have nothing to govern anymore. Ma'am!"

Disturbed by the heavy sarcasm, Natas offers Madeline a relaxing smile, while hiding his concern.

I can see this attractive young woman needs to be reigned in.

"Where have you come from?"

"Oh – er - on my own mostly. I did pass some folks in New Mexico."

Natas does not believe her.

She is lying. why?

Still uncomfortable with this woman, Julie digs a little deeper.

"Why didn't you stop and join them?"

To answer, Madeline becomes nervous and gazes at Natas for support.

"It is this dream telling me I had to come here."

His patience dwindling, James leans toward his boss and is discreet as he whispers in her ear.

"I think I ought to rally everyone. Get us all together to form a proper safe convoy."

Weighing up the situation, his boss agrees.

"Excellent thinking James."

James indicates to Peter as he walks toward the main group. They both stand together while James addresses everyone.

"I would like you all to join us to make a more organized convoy, which will be safer and..."

A voice shouts out.

"Safer from whom? There 'is' nobody."

Understanding their point, James turns to Peter for help.

"Ask them what type of dreams they've been having?"

Willing to help, Peter nods and turns to his group.

"Hands up who dreamt of this crater?"

As about thirty hands go up, Peter asks again.

"Okay. Right, how many of you had another type of dream?"

A young boy of about thirteen is eager to raise his hand.

"I dreamt I was going down a long straight road, and at the end the sun is changing color and each side of the road is miles of sand."

Peter acknowledges the boy with a smile, and asks the rest another question.

"Who else had a similar dream?"

Another thirty raise their hands. Peter thanks them and turns to James.

"Seems fairly equal. What do you think?"

Wanting to get organized into on convoy as soon as possible, James bites his bottom lip from impatience.

"Let me talk to them."

As James takes a step nearer to the group, he hides his agitation and acts casual.

"Most of our convoy has had the sun dream from the start, but quite recently a few of us dreamt about this crater. This is the reason we came here, because we suspected there might be some more survivors. Now we are all together, I suggest we all join together on this momentous journey."

Disturbing the silence, a skeptical voice reverberates out of the center of the group.

"How do you know where it is? What is the point of us all going there anyway?"

Sensing James floundering, Natas comes and stands next to him. As a token of support, Natas touches James's forearm as a signal he wants to address the group. Relieved and glad of the help, James lets him go forward. Taking charge being natural to Natas, he clears his throat while scanning the curious faces.

"Fellow survivors. Do any of you remember Gus? He was on television with the Pope and flew on Air force One by kind permission of our gracious President..."

Before he can finish, almost everyone raises their hands. Suppressing his normal irritation Natas, offers them his sincerest smile.

"That is excellent! Because you see, I am closely connected to him. We go back a long way. These dreams we have all been having are closely connected to him, and what is happening here..."

While a lot of the group are not reassured, he pauses while he needs to get across his message.

"So, to answer your questions. We know exactly where we are going. The point of us all going there is because of a higher calling. It is going to determine the rest of our lives, and the future prosperity of our new world."

While his words sink in, there is a thoughtful pause. Thinking it through,

Peter gives his opinion.

"As you have all trusted me so far, I think we ought to join our new friends here. What do we have to lose? There is nothing here - especially water."

Among the murmurs of agreement as the people begin to organize to join up with Natas, James expresses his thanks by shaking his hand, and then joining his relieved, but tired boss.

In the meantime, Natas feels a tug on his arm. He turns to find Madeline glaring at him with a hint of sarcasm.

"If they believe that, they'll believe anything."

Becoming annoyed by this woman who is disturbing his emotions, he is discreet as he moves her away from the others.

"What are you talking about? I meant every word."

"Oh, come on! You and Gus go back a long way? What does that mean?"

"It means what I said."

"Why aren't you with him then?"

He hesitates.

She knows Gus?

"I would, if he was alive."

"He 'is' alive. I've been with him the last few days."

All of a sudden he feels sick to the stomach. Picturing Gus falling at the UN building, he tries to appear relaxed. Not wanting to give this woman the impression he and Gus are the ultimate in enemies, he acts caring.

"You say he is alive? How do you know I am talking about the same person?"

"He's the same guy all right! Everyone called him Gus, and he performed a miracle while I was there."

Knowing Gus's power, his stomach is becoming more unsettled.

"What type of miracle?"

"An old Indian chief had been blind for years. So, Gus healed him and restored his sight."

Feeling as if he is about to explode, Natas has to turn away to gain some sort of control over his anger and disappointment .

Becoming confused by his actions, she senses his distaste.

"Are you okay? It's as if you don't want to hear any of this?"

He turns back to her with tears of anger running down his face. However, he makes it look like tears of joy.

"Yes! I am fine. I am so relieved to hear that he is all right. Tell me, why did you leave his group? I would have thought it being be more practical for you to stay."

Her response is to take his hand and stand closer to him. He can smell her natural perfume, which is beginning to arouse his basic sexual desire. Sensing the affect she is having on him, she gazes deep into his eyes for a reaction.

"I'm not a very practical woman. I have a tendency to do things on a whim. I also dreamt of you. It was so powerful - I had to find you."

Before he can react, she stands up on her toes and plants a soft kiss on his unsuspecting mouth. As he is not resisting, she holds the kiss for a few seconds, and then takes her time in withdrawing. Relishing the electricity rushing through him, all thoughts of Gus leave his mind.

"I dreamt of you as well."

"You did? What does that tell you?"

"It tells me we are to be as one."

Still holding his hand, she still gazes up at him. Her smoky gray-green eyes brighten with excitement, as she brings his hand up to her breast.

"When? I want to be as one 'now'."

Imagining this beautiful woman naked and within his grasp, his torrid emotions and desire is getting the better of him.

She must be here to take me back. God has sent her to me!

His eyes blazing with passion, he releases her breast, grabs her by the shoulders and looks straight into her eyes.

"I've been waiting for you. Tonight we will reach paradise together. Meanwhile, stay close to me. I need your help and support while traveling with these people. When we have finished with them, we shall be free to be as one, and then go back."

To her disappointment, he releases his grip, and leaves her to join the others. While glaring at him helping some children into her truck, her yearning for him turns to irritation.

Go back where? You're mine buddy! You and I are going to run this new world.

61

More Survivors

Gus' convoy is now approaching Flagstaff. The Interstate Forty is so cluttered with damaged cars and deserted trucks, the convoy has to weave in and out of the stranded vehicles to make it's way to the nearest block of crumbling buildings.

As Garth stops the bus, the afternoon sun appears hypnotic by casting long eerie shadows everywhere. To him, the whole scene looks like the aftermath of a battle zone. There is a tap on the door of the bus ripping Garth from his imagination. Gus is outside indicating to him to open the door. Sensing an urgency, Garth pulls the lever that opens the door, while rising from the driver's seat. Adding to the seriousness, there is an air of anxiousness in the bus, as he looks around at the crammed passengers.

"Stay here everyone. Gus and I are going to look around."

Tizzy, who is sitting behind the driver's seat, stares at him with eyes taut with fear.

"Be careful."

Hesitating for a second, he offers her a reassuring smile, and then exits the bus.

Meanwhile, Gus indicates to Garth to come with him, so they are out of earshot from the bus. His face stiff with anxiety, Gus points to a thin trail of smoke rising over the ruins.

"What do you think?"

"It could be people or it could be a broken gas main. Let's check."

While they trek through the rubble until they are quite near the smoke, Gus stops behind a tall wall and signals Garth to listen. Concentrating, they can both hear voices and the sounds of animals. Not sure what they are facing, they become cautious as they step out from the shelter of the wall. Now standing in a clearing, they stare in amazement at a scene of several hundred men, women, and children with an abundance of domestic and farm animals roaming nearby. Surprised at such a gathering, Gus looks at Garth for a reaction. At the same time, a startled voice from the group shouts out.

"Look! There's someone there."

The crowd showing no fear as they inspect these two strangers, a heavyset woman in her fifties separates from her group and takes a few steps forward. In a welcoming manner she invites the new visitors to join her.

Reassured by the warm welcome, the two men scramble down a bank of rubble to meet up with the woman. Not hesitating, she puts out her hand and offers them a warm, welcoming smile.

"Hi, there! Welcome to our humble dwelling. My name is Susan and these are all my friends."

Still not believing their luck, the two men introduce themselves. Before they can explain their circumstances, a deep voice bellows out from the center of the crowd.

"Master? Is that you?"

Gus shelters his eyes from the sun to see who is the owner of the familiar voice.

"My God! Is that you Will?"

To the amusement of the crowd, Will strides through another group to greet his old friend. As he comes up to Gus, tears of gratitude fill his joyful eyes. He pauses, as if he can't believe his eyes, smiles and then wraps his heavy arms around Gus. Not satisfied with that, he lifts his friend up a couple of feet above the ground. In the meantime, Garth is amazed at the sight of this giant of a man lifting his friend as if he is a rag doll.

When Will decides to let Gus down, he turns to the crowd, and shouts.

"This is Jesus. The one I have been telling you about."

Susan's reaction is to chuckle with affection.

"So you're his Jesus? How sweet. He has done nothing but talk about you ever since we found him wondering with a bunch of children on our way here."

In seeing Gus, the 'bunch' of children appear out of the crowd and come running up to Gus. Witnessing this delightful scene, Garth is amazed at the way these twenty odd children hold their arms out wide to greet him. Enthralled by seeing Gus, another voice bellows out from the center of this community.

"You were right all the time."

Gus looks up to see Walter Cameron, the television personality who almost bled to death in the green room at the Television studio. Still hanging onto the children with one hand, Gus puts out his free hand to Walter who is glad to take it.

"It's so good to see you young man. I hope you can explain all this to the likes of me and all these fine people here."

On being introduced to Garth, Susan is listening to Walter, and has become curious about these new additions to their community.

"Yes! Please explain all this to us. One minute we are living our normal, every day lives and the next is like hell has come to take us over."

Taking a step forward to reassure, Gus grips her hand and conveys to her a grateful smile.

"This certainly isn't hell. It's a new beginning. A second chance."

Meanwhile, Tizzy is becoming worried and looks at Silver Eagle for reassurance.

"They've been gone a long time. I hope everything is okay?"

The Chief groans a little as he releases his stiff joints from his seat as the same time as Eva rises from hers. Being the man he is, he indicates to Eva to stay put.

"I will go. The children will need you if anything happens."

Her mind still disturbed about Madeline leaving, she is reluctant to agree, and sits back down.

I will never leave you Gus.

Realizing he has kept his own group waiting, he touches Garth's arm as a gesture that he is going back to the bus. Garth acknowledges. As Gus turns and begins to scramble back up rubble slop, he almost bumps into Silver Eagle. Gripping Gus's arm, the chief appears anxious.

"We were getting worried. Maybe more slip ups?"

Understanding the sarcasm, Gus has to laugh.

"Not here! These are all good people...."

"As far as you know."

Supporting each other, they both carry on toward the bus.

Eva and her son Ryan hold their breath with relief as they observe the two men appear out of the ruins.

"Mom? We just have to get used to seeing good people all the time. We don't have to worry if there are any bad guys waiting around every corner."

Amazed by his wise words, she rubs his head and smiles in gratitude.

Meanwhile, as Gus and the Chief arrive back at the bus, Gus sits in the driver's seat and turns to all the passengers.

"I apologize for being so long. There is a whole community behind that ruin, so we're going to join them and rest for tonight. Then tomorrow we shall all depart for our final destination. Eva? Can you drive the fueled truck for me and lead the others? Just follow the bus."

In the next thirty minutes, the convoy is cautious as it makes its way around the flattened buildings to join the new community.

Over an hour has passed. The air becomes cool as the sun goes down creating long shadows, as everyone gets warm comfortable as possible around several new bonfires. Many sit on the ground, near the fires, especially the children, some older adults sit in makeshift chairs and seats consisting of upturned boxes, buckets and small metal drums. The remainder sits or stands in small groups on the nearby trucks.

Gus and Garth have been given folding picnic chairs near one of the fires, among the children. Will and Ryan are sitting together on the ground near Gus. Susan, who seems to have been given the authority to organize these proceedings, is standing behind Gus. Her hands resting on his shoulders, she scans the whole area with a sense of satisfaction.

Keeping her hands on Gus's shoulders, she signals everyone to be quiet so she can give her opening address.

"I want to thank you all for introducing me to Gus and his friends on this calm and pleasant evening. I hear from some of you that Gus is quite a celebrity, especially from the last few weeks before all this turmoil happened. Please accept my apologies Gus for not of having heard of you. Possibly, because I live out in the wilds of Oklahoma, miles from anyone, and I don't ever watch TV. I'm always busy looking after my farm since my dear spouse died three years ago..."

She is reluctant to withdraw her hand from Gus's shoulder to wipe an escaping tear. Keeping her pride in tact, she replaces her hand on the neglected shoulder and continues.

"Then, I kept getting this strange dream about following the sun down this long sandy road. Also, for the first time in my life, I experienced an earthquake, which flattened my house and farm. The power went out, never to return. That wasn't all! The thing that frightened me the most was the bright beams of light coming from the sky. The horizon was full of them. I felt lucky that none came near me. I have learnt since that these beams of light actually sort of vaporized people, like science fiction. It seems that Gus can explain all this to us and put our minds at rest."

As if to signal Gus, she withdraws her hands, and steps back to her own improvised seat. On standing, Gus looks down to Susan, smiles in appreciation and then prepares to talk.

"Thank you Susan. On behalf of my fellow travelers and myself, I would like to thank you all for your hospitality and kindness. Some of you here already know me or know about me. However, I am going to address the good people who do not. First, I will try to explain what is going on, and why it's happening."

Aware of the apprehensive faces looking up to him, he pauses for a few seconds to gather his thoughts.

"A couple of weeks ago I went on television, had a rally and did various things to warn the world how it would end in one year if all the greed, corruption and persecution didn't stop. Well, as you might have expected, I was jeered and laughed at, as if I was a mad man. Not by every one, but by most people. Therefore, it was taken out of my hands and today is the result. All I can see on your faces is utter confusion. That being so, I will explain where we are right now. You and whomever you've met and will meet on this planet since the earthquake - are the chosen ones. These are good and genuinely righteous people left behind to look after this delicate world of ours..."

Sensing their continuing confusion, he pauses to to look at Garth for support. Knowing by his friend's encouragement he has all his support, he carries on.

"From now on there will be only 'one' law. That being so, we do not need police or military to keep order because we do it all ourselves. We have all had the same dream, which is why we are here on our way to a destination that will decide our final future..."

A young girl of about ten, raising her hand, breaks the silence.

"Why were you chosen to lead us?"

Reticent in announcing his true identity, Gus hesitates. Instead, Garth stands up and answers the girl.

"He was chosen - because he is Jesus! He has returned to save us."

Expecting disbelief, he now turns to face the rest of the group to survey the stunned faces.

"I know this for a fact. I have seen him work and help people as he did over two thousand years ago. We have all had the same dream of traveling down this desert road towards the sun that changes color. It appears a bit scary, but it's not. I 'believe' in this man and so must you. That's why you have all been spared."

Having said his piece, Garth sits. The reaction from the crowd is still quiet and tense. An older man standing at the rear calls out.

"Why so much desolation and killing, just for us fortunate few?"

Gus, still standing, scans the curious faces who are still looking for answers.

"What I'm going to say is going to shock most of you. However, first I will give you some valuable history so you will be prepared for what's to come."

He turns to his right, takes three steps, and scans his audience.

"As you know, it says in the bible that Jesus was the Son of God who died on the cross to take on all our sins. That is an underestimation of the whole situation. He was the Son of God, as we 'all' are God's children. He was resurrected by his soul remaining alive and going to God..."

As the memories come flooding back from that precarious time, he pauses before going into the final onslaught.

"That was a graphic demonstration of what happens to a person who has God inside them. It explains that when we die, by whatever method, our souls live on. Look at me, I have the soul of Jesus. I have been given the task again to take away the sins of man. With one difference, I had more help this time..."

He stops to look up into the night sky. Closing his eyes, he takes a deep breath, and then looks back at the people.

"All of you plus - everyone else alive in the world tonight has been chosen to take away the sins of man, because you 'all' have the soul of God. These souls go back since time began, and will continue forever. What has happened over the years is that people were being born with evil in their genes and eventually that evil took everything over. Sometimes in big ways, but many times in subtle ways. I could give you a million examples of selfishness, hypocrisy and not caring. It is all evil, and after a time it becomes the norm. Now you will ask, why wasn't this evil wiped out years ago? It was. Way back there has always been famines, petulance and disease, which remain with us up to now. We know it today as virus' bacteria and pollution disease, as well as hurricanes, tornadoes,

563

floods, volcanic eruptions and earthquakes. Unfortunately, this type of mechanism is crudely ineffective. Good people died as well as bad. In the meantime, with some evil men prospering at the expense of the majority, this evil has become increasingly prevalent. In the last two thousand years alone, there has been more murder and carnage in the name of 'God' than at any other time. This is classic Satan doing his work..."

The intense curiosity filling the air, he pauses again to study the crowd. Sensing they are warming toward him, he continues.

"Back to the present. Now is everyone's second and final chance. The light beams and the earthquakes were the first of the final stages. Then, if there was still any more evil, the fire, followed by the storms, should have cleaned up what was left. However, there is still the 'final' conclusion to come. That is why we are all on this journey. I am unable to give you anymore information, because that's all I know."

Knowing he has not convinced everyone, he turns to his left and walks three steps back to his original position.

"God is love! So, all of you here are full of that love for your fellow Citizens - the sons and daughters of God. Those who did not have love in their hearts are the sons and daughters of Satan - the Devil's messiah."

Becoming weary, he places his hand on Garth's shoulder for support, but still gazes at his audience.

"You all have a direct line to God. From now on there is no need of 'Religion' and church hierarchy, because you're 'all' the children of God. Tomorrow we 'all' take that final journey to the desert in California, so we can start building the final Garden of Eden."

Fatigue taking over, he bows his head in respect. Succumbing to his message, they all respond by giving him a heartfelt applause.

In the meantime, Natas' expanding convoy is parked in a desolate area of Blythe in the Californian desert. Everyone is cheerful as they settle down for the evening around several campfires. Not wanting to be here, Natas has walked away from the main group to have some solitude. He finds a small boulder to sit on so he can look up at the clear moonless desert sky.

"Why do I have to continue with this journey? It all seems so senseless, traveling to a - excuse the expression, 'God forsaken place'. For what? Why do you not take me back now?"

"Maybe we still need you."

Julie is standing behind him. As she places her delicate hand on his left shoulder, he freezes. Sensing his insecurity, she removes her hand and stands next to him.

Her smell filling his nostrils, his instinct is to grab her forearm while looking up to her.

"Do you really think so? What use have I been so far?"

Relishing the warmth of his hand, she crouches down to his level, so their eyes meet.

"We would not have got this far without you. I know I could not have done it without you."

His response to her compliment is to release his grip on her arm and bring her hand up to his lips.

"I appreciate that vote of confidence, but you know I shouldn't even be here..."

Feeling her shudder by his soft kisses, his eyes seem to penetrate.

"I am not one of the 'good' guys like all those people sitting there. I am the worst there is. A mistake! I should have been taken with all the other scum."

Not believing him, and her heart palpitating from her desire, she rests her other hand on his head.

"God doesn't make mistakes. You're here for a good reason. Perhaps it is to love me? You have been forgiven and given this chance to redeem yourself. When you have and love me, you will be taken back."

"You have it all worked out my dear."

Madeline is standing behind them both. Julie almost jumps out of her skin, when Madeline places her hand on her head.

"What pretty hair you have."

She moves around and sits on the dirt facing them both, but looking straight at Julie.

"So you know who he really is, and you love him? So, what do we do now? Tell everyone?"

Not letting go of Natas's hand, Julie is stuck for words. Not wanting Julie to be hurt, Natas speaks instead.

"No, we do not! Julie is the only one who knows who I am. She is helping me to get back. It must stay that way."

Madeline suppresses a smirk and takes hold of Julie's hand.

"That is very noble of you. Now we have a secret between the three of us, which must be kept. Perhaps we could enjoy this 'threesome' in other ways."

His imagination going awry, he releases Julie's hand with a final kiss.

"You better go. Your mother will be looking for you. I'll talk to you later."

Confused by Madeline's suggestion, Julie is reluctant to leave. Still looking at Natas for some reassurance, he offers her a nod and a smile as she leaves.

Witnessing all this with a continual smirk, Madeline remains in the same position, while she watches Julie head toward the crowd to look for her mother.

Madeline now turns her eyes to Natas who is now becoming uncomfortable in this woman's presence.

"You are not going back anywhere. You and I are going to run this new world between us."

She stands and places both of her hands on each of his shoulders. Now inches apart, she pulls his head is up against her stomach.

"That my love is my womb. It is waiting expectantly for your seed to produce the 'ultimate' Messiah."

Even though he is weakening toward her by her her smell and closeness, he pushes her away.

"You are crazy. I do not need anything like you. I have the power myself. Yes, we could have fun in a physical way, hence your suggestion of a threesome with Julie, of which I do not approve. The only reason I am here is that I have been allowed to stay, so I can redeem myself and go back. However, I am still wondering why you have been allowed to stay as you crave evil so much."

Madeline's answer is to release a humorless laugh.

"It just goes to prove how your God is not so clever after all. I tried to love Gus. I was even willing to mend my ways, but he refused me saying that his 'mission' was more important. Now, young Julie I can do something with. I can see how she worships you."

"She is an innocent young girl who loves me and is trying to help. She accepts me for what I am."

"That's perfect! She'll be our first disciple."

Troubled by his rising desire, he is becoming more nervous of this woman and wants to get back with the others. He begins to rise, but before he is able, she grabs his head in her hands, and peers into his eyes.

"Don't resist what is inevitable."

She lowers her head and plants a warm soft kiss on his pensive mouth. Him not resisting, she parts her lips and explores with the tip of her tongue. Him now weakening, she straddles his lap and positions his head against her full breasts.

"Come my love. I will raise you to the extreme heights of pleasure you would never find with any another woman."

Without saying a word and his eyes glazed with yearning, he pulls his head back a little and strokes her breasts. Expectant of what is to come, she moans with pleasure as he cradles her in his arms. After a few seconds they stand, and with one sweeping movement, he carries her further out into the dark desert.

Having found a secluded spot, she whispers in his ear.

"Now my darling! NOW…"

Still shaking off Madeline's offer, Julie is becoming anxious about Natas' absence.

It's over an hour since I spoke to him.

While her mother is standing next to her observing the secure atmosphere of the crowd, she senses her daughter's unease.

"What is it my dear? You've been on edge for the last hour."

"It's nothing mother. I haven't seen Nat for a while. The last time I saw him he was talking to that Madeline woman."

"Do I sense some jealousy in your voice? He is very capable that one. So, I wouldn't worry if I were you."

Half listening to her mother, Julie's heart lifts as she notices Natas coming toward them. She also is observing Madeline walking two paces behind looking relaxed with a satisfied grin on her face. As Natas approaches her with a pensive smile, she notices he appears flushed and disheveled. Madeline, on the other hand is calm as she smiles at Julie.

Now noticing Natas, the President gazes at him with a curious expression.

"There you are! We thought you had wondered off in the desert and got lost."

Meanwhile, Madeline comes up to Julie and slides her hand around her waist.

"He was quite safe. He was with me - working on his future."

Cringing at the thought, Julie grips hold of Madeline's hand to remove it from her waist.

"Oh? Is that what you call it? And what is his future?"

Not disturbed by Julie's rejection, she plants a soft kiss on Julie's cheek and whispers.

"Come, I'll show you."

Madeline then looks at Julie's mother and raises her voice.

"Do you mind if I borrow your daughter for a moment - Madam President?"

Before Julie's mother can answer, Madeline is whisking Julie away toward the desert. Observing the President's unease, Natas puts out a reassuring hand.

"She is in fine hands Ma'am. I totally underestimated that woman."

Hiding her confusion at what is going on, she takes the initiative.

"Tell me Nat, on behalf of all these people, what is 'your' future, and further more what is 'ours'?"

568

Without answering, he looks into her eyes as if searching for something, gives her arm a gentle squeeze, and then leaves to go to one of the fires.

Meanwhile, Madeline is trying to make conversation with a reluctant Julie.

"Julie? I want to apologize to you about my behavior. You are a very sweet girl and in no way do I want to hurt or upset you, especially, when it concerns Nat.

As I see it, you care for him and want to make sure he comes to no harm. Am I correct?"

A skeptical Julie hesitates, and then answers.

"Yes! I do care and love him. So much that I want to make sure that he will be good enough to go back to God."

Looking into Julie's defiant eyes, Madeline softens her tone and gives Julie a hug.

"That is how I feel. I love him too. I love him so much that I am willing to give up everything - so he will go back. If he doesn't redeem himself, he will be taken from us. If that happens, I will go with him anyway."

Sidetracked by this woman's warmth and softness, Julie does not resist the hug.

"We seem to want the same thing."

Madeline takes Julie's hand and brings it up to her lips, gives it a gentle kiss and lowers it to her stomach.

"We do. We both love him and still have his interest at heart. I want us to be close and keep with him all the time so we can guide him to make the right decisions, especially in the next few days. As a sign of our closeness, I want you to be the first to know. In time, my womb is going to grow to bear his child..."

"You can't! You will be having a child of the...."

"The Devil? No, my dear. Not if he goes back."

Still in Madeline's arms, Julie is becoming confused, her mind in turmoil. *What is happening to me? This woman appears sincere, but there's something not quite right.*

"All right! You and I will do as you say, but this has to be 'our' secret."

Madeline's response is to tighten her hug, while her appreciating lips plant a soft kiss on Julie's cheek. To Julie's surprise, her mouth is then covered by the same soft lips. After a couple of seconds, Madeline withdraws and gazes into Julie's eyes.

Got you my sweet. I see you enjoyed that. Plenty more where that came from. From now on, you're mine!

"Yes, my sweet. Our secret."

Tingling with excitement, she kisses Julie's forehead, cheeks, and then her lips.

Receiving an even longer kiss from this other woman, Julie is becoming more confused and aroused.

While this is going on, Natas feels the need to explain to these people they are leaderless, and need to be guided until they reach the final destination.

God? Why have you not contacted me? I am confused. A woman who suddenly has a strong influence over me has just seduced me. Did you send her, or is she on her own agenda?

Standing by and looking down into one of the fires, he ponders.

What do I say that they do not know already? Am I worthy of them? Will they even follow me?

As the crowd become aware of his need to talk, he lifts up his head and begins to address them.

"Friends? I wish to inform you of a few important things. After that I would appreciate any questions or comments you might have."

Now attracting their attention, he moves to a position in which he is in the center of the whole area with the fires surrounding him. Beginning to feel at ease from their heat, he scans the curious faces.

"It seems we have discovered that our friend and possible savior - Gus, is alive and heading to the same destination as us."

As a sense of excitement and anticipation fills the air, Natas continues.

"I found this out from our friend Madeline, who joined us at the crater. She had come from the group that contained Gus. By all accounts, he is still doing his miracles. That only goes to prove that God or some higher authority is guiding us all with the same dream..."

Waiting for the enthusiasm of the crowd to calm, he then continues.

"After all our experiences of these last few days, there are many questions to be answered. As I see it, and many of you may feel the same, a force beyond our control has almost annihilated the human race leaving small groups like us. I hope there is more, but we have no way of knowing. There is a thought among you that we few have been chosen by God, and all those who were vaporized were all - evil. Then the fire, and the mother of all storms followed, thinning us out even more, and we still do not know how it is all going to end..."

Listening to the murmurs and expressions of doubt, Natas takes advantage by raising his voice.

"Listen my friends! Do you really think a merciful God would kill his own like this, just to get control? Somehow I don't think so. I think there is something 'else' up there that we cannot even imagine. Something evil, like aliens or even our own military testing a new secret weapon that went terribly wrong. The thing is, we 'still' do not know. However, do not forget we have our gracious President here. Perhaps she can enlighten us all."

Nervous at being put on the spot, the President suppresses her anxiety, as she steps forward into the light of the fires.

"I can only tell you what I know. All the time I was in the White House, either as your President or as the Vice President, there were no secret military weapons of this magnitude being developed. However, I can confirm that Gus informed me and my daughter that if humankind didn't stop all the greed, corruption, exploitation and bigotry that was ruining millions of peoples lives, causing unemployment, bad health care, bankruptcies and climate change, things would be taken out of our hands. Everything that has happened in the last few days - he predicted."

Now finished, she does not attempt to go back to her former seat. As Natas glares at her in mock respect, he can see the crowd is acknowledging her speech. So, to keep favor with this crowd, he offers her a sincere smile.

"Thank you Madam President. That reassures us that it is not the military that is trying to kill us. In addition, thank you for the informative news about Gus' prediction. However, that is all it was ladies and gentlemen, a mere prediction.

People have been making predictions for thousands of years to no avail. Gus was right in one sense: man cannot treat his fellow man the way he has been doing without repercussions. Therefore, what have we learnt here? Precisely nothing! My humble opinion is, we all stick together and wait to see what happens. Our very survival? Is it our destiny or is it all just luck? What ever it turns out to be, I would be honored to lead you in that journey. Are there any questions?"

Not far from Natas, an attractive woman in her early thirties stands up. Stirring his interest, he notices she has a tailored suit that emphases her hour glass figure. She also looks well educated. She glares straight at him.

"By your attitude you're suggesting that all these events do not seem to be designed in a deliberate way. How come that all of us here, who are fundamentally good people, have been chosen to survive? Surely, sir, this is fortuitous, as Gus originally forecasted and not as you suggest - just luck."

Not expecting this challenge, Natas is becoming irritated by this woman. However, he hides his annoyance and conveys to her a beaming smile.

Okay you smart bitch! Do not play with me.

"You could be perfectly right! However, we do not 'really' know, only speculate. Let us suppose that Gus and all you here are right, and all the bad guys are gone and only kind, gentle, loving people are left. It means 'one' thing and 'one' thing only. You are 'not' in charge of your own destiny any more. Your freedom of choice has gone. Your kind gentle lives are going to be run by a dictator. And who is that dictator? It is God. It will be the new Garden of Eden with God in charge of your every move. With you not having a say in anything about your own existence, is that what you really want?"

The woman is quick to answer him back.

"Is that so bad? Considering what we've all been living with - a world engulfed in evil - caused by freedom of choice."

Not letting her get to him, Natas keeps right on smiling, and is relieved as a teenage boy raises his hand. Natas turns away from the woman, and acknowledges the boy, as he puts forward his question.

"If we all obey the Ten Commandments, will God be happy and not punish us?"

As Natas observes murmurs of agreement amongst everyone, he realizes he has to play clever, otherwise they will ignore him and he will lose face.

"All right my young friend. If that is what you want, that's fine. I agree, you will have peace on God's terms. And if you obey the rules you will have happy but suppressed lives. I am the last person here to stop you. I will accompany you to your final destination where you will 'have' to choose between having a good life, making your own decisions, or living a secure, but dictated life. What ever you all decide, I will support you. Thank you for listening to me."

Suppressing his frustration, he is abrupt when leaving. While wanting to get away into the desert to search for some solitude, he finds a large boulder to lean against. Staring at the distant fires, he shuts his eyes and concentrates his mind.

Why do you not contact me? I am not even dreaming about you anymore. Why? Do you have something else lined up for me, now we know that your prodigy Gus is alive and well? What do I do with these people..?

The sound of feet on the gravelly sand coming toward him interrupts his thoughts. He opens his eyes to find Madeline, with her arm around Julie's shoulder. Both of them looking worried, Julie is the first to talk.

"There you are. Madeline and I were wondering why you left so abruptly."

His energy dissipating, he leans against the boulder for support. He offers the two women a confident smile, but inside, he wants to vomit.

"My dear ladies! I left abruptly, as you put it, because I felt I would have a lesser headache if I had a brick wall handy to bang my head against."

Concerned by his attitude, Julie is becoming puzzled.

"What do you mean?"

He is becoming restless with agitation as he stands away from the boulder.

"They are not listening to me! All I want is to help them so they do not make the same old mistakes."

Noticing the tears forming in his eyes, Julie is the first to come to him and take hold of his forearm. She can see, even in the night light he appears to be on the verge of breaking down.

"The only mistake they would make if they ignored the dreams and not go to where we have been called. The final destination is where we all can start afresh."

His response to such an innocent statement is to bring her hand to his mouth and smother it with soft kisses. Feeling her shudder with emotion, he then focuses his eyes on hers. Her irrational passion for him is causing her heart to pound, and the warmth of his mouth is sending even stronger signals of desire through her. At the same time, his voice seems to be coming from inside her head.

"My love. Tomorrow we will be there. I need you by my side to help me guide these poor souls."

Her breathing becomes heavy as she feels Madeline hands sliding under her armpits and begin stroking her breasts. Julie's desire now reaching a new height, she is at the stage of giving in to this mysterious experience, when her mind clears and she pulls away. Her heart still pounding, she grips Madeline's hands and glares at Natas as sweat appears on her forehead. She takes a deep breath, and then howls a cry from deep inside her throat.

"Oh my God! What are we doing?"

Not waiting for a reply, she turns and runs off toward the glowing campfires.

Madeline's reaction is to burst out laughing.

"We almost had her! She could now be carrying your seed. Maybe next time?"

Shocked by her morbid utterance, he reacts.

"What 'are' you saying?"

"I'm saying you got her so aroused, it frightened her. Don't worry she will go away and coolly think about what she has discovered, and how she enjoyed these new sensations. Then she will conclude that her passion for you is so powerful, she will be willing to accept your seed."

Shocked, but seeing the sense in this discussion, Natas ponders.

"She is a mere child. The whole thing is ridiculous! I keep telling you she only wants to help me to go back..."

Knowing he is lying, she wraps both her arms around his neck and stares hard into his eyes.

"It's not as ridiculous as it seems, and you damn well know it! You almost had her. You have always had this effect on women. So, with my help and joining in the fun, you could have a harem in our new destination in no time."

His ego being stroked, and becoming weakened by her touch, as her hand rests against his yearning crotch, he is unable to resist her present intentions.

Meanwhile, the President becomes concerned as her daughter comes rushing up to her and James.

"Are you all right my dear?"

Appearing disoriented, Julie does her best to answer.

"I think so Mother. I am going lie down somewhere."

James studies his boss's daughter as she leaves and heads toward one of the trucks.

"I have a nagging feeling your daughter has just experienced her first time at being a young woman."

"What the hell do you mean James?"

Instead of answering, he indicates to a flush looking Natas as he scurries past them with Madeline following.

"It's something to do with him, and maybe her as well."

"How do you know?"

"Just a feeling Ma'am. Just a feeling."

Gripping his arm for support, the President looks concerned.

"I think I will have a little heart to heart with my daughter. Keep an eye on things for me."

"Yes, Ma'am."

With a worried expression, he watches his boss hurry amongst the vehicles until she comes to the Hummer. On arriving, she looks inside, stops and listens. She can hear quiet sobbing coming from the rear, but cannot see anything.

"Julie? Is that you?"

Reacting to her mother's request, the sobbing becomes louder. The President then enters the vehicle and makes her way to the rear. Finding her daughter lying face down on the long back seat crying her heart out, she kneels down on the floor and strokes her daughter's hair.

"What is it my dear that can upset you so much?"

The crying pauses, and then Julie wraps her arms around her mother's neck.

"Mother? I really wanted him to...."

"What dear?"

"I wanted Nat to take me. He just kissed my hand and looked right into me with those eyes of his. I felt overwhelmed. Oh Mother, I feel terrible. One side of me feels ashamed, but the other side...."

Trying to keep her voice calm, the President hugs her daughter.

"Yes, dear. Don't worry. It will soon pass. I will have a little chat with our friend Nat."

Becoming agitated, Julie sits up.

"Mother? It's not him. Its me. I'm the one who's at fault."

"You're a child who is being manipulated by a...."

"No! He has never used or taken advantage of me. It has always been me who has taken the initiative."

"Why? He is almost old enough to be your father."

"I don't know! I can't help it. But he has told me secrets – and..."

Shaking with surprise, Julie's mother gets up off the floor and sits next to her daughter.

"Yes? What secrets?"

"He has told me that he loves me, and God has asked him to go back."

"Go back where?"

"To God, of course! Where else?"

Now more confused than ever, Julie's mother gives her daughter an extended hug, and then lays her back down on the seat.

"You sleep for a while. I'm going to see James."

As she weaves her way through the cheerful crowd, she has the overwhelming feeling that they do not accept her as the President anymore, because of the circumstances. In a way, it is a relief, but at the same time, she still feels some sort of responsibility.

Seeing James standing not far from where she left him, she notices how lonely he looks, staring into the fire, and deep in his own thoughts. She stops a few feet away and gazes at him wondering how long he can be loyal to a nobody without a country or government. She steps closer and grips his forearm. He returns her gesture with a warm smile.

"How is she?"

"She is rightly confused. I'm confused, and angry."

"What do you mean?"

"She has a crush on Nat, and he is telling her all his secrets. Reading between the lines, I think she has just experienced her first sexual passion. He must have encouraged her in some way."

"Oh, dear."

His reaction is to grip her forearm and guide her through the crowd until they reach a quiet spot. James then lets go of her arm and looks up into the star filled desert sky.

"Why are you confused? Do you want me to have a quiet word with him?"

"No! I'll do it later."

Needing his support more than ever, she grips his hand with both of hers and stands closer to him.

"James? I 'am' confused about many things lately. First, I don't know what to do about the role as President. Second, I wish Gus were here, so he can explain what is going on; and third, this Nat guy having so much influence over my only child. Julie says he is telling her that he wants to go back to God, and it seems he wants her to help him. What the heck does all that mean?"

Rubbing his accumulating stubble in thought, James tries his best to comfort her.

"We will soon be at the final destination. I hope then Gus will explain it all, so we can get on with our new lives."

On impulse, he places his free hand onto hers and brings it up to his cheek.

"Ma'am? I'm afraid what I am about to tell you is strictly between us."

He lets go of her hands and takes a step backwards as if he needs space to explain.

"Ever since you were Vice President, I have often felt sympathy for you and done my utmost to help you. However, when the late President was assassinated and you were literally thrown into the Presidency, I developed a deep admiration for you as well."

Her response is to reach out to him. Not finished, he ignores the gesture and continues.

"Now, since this latest turn of events that admiration has turned into - love."

Her reaction is to reach out to him again. This time he takes her hand and brings it to his lips. On letting go of her hand, he can see tears forming in her eyes reflecting from the light of the campfires.

"Oh James."

He resists the temptation to hold her so he can carry on explaining.

"You see Ma'am...."

"Call me Joan."

"Well, you see - Joan, this is why I stayed with you and Julie. Working hard to get us this far is because I love you. I know the Presidency is now gone, and I pretended to act as your Secret Service agent, but I didn't do it for the Presidency. I did it for you."

Tears now running down his cheeks, she goes to him, wraps her arms around him and rests her head against his chest.

"Oh, James!"

62

The Last Stage

It is the next day. Gus's new larger convoy is traveling on Interstate Ten heading toward the California desert. The evening sun glows deep orange as it lowers toward the horizon.

The bus leading the convoy, Garth is driving while Gus is in deep conversation with Walter Cameron, seated behind him. Noticing something unusual, Garth shouts and points to some debris near the roadside.

"That looks like an abandoned campsite."

On impulse, he stops the bus. Curios, Gus peers out of the window.

"Silver Eagle and I will take a look."

The two men climb out of the bus and make their way to investigate several extinguished bonfire sites. Silver Eagle is the first to squat down and feel the ashes. His face expressing concern, he then and scans the whole area.

"The fire is still warm. I would say they left early this morning. I estimate that by the tracks left behind there are at least five to six hundred people and about thirty to forty vehicles"

Gus not reacting, the Indian stands and walks a few paces.

"Good place to camp."

Taking his friend's advice, Gus turns to the bus and gives a thumbs up gesture.

"I wonder how many more groups like this are traveling in the same direction?"

Sniffing the air like tracker dog, Silver Eagle offers his opinion.

"I have a strong feeling it is only us and these people."

"What makes you think that?"

His face stoic, Silver Eagle walks back to the ashes.

"I just feel it."

As if caught up in some sort of trance, he begins to amble around the ashes, shuts his eyes and sniffs the air again. Mesmerized by this man's actions, Gus goes to him.

"Can you sense anything else?"

His face still not showing any emotion, the chief carries on pacing around the whole site, and then stops.

"*Bilh-he-neh.* A warning. Everything is *al-tkas-ei,* mixed. I feel two *na-ne-klah,* difficult conflicting emotions. All good, but the other is *al-cha-lil,* detached, and separate. This is the one to fear, because it is an *a-tkel-el-ini,* troublemaker, *jish-cha,* among devils."

"You mean you can sense someone evil amongst these people?"

"That is what I sense. Good will fly with the wind, but evil hangs around like a bad smell. All the good spirits have gone leaving no trace, clean and pure, but the remnants of evil are still here, dirty and foul. It is still okay to camp here."

Admiring this chief for his intuitive skills, and Gus beginning to feel concern, they are somber as they make their way back to the convoy.

It is now dark and fires have been lit. Everyone is in good spirits, and waving at Gus as he walks around and checks everyone's welfare. He smiles with delight as he notices Garth and Tizzy are now inseparable.

Will has offered to dig the latrine trenches - much to everyone gratitude as this hard desert ground can be a tough job to dig. Full of appreciation, Gus wanders up to the latrines and admires the square upright walls in the long straight trenches. As he stands and gazes into the long black holes, he feels a large hand lean on his shoulder.

"Good job, eh."

Grinning, Gus turns to face Will.

"Wonderful. Will, we all appreciate you doing this for us. In addition, I personally want to thank you for looking after the children that got separated when all this devastation occurred ."

Will looks down, as if recollecting.

"They're my family. They look on me to take care of them."

While placing a grateful hand on Will's powerful shoulders, Gus notices this kind giant has lost his stammer.

"We are all your family now."

Both men now consumed by their own thoughts, begin to amble away from the latrines and into the desert. Still within sight of the fires, Will's eyes appear curious as if his mind is gravitating toward a serious thought. He stops walking and looks straight at his mentor.

"What is heaven like when I die?"

Taken aback by such an innocent question, Gus ponders for a few seconds before answering.

"You do not have to die to experience Heaven. Heaven is when God is inside you and you are at peace with yourself and the world around you. When you die, your soul goes on a voyage entering a new life so it can carry on God's love in everything it does."

Looking down at the ground, Will turns this revelation over in his mind.

"What about Hell then?"

"There is no Hell as such. Stories of a cold dark place where bad people's souls go when they die was started way back in the dark ages when the early 'Christian leaders' told there flocks that if you were bad, you would go straight to Hell. The story also went on to say if these 'leaders' were undecided in judging you, your soul would hang around in purgatory until it was decided whether to send it to Heaven or Hell. This is total nonsense. Hell is inside you when you have been taken over by evil, and become bitter, twisted and mean. You can no longer experience true joy and peace."

His eyes softening with gratitude,Will looks into Gus's eyes.

"Good! I haven't been to Hell yet."

The two men laugh with relief. With unspoken words of understanding, they saunter back to the others.

The children become excited as Will sits down with them next to one of the fires.

Looking up at the clear night sky, Gus inhales with a sense of satisfaction, tinged with concern, as he makes his way toward the bus where Eva is waiting. Leaning against the front fender for support, her weary face offers him a reticent smile when he approaches.

"Hi you. I thought you'd got lost. I've been missing you."

Touched by her concern, he reaches out to grip her hand, and conveys a melancholy smile.

"I have been inspecting the latrines and congratulating Will on doing a great job."

Becoming troubled by his weary and depressed expression, she indicates for him to enter the bus. Taking her advice, he wanders to the back of the bus where he sits and releases a heavy sigh. Anxious, she sits close to him and plants a soft kiss on his left cheek.

"What's up my love?"

Appreciating the kiss, he puts out a hand to stroke her cheek.

"I love you Eva. When this is all over, we will be together always."

Reacting with tears stinging her tired eyes, she takes hold of his hand and smothers it in soft kisses.

"You know how much I love you. Right now, I'm worried about you appearing so depressed."

Still holding her hand, he leans back in the seat.

"Not so much depressed, more like being anxious. I have Silver Eagle telling me that the group who is ahead of us has some evil troublemakers. Then I have Will getting concerned about Heaven and Hell. Moreover myself, I don't have a clue what's going to happen to us all tomorrow. Because I don't have a clue about the place at the end of this journey, and what we do when we get there, I am in the dark of how its all going to end."

He lets out another heavy sigh. She gives his hand another kiss as a gesture to try to calm him. However, in her mind, she would rather take him in her arms and sooth away his troubles.

"How does Silver Eagle know about the evil trouble makers?"

"He says he can feel it. I believe him, because he is an exceptional man. He uses his ancient intuitive powers we all have, but rarely use."

"Do we have to worry about some sort of showdown?"

"Maybe. What I fear most is someone stirring up doubt and dissension, which will cause these good people to feel insecure and troubled."

She gives him back his hand, and then strokes his cheek.

"Nothing is going to go wrong. We have God on our side! Do you think after all that has happened so far, God will allow it all to end in a mess?"

He grips her hand in appreciation, and gives it a gentle kiss.

"I hope not. Sometimes I feel that your faith is stronger than mine."

Her insides turn over as she feels his tears of apprehension dripping on her skin.

Meanwhile, Garth leans inside the bus door opening.

"There you are. I was getting worried as I hadn't seen you for a while."

Gus's reaction is to release Eva's hand, and wipe his eyes. Conveying a reassuring smile to his good friend, he rises out of his seat.

"I'm sorry. I'm just taking a breather."

Not convinced, Garth steps further into the bus and surveys his friend's tense face.

"You all right?"

Gus hesitates for a second, and then replies.

"Yes. I'm fine. What do you need?"

"The people want you to talk to them. They're curious, excited, and a little anxious about tomorrow."

"I feel the same. I'm in the dark about it all - the same as them."

Observing Gus floundering, Eva grips his hand.

"You're our leader. We need some sort of reassurance!"

Searching her eyes for some sort of strength, he hesitates.

"I'll – I'll do my best."

Carrying anxious expressions, the three of them leave the bus and work their way to the center of the group.

While Garth and Eva sit down nearby, Gus remains standing as he prepares for the challenge ahead. His face stoic, he looks around at the reticent crowd, forces a smile, and tries to appear relaxed.

"Tomorrow is going to be the beginning of the rest of our lives. Lives that will be the stewards of the new world. A new world full of love and fulfillment. I understand if some of you might feel a touch of anxiety. To be honest I feel the same in my mind, but in my heart, I cannot wait to get started. Just think, a world without any evil. A place where your children can grow up without fear and persecution. However, like anything as precious as this, there is always a price and in this case, it is living under God's law instead of artificial laws. I know many of you still do not understand what has happened. The only thing that you really need to know for now is that you all have been chosen to start the new Garden of Eden..."

Before he can finish, several questioning arms are being raised. His nerves tingling, Gus puts on a smile and points to a teenage girl who stands.

Nervous and self-conscious in front of a crowd, she speaks with emphasis.

"Is it 'really' true that you are Jesus' come to save us all?"

Not waiting for a reaction, she sits back down as other anxious faces gaze at Gus for an answer. As if taken by surprise, Gus raises his head and looks into the night sky. After a few seconds and sensing the pressure, he lowers his head to speak.

"As the same as over two thousand years ago, I have been given the task of guiding and teaching you, that if you live by the word of God your lives will be completely fulfilled. I have previously explained that good souls never die. Your souls go back to the beginning of time when man first set foot on this wonderful creation of Mother Earth. This is why you are here. I have the soul of Jesus and the responsibility of leading you, so you can start building a civilization that will be devoid of discrimination, prejudice and selfishness. You have all survived so far, because you have this love already inside of you. So, building this perfect society will not be a problem, burden or a hardship."

Happy with that explanation, the girl smiles at Gus. Still unsettled, a middle aged, tall slender man stands near the rear of crowd. His bright eyes reflecting the glow of the fire, he puts forward his question.

"Once we arrive at this place tomorrow, what happens then? And what has happened to all the wildlife of the world?"

Not wanting to stand anymore, the man sits. Meanwhile, Gus ponders over this question.

"When we arrive tomorrow, I expect there will be everyone there that has been chosen. I have no idea why this particular spot. All I can say is trust that there is a good reason for it, and it will be a rallying point for us to start afresh. I will be better prepared to tell you more tomorrow. As far as the world's wildlife is concerned, I think you will find that it is already being sorted out. Evil has run among animals as well as humans, so you will find that the surviving species will have been chosen for good reason."

Just as Gus is finishing, Walter Cameron stands. As he is near the rear of the crowd leaning against a truck, his clear crisp echoes through out the area.

"I think I speak for everyone here. We would like to thank you for giving us all hope, inspiration, and to have got us to where we are now to build this new world. Myself, and most of you will say it is about time. I am sure we have all felt the despair that the world could not go on as it was..."

There is an immediate applause. Humbled and honored at this impulse, Gus can't hide his tears. In the meantime, Walter continues.

"I do have one question which I think is important. After tomorrow's conclusion will you be our leader in building this new utopia?"

Finding it difficult to give the answers these people are looking for, Gus bites his lip before answering.

"I will be with you at the start. Then I must go and help other groups, spread out all over the world. I don't know how I'll manage this, but we all have to remember that none of this just happened, it was planned. For example, you will find plenty of food and supplies everywhere to give you a start. There is also a variety of skilled people among you. They will lead in various fields for you to survive and flourish."

Susan, who is quite near Gus, raises her hand.

"If you're not going to stay and lead us how will we govern ourselves?"

Astonished by the question, Gus conveys to her a confident smile.

"You won't need to 'govern' yourselves. You all have God within you, so there will not be any selfishness or self-interest. You will choose your own leaders who will be responsible to only you. Working to God's law simplifies things. If anyone does lose their way, it is up to you all to help that individual. If that doesn't work it will be taken out of your hands - and dealt with."

Hearing such a direct solution, there is a stunned silence. Once understood, everyone knows what that means. In the meantime, Gus continues.

"I assure you, this will only happen as a finality, because you are all being cared for to protect you against evil. I suggest for now that we all get plenty of sleep tonight, for tomorrow is going to be quite a day. Thank you everyone."

63

Unbelievable

Natas' group stops for a break on Interstate Ten. In the distance, the mass of turbine windmills spin in the light breeze. Curious by this man-made spectacle, people clamber out of their vehicles to admire and inspect further.

Natas is amused to hear someone near to him explaining to some children the design of the windmills and how they produce electricity. He feels a tug on his sleeve to find Madeline standing behind him.

"Nearly there?"

"I think so. My feeling is that there will already be some people at the designated area."

"Perhaps Gus is there."

His insides stiffen at the thought.

"I don't think so. My thoughts are that he is behind us and will arrive tomorrow or tonight."

"What are you going to do when he arrives and convinces these people?"

He is becoming aware of his nerves tingling in anticipation.

What am I going to do? I'll have to act fast.

"I am going forward to find our Eldorado, and then persuade these fools I am the way forward. So, by the time his lordship arrives, I will have these idiots in my pocket, eating out of my hand, or whatever."

Frowning, she makes a point of sliding her arm around his waist, and pressing her breasts against his arm.

"Don't you mean – 'we' will have them eating out of 'our' hands?"

"Something like that."

Becoming restless and irritated by Madeline's advances toward Natas, Julie goes to Natas.

"Why are we stopping? This is not the place!"

Madeline smirks at her, and then at him.

"She's right Nat.Let's get moving. The quicker the better. Don't you agree?"

His jaw muscle twitching with tension, he ignores Madeline and offers Julie his best smile.

"You are quite right my dear. We stopped awhile, just to admire the windmills. One of man's creations that seems to have stood up against the anger of God. Well, as I am driving today and the leader of the convoy, I will begin thereof."

Still ignoring Madeline, Natas climbs back into the Hummer and sits in the driver's seat. At the same time, James is checking the GPS with Joan behind him looking over his shoulder.

"Do you think it's very far?"

"I don't think so. By my reckoning and from various details of the dreams we've been having, I think we need to turn north for about ten miles to find the right place."

Demonstrating her affection and trust toward this man, she places her hands on his shoulders.

"Our dreams are facing west, and then looking at the sun changing color."

"You're correct. However, we still have to go north into the desert to find the road with the sand each side that goes west. You see, if we keep going west on Interstate Ten there is no desert sand, only mountains and scrub."

Listening to this conversation, Natas notices a road on his right pointing north. Using his instincts he obliges by turning his steering wheel so the convoy is now heading in the right direction. He smiles with sarcastic satisfaction at the windshield, but talks to James.

"How ironic! We have the wonders of modern science, using GPS from man-made satellites, and yet we all use our premonition dreams to guide us here."

Taking in Natas's observations, Joan leans further over James and whispers in his ear.

"How will Gus make it then?"

Before James can answer, Natas interrupts.

"Madam President! Do not whisper, it is bad manners. How are we all to get along if you start whispering in secret so we cannot hear. To answer your question, do not forget, Gus has super natural powers. He will be with us by tomorrow. Does that help you?"

Sitting back in her chair, uncomfortable at his sarcasm, a soothing hand on her shoulder relieves her a little. Julie, sitting behind her, leans forward to 'whisper' in her ear.

"Won't be long now Mother."

Appreciating her daughters comfort, she pats Julie's hand, and smiles with satisfaction as Natas becomes more agitated.

An hour goes by. Everyone is quiet. The driving is difficult as there are many upturned deserted vehicles, and rubble to drive around. As James is still checking the GPS and almost sure they are in the right area, Natas suppresses his anxiety.

In the meantime, young man jumps out in front of their Hummer waving his arms in the air. Causing more irritation, Natas puts his foot down on the brakes. His agitation heightens as he hears the deafening screech of brakes, as the whole convoy has to grind to a stop. Suppressing his intolerance at the disheveled young man, he winds down the driver's window.

"You damn fool! You nearly got run over."

Ignoring Natas's protest, the young man begins to weep with joy as he leans against the door.

"Are yer the rescue team? We're up there. What's left of us."

Needing to be included, Madeline winds down her window.

"How many of you?"

"Well, thuh's only about a dozen of us from around here, but folks have been showin up here from everywhere ever since thuh quake, and other people just disappearin. What thuh hell's goin on?"

Annoyed by Madeline interfering, Natas does not bother to answer the young man's question. Instead, he asks his own.

"Can you take us to where these people are?"

"Oh yeah. We've bin takin it in turns ter keep watch fer the emergency people ter show up."

Natas is reluctant to let the lad squeeze into the truck, but has no choice. Letting the lad kneel down in between the driver's seat and James, he can look out of the windshield.

"If yer carry on fer about two miles, yer go up to the last crossroads. Turn left and yer will see everyone. Be careful, there's a ton a rubble everywhere and the roads are cracked real bad."

Frowning at the lad's obvious observations, Natas begins to drive with the right amount of caution to satisfy his own instincts. Meanwhile, he can see in his rear view mirror, the rest of the convoy has the sense to follow.

While all this all happening, James is becoming concerned, as he again checks his GPS.

"We're right on the San Andrea's fault line. This is one of the most unstable earthquake areas in the country.Why on earth was 'this' place chosen for us all to start afresh?"

While concentrating on his driving, Natas can't help but smile.

"Perhaps all is not what it appears!"

Joan is becoming nervous and irritated by Natas's sarcasm.

"What do you mean by 'that' statement?"

Enjoying the conflict, Natas continues to smirk while answering.

"My dear Madam President. We are all pawns on this particular chess board. We have all realized that we are here for a specific purpose. What that purpose is? We do not know. However, it is for us to find out, and come to terms with the outcome one way or another."

As Joan is becoming more confused, and annoyed at Natas, James senses her distress.

"It's okay Joan. We'll sort it out."

The two-mile journey seems to be taking forever. They seem to be on Main Street. Each side, there is flattened buildings, stores and shops. It looks as if a giant roller has run over everything, leaving nothing in its wake. The road is beginning to incline. His patience running low, Natas glares in his rear view mirror to find the rest of the convoy is lagging well behind. Releasing a heavy sigh, he decides to stop at a junction. Up ahead on his left there is a ruin of a large hotel. The swimming pools and spas are full of debris. Deck chairs are sprawled across grass areas as if they have just been thrown.

At last, the convoy catches up. Hiding his frustration, Natas starts his engine and moves forward at a slower pace. As the incline increases, they pass an even larger hotel located on their left. Natas can't help noticing everything has caved in on itself. The hotel sign is just visible from the road saying, 'Springs & Spa Hotel.'

Ignoring Natas's heavy breathing of impatience, James comments.

"This whole area is famous for its hot mineral springs, but I still don't see any connection to why we're here."

Concentrating on the road ahead, the young man points to a nearby crossroads. .

"There it is! Turn left here."

Checking his rear view mirror, Natas turns on his indicator to bear left. On checking his mirrors, he is relieved that the convoy has the sense to follow him.

The road begins with ruined houses on either side, and then opens out into clear open desert. As all the passengers in the Hummer stare out of the windows in amazement, Julie shouts out.

"It's our dream!"

The long straight road with desert sand both sides, and the sun facing them, Julie shouts out with further excitement.

"There they all are!"

Natas becomes hesitant as they get closer to a large community, consisting of a variety of transportation and temporary shelters. Various breeds of domestic animals wander around as groups of people come to the road waving with enthusiasm to greet the new convoy.

Look at these pathetic creatures! Give me a few hours and I'll have them eating out of my hands before his lordship arrives.

As Natas stops by the first group, a tall slim man approaches him. He pushes away his long fair hair from his forehead exposing bright blue eyes that seem to look right into you. He presence Natas with a broad genuine smile, showing well-formed white teeth.

"Hi guys! The name's Jim. Are you the rescue team? Are we glad to see you. People have been showing up here in dribs and drabs for the last three days. All of them having the same dream. Do any of 'you' know why this is happening?"

Before answering, Natas clambers out of the Hummer and turns to James.

"Can you take over the driving while I talk to these people?"

A touch annoyed at being treated as an insubordinate, James glances at Joan for reassurance. When she offers him a confident smile, and then nods to Natas, the disheveled young man still sitting in between the front seats, jumps out. Becoming more irritated, James moves into the driver's seat, and glances at Joan again.

"I hope he knows what he's doing?"

Meanwhile, Natas takes a good look at all the bustling community around him, and then answers Jim's original question.

"To answer your question my friend, we are not a rescue team. We are survivors like you. Anyway, to reassure your anxiety, I will talk to you all and explain everything. By the way, how many of you are here?"

Conveying a smile of cautious optimism, Jim answers.

"Must be at least five to six hundred, plus a group of soldiers that came in this morning. They parked themselves back yonder."

Natas can see a variety of military transport parked in a neat and precise order on the edge of the camp. A group of about fifty personnel are waiting in several casual lines, looking out of place. Sensing Jim's mood, Natas places a reassuring on his shoulder and offers him his best smile.

"We have about the same. Are you their leader?"

"Hell, no! I am or I was the general manager of that Hotel you passed back there so I just sort of wound up helping everyone. So, now they automatically come to me. I guess you could say I've become their unofficial leader."

Withdrawing his hand from Jim's shoulder, Natas puts out his hand for the courteous hand shake.

"I am Nat. I suppose I am 'our' leader. We need to get our heads together and organize."

"Organize what? Surely, this is not a permanent situation? Our supplies of food and water are not going to last very long. Do you think there will be any more people show up?"

Irritated that Jim is standing so close, Natas is reluctant to answer.

"It so happens, there is another convoy on its way. I estimate it will be here by tonight or early tomorrow. The reason I know this, because we have someone traveling with us from that convoy. As far as supplies, I think we should just merge in and share our resources, don't you?"

"Sounds good to me. You're all very welcome."

Nauseated by all this sincerity, Natas begins to walk away toward James, and then decides to stop and turns back to Jim.

"Tell your people I will talk to them tonight when everyone is settled."

Jim acknowledges and shakes his head a little, as they go to each of their groups.

It is becoming dark, and too dangerous to travel further. Gus is disappointed that the convoy did not make such good time as they would have liked. So, they all decided to camp on the side of the road within site of the famous electric generating windmills. The sun going down transforms

594

the windmills into black silhouettes against a golden-red sky.

Staring at the glorious spectacular, Gus is looking worried while standing alone away from the group. He feels a hand slide around his waist, and the familiar perfume of Eva as she stands close to him. Hugging him and resting her head on his shoulder, she asks the obvious.

"Watching the sunset?"

"Yes. And marveling at the windmills still standing, working and producing electricity to nowhere."

"Perhaps to somewhere, now we're here. I bet we have some electricians with our people who can make it all work."

"Perhaps."

Sensing his mood, she reaches up and plants a soft kiss on his cheek.

"Are you getting despondent now we are almost there?"

He turns to face her. She can see tears forming in his eyes, as he wraps his arms around her, searching for the strength he needs.

"Not despondent – 'scared'. I have been telling everyone that we would be there today, instead of camping here tonight. All of us have come so far, I don't want it all go wrong."

Becoming concerned by his fatalism, she pulls away, grabs him by the shoulders and looks him straight in the eye.

"What are you talking about? It's not your fault we're a little behind. Do you see anyone complaining? Why should you feel scared? God has chosen us all for a good reason. No way is it all going to go wrong and be wasted. I bet we have every skill in the book amongst these people. Skills to build a great new world."

"I'm not worried about the people, they're all wonderful. I'm worried that evil is not yet defeated. All you need is one bad seed and it will become contagious and spread like a malignant weed."

Garth being nearby and overhearing these doubts, joins them.

"I have come to tell you that everyone is settling down for the night. What's up with you two?"

Eva looks at him and conveys a cautious smile.

"Gus is nervous about tomorrow?"

595

"Nervous? What about? Things are going so good right now."

With tension in his eyes, Gus grips Garth's forearm. .

"Garth? Can you ask everyone I would like to say a few words before they turn in for the night? Tell them I just want ten minutes of their time."

Becoming concerned by his friend's unease, Garth hesitates before acknowledging. Not wanting to inflame the situation by enquiring even more, Garth leaves in a hurry to carry out the request.

In the meantime, Eva reaches out both arms for Gus, and pulls him tight toward her. Sinking into her warmth and holding her tight, her familiar smell brings back recent memories. Sensing his desperation, she grips him even tighter.

"Oh my love! I don't ever want to be separated from you again. Even though you'll leave here and travel to find and help others, I must be with you."

His reaction is to hug her tighter and begin stroking her hair.

"In that case, would you and Ryan like to come with me? Better still, will you be my wife?"

"Would I? Oh Gus!"

She pulls away, gazes into his eyes, and slides both her hands around his neck. Her heart palpitating with delight, she goes to pull his head down with the intention of sealing the contract with a kiss. His eyes filling with tears, he holds back.

"I take that as a yes?"

She is too happy to answer as she continues to pull him toward her to fuse their lips together. Deep coughing from nearby is suggesting an interruption. The happy couple aren't aware. The coughing becomes more exaggerated. Now aware, Gus is reluctant to separate to notice Irwin and Max standing nearby. Happy for Eva, Max produces a wide smile.

"Sorry to interrupt. Everyone is waiting."

With a mixture of emotions, Gus smiles at the the two men with appreciation.

"Okay! Tell everyone I'll be right there."

As Irwin leaves to deliver the message, Gus begrudges withdrawing from

Eva, but still holds one of her hands.

"We're going to be married."

Max's smile becomes broader as he takes Gus' hand.

"Well done you two. I knew you were both meant for each other and greater things. Enjoy it! I must get back to the others."

As Max leaves, Gus pulls Eva to him.

"Stay with me."

"Always."

Being there is one fire tonight as the evening is mild, Gus can make out most of the several hundred faces reflecting off the flames as they all sit or stand in a wide semicircle around the fire. Eva, Garth, Tizzy and Silver Eagle are sitting on a makeshift bench behind Gus. Max, Irwin and many of the children are in front of Gus, as all are focusing on him with a mixture of apprehension and curiosity.

The air is still. Aware of the silence and cracking of the fire, Gus lifts his head and gazes at the glistening stars, as if asking for strength. After a short pause, he lowers his head. Now scanning his audience, he makes sure his voice is clear and sharp.

"I wish to apologize for not getting you to your destination on time. However, we will be there tomorrow. I expect you're wondering why I needed to talk to you..."

His stomach churns as all the anxious faces focus on him.

"The last day or two I have been getting a feeling that not all is well. I tried to shrug it off by telling myself that I was probably a bit tired after all we've been through. Unfortunately, our good friend Silver Eagle feels it even more than me. There is a group traveling in front of us. When we stopped at their abandoned campsite, Silver Eagle told me then that he could still smell the evil that was left behind. He and I feel and suspect there is a troublemaker among that group already spreading evil."

Murmurs of confusion come from the group, as Susan raises her hand.

"I thought all the evil of this world had gone. How come it 'may' still be with us?"

Troubled by her concern, Gus takes two paces to his right so he can be nearer to her.

"I honestly don't know. Maybe someone slipped through the cracks or it may not be as bad as we might think. I just want you all to be aware that there 'might' be some sort of conflict. Whatever happens, I will make sure that it is solved quickly, and our new life will start as planned."

Several hands are raised in reaction. Gus points to Ryan who is sitting with Will and the children.

"Is it true we are all supposed to be born good and only become evil when we mix with bad people?"

Eva smiles with pride at her son's interest, as Gus answers.

"That is a good question Ryan. Unfortunately, many people 'are' born evil and go on to influence the ones born good. The new evil, then go to infect others. However, most people are born with a mixture of good and evil. They struggle all their lives with temptation. Many succumb to evil because it is easiest and offers cheap pleasure. Happily, some do remain good and join the souls that are born good and have remained good. These are the souls you have here."

Happy with Gus's explanation, Ryan smiles at his mother. Meanwhile, Gus points to another raised hand, which belongs to a young woman in her late teens. Her pale blond hair reflecting off the fire, makes it look like metallic gold. She hesitates before she speaks.

"If what you say is true then we have no fear in the future of Armageddon or an Antichrist?"

Taken aback by such a profound question, Gus looks up to the night sky, and closes his eyes.

I'm so tired! I want to go somewhere quiet to pray and gather my thoughts, but I can't, I have a mission to complete. These trusting souls need me, at least until tomorrow.

His insides tightening, he lowers his head, and then opens his eyes looking straight at the bright blue inquisitive eyes of the young woman.

"We have just experienced Armageddon these last few days. 'We' have been left to carry on. As far as an Antichrist, either God is inside you –

God being love, or Satan masquerading as God is the Antichrist inside you. Satan was inside those people, who were bleeding and raping poor Mother Earth, creating havoc, greed, bigotry, cruelty, selfishness and hypocrisy. This is what caused all the misery and suffering over thousands of years. Evil beating good into the ground by causing global and local wars, with millions of people dying unnecessarily. Then you get the age-old question.Where was God when this all happened?"

Still gazing at the unflinching eyes, he continues.

"We decided in the beginning we wanted to be free and independent, and only call on God when we couldn't manage or were having a bad day. Okay, that's fine to a certain degree; God is always there to help. However, do not expect God to intervene in man's own troubles, that he has caused himself. So, the big question is, why has God intervened now? Because enough is enough. It is the straw that broke the camel's back. The world was on the brink; mass starvation, high unemployment among the working people while the elite rich became mega-rich, all bringing global warming and disease to dangerous levels. They were warned, but they wouldn't listen. Corporate greed carried on. Now we are rid of them. I tried to teach this lesson to everyone over two thousand years ago, but the majority didn't understand or care. Now there is no choice. It is the true way or nothing. In my humble opinion, this is the best way. Tomorrow is going to be the day of finality, when we will all come together and build the real kingdom of God. I'm looking forward to that. Thank you for listening to me and God bless."

There is a thoughtful silence in the group as he moves away and heads out toward the open desert. His mind in Turmoil, he wants to find a boulder and sit down on the sand.

As he leans over the boulder to support his arms, he clasps his hands together in silent prayer. At the same time, his fatigue is overwhelming.

Oh God, what now? All I feel is fear and apprehension for tomorrow, as if something terrible is going to happen. Whatever it is, stay with me so I can carry

on and be of help to these trusting souls that you have saved...

His heart misses a beat, as he hears footsteps approaching. He opens his eyes to strain in the dark to find Garth coming toward him. Gus sits up on the boulder, while Garth crouches in front of him.

"I was wondering where you were? Are you all right? Silver Eagle is becoming concerned."

Observing the dark shadows under Gus's eyes, Garth places his hand with affectionate on his friend's shoulder.

"Have you prayed?"

"Yes. I have asked for help – like I usually do."

"Well, that's fine then. Tomorrow is going to be great. So, let's join the others and get some sleep. Okay?"

Welcoming Garth's strength of character, Gus stands and slides his arm around Garth's shoulder for support.

"Okay – my dear friend."

Natas' enlarged community sits in anticipation to hear him explain what is going to happen to them now and possibly their future.

As its warm, there is one main fire. Everyone is seated on the ground in a large semicircle behind the fire while Natas is standing on a raised makeshift platform facing them. The fire is reflecting off his black and gold robes giving him a surreal look. His eyes sparkle like emeralds with excitement as he paces back and forth on the platform, and his voice booms in the still desert air.

"Welcome to the New World. As from tomorrow, all of you here will run this new life we have been granted. You will organize yourselves and decide how you are going to achieve this – despite the devastation you have recently experienced. You ask yourselves, why has all this happened? Why are we the only survivors? I do not think anyone can really answer those questions."

He makes a point of focusing on Julie.

"Even if some of you think you know, let us just be thankful that we have survived. Survived to create a world that is going to be far better than the one we left behind."

Being caught up in his magnetism, he is received by a spontaneous applause. Sensing he is getting somewhere with these people, Natas is becoming more confident so he can stand up to Gus.

Let me lead you my sheep!

He continues talking.

"Tomorrow, another community will be joining us to expand our new world. On the surface that sounds fine, but I have to warn you that the leader of this other community claims he is Christ come back to lead us all to a life to live only under God's law. I expect the man feels sincere in his beliefs and has all our interests at heart. However, be prepared for some conflict, especially between him and myself."

As Julie and her mother grip each other in alarm, Julie shouts out.

"How can you say that when you 'know' the truth?"

Suppressing his anger at Julie's challenge, Natas' eyes turn crimson from the fire.

"My dear girl, I am the 'only' truth. Now, where was I? Ah, yes! Now, myself, I am a great believer in handling my own life. I have always said: if it does not hurt anyone else, then there is no harm in it. What ever 'it' is..."

Biting his lip and his jaw muscles twitching in frustration, he is determined to carry on.

"Religion has always been the downfall of society. Most of the wars we have had over thousands of years were all caused by religion. Only the last few years we have seen extremists on the 'Christian' side confronting 'Moslem' extremists on the other. Now for the first time on this fine planet of ours, we can prevent this from ever happening again. We are free. Free from meddling governments, bureaucracy and stupid 'religious' leaders who only had their own interest at heart and not yours. From now on, 'you' decide what is good for you. Do not let anyone else do it for you. Anyway, thank you for letting me speak. I am with you people all the way."

As he steps down off the platform, there is a muted, but sporadic applause, and a fair amount of mumbling and discussion among the crowd. Much to his annoyance, Natas can see several people pointing at him as he makes his way out into the desert to collect his thoughts.

He stops some distance from the camp. Sensing someone is following him, he notices the familiar black silhouette of Madeline against the glow of the now dwindling fire. As she steps nearer, he is not in the mood for conversation, especially hers. However, not to show his true feelings, he presence her with enthusiastic demeanor. At the same time, her manic excitement disturbs him.

"Well, it's started."

"Do you think so?"

"Your little chat was good."

Becoming disturbed by her sexuality, he turns away. The pit in his stomach is making him feel sick.

"Some chat! I felt I was not getting through. Then of course, there is Julie and her highness - Madam President to still convince. However, tomorrow is the big day."

Becoming exasperated by his attitude, and her eyes shimmering with mania, she grabs him by the shoulders.

"What's the matter with you? Where's your strength and cunning? These people are simpletons compared to us. In time you can get them eating out of your hand and..."

"Yes! I am aware of that. 'If' I keep at them, but unfortunately I do not have that time. Another thing your pretty little head has yet to realize, these people have been chosen because they are 'good' and 'kind', totally the opposite of US!"

Not disturbed by his hesitancy, she continues her determination.

"Do you really believe that? I don't! I think we have totally underestimated this whole situation. I'm not saying these people aren't good. What I am saying is that 'good' people are more gullible and easier to manipulate."

He stares at her in astonishment.

"I am 'nothing' compared to you. You are 'completely' evil. There is not one grain of decency in you."

Not disagreeing, she offers him a provocative smile that any normal man would be powerless to resist. Tuning in to his weakness, she steps closer until her softness and warmth of her tempting body is pressing against him. Without any resistance, he lets her slide her arms around his neck. She then pulls his head down so her hungry lips ravage his pensive mouth. Him now surrendering, and her eyes blazing with excitement, she places his hands on her breasts.

"This is why you can never resist me. We are the perfect pair – made in Hell!"

The setting sun is turning to a pale purple. A black silhouette is floating toward him with hands held out.

"Take my hand, I will take you there."

Take me where? I have to reach the people.

The silhouette comes closer. He can now see the face.

"Mary? What do you want?"

She replies as she comes closer.

"I have come to take you home my darling. Where you belong."

She kisses him, causing his body to ache for her. He is disappointed by her easing away and gazing at him. The face is now Eva's. Her voice soft.

"I love you Gus. I always have. We all need you."

Oh, Eva.

She kisses him gentle at first, and then her passion turns to hunger and wanting. While his body is burning with longing, she laughs and withdraws. Her teasing arms so close, he is desperate to reach out to her. Seeing it is Madeline, he feels sick and screams at her, while everything begins to shake and tremble.

Oh God! Not another quake. Haven't you finished punishing us yet?

Gus wakes up with a start to find Garth is shaking him.

"I'm sorry Gus, but you were on the verge of screaming."

As Gus comes to, he looks up at a concerned Garth. Gus's hands tremble as he wipes the sweat from his forehead.

"I had the most awful nightmare, but I'm all right now."

"Are you sure? You look awful. I'll get you a cup of tea."

603

"Thanks."

Still appearing concerned, Garth unzips his own sleeping bag and walks toward where breakfast is being served. After a minute, Gus decides to vacate his sleeping bag and begin pacing to relieve his mind. Unable to get the image of Madeline from his brain, he stops and looks up at the clear morning sky.

Is she going to be there? Are 'you' going to be there to guide us?

Still mournful, he rolls up his sleeping bag when he sees Garth coming back holding a couple of paper cups. Observing Garth smiling and nodding at the other early risers, Gus is thankful for such a friend.

On receiving the tea, he welcomes the warm, sweet liquid as he puts it to his lips. While Garth stands next to him, his concern is still apparent.

"You okay now?"

Gus hides his fears, as he nods and smiles back.

"I'm fine! Good tea."

While both men sip their tea in thoughtful silence, Garth attempts some light conversation.

"I've been teaching Tizzy how to make tea. As you can see, she does a great job."

Aware that Garth is trying to make light of everything, he pats Garth's upper back in appreciation.

"I can feel an air of excitement among the people."

"Yes, I think they feel everything is coming to a head, and we will all start to plan some sort of life for us all. All the kids think this is quite an adventure."

Absorbing his friend's words, Gus finishes his tea and pats Garth on the shoulder.

"I'm going to walk around and check everyone. I'll see you at the bus."

Still worrying about his mentor's sullen mood, Garth nods and begins to roll up his sleeping bag.

As he wanders among the people, Gus heart lifts as he notices Eva helping to organize the children. He pauses to watch her and young Ryan serve out food and drink to the line of well behaved, but excited children. On seeing Gus, Eva offers him a smile and points behind her. Gus can see Silver Eagle in deep discussion with a small group of men. One of them is a vocal Walter Cameron.

Not showing his unease at the men's troubling expressions, Gus walks up to the group and puts his hand on Walter's shoulder.

"What's up guys?"

His eyes looking serious,Walter turns to him.

"Ah, Gus. We're getting short of everything. Only enough gas for today. Food, and water for the next two days."

Still hiding his own anxiety, Gus conveys to them a reassuring smile.

"Is that all? I thought it was something serious."

The men stare at Gus as if he is not quite aware of the reality of the situation. Gus is aware, but wants to keep everyone calm. The last thing he wants is panic.

"We are coming into a town that will have filling stations with under-ground fuel tanks. Also, there will be at least two supermarkets where we can scavenge food and drink. The people that we are going to meet up with will help us also."

Still doubtful, the men glance at each other for support, while Gus places his other hand on Silver Eagle's shoulder.

"Have faith people. You don't think that we've come this far and not be looked after?"

Seeing sense, Silver Eagle pats Gus' hand.

"You are so right my friend. What are we all thinking of?"

The men lower their heads as if embarrassed by their own insecurity. Offering Gus smiles of appreciation, they walk away leaving Silver Eagle. Silver Eagle's reaction is to slide his arm around Gus' shoulder.

"My friend, we are ready to go. Garth thinks he knows the way using his map. We should be there in under an hour - if there aren't too many obstacles."

He withdraws his arm from Gus and looks him straight in the eye.

"I had a dream last night about today. The 'Chindi'will be there - the devil. 'Yeh-wol-ye hi-he a-din' - we know of no fear. 'Hozo-go nay-yeltay to' - may we live in peace hereafter. I am letting you know that when you have conflict with this man, you will have no fear. We will be supporting you because this is 'to-altseh-hogan' - a temporary place. You will beat this man, and then we will all 'ah-hi-di-dail' - come together, and then 'yah-tay-go-e-elah' - make good."

Hearing these words of encouragement, tears of appreciation fill Gus's eyes as he hugs the Chief.

"Thank you."

As they separate, Gus wipes his eyes. To demonstrate his faith in Gus, Silver Eagle puts a hand on his shoulder.

"You are the Great Spirit. It is us thanking you."

Without any more words spoken, they leave; each knowing what they have to do.

It is just under an hour later. Garth is driving the bus with Gus sitting behind him, when a young man jumps out into the road and waves the convoy to stop. Winding down the window, Garth can see that the lad is covered with dust and cement. Remembering Silver eagle's prophetic words, Gus taps his shoulder.

"Perhaps he is from another group."

"We'll soon find out."

While the convey grinds to a halt, the young man appears extra eager as he approaches the bus.

"Are yer the other party?"

Garth becomes curious at the grimy face.

"Are you expecting us?"

"I've been waitin fer yer since yesterday."

Becoming enthralled by this young man, Gus signals Garth to open the door. The lad's enthusiasm is obvious as he climbs aboard, stands by Garth and surveys everyone seated.

"How manis of yer?"

Still engrossed, Gus answers.

"At least a couple of hundred. We haven't counted."

"Wow, that's a lot a people, when yer add the last party that came two days ago..."

Gus has to interrupt.

"Where are they all now?"

The lad points straight ahead.

"Carry on straight ahead, and then take a left at the top of thuh hill. I'll tell yer when we git there."

Fifteen minutes have gone by. The lad points at the windshield.

"Turn left here."

Checking the bus's mirrors, Garth can see the convoy is following without any snags. As they proceed, everyone looks out of their windows to observe the flattened houses giving way to desert sand. Meanwhile, Gus hears Mary Morning star's voice.

"Look at that!"

As the bus creeps along, a large community is coming into view on their left. Gus feels his stomach tighten as more of the improvised settlement is exposed. Garth stops driving when the young man taps his arm. His enthusiasm heightens as he beckons to the welcoming few that step out into the road in front of them.

The bus door opens to a buzz of excitement. Garth and Gus can hear the muted cheers of people as they gather to see the new arrivals. Garth is the first to step outas a tall slim man welcomes him.

"You're here then? Not too many hazards?"

Intrigued by such a question, Garth shakes his hand. Watching Garth and the tall man wander toward the rest of the convoy behind the bus, Gus decides to get off the bus. On stepping onto the sand, he hears a familiar voice above the noise.

"Gus? Is that you?"

He strains his eyes in the bright sunshine to search for the voice, when Julie appears, followed by her mother. Her relief obvious, Julie runs to him as he opens his arms. Wrapping her arms around him, her relief turns to tears.

"Oh Gus! You 'are' alive. I just knew you would be all right."

"Yes, Julie. I'm fine. How are you both?"

Not answering straight away, Joan reaches out and grips one of his hands. Gus can see tears of relief flowing down her face, as she steps closer and leans toward his right ear.

"Thank God you are safe."

Becoming caught up in all the emotion, and trouble by Joan's unkept appearance, Gus swallows hard in trying to keep calm.

"Yes, Madam President. Thank God we are all safe."

As Joan wraps her arm around his, and Julie does the same with his other arm, James comes up to him, and stands next to Joan.

"Hi, I'm James. I am the President's – err - Joan's Secret Service agent. She has told me much about you."

Sensing James is far more to 'Joan' than a formal agent, Gus is warmed by the man's sincerity and obvious protective manner.

"All good, I hope?"

James smiles back, as Joan reaches out to him with her spare hand.

"Oh yes, all good."

Becoming more aware of the strong bond between them, Gus indicates to James.

"Is there any form of leadership, or is everyone waiting for yours truly?"

James's face drops its smile, as he takes the lead by walking ahead toward a more central point in the array of vehicles and shelters.

"There is one guy who seems to have taken over the responsibility."

As they arrive at the Hummer, James is still serious as he climbs inside. Beckoning all to follow, Gus, James, Joan and Julie arrange their seating so they can all look at each other. Sensing an urgency amongst them, Gus stiffens as James talks first.

"Its great that you guys got here okay. How are your supplies?"

His stomach tightening, Gus pauses and takes a breath before telling him the worrying news.

"Not so good. We are almost out of fuel, and only have food and water for two days."

Becoming more anxious, Joan speaks.

"About the same as us. Our people have been good and not wasted anything. The few survivors that were here when we arrived say there is plenty of bottled water, canned and dried foods down town in some of the stores and supermarkets."

On hearing this, Gus is relieved there is no immediate danger.

"I think after today, people will be leaving in their chosen groups to make it on their own."

Joan thinks otherwise

"Why? We all need to stick together! Safety in numbers and all that."

Gus is surprised and a little disheartened by her insecurity.

"Safety from what? All the survivors are good people. So, where ever you go on this planet you will be welcomed without 'any' fear."

Embarrassed by her mother's lack of faith, Julie speaks.

"We know you're right, but some of us have still got some doubts."

"What sort of doubts?"

James answers Gus with a question.

"Do you know a woman calling herself Madeline?"

His dream returning, Gus' stomach tightens.

"Yes I do. We had a young woman of that name with us, but she left us several days ago. Why?"

"She's here with us. She just showed up about two days ago and straightaway got involved with a man called Nat. This guy is a weird one. He has a way of stirring the pot, while causing a lot people to become confused about their future."

"Can you describe this man?"

"About six feet, slim, and in good shape. He has dark curly hair with a tanned complexion, and bright green eyes. He is wearing black and gold robes."

As Gus is building a picture in his mind, his insides turn over even more.

It's him.

Trying to act calm, he gets up and steps out of the Hummer. Wondering what he is up to, the others stare at him. Observing their confused faces, Gus puts on the best smile he can muster.

"I'll be back. I have to see someone."

Becoming anxious, they watch him walk away with his head down and a determination in his step. When out of sight they gaze at each other as if searching for an answer. Understanding Gus, Julie speaks first.

"I know what he has to do."

Becoming disappointed by this tenuous situation, Joan gazes at her daughter.

"What is that my dear?"

"He has to do something about Nat."

Gus has found Silver Eagle with his daughter Mary, talking with enthusiasm to a group of children. Gus pauses while observing this happy sight, and how gracious the Indian chief comes across.

All this good must never be destroyed.

Mary's face tightens when she sees Gus carrying a serious expression. She prods her father. Him turning around, he smiles at Gus, but notices distress. He apologies to the children for having to leave, but promises to return. Meanwhile, he is worried about Gus's appearance.

"My dear friend. What is it? You have pain in your heart."

Doing his best to hide his anguish, Gus leads father and daughter to a quiet spot behind an army truck.

"He's here! You were right."

As Mary gasps, Silver Eagle thinks.

"Have you seen him?"

"No."

"Then how do you know he's here?"

"The leader of one of the groups described him - and Madeline."

The chief's eyes harden as he rubs his chin, while staring into space.

"Don't make a move to find him. Let him 'altseh-e-jah-he' - strike first. Then we will 'de-ji-kash' - .bunch together and protect you."

Sick with apprehension, Gus hugs the old man on impulse.

"He's very clever. He will appear when we are least expecting him."

Silver Eagle places an affectionate hand on Gus's shoulder, and presence him with a confident grin.

"What ever happens, we will be ready. I am going prowl and sniff like the wolf to see what I can smell."

He offers them a sly smile as he leaves to blend in with the surroundings. Mary Morning star's reaction is to grip hold of Gus's hand.

"My father is a great man."

"I know."

"He can speak excellent English, but he is still proud of his Navajo language."

"So he should be."

She now grabs his hand with both of hers.

"You are also a great man."

"What makes you think that?"

"Because I have been studying you ever since we met."

Flattered and amused by her compliment, he smiles with affection.

"So, what is the result of your studies?"

Slow in answering, and still holding his hand, she brings it up to her face, shuts her eyes and strokes it against her cheek. She then gives his hand a gentle childlike kiss, and lowers it. Still holding on, she then looks straight up at him.

"That we all love you, and believe in what you're doing."

While hope rises in him, he notices her bright hazel eyes are dotted with little green flecks, which are now moist with tears.

"Never fear the future. I will always be with you..."

Now his eyes become moist with tears, the fear is still gnawing away at the back of his mind. He releases the tension by giving her a hug...

"Am I missing something?"

Recognizing the voice, Gus wipes his eyes and stretches out an arm to Eva while still holding Mary. Without any hesitation, Eva is eager to wrap her arms around both of them.

"I was worried! I couldn't find you. Mary's father told me you were here."

Relishing the warmth of the two women, Gus kisses her forehead.

"We've been having an important conversation about studying."

"What sort of studies?"

Reluctant to withdraw, he winks at Mary.

"Oh, life as it should be."

Having more serious things to convey, Eva separates.

"Well? Life as it is at the moment is that some of the men are getting together to talk to you about the next move."

Being brought back down to reality, Gus's insides tighten again.

"Can you talk to these people for me and tell them I'll see them all in a while? I need to think and get my act together."

Ill-at-ease with what he has to do, Gus wanders off behind some trucks and finds a quiet spot behind the bus. He sits down on the sand and leans back to rest his head against the side of the bus. He is finding it difficult to relax, as he shuts his eyes and forces his mind back over the last few days.

What now? What do I tell them? What about 'him', who tried to kill me? He is here ready to do it again. Why did you not dispose of him like you did everyone else? Or do you still have a last surprise up your sleeve? Right now, I've run out of energy. I'm running on instinct and not logic. Perhaps that's what you want? I'm more receptive to you..?

"Hi, Gus. I hope I'm not disturbing you."

He jumps inside at the sudden intrusion. He opens his eyes to find Madeline standing in front of him. Before he has time to respond, she moves around so she can sit down next to him.

"I've been looking for you."

Stunned by her audacity, his stomach tightens even more.

"Now you've found me. How can I help you?"

"Oh! We are formal all of a sudden."

Controlling his rage as she sidles up to him, Gus doesn't answer.

Determined to get his full attention, she places her hand on his forearm, and keeps it there.

"Look. I'm sorry about leaving you guys, but I had this dream that I was going to meet my lover for life. I was supposed to meet him at a crater..."

"Did you?"

"Yes, I did."

"So? What is the problem?"

"Who said there is a problem?"

Irritated by her closeness, he stands and raises his voice.

"Because you said you were looking for 'me'! Why is that?"

She takes her time to stand. While brushing some sand off her arms, and then her breasts, she gazes at him as if to tease. Stepping closer to him, she can tell his emotions are getting the better of him. Her face tightens as he tries to move away. Aware of his antagonism toward her, she blocks his path and becomes more conciliatory.

"Look, I know we haven't exactly hit it off, but I don't want us to be enemies."

His pulse increasing, he knows different.

We're already enemies.

"You've made your point! So, what is it you want?"

Still close, her eyes pierce into him.

"In the beginning I wanted 'you'. A lover that would have transcended anything you have experienced - the mother of God! But no, you spurned me. Now, I don't want anything from you. I have who I need. You know him. In fact, you know him quite well. You guys are supposed to have gone back a long way."

As realization hits home that she is in love with 'him', he wants to vomit.

"So, the whole object of this conversation is that you - and 'him' are...."

"Lovers! Sex you wouldn't believe! I have 'his' seed in me. Me, the mother of all evil."

Needing to get away, he cannot bear to breath the same air, as well being in the same area as her. Sensing his revulsion, she grabs him by the collar, while her manic eyes blaze.

"I wanted 'your' seed in me. Oh no, you didn't want to know 'me'. I was too low for you, so I got up and left. You've always preferred that black bitch..."

Amazed by her strength and bringing Eva into this confrontation in such a derogatory way, he tries hard to control the natural human urge of knocking her down.

"You're not just evil, but crazy with it! You make satan look credible compared to you."

Taking this as a compliment, she lets go of his collar and bursts out laughing.

He stares in fear and amazement as her handsome features become ugly and distorted.

This is total madness. She has to be stopped!

While she backs away from him, her laugh winds down into a whimper. She then turns and runs off, disappearing out of sight behind some vehicles. For a minute, he feels at a loss. The sound of a familiar voice distracts him.

"That woman is the ultimate in evil. If I didn't know different, I would say she is Satan."

Garth is holding hands with Tizzy, while she is struggling to hold a cup of coffee and a paper plate consisting of a small serving of beans and vegetables. While handing Gus the food, she offers him a cautious smile.

"Perhaps we've got it all wrong about Satan being a male? Anyway, I'm afraid the food is not much for now, but later this evening we will be putting on a proper spread to celebrate us all coming together."

Being so shaken by Madeline, Gus has to place the plate on the step of the bus.

He chokes on his coffee and has to put that down as well.

"Interesting in what you say about Satan being female, but I think that might be a wee bit premature. Unless this last bastion of evil is totally eradicated by this afternoon, we might find out."

After pausing for a minute to gather his momentum, Gus lifts up the plate and becomes grateful as he chews on a mouthful of beans.

Meanwhile, Tizzy taps Garth on the arm and indicates that she has to leave. Garth nods in agreement, as

Gus appears puzzled at her leaving.

"Something I said?"

Having never seeing his friend and mentor being so edgy and distressed like this before, Garth keeps his voice cheerful.

"No. Don't be daft. She's still helping with the food."

Still dreadful at feeling on edge, and the last thing he wants is to hurt any of his dear friends, he looks at Garth in earnest.

"Garth? Do you remember clearly the moment we were shot at in the UN Building?"

"Do I? That is something I'll never forget! The guy in the black robes. Why?"

"Because the man who did that shooting is right here."

The color drains from Garth's face.

"What? Are you sure?"

"Positive! That evil woman is with him!"

"What are we going to do?"

"Face him of course and defeat him. With any cohorts he might have with him."

Coming to terms with the shock, Garth feels a little shaky.

"I thought all the bad people were supposed to have been dealt with? We shouldn't even have to be in this situation."

Gus thinks the same.

This shouldn't be happening. Or is it for a reason?

"I agree."

As if by an illusion, Silver Eagle appears.

"I have just come from him, and that woman. He never saw me."

Relieved that the chief is helping by his intriguing unorthodox methods, Gus asks the obvious.

"Where did you see them?"

"On the North edge of the camp, behind the army trucks. He is dressed in black robes."

"What were they doing?"

"They were arguing. He was telling her not to interfere in what he has to do. What ever it is, he must be stopped."

Garth joins in the discussion.

"What do you suggest? Killing him?"

His eyes hardening, Silver Eagle nods.

"That is the only way of dealing with vermin. It is her I'm more worried about."

Gus has heard enough.

"There will be none of that talk! This is the 'new' world, not the old. I'm going to face him and 'win'. I have to, otherwise all this struggling has been for nothing.

Anyway, you cannot just 'kill' something like that."

The Indian's reaction is to grab hold of Gus' arm and looks him in the eye.

"Which ever way you go, we know it will be the right way, and we will be there with you."

As the two men hug, the chief withdraws, squeezes Gus's forearm and leaves.

All of a sudden, Gus feels lonely, even though Garth is standing right next to him. His mind troubled, but focused, Gus looks down at the ground. Sensing his mentor needs to be alone, Garth takes one step back.

"Do you need any help or do you want me to go?"

Looking tired, Gus looks up toward his friend.

"The sort of help I need, no man can give me. However, there is one thing you can do for me…"

"Anything."

"Tell everyone I will talk to them in fifteen minutes. Tell them also, that I will explain everything, and then it will be up to them to decide what they want."

"What if 'he' comes and causes trouble?"

"Let him come. I will challenge him, and then the people can decide. I have a feeling this is meant for a reason."

Garth is not so sure.

"All right. I'll tell them. I'll see you in fifteen minutes."

As Gus watches a skeptical Garth turn and leave, his fatigue becomes overwhelming. Also plagued with nerves, he leans back against the bus, looks up, and closes his eyes.

Oh, God, what do you want me to do now? Is all this part of the master plan? Do I have to die again to prove something?

Fifteen minutes has passed. Gus is now standing on a low makeshift platform in front of the large crowd, which is split up into various size groups dotted around in a large semi circle. Many of the children are sitting together on the ground in front of him. Other people are leaning against or sitting in many of the parked vehicles. The rest are sitting in different sized groups behind the children.

While the whole crowd is alive with speculation, Max turns to Irwin.

"Truly, a TV moment, but I haven't a camera."

Seeing the irony, Irwin smiles back.

"Truly a newspaper moment, but I have no newspaper or press. Or come to that, no social media"

A cooling light breeze appears. The air from the late afternoon heat is now more comfortable. Standing with the western horizon behind him, Gus senses a congenial atmosphere from the expectant crowd. This gives him a small boost to his flagging confidence as he scans the whole area.

No sign of him or Madeline.

Taking a deep breath and clenching his fists by his side, he walks a few steps back and forth on the creaking platform as if to prepare.

"Some of you know me and some of you have heard about me. For those who haven't neither, my name is Gus. Some of you must be wondering why we are here? It is great that we have all made it this part of the world without any major obstacles. There is a good reason for that, and I aim to tell you why..."

Because of the crowd being attentive and quiet, this gives Gus more confidence to continue.

"First, I will go back a couple of weeks. I was sent here to warn everyone that the world as we have always known it, would end in one year if the human race did not change and improve its ways. Some of you here conversed with me about that situation. Many others I spoke to rejected me. They're not here today. Why we had to come here to this particular spot? I don't know. However, I'm sure that we'll find out soon enough. I expect a lot of you will be saying to yourselves, why has this all happened? And why wasn't the human race not given the chance of one year to rectify all the problems? In my opinion, God decided it wasn't going to happen... "

Even though he is more self-confident, he still has to pause to gather his dwindling energy...

"The amount of evil in the world was so overwhelming, God decided to go ahead much earlier and rid the world of that evil - before it had a chance to consume and destroy 'everything'. Hence, there are only a few of us left. Therefore, from this moment on, you are 'really' free. Free from tyranny and fear. There are no man made laws, no military and police to uphold those laws. There's no need, because now we live only by God's law. This is how it was meant to be from the very beginning. Five thousand years ago, the Jewish race was formed and chosen. They were to live by God's law, and yet over the years, they didn't get it right. All the trappings of evil prevailed, such as greed, power, and hypocrisy. The small minority owning the majority of the wealth, created extreme hardship for everyone else. Then two thousand years ago, I appeared..."

Some of the crowd begin to exchange words of doubt. Expecting this, Gus holds up his hand to reassure.

"I came to show everyone a better way, but the ones running things didn't want that. It interfered with all their power and greed. I was becoming a thorn in their side. I was being called a 'revolutionary'. Me? A leader of a revolution? Don't make me laugh. All I spoke of was love. For that I was brutally beaten and flogged, and then strung up on a rough wooden cross to suffer the most horrific death ever invented by man..."

He has to pause to calm his fraying nerves, as some of the crowd are becoming confused.

"However, it did not quite work out, as they wanted. I beat them and God's word flourished - for a while, but evil was never far behind. Wars, often in God's name has raged through the centuries slaughtering millions of people. Do you know how that made me feel? So, here we are on the threshold of a new world. A world of love and giving, working within a framework of protection against evil..."

As his fatigue increases, he surveys their awe stricken faces. His legs now beginning to tremble and ache, he becomes more aware of his audience needing to know more. He looks down, turns, and takes some small steps to his right on the small platform. He stops and gazes at the pale orange sun between the two mountains.

I estimate it is about two more hours to sunset. This day has to be the day of reckoning, but nothing is happening. I can't say anymore. I'm going to open up and ask questions.

"I 'hope' I have explained it enough. Is there any questions?"

"Yes! I have some questions."

It is Natas. Him standing on the roof of the bus in a flamboyant manner, makes the crowd looks up in his direction. Continuing his flamboyance, he strides up and down the length of the bus, causing his Pharisee's robes to flap in the breeze.

Gus freezes, as Natas surprises everyone by jumping off the bus. His black robes flowing high, gives the appearance of a giant bird as he seems to glide in slow motion down toward the back of a nearby open pick up truck. Mesmerized by this spectacle, the crowd is becoming more confused. As Natas is crouching, letting his robes settle around him, he becomes aware of his audience's full attention. He responds by rising to his full height. Creating the effect he wants, he takes advantage by raising his voice.

"Yes! I have 'many' questions. First, how do you 'really' know that God, the 'great creator', produced all this carnage? Second, how do we all know that 'you' are whom you say you are?"

The confused crowd turns to look at Gus for his reaction. Gus feels the bile coming to his throat as the fear of this evil grips his insides. Without letting the crowd sense his fear, he takes a deep breath to prepare his defense.

"Because it is written that God will scourge the world of evil so the meek shall inherit..."

Natas interrupts by bellowing out an exaggerated laugh.

"Well! That doesn't say much for these good folk here. I do not see any 'meek' souls? I see strong, decent people. I think that myth ought to be thrown out."

Meanwhile, Garth, Eva and Silver eagle, who are standing just to the left of Gus, glance at each other with worried frowns. At the same time, Natas continues.

"As far as 'your' true identity is concerned, it is very questionable."

Gus's fear now turning to anger, gives him the strength to survive this heinous onslaught. He points to his archenemy, and makes sure he is heard.

"You 'know' who I am, because you tried to kill me just before this all happened.

Incidentally, you committing that evil deed 'caused' all this to happen."

Not swayed by the accusation, Natas lets out another loud laugh.

"I attempted to dispose of you, because of the 'lies' you were telling the world.

The lies about you being the Christ returned. How on earth can 'you' be Jesus of

Nazareth? You are a mere man who has no power to do anything Godly?"

Confused murmurs are now erupting from the crowd. In the meantime, Silver Eagle wells up with anger, points to Gus, and shouts above the crowd.

"This 'is' the great one. You, 'yah-tay-go-e-elah' - make talk. You are 'do-ya-sho-Da' - no good, a 'a-tkel-el-ini' – troublemaker! This great man healed me from years of blindness, so I can now be able to see you. The 'chindi' - the devil."

Gus's eyes sting with tears of appreciation, as he watches this good honest man stand up to this ultimate in evil. Meanwhile, Natas is not at all disturbed by the Chief's statement.

"Come on old man! Don't fool me or any of these good people..."

Seething with anger, Mary, Silver Eagle's daughter interrupts him by shouting.

"I know, because he's my father! He is one of the kindest and strongest men in the world."

Cheers irrupt from the Navajo people sitting in front of Gus' platform, while Silver Eagle turns to gaze at his daughter with pride. Witnessing this show of loyalty causes Natas to pause for a minute.

Seeing her opportunity, Joan the President comes forward and looks up to face Natas. All observing their President, the crowd goes silent. Smirking, Natas stares down in fascination.

"Well? If it isn't our 'ex' President to say a few words."

Unperturbed by the cutting sarcasm, Joan challenges him.

"You are quite wrong in everything you say. I 'know' Gus, and I know what he has done. There are people here who also know who he is..."

Some cheers coming from the crowd interrupt. Not letting the cheers slow her down, she continues.

"...and have witnessed his greatness first hand, so if I were you..."

Not letting her have the final word, Natas seems to fly off the truck and land on the sand. He then glides up to Joan in a threatening manner, raising both arms, making him appear like a huge bat. Refusing to be intimidated, Joan stands her ground. Seeing he is not getting anywhere, Natas lowers his arms and conveys to her his best disarming smile. As if the whole event is nothing but a piece of grand theater, Natas leaves Joan and moves toward the platform. He stands in front of it, blocking the lower half of Gus's body. As Gus is finding it hard to control his anger, Natas stares hard at Joan.

"Now if you 'were' me, you would do 'what'? Don't make threats - bitch if you cannot carry them out. That is why 'you' ended up being President."

As he laughs at his own joke, the audience does not reciprocate. He lowers his head as if he is studying the sand, and then begins to saunter to the end of the platform. Keeping up his 'act', he stops, raises his head to the sky, and then lowers it to face the crowd.

"As I see it, we seem to have a difference of opinion. However, we always have a choice. Isn't that the democratic way? I tell you, I am not the bad person some of you think I am. Therefore, I will put 'my' case to the people, and then Gus here can put 'his' case forward. I think that is fair. Don't you?"

Somewhere at the back of the crowd, Madeline shouts.

"You tell em Nat!"

Not sure if he wants Madeline's support, Natas smirks.

"I seem to have one fan so far. Well, as I seem to have the floor, I will begin."

Unable to move a muscle, Gus stands transfixed and sick to his stomach while watching this evil walk back and fourth in front of his raised platform. At the same time, Natas begins.

"I'll start off with the basics. First, - we are 'supposed' to be created in God's image. We could not even run this planet properly, so how would you expect someone like us - in God's image to run the universe. Someone far greater created this universe. Someone far superior than anything you can imagine."

Becoming excited at having the crowds full attention, he pauses to take a breath, and then continues.

"That brings us to the present predicament. Was it 'God' who killed most of the human race these last few days or was it something or someone else that we cannot even imagine? If God is love, as they tell me, why would God kill and completely obliterate the Planet - God's own creation? The whole thing doesn't add up. There is no logic, except God is 'not' love, but a harsh dictator."

The crowd becomes disturbed and murmurs in confusion. In his determined mind Natas thinks he is beginning to regain their support.

"Anyway! What about us few survivors that remain? How are we going to run 'our' lives? There has to be order of some sort. It's obvious we cannot go back to the way things were. So what do we do? In my humble opinion, we have to have leadership. Leaders of some sort that will keep everything going and make us all happy. Don't you agree?"

His eyes glisten as he hears some muted agreements among the crowd.

Their listening to me! I'll soon have them eating out of my hands.

"So, how do we keep everyone happy? First thing - people need good food in there bellies, a decent place to live, and some 'real' fun to bring it all together. Fun is fun. Right? Different people like different types of fun. You know what I mean?"

He senses the younger people are agreeing with him.

Keep going, it will not be long now.

"That is where good leadership comes in. Someone who can supply you with these things and give you that nice feeling of security - without dictatorship!

You know as well as I do that 'everything' comes at a price. The only price 'I' ask for is loyalty. Loyalty to me! So I can look after 'you'. I think that is a good deal."

Still flamboyant, he turns to Gus.

"The floor is yours squire."

The crowd now silent as well as confused, watch Gus who is numb with fury as he glares at Natas strolling through the crowd. Still glaring, his stomach churns as his arch enemy ends up with Madeline. Aware of still being watched, Natas continues his theatricals by sliding his arms around Madeline, and making a big show of kissing her cheek, and then her lips.

Eva's heart goes out to Gus as he attempts to control his rage. She can feel his pain and hopelessness as she witnesses him shuffle up and down his makeshift platform determined not to show his vulnerability. Also witnessing this exhibition, the crowd become a little anxious, and restless, while they wait for Gus to retaliate.

Meanwhile, Garth squeezes Tizzy's hand while he wills Gus to be strong.

Show them Gus. Show them the real truth.

Digging deep into his reserves, Gus looks west into the warm evening sky. The sun is glowing to a deep orange as it drops nearer to the horizon. He now looks upward, shuts his eyes, pauses, opens them, and then faces the crowd.

"The only thing that we 'all' agree on is we cannot go back to how things were. You have to choose yourself. I can only tell you what 'will' happen if you don't choose the right way. Each one of you was chosento stay. This isn't an accident or a matter of luck, even though you have been told otherwise. As I've been continually saying, we are going to live by God's law now. You all know that deep in your hearts..."

There is a loud shout coming from the Bus. It is Natas. He is standing on the roof again.

"It will be a dictatorship! No freedom of choice. God's way or the highway. The highway to extinction. One zap, and you are gone. Is that what you really want? It sound like to me that you have no choice. All this suffering, for what?"

Gus now seeing on Natas's face that he is losing this final battle, Gus's fear has gone. The feeling for this evil individual is now sadness, as Gus replies in earnest.

"You have no idea! God is not a dictator, but a loving parent."

His confidence showing, he now focuses on the crowd.

"We are the children of God's family. You will be cared for and you will not suffer if you love each other as God loves you. That is why you're here and not dust like the all the others who were not worthy..."

Someone in the crowd shouts.

"Look! There is someone standing out there alone in the desert."

Hoping this is not another evil ploy, Gus joins the the crowd in observing the stranger.

As Gus steps down from his platform, he is met by Garth and Tizzy accompanied by Silver Eagle and Eva. Becoming caught up in all the emotion, Garth is the first to question.

"Do you think it has started? Look at the sun, it is almost at the base of the mountains."

Unable to answer, Gus waits, and then begins to follow the crowd.

"One way to find out."

Each of them becoming curious at the figure standing not far from the settlement, they are also a little anxious. As the figure becomes clearer, they focus on a young woman dressed in a single fawn robe and her feet are bare. Her long thick dark wavy hair does not move in the light breeze. Her back to the sun, Garth notices a young girl running up to this woman. Silver Eagle gasps when he recognizes her.

"My daughter Mary! What is she doing?"

The answer comes when the chief's daughter opens her arms to greet this stranger and embrace. Gus' heart almost stops when he recognizes the woman.

It's Mary Magdalene! God? What is going on?

Gus and the crowd can see that Mary Magdalene does not appear solid, as if a hologram. Mary Morning Star's hands seem to melt into her form.

Amazed by this 'illusion', the crowd gathers round within a few feet of this wonder, and one by one, they begin to sit on the sand.

Demonstrating anger, Natas comes rushing to the front of the crowd holding Madeline's arm. As the setting sun reflects off his robes and green eyes,

Madeline turns away from the sun. His anger still apparent, Natas points at Mary Magdalene.

"What are you doing? Is this another trial these people have to go through?"

There is no answer. Instead, the Indian girl turns to face Natas and points at Madeline.

"You and your unequaled whore are the only ones on trial, not these good souls."

As Mary Morning Star's mouth is shaping the words, the voice is not hers. The actual female sound fills the whole area. Demonstrating his true nature, and determined not to be undermined, Natas spits back.

"You are a nobody! Just a redskin kid."

The strong female voice continues to echo throughout.

"You 'know' who I am. I am the 'ultimate' authority. The rule of law you will all live by. You are all my children. I will love, cherish and take care of you."

The Indian girl points at Madeline.

"You, the 'real' evil, not him, are finished."

She now points back to Natas.

"I gave you many chances to redeem yourself, but to no avail. You always had your weaknesses. You have never realized your true potential. That is why I gave you those chances. Now you have been influenced by the 'true' devil, you are beyond redemption. Therefore, you and 'her', and anyone connected with her, are finished."

While Natas glares at Madeline, and appears shocked, the crowd is enthralled, but silent.

Sympathizing with Natas, Julie comes forward, steps up to Natas, and looks at Mary.

"I'm not sure who you are, but isn't there any chance he can repent and be like us?"

Natas glares at her in astonishment, as if she is insane. On the other hand, always seeing Julie as his first disciple, his eyes soften a little.

"Julie my dear, I had no intention of going back. I was just playing with you lik a toy."

Her eyes now filling with tears of betrayal, Julie cannot believe her ears.

"You were really serious about going back. I could feel it. And you said you loved me."

As if ashamed, Natas lowers his head. Presuming she is still getting through to him, Julie grips his forearm.

"Didn't you 'ever' love me?"

Witnessing this farce, before Natas can reply,Madeline spits at Julie.

"You stupid bitch! He had no intentions about going back or wanting you to help him in doing so. Can't you see he's mine! Always has been, and always will be?"

Natas glares at Madeline and tightens his grip on her arm causing her to squeal in pain.

"Don't you 'dare' to presume what intentions I had or did not have? Julie only had my interest at heart. At least I know what I am, but you are far worse. For a short while, I did think about going back, but your seductive evil is so beyond any sin I have ever committed, I admit to failure."

Still in pain, Madeline is defiant.

"Don't forget I have 'your' child growing in me. You didn't mind performing that little sin."

His weakness showing, he hesitates, and looks at young Mary as if he now knows his final fate.

"I can understand why you are dealing with me...." He pulls Madeline and throws her at the feet of Mary Morning star. "....but how did 'this' - ever get by you?"

"We have always known about her, because she is the 'real' devil. You are just the fallen one who has unwittingly been carrying out her evil commands over the millenniums. Knowing how you were pondering about a final decision in coming back to us, we needed to test your sincerity by letting her tempt you otherwise. Because of your weak disposition, you failed."

Her eyes glaring crimson, Madeline, wrenches free of Natas's grip. Everyone now focusing on this woman, they gasp as Madeline haunches onto her hands and knees, hisses at Silver Eagles daughter, and pounces at her like a cat. Horrified, Silver Eagle runs up to Madeline just as she grips his daughter's throat. Mary gives out a muted scream as the grip becomes tighter. As the crowd stare in horror, at the same time the ground begins to rumble and shake. Everyone screams in fright. Many scramble to the safety of the vehicles. Madeline loses her balance and falls, losing her grip from Mary's throat. At the same time, Silver Eagle loses his balance and falls upon Madeline.

The ground begins to crack, running from north to south just in front of Mary Morning star. As everyone in the crowd tries to gather their momentum, the earthquake stops, and everything is quiet. Becoming fatalistic, Natas falls down on his knees. Not realizing the thin crack is right underneath him, he lets Julie stand close to him. Relishing her warmth in this time of crisis, he slides his arm around her waist and rests his head against her young breasts.

"Ignore her. She is the devil incarnate. I do have feelings for you, but..."

He is interrupted by a manic Madeline struggling against Silver Eagle who is now trying to restrain her. With abnormal strength, she brakes free and makes another pounce at Mary. The ground shakes again, causing the crack to open up. Instead of clutching onto Mary, Madeline loses her footing as one of her legs catch into the expanding opening. Frustrated, she screams with rage as she opens her arms for Natas to help. Taking Julie with him, he manages to roll over to clear the crack. His response to Madeline's plea is to release Julie, and then crouch down on his knees. As Madeline keeps pleading, Natas becomes an obedient disciple by reaching over and gripping both of her hands. The crowd watch in fascination as the earth rumbles again and the crack widens, causing Madeline's other leg to dangle into open space. Now hanging over the chasm with Natas bent over on his knees struggling to hold each of her hands, and not quite knowing what to do, Julie comes up to Natas offering to help.

Meanwhile, making sure the two Mary's are safe, Gus comes to the other side of Natas and peers down the bottomless pit.

"Hang on, I'll help you."

As he goes to grip Madeline's forearm, Julie does the same her side.

"We need more help!"

While this is happening, Madeline is cursing and spitting at Gus as she becomes desperate in trying to establish a foothold on the smooth wall of the chasm.

Observing Natas's arms are tiring, Gus indicates to Silver Eagle for help. For obvious reasons, the Indian is reluctant to assist, as he signals Julie to move to safety. Before Gus and the chief can sustain a grip, Natas eyes become blank as if his mind is elsewhere. He then gazes at Gus, blinks and let's go of Madeline.

While Madeline's pitiful screams echo, and then diminish, the remain sound to be heard is the soft howl of the desert breeze. All eyes now on Natas, he is still staring at Gus, he blinks again, and then turns his head toward Mary Magdalene. Watching him with a dispassionate expression, she leans her head to one side, as her eyes change to a more commanding stare. Reading this as a command, Natas turns back to Gus.

"See you in Hell brother. I am going home."

Without any emotion or regret, he rolls off the edge and falls into the chasm without a sound. Horrified, Gus peers over the edge and witnesses Natas appearing to float until he is out of sight in the dark depths. Controlling his emotions, Gus steps back from the gap as the ground rumbles again and the gap begins to close. A plume of hot water gushes out of the closing crack behind the two Mary's. The crack now closed, the plume of hot water continues and has now changed into a tall majestic fountain of warm blue mineral water. The crowd stare in fascination as the setting sun shines through the blue water causing the sun to appear purple.

Someone shouts out.

"The dream!"

Then there is stillness as the sun touches the horizon. Mary Magdalene's back still to the fountain, the purple seems to shine through her, while she raises her arms.

As if to call everyone, Mary Morning Star stands in front of Mary Magdalene as Garth comes forward and kneels in front of the chief's daughter. Her silhouette appears dark against the sinking desert sun. Acting as a signal of faith, the crowd come forward to be nearer young Mary. Garth now taking the lead, Eva, Julie and her mother do the same, and then followed by the rest of the crowd.

Still standing, and overcome by his daughter's new 'authority', Silver Eagle begins to sing and chant in Navajo. His soft penetrating voice filling the surrounding desert is the signal for this new world order to begin.

After a minute the song ends. His daughter's lips begin to move again. The same deep soft female voice reverberates.

"It is finished. Evil is no more. This is the 'Final Testament' to be written. You are all free to travel and settle anywhere. There are good people of all nations at this moment receiving this same message. Go, unite, and live under the law of God. My law!"

Overcome by his daughter being the messenger for God, Silver Eagle's eyes fill with tears, as he kneels down next to Gus. The message continues toward Gus.

"....as for you my son, your mission is almost over. Now you need to go to the other nations and bless them with my love, a mother's love, and then inform and guide them in bringing a better life for all humankind."

In the brief silence that follows, Gus can hear people in the crowd praying. Sensing everyone is of the same mind, Silver Eagle looks up to his daughter, as she rests her hand on his head. Gus can see she has her eyes closed and is praying in her own voice. He then gazes up to Mary Magdalene. As her olive eyes meet his, she places both her hands on his head. The warmth radiating, but the hands not touching, all the memories of them as lovers come flooding back. From her first kiss at the well to when he had to leave her. Her voice fills his head.

"My love! We are never apart. That is why I am always in your dreams. I have been with you through every turmoil and every ecstasy. I have cried when you cry, I have laughed when you laugh and most of all I love you when you love. You are God's son as we are all 'Her' children. She sends me as her messenger to you because of our love. 'She' is the Mother of us all, and will not cry anymore at man's inhumanity. She will not now despair at the pain her children have had to suffer. Lead them my love and this world will finally be the true Garden of Eden."

The sun has almost set. The purple light is dwindling. Silver Eagle stands, wipes his eyes and slides his arm around his daughter's shoulders, as he turns to face the crowd. Gus is still kneeling with his eyes closed. The Chief and his daughter join Garth and Tizzy who is still in the front of the crowd. All are thoughtful as they watch Gus still kneeling. The apparition has gone, but Gus can still feel and hear her.

"Go now with all my love."

Minutes pass. Feeling energized, Gus stands. Still looking at the dwindling sunset through the fountain, he is conscious of a surrounding heavy silence. He turns to find the crowd waiting, and staring at him with expectation. Breaking the spell, Eva runs up to him, wraps her arms around him and rests against his chest.

"You did it! Mission completed."

Enjoying her familiar warmth and smell, he strokes her hair.

"Almost there."

Julie, followed by a group of children, runs up to them and gives Gus and Eva a hug. A young girl with bright red curly hair and curious bright blue eyes, gazes up to Gus.

"I never knew God was a woman?"

Young Ryan interrupts.

"I always knew! You have Mother Nature. Mother Earth. Also, the hand that rocks the cradle, rules the world. So to me, God must be a woman!"

The young girl's reaction is to kiss Ryan's cheek, and then question Gus.

"Can we go home now?"

For the last time he gazes up to the twilight sky. Observing a lone star blinking, he is sure he can feel a hand stroke his face, as a light breeze develops.

"Yes. We can 'all' go home now."

THE END

Made in the USA
Las Vegas, NV
01 March 2022

44847447R00374